PRIESTESS *of the* WHITE

By Trudi Canavan

The Black Magician Trilogy
THE MAGICIANS' GUILD
THE NOVICE
THE HIGH LORD

Age of the Five
PRIESTESS OF THE WHITE

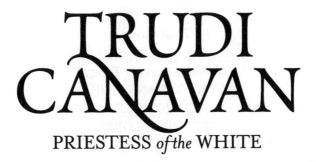

TRUDI CANAVAN

PRIESTESS *of the* WHITE

AGE OF THE FIVE: BOOK ONE

www.orbitbooks.co.uk

ORBIT

First published in Great Britain in February 2006 by Orbit

A CIP catalogue record for this book
is available from the British Library.

ISBN 1 84149 386 4

Typeset in Garamond 3 by Palimpsest Book Production Limited,
Polmont, Stirlingshire
Printed and bound in Great Britain by Mackays of Chatham, Chatham, Kent

Orbit
An imprint of
Time Warner Book Group UK
Brettenham House
Lancaster Place
London WC2E 7EN

www.orbitbooks.co.uk

TO PAUL

ACKNOWLEDGEMENTS

Many thanks to:
'The Two Pauls' and Fran Bryson who read the roughest of the rough drafts. Also to Jennifer Fallon, Russell Kirkpatrick, Glenda Larke, Fiona McLennan, Ella McCay, Tessa Kum for their feedback. To all the readers, especially all my friends on Voyager Online. And, finally, to Stephanie Smith and the Voyager team.

ARBEE

MIRROR STRAIGHT

AIME

GENRIA

NORTHERN
ITHANIA

PORIN   TOREN

THE OPEN

JURAN

SI

BORRA   PORTL

SOUTHERN
OCEAN

RIAN   MAIRAE

SOMREY

SEA OF CHAIA

ARIME

HANIA

CHON

DUNWAY

GULF OF LORE

SENNON

KARIENNE

MUR

HANNAYA

GLYMMA

SOUTHERN
ITHANIA

AVVEN

KAVE

DEKKAR

DYARA

AURAYA

PROLOGUE

Auraya stepped over a fallen log, taking care that no crinkle of crushed leaves or snapping of twigs betrayed her presence. A tug at her throat warned her to look back. The hem of her tawl had caught on a branch. She eased it free and carefully chose her next step.

Her quarry moved and she froze.

He can't have heard me, she told herself. *I haven't made a sound.*

She held her breath as the man rose and looked up into the mossy branches of an old garpa tree. His Dreamweaver vest was dappled with leafy shadows. After a moment he crouched and resumed his examination of the underbrush.

Auraya took three careful steps closer.

'You're early today, Auraya.'

Letting out a sigh of exasperation, Auraya stomped to his side. *One day I'm going to surprise him*, she vowed. 'Mother took a strong dose last night. She'll sleep late.'

Leiard picked up a piece of bark, then took a short knife from a vest pocket, slid the point into a crack and twisted it to reveal tiny red seeds inside.

'What are they?' she asked, intrigued. Though Leiard had been teaching her about the forest for years there was always something new to learn.

1

'The seed of the garpa tree.' Leiard tipped out the seeds and spread them in his palm. 'Garpa speeds the heart and prevents sleep. It is used by couriers so they can ride long distances, and by soldiers and scholars to keep awake, and . . .'

Falling silent, he straightened and stared into the forest. Auraya heard a distant snap of wood. She looked through the trees. Was it her father, come to fetch her home? Or was it Priest Avorim? He had told her not to speak to Dreamweavers. She liked to secretly defy the priest, but to be found in Leiard's company was another matter. She took a step away.

'Stay where you are.'

Auraya stilled, surprised at Leiard's tone. Hearing the sound of footsteps, she turned to see two men step into view. They were stocky and wore tough hide vests. Both faces were covered in swirls and dashes of black.

Dunwayans, Auraya thought.

'Stay silent,' Leiard murmured. 'I will deal with them.'

The Dunwayans saw her and Leiard. As they hurried forward she saw that each carried an unsheathed sword. Leiard remained still. The Dunwayans stopped a few steps away.

'Dreamweaver,' one said. 'Are more people in the forest?'

'I do not know,' Leiard replied. 'The forest is large and people seldom enter.'

The warrior gestured with his sword toward the village. 'Come with us.'

Leiard did not argue or ask for an explanation.

'Aren't you going to ask what's going on?' Auraya whispered.

'No,' he replied. 'We will find out soon enough.'

Oralyn was the largest village in northwestern Hania, but Auraya had heard visitors grumble that it wasn't particularly big. Built on the summit of a hill, it overlooked the surrounding fields and forest. A stone Temple dominated the rest of the buildings and an ancient wall encircled all. The old gates had been removed over half a century ago, leaving misshapen stumps of rust where hinges had once been.

Dunwayan warriors paced the wall and the fields outside were empty of workers. Auraya and Leiard were escorted along equally empty streets to the Temple, then directed inside. Villagers crowded the large room. Some of the younger men wore bandages. Hearing her name, Auraya saw her parents and hurried to their side.

'Thank the gods you're alive,' her mother said, drawing Auraya into an embrace.

'What's happening?'

Her mother sank to the floor again. 'These foreigners made us come here,' she said. 'Even though your father told them I was sick.'

Auraya undid the ties of her tawl, folded it and sat down on it. 'Did they say why?'

'No,' her father replied. 'I don't think they intend to harm us. Some of the men tried to fight the warriors after Priest Avorim failed, but none were killed.'

Auraya was not surprised that Avorim had been defeated. Though all priests were Gifted, not all were powerful sorcerers. Auraya suspected there were farmers with more magical ability than Avorim.

Leiard had stopped by one of the injured men. 'Would you like me to look at that?' he asked quietly.

The man opened his mouth to reply, but froze as a white-clad figure moved to stand beside him. The injured man glanced up at Priest Avorim then shook his head.

Leiard straightened and looked at the priest. Though Avorim was not as tall as Leiard, he had authority. Auraya felt her heartbeat quicken as the two men stared at each other, then Leiard bowed his head and moved away.

3

Fools, she thought. *He could stop the pain at the least. Does it matter that he doesn't worship the gods? He knows more about healing than anyone here.*

Yet she understood the situation wasn't that simple. Circlians and Dreamweavers had always hated each other. Circlians hated Dreamweavers because Dreamweavers didn't worship the gods. Dreamweavers hated the gods because they had killed their leader, Mirar. *Or so Priest Avorim says*, she thought. *I've never heard Leiard say so.*

A metallic clunk echoed through the Temple. All heads turned toward the doors as they swung open. Two Dunwayan warriors entered. One had lines tattooed across his forehead, giving the impression of a permanent scowl. Auraya's heart skipped as she recognised the pattern. *He is their leader. Leiard described these tattoos to me once.* Beside him was a man in dark blue clothing, his face covered in radiating lines. *And he is a sorcerer.*

The pair looked around the room. 'Who leads this village?' the Dunwayan leader asked.

The village head, a fat merchant named Qurin, stepped forward nervously.

'I do.'

'What is your name and rank?'

'Qurin, Head of Oralyn.'

The Dunwayan leader looked the plump man up and down. 'I am Bal, Talm of Mirrim, Ka-Lem of the Leven-ark.'

Leiard's lessons were coming back to Auraya. 'Talm' was a title of land ownership. 'Ka-Lem' was a high position in the Dunwayan military. The latter ought to be linked to the name of one of the twenty-one warrior clans, but she did not recognise the name 'Leven-ark'.

'This is Sen,' Bal continued, nodding to the sorcerer at his side. 'Fire-warrior of the Leven-ark. You have a priest with you.' He looked at Avorim. 'Come here and speak your name.'

Avorim glided forward to stand beside the village head. 'I am Priest Avorim,' he said, the wrinkles of his face set in an expression of disdain. 'Why have you attacked our village? Set us free at once!'

Auraya suppressed a groan. This was not the way to address a Dunwayan, and definitely not the way to address a Dunwayan who had just taken a village hostage.

Bal ignored the priest's demand. 'Come with me.'

As Bal turned on his heel, Qurin looked desperately at Avorim, who put a hand on his shoulder in reassurance. The pair followed Bal out of the Temple.

Once the door had closed the villagers began speculating. Despite the village's close proximity to Dunway, its people knew little about the neighbouring land. They didn't need to. The mountains that separated the two countries were near impassable, so trade was undertaken by sea or through the pass far to the south.

The thought of what Qurin and Avorim might say to upset Bal sent a shiver of apprehension down Auraya's spine. She doubted there was anyone in the village, other than Leiard, with enough understanding of Dunwayans to negotiate a way out of this situation. But Avorim would never allow a Dreamweaver to speak for them.

Auraya thought back to the day she had first met Leiard, nearly five years before. Her family had moved to the village in the hope that her mother's health would improve in the clean quiet of the country. It hadn't. Auraya had heard that Dreamweavers were good healers, so she sought out Leiard and boldly asked him to treat her mother.

Since then she had visited him every few days. She'd had a lot of questions about the world that nobody could answer. Priest Avorim could only tell her about the gods, and he was too weak to teach her many magical Gifts. She knew Leiard was strong magically because he had never run out of Gifts to teach her.

Though she disliked Avorim she understood that she ought to learn Circlian ways from a Circlian priest. She loved the rituals and sermons, the history and laws, and counted herself lucky to be living in an age the gods had made peaceful and prosperous.

If I was a priestess, I'd be much better than he is, she thought. *But that's never going to happen. So long as Mother is sick she'll need me to stay here and look after her.*

Her thoughts were interrupted by the opening of the Temple doors. Qurin and Avorim hurried inside and the villagers moved close.

'It appears these men are trying to stop the proposed alliance between Dunway and Hania,' Qurin told them.

Avorim nodded. 'As you know, the White have been trying to form an alliance with the Dunwayans for years. They're having some success now that suspicious old I-Orm has died and his sensible son, I-Portak, is ruler.'

'So why are they here?' someone asked.

'To prevent the alliance. They told me to contact the White to communicate their demands. I did, and I . . . I spoke to Juran himself.'

Auraya heard a few indrawn breaths. It was rare for priests to speak telepathically to one of the Gods' Chosen, the four leaders of the Circlians known as the White. Two spots of red had appeared on Avorim's cheeks.

'What did he say?' the village baker asked.

Avorim hesitated. 'He is concerned for us and will do what he can.'

'Which is what?'

'He didn't say. He will probably speak to I-Portak first.'

Several questions followed. Avorim raised his voice. 'The Dunwayans do not want a war with Hania – they made that clear to us. After all, to defy the White is to defy the gods themselves. I don't know how long we will be here. We must be prepared to wait for several days.'

As questions turned to matters of practicality, Auraya noticed that Leiard wore a frown of worry and doubt. *What is he afraid of? Does he doubt that the White can save us?*

Auraya dreamed. She was walking down a long corridor lined with scrolls and tablets. Though they looked interesting, she ignored them; somehow she knew that none of them contained what she needed. Something was urging her forward. She arrived in a small circular room. On a dais in the centre was a large scroll. It uncurled and she looked down at the text.

Waking, she sat bolt upright, her heart pounding. The Temple was quiet but for the sounds of the villagers sleeping. Searching the room she found Leiard asleep in a far corner.

Had he sent her the dream? If he had, he was breaking a law punishable by death.

Does that matter, if we're all going to die anyway?

Auraya drew her tawl back up around herself and considered her dream and why she was now so certain the village was doomed. On the scroll had been one paragraph:

'Leven-ark' means 'honour-leaver' in Dunwayan. It describes a warrior who has cast aside all honour and obligations in order to be able to fight for an idealistic or moral cause.

It hadn't made sense to Auraya that a Dunwayan warrior would dishonour his clan by taking unarmed villagers hostage or killing defenceless people. Now she understood. These

Dunwayans no longer cared for honour. They could do anything, including slaughter the villagers.

The White were powerfully Gifted and could easily defeat the Dunwayans in a fight, but during that fight the Dunwayans might kill the villagers before the White overcame them. However, if the White gave in to the Dunwayans' demands others might copy them. Many more Hanians could be imprisoned and threatened.

The White won't give in, she thought. *They'd rather some or all of us were killed than encourage others to take a village hostage.* Auraya shook her head. *Why did Leiard send me this dream? Surely he wouldn't torment me with the truth if there wasn't anything I could do about it.*

She considered the information in the scroll again. *'Levenark'. 'Cast aside all honour'. How can we turn that to our advantage?*

For the rest of the night she lay awake, thinking. It was only when the dawn light began to filter softly into the room that the answer came to her.

After several days, tempers were thin and the stale air was heavy with unpleasant odours. When Priest Avorim wasn't settling disputes among the villagers he was bolstering their courage. Each day he gave several sermons. Today he had told of the dark times before the War of the Gods, when chaos ruled the world.

'Priest Avorim?' a young boy asked as the story ended.

'Yes?'

'Why don't the gods kill the Dunwayans?'

Avorim smiled. 'The gods are beings of pure magic. To affect the world they must work through humans. That is why we have the White. They are the gods' hands, eyes and voices.'

'Why don't they give *you* the power to kill the Dunwayans?'

'Because there are better ways to solve problems than killing. The Dunwayans . . .' The priest's voice faded to silence. His eyes fixed on a distant point, then he smiled.

'Mairae of the White has arrived,' he announced.

Auraya's stomach fluttered. *One of the White is here, in Oralyn!* Her excitement died as the door to the Temple opened. Bal stepped inside, flanked by several warriors and his sorcerer, Sen.

'Priest Avorim. Qurin. Come.'

Avorim and Qurin hurried out. Sen did not follow. The radiating lines on his face were distorted by a frown. He pointed at the blacksmith's father, Ralam.

'You. Come.'

The old man rose and staggered toward the sorcerer, hampered by a leg that had been broken and badly set years before.

The sacrifice, Auraya thought. Her heart began to race as she moved forward. Her plan relied on the Dunwayans being reluctant to break their customs, despite their intentions. She stepped in front of Ralam.

'By the edicts of Lore,' she said, facing Sen, 'I claim the right to take this man's place.'

The sorcerer blinked in surprise. He glanced aside at the warriors guarding the door and spoke in Dunwayan, gesturing dismissively at her.

'I know you understood me,' she said, striding forward to stand a pace from the sorcerer. 'As did your warrior brothers. I claim the right to take the place of this man.'

Her heart was hammering now. Voices called out to Auraya, telling her to come back. The old man tugged at her arm.

'It's all right, girl. I will go.'

'No,' she said. She made herself meet Sen's eyes. 'Will you take me?'

9

Sen's eyes narrowed. 'You choose freely?'

'Yes.'

'Come with me.'

Someone among the audience shrieked her name and she winced as she realised it was her mother. Resisting the urge to look back, she followed the Dunwayans out of the Temple.

Once outside, Auraya felt her courage weakening. She could see Dunwayan warriors gathered in a half-circle around the gap in the village wall. Late-afternoon light set their spears glittering. There was no sign of Qurin or Priest Avorim. Bal stepped out of the half-circle of warriors. Seeing Auraya, he scowled and said something in his own language.

'She offered herself in exchange,' Sen replied in Hanian.

'Why didn't you refuse?'

'She knew the ritual words. I was honour-bound to—'

Bal's eyes narrowed. 'We are the Leven-ark. We have abandoned all honour. Take—'

A warning was shouted. All turned to see a priestess standing in the gap in the wall.

The priestess was beautiful. Her gold-blonde hair was arranged in an elaborate style. Large blue eyes regarded all serenely. Auraya forgot all else but the fact that she was looking at Mairae of the White. Then Sen took her wrist in an iron grip and pulled her after Bal, who was marching toward the woman.

'Stay there, or she dies,' the Dunwayan leader barked.

Mairae regarded Bal intently. 'Bal, Talm of Mirrim, Ka-Lem of the Leven-ark, why are you holding the people of Oralyn prisoner?'

'Did your priest not explain? We demand you stop your alliance with Dunway. If you do not we will kill these villagers.'

'I-Portak does not sanction this action you have taken.'

'Our argument is with you *and* I-Portak.'

Mairae nodded. 'Why do you seek to prevent the alliance when the gods want our lands to unite?'

'They did not proclaim that Dunway should be ruled by the White, only that our lands be allies.'

'We do not wish to rule you.'

'Why, then, do you ask for control of our defences?'

'We do not. Your land's army is and will always be for I-Portak and his successors to control.'

'An army without fire-warriors.'

Mairae's eyebrows rose slightly. 'Then it is the dismantling of the Sorceror Clan that you protest against, not the alliance itself?'

'It is.'

She looked thoughtful. 'We believed dismantling the Sorceror Clan had the support of its sorcerers. I-Portak saw great benefits in sending Gifted Dunwayans to the priesthood. There is much that we can teach them that they would not learn in the clan house. Healing, for example.'

'Our fire-warriors know how to mend a wound,' Sen snapped, his voice loud in Auraya's ear.

Mairae's attention shifted to him. 'Not how to cure a child's illness, or assist in a difficult birth, or clear an old man's sight.'

'Our Dreamweavers tend to those duties.'

Mairae shook her head. 'There cannot be enough Dreamweavers in Dunway to tend to those needs.'

'We have more than Hania,' Sen said stiffly. 'We did not seek their deaths as Hanians did.'

'A hundred years ago Dunwayans were as eager to be rid of the Dreamweaver leader, Mirar, as Hanians were. Only a few misguided Hanians sought to kill his followers. We did not order it.' She paused. 'Dreamweavers may be Gifted healers, but they do not have the power of the gods to call upon. We can give you so much more.'

'You would steal from us a tradition that we have kept for over a thousand years,' Bal replied.

'Would you make yourself an enemy of the gods for that?' she asked. 'Is it worth starting a war? For that is what you will do if you execute these villagers.'

'Yes,' Bal replied heavily. 'It is what we are prepared to do. For we know that it is not the gods who demand the end of the Sorceror Clan, but I-Portak and the White.'

Mairae sighed. 'Why did you not speak out earlier? The terms of the alliance might have been altered, had you approached us peacefully. We cannot accede to your demands now, for if others were to see that you had been successful, they, too, would threaten innocents in order to get their way.'

'So you will abandon these villagers to their fate?'

'That is on your conscience.'

'Is it?' Bal asked. 'What will people think of the White when they hear they refused to save their own people?'

'My people's loyalty is strong. You have until the end of the day to leave, Talm of Mirrim. May the gods guide you.'

She turned away.

'Our cause is just,' Bal said quietly. 'The gods see that it is so.' He gave Auraya a disturbingly impersonal glance, then nodded at Sen. Auraya went cold as she felt Sen's hand grasp the back of her head.

'Wait!' she gasped. 'Can I speak before I die?'

She felt Sen pause. Mairae stopped and looked over her shoulder at Bal. The Dunwayan smiled.

'Speak,' he said.

Auraya looked from Mairae to Bal and drew up the words she had practised silently for days. 'This can go one of four ways,' she said. 'Firstly, the Dunwayans could give in and let the White have their way.' She glanced at Bal. 'That's not likely. Neither is it likely that the White will give in and wait for a better time to make an alliance, because they don't want anyone copying you.'

Her mouth was so dry. She paused to swallow.

'It seems like the White have to let the Leven-ark kill us. Then either the White or I-Portak will kill the Leven-ark. We'll all be seen as martyrs to our land or cause.' She looked at Bal again. 'Or will we? If you die, the Sorceror Clan will still end. You fail.' She looked at Mairae. 'There must be another way.'

Everyone was staring at her. She forced herself to look at Bal once more. 'Make it *look* as if the Leven-ark failed. You cast aside all honour and came here prepared to sacrifice your lives to save the Sorceror Clan. Are you prepared to sacrifice your pride instead?'

Bal frowned. 'My pride?'

'If you let the White escort you out of Hania in shame – if you appear to have failed – then we need not fear others will copy you.' She looked at Mairae. 'If he agrees, will you change the terms of your alliance?'

'To allow the Clan to continue?'

'Yes. Even I, living in this tiny village, know of the famous Dunwayan Fire-Warrior Clan.'

Mairae nodded. 'Yes, if the Dunwayan people wish to keep it.'

'Alter the terms of the alliance – but not straightaway or others will still see a connection between the Leven-ark coming here and the change. Arrange for something else to prompt the change.'

Bal and Mairae looked thoughtful. Sen made a low noise, then said something in Dunwayan. At Bal's reply he stiffened, but said nothing more.

'Anything else you wish to say, girl?' Bal asked.

Auraya bowed her head. 'I'll be grateful if you don't kill my family and neighbours.'

Bal looked amused. He turned to regard Mairae. Auraya fought a growing suspicion that she had just made a fool of herself.

I had to try. If I thought of a way to save the village and didn't try it, I'd . . . I'd end up dead.

'Are you willing to let the world believe you failed?' Mairae asked.

'Yes,' Bal replied. 'My men must agree, though. If they do, will you change the terms of the alliance?'

'If my fellow White and I-Portak agree. Shall we consult our people and meet again in an hour?'

Bal nodded.

'You will not harm any of the villagers before then?'

'I swear, in the name of Lore, they will remain unharmed. But how can we trust that you *will* change the alliance after we have left?'

Mairae's mouth relaxed into a smile. 'The gods do not allow us to break our promises.'

Bal grunted. 'We must be satisfied with that. Return in an hour. We will give you our answer.'

As Mairae entered the Temple the villagers fell silent.

'A peaceful solution has been found,' she announced. 'The Dunwayans have left. You may return to your homes.'

At once the Temple filled with cheers.

Auraya had followed Mairae, Avorim and Qurin into the room. 'You little fool!' a familiar voice cried. Her mother rushed forward to embrace her tightly. 'Why did you do that?'

'I'll explain later.' Auraya looked for Leiard but he was nowhere in sight. As her mother released her she suddenly realised that Mairae was standing beside her.

'Auraya Dyer,' the White said. 'That was bravely done.'

Auraya felt her face heat up. 'Brave? I was scared the whole time.'

'Yet you didn't let fear silence you.' The woman smiled. 'You demonstrated a rare insight. Avorim tells me you are an intelligent and exceptionally Gifted student.'

Auraya glanced at the priest, surprised.

'He did?'

'Yes. Have you considered joining the priesthood? You are older than our usual initiate, but not too old.'

Auraya's heart sank. 'I would love to, but my mother . . .' She glanced at her parents. 'She is ill. I look after her.'

Mairae looked at Auraya's mother. 'The healers in the Temple are the best in the land. If I send one here to tend you, would you allow Auraya to join us?'

Feeling light-headed, Auraya looked back at her parents, whose eyes were wide with astonishment.

'I would not like to cause so much trouble,' her mother began.

Mairae smiled. 'Consider it an exchange: a new priestess for a fully trained one. Auraya has too much potential to be wasted. What do you think, Auraya?'

Auraya opened her mouth and let out an undignified squeal that she would recall with embarrassment for years to come. 'That would be *wonderful*!'

PART ONE

CHAPTER 1

Though Danjin Spear had entered Jarime's Temple on several occasions before, today he felt as if he were arriving for the first time. In the past he had visited on behalf of others or in order to perform minor services as a translator. This time was different; this time he was here to begin what he hoped was the most prestigious job of his career.

No matter where this led him, even if he failed or his duties proved tedious or unpleasant, this day would be imprinted on his memory forever. He found himself taking more notice of his surroundings than he usually did – perhaps in order to memorise them for future reflection. *Perhaps only because I'm so anxious*, he thought, *this journey feels as if it's taking forever*.

A platten had been sent for him. The small two-wheeled vehicle rocked gently in time with the gait of the arem pulling it, slowly passing other vehicles, servants and soldiers, as well as rich men and women strolling about. Danjin bit his lip and resisted asking the man perched in the small driver's seat to urge the docile creature into a faster pace. All of the Temple servants had a quiet dignity that discouraged most people from ordering them about. Perhaps this was because their demeanour reminded one of priests and priestesses, and one certainly didn't order *them* about.

They were nearing the end of a long, wide road. Large two- and three-storey houses lined both sides, a contrast to the jumble of apartments, shops and warehouses that made up most of the city. Houses on Temple Road were so expensive that only the most wealthy could afford them. Though Danjin was a member of one of the wealthiest families in Jarime, none of his relatives lived here. They were traders and had as much interest in the Temple and religion as they had in the market and their dinner: a basic necessity not worth making a fuss over, unless there was wealth to be made from it.

Danjin thought differently, and had for as long as he could remember. Value could be measured in things other than gold, he believed. Things like loyalty to a good cause, law, a civilised code of behaviour, art, and the pursuit of knowledge. All things which his father believed could be bought or ignored.

The platten reached the White Arch that spanned the entrance to the Temple and relief carvings of the five gods loomed over Danjin. Grooves filled with gold did a pretty job of depicting the glowing light that spilled from them when they took their visible forms. *I know what Father would say about this: If money doesn't matter to the gods, why isn't their Temple made from sticks and clay?*

The platten continued through the arch and the full glory of the Temple appeared. Danjin sighed with appreciation. He had to admit he was glad it wasn't made of sticks and clay. To his left was the Dome, an enormous half-sphere in which ceremonies were held. High arches around its base allowed access to the inside, and gave the impression that the Dome was floating just above the ground. Inside the Dome was the Altar, where the White communed with the gods. Danjin had not seen it, but perhaps in his new role he would gain the opportunity.

Beside the Dome stood the White Tower. The tallest building

ever to have existed, it appeared to stretch up to the clouds. It didn't, of course. Danjin had been in the highest rooms and knew the clouds were far out of reach. The illusion must make a strong impression on visitors, however. He could see the benefits of impressing and humbling both commoner and foreign ruler.

To the right of the Tower lay the Five Houses, a large hexagonal building that housed the priesthood. Danjin had never entered it and probably never would. While he respected the gods and their followers, he had no desire to become a priest. At fifty-one years of age he was too old to be giving up some of his bad habits. And his wife would never have approved.

Then again, she might like the idea. He smiled to himself. *She's always complaining I mess up her house and plans when I'm home.*

A generous spread of open land surrounded the Temple buildings. Paved paths and garden beds had been laid out in patterns of circles within circles. The circle was the sacred symbol of the Circle of Gods, and some of the ways it had been incorporated into the Temple made Danjin wonder if the original designers and architects had been demented fanatics. Did they need to decorate the communal toilets with circular designs, for instance?

The platten rolled ever closer to the Tower. Danjin's heart was beating a little too fast now. White-clad priests and priestesses strode back and forth, a few noting his arrival and nodding politely, as they probably did to anyone as richly dressed as he. The platten came to a halt beside the Tower and Danjin climbed out. He thanked the driver, who nodded once before urging the arem into motion again.

Taking a deep breath, Danjin turned to face the Tower entrance. Heavy columns supported a wide arch. He moved inside. Magical lights within revealed the entire ground floor of the Tower to be a densely columned hall. Here, gatherings were held and important visitors entertained. Since the White were the rulers of Hania, as well as heads of the Circlian religion, the Temple was as much palace as religious centre. Rulers of other lands, their ambassadors and other significant personages congregated here on important occasions, or visited to negotiate political matters. This was a unique situation; in all other lands the priesthood was secondary to the ruling power.

The hall was filled with people and buzzed with voices. Priests and priestesses hurried about or mingled with men and women dressed in tunics made of luxurious fabrics, covered in generous tawls despite the heat, and glittering with jewellery. Danjin gazed around at the faces, feeling something akin to awe. Nearly every ruler, every famous, wealthy and influential man and woman of Northern Ithania was here.

I can't believe I'm seeing this.

What had brought them to the Temple of Hania was a desire to witness the gods choose the fifth and final White. Now that the ceremony had taken place, they all wanted to meet the new member of the Gods' Chosen.

Danjin forced himself to continue on his way, walking between two rows of columns. They radiated toward the centre of the building, drawing him ever inward to a thick circular wall. It encompassed a spiralling staircase that curved upward to the highest level. The climb to the top of the Tower was a strenuous one, and the creators of this place had come up with a startling solution. A heavy chain hung in the stairwell, descending into a hole in the floor. A priest stood at the base of the stairs. Danjin approached the man and made the formal sign of the circle: holding forefingers and thumbs of both hands together.

'Danjin Spear,' he said. 'I am here to see Dyara of the White.'

The priest nodded. 'Welcome, Danjin Spear,' he replied in a deep voice.

Danjin watched for some indication of the mental signal the priest was communicating to others, but the man did not even blink. The chain in the stairwell began to move. Danjin held his breath. He was still a little frightened of this contraption in the centre of the White Tower. Looking up, he saw a large metal disc descending toward them.

The disc was the base of a metal enclosure as wide as the stairwell. Everyone referred to this contraption as 'the cage', and the reason was obvious. It looked just like the bent-reed cages used to hold animals in the market – and probably inspired a similar feeling of vulnerability in its occupants. Danjin was grateful that this was not his first ride in the contraption. While he did not think he would ever feel comfortable using it, he wasn't as terrified as he had once been. He did not need terror added to the anxiety of beginning an important job.

When the metal enclosure had settled at the bottom of the stairwell, the priest opened the door and ushered Danjin inside. As the cage rose Danjin soon lost sight of the man. The stairwell appeared to spiral around him as the cage gained height. Men and women dressed in circs, servant uniforms or the sumptuous clothes of the rich and important populated the treads. The lower levels contained accommodation and meeting rooms for visiting dignitaries. The higher the cage rose, however, the fewer people Danjin saw. Finally he reached the highest levels, where the White lived. The cage slowed, then came to a halt.

Opening the door, Danjin stepped out. Two steps away, in the wall opposite, was a door. He hesitated before moving to it. Though he had spoken to Dyara, the second most powerful White, several times now, he was still a little overwhelmed in her presence. He wiped his sweaty hands against his sides, took a deep breath and lifted a hand to knock.

His knuckles met with nothing as the door swung open. A tall, middle-aged woman smiled at him.

'Right on time, as usual, Danjin Spear. Come in.'

'Dyara of the White,' he said respectfully, making the sign of the circle. 'How could I be late when you so kindly sent me a platten?'

Her eyebrows rose. 'If all it took to guarantee punctuality was sending a platten then there are more than a few people I've summoned in the past who have a lot to explain. Come in and sit down.'

She turned and strode back into the room. Her height, coupled with the garb of a Circlian priestess, would have made her an imposing figure even if she hadn't been one of the immortal White. As he followed her into the room he saw that another of the White was present. He made the sign of the circle again. 'Mairae of the White.'

The woman smiled and Danjin felt his heart lighten. Mairae's beauty was renowned throughout Northern Ithania. In songs of tribute her hair was described as sunlight on gold and her eyes were compared to sapphires. It was said she could charm a king out of his kingdom with a smile. He doubted any of the current kings could be made cooperative with a mere smile, but there was an appealing sparkle in Mairae's eyes and warmth in her manner that always put him at ease.

She was not as tall as Dyara and she did not exude stern confidence in the way the older woman did. Of the five White, Dyara had been chosen second. Her Choosing had occurred seventy-five years ago, when she was forty-two years of age, so she had more than a century's knowledge of the world. Mairae, chosen at twenty-three a quarter of a century ago, had less than half Dyara's experience.

'Don't let King Berro take up all your time today,' Dyara said to Mairae.

24

'I'll find something to distract him,' Mairae replied. 'Do you need help with the preparations for tonight's celebrations?'

'Not yet. There's a whole day in which disasters could develop, however.' She paused as if something had just occurred to her, then glanced at Danjin. 'Mairae, would you keep Danjin Spear company while I check something?'

Mairae smiled. 'Of course.'

As the door to the room closed behind Dyara, Mairae smiled. 'Our newest recruit is finding it all a bit overwhelming,' she said in a conspiratorial tone. 'I still remember what it was like. Dyara kept me so busy I didn't have time to think.'

Danjin felt a twinge of apprehension. What would he do if the newest White was incapable of performing her duties?

'Don't be alarmed, Danjin Spear.' Mairae smiled and he remembered that all of the White could read minds. 'She's fine. She's just a bit surprised to find herself where she is.'

Danjin nodded, relieved. He considered Mairae. This might be an opportunity to gain a little insight into the newest White.

'What is she like?' he asked.

Mairae pursed her lips as she considered her answer. 'Smart. Powerful. Loyal to the gods. Compassionate.'

'I mean, how is she different to the rest of the White?' he amended.

She laughed. 'Ah! Dyara didn't tell me you were a flatterer. I like that in a man. Hmm.' Her eyes narrowed. 'She tries to see all sides of an argument, and naturally looks for what people want or need. I think she will be a good peacemaker.'

'Or negotiator? I heard she had something to do with that incident with the Dunwayans ten years ago.'

'Yes. It was her village they took hostage.'

'Ah.' *Interesting*.

Mairae abruptly straightened and looked at the wall behind

25

him. *No*, he corrected, *she's not looking at the wall. Her attention is elsewhere.* He was beginning to recognise mannerisms that hinted at mental communication passing between the White. Her gaze shifted to him again.

'You're right, Danjin Spear. I have just received notice that King Berro has asked to see me. I'm afraid I must leave you. Will you be fine here on your own?'

'Yes, of course,' he said.

Mairae rose. 'I'm sure we will meet many times again, Danjin Spear. And I am sure you will make a fine adviser.'

'Thank you, Mairae of the White.'

When she had gone, the silence was unusually intense. *That's because there is no noise from the outside*, he thought. He looked toward the window. It was large and circular, and gave a view of the sky. A shiver of cold ran down his spine.

Standing up, he forced himself to move closer. Though he had seen it before, the view from the White Tower still unnerved him. The sea appeared. A few steps more and he could see the city below – a toy city of tiny houses and tinier people. Taking another step, he felt his heart begin to race as the Dome came into view, like a massive egg half-buried in the ground.

The ground. Which was a long, long way below.

The world tilted and began to revolve. He backed away until all he could see was the sea and sky. At once his head stopped spinning. A few deep breaths later his pulse started to slow.

Then he heard the sound of the door opening behind him and his heart lurched. He turned to see Dyara entering the room. A priestess accompanied her. As he realised who this must be his apprehension was replaced by curiosity.

The new White was as tall as her companion but her arms were thinner and her face was all angles. Her hair was a shade lighter than Dyara's earthy brown. Large eyes were tilted upward

26

at the outer edges, giving her a birdlike appearance. Those eyes regarded him with intelligence and her mouth quirked with amusement. She was probably watching him assessing her, reading his every thought.

Habits were hard to break. He had learned over the years to gauge a person's character at first glance, and could not stop himself now. As she and Dyara walked toward him he noted that the way the new White held her shoulders betrayed her nervousness. Her unwavering gaze and strong mouth suggested a natural confidence would replace it soon, however. He had been told she was twenty-six, and his eyes confirmed it, but there was a maturity in her expression that hinted at a greater knowledge and experience of the world than the average noble-woman would have at that age.

She must have studied hard and learned quickly to become a high priestess by this age, he thought. *Her Gifts must be strong, too. If she is the one who came from that little village the Dunwayans took hostage, she has come a long way.*

Dyara smiled. 'Auraya, this is Danjin Spear,' she said. 'He is to be your adviser.'

Danjin made the formal sign of the circle. Auraya began to raise her hands in reply, then stopped and let them fall to her side again.

'Greetings, Danjin Spear,' she said.

'Greetings, Auraya of the White,' he replied. *She sounds confident*, he noted. *At least she keeps her nervousness from her voice. She just needs to work on her bearing.* She straightened and lifted her chin. *That's better*, he thought. Then he realised that she would have read his thoughts and adjusted herself in response. *It is going to take some time to get used to this mind-reading*, he mused.

'I can see you two will work well together,' Dyara said. She ushered them toward the chairs. 'Danjin has been useful to us in the past. His assessment of the Toren situation was particularly insightful and helped us achieve an alliance with the king.'

Auraya looked at him with genuine interest. 'Is that so?'

He shrugged. 'I only related what I learned from living in Toren.'

Dyara chuckled. 'He is refreshingly humble, too. You'll find his knowledge of other peoples as useful. He can speak all the languages of Ithania.'

'Except those of the peoples of Siyee and Elai,' he added.

'He is a good judge of character. He knows how to deliver advice to powerful men and women discreetly and without causing offence.'

Auraya's attention moved from Dyara to him as they spoke. Her lips twitched at Dyara's last comment.

'A useful skill indeed,' she said.

'He will accompany you whenever you hold an audience. Pay attention to his thoughts. They will guide you in your responses.'

Auraya nodded and looked at Danjin, her expression apologetic.

'Danjin is well aware that having his mind read constantly is part of his role,' Dyara assured her. She turned and smiled at Danjin while continuing to speak to Auraya. 'Though that doesn't mean you should ignore the rules of good manners about which I told you.'

'Of course not.'

'Now that introductions are over, we must get you to the lower levels. The Toren king is waiting to meet you.'

'I'm meeting kings already?' Auraya asked.

'Yes,' Dyara said firmly. 'They came to Jarime to witness the Choosing. Now they want to meet the Chosen. I wish I could give you more time, but I can't.'

'That's fine,' Auraya said, shrugging. 'I just hoped to have time to familiarise myself with my new adviser before demanding work of him.'

'You will familiarise yourselves as you work.'

Auraya nodded. 'Very well.' She smiled at Danjin. 'But I do hope to get to know you better when I have the chance.'

He bowed his head. 'And I look forward to making your acquaintance too, Auraya of the White.'

As the two White rose and moved toward the door, Danjin followed. he had met the woman he would be working for, and nothing about her suggested his role would be difficult or unpleasant. His first task, however, was another matter.

Helping her deal with the Toren king, he thought. *Now this will be a challenge.*

Tryss changed his position slightly, his toes curling and uncurling around the rough bark of the branch. Staring down through the tree's foliage he saw another movement in the undergrowth below and felt a rush of anticipation. But though he longed to lean forward, stretch his wings out and dive, he held himself still.

His skin itched as sweat ran over him, wetting the woven string-reed cloth of his vest and trousers and making the membrane of his wings itch. Straps about his hips and neck felt restrictive and uncomfortable and the spikes hanging against his belly felt heavy. Too heavy. They would drag him to the ground the moment he tried to fly.

No, he told himself. *Fight your instincts. The harness won't restrict you. It won't weigh you down. There's more danger on the tips of these spikes.* If he scratched himself with them . . . He did not like his chances of surviving if he succumbed to a sleep drug while perched on a thin bough many man-heights above the ground.

He stiffened at another movement below. As three yern

stepped out into the clearing beneath him, he held his breath. From above they were narrow barrels of brown hide, their sharp horns foreshortened to mere stubs. Slowly the creatures approached the glistening creek, snatching mouthfuls of grass as they moved. Tryss ran his hands over the straps and wooden levers of the harness, checking that all was set correctly. Then he took a few deep breaths and let himself fall.

Yern were herbivorous herd animals with fine senses that allowed them to detect the position and mood of every member of their herd. Those senses could also detect the minds of other animals nearby and know if any were intending to attack. Yern were swift runners. The only predators who succeeded in catching one were those that used the advantage of surprise or had canny mind-deception Gifts of their own – like the dreaded Ieramer – and even then they could only hope to catch the old and sick animals of the herd.

As Tryss fell, he saw the yern – sensing the approach of a mind set on attack – tense and cast about, confused and unsure which direction to flee in. They could not comprehend that a predator might attack from above. Halfway to the ground, Tryss spread his arms wide and felt the membranes of his wings collect and resist air. He shot out of the tree and swooped toward his prey.

Sensing him almost upon them, terror overcame the beasts. They scattered in every direction, hooting loudly. Tryss followed one, ducking under the branches of other trees. He chased it into the open, then, when he judged himself in the right position over the beast, he tugged at the strap wound around his right thumb. One of the spikes at his waist fell.

At the same time the yern abruptly changed direction. The spike missed and disappeared in the grass. Biting back a curse, Tryss banked and followed the creature. This time he tried not to think about being ready to strike. He cleared his mind of all thought but matching his flight with the yern's, then jerked his left thumb and felt the small weight of the spike fall.

It struck the beast's back just behind the withers. Tryss felt a surge of triumph. As the animal continued running, the spike flicked back and forth against its hide. He watched anxiously, afraid that it hadn't sunk deep enough for the drug to enter the bloodstream, or that it might fall out again.

The spike remained lodged in the yern's back. The beast's run slowed to a stagger, then it stopped and Tryss found himself circling like a carrion bird. He searched the surrounding area carefully for leramer or other big predators. They would steal his prize if he was not careful.

The yern below him swayed, then toppled onto its side. Judging it safe to land, Tryss dropped lightly to the ground a few strides from the animal. He waited until he saw the yern's eyes glaze over before approaching. The animal's horns were sharp and could easily ruin a Siyee's wings.

The animal looked huge up close. Tryss doubted his head would have reached the height of its shoulders, had it been standing up. He ran his hand over the yern's hide. It was warm and had a strong animal smell. He realised he was grinning with excitement.

I've done it! I've single-handedly brought down one of the big animals of the forest!

Siyee did not hunt the large animals. They were a small race, light and fragile with few magical Gifts. Their bones were delicate and easily broken. Their legs were not suited to running long distances, and the movement of their arms – their wings – was limited. Even if they could have hefted a spear or sword, their grip on it would have been too precarious. With all but thumb and forefinger included in the structure of their wings, their hands were useless for tasks that required strength. Whenever Tryss regarded his body, he wondered if the goddess Huan who had created his people out of landwalkers – the humans that occupied the rest of the world – so many hundreds of years ago had forgotten to consider how they would defend or feed themselves.

It was accepted that, since there was no weapon the Siyee could use while flying, the goddess had never intended them to be a people that hunted or fought. Instead they must gather and grow grain, vegetables, fruit and nuts. They must trap and breed small animals and live where no landwalkers could reach them: in the harsh, impassable mountains of Si.

There were only a few small pockets of workable land in the mountains, and many of the animals they ate were increasingly hard to trap. Tryss was sure Huan had not intended for the people she had created to starve. That was why, he reasoned, some had been given inventive minds. He looked down at the contraption he had strapped to his body. It was a simple design. The challenge had been to create something that allowed all the movement needed in flight while providing a simple means of releasing the spikes.

With this we can hunt! We might even be able to defend ourselves – perhaps take back some of the places the landwalkers have stolen from us. He knew they would not be able to fight large groups of invaders this way, but the odd group of landwalker outlaws venturing into Si could easily be dealt with.

But two spikes aren't nearly enough, he decided. *I'm sure I can carry four. They don't weigh that much. But how to release them? I've only got two thumbs.*

That was something to consider later. Looking at the sleeping yern, he realised he had a problem. He had brought a length of rope, intending to hoist it up a tree to keep it out of the reach of most predators while he flew home to bring others back to admire his achievement and help butcher it. Now he doubted he had the strength even to drag it to the nearest trunk. He had no choice but to leave it there and hope predators didn't find it. That meant he must fetch helpers quickly. He'd fly faster without the harness. Unbuckling it, he shrugged out of the contraption and hung it up in a nearby tree. He drew his knife and cut a handful of hair from the yern's mane and tucked it into a pocket. Judging the direction of the wind, he began to run.

Becoming airborne from the ground took a great deal of energy. Tryss leapt into the air and beat his wings, and was gasping with exertion by the time he had reached a height where the winds were stronger and allowed him to glide and soar. Once he had caught his breath, he sped himself along with strong wing-beats, following favourable currents of air.

It was at these moments that he could forgive the goddess Huan for the hardship and difficulties his people faced. He loved to fly. Apparently landwalkers loved using their legs, too. They enjoyed an entertainment called 'dancing' in which they walked or ran in set patterns, alone or in groups of two or more. The closest Siyee equivalent was trei-trei, which could be a part of Siyee courtship or a sport for testing skill and agility.

Tryss's musing ended as he sighted a stretch of bare rock ahead, like a long, narrow scar dividing the mountain's pelt of trees. It was broken into three steps that descended the mountain slope. This was the Open, the largest Siyee settlement. Countless Siyee came and went from this steep clearing every day. Tryss descended slowly, searching for familiar faces. He had almost reached his parents' bower when he spotted his cousins. The twins were sitting on the warm rocks of the lower slope on either side of a girl.

Tryss felt his chest tighten as he recognised the fine-boned, glossy-haired girl: Drilli, whose family recently became his neighbours. He circled and considered flying on. In the past he had got along well with his cousins – if he was prepared to weather a lot of teasing for his strange ways.

Then Drilli's family had moved to the Open. Now his cousins competed for her attention, often at Tryss's expense. He had learned to avoid their company when she was around.

They had once respected his inventiveness, and he still wanted to share his victories with them, but he couldn't tell them about his successful hunt while Drilli was there. They would turn it into something to taunt him about. Besides, his tongue always tied itself in knots when she was near. No, he should find someone else.

Then he noticed that, from above, the cut of her vest revealed that fascinating small hollow between her breasts and he found himself circling one more time. His shadow passed over her and she looked up. He felt a dizzying thrill of pleasure as she smiled at him.

'Tryss! Come down and join us. Ziss and Trinn just told me the funniest joke.'

The two boys looked up and scowled, clearly wanting her attention all for themselves. *Well, too bad*, Tryss thought. *I just brought down a yern. I want Drilli to see it*. Swooping down, he folded his wings and landed lightly before them. Drilli's eyebrows rose. At once his throat sealed up and he couldn't speak. He stared at her, feeling his face begin to tingle the way it did whenever it turned red.

'Where have you been?' Ziss demanded. 'Aunt Trill's been looking for you.'

'You'd better go see what she wants,' Trinn warned. 'You know what she's like.'

Drilli laughed. 'Oh, she didn't seem all that worried. I don't

34

think you need to go right away, Tryss.' She smiled again. 'So, where have you been all morning?'

Tryss swallowed hard and took a deep breath. He could manage one word, surely.

'Hunting,' he choked out.

'Hunting what?' Ziss scoffed.

'Yern.'

The two boys snorted with disbelief and amusement. Trinn turned to Drilli and leaned close as if to share a secret, but his voice was pitched loud enough for Tryss to hear.

'Tryss has got these strange ideas, you see. He thinks he can catch big animals by tying rocks to himself and dropping them on them.'

'Rocks?' she said, frowning. 'But how—?'

'Spikes,' Tryss blurted out. 'Spikes with florrim juice on the tips.' He felt his face heat up, but when he thought of the unconscious yern a cool rush of pride came over him. 'And I *have* caught one.' He dug into his pocket and drew out the lock of yern hair.

The three Siyee regarded the hair with interest. Ziss looked up at Tryss with narrowed eyes. 'You're having us for a joke,' he accused. 'You got this from a dead one.'

'No. It's asleep from the florrim. I'll show you.' Tryss glanced at Drilli, amazed and relieved that he was finally managing to form whole sentences around her. 'Bring your knives and we'll have a feast tonight. But if you wait too long a leramer will find it and we'll get nothing.'

The boys exchanged glances. Tryss guessed they were weighing the chances of this being a joke against the possibility of meat for dinner.

'Fine,' Ziss said, rising and stretching. 'We'll see this yern for ourselves.'

Trinn stood up and flexed his wings. As Drilli got to her feet, clearly intending to follow, Tryss felt his heart skip. She

35

was going to be impressed when she saw the yern. He grinned, broke into a run and leapt into the sky.

Leading them away, he scowled with annoyance when the twins flew over to a group of older boys near the end of the Open. Tryss recognised Sreil, the athletic son of Speaker Sirri, the leader of his tribe. His mouth went dry as the group swooped toward him, whistling shrilly.

'Got yourself a yern, have you?' Sreil called as he passed.

'Might have,' Tryss replied.

More questions came, but he refused to explain how he had brought the animal down. He'd been unable to persuade many Siyee to look at his harness before this. If he started describing it now, they would get bored and lose interest. Once they saw the yern, however, they would want to know how he'd caught it. He would demonstrate the harness. They'd start to take his ideas seriously. After several minutes he glanced behind. To his consternation, the group following him had doubled in size. Doubts began to eat at his confidence, but he pushed them away. Instead, he let his imagination take him into the future. Sreil would take meat back to Speaker Sirri. The Siyee leader would ask to see Tryss's invention. She would have Tryss make more and teach others to use them.

I'll be a hero. The twins will never mock me again.

He roused himself from his daydream as he neared the place he had left the yern. Circling around, he searched the area but found nothing. Feeling eyes on him, he dropped to the ground and paced about. There was a hollow in the grass the size of a large beast, but no yern.

He stared at the hollow in disappointment, then felt his stomach sink as Siyee dropped to the ground all about him.

'So, where's this yern, then?' Ziss asked.

Tryss shrugged. 'Gone. I told you if we took too long a leramer would find it.'

'There's no blood.' This came from one of the older boys. 'If a leramer took it, there'd be blood.'

'And there's no sign anything was dragged away,' another added. 'If it stayed to eat, there'd be a carcass.'

He was right, Tryss realised. So where had the yern gone?

Sreil stepped forward and examined the ground thoughtfully. 'But something big did lie here not long ago.'

'Having a nap, probably,' someone said. There was a snigger from a few of the watchers.

'So, Tryss,' Ziss said, 'did you find a sleeping yern and think you could convince us you'd killed it?'

Tryss glanced at his cousin, then at the amused faces of the Siyee around him. His face burned.

'No.'

'I've got things to do,' someone said. The Siyee began to move away. The air hummed with the sound of their wings. Tryss kept his eyes on the ground. He heard footsteps approach, then felt a pat on his shoulder. Looking up, he found Sreil standing beside him, holding out the spike that had struck the yern.

'Good try,' he said. Tryss winced. He took the spike from Sreil, then watched as the older boy sprinted into the open and leapt into the air.

'You used florrim, didn't you?'

Tryss started. He hadn't realised Drilli was still there.

'Yes.'

She looked at the spike. 'It's got to take a lot more florrim to put a big animal to sleep than a person, and that wouldn't have got far through a yern hide. Maybe you should try something stronger, or deadlier. Or make sure it can't wake up again after it falls asleep.' She patted the sheathed knife buckled to her thigh meaningfully.

She has a point, he thought.

37

Drilli grinned, then turned away. As she leapt into the sky, Tryss watched her in admiration.

Sometimes he wondered how he could be so stupid.

CHAPTER 2

Auraya sat before the polished silver mirror, but she did not see her reflection. Instead she was captivated by a recent memory.

In her mind she could see thousands of white-garbed men and women congregated before the Dome. She remembered how she had never seen so many priests and priestesses gathered in one place. They had travelled to the Temple from all the lands of Northern Ithania in order to attend the Choosing Ceremony. Every priest and priestess living in the Five Houses had been sharing their rooms with those from outside the city and country.

She had glimpsed the size of the crowd as she had left the Tower, walking with her fellow high priests and priestesses to the Dome. Beyond the sea of white figures there had been an even larger crowd of ordinary men, women and children come to witness the event.

Only high priests and priestesses had been candidates for the last position among the Gods' Chosen. Auraya had been one of the youngest of these. Some had said she had ascended the ranks only because of her strong Gifts. Her stomach still tensed with anger at the memory.

It is unfair of them. They know it took me ten years of hard work and dedication to reach the position so quickly.

What did they think now that she was one of the White? Did they regret their judgement of her? She felt a mingled sympathy and triumph. *They were victims of their own ambition. If they thought the gods would pay attention to their lies they were fools. Instead it probably proved they were unworthy. A White shouldn't have a habit of spreading untrue gossip.*

Returning to her memory, she replayed the walk from the Tower to the Dome in her mind. The high priests and priestesses had formed a ring around the dais inside. The Altar, the most sacred place in the Temple, stood at the centre. It was a large five-sided structure three times as high as a man, each wall a tall triangle that sloped inward to meet its fellows. On occasions when the White entered it, the five walls hinged outward until they rested on the floor, revealing a table and five chairs within. When the White wished to converse in private the walls folded upwards to enclose them in a room from which no sound could escape.

The Altar had folded open like a flower as the four White climbed the steps of the dais and turned to face the crowd. Auraya closed her eyes and tried to recall Juran's exact words.

'Chaia, Huan, Lore, Yranna, Saru. We invite you, our divine guardians and guides, to meet with us today, for the time has come for you to choose your fifth and last representative. Here stand those who have proven themselves your worthy, capable and devoted followers: our high priests and priestesses. Each is ready and willing to dedicate their life to you.'

The air had seemed to shimmer briefly. Auraya shivered as she remembered. Five figures had appeared on the dais, each a being of light, each a translucent illusion of humanity. A low sound had risen from the watching priests and priestesses. She had heard faint shouts of 'The gods have appeared!' in the distance.

And what a sight they were, she thought, smiling.

The gods existed in the magic that imbued all the world, in every rock, every drop of water, every plant, every animal, every man, woman and child, in all matter, unseen and unfelt unless they wished to influence the world. When they chose to reveal themselves they did so by changing magic into light and shaping it into exquisitely beautiful human forms.

Chaia had been tall and dressed like a statesman. His face was noble and handsome, like a kingly figure chiselled from polished marble. His hair had moved as if stirred by an affectionate wind. *And his eyes* . . . Auraya sighed. *His eyes were so clear and unbearably direct, but also somehow warm and . . . affectionate. He really does love us all.*

Huan, in contrast, had been intimidating and stern in appearance – beautiful but fierce. With her arms crossed over her chest she had radiated power. She had swept her eyes over the crowd as if looking for something to punish.

Lore's stance had been casual, though his build was heavier than the rest of the gods. He wore glittering armour. Before the War of the Gods he had been worshipped by soldiers.

Yranna had been all smiles, Auraya recalled. Her beauty was more feminine and youthful than Huan's. She was a favourite among the younger priestesses, still a champion of women, though she had put aside the role of goddess of love when joining the other gods.

The last god Auraya had noticed was Saru, a favourite of merchants. It was said he had once been the god of thieves and gamblers, but Auraya was not sure it was true. He had taken on the slimmer physique fashionable among courtiers and intellectuals.

At the gods' appearance all had prostrated themselves. Auraya could still remember the smoothness of the stone floor against her forehead and palms. Silence had followed, then a deep, melodious voice filled the Dome.

41

'Rise, people of Ithania.'

As she had climbed to her feet with the rest of the crowd, Auraya had been trembling with awe and excitement. She hadn't felt so overwhelmed since she had first arrived at the Temple ten years before. It had been strangely delightful to feel so inspired again. After so many years living in the Temple, little about it stirred such exhilaration any more.

The voice spoke again and she realised it belonged to Chaia.

'A few short centuries ago gods fought gods and men fought men, and much grief and ruin was caused. We five were saddened by this and undertook a great task. We would make order from the chaos. We would bring peace and prosperity to the world. We would release humankind from cruelty, slavery and deceit.

'So we fought a great battle and reshaped the world. But we cannot shape the hearts of men and women. We can only advise you and give you strength. In order to help you, we have selected representatives from among you. Their duty it is to protect you and be your link to us, your gods. Today we will choose our fifth representative from those you have deemed most worthy for this responsibility. To the one we choose we bestow immortality and great strength. When our gift is accepted, another stage of our great task will be completed.'

He had paused then. Auraya had expected a longer speech. A silence had filled the hall so complete that she had been sure every man and woman was holding their breath. *I was holding mine*, she remembered.

Then came the moment she would never forget.

'We offer this gift to High Priestess Auraya, of the family Dyer,' Chaia had said, turning to face her. 'Come forward, Auraya of the White.'

Auraya took a deep, shuddering breath as joy swept over her again. At the time it had been tempered by sheer terror.

She'd had to approach a god. She'd been the focus of attention – and probably jealousy – of several thousand people.

Now it was tempered by the reality of her future. From the moment she had been chosen she'd barely had a moment to herself. Her days were filled with meetings with rulers and other important people – and the difficulties had ranged from language barriers to avoiding making promises the other White were not yet ready to make. The only time she was left alone was late at night, when she was supposed to sleep. Every night so far she had lain awake, trying to sort through all that had happened to her. Tonight she had paced her room, finally sitting down in front of the mirror.

It's a wonder I don't look like a wreck, she thought, making herself regard her reflection again. *I shouldn't look this good. Is this another of the gods' Gifts?*

She looked down at her hand. The white ring on her middle finger almost seemed to glow. Through it the gods gave her the Gift of immortality and somehow enhanced her own Gifts. They had made her one of the most powerful sorcerers in the world.

In return she gave her will and her now never-ending life to their service. They were magical beings. To affect the physical world they must work through humans. Most of the time this was through instruction, but if a human gave up their will the gods could take over their body. The latter was rare, as it could, if maintained too long, affect the owner's mind. Sometimes their sense of identity was confused, and they continued believing they were the god. Sometimes they simply forgot who they were.

Best not think about that, she thought. *The gods wouldn't wreck the mind of one of their Chosen anyway. Unless they wanted to punish them . . .*

She found herself looking at an old trunk that stood against one wall. The servants had obeyed her instruction to leave it unopened, and so far she hadn't had the time or courage to open it herself. Inside were the few belongings she owned. She couldn't imagine the quaint, cheap trinkets she had bought over the years looking anything more than tacky in the austere rooms of a White, but she didn't want to throw them away. They reminded her of times in her life and people she loved or wanted to remember: her parents, friends in the priesthood, and her first lover – how long ago that seemed now!

At the base of the trunk was something more dangerous. There, in a secret compartment, were several letters she ought to destroy.

Like the trinkets, she didn't want to. However, unlike the trinkets, the letters might now cause a scandal if they were discovered. *Now that I have some time to myself, I may as well deal with them.* Rising, she moved to the trunk and kneeled in front of it. The latch clicked open and the lid creaked as she lifted it. Just as she had suspected, everything within it looked too rustic and humble. The little pottery vase her first lover – a young priest – had given her looked artless. The blanket, a gift from her mother, was warm but looked dull and old. She took these out, uncovering a large white circle of cloth – her old priestess's circ.

She had worn a circ every day since she had been ordained. All priests and priestesses wore them, including the White. Ordinary priests and priestesses wore a circ trimmed in blue. The circ of a high priest or priestess was trimmed in gold. The White's bore no decoration to show that they had put aside self-interest and wealth in order to serve the gods. It was also why people called the Gods' Chosen the 'White'.

Looking over her shoulder, Auraya regarded her new circ, hanging on a stand made for that purpose. The two gold clasps pinned to the edge marked where the top third of the circle folded back against the rest. It was draped around the shoulders, the clasps attaching to opposite sides.

The circ in her hands was lighter and coarser than the one on the stand. *The White might not embellish their circs*, she mused, *but they do have them made from the best cloth.* The softer white garments she had been given to wear beneath her new circ were also better quality. As with lesser priests and priestesses, the White could change their garments to suit the weather and their gender but everything was well crafted. She now wore sandals made of bleached leather with small gold clasps.

She put the circ aside. She hadn't worn it for over two years – not since she had become a high priestess and received a circ with a gold edge. That had disappeared, whisked away by servants the day she had been chosen. Would this, too, be removed if the servants found it? Did she care? She had only kept it out of a sense of sentimentality.

Auraya turned back to the trunk. Taking out the rest of the objects within, she laid them on a seat nearby. When the trunk was empty she reached inside and levered open the secret compartment. Small rolls of parchment lay within.

Why did I even keep these? she asked herself. *I didn't need to. I guess I couldn't make myself throw away anything that my parents sent.*

Taking out a scroll, she unrolled it and began to read.

My dear Auraya. The harvest has been good this year. Wor married Dynia last week. Old Mulyna left us to meet the gods. Our friend has agreed to my proposal. Send your letter to the priest.

The next letter read:

Dearest Auraya. We are glad to hear you are happy and learning fast. Life here is the same as always. Your mother has improved greatly since we took your advice. Fa-Dyer.

45

Her father's letters were, by necessity, short. Parchment was expensive. She felt a wary relief as she read more of them. *We were careful*, she thought. *We didn't say exactly what we were doing. Except for that first letter I sent, in which I had to make it plain what I wanted Father to do. Hopefully he burned that one.*

She sighed and shook her head. No matter how careful she and her father had been, the gods must know what they had done. They could see into the minds of all.

Yet they still chose me, she thought. *Of all the high priests and priestesses, they chose someone who broke the law and used a Dreamweaver's services.*

Mairae had been true to her promise ten years ago. A healer priest had travelled to Oralyn to care for Auraya's mother. Leiard could hardly continue treating Ma-Dyer, so Auraya had sent him a note thanking him for his help and explaining it was no longer needed.

Despite the healer priest's attention, Auraya's mother had grown sicker. At the same time Auraya had learned through her studies that healer priests did not have half the skill or knowledge that Dreamweavers possessed. She realised that by causing Leiard's treatments to be replaced by those of a healer priest she had effectively doomed her mother to an earlier, more painful death.

Her time in Jarime had also shown her how deeply Circlians despised and distrusted Dreamweavers. She asked careful questions of her teachers and fellow priests and soon came to the conclusion that she could not openly arrange for Leiard or any other Dreamweaver to treat her mother again. She would meet resistance from her superiors if she did and she did not have the authority to order the healer priest home. So she had to arrange it surreptitiously.

She had suggested in a letter to her father that her mother exaggerate her symptoms in order to convince everyone she was close to death. In the meantime, her father ventured into the forest to ask Leiard if he would resume his former treatment. The Dreamweaver had agreed. When Auraya received the news that her mother was dying, she suggested to the healer priest that he return to Jarime. He had done all he could.

Leiard's treatment had revived her mother, as she'd hoped. Her mother had played down her miraculous recovery, staying in the house and seeing few visitors – which was her inclination anyway.

I was so sure this would stand against me being chosen. I wanted so much to be a White, but I couldn't make myself believe that the Dreamweavers are bad or that I had done anything wrong. The law against using a Dreamweaver's services is ridiculous. The plants and other remedies Leiard uses are not good or evil depending on whether a heathen or believer uses them. I haven't seen anything to convince me that Dreamweavers, in general, deserve to be hated or distrusted.

Yet the gods still chose me. What am I to make of that? Does this mean they are willing to tolerate Dreamweavers now? She felt a thrill of hope. *Do they want Circlians to accept Dreamweavers too? Am I meant to bring this about?*

The feeling faded and she shook her head. *Why would they do that? Why would they show any tolerance for people who do not follow them and discourage others from doing so? More likely I will be told to keep my sympathies to myself and do my job.*

Why did that bother her? Why should she feel any sympathy for the members of a cult that she did not belong to? Was it simply because she still felt a debt of gratitude to Leiard for all that he had taught her, and for helping her mother? If that were so, it made sense that she would be concerned for his well-being, but not that she was concerned for Dreamweavers she had never met.

It's the thought of all the healing knowledge that would be lost if the Dreamweavers no longer existed, she told herself. *I haven't seen Leiard in ten years. If I'm concerned about him, it is probably only because my mother's life depends on him.*

Taking all the letters out of the compartment, she placed them in a silver bowl. She held one up, drew magic to herself and sent it out as a little spark. A flame snapped into life, then ate its way down the parchment. When it had nearly reached her fingers she dropped the letter back into the bowl and picked up another.

One by one the letters burned. As she worked she wondered if the gods were watching. *I arranged for a Dreamweaver to treat my mother. I won't willingly end that arrangement. Nor will I make it publicly known. If the gods disapprove, they will let me know.*

Dropping the last burning corner of parchment into the bowl, she stepped back and watched it turn to ash. She felt better. Holding onto that feeling, she returned to her bedroom and lay down.

Now, maybe, I can get some sleep.

The cliffs of Toren were high, black and dangerous. During storms the sea flung itself against the rock wall as if determined to batter it down. Even on quiet nights the water appeared to resent the presence of the natural barrier, foaming where it touched rock. But if this war between land and water was leading to a victory, it was coming too slowly for mortal eyes to guess the winner.

In the distant past, many watercraft had become casualties of this battle. The black cliffs were difficult to see most nights and were a hidden peril if the moon was obscured by cloud. More than a thousand years ago, when the lighthouse had been built, the shipwrecks had stopped.

Made from the same rock as the cliff wall it topped, the round stone walls of the tower were resisting time and weather.

The wooden interior, however, had succumbed to rot and neglect long ago, leaving only a narrow stone stair curving up the inside of the wall. At the top was a room floored with a huge circular slab of rock through which a hole had been carved. The walls built upon this slab had suffered worse; only the arches still remained. The roof had fallen away years ago.

Once the centre of the room had been occupied by a floating ball of light so bright that it would blind anyone foolish enough to stare at it for more than a few moments. Sorcerers had maintained it, keeping the sea safe for centuries.

Emerahl, wise woman and sorceress, was the only human visitor to that room these days. Years ago, when clearing some of the rubble that filled the hollow structure, she had found one of the masks those long-dead sorcerers had worn. The eyeholes were filled with dark gems to filter the dazzling light they had fed with magic.

Now the lighthouse stood crumbling and unused and ships must judge the passage past the black cliffs without its help. As Emerahl reached the topmost room she paused to catch her breath. Placing a wrinkled hand on the column of an arch, she looked out at the sea. Tiny specks of light drew her eye. Ships always waited until daylight before navigating the passage between the cliffs and the islands.

Do they know this place exists? she wondered. *Do people still tell stories of the light that burned here?* She snorted softly. *If they do, I doubt they know it was built by a sorcerer at the bidding of Tempre, the fire god. They probably don't even remember Tempre's name. It's only a few centuries since he died, but that's plenty of time for mortals to forget what life was like before the War of the Gods.*

Did anyone know the names of the dead gods these days? Were there scholars who studied the subject? Perhaps in the cities. Ordinary men and women, struggling to make the best of their short lives, did not care about such things.

Emerahl looked down at the cluster of houses further along the shore. As she did a movement closer to the lighthouse caught her eye. She groaned quietly in dismay. It had been weeks since anyone had dared to visit her. A thin girl dressed in a ragged tunic scrambled up the slope.

Letting out a long sigh, Emerahl looked at the houses again and thought back to when the first people had arrived. A few men had found their way up the cliffs from a single boat and camped in the area. Smugglers, she had guessed. They had erected makeshift huts, dismantling and rebuilding them several times over the first months until they found an area sheltered enough from the regular storms for the huts to remain standing. They had approached her once, thinking to rob her, and she had taught them to respect her desire to be left alone.

The men had left and returned regularly, and soon the single boat was accompanied by another, then more. One day a fishing boat arrived full of cargo and women. Soon there was the thin cry of a baby at night, then another. Babes became children and some lived to become adults. The girls became mothers too young, and many did not survive the experience. All villagers were lucky to live into their forties.

They were a tough, ugly people.

Their rough ways mellowed with each generation and with the influence of outsiders. Some newcomers came to establish trade, and a few stayed. Houses made of local stone replaced the huts of scavenged materials. The village grew. Domestic animals were let loose to graze on the tough grasses of the cliff top. Small, carefully maintained vegetable plots defied the salt air, storms and poor soil.

Occasionally one of the villagers would trek up to the lighthouse seeking cures and advice from the wise woman there. Emerahl tolerated this because they brought gifts: food, cloth, small trinkets, news of the world. She was not

50

averse to a little trade if it brought a small variation to her days and diet.

The villagers did not always make good use of Emerahl's remedies, however. One wife came for velweed for her haemorrhoids, but used it to poison her husband. Another man was sent to Emerahl by his wife for a cure for impotence, then, after his next journey away, came in search of a cure for genital warts. If Emerahl had known that the Gifted boy who wanted to learn how to stun fish and make fires was going to use these abilities to torment the village simpleton she would not have taught him anything at all.

But she was not to blame for any of this. What people decided to do with what they bought from her was their problem. If a wise woman hadn't been available, the wife would have found another way to kill her husband, the unfaithful husband would have strayed anyway – though perhaps with less gusto – and the Gifted bully would have used stones and fists.

The village girl was getting closer now. What would she ask for? What would she offer in return? Emerahl smiled. People fascinated and repelled her. They were capable of being amazingly kind and ferociously cruel. Emerahl's smile twisted. She had placed the villagers somewhere closer to the cruel side of humanity.

She moved to the top of the stairs and began to descend. By the time the girl appeared, panting and wide-eyed, in the doorless entrance of the lighthouse, Emerahl was most of the way down. She stopped. A quick channelling of power set the small pile of sticks and branches in the centre of the floor burning. The girl stared at the fire, then looked up at Emerahl fearfully.

She looks so scrawny and worn out. But then, so do I.

'What do you want, girl?' Emerahl demanded.

'They say . . . they say you help people.'

The voice was small and subdued. Emerahl guessed this girl did not like to attract attention to herself. Looking closer, she saw the signs of physical development in the girl's face and body. She would become an attractive woman, in a thin, scrawny way.

'You want to charm a man?'

The girl flinched. 'No.'

'You want to un-charm a man, then?'

'Yes. Not just one man,' the girl added. 'All men.'

Emerahl cackled quietly and continued down the stairs. '*All* men, eh? One day you might make an exception.'

'I don't think so. I hate them.'

'What about your father?'

'Him most of all.'

Ah, typical teenager. But as Emerahl reached the bottom of the stairs she saw a wild desperation in the girl's eyes. She sobered. This was no sulky rebellious child. Whatever unwanted attentions the girl was enduring had her terrified.

'Come over by the fire.'

The girl obeyed. Emerahl waved to an old bench she had found on the beach below the cliffs after a shipwreck, long before the village existed.

'Sit.'

The girl obeyed. Emerahl lowered herself onto the pile of blankets she used as a bed, her knees creaking.

'There are potions I can make that will take the wind out of a man's sails, if you know what I mean,' she told the girl. 'But dosing a man is dangerous, and temporary. Potions are no use unless you know what's coming and can plan for it.'

'I thought you might make me ugly,' the girl said quickly. 'So they don't want to come near me.'

Emerahl turned to stare at the girl, who flushed and looked at the ground.

'There's no safety in ugliness, if a man is drunk and capable of closing his eyes,' she said in a low voice. 'And, as I said, one day you might want to make an exception.'

The girl frowned, but remained silent.

'I'm guessing there's nobody down there willing or able to defend your virtue, or you wouldn't have come,' Emerahl continued. 'So I'll have to teach you to do it yourself.'

She caught at a chain around her neck and drew it over her head. The girl caught her breath as she saw the pendant hanging from it. It was a simple hardened droplet of sap, taken from a dembar tree. In the light of the fire it glowed a deep orange. Emerahl held it at arm's length.

'Look at it closely.'

The girl obeyed, her eyes wide.

'Listen to my voice. I want you to keep your eyes on this droplet. Look inside it. See the colour. At the same time, be aware of the warmth of the fire beside you.' Emerahl continued talking, watching the girl's face carefully. When the intervals between the girl's blinks had lengthened, she moved her foot. The eyes fixed on the pendant did not shift. Nodding to herself, she told the girl to reach toward the droplet. Slowly the girl's hand extended.

'Now stop, just there, close but not quite touching the droplet. Feel the heat of the fire. Can you feel the heat?'

The girl nodded slowly.

'Good. Now imagine that you are drawing heat from the fire. Imagine that your body is full of its gentle warmth. Do you feel warm? Yes. Now send that warmth to the droplet.'

At once the sap began to glow. The girl blinked, then stared at the pendant in amazement. The glow faded again.

'What happened?'

'You just used a little magic,' Emerahl told her. She lowered the pendant and put it back around her neck.

'I have Gifts?'

'Of course you do. Every man and woman has Gifts. Most don't have much more than what it takes to light a candle. You have more Gift than that, however.'

The girl's eyes were bright with excitement. Emerahl chuckled. She had seen that expression many times before. 'But don't go thinking you're going to be a great sorceress, girl. You're not *that* Gifted.'

That had the desired sobering effect. 'What can I do?'

'You can persuade others to think twice before paying you more attention than you want. A simple shock of pain as a warning, and a numbing for those who don't take it or are too drunk to feel pain. I'll teach you both – and give you a little piece of advice to go with it. Learn the art of the flattering or humorous refusal. You might wish to see them robbed of their dignity, but a wounded pride will crave revenge. I have no time to teach you something as complex as how to unlock a door or stop a knife.'

The girl nodded soberly. 'I'll try, though I'm not sure it'll work on my father.'

Emerahl hesitated. So it was like that. 'Well, then. I'll teach you these tricks tonight, but you must practise them afterwards. It's like playing a bone whistle. You might remember how a tune goes, but if you don't practise playing it your fingers lose the knack.'

The girl nodded again, this time eagerly. Emerahl paused to regard her student wistfully. Though this one's life had been hard, she was still so blissfully ignorant of the world, still full of hope. She looked down at her own withered hands. *Am I any different, despite all the years I have on her? My time is long past and the world has moved on, but I'm still clinging to life. Why do I, the last of my kind, continue on like this?*

Because I can, she replied to herself.

Smiling crookedly, she began to teach yet another young girl how to defend herself.

CHAPTER 3

The Temple did not post guards at its entrance. In principle, all were free to enter. Once inside, however, visitors needed directing to those who could best serve their needs, so all initiates to the priesthood spent some of their time employed as guides.

Initiate Rimo didn't mind this part of his duties. Most of the time it involved wandering along the paths of the Temple, basking in the sunshine and telling people where to go, which was much easier and more satisfying than lessons on law and healing. Something amusing happened during nearly every shift, and afterwards he and his fellow initiates would gather together and compare stories.

After several days of greeting visiting monarchs, nobles and other dignitaries, none of the initiates were particularly impressed by tales of meeting important people any more. Stories of the strange antics of ordinary visitors hadn't regained their popularity, either. Rimo knew that only something as extraordinary as meeting Auraya of the White would gain him any admiration, and there was as much chance of that as . . .

Rimo stopped and stared in disbelief as a tall, bearded man walked through the White Arch. *A Dreamweaver? Here?* He had never seen one of the heathens in the Temple before. They wouldn't dare enter the most sacred of Circlian places.

Rimo glanced around, expecting to see someone hurrying after the Dreamweaver. His stomach sank as he realised he was the only guide standing close by. For a moment he considered pretending he hadn't noticed the heathen, but that might be regarded as being just as bad as inviting the man into the sacred buildings. With a sigh, Rimo forced himself to go after the man.

As he drew near, the Dreamweaver stopped and turned to regard him. *I only have to find out what he wants,* Rimo told himself. *And then tell him to leave. But what if he won't go? What if he tries to force his way in? Well, there's plenty of priests about to help if it comes to that.*

'May I assist you?' Rimo asked stiffly.

The Dreamweaver's gaze fixed somewhere past Rimo's head. Or perhaps *inside* his head.

'I have a message to deliver.'

The heathen drew a cylinder out from under his robes. Rimo frowned. A message to deliver? That would mean allowing the heathen to continue further into the Temple grounds, perhaps even enter the buildings. He couldn't let that happen.

'Give it to me,' he demanded. 'I will see that it is delivered.'

To Rimo's relief, the Dreamweaver handed him the scroll. 'Thank you,' he said, then turned and walked back toward the gate.

Rimo looked down at the cylinder in his hands. It was a simple wooden message-holder. As he read the recipient's name inked onto the side he drew in a quick breath of astonishment. He stared at the Dreamweaver. This was just too strange. The recipient was 'High Priestess Auraya'. Why was a heathen delivering messages to Auraya of the White?

Perhaps the man had stolen it in order to see the contents.

Rimo examined the cylinder carefully, but the seal was whole and there were no signs of tampering. Still, it was too strange. Other priests might ask questions. He considered the retreating man's back, then made himself stride forward in pursuit.

'Dreamweaver.'

The man stopped and looked back, and his brow creased with a frown.

'How is it that you were charged with the delivery of this message?' Rimo demanded.

The man's lips thinned. 'I wasn't. I encountered the courier a few days ago, drunk and unconscious beside the road. Since I am acquainted with the recipient, and was headed in this direction, I decided to bring it myself.'

Rimo glanced at the name on the scroll. Acquainted with the recipient? Surely not. Still, it was always better to be cautious.

'Then I will see she gets this immediately,' he said.

Rimo turned away quickly and started toward the White Tower. After several steps he glanced back and saw that, to his relief, the Dreamweaver had passed through the arched entrance of the Temple and was walking toward the west side of the city. He looked at the recipient's name again and smiled. If he was lucky, he might get to deliver this personally. Now *that* would be a story to tell.

Feeling excitement growing, he lengthened his stride and hurried toward the entrance of the White Tower.

The Sennon ambassador began another long digression into a story from his land's history – something his people were in the habit of doing when making a point. Auraya's expression shifted slightly. To all who had observed this meeting she would have appeared absorbed by the man's conversation. Danjin was beginning to read her better and saw signs of forced patience. Like most plain-speaking Hanians, she was finding the Sennon's endlessly embellished conversation tedious.

'We would be honoured, indeed pleased beyond rapture, if you were to visit the city of stars. Since the gods chose the great Juran a century ago we have been blessed with only nine opportunities to receive and accommodate the Gods' Chosen. It would be wonderful, do you not agree, if the newest of the gods' representatives should be the next to walk the streets of Karienne and climb the dunes of Hemmed?'

That's all? Danjin suppressed a sigh. The ambassador's elaborate speech had been leading to nothing more than an invitation to visit his country. *Though he is also pointing out that the White rarely visit Sennon. It would be no surprise if the Sennons were feeling a bit neglected.*

The trouble was, Sennon was separated from Hania by a mountain range and a desert, and the road to Karienne was a long and difficult one. Dunway was also located across the mountains, but could at least be reached by sea. Sennon's main port was situated on the opposite end of the continent. In good weather a sea journey could take months. In bad, it could take longer than the overland route. If Sennon did eventually become an ally, the White would have to make that journey more often.

Danjin suspected that the other reason the White were reluctant to invest time in the journey was that a large number of Sennons still worshipped dead gods. The emperors of Sennon, past and present, had always supported the belief that their people should be free to worship whoever and whatever they wanted, and that whether the gods these people worshipped were real or not wasn't for rulers to decide. They would probably continue to do so as long as the Sennon 'religion tax' added to their wealth.

Only one cult objected to the situation as loudly as Circlians.

They called themselves the Pentadrians. Like the Circlians, they followed five gods, but that was the only similarity. Their gods did not exist, so they beguiled their followers with tricks and enchantments. It was said the Pentadrians sacrificed slaves to these gods, and indulged in orgiastic fertility rituals. No doubt these acts ensured that their followers did not dare to doubt the existence of their gods, lest he or she find there had been no justification for their depravity.

Auraya glanced at Danjin and he felt his face heat with embarrassment. He was supposed to be paying attention to the ambassador's continuing ramble in order to provide her with a ready source of insight. *I guess I was providing insight – just not the kind she can use right at this moment.*

The door to the room opened and Dyara entered. Danjin noted with amusement the way the older woman examined Auraya critically, like a mother looking for faults in her child's behaviour. He resisted a smile. It would take time before Auraya carried herself with the same air of self-assurance that Dyara had. Auraya was in an interesting position, having moved from one of the highest positions a mortal priestess could attain to what was, as far as age and experience went, the lowest position among the immortals.

'A message has arrived from your home, Auraya,' Dyara said. 'Do you wish to receive it now?'

Auraya's eyes brightened. 'Yes. Thank you.'

Dyara stepped aside, allowing an initiate of the priesthood to enter and hesitantly present a message cylinder.

Auraya smiled at the young man, then blinked in surprise. As Dyara ushered the messenger from the room Auraya broke the seal and tipped out a slip of paper. Danjin could see that there were few marks on the vellum. He heard a sharply indrawn breath and looked at Auraya closely. She had turned pale.

Auraya glanced at Dyara who frowned and turned to the

ambassador. 'I trust you have enjoyed your visit to the Temple, Ambassador Shemeli. Might I accompany you on your way out?'

The man hesitated, then bowed slightly. 'I would be most honoured, Dyara of the White.' He formed a circle with both hands and bowed his head to Auraya. 'It was a pleasure speaking to you, Auraya of the White. I hope that we may continue our acquaintance soon.'

She met his eyes and nodded. 'As do I.'

As Dyara drew the man out of the room, Danjin studied Auraya closely. The newest White was gazing intently at a vase, but he was sure it was not the subject of her attention. Was that a glitter of tears in her eyes?

Danjin looked away, not wanting to discomfort her by staring. As the silence continued he began to feel uncomfortable. There was something a little unsettling about seeing one of the White tearful, he mused. They were supposed to be strong. In control. *But she isn't exactly an old hand at this*, he reminded himself. *And I'd prefer that those who guided humans in matters of law and morality still had human feelings rather than none at all.*

The door opened and Dyara stepped inside again, her hand lingering on the door handle.

'I'm sorry, Auraya. Spend the rest of the day as you wish. I will come and see you this evening when I am free.'

'Thank you,' Auraya replied softly.

Dyara looked at Danjin then nodded toward the door. He rose and followed her out of the room.

'Bad news?' he asked when the door had closed.

'Her mother has died.' Dyara grimaced. 'It is unfortunate timing. Go home, Danjin Spear. Come back tomorrow at the usual time.'

Danjin nodded and made the sign of the circle. Dyara strode

away. He looked down the corridor toward the staircase, then back at the door of the room he had just left. A free afternoon. He hadn't had a moment to himself for several days. He could visit the Grand Market and spend some of the money he was earning on gifts for his wife and daughters. He could do some reading.

A memory of Auraya's pale face slipped into his mind. *She will be grieving*, he thought. *Is there anyone here to comfort her? A friend? Maybe one of the priests?*

All ideas of visiting markets and reading evaporated. He sighed and knocked on the door. After a pause, the door opened. Auraya looked at him questioningly, then smiled wanly as she read his mind.

'I'll be fine, Danjin.'

'Is there anything I can do? Someone I can fetch?'

She shook her head, then frowned. 'Perhaps there is. Not to fetch, but to locate. Find out where the man who delivered the message to the Temple is staying. The initiate, Rimo, should be able to describe him. If he is who I suspect he is, his name is Leiard.'

Danjin nodded. 'If he's still in the city, I'll find him.'

Not far to his left, three women were standing at a table preparing the night's meal. They were barely aware of their hands deftly kneading, stirring or slicing as they chatted among themselves, discussing the coming marriage of their employer's daughter.

Behind, and further away, a man had reached an almost meditative state of mind as he shaped the clay between his hands into a bowl. Satisfied, he cut it from the wheel with a length of wire and set it down among the others he had made, then reached for some more clay.

To the right, a youth hurried past, tired and dispirited. His parents had fought yet again. As always, it had ended in the dull thud of fists on flesh and whimpers of pain. He considered the foreigners who still filled the market, seemingly oblivious to the existence of pickpockets, and his heart lightened. Easy pickings tonight.

Far to the right, but louder, a mother was arguing with her daughter. The fight ended with a surge of satisfaction and anger as the daughter slammed the door between them.

Leiard drew in a deep breath and let these and other minds fade from his senses. The ache in his body had changed to a more bearable weariness. He was tempted to lie down and sleep, but that would leave him wakeful in the evening, and he had already endured enough restless nights wondering if he had made the right decision in taking the message from the courier.

Someone had to take it, he thought. *Why did Fa-Dyer trust that boy to deliver it?*

The harvest was probably underway. Few could be spared for the task of delivering a message. The boy might have offered to take it in order to get out of the hard work, Fa-Dyer must not have known of his lazy nature.

Leiard had managed to extract enough from the drink-befuddled boy to work out why Auraya's father had sent a message rather than ask Priest Avorim to communicate it mentally. The priest was sick. He'd collapsed several days before.

So, with the priest ill, Fa-Dyer had no choise but to send a courier. Leiard had no idea how ill Priest Avorim was. The old man could be dying. If he didn't find another courier Auraya might not receive the news of her mother's death.

Ironically, Leiard had only encountered the drunken courier because Ma-Dyer's death had freed him to leave. Every year he travelled to a town a few days' walk from Oralyn to buy cures he could not make himself. The boy had given him what remained of the money Fa-Dyer had provided for food and board, but when Leiard reached the town he discovered it was not enough to buy another courier's services.

Leiard had considered taking the message to the town's priest, but when he imagined himself explaining how he came by it he could not see any priest believing him. That left him with two choices: take the message back to Fa-Dyer, who did not need an extra source of disappointment and distress right now, or deliver it himself. He only had to hand it over to one of the gatekeepers of the Temple, he'd reasoned.

But there hadn't been any gatekeepers or guards. Remembering the moment when he had arrived at the Temple entrance, Leiard felt his skin prickle. He had been too preoccupied with the bustle of people around him to notice the great white Tower stretching above the city buildings. Only when he had reached the archway over the Temple entrance did he see it.

Something about it chilled him to the core. A part of him had felt wonder and admiration for the skill that must have gone into its creation. Another part of him shrank away, urging him to turn and leave as quickly as possible.

His determination to deliver the message kept him there. He hadn't travelled this far only to scurry away. But there had been nobody at the entrance for him to give the message to, and none of the priests and priestesses within looked inclined to approach him. He'd had to pass through the arch in order to gain anyone's attention. After he had passed the message to a young priest he had left quickly, relieved to be free of it at last.

Jarime had grown and changed since he had last visited, but that was the nature of cities. The dense mix of people was both stimulating and wearying. It had taken several hours of walking before he found a boarding place for Dreamweavers.

It was owned by Tanara and Millo Baker, a couple of modest income who had inherited a small apartment block. Their son, Jayim, had chosen to become a Dreamweaver, inspiring them to offer lodging to Dreamweavers who passed through the city. They lived on the first floor and rented the ground floor to shopkeepers.

Tanara had shown him to a room and left him there to rest. Leiard could not resist the temptation to enter a trance in order to skim the thoughts of the urban dwellers around him. They were like people everywhere, immersed in lives that were as varied as the fish in the ocean. Bright and dark. Hard and easy. Generous and selfish. Hopeful. Determined. Resigned. He had also sensed the mind of his hostess in the kitchen below, thinking she must call Leiard to dinner soon. She was also hoping he would help her son.

Taking another deep breath, Leiard opened his eyes. Jayim's teacher had died last winter and no Dreamweaver had chosen to replace him. Leiard knew he must disappoint them again. He would be returning to the village tomorrow. Even if he had wanted to take on another student, Jayim would have to return with him. The Bakers would probably rather Jayim remained untaught than have him leave them.

If Jayim wanted to come with me, would I take him? Leiard felt the pull of obligation. Dreamweavers were few in number now, and it would be a shame if this youth gave up for lack of teachers. Perhaps when he met the boy he would consider it. He had, after all, been prepared to teach Auraya if she had wanted it.

Standing up, he stretched and moved to a narrow bench where Tanara had placed a large basin of water and some rough towels. He washed himself slowly, dressed in his spare set of tunic and trousers and shrugged into his Dreamweaver vest. Leaving the room, he moved into the communal area at the centre of the house and found Tanara sitting on an old cushion, her brow furrowed with concentration. Bread was cooking on a large flat stone suspended on two bricks. There was no fire beneath the stones, so she must be using magic to heat them.

'Dreamweaver Leiard,' she said, the wrinkles deepening around her eyes as she smiled. 'We don't have any servants and I prefer to cook than buy that muck from the shop next door. I've only eaten their food twice, and was sick both times. They are prompt with the rent, though, so I shouldn't complain.' She nodded toward a doorway. 'Jayim has returned.'

Leiard turned to see a young man sprawled on an old wooden bench in the next room. His Dreamweaver vest lay on the floor beside him. Sweat stained his tunic.

'Jayim, this is Dreamweaver Leiard,' Tanara called out. 'Keep him company while I finish here.'

The young Dreamweaver looked up and, seeing Leiard, blinked in surprise. He straightened on the bench as Leiard moved into the room. 'Hello,' he said.

'Greetings,' Leiard replied. *No traditional welcome from this one, then. Was it lack of training, or simply disdain for ritual?*

Leiard sat in a chair opposite Jayim. He looked at the vest. The boy followed his gaze, then quickly picked it up and draped it over the back of the bench.

'Bit hot today, isn't it?' he said. 'Have you been to the city before?'

'Yes. Long ago,' Leiard replied.

'How long ago?'

Leiard frowned. 'I'm not sure exactly.'

The boy shrugged. 'Then it must be a long time ago. Has it changed a lot?'

'I noted a few changes, but I cannot judge well as I have seen only part of the city since I arrived this afternoon,' Leiard replied. 'It sounds as though eating at the street shops is as perilous as it has always been.'

Jayim chuckled. 'Yes, but there are some good ones. Will you be staying long?'

Leiard shook his head. 'No, I leave tomorrow.'

The boy did not hide his relief well. 'Back to . . . where was it?'

'Oralyn.'

'Where is that?'

'Near the Dunwayan border, at the base of the mountains.'

Jayim opened his mouth to speak, but froze at the sound of knocking. 'Someone's at the door, Mother.'

'Then answer it.'

'But . . .' Jayim looked at Leiard. 'I'm keeping our guest company.'

Tanara sighed and stood up. She crossed to the main door, out of sight. Leiard listened to the slap of her sandals on the tiled floor. He heard the sound of a door opening, then female voices. Two sets of footsteps returned.

'We have a customer,' Tanara announced as she entered the room. A woman wrapped in a generous swathe of dark cloth entered. The cloth was draped over her head, hiding her face.

'I haven't come for healing,' the woman said. 'I am here to see an old friend.'

The voice sent a shiver up Leiard's spine, but he was not sure why. He found himself rising to his feet. The woman pulled back the cloth from her head and smiled.

'Greetings, Dreamweaver Leiard.'

Her face had changed. She had lost all the roundness of childhood, revealing an elegant jaw and brow and high cheekbones. Her hair had been dressed into an elaborate style favoured by the rich and fashionable. She seemed taller.

But her eyes were the same. Large, expressive and bright

with intelligence, they gazed at him searchingly. *She must be wondering if I remember her*, he thought. *I do, but not like this.*

Auraya had grown into a strikingly beautiful woman. It would never have been apparent in the village. She would have seemed too fragile and thin. The fashion of the city suited her better.

The fashion of the city? She did not come here to be fashionable, but to become a priestess. At that thought he remembered his hosts. Knowing they had a Circlian priestess in their house might frighten them – especially a high priestess. *At least Auraya had the sense to cover her priestess's clothes.* He turned to Tanara.

'Is there a place the lady and I might talk privately?'

Tanara smiled. 'Yes. On the roof. It's nice out there on a summer evening. Follow me.'

The woman led them through the communal room to the staircase opposite the main door. As he emerged onto the roof, Leiard was surprised to find it was covered with potted plants and worn wooden seats. He could see neighbouring apartments and other people relaxing in rooftop gardens.

'I'll get you some cool drinks,' Tanara said, then disappeared downstairs.

Auraya sat down opposite Leiard and sighed. 'I should have sent you a message warning that I was coming. Or arranged to meet you somewhere. But as soon as I learned you were here . . .' She smiled crookedly. 'I had to come straightaway.'

He nodded. 'You need to talk about your mother with someone who knew her,' he guessed.

Her smile faded. 'Yes. How did she . . . ?'

'Age and sickness.' He spread his hands. 'Her illness took a greater toll as she grew older. Eventually it was going to defeat her.'

Auraya nodded. 'So that was all? Nothing else?'

He shook his head. 'It is easy, after a long time keeping a sickness at bay, to be surprised when it claims a person.'

She grimaced. 'Yes – especially when the timing is . . . unfortunate.' She let out a long sigh. 'How is Father?'

'He was well when I left. Grieving, of course, but also accepting.'

'You told the initiate that you found the message in the hands of a drunken courier. Do you know why Priest Avorim has not contacted me?'

'The courier claims he is sick.'

She nodded. 'He must be so old now. Poor Avorim. I gave him such a hard time during his lessons. And you.' She looked up and gazed at him, smiling faintly. 'It's strange. I recognise you, but you look different.'

'How so?'

'Younger.'

'Children think all adults are old.'

'Especially when those adults have white hair,' she said. She pulled at the cloth covering her. 'It's a bit hot to be so dressed up,' she continued. 'I was worried that if people saw me arrive it would bring your hosts trouble.'

'I'm not sure what it is like for Dreamweavers in the city.'

'But you believe your hosts would be frightened if they knew who I was,' she guessed.

'Probably.'

She frowned. 'I don't want them to fear me. I don't like it. I wish . . .' She sighed. 'But who am I to want to change the way people are?'

He regarded her closely. 'You are in a better position than most.'

She stared at him, then smiled self-consciously. 'I guess I am. The question is: will the gods allow it?'

'You're not thinking of asking, are you?'

Her eyebrows rose. 'Maybe.'

Seeing the bright glint in her eye, Leiard felt an unexpected affection for her. It seemed some of the curious, relentlessly questioning child remained in her. He wondered if she let her peers encounter it, and how well they coped.

I can even imagine her drilling the gods about the nature of the universe, he thought, laughing silently to himself. Then he sobered. *Asking questions is easy. Making change is harder.*

'When do you plan to leave?' she asked.

'Tomorrow.'

'I see.' She looked away. 'I had hoped you might be staying longer. Perhaps a few days. I'd like to talk to you again.'

He considered her request. *Just a few days.* Footsteps from the staircase hailed the return of Tanara. She appeared carrying a tray bearing pottery goblets and a dish of dried fruit. She lowered the tray and offered it to Auraya. As Auraya reached out to take a goblet Tanara gasped and the tray dropped.

Leiard noticed Auraya's fingers flex slightly. The tray stopped, the contents of the goblets sloshing, and remained suspended in the air. He looked up at Tanara. The woman was staring at Auraya. He realised that the cloth covering Auraya's shoulders had slipped and the edge of her circ was showing.

He stood up and placed his hands on Tanara's shoulders. 'You have nothing to fear,' he said soothingly. 'Yes, she is a priestess. But she is also an old friend of mine. From the village near my—'

Tanara gripped his hand, her eyes wide. 'Not a priestess,' she gasped. 'More than a priestess. She's . . . she's . . .' She stared at Leiard. 'You're a friend of *Auraya of the White?*'

'I . . .' Auraya of the *what?* He looked down at Auraya, who wore a grimace of embarrassment. He looked at the circ. It bore no gold edging of a high priestess.

70

It bore no edging at all.

'When did this happen?' he found himself asking.

She smiled apologetically. 'Nine, ten days ago.'

'Why didn't you tell me?'

'I was waiting for the right moment.'

Tanara let go of Leiard's hand. 'I'm sorry. I did not mean to spoil the surprise.'

Auraya laughed ruefully. 'It doesn't matter.' She took the tray and put it on the bench beside her. 'I should be apologising for causing you so much distress. I should have arranged to meet Leiard elsewhere.'

Tanara shook her head. 'No! You're welcome here. Any time you wish to visit please don't hesitate to—'

Auraya's eyes narrowed a fraction, then she smiled broadly and stood up. 'Thank you, Tanara Baker. That means more to me than you can know. But for now I feel I must apologise for disrupting your evening.' She drew the cloth close around herself. 'And I should return to the Temple.'

'Oh . . .' Tanara looked at Leiard apologetically. 'I'll take you to the door.'

'Thank you.'

As the two women left, Leiard slowly sat down. *Auraya is one of the White.*

Bitterness overwhelmed him. He had seen the potential in her. She was intelligent but not arrogant. She was curious about other peoples, but not contemptuous of them.

Her ability to learn and use Gifts was greater than any student he had taught.

Of course they had chosen her. He'd even told himself that it was better that she had joined the Circlians, because with the restrictions of a Dreamweaver life much of her potential would be wasted.

And how much better is it now that she is one of the immortal

71

White? he asked himself bitterly. *The world can benefit from her talents for evermore.*

And her loss will torment you for all eternity.

The thought startled him. It sounded like his own mental voice, yet it felt like the mental voice of another person.

'Leiard?'

He looked up. Tanara had returned.

'Are you well?'

'A little surprised,' he said dryly.

Tanara moved to the opposite seat. The one Auraya had been sitting in. 'You didn't know?'

He shook his head. 'It seems my little Auraya has come much further in the world than I thought.'

'Your *little* Auraya?'

'Yes. I knew her as a child. Taught her, too. She probably knows more about Dreamweaver healing than any priest or priestess.'

Tanara's eyebrows rose. She looked away, her expression thoughtful. Then she shook her head. 'I can barely comprehend this,' she said in a hushed voice. 'You're a friend of Auraya of the White.'

From behind them came a choking sound. Leiard turned to find Jayim standing on the staircase, his eyes wide in surprise at what he'd overheard.

'Jayim,' Tanara said, leaping up and pushing her son back inside. 'You can't tell anybody about this. Listen—'

Leiard rose and followed them down the stairs, going into his room. His dirty clothes still hung over the back of a chair. His bag was half empty, its contents spread over the bed.

Sitting down, he swiftly stowed everything away again. As he placed the dirty robe in the top of his bag, he heard footsteps and turned to see Tanara stop in the doorway. She glanced at the bag and her expression hardened.

'I thought so,' she muttered. 'Sit down, Leiard. I want to talk with you before you run off to your forest home.'

He lowered himself onto the bed reluctantly. She sat down next to him.

'Let me just check what I have heard. You said you taught Auraya when she was a child. You mean Dreamweaver lore?'

He nodded. 'I had hoped she might join me.' He shook his head. 'Well, you can see how *that* turned out.'

Tanara patted him on the shoulder. 'It must have been frustrating. Strange that the gods would choose her, then. Surely they must know she was taught by a Dreamweaver.'

'Perhaps they knew where her heart truly lay,' he muttered bitterly.

Tanara ignored that. 'It must have been odd talking to her again, even when you thought she was merely a high priestess. You sounded like you were getting along well enough when I arrived. Obviously you didn't notice any change. You would have if this Choosing had turned her into someone different.'

'I know I said we were friends,' he replied. 'But I said that to reassure you. Until today I hadn't seen her in ten years.'

Tanara absorbed that silently.

'Consider this, Leiard,' she murmured after a while. 'Auraya obviously wants to continue to be your friend. One of the White wanting to be friends with a Dreamweaver ought to be impossible, but it clearly isn't. And if Auraya of the White is friends with a Dreamweaver, maybe other Circlians will treat Dreamweavers better.' Her voice lowered. 'Now, you've got two choices. You can leave and return to your forest, or you can stay here with us and keep this friendship going.'

'It's not that simple,' he argued. 'There are risks. What if the other White disapprove?'

'I doubt they'd do anything more than tell you to leave.' She leaned closer. 'I think that's worth the risk.'

'And if the people decide they don't like it? They might take matters into their own hands.'

'If she values your friendship she'll stop them.'

'She might not be able to – especially if the White will not support her.'

Tanara leaned back to regard him. 'I don't deny there are risks. I only ask that you consider. You must do what your heart tells you.'

Standing up, she left the room, drawing the door shut behind her. Leiard closed his eyes and sighed.

Tanara is ignoring one simple fact: the gods would not have chosen anyone sympathetic to Dreamweavers, he told himself.

But they *had* chosen Auraya. Either she had developed a dislike of Dreamweavers, or they were playing a different game. He considered the possibilities. If they took an intelligent and Gifted woman who was sympathetic to Dreamweavers and caused her to turn against them, she might bring a new and fatal force to the Circlian hatred of heathens. She might be the one to destroy the Dreamweavers completely.

And if he ran away and left her, alone and grieving, he might be the first to give her a reason to resent his people.

Curse the gods, he thought. *I have to stay. At least until I know what's going on.*

CHAPTER 4

The heat from the summer sun was stronger on the upper slopes of the mountains. As Tryss felt sweat beginning to run down his brow again, he straightened and shook his head. Droplets landed on the frame of the harness and were quickly absorbed by the dry wood. He pulled off his string-reed vest and laid it aside. Then, bending closer, he carefully stretched strips of flexible gut between the harness joints.

Much of the harness lay in pieces. He was trying to duplicate the lever system so he could carry four spikes instead of two. Already he was beginning to doubt that he could get off the ground while carrying something this heavy. Perhaps he would have to haul it up a tree or a cliff before launching himself into the air.

That wouldn't impress people, however. He had decided he wasn't going to show anyone this new harness until he'd had several successful hunts. Whenever he brought a creature down he would let it sleep off the drug, but when the time came to prove himself he would butcher his catch and carry meat back to the Open. When the other Siyee saw his family feasting, their jeers and mockery would stop.

He paused to sigh. If only his cousins had followed him quietly instead of telling other Siyee what Tryss had claimed to have done. Then only they and Drilli would have been present when Tryss arrived to find the yern gone. Since that day the story of his wild claim had spread throughout the Open. He was teased constantly, sometimes by Siyee he didn't even know.

A prick of pain stung his arm and he jumped. The gut string slipped from between his fingers and flicked away. He cursed and examined his arm. A small red dot had appeared. Had something stung him? He looked around, but could see no insect buzzing nearby that might have made such a bite.

Just as he was searching the ground for crawling insects he felt another sting, this time on his thigh. He looked down in time to see something small and round fall to the ground. Bending closer, he noticed a winnet seed among the stones of the rock face. They were bright green and hard to miss, especially as winnet seeds weren't found this high up in the mountains. The small tree grew alongside creeks and rivers, not on dry rocky slopes.

A small click brought his attention back to the harness just in time for him to see another seed fall from the frame to the rocks, then roll away. He slowly disentangled himself from his invention and stood up, casting about. In the corner of his eye he saw a movement and felt a sting on his shoulder. He spun around and started toward a large rock near where he had seen the movement.

Then he heard his name whistled from above.

Looking up, he felt his heart jump as he recognised Drilli's wing markings. He searched the sky quickly, but there was no sign of his cousins. His heart began to beat faster as she circled lower.

There was a broad grin on her face. 'Tryss!' she called. 'I think I lost . . .' Her gaze shifted away and he saw her smile change to a look of outrage. At the same time he felt another sting, this time on his cheek. He cursed in pain and put a hand to his face.

'Fools!' she shrieked. Tryss caught his breath as she dropped into a dive and landed beside the rock he had been heading toward. She disappeared and Tryss heard a slap, then a Síyee staggered out from behind the rock, arms raised to protect his head as Drilli swiped at him again and again.

Ziss! Tryss heard laughter from behind him and turned to find Trinn climbing up the rock shelf toward them. Drilli stormed over to him and snatched something out of his hands.

'I told you not to use them on Siyee!' she said. 'What if you tore his wings? Stupid girri-brain! If I'd known you'd do something like this I'd never have made them for you.'

'We wouldn't have got his wings,' Trinn said. 'We've been practising.'

'What on?' she demanded.

Trinn shrugged. 'Trees. Rocks.'

'Girri?'

He looked away. 'No.'

'It was you, wasn't it? And you watched me spend half the night weaving string-reed mats to console Aunt Lirri. She thinks her girri died from neglect.'

'She was going to eat them anyway,' Ziss protested.

Drilli whirled around to glare at him. 'You two disgust me. Go away. I don't want to see you again.'

The cousins exchanged a look of dismay, though it was clear Ziss wasn't as bothered by her words as Trinn. He shrugged and turned away, running a few steps then leaping into the sky.

'Sorry,' Trinn offered. When Drilli turned to glare at him he winced, then followed his brother.

Drilli watched them until they were small dark marks against the distant clouds near the horizon, then she turned to Tryss and grimaced.

'I'm sorry about that,' she said.

He shrugged. 'Not your fault.'

'Yes, it is,' she replied, anger returning to her voice. 'I know what they're like. I shouldn't have shown them what the pipes were for, let alone made them a set.'

He looked at the object in her hand. It was a long piece of reed. 'Pipes?'

'Yes.' She smiled and held the tube out to him. 'A blow-pipe. We started using them in our village to hunt small animals. You put a missile in here and—'

'I know how they work,' Tryss said, then winced at his own terseness. 'But I haven't seen one used before,' he added in a more encouraging tone. 'Could you show me?'

She smiled and plucked the tube from his hands. Taking something from her pocket, she slipped it into the pipe. He heard a faint click as it met with something else inside that must have prevented it from coming out the other end. She turned and pointed.

'See that rock over there that looks a bit like a foot?'

'Yes.'

'See the black stone on the top?'

'Yes . . .' He glanced at her doubtfully. It was a long way away.

She put the pipe to her lips and blew into it quickly. Tryss barely saw the missile, but a moment later the black stone bounced off the rock and disappeared over the other side.

Tryss stared at Drilli in surprise. *She's not just pretty and strong*, he thought. *She's clever as well*. She looked back at him and grinned, and suddenly he didn't know what to say. He felt his face beginning to heat.

'So is this where you disappear to?' she asked, her gaze sliding to the harness.

He shrugged. 'Sometimes.'

She moved over to the harness and gazed down at it. 'This is how you caught the yern, isn't it?'

So she believed he'd actually caught one. Or was she just saying so to be nice?

'Um . . . yes.'

'Show me how it works.'

'It's . . . it's . . .' He waved his hands uselessly. 'I'm changing it. It's all in pieces.'

She nodded. 'I understand. Another day, then. When you're finished.' She sat down beside the harness. 'Mind if I watch you work?'

'I suppose. If you want.' He dropped into a crouch and, conscious of her attention on him, rummaged in his pockets for more gut strings. She watched silently, and soon he began to feel uncomfortable.

'How long have your people been using blowpipes?' he asked.

She shrugged. 'Years. My grandfather came up with the idea. He said we have to go backward instead of forward. Rather than trying to find a way to use swords and bows like the landwalkers, we should go back to simpler weapons.' She sighed. 'It didn't help, though. The landwalkers still drove us out of our village. We got a few with poisoned darts and traps, but there were too many.'

Tryss glanced at her sideways. 'Do you think it would have turned out differently if you had been able to attack them from the air?'

She shook her head. 'I don't know. Maybe; maybe not.' She looked at the harness. 'Don't know until we try. Are you . . . are you going to the Gathering tonight?'

Tryss shrugged. 'I don't know.'

'I've heard a landwalker arrived last night. Climbed over the mountains to get here. He'll be at the Gathering.'

'They didn't kill him?' Tryss asked, surprised.

'No. He's not one of the people taking our land. He's from far away.'

'What does he want?'

'Not sure exactly, but my father said something about this man being sent by the gods. To ask us to join something. If we do, other landwalkers might help us get rid of the ones taking our lands.'

'If they can do that, then they can take our lands themselves,' Tryss pointed out.

Drilli frowned. 'I hadn't thought of that. But the gods sent him. Surely Huan wouldn't allow that if it meant we'd all be killed.'

'Who knows what the goddess intended?' Tryss said dryly. 'Maybe she's realised making us was a mistake, and this is a way to get rid of us.'

'Tryss!' Drilli said, shocked. 'You shouldn't speak of the goddess so.'

He smiled. 'Perhaps not. But if she is watching, she will have heard me thinking that. And if she can hear me thinking that, then she can see that I don't believe what I said.'

'Why say it then?'

'Because the possibility occurred to me, and I need to speak of it in order to realise I don't believe it.'

Drilli stared at him, then shook her head. 'You *are* a strange boy, Tryss.' She nodded at the harness. 'Are you taking that to the Gathering tonight?'

'This? No. They'd laugh at me.'

'They might not.'

'I've shown people before. They think it'll be impossible to fly with it, or that it will make flying clumsy and dangerous, and even if I prove them wrong they won't believe it's possible to hunt with one. And at the moment I'm not sure it's going to work anyway. Two spikes don't seem like enough. I've been trying to change it so it carries more, but . . . but . . . it's complicated.'

'It looks it. But I'd give it a try. I wonder . . . could you make something that would allow me to use the blowpipe while flying?'

He looked at the pipe in her hands, then at the harness. She'd need some sort of frame to hold the pipe steady and a way to reload it with missiles. She could suck the missiles into the pipe from out of a bag. And the missiles were much smaller and lighter than spikes, so she could carry more . . . He sucked in a breath. But that was brilliant! As possibilities rushed through him, he felt his hands beginning to shake with excitement.

'Drilli,' he said.

'Mmm?'

'Can I . . . can I borrow that pipe?'

Auraya watched, fascinated, as her new pet chased an imaginary spider up the wall. He was a veez – a small, slim creature with a pointy nose, fluffy prehensile tail and large eyes that gave him excellent night vision. His soft toes splayed out across the painted surface, somehow allowing him to cling effortlessly to the wall – and now the ceiling. Stopping just above her, he suddenly dropped onto her shoulder.

'No fug,' he said, then leapt onto a chair and curled up with his speckled grey fluffy tail across his nose.

'No bug,' Auraya agreed. The animal's most remarkable trait was the ability to speak, though he talked only of the matters that concerned a small creature, like food and comfort. She doubted she'd have any enlightening philosophical discussions with him.

A knocking came from the door. 'Come in,' she called.

Dyara stepped inside. 'Auraya. How are you this morning?'

81

'Owaya,' a small voice repeated. Dyara's gaze shifted to the veez. 'Ah, I see the Somreyan Council of Elders have delivered their customary gift for a new White.'

Auraya nodded. 'Yes. Along with an amazingly elaborate array of toys and instructions.'

'Have you named him yet?'

'No.'

The older woman moved to the chair and extended a finger toward the veez. He sniffed, then cocked his head to one side and allowed Dyara to scratch behind his tiny pointed ears.

'Once you've learned to link your mind with his you'll find him useful. Just show him a mental picture of an object and he'll fetch it for you. He can find people, too, though it's easier if you give him something they've touched to catch a scent from.'

'The instructions said they make good scouts.'

Dyara smiled. 'Scouts being the polite term for spies. When you link with his mind you'll be able to see what he sees – and since their night vision is excellent and they can get into places humans can't, they do make good, ahem, scouts.' The veez's eyes were closed in bliss at her scratching. 'But you'll find you'll appreciate them as much for their nature. They're affectionate and loyal.' She stopped scratching and straightened. The veez's eyes opened wide and he stared up at her intently.

'Scatch?'

She ignored him and turned to Auraya. 'We'll be—'

'Scatch!'

'Enough,' she told him firmly. He ducked his head like a chastised child. 'They can also be a bit demanding at this age. Just be firm with him.' She moved away from the chair, then looked at Auraya sidelong, her expression unreadable. Not for the first time, Auraya wished she could read the other woman's mind as easily as she could now read most people's.

'You said last night that you had visited an old friend in the afternoon,' Dyara said. 'There are more than a few "scouts" in the city who are anxious to prove themselves and gain work from me, who take it upon themselves to report what they see. This morning one of them claims that this friend you visited is a Dreamweaver. Is this true?'

Auraya regarded Dyara carefully. What should she say? But she would not lie to one of the White. Nor would she pretend to feel guilty for visiting her old friend.

'Yes,' she replied. 'He is Dreamweaver Leiard, from my home village. I haven't seen him in ten years. He brought the message of my mother's death to the Temple. I wanted to thank him for that.'

'I gather he will be returning to his home again now that the message is delivered.'

'Probably.' Auraya shrugged. 'I doubt he'll stay here long. I can't imagine city life would suit him. He has always been a solitary type.'

Dyara nodded. 'The others will be at the Altar by now. We should not keep them waiting.'

Auraya felt her stomach flutter with both anxiety and excitement. For the first time she would sit with the other four White as they discussed their duties and responsibilities. They might give her a task to perform. If they did, she expected it would be a minor responsibility. Even if they didn't, it would be interesting to hear what worldly matters they were involved in.

Dyara's circ flared as she turned on her heel and strode to the door. Auraya followed. The cage was waiting for them. As they descended Auraya considered the 'scouts' Dyara had spoken of. She was disturbed by the news that strangers were watching her, but wondered if they truly had done so voluntarily. What was worse: that they had spied on her out of their own initiative, or that someone had asked them to?

Are my fellow White keeping an eye on me? If I arrange to meet Leiard again, will they try to discourage me? Should I let them? As the cage settled at the bottom of the stairwell, Auraya followed Dyara out. *The gods chose me. They knew everything about me, including my friendship with Leiard and sympathy for Dreamweavers. If they hadn't approved, they would have chosen someone else.*

Or would they? Perhaps they tolerated that one aspect of her character in order to make use of others. However, until they told her not to, she would continue associating with Dreamweavers.

She shivered. When the news of her mother's death had arrived she had feared the gods were making a point – that they were making it clear they disapproved of her use of a Dreamweaver's services by killing her mother.

Ridiculous, she thought. *The gods don't work that way. When they want something, they tell you.* Despite knowing this, she hadn't been able to shake the fear until Leiard had assured her that her mother's illness had been the cause of her death.

The air outside the Tower was warm and the sun's heat promised a hot day to come. Dyara's pace quickened. They reached the Dome, entered it and strode toward the dais and Altar at the centre.

The other three White were waiting for them, seated at a circular table. Auraya felt her pulse racing as she drew closer, and memories of the Choosing Ceremony flashed through her mind. She followed Dyara onto the Altar.

'Welcome, Auraya,' Juran said warmly.

She smiled and nodded. 'Thank you, Juran.'

As Dyara slipped into a seat, Auraya took the remaining chair. The five sides of the Altar began to move, hinging upward until their triangular points met. The walls glowed with a diffuse light.

Auraya glanced at the other White. Rian sat straight in his

chair, but his gaze was distant. Even when he looked at Auraya, and acknowledged her with a nod, he seemed distracted. Mairae looked exactly as she had ten years before when she had come to Oralyn to negotiate with the Dunwayans. This evidence of the White's immortality sent a shiver down Auraya's spine. *One day*, she thought, *someone will look at me and marvel at this sign of the god's powers.*

Meeting Auraya's gaze, Mairae smiled, then turned to look at Juran. The leader of the White had closed his eyes.

'Chaia, Huan, Lore, Yranna, Saru. Once again, we thank you for the peace and prosperity you have brought. We thank you for the opportunity to serve you. We thank you for the powers you have given us, that allow us to guide and help the men and women, old and young, of this world.'

'We thank you,' the others murmured. Auraya joined them, having been taught the ritual by Dyara.

'Today we will use the best of our wisdom in your service, but should we err in our judgement or work contrary to your great plans we ask you to speak to us and make your wishes known.'

'Guide us,' Auraya recited along with the others.

Juran opened his eyes and looked around the table.

'The gods have made it known to us that they wish for all of Northern Ithania to be united,' he said, looking at Auraya. 'Not by war or conquest, but through a peaceful alliance. They wish for all the lands to choose and negotiate the terms of their alliance with us. Those lands that are not predominantly Circlian are more likely to ally with us for reasons of politics and trade rather than obedience to the gods. Peoples like the Siyee and Elai, who are suspicious of landwalkers, need to learn to trust us. Those peoples who are predominantly Circlian would obey an order from the gods, but if they felt an alliance was not fair or beneficial they would cause trouble for other lands.'

Juran looked at Dyara. 'Let us discuss those allies we already have. Dyara?'

Dyara sighed and rolled her eyes. 'The Arrins of Genria and the King of Toren are still antagonising each other. Every time one of the Arrin families produces a son – which they seem to be doing every few months – Berro puts restrictions on imports from Genria. The royal high priest reminds him of the terms of the alliance, but it always takes several weeks for the restrictions to be lifted.'

'And the Genrians? How are they taking this?'

'With gritted teeth.' Dyara smiled. 'It's hardly their fault that Berro hasn't produced a male. So far there have been remarkably few retaliatory moves. Every family with a boy is anxious to avoid offending the gods. Evidence, perhaps, that they have realised that Guire chose Laern as his successor because he was the only prince who hadn't tried to murder another. But someone is making sure Berro hears promptly of the birth of every Arrin male.'

'Sounds like that someone ought to be found,' Juran said.

'Yes. The royal high priest is also encouraging Berro to adopt an heir, even if it is a temporary arrangement until he sires one. That might settle him down for now.'

Juran nodded, then turned to Mairae. 'What of the Somreyans?'

Mairae grimaced. 'They turned us down again.'

He frowned. 'What was their reason this time?'

'A minor detail of the alliance terms. One member of the council protested against it, and others supported her.'

'It's a wonder their country doesn't fall apart,' Dyara said darkly. 'Their council never agrees on anything. What was it this time?'

'The restriction that their Dreamweavers must only treat their own soldiers.'

'And this council member who protested is the Dreamweaver representative?'

Mairae nodded. 'Yes. Dreamweaver Elder Arleej.' Auraya knew that this Dreamweaver elder was not only a member of the Council of Elders in Somrey, but the leader of the Dreamweavers. 'I was surprised that others supported her. It is a minor point, and most of the council are keen to see this alliance signed. Keen enough to overlook something like this.'

'We knew Somrey would be difficult,' Rian said. 'We can't please every member of the council. Doing so would mean making too many compromises. I say we stand firm on this.'

Juran frowned and shook his head. 'I don't understand. We haven't asked them to change any of their ways. Why can't they do the same for us?'

The others shrugged or spread their hands helplessly. Juran looked at each, then his gaze settled on Auraya and his expression became thoughtful.

'You knew a Dreamweaver during your early years, didn't you, Auraya?'

His question was not accusatory, or even disapproving. She nodded slowly, aware that Dyara was watching her closely.

'You probably have a better understanding of their ways than the rest of us. Can you explain why they're resisting this term of the alliance?'

Auraya glanced around the table, then straightened.

'All Dreamweavers make an oath to heal any person who needs and wants it.'

Juran's eyebrows rose. 'So this term of the alliance requires Dreamweavers to break their oath. The council doesn't want to force them, so they refuse to sign the treaty.' He looked at Dyara. 'Does Auraya have time to read the proposed treaty?'

Dyara's shoulders lifted. 'I can make time for it in her schedule.'

Juran smiled. 'I look forward to hearing any suggestions you have, Auraya.' She smiled back, but he had already turned away. 'Rian. What of Dunway?'

Rian smiled faintly. 'The alliance is holding firm. I have nothing to report.'

'And Sennon?'

'The emperor is still considering our proposal. I don't believe he is any closer to a decision than he was five years ago.'

'That's no surprise,' Dyara said, chuckling. 'Nothing in Sennon ever happens quickly.'

Rian nodded. 'Sennon was always going to be more difficult to court than Somrey. How much value can we place in an alliance with a country that cannot decide who or what to worship?'

Juran nodded in agreement. 'I still feel it is best left to last. Perhaps, in the end, Sennon will fall into line when all the rest of Northern Ithania is united.' He straightened and smiled. 'That leaves us with two more nations to discuss.'

Auraya noted that Mairae's gaze had brightened, while Dyara's lips had compressed into a sceptical smile.

'Si and Borra.' Juran linked the fingers of his hands together. 'Several months ago I sent a courier to each country to deliver invitations for an alliance.'

Auraya felt a twinge of excitement. Stories of the winged people of the southern mountains and the water-breathing sea folk had always fascinated her. As she had grown older they had seemed too fantastic to be true, but both Priest Avorim and Leiard had assured her that such peoples did exist, though their description was often exaggerated.

'I'll be impressed if any of those messengers arrive,' Dyara muttered darkly. Auraya looked at her in surprise. 'Not that I think they'll murder them,' she assured Auraya. 'But the homes of the Siyee and Elai are not easy to reach, and they are suspicious and shy of ordinary humans.'

'I have chosen my couriers carefully,' Juran said. 'Both have visited or traded with these peoples previously.'

At that, Dyara looked impressed. Juran smiled, then placed both hands on the table. His expression became serious.

'We have not yet considered the three lands of Southern Ithania: Mur, Avven and Dekkar.'

'The lands of the Pentadrian cult?' Rian asked, his expression disapproving.

'Yes.' Juran grimaced. 'Their way of life and ethics may be incompatible with ours. The gods want all Northern Ithania united, not all Ithania. However, once Northern Ithania is united, the southern lands will be our neighbours. I have had our advisers gather information about these lands. Maps, drawings and reports of their beliefs and rituals.'

'Are there any descriptions of orgies?' Mairae asked.

'Mairae!' Dyara said reproachfully.

Juran's lips had twitched into a smile at the question. 'You'll be disappointed to hear that the rumours of orgies are exaggerated. They have fertility rites, but only for married *couples*. Two does not make an orgy.'

Mairae shrugged. 'At least I know I'm not missing out,' she murmured. Rian's eyes rolled.

'Thinking of becoming a Pentadrian?' he asked, amused, then continued without waiting for an answer, 'Then you'll need to know you're expected to obey the five leaders of the cult, who call themselves by the pretty title of "the Voices of the Gods", and the hierarchy of their followers known as "the Servants of the Gods". You'll need to believe in their gods. You have to wonder how a cult so powerful can arise from a belief in gods that do not exist. You might expect them to fear the influence of other cults, but they actually encourage tolerance of them.'

Mairae pulled a face in mock disappointment. 'I'm afraid

that without the orgies Southern Ithania has no attraction for me.'

Juran chuckled. 'That is a relief to hear. We would so hate to lose you.' He paused, then sighed. 'Now, lastly, there is a darker matter to attend to. A few weeks ago I received several reports from eastern Toren of attacks by a hunt of vorns. These are no ordinary vorns. They're twice the size of the usual creatures. Travellers, farmers and even merchant families have been killed by them.

'Several hunting teams were sent, but none have returned. A woman who witnessed them kill her husband outside her home claimed that a man was riding one of the creatures, and appeared to be directing them. I thought at first she had made a mistake. Vorns work so well together that they can appear to be directed by an outside force. Perhaps she imagined a man-shape in the darkness. There seems to be no human purpose to the attacks, either. The victims have nothing in common except that they were outside at night.

'But other witnesses have now confirmed her story. Some say he is directing them telepathically. If that is true, he must be a sorcerer. I have sent three village priests to investigate. Should this man prove to be a sorcerer I will contact you all telepathically so that you may witness the confrontation.' Juran straightened. 'That is all I have to present today. Does anyone else have a matter to raise?'

Mairae shook her head. As Rian voiced a negative, Dyara glanced at Auraya, then shrugged.

'Nothing, for now.'

'Then I declare this meeting ended.'

CHAPTER 5

*T*he tower was taller than any she had seen. It was so high that clouds tore themselves upon it as they passed. Conflicting emotions warred within Emerahl. She should flee. Any moment they would see. But she wanted to look. Wanted to watch. Something about that white spire fascinated her.

She moved closer. As she did, the tower loomed over her. It seemed to flex. She realised too late that this was no illusion. Cracks had appeared, zigzagging along the seams of the huge stone bricks the tower had been built from. The tower was going to fall.

She turned and tried to run but the air was thick and syrupy and her legs were too weak to move through it. She could see the shadow of the tower lengthening before her. As it widened, she wondered why she hadn't had the sense to run sideways, out of its path.

Then the world exploded.

Everything was abruptly dark and silent. She could not breathe. Voices called her name, but she could not draw enough breath to answer. Slowly the cold darkness crept in.

'Sorceress!'

The voice of the speaker was dark with anger, but it was a chance of rescue nonetheless.

'Come out, you meddling old bitch!'

Emerahl started out of the dream and opened her eyes. The

round interior wall of the lighthouse disappeared into darkness above. She heard the sounds of approaching footsteps and the muttering of several voices coming from the opening in the wall where, in the past, two great carved doors had been. A broad-shouldered shape stood beyond.

'Come out, or we'll come in and get you.'

The voice was full of threat and anger, but also a hint of fear. She shook off the lingering nightmare reluctantly – she would have liked time to analyse it before the details faded – and scrambled to her feet.

'Who are you?' she demanded.

'I am Erine, Head of Corel. Come out now, or I'll send my men to fetch you.'

Emerahl moved to the doorway. Outside stood fourteen men, some looking up at the lighthouse, some glancing behind, and the rest watching their leader. All wore a scowl and carried some kind of rough weapon. Clearly none could see her, as they were standing in the bright morning light and she was hidden in the shadows of the lighthouse.

'So that's what you're calling that ring of hovels nowadays,' she said, stepping into the doorway. 'Corel. A pretty name for a place founded by smugglers.'

The broad-shouldered man all but bared his teeth in anger. 'Corel is our home. You'd better show some respect or we'll—'

'Respect?' She stared up at him. 'You come up here shouting and putting out orders and threats, and you expect me to show you some respect?' She took a step forward. 'Get back to your village, men of Corel. You'll get nothing from me today.'

'We don't want any of your poisons or tricks, sorceress.' Erine's eyes gleamed. 'We want justice. You've meddled one time too many. You won't make any more women in our village into sorceress bitches. We're turning you out.'

She stared at him in surprise, then slowly began to smile.

'*So you're* the father?'

His expression shifted. A moment's fear, then anger.

'Yes. I'd kill you for what you did to my little Rinnie, but the others think that'll bring bad luck.'

'No, they just don't feel like they've lost as much as you,' she said. 'They were just trying their luck with Rinnie. Seeing what you'd let them get away with. But you,' she narrowed her eyes, 'you've been enjoying her for years and now you can't touch her. And you *so* like getting your way. It drives you crazy you can't have her any more.'

His face had turned red. 'Shut your mouth,' he growled, 'or I'll—'

'Your own daughter,' she threw at him. 'You come up here calling her "my little Rinnie" like she's some innocent child you love and protect. She stopped being an innocent child the first time she realised her own father was the man most likely to harm her.'

The other men were eyeing their leader uneasily now. Emerahl was not sure if their discomfort was from what she accused Rinnie's father of, or because they had known what he was doing to his daughter and hadn't stopped him. Erine, aware of their stares, controlled himself with an effort.

'Did she tell you that, you foolish old woman? She's been making up such stories for years. Always looking for—'

'No, she didn't,' Emerahl replied. She tapped her head. 'I can see the truth, even when people don't want me to.'

Which was not true; she hadn't read the girl's mind. Her skill in mind-reading was nothing like it had once been. All Gifts needed to be practised and she had lived in isolation for too long.

But her words had the desired effect. The other men exchanged glances, some regarding Erine with narrowed eyes.

'We don't want your lies or your cursed sorceries any more,'

Erine growled. He took a step forward. 'I'm ordering you to leave.'

Emerahl smiled and crossed her arms. 'No.'

'I am Head of Corel and—'

'Corel is down there.' She pointed. 'I have lived here since before your grandfathers' fathers built their first shack. You have no authority over me.'

Erine laughed. 'You're old, but you're not that old.' He looked at his companions. 'See how she lies?' He turned back. 'The village doesn't want you harmed. They want to give you the chance to pack up and leave in peace. If you're still here when we come back in a few days, don't expect us to be nice about it.'

At that, he turned and stalked away, gesturing for the others to follow. Emerahl sighed. *Fools. They'll come back and I'll have to teach them the same lesson I taught their great-grandfathers. They'll sulk for a while and try to starve me out. I'll miss the vegetables and bread, and I'll have to go fishing again, but in time they'll forget and come looking for help once more.*

Six men waited outside the Forest Edge Wayhouse: three priests and three locals. The blue trim of the priests' circs looked black in the fading light. The other men wore the simple clothes of farmers and carried packs.

Adem flexed his shoulders to shift the weight of his gear into a more comfortable position, then stepped into the street. From behind him came the reassuring footsteps of his fellow vorn-hunters. One, then all of the priests and their companions turned to regard the newcomers. He smiled as they eyed his clothing with obvious dismay. Hunters travelled light, especially in the forest. They might carry one spare set of clothes to change into after a day's butchering, but those, too, quickly became stained with blood and dirt.

In the trade, clean clothes were a sign of a failed hunter. Adem wryly noted the spotless white circs of his employers. He supposed dirty garments would not be an encouraging sign on a priest. It must be a chore keeping them clean.

'I'm Adem Tailer,' he said. 'This is my team.' He didn't bother introducing the men. The priests would not remember a list of names.

'I am Priest Hakan,' the taller of the priests replied. 'This is Priest Barew and Priest Poer.' He gestured to a grey-haired priest, then a slightly portly one, and then waved at the three locals. 'These are our porters.'

Adem made the quick one-handed gesture of the circle to the priests and nodded politely at the porters. The locals looked apprehensive. As well they might.

'Thank you for volunteering your services,' Hakan added.

Adem gave a short bark of laughter. 'Volunteer? We're no volunteers, priest. We want the skins. From what I hear these vorns are big bastards and all black. Pelts like that will fetch a high price.'

Priest Hakan's mouth twitched up at one corner but his two companions grimaced in distaste. 'I'm sure they will,' he replied. 'Now, how do you recommend we proceed?'

'We look for tracks where the last attack happened.'

Hakan nodded. 'We'll take you there.'

Faces appeared in windows as they passed through the village. Voices called out, wishing them luck. A woman hurried out of a door with a tray of small cups, each brimming with tipli, the local liquor. The hunters downed theirs cheerfully, while the porters gulped their share with telling haste. The priests took one sip before returning their cups to the tray unfinished.

They moved on out of the village. The dark shapes of trees pressed in on either side. The portly priest lifted a hand and everyone was dazzled as a bright light appeared.

'No light,' Adem said. 'You'll frighten them off if they're close. The moon will rise soon. It should give us enough light once our eyes are used to it.'

The priest glanced at Hakan, who nodded. The light blinked out, leaving them to stumble forward in darkness until their eyes adjusted. Time passed slowly, measured by the tread of their boots. Just as the moon struggled up from the tops of the trees Priest Hakan stopped.

'That smell . . . this must be the place,' he said.

Adem looked at the portly priest. 'Can you make a soft light?'

The priest nodded. He extended a hand again and a tiny spark of light appeared. Adem saw the remains of a platten ahead. They walked over to the vehicle, which was listing to one side on a broken wheel. The stench grew stronger as they approached and its source proved to be the corpse of an arem, gouged out where the vorns had eaten part of it.

The ground was covered in tracks – huge pawprints that set Adem's heart pounding with excitement. He tried to estimate the number of them. Ten? Fifteen? The prints congregated in a mass of churned ground. Fresher human ones crossed them. Adem noticed something glittering. He reached down and plucked a short length of gold chain from the trampled soil. It was covered in a crusty substance he suspected was dried blood.

'That's where they found the merchant,' Hakan murmured. 'Or what was left of him.'

Adem pocketed the links. 'All right, men. Scout about and find tracks leading away.'

It did not take long. Soon Adem was leading the priests into the forest, following a trail that wouldn't have been easier to follow had the giant footprints glowed in the dark. They were a day behind the hunt, he estimated. He hoped the priests were prepared for a long trek. He did not call for a stop until the moon was directly overhead, then gave them only a few minutes to rest.

After a few more hours they reached a small clearing. Vorn tracks filled the space – and human. A single set of bootprints marked the forest floor. They had found no human footprints since the site of the attack. Adem's men scurried through the forest.

'Looks like they stopped last night,' he murmured.

'They went this way,' one called softly.

'Any human footprints leading away?' Adem asked.

There was a long pause.

'No.'

'Witnesses say he rides one of them,' Hakan said.

Adem moved to Hakan's side. 'Wouldn't have thought it possible. But I guess they're big enough. I—'

'Sentry!' one of his men hissed.

The hunters froze. Adem cast about, searching the forest and listening.

'Sentry?' Hakan whispered.

'Sometimes the hunt leaves a single member behind to wait and see if they're being followed.'

The priest stared at Adem. 'They're *that* smart?'

'You'd better believe it.' A faint sound drew Adem's attention to the right and he heard his men suck in a breath as they, too, saw a shadow slink away. A huge shadow. Adem cursed.

'What's wrong?' Hakan asked.

'The hunt knows we're coming, I doubt we'll catch them now.'

'That depends,' the priest murmured.

'Oh?' Adem couldn't hide the scepticism in his voice. What did priests know of vorns?

'On whether the rider slows them. Or wants us to find him.'

He has a point. Adem grunted in reluctant agreement.

'Let us continue,' Hakan said.

For the next few hours they crept through the forest, following a trail now half a day fresher. The darkness thickened as the night reached that time, just before morning, when all was still and cold. The priests yawned. The scouts trudged after them, now too tired to fear. Adem's fellow hunters walked with a distinct lack of enthusiasm. He had to agree. Their chances of catching the hunt were slim now.

Then a human scream tore through the silence. Adem heard several curses and unslung his bow. The sound had been close. Perhaps one of the trackers . . .

The forest filled with leaping shadows and snapping teeth.

'Light!' Adem shouted. 'Priest! Light!'

More screams came. Screams of terror and pain. Adem heard a soft patter and turned to see a shadow leap toward him. There was no time to nock an arrow. He grabbed his knife, ducked and rolled, and thrust upward. Something caught it, ripping the blade from his grip. There was an inhuman garbled cry of pain and the sound of something landing heavily nearby.

Then light finally flooded the forest. Adem found himself staring into the yellow eyes of the largest vorn he had ever seen. In the corner of his vision he could see white figures. Adem dared not take his eyes from those of the beast to look. The vorn whined as it got to its feet. Blood dripped from the matted hair of its belly. Adem weighed his chances. It was close, but in pain and perhaps weakened from blood loss. There was no use running away. Even wounded these creatures could outrun a man in ten strides. He groped for an arrow.

The vorn slunk toward him, pink tongue lolling from its mouth. *A mouth large enough to encompass a man's head,* Adem couldn't help thinking. He got the arrow nocked, aimed between the eyes of the beast and released.

The arrow bounced off the vorn's skull.

Adem stared at it in disbelief. The animal had leapt backwards in surprise.

'Where are you, sorcerer?' Hakan shouted. 'Show yourself!'

Sorcerer? Adem thought. *Magic? The vorns are protected with magic? That is not fair!*

'You do not order *me*, priest,' a voice replied in a strange accent.

The vorn whined again and dropped to the ground, rolling onto its side. Adem could see his blade lodged in its belly. He decided he could risk looking away.

Priests, hunters and porters stood in a group under a hovering spark of light. Vorns ringed them all.

The elderly priest was crouching at the side of another. Hakan stood staring into the forest. As Adem watched a stranger stepped into the light. *Foreign*, Adem thought. *No race I've ever seen.* Long pale hair spilled over a black many-layered garment. On his chest lay a large silver pendant in the shape of a five-pointed star.

'You have killed innocent people, sorcerer,' Hakan accused. 'Give yourself up and face the gods' justice.'

The sorcerer laughed. 'I don't answer to your gods.'

'You will,' Hakan said. Sparks of light flashed from the priest toward the foreigner. Just before they reached their target they skittered aside and struck the trees, tearing bark from the trunks. Adem backed away. It was never wise to remain close to a magical battle. The injured vorn growled, reminding him that other vorns were about. He stopped, uncertain as to whether he should take his chances with a hunt of overgrown vorns or remain near the magical contest.

'Your magic is small, priest,' the foreigner said.

The air rippled and Hakan staggered backwards and threw up his hands. Adem could see a faint shimmer in the air forming an arc that surrounded the priest and his men. Hakan didn't return the attack. It looked as if all his effort was going into protecting himself and the men around him.

One of the trackers standing behind the priests turned and bolted. He took only two steps before he screamed and fell to the ground. Adem stared in horror at the man's legs. They were twisted in odd directions and blood was quickly soaking through his trousers.

Adem felt his mouth go dry. *If this is what the sorcerer does to those outside the barrier, perhaps I had better stay still and hope he doesn't notice me.* He slowly crouched beside a bush, where he could still see the battle. The arc around the priests and hunters had spread to form a sphere encompassing all. The foreign sorcerer chuckled quietly to himself, a sound that sent a shiver down Adem's spine.

'Surrender, priest. You will not win.' He extended a hand and curled his fingers as if clutching something before him.

'Never,' Hakan gasped.

The sorcerer shook his hand. Adem went cold as the sphere jerked about. The men within stumbled and fell to their knees. Hakan clutched his head and gave a wordless cry. The elderly priest jumped to his feet and grabbed Hakan's shoulder. Adem saw Hakan's face relax a little and heard the other priest gasp. At the same time the sphere flickered.

Hakan collapsed. Looking closely, Adem felt his heart freeze as he saw the elderly priest's lips moving. He caught snatches of a prayer and felt the despair in the words.

The priest believed they were going to die.

I have to get out of here.

Rising, Adem took a few steps away from the battle.

'That is your choice,' the sorcerer said.

Adem glanced back in time to see the sorcerer's extended hand flex then close into a fist. There was a cry from the elderly priest. A cry that was cut off. The light went out and a deathly silence followed.

Slowly Adem's eyes adjusted to the faint glimmer of early dawn. He found himself staring at the silent place where priests and hunters had stood, and could not persuade his eyes to move away from the bloody mound of crushed limbs, weapons, packs and priests' circs, not even as his stomach heaved its contents onto the ground.

There was an animal whine nearby. A voice spoke strange words in soothing tones. Adem watched as vorns gathered around the sorcerer to be petted. Then the injured vorn whined again and the sorcerer looked up, straight into Adem's eyes.

Though he knew there was no hope, Adem ran.

As Auraya enterd Juran's room she met the eyes of each of the other White. Juran had woken her a short while before so that she could link with the priests fighting the sorcerer. She had sensed the minds of the other White, and felt their shock and dismay.

'I'm sorry, Auraya,' Juran said. 'If I had known the confrontation was going to end so badly I would not have woken you.'

She shook her head. 'Don't apologise, Juran. You could not have known how it would turn out, and it's no revelation to me that terrible things happen in this world – though I do appreciate your concern.'

He ushered her to a chair. 'Such a waste,' he murmured. He began to pace the room. 'I should not have sent them. I should have investigated myself.'

'You could not have known this sorcerer was so powerful,' Dyara repeated. 'Stop blaming yourself and sit down.'

Auraya glanced at Dyara, amused despite the seriousness of

the moment to hear her take such a stern tone with Juran. The White leader did not appear to mind. He dropped into his chair and sighed heavily.

'Who is this sorcerer?' Rian asked.

'A Pentadrian,' Mairae replied. 'There is a sketch of the star pendant in the report. They're worn by Servants of the Gods.'

'A powerful sorcerer priest,' Dyara added.

Juran nodded slowly. 'You're right. So why is he here?'

'Not to propose trade or forge an alliance, it seems,' Mairae said.

'No,' Dyara agreed. 'We have to consider whether he was sent here or is acting on his own. Either way, he must be dealt with, and we cannot risk sending a high priest or priestess to confront him.'

Rian nodded. 'One of us must go.'

'Yes.' Juran glanced at each of the White in turn. 'Whoever does will be absent some weeks. Auraya hasn't completed her training yet. Mairae is occupied with the Somreyans. Dyara is training Auraya. I would go myself, but . . .' He turned to Rian. 'You have not dealt with a sorcerer before. Do you have the time?'

Rian smiled grimly. 'Of course not, but I will make time. The world needs to be rid of this Pentadrian and his vorns.'

Juran nodded. 'Then take one of the Bearers and go.'

Rian straightened. A gleam had entered his gaze. As the young man rose and stalked from the room, Auraya felt a moment's wry sympathy for the Pentadrian sorcerer. From what she had seen so far, all but the more severe rumours of Rian's ruthless fanaticism were true.

CHAPTER 6

'What do you think of Dreamweavers, Danjin Spear?'
Danjin looked up in surprise. He was sitting opposite Auraya at the large table in her reception room, helping
her examine the terms of the proposed alliance with Somrey.

Auraya met his eyes steadily. He thought back to the day
news of her mother's death had arrived. At her bidding he
had sought the location of the man who had delivered the
message to the Temple. To his surprise, the man was a
Dreamweaver.

Later he had been even more surprised to learn that Auraya
had visited the man in disguise. He wasn't sure if he was more
disturbed by the idea of a White paying a social visit to a
Dreamweaver, or that Auraya had tried to do so secretly –
which indicated she knew she was doing something that might
be considered ill-advised or inappropriate.

Of course, she was reading all this from his mind right now.
She must also know that he had looked into her past and
learned of her childhood friendship with Dreamweaver Leiard
and that she had been known in the priesthood for her sympathetic view of the heathens. She would have seen that her
second meeting with the Dreamweaver had been noted, and
that he had heard people, inside and outside the Temple,

gossiping about it. She also had to know that he didn't respect or like Dreamweavers.

In the weeks since he had found Leiard she had not discussed Dreamweavers with him at all. Now she was working on the Somreyan problem they could not avoid the subject any longer. He had to be honest. There was no point pretending he agreed with her.

'I don't think much of them, I'm afraid,' he admitted. 'They are at best pitiful, and at worst untrustworthy.'

Her eyebrows rose. 'Why pitiful?'

'I guess because they are so few and so despised. And misguided. They do not serve the gods, so their souls die when their body does.'

'Why untrustworthy?'

'Their Gifts – some of them – enable them to mess about with people's minds.' He hesitated as he realised he was repeating what his father had always said. Were these truly his own opinions? 'They can torment their enemies with nightmares, for example.'

She smiled faintly. 'Have you ever heard of a Dreamweaver doing so?'

He hesitated again. 'No,' he admitted. 'But then there are so few now. I don't think they'd dare.'

Auraya's smile widened. 'Have you ever heard of a Dreamweaver doing something to earn them the label "untrustworthy"?'

He nodded. 'Some years ago a Dreamweaver poisoned a patient.'

The smile vanished and she looked away. 'Yes, I studied that case.'

He looked at her in surprise. 'As part of your training?'

'No.' She shook her head. 'I've always taken an interest in crimes that involve Dreamweavers.'

'What . . . what did you make of it?'

She grimaced. 'That the Dreamweaver was guilty. She confessed to it, but I wanted to be sure she wasn't blackmailed or beaten into doing so. I looked to the reaction of other Dreamweavers for clues. They turned from her. I found that to be the most convincing evidence of her guilt.'

Danjin was intrigued. 'They might have turned from her to protect themselves.'

'No. I think Dreamweavers know when another is guilty of a crime. When one is falsely accused – and some of the trials have been disgustingly transparent – they defend them in their own way. The accused is calm, even when they know they are to be executed. But when the accused is guilty, not a word is spoken in their defence. This woman was frantic,' Auraya shook her head slowly, 'and angry. She raged against her own people.'

'I heard that she asked for garpa so she could avoid sleeping.' Danjin shuddered. 'If they are willing to torment one of their own, what might they do to an enemy?'

'Why do you assume they were tormenting her? She might have wanted to avoid her own dreams.'

'She was a Dreamweaver. Surely she had control of her own dreams.'

'Again, you can only assume so.' Auraya smiled. 'You judge them untrustworthy because they have the ability to harm others. Just because they can, doesn't mean they will. I could snuff out your life with a thought, but you trust me not to.'

He stared at her, disturbed at her casual mention of her gods-given powers. She held his gaze. He looked down at the table. 'I know you wouldn't.'

'So perhaps you should reserve your judgement of each Dreamweaver until you know him or her personally.'

He nodded. 'You're right, of course. But I cannot trust them any more than I would trust a stranger.'

105

She chuckled. 'Nor I. Or even those I think I know, as sometimes people I thought I knew well have demonstrated a meanness or callousness that I hadn't realised they were capable of.' She looked down at the scroll spread before her. 'I value your views even if I don't agree with them, Danjin. I am finding myself alone in my perspective on this matter. I am no Dreamweaver. My understanding of them is proving to be limited. Neither am I a typical Circlian, who distrusts Dreamweavers at best and actively persecutes them at worst. I need to understand all perspectives if I am to suggest ways for Mairae to persuade the Somreyans into forming an alliance with us.'

Danjin noted the crease that had formed between her brows as she spoke. When he had been offered this position, Dyara had assured him that Auraya would not be given any difficult tasks during her first few years as a White. It seemed this task had found her.

Her knowledge of Dreamweavers made her the best White for it, however. Maybe this was why the White were allowing it to become common knowledge that the newest White was tolerant of, if not supportive of, heathens. What effect would that have in the long term? While the law dictated that seeking a Dreamweaver's services was a crime, so many people ignored it that few were ever punished. Would Auraya's tolerance of Dreamweavers encourage more people to defy the law?

Auraya said nothing. Her attention had returned to the alliance.

'Which terms did the Somreyans initially protest against?'

Danjin had anticipated this question. Bringing a wax tablet closer, he recited a long list of changes to the terms of the alliance. The last third were entirely to do with Dreamweaver matters.

'These aren't new terms, are they? They've always been in the alliance.'

'Yes.'

'Why didn't the Somreyans protest about them in the beginning?'

Danjin shrugged. 'As larger matters are settled, smaller ones become more noticeable. Or so they say.'

'And they have been noticing them one at a time?' Her voice was heavy with scepticism.

He chuckled. 'Every time one matter is resolved, they protest against another.'

'Are they delaying, then? Is there any reason you can see for the Council of Elders to put off signing? Or is it only the Dreamweavers who want to delay or stop the alliance?'

'I don't know. Mairae feels certain that most of the council want the alliance.'

Auraya drummed her fingers on the table. 'So either they are unhappy with the small matters and are presenting them one by one in order to avoid any being tackled with less seriousness in the shadow of others, or they are simply messing us about. Patience will overcome the first possibility. To overcome the other . . .'

'Nothing will overcome the other. Nothing but direct interference in Somreyan politics.'

'I don't think we have to go that far. We simply have to reduce the power of the Dreamweaver elder.'

Danjin stared at her in surprise. This was not something he'd expect from a Dreamweaver sympathiser.

'How?'

'By giving some of that power to another Dreamweaver.'

'The council can only contain one representative of each religion. How can you change that without influencing Somreyan politics?'

'I don't mean to put two Dreamweavers in the council, Danjin. This would be a separate position.'

'Chosen by whom?'

'By the White.'

'The Somreyans wouldn't accept it!'

'They'd have no choice. It would have nothing to do with them.'

Danjin narrowed his eyes. 'All right. You have me mystified. Just tell me.'

She chuckled. 'Clearly the White need an adviser on Dreamweaver affairs.'

'And this adviser would be a Dreamweaver?'

'Of course. The Somreyan Dreamweavers would never listen to a Circlian elected to the position.'

Danjin nodded slowly as he considered the advantages of this arrangement. 'I see. First, the Dreamweavers will be mollified. By hiring one of them as an adviser, the White acknowledge that Dreamweavers have some value. The adviser tackles face-to-face discussion over the terms of the alliance so that, faced with one of their own, the Dreamweaver elder is forced to negotiate sensibly rather than reactively.'

'And our adviser could make suggestions on how the terms of the alliance might be altered to reduce the number of protests, and therefore speed the process,' Auraya added.

What are the disadvantages, then? Danjin asked himself. *What are the weaknesses in this plan?*

'You will have to take care that this adviser's goals are not contrary to your own,' he warned. 'He or she might suggest changes to the alliance that benefit their people and prove to have ill consequences for us.'

'He or she would have to be as unaware of those consequences as I,' she replied, tapping her forehead. 'There are only four people in the world who can lie to me.'

Danjin felt a thrill at this piece of information. So the White could not read each other's minds. He had always suspected it was so.

'Of course, it may be that no Dreamweaver will agree to work with us,' he warned.

She smiled.

'Do you have anyone in mind?' Even as he asked, he knew the answer.

'Of course. Naturally, I'd want to work with someone I feel I can trust. Who better, then, than the Dreamweaver I know personally?'

As the platten trundled away, Auraya took in her surroundings. She and Dyara were in a wide, flat space between rows of cultivated trees. Long grass swayed in the breeze. In the distance a priest and priestess cantered around a field on large white reyna. Both looked familiar.

'Is that . . . ?'

'Juran and Mairae,' Dyara answered. 'We call the last day of the month Training Day because it's the day we work with the Bearers. Once you have established a link with one, you need to maintain it.'

'Is that what I'll be doing today?'

Dyara shook her head. 'No. You will have to learn to ride eventually, but it is not a high priority. It is more important to teach you how to use your new Gifts.'

The two reyna in the distance wheeled in a complicated-looking manoeuvre, their legs moving in unison. Auraya could not imagine herself managing to remain on a reyna's back while it twisted about like that. She hoped her relief at the news her feet would remain on the ground wasn't too obvious.

'The shield I taught you to make last time will hold off

most types of attacks,' Dyara said, her voice taking on a now-familiar lecturing tone. 'It will deflect projectiles, flame and force, but it won't stop lightning. Fortunately, lightning is naturally attracted to the ground. It will take the easiest route – through you. To prevent that you have to give it an alternative route, and you have to do it quickly.'

Dyara held out a hand. A tortured ribbon of light flashed from her fingers to the ground and a deafening crack echoed across the field. A burn marked the grass. The air sizzled.

'When do I get to do that?' Auraya breathed.

'Only when you've learned to defend against it,' Dyara replied. 'I will begin with small strikes, aiming at the same place. You must try to alter its course.'

At first Auraya felt as if she had been ordered to catch sunlight in her hand. The lightning strikes happened too quickly for her to sense anything about them. She noticed the wriggly line of light was never the same. It must have a reason to follow a different path. Something about the air.

:Dyara? Auraya? a voice said in Auraya's mind.

Dyara's head snapped up. She had obviously heard it too.

:Juran? she replied. Auraya glanced toward the field, but the two riders were no longer there.

:Rian has found the pentadrian. Focus on his mind through mine.

Dyara looked at Auraya, then nodded. Closing her eyes, Auraya sought Juran's mind. As she linked with him she sensed Mairae and Dyara, but Rian's thoughts demanded attention. From him came sounds and images. A forest. A half-ruined stone house. A man in black clothing standing in the doorway. She drew in a breath in wonder as she discovered she could see what Rian was viewing as clearly as if she were standing in his place. She could also sense him drawing magic in order to feed the shield of protection around him.

The Pentadrian was watching Rian approaching. Vorns were

all around him. He reached out and stroked the head of one sitting beside him, murmuring in his strange language.

Rian stopped and dismounted. He sent an instruction to the mind of his Bearer. It galloped away.

The sorcerer crossed his arms. 'You come to catch me, priest?'

'No,' Rian said. 'I have come to kill you.'

The sorcerer smiled. 'That not polite.'

'It is what you deserve, murderer.'

'Murderer? Me? You speak of priests and men, yes? I only defend myself. They attack first.'

'Did the farmers and merchants you killed attack you first?' Rian asked.

:I can't read his mind, Rian said. *His thoughts are shielded.*

:Then he could be dangerous, Juran said.

:As powerful as one of the immortals of the past Age. This will be an interesting fight, Rian replied.

'I not attack farmers and merchants,' the sorcerer said. He scratched the head of a vorn. 'My friends hungry. They not given respect or food. You people not polite or respect me and my friends from day I here. Now you say you kill me.' He shook his head. 'You people not friendly.'

'Not to murderers,' Rian said. 'Perhaps in your land savagery is no crime, but in ours it is punishable by death.'

'You think you can punish me?'

'With the gods' blessing and power.' Auraya felt the surge of adoration and determination that Rian felt. *He is utterly dedicated to the gods*, she found herself thinking. *In comparison the rest of us are merely loyal. Yet the gods must find that acceptable, or all White would be like Rian.*

The sorcerer laughed. 'The gods would never bless you, heathen.'

'Not your false gods,' Rian replied. 'The Circle. True, living

111

gods.' He drew magic and channelled it out, shaping it into a streak of white heat. The air before the sorcerer suddenly became a wall of violent ripples. A wave of warm air washed back over Rian. The sphere of protection Rian had set about himself buckled inward. He strengthened it instinctively, warding off the force buffeting it. Auraya heard the snap of wood as the trees around Rian bore the brunt of reflected power.

Rian attacked again, this time shaping magic into darts that assailed the sorcerer from all sides. The Pentadrian's defence held, and he returned with strikes of lightning that Rian guided to the ground.

So that's how it's done, Auraya thought.

The ground beneath Rian bucked and jumped. He sent magic down, steadying it. At the same time he drew air from around the sorcerer, trapping him in a vacuum. The sorcerer wrested air back.

:He's testing me, Rian observed.

:I agree, Juran replied.

Rian felt a force envelop him, pressing upon the protection around him. He fought it, but it grew ever stronger. Auraya was not surprised to see that the sorcerer was standing with one hand extended and curved into a claw, just as he had during the fight with the priests.

:Now comes the test of strength, Rian said. He resisted the crushing, matching force with force. At the same time he watched for other forms of attack. Time slid by. The sorcerer's attack grew steadily more powerful. Rian slowly increased the strength of his defence.

Abruptly, the crushing force eased.

Though Rian reacted quickly, a great wave of force rushed out from him. Trees shattered. The ruined house flew apart. Dust and rocks filled the air, obscuring all. Rian threw out a gentler magic, pushing the dust to the ground.

The sorcerer was gone. Casting about, Rian saw a huge black beast loping away, carrying a man. He sent a bolt of lightning toward it, but the energy skittered around the fleeing sorcerer and sank into the ground.

'Gods strike him,' Rian hissed as the man and beast disappeared into the trees. He sent a mental call to his Bearer. The mount was not far away.

:Take care, Juran warned. *Follow him, but be wary. He is powerful, and a surprise attack could be deadly.*

Auraya felt a chill run down her spine. Deadly to Rian? But surely nothing could harm him.

:Not as powerful as I, Rian replied, his thoughts dark with anger and determination. *There will be no opportunity for ambush. I will not sleep or rest until I know he is dead.*

Then his thoughts faded from Auraya's senses. She opened her eyes. Dyara met her gaze.

'That was enlightening,' the woman said dryly. 'We have not encountered an enemy this powerful for a long time.' Her eyes narrowed. 'You look puzzled.'

'I am,' Auraya replied. 'Is Rian in any danger?'

'No.'

'Then why did Juran warn him to watch for a surprise attack? Surely he cannot be killed.'

Dyara crossed her arms. 'Only if he makes a foolish mistake – and he won't. I taught him well.'

'So we're not invulnerable. Or immortal.'

Dyara smiled. 'Not exactly. Most would say we're close enough to it. We do have limitations. One is access to magic. Remember what I taught you: when we draw in magic we use up some of what is around us. If we use a lot it becomes harder to draw in as the magic around us thins and we have to reach further from our position to get to it. Magic will flow back into the place we have weakened, but it happens slowly. To

113

gain a fresh, strong source we must move to a new position.

'It is rare for us to use that much magic,' Dyara continued. 'But the most likely situation to cause us to is battle with another sorcerer – an exceptionally powerful sorcerer. The depletion of an area may cause you to weaken at an inopportune moment.' She paused and Auraya nodded to show she understood.

'Your own ability to learn and use Gifts is your other limitation. The gods can only enhance our Gifts. Each of us is as strong as the gods can make us. That is why we are not equal in strength. Why Mairae is the weakest and Juran is the strongest.'

'Is it possible for a sorcerer to be stronger than us?'

'Yes, though sorcerers of such strength are rare indeed. This is the first one I've learned of in nearly a hundred years.' She smiled grimly. 'You have joined us during interesting times, Auraya. Lack of training is another limitation, but one I'm sure you'll overcome quickly considering the rate at which you're learning. Don't worry. We would never send you out to deal with a sorcerer of such strength until your training was complete.'

Auraya smiled. 'I'm not worried. And I had wondered how we could be invulnerable when the gods aren't.'

Dyara frowned. 'What do you mean?'

'Many gods died in the War of the Gods. If gods can die, then so can we.'

'I suppose that is true.'

Hearing the beat of hooves on the ground, they both turned to see Juran and Mairae riding toward them. As the reyna came to a halt Auraya realised that neither wore reins. She remembered what Dyara had told her: that Bearers were directed by mental commands.

Juran looked down at Auraya.

114

'I have a question for you, Auraya. Mairae tells me you've finished looking over the Somreyan alliance proposal. Would you make any changes to the terms?'

'A few, though I suspect even more changes need to be made. As I was reading I found that I didn't know as much about Dreamweavers as I thought. I know how they'd treat woundrot, but not how they fit into Somreyan society. I began to wish I had an expert to call upon, and a possible solution came to me. Perhaps what we need is an adviser on Dreamweaver matters.'

Juran turned to regard Mairae. 'You tried this, did you not?'

Mairae nodded. 'I could not find anyone with the appropriate knowledge.'

Auraya felt her heartbeat quicken a little, but did not pause. 'Did you try a Dreamweaver?'

'No. I did not expect them to cooperate.'

Juran's eyebrows had risen, but his expression was not disapproving. 'You believe they might, Auraya?'

'Yes, if they felt our purpose was not contrary to their well-being. The alliance isn't, as far as I can see.' She smiled crookedly and touched her forehead. 'And we have our own safeguards against the possibility that their purpose is contrary to ours.'

'Which they will be quite aware of.' Juran reached forward and rubbed his Bearer between the ears, around the stub of one horn. 'I would be surprised if any agreed to it, but I can see the advantages we will gain if one did.'

Mairae smiled. 'The Somreyan Dreamweaver elder would not so easily defy one of her own.'

'No,' Juran agreed.

'We would be admitting they have power and influence,' Dyara warned.

Mairae shrugged. 'No more power than they actually have.

115

No more than we have already acknowledged in the terms of the alliance.'

'We will signal to our people that we approve of them,' Dyara persisted.

'Not approve. Tolerate. We can't pretend they don't have power in Somrey.'

Dyara opened her mouth, then closed it again and shook her head.

Juran looked at Auraya. 'If you can find a Dreamweaver willing to do this, then I will send you and Mairae to Somrey together.'

'But Auraya has barely begun her training,' Dyara protested. 'This is too much to expect of her so soon.'

'The only alternative I see is to abandon negotiations.' Juran looked at Auraya and shrugged. 'If you fail, people will assume it was through inexperience rather than a fault in our strategy.'

'That's hardly fair on Auraya,' Dyara pointed out.

Auraya shook her head. 'I don't mind.'

Juran looked thoughtful. 'If Mairae were to behave as if she didn't expect to gain any ground, but has taken you there to educate you in other systems of government . . . Let them underestimate you.' His attention returned to her. 'Yes. Do it. See if you can find us an adviser.'

'Do you have anyone in mind?' Mairae asked.

Auraya paused. 'Yes. The Dreamweaver I knew as a child. He is living in the city temporarily.'

Juran frowned. 'An old friend. That could be unpleasant for you, if he proves troublesome.'

'I know. However, I'd rather work with someone I know well, than not.'

He nodded slowly. 'Very well. But be careful, Auraya, that you do not compromise yourself for the sake of friendship. It is far too easy to do.' His tone was regretful.

'I will be careful,' she assured him.

Juran patted his Bearer's neck and it pawed the ground. Auraya resisted the urge to back away. They were such big creatures.

'We must return to our training,' Juran said. As he and Mairae rode away, Auraya wondered what had happened to cause him to feel such obvious regret. Perhaps she would find out, one day.

There was so much she didn't know about her fellow White. But there was plenty of time to learn about them. Maybe not all of eternity, but, as Dyara had said, close enough.

CHAPTER 7

Five sat on benches within the communal room of the Bakers' house. Another Dreamweaver, Olameer, had arrived that morning. She was a middle-aged Somreyan journeying south to gather herbs that would not grow in the colder climate of her homeland. Jayim had been quiet for most of the meal.

'Have you visited Somrey, Leiard?' Tanara asked.

Leiard frowned. 'I am not sure. I have memories of it, but I do not recall where they fit into my past.'

Olameer looked at him closely. 'They sound like link memories.'

'Probably,' Leiard agreed.

'But you are unsure,' Olameer stated. 'Do you have other memories that you are not certain are yours?'

'Many,' he admitted.

'Forgive me, but what are link memories?' Tanara interrupted.

Olameer smiled. 'Dreamweavers sometimes link minds in order to communicate concepts and memories to each other. It is quicker and easier to explain some things that way. We also occasionally use links as a part of our rituals and a way to get to know another person.' She looked at Leiard and her smile changed to a thoughtful frown. 'We tend to accumulate memories that are not our own, but usually we can tell which are ours and which are not. If a memory is old, however, it is easier to forget that it was not ours. And in rare instances, where a Dreamweaver endures a traumatic event, his or her memories will mix with link memories.'

Leiard smiled. 'I have not suffered such an event, Olameer.'

'None that you remember,' she replied softly.

He shrugged. 'No.'

'Would you . . . would you like to perform a linking tonight? I could examine these link memories and try to find the identity behind them.'

Leiard nodded slowly. 'Yes. It has been too long since I have performed the ritual.' He noticed Jayim staring at him and smiled. 'And Jayim should join us. He has remained untrained since his teacher died six months ago.'

'Oh, don't put yourselves out for me,' Jayim said hastily. 'I'll only . . . get in the way.'

Tanara stared at her son in surprise. 'Jayim! You should take advantage of such a generous offer.'

Leiard looked at Olameer. Her expression was knowing.

'I can't. I'm visiting a friend tonight,' Jayim told his mother.

Millo frowned at his son. 'You did not mention this earlier. Are you planning to go alone? You know it's dangerous.'

'I'll be fine,' Jayim said. 'It's not far to Vin's place.'

Tanara's lips pressed together. 'You can go in the morning.'

'But I promised,' Jayim protested. 'He's sick.'

Tanara's eyebrows rose. 'Again?'

'Yes. The breathing sickness. It gets worse in summer.'

'Then I had best go with you,' Leiard said. 'I know many treatments for illnesses of the lungs.'

'I—'

'Thank you, Leiard,' Tanara said. 'That is kind of you.'

Jayim glanced from his mother to Leiard, then his shoulders slumped. Tanara stood and started gathering the dirty dishes. Olameer yawned delicately, then rose to help.

'Just as well,' she murmured. 'I am probably too tired to be of any use to you, Leiard. I never sleep well on ships.'

He nodded. 'Thank you for the offer. Perhaps another time?'

'I will be leaving in the early morning, but if you are here on my return we will perform the ritual then. In the meantime, be well.' She rose, then touched her heart, mouth and forehead. Leiard returned the gesture, and saw in the corner of his eye Jayim hastily following suit.

As Olameer left the room Leiard rose and looked expectantly at Jayim.

'What does your friend do for a living?'

The boy glanced up, then stood. 'His father is a tailor, so he's learning to be one too.'

'Will his family protest if I come to their house?'

Jayim hesitated, obviously considering this opportunity to be rid of Leiard, then shook his head.

'No. They won't mind. My teacher helped them since Vin was a baby. That's how I met him. I'll just get my bag.'

Leiard waited as Jayim fetched a small bag from his room. Once outside, the boy set a rapid pace. The street was dark and quiet. The windows of the houses on either side were bright squares of light and Leiard could hear the sound of voices and movement inside.

'Why did you decide to become a Dreamweaver, Jayim?' Leiard asked quietly.

Jayim glanced at him, but it was too dark to read his expression.

'I don't know. I liked Calem, my teacher. He made it sound so noble. I'd be helping people in ways the Circlians never can. And I hated the Circlians.'

'You no longer hate them, then?'

'I do, but . . .'

'But?'

'Not like I did then.'

'What has changed, do you think?'

Jayim sighed. 'I don't know.'

Sensing that the boy was thinking hard, Leiard remained silent. They turned into a narrower street.

'Maybe it isn't all the Circlians I hate. Maybe it's just a few of them.'

'Hate for a person is different to hate for a group of people. Usually it is harder to hate a group of people once you have realised you like an individual from that group.'

'Like Auraya?'

Leiard felt a strange thrill at the name. He had met with Auraya twice since her initial visit. They had talked of people they both knew in the village, and of events that had happened since she had left. She had told stories of her time as an initiate and then as a priestess. At one point she had admitted she was still surprised that the gods had chosen her. 'I didn't always agree with my fellow Circlians,' she had said. 'I guess that's your fault. If I had grown up in Jarime I'd probably have turned out as narrow-minded as everyone else.'

'Yes,' he said. 'Auraya is different.'

'But it's the other way around for me,' Jayim continued. 'I can see now that I don't hate all Circlians just because some of them are bad.'

And I don't hate Circlians – just their gods, a voice said from the depths of Leiard's mind. He drew in a quick breath at the surge of intense emotion that came with it. *Why have I buried such hatred?* he wondered. *Why has it only surfaced now?*

'I . . . I'm having doubts, Leiard.'

Leiard dragged his attention back to the boy at his side.

'About?'

Jayim sighed. 'Being a Dreamweaver. I'm not sure I want to any more.'

'I guessed as much.'

'What do you think I should do?'

Leiard smiled. 'What do you want?'

'I don't know.'

'What do you want from your life, then?'

'I don't know.'

'Of course you do. Do you want love? Children? Wealth? What about fame? Or power? Or both? Or do you want wisdom and knowledge more? What are you willing to work toward, Jayim? And what would you forsake in pursuit of it?'

'I don't know,' Jayim gasped despairingly. He moved into an alley. It was narrow, forcing Leiard to walk behind the boy. The sour smell of rotting vegetables filled the dark, close space.

'Of course you don't. You're young. It takes time for anyone to . . .'

A feeling of threat swept over Leiard. He caught hold of Jayim's shoulder.

'What?' the boy said tersely.

A wheezing exhalation echoed in the alley, then spluttered into a laugh. Two more voices joined in this merriment. As three shapes appeared in the gloom, Jayim cursed quietly.

'Where are you going this time of night, Dreamer?'

The voice was young and male. Leiard let these strangers' emotions flow over him. He felt a mix of predatory intention and cruel anticipation.

'He's got a friend,' a second voice warned.

'A friend?' the first boy scoffed, though his thoughts were immediately tempered by caution. 'Dreamers don't have friends. They have lookouts. Someone to watch in case a person happens upon them while they're seducing other people's wives and daughters. Well, that's too bad for you, Dreamer. We got here first. You're not going anywhere near Loiri.'

Seducing wives and daughters . . . An image flashed through Leiard's mind. He faced two men, both angry, both holding weapons. In a window above, a woman appeared. Though her face was in shadow he knew she was beautiful. She shouted angrily, but not at him. Her curses were directed at the men below.

'I'm not here to see Loiri, Kinnen,' Jayim said between gritted teeth. 'I'm here to see Vin.'

Leiard shook his head as the image faded. Another link memory? He could not remember ever being so intent on seduction. Something like that would surely stick in one's memory. *But then link memories also did that.*

'Vin ought to know better,' a third voice said, 'than to associate with Dreamweavers. What's in the bag, Jayim?'

'Nothing.'

Jayim's voice was steady, but Leiard could feel his fear increase abruptly. As the three bullies drew closer, Leiard channelled a little magic into his palm. Light blossomed between his fingers, setting his hand aglow. He stepped past Jayim and uncurled his hand.

The light filled the alley. To Leiard's dismay, three Circlian priests stood before him.

No, he corrected himself. *Initiates. They're not wearing rings.*

They stared at the light, blinking rapidly, then their eyes shifted to his face. Leiard regarded them impassively.

'I am unsure what your intention is by meeting us here in this manner. Jayim has informed you of the identity of our host and assured you that we are welcome. If that is not enough to satisfy you, then perhaps you should accompany us to our destination. Or . . .' he paused, then lowered his voice '. . . did you meet us here in order to acquire our services?'

The boys exchanged alarmed looks at the suggestion.

123

'If you have,' Leiard continued, 'and the matter is not urgent, we can arrange to visit you tomorrow. Would you prefer we came to the Temple or your homes?'

At that, the three boys began to back away.

'No,' the first said stiffly. 'That's fine. We're fine. No need to visit.'

After several steps they turned and swaggered off, making a show of indifference. Jayim let out a long, quiet sigh.

'Thanks.'

Leiard regarded the boy soberly. 'Does this happen often?'

'Now and then. Not for a while, actually, but I think they've been busy with all the visitors who came to the Choosing Ceremony.'

'Probably,' Leiard agreed.

'You frightened them off, though,' Jayim said, grinning.

'I bluffed them. It will not work again. They will remember that the law is against anyone using our services. You need to learn to protect yourself.'

'I know, but . . .'

'Your doubts have prevented you seeking a new teacher.'

'Yes.' Jayim shrugged. 'I have Dreamweavers like you, who come to stay with us. They all teach me things.'

'You know that is not enough.'

The boy bowed his head. 'I think becoming a Dreamweaver was a mistake. I wanted to *be* someone.' He looked down the alley. 'Like them, but not a priest. They would have made my life terrible. And . . . and Father kept pushing me to be a scribe, like him, but I wasn't any good at it.' He sighed. 'Becoming a Dreamweaver only made things worse with Kinnen's lot. And my parents.' He gave a bitter laugh. 'They were so eager to show they'd accept whatever choice I made that they turned our home into a safehouse.' He sighed. 'So I can't stop now.'

'Of course you can,' Leiard told him.

Jayim shook his head. 'Kinnen's lot will think I gave in. And my parents will be disappointed.'

'Which is not reason enough for you to be allowed to continue wearing the vest.'

Jayim frowned, then his eyes widened. 'You're . . . you're here to kick me out!'

Leiard smiled and shook his head. 'No. But I see much about you that concerns me. By our laws, if three Dreamweavers of each of the three ages agree that another must be cast out, it can and must be done.' He let his voice soften. 'You are full of doubts, Jayim. That is reasonable in a boy of your age, in your situation. We will give you time to consider. But you cannot neglect your training while you consider, and you have taken no steps to acquire a teacher.'

Jayim stared at the light in Leiard's hand. 'I see,' he said quietly.

Leiard paused, then put aside the last shreds of his fading need for solitude. 'If you decide to remain with us, Jayim, and you wish it, I will take up your training. I cannot promise that you will always remain in Jarime, so you must be prepared to leave your parents and accompany me into an uncertain future. But I will promise that I can make a Dreamweaver of you.'

The boy's gaze shifted to Leiard's, then he looked away, his thoughts in turmoil.

Leiard chuckled. 'Think about it. Now we had best visit this sick friend of yours.'

Jayim nodded, and pointed along the alley. 'We go in the back way. Follow me.'

Flying over the Open, Tryss felt a shiver of excitement. A great half-circle of lights had formed near the centre where a sheet of rock known as the Flat provided space for many Siyee to stand together. The leaders of every tribe – the Speakers – stood above this, along the edge of a low natural wall of rock. The air was thick with Siyee arriving for the Gathering.

As his father began to descend, Tryss followed. His mother was a presence not far behind. They joined the Siyee circling down and, once their feet were on the ground, quickly moved out of the way to allow others room to land. As they joined their tribe, Tryss looked for Drilli's. They stood close by. Drilli caught his eye and winked. He grinned in reply.

There were fifteen tribes of Siyee this year. One less than the last. The West Forest tribe had been butchered by land-walkers last summer. The few surviving members, unable to return to their territory, had joined other tribes. Drilli's people, the Snake River tribe, had been driven from their village, but enough members had survived for them to still be considered a tribe. They had settled temporarily among other tribes until a new village site could be agreed upon.

Tryss looked up at the Speakers. A strangely garbed man was sitting among them. His clothing covered his arms, but this only drew attention to the absence of membranes between his arms and body. No Siyee could ever wear clothing like that.

His size more than made up for his lack of wings. Tryss could finally see why these landwalkers, despite their inability to fly, were such a danger to his people. The man was sitting on the rock ledge, yet his head was on an equal level to the Speakers'. His arms were thick and his legs long. His body was a great barrel, made even bigger by the thick layers of clothing he wore.

He was enormous.

His head, however, was small. Or was it? Tryss did a quick comparison to one of the Speakers, then nodded to himself. The landwalker's head was the same size as a Siyee's. It just looked smaller because it was attached to such a large body.

The Speakers were moving now. They formed a line along the ledge and each gave a piercing whistle. The landwalker, Tryss noted, winced at the sound. The Siyee quietened.

Sirri, the Speaker of Tryss's tribe, stepped up onto an outcrop known as Speakers' Rock. She lifted her arms and spread her wings wide.

'People of the mountains. Tribes of the Siyee. We, the Speakers, have called you here tonight to hear the words of a visitor to our lands. He is, as you have heard and can see, a landwalker. A landwalker from a distant land called Hania, not a landwalker from among those who have killed our kin and taken our lands. We have spoken with him at length and are satisfied that this is true.'

Sirri paused, her eyes moving from face to face as she judged the mood of the Gathering.

'Landwalker Gremmer has climbed our mountains and crossed our rivers in order to reach us. He has come alone, on a journey that, for a landwalker, takes months. Why has he done this? He has brought an offer of alliance. An alliance with the White, the five humans that the gods have chosen to be their representatives in the mortal world.'

The Siyee stirred, exchanging glances. Talk of a group of landwalkers chosen by the gods had been repeated among the Siyee for years. Over the last century individual Siyee had been visited by the goddess Huan, who had spoken of the Gifted humans who had been selected. In time, the goddess had promised, these chosen ones would help the Siyee defend themselves from invaders.

In the last five years the landwalker incursions had increased dramatically, prompting many to hope that these promised protectors would arrive soon. *A whole tribe was lost last summer*, Tryss thought. *They'd better hurry up, or there might not be any of us left to protect.*

'Gremmer has spent many days with us now,' Sirri continued, 'and has learned a little of our language. He wishes to speak to you tonight, to tell you of the Gods' Chosen.'

Sirri turned and nodded to the landwalker. The man slowly rose and stepped up onto Speakers' Rock. There was a murmuring among the watching Siyee, half wonder, half fear, as his full height was revealed.

The landwalker moved to the edge of the outcrop and smiled self-consciously at the crowd. He towered over all. Then, to Tryss's surprise, Gremmer sat down, crossing his legs like a child.

He did that deliberately, Tryss mused. *To look less imposing.*

The man was holding a piece of paper in his large, stumpy fingers. He looked down at it and coughed quietly.

'People of the sky. Tribes of the Siyee. Let me tell you of the men and women the gods have chosen as their representatives.' His way of speaking was strange, and it was obvious that he was taking care with every word.

'The first was Juran, chosen a century ago. He is our leader and the one who gathered the first priests and priestesses together and called them Circlians. The second was Dyara, chosen to be the law-maker. Then Rian, the pious one, joined them; and Mairae, a maid of beauty and compassion, followed. The last was chosen but a month ago. I do not yet know his or her name as I left before the Choosing Ceremony.'

Gremmer looked up from his sheet of paper. 'For a hundred years Hania has seen good work from the Gods' Chosen. Law and justice have been fair. Those who meet with misfortune are helped. Those who fall ill are cared for. Children are taught to read, write and understand numbers. There has been no war.'

He straightened now, and his eyes moved across the faces of the Siyee before he looked at his notes again.

'Circlian priests and priestesses have served in many lands since the beginning, but Hania is the only land the White rule. Toren and Genria in the east have been our allies for over fifty years. Dunway, the warrior nation in the northwest, became an ally ten years ago. The White are negotiating with the Council of Elders in Somrey, and now we bring an offer of alliance to Si.'

He smiled and glanced up at the Siyee. 'I have found you to be a noble, peaceful people. I know the White can help you with your troubles. Your land is being taken by Toren settlers. Laws need to be made and enforced to stop them. You need to look to your defence. If you cannot stop Toren settlers, how would you ever stop an army?

'The White protect their allies. In return, they ask that allies send fighters to help them if they are invaded. Since they are powerful and bring peace wherever they go, that help will probably not be needed.

'If Si and the White were allies, we could help each other in many ways. You know of Huan and a little of the other gods. Our priests and priestesses can teach you more. They can also increase your knowledge of magic, writing, numbers and healing. If you wished, the Temple would send a few priests to Si to live among you. Siyee might come to the Temple to become priests and priestesses themselves. There are many advantages to this. Messages can be sent telepathically by those priests and priestesses, so you would know what is happening in the world outside. Reports of attacks upon Siyee would reach the White quickly and be dealt with. People – landwalkers – would understand the Siyee better, and Siyee would understand landwalkers, too. Understanding brings respect and friendship. Friendship brings peace and prosperity.' He smiled and nodded several times. 'Thank you for listening.'

The Siyee remained silent as Gremmer stood up and backed

away from the edge of the outcrop. Tryss found that his heart was racing. *We could learn so much from these landwalkers*, he thought. *Things we lost when we came to the mountains. Things the landwalkers have invented since*. But Tryss read doubt in the faces of his people. Sirri stepped forward.

'We, the Speakers, will now talk with our tribes.'

The Speakers leapt off the outcrop and glided down to their tribes. As Sirri landed and joined Tryss's tribe several people spoke at once. She raised her hands to stop them.

'One at a time,' she said. 'Let us sit in a circle and speak our minds in turn.'

Tryss's mother and father sat down and he settled behind them. Sirri nodded to the man sitting to her left, Tryss's uncle, Till.

'It is a good offer,' he said. 'We could use their protection. But we have nothing to offer in return. Gremmer speaks of fighters. We have none.'

Sirri turned her attention to the next Siyee in the circle. He repeated the same doubts. As the rest of the tribe spoke, Tryss felt frustration building. Then Tryss's aunt spoke up.

'Does it matter?' Vissi said darkly. 'They are the Gods' Chosen. Who would dare to fight them? Gremmer is right. We would probably never need to fight. We should agree to this alliance.'

'But what if there is a small war? Between countries allied with the White. Or a rebellion,' Tryss's father asked. 'What if they ask for our help then? Do we send our young men and women to a certain death?'

Vissi looked pained. 'Not certain. Possible. It is a risk, yes. A gamble. We are losing young men and women to these settlers all the time. And older men and women. And their children. We will keep losing them – and our land, too. That is more certain than the chances of us being called to war.'

There were reluctant nods from the gathered Siyee. Tryss bit his lip. *We can fight*, he thought at them. *You keep thinking that you have to fight like landwalkers. We have to fight like Siyee – from the air. With my hunting harness. With Drilli's blowpipe.*

'Perhaps we will learn how to fight before then.'

This had come from Sreil. Tryss felt his heart lift. Had Sreil remembered Tryss's harness?

'If landwalkers come here, they can teach us,' Sreil added. Tryss's heart sank.

'But then we will have to admit we can't fight,' Vissi warned.

'I think we must be honest with these White,' Sirri said. 'After all, they are closer to the gods than any mortal, and the gods can see our minds. They will know if we are dishonest.'

The tribe was silent. Then Tryss's father spoke.

'Then they will know that we cannot fight with sword or spear. They would not have asked this of us, if they felt we had no value to them in war.'

The meaning behind his father's words struck Tryss like a physical blow. He felt a rush of cold, and shivered. Slowly he lifted his head to stare up at the stars.

Have you seen my mind? he asked. *Have you seen my ideas? Is this what you mean to have happen – for me to give my people a way to fight?*

He held his breath. *What if the gods answer?* he suddenly thought. *That would be . . . wonderful and terrifying.*

But no answer came. Tryss felt a moment's disappointment. Had they heard, but were ignoring him? Did this mean he shouldn't continue with his inventions? Or were they just not paying attention?

I could go mad thinking like this, he decided. *They didn't say 'yes'. They didn't say 'no'. I'll take that as meaning they weren't listening, or don't care, and do what I want.*

All he wanted was to perfect his harness and see the Siyee

using it to hunt. If his inventions led to the end of his people's troubles . . . well, that would be even better. He'd be famous. Respected.

Tomorrow, he decided, *I'm going to finish making my changes. After that I'll test it. When I'm sure it's working perfectly, I'll present it to the Speakers.*

CHAPTER 8

Jarime was a city with many rivers. They carved the city into districts, some more affluent than others, and were utilised by watercraft carrying people and goods. Water was drawn from them for use, then channelled away to the sea through underground tunnels.

One half of the Temple boundary was formed by a river, and a tributary of it flowed through the holy ground. There were many pleasant leafy places along this tributary where a priest or priestess could find quiet and solitude for contemplation and prayer. The mouth of it was guarded to prevent outsiders disrupting the quiet, but if a visitor carried the right permission token he or she could ride the shallow Temple boats into the grounds.

Auraya's favourite place on the river was a small whitestone pavilion. Stairs led down to the water on one side, where bollards allowed boats to be tied up. At the moment a veez was balancing on the rounded top of one bollard, investigating it closely. He looked up at the next post and Auraya caught her breath as he sprang toward it. Landing neatly, he leapt again, jumping from one bollard to the next.

'I do hope you can swim, Mischief,' she said. 'One mistake and you're going to fall in the river.'

Having reached the last bollard, he stood up on his hind legs and blinked at her.

'Owaya,' he said. In a blur of movement, he jumped down from the post, bounded to her seat and leapt into her lap.

'Snack?' he asked, gazing up into her eyes.

She laughed and scratched his cheeks. 'No snacks.'

'Tweet?'

'No treats.'

'Food?'

'No food.'

'Titfit?'

'No titbits.'

He paused. 'Niffle?'

'No nibbles.' She waited, but he stayed silent, gazing imploringly at her. 'Later,' she told him.

The veez's sense of time was limited. He understood 'night' and 'day', and the phases of the moon, but had no understanding of smaller units of time. She could not tell him 'in a few minutes' so she made do with 'later', which simply meant 'not now'.

He was a strange and amusing companion. Whenever she returned to her rooms he bounded up to her, saying her name over and over. It was hard to resist such a welcome. She tried to find an hour each day to work on his training, as the Somreyans recommended, but she was lucky to manage more than a few minutes. Yet he learned quickly, so perhaps this was enough.

Finding a name for him had been a challenge. After she had heard that Mairae's veez was named Stardust she decided she must find something less fanciful. Danjin had told her of a rich old lady who had named hers Virtue – apparently so she could always end a conversation with 'but I do treasure my Virtue'. Now, when Auraya discussed her plans each morning with Danjin, he always smiled when she told him: 'I must put aside some time for Mischief.'

This morning, however, her reason for bringing Mischief with her was not to continue his training but as a distraction if the conversation she was planning proved awkward. She was curious to see how the veez would react to her visitor, though he had a habit of pronouncing judgement of people loudly while in their presence, which she hadn't yet managed to break.

Opening her basket, she took out an elaborate toy from the collection the Somreyans had provided. Setting it down, she began reading the instructions on its use. To her surprise it appeared to be a toy designed to teach the veez how to unpick locks with its mind. She wasn't sure what was more amusing, that the creature was capable of it, or that the Somreyans thought it an appropriate trick to teach it.

She heard a splash and looked upriver. A punt drifted into sight, guided by two pole men. As she saw the passenger, she sighed with relief. She had not been sure if Leiard would accept her invitation. They hadn't met in the Temple grounds before, but in quiet and private places in the city. Knowing how all things Circlian made him nervous and fearful, she had wondered if he would dare enter the Temple again.

But here he was.

Which was just as well. If he had been unable to bring himself to enter the Temple he would not be able to perform the role she wanted to offer him. She watched the punt draw closer. Mischief leapt out of her lap and scampered up a post of the pavilion into the roof. The pole men manoeuvred the punt out of the current, and when the craft neared the stone steps one jumped out and tossed ropes around the bollards.

Leiard rose in one graceful movement. He stepped ashore and climbed the stairs. Watching him, Auraya felt a wistful admiration. There was something appealing about his perpetual air of dignity and calm, and the way he moved with unhurried ease.

Yet as she met his eyes she saw that this impression of calm was only external. His gaze wavered, leaving hers and returning only to slip away again. She hesitated, then looked closer. Fear and hope warred in his thoughts.

She was glad she had insisted that she meet him alone. Dyara had wanted to supervise, as always, but Auraya had guessed that the presence of another White would intimidate him. Especially one who radiated disapproval at the mere mention of Dreamweavers.

As she observed she saw that hope appeared to be winning the battle with fear. Leiard saw in Auraya a potential for change for his people that made dealing with the fear the Temple aroused in him worthwhile. She noted his trust only extended to her. He believed she would not harm Dreamweavers willingly. Nor would she be happy should the other White do so. She was the best opportunity for peace the Dreamweavers had encountered.

However, she saw that he did not entirely believe this. Circlians cared only for their gods and themselves. They despised and feared Dreamweavers. He wondered if he was a fool for trusting her. It was frustrating being unable to sense her emotions. She might have changed since becoming a White. This might all be a trap . . .

Auraya frowned. She had seen hints that he had an ability to sense emotions with his mind when they had met before, but this was the first time he had thought about it specifically, confirming that it was true. He had never mentioned this ability previously, not even when she was a child.

So he didn't tell me everything back then, she thought. That isn't surprising. The villagers would not have liked the idea he could sense something of their thoughts, even if only emotions. I wonder if other Dreamweavers have this ability, too.

All this flashed through her mind as he climbed into the pavilion. She smiled as he stopped a few steps below her, his eyes level with hers.

'Auraya,' he said. 'Auraya the White. That is how I should address you, isn't it?'

She shrugged. 'Officially, yes. Privately you can call me whatever you feel comfortable with. Except dung-breath. I'd take exception to that.'

His eyebrows rose and his lips twitched into a smile. Seeing the pole men raise hands to cover their mirth, she turned and waved at them.

'Thank you. Could you return in an hour?'

They nodded, then made the two-handed gesture of the circle. Unwinding the ropes from the bollards, they stepped back onto the punt, picked up their poles and guided the craft downstream.

Auraya moved into the shade of the pavilion, conscious of Leiard as he followed her.

'How are you?' she asked.

'Well,' he replied. 'And you?'

'The same. Better. I'm glad you changed your mind about leaving the city.'

He smiled. 'As am I.'

'How are your hosts?'

'Well. Their son's teacher died last winter and he found no replacement. I have taken on the task, for now.'

She felt a small pang of envy. Or was it simply longing for the past? Whatever the reason, she hoped the boy realised how lucky he was having Leiard for a teacher.

'I'd have thought it would be easier to find Dreamweaver teachers in the city than out of it,' she said. 'Surely there are more here than you and this boy?'

Leiard shrugged. 'Yes, but none were free to take on a student.

137

We do not teach more than one at a time, and even those of us that like to teach need some time free from the constant demands of a student.'

Constant demands? Did this mean Leiard was going to be occupied for the next few years?

'So will this new student take up all of your time?' she asked.

He shook his head. 'Not all.'

'Will he keep you in Jarime?'

'Not if I decide to leave. A student goes wherever his teacher does.'

'You wouldn't happen to be thinking of visiting Somrey, would you?'

His eyebrows rose. 'Why?'

She made her expression sober and her voice businesslike. 'I have a proposal for you, Leiard. A serious proposal from a White to a Dreamweaver.'

She watched him react to the change in her manner. He leaned away from her and his expression became wary, but his mind was full of hope.

'Don't feel you have to accept it,' she told him. 'If what I propose doesn't suit you, it might suit another Dreamweaver. If you don't think any Dreamweaver would agree to what I'm proposing, please tell me. Either way, I'd appreciate your advice.'

He nodded.

'The White are seeking an alliance with Somrey,' she told him. As she explained the situation he said nothing, only listened and occasionally nodded to show that he understood. 'Juran asked me to look over the terms of the alliance,' she continued, 'and I realised I didn't know as much about Dreamweavers as I thought. The questions I had . . .' She smiled. 'I wished you were there to answer them for me. I realised that what we need is a Dreamweaver adviser. Someone to tell us which terms of the alliance are likely to cause offence. Someone to help us negotiate. Someone who might come to negotiate on behalf of Dreamweavers everywhere.' She paused and watched him closely. 'Would you be our Dreamweaver adviser, Leiard? Will you come with me to Somrey?'

He regarded her silently. As he recovered from his surprise he began to consider her offer, debating with himself.

This is the opportunity Tanara thought might come. I can't let it pass by. I will accept.

No! If you do this you will have to enter the White Tower. Juran will be there. The gods will be there!

I can't let this opportunity pass out of fear.

You must. It is dangerous. Let her choose another. Find her another.

There is nobody better than myself for this position. I know her. She knows me.

She is a slave to the gods.

She is Auraya.

It was strange to be watching someone else's internal struggle. Reason and hope were winning the fight against his fear, but she saw that the fear ran deep. What had caused this powerful terror of the gods? Had something happened to him to fill him with such dread? Or was this fear common among Dreamweavers? The stories she had heard of times when the Dreamweavers had been brutally persecuted were enough to make anyone's skin prickle with horror.

He would have to fight this fear every time he entered the Temple. Suddenly she knew she could not ask this of him. She would have to find another Dreamweaver. She could not ask a friend to face this terror.

'It doesn't have to be you,' she told him. 'You may be too busy training this boy, anyway. Can you recommend another Dreamweaver?'

'I . . .' He paused and shook his head. 'Once again, you have surprised me, Auraya,' he said quietly. 'I thought, at first, that you only wanted advice on this alliance. Your offer is too great a thing to decide without spending some time in consideration.'

She nodded. 'Of course. Think about it. Let me know in . . . well, I'm not sure how long I can give you. A week. Maybe more. I'll let you—'

They both jumped as something dropped onto her shoulder.

'Tweet!' a shrill voice trilled in her ear.

'Mischief!' she gasped, holding a hand to her pounding heart. 'That was not polite!'

'Tweeeeeet!' the veez demanded. He leapt off her shoulder onto Leiard's. To Auraya's relief, Leiard was smiling broadly.

'Come here,' he said, slipping his fingers around the veez's body. Mischief gave a mew of protest as Leiard lifted him down and turned him onto his back. As the Dreamweaver began scratching his belly, the veez relaxed and closed his eyes. Soon he was lying, limp, in one of Leiard's hands, his little fingers twitching.

'That's pathetic,' she exclaimed.

He grinned and held the veez out to her. For a moment his gaze met hers over the creature. She felt a strange delight at the sparkle that had come into his eyes. She had rarely seen him look so . . . *playful*.

Suddenly she remembered something her mother had said, years before. That the women in the village were worried she fancied Leiard. That he was not as old as he appeared.

I can see why they were worried. I thought he was ancient, but then I was a child and only saw the white hair and long beard. He can't be older than forty, and if he shaved and cut his hair I think he'd be quite good-looking, in a weathered sort of way.

The veez roused himself from his trance and lifted his head. 'More scratch?'

They both chuckled. Leiard set the veez down on the seat.

Mischief began to beg for food again so Auraya opened her basket and brought out refreshments for them all. Then she read aloud the instructions for the toy and they speculated on the wisdom of teaching such tricks to the creature.

Too soon, the punt reappeared. Leiard waited until it was tied to the bollards before standing. He paused and looked down at her.

'When do you sail for Somrey?'

She shrugged. 'That depends on whether I find an adviser. If I don't, Mairae will probably go alone in a month or so.'

'If you do?'

'Sooner.'

He nodded, then turned and walked toward the punt. After a few steps he paused and looked back, smiled faintly and inclined his head.

'It was a pleasure talking to you, Auraya the White. I will accept this position you have offered me. When would you like me to meet with you?'

She stared at him in surprise. 'What happened to spending some time in consideration?'

His shoulders lifted. 'I just did.'

She looked at him closely. There was no sign of the turmoil that had filled his mind earlier. It seemed reason had overcome his fear, now that he'd had a chance to think about it.

'I'll tell Juran you have accepted. When I need you to come to the Tower, I'll send you a message.'

He nodded once. Turning away, he stepped down to the punt and folded himself onto the low seat. She nodded to the pole men, who tossed ropes onto the craft and stepped aboard. Soon they were pushing their way upstream, Leiard sitting calmly between them.

Watching them, Auraya considered the doubts she'd had. She'd feared he wouldn't meet with her, but he had. She'd worried that the meeting would be awkward, but she'd felt as at ease with him as she always had. At the same time, she had anxiously wondered what his answer would be.

Now she had only to fret about the possibility that this whole arrangement might ruin their friendship.

When the punt had moved out of sight, Auraya called to Mischief, picked up her basket and started back toward the White Tower.

Fiamo swallowed the last of the spicewater and leaned back against the mast. He was feeling particularly pleased with himself, and it wasn't just the effect of the liquor. Summer always brought bigger catches, but today's had been better than the season's average. He'd made a good sum of money.

He smiled to himself. Most would go to the crew when they got back – and his wife. But he had a mind to put a little aside to buy presents for his sons when he next took a trip northeast.

For now there was nothing to do but lounge around the pier of Meran. The wind had dropped off, and probably wouldn't return until late afternoon. In the meantime it was promising to be one of those warm, lazy afternoons good for nothing but drinking with his crew.

His men were neighbours and family. He had worked with them for years, first as crew working with his father, now as captain since his father had died of lungrot five years before.

Fiamo felt the boat tilt fractionally and heard the sound of boots on the gangplank. He looked up and grinned as Old Marro stepped onto the deck, carrying an earthenware jug and a large flatloaf of bread.

'Supplies,' the man said. 'Like you ordered.'

'About time,' Fiamo said gruffly. 'I thought you'd—'

'Captain!' This came from Harro, the youngest of Fiamo's

crew – a neighbour's son. Fiamo looked up at the boy, hearing uncertainty and warning in the young voice. Harro was standing at the prow, his eyes fixed on the small village.

'Eh?'

'There's a . . . there's a hunt of vorns coming down the road. Maybe ten of them.'

'There's *what*?'

Fiamo clambered to his feet, and for a moment his vision blurred from spicewater and the sudden movement. As his sight cleared he saw what the boy had noticed. Meran was the largest port a local could reach in a day's sailing, but it was small as far as villages went. A road began at the end of the pier and climbed steadily up into rolling hills. Coming down that road was a surging, leaping mass of black creatures.

'Gods protect us,' he gasped, and made the one-handed symbol of the circle. 'Untie us. Ring the bell.'

He had seen a vorn once in the light of a full moon. It had been big, most likely enlarged in his eyes by his fear. These vorns were larger than his imagination had ever painted them. They seemed unperturbed by the sunlight, too. They were running down the road toward him in one sinuous black mass.

'Hurry up,' he snapped.

The crew had risen to see this impossible sight. At his words, they sprang to the ropes. Fiamo moved to the rail and shouted a warning to the other fishermen tied there. He felt his own boat rock as his men pushed it away from the pier. Harro rang the warning bell urgently.

Sails were unfurled, but remained slack. Fiamo realised his heart was pounding. He watched as the few villagers still outdoors in the small town sighted the coming mass of animals and fled inside their houses. The gap between his boat and the pier widened slowly. The length of road between the vorns and the pier was shrinking much faster.

'Oars!' he shouted.

Men scrambled to obey. As Fiamo stared at the advancing creatures they reached level ground. A shape appeared in the middle of them and he heard himself gasp in disbelief.

'A man! A man riding one of them!' Harro yelled.

At the same time, Fiamo felt the boat's progress speed as oars dipped into the water on either side. He looked around the pier. The other boats, smaller and lighter, had made better progress. His was now the closest to the pier. Though he doubted even vorns of that size could leap the gap, something told him he was not out of danger yet.

The hunt spilled through the village like a black flood. Fiamo could see the rider better now, a man dressed in clothes like no commoner would wear. The boat was more than twenty strides from the pier and gathering speed as fear lent strength to the crew. The vorns ignored the houses. They loped onto the pier, then milled at the edge. The rider looked around at the fleeing boats, and his gaze returned to Fiamo's. He raised a hand.

Fiamo drew in a breath, ready to defy the stranger's order to return. No voice came across the water. Instead, the boat shuddered to a halt.

Then it rushed backwards.

The oars jammed in their rings. Crew struggled uselessly with them. The boy gave a high-pitched shriek. Others cried out names of the gods. Fiamo crouched, paralysed by terror, as his boat raced back to the shore like a woman who had just laid eyes on her lost love.

We're going to smash into the pier, he thought.

At the last moment, the boat slowed. Even before it bumped into the pier, vorns were leaping aboard. There were splashes on either side as those men who could swim dived into the water. *I should go too*, he thought, but he remained where he

144

was. *Cursed fool I am. I can't bring myself to give up my boat so easily.*

A thought had burrowed its way into his mind. If this man could control these beasts, then he had only the man to fear. A man could be bargained with.

Still, Fiamo's heart thundered in his chest as the vorns surged past him, their tongues lolling in mouths lined with sharp teeth. A few circled him, but they did not leap for his throat. He turned as yells of pain came from behind, and cried out in dismay as he saw vorns with their jaws fixed on the arms and legs of crew, but they were dragging the men away from the railing, not pulling them to the deck. With their added weight the boat floated low in the water.

Hearing the sound of wood sliding over wood, Fiamo turned back to see the gangplank move, unaided by any human, to the edge of the deck. As it settled on the pier the stranger rode aboard. He slid off the back of his mount and turned to stare at Fiamo.

'Captain,' the man said in a strange accent. 'Tell crew take oars.'

Fiamo forced himself to look at his remaining crew, huddled together, ringed by vorns. Some, he heard, were murmuring prayers to the gods.

'You heard him, boys. Back to the oars.'

His voice shook, but held enough command to send the crew edging around the vorns to their former places.

'Pull up oars and keep them up,' the sorcerer ordered.

As the crew obeyed, the boat began to move away from the pier. The gangplank slid into the water like a bad omen. Fiamo stared in amazement as his boat picked up speed, cutting through the water despite the idle rowers and lack of wind.

Magic, he thought. He turned to find the stranger looking back to the shore. Following the man's gaze, Fiamo saw a distant figure riding down the road to the village. A white figure on a galloping white mount.

Could it be . . . ?

The newcomer pulled up at the end of the pier and leapt to the ground. The boat shuddered to a stop, knocking Fiamo and many of the vorns off their feet. Fiamo felt his heart lift as the craft began to move backwards. He gazed at the white figure.

It is! It's one of the White. We're saved!

The stranger muttered something and the force pulling them backwards lost its hold. Released, the boat drifted to a halt.

'Row,' the stranger growled. 'Now.'

The men hesitated, glancing doubtfully at Fiamo.

Vorns growled.

Men grabbed oars and began to row. Fiamo climbed to his feet again. Slowly the boat moved away from the coastline. When the distant figure was a mere speck of white, the black sorcerer chuckled quietly. He turned his back on the coast and swept his gaze over the boat and its crew. When he met Fiamo's eyes he smiled in a way that turned the captain's blood to ice.

'Captain, do you have more oars?'

Fiamo looked around. Harro and Old Marro stood empty-handed. The boy whimpered as two of the vorns approached him.

'No,' Fiamo admitted. 'But we—'

At some unspoken signal, the animals leapt up and seized the pair's throats. As blood gushed forth, Fiamo felt all strength drain from his legs and he sank to the deck. There were no screams, but he could hear arms and legs flailing.

'Keep rowing,' the sorcerer barked. Fiamo heard him moving along the deck toward him. The sounds of the animals feasting was all too audible in the windless silence.

146

Old Marro. My neighbour's boy. They're dead. Dead.

The sorcerer loomed over him.

'Why?' Fiamo heard himself croak.

The man looked away. 'They hungry.'

Then a rustle of cloth drew Fiamo's eyes upwards. The sails were billowing with air. The afternoon wind had arrived.

Where it would take them today, he did not like to guess.

The tower was taller than any she had seen. It was so high that clouds tore themselves upon it as they passed . . .

No. Not again.

Emerahl wrenched herself out of the dream and opened her eyes. It had come to her nearly every night for the last month. Each time it was the same: the tower fell on her and she slowly suffocated under the rubble. If she let it run to its end she woke up feeling shaken and frightened, so she had started waking herself up as soon as it began.

After all, it's going to wake me up anyway. I may as well do so on my terms.

Sighing, she rose and poured some water into a kettle and started a fire. The flames cast eerie shadows on the walls of the lighthouse – the most menacing being that of herself with hunched shoulders and mussed hair.

Old witch woman, she thought at the shadow. *No wonder the villagers fear you.*

She hadn't seen any of them for several days. Occasionally she wondered if 'little Rinnie' was still evading the clutches of her father and his cronies. Mostly she enjoyed the peace.

Then why these dreams? she asked herself. Taking a few dried leaves from a jar, she sprinkled them into a cup. The kettle whispered as the water grew hot. She linked her fingers together and considered the dream.

It was always the same. The details never varied. It was

more like a memory dream than an ordinary dream, but she had no memories like it. She prided herself on her memory and that she had never suppressed any of her recollections of the past. Good or bad, she accepted them as part of who she was.

This dream had a purposeful feel to it. Something she had not felt for a long time. It reminded her of a . . . *of a dream sent by a Dreamweaver*!

This revelation sent a rare thrill of surprise through her. It was possible that a sorcerer had learned the skill, or even a priest, but something told her it was a Dreamweaver's work.

But why send it? Had it been sent solely to her, or projected out to anyone sensitive enough to receive it? She drummed her fingers on her knees. The contents of a dream could be a clue to its origins. She considered the towers that she knew had existed in the past. None looked similar, but the dream tower could simply represent some other one. Or another building that had collapsed. She felt a chill run down her spine. Mirar had been killed when Juran, the leader of the Circlians, had destroyed Jarime's Dreamweaver House and buried him in the rubble. It was said his body was crushed so badly he was barely recognisable.

Did this mean someone was dreaming about the death of Mirar? Someone with Dreamweaver skills so powerful that he or she was projecting the dream loud enough for Emerahl, in her remote location, to receive them. It made sense that a Dreamweaver would dream of the death of his or her leader, but why was he or she dreaming of it over and over. And why project it?

The kettle had begun to rattle softly now. Suddenly she was in no mood for a soporific. She wanted to think. Taking the kettle from the fire, she set it aside. As its bubbling subsided she heard the faint sound of voices outside.

She sighed. So they were coming at last. Time to show these upstart villagers why they should respect their elders.

Rising, she moved to the entrance of the lighthouse. Sure enough, a column of men was winding its way up the path to the lighthouse. She smiled sadly and shook her head.

Fools.

Then her amusement fled. At the head of the column was a man dressed entirely in white.

Priest! Turning away, she cursed loudly. No priest of the Circlians was strong enough to best her, but each was a conduit to their gods. And should the gods see her through this priest's eyes . . .

She cursed again, then hurried back inside. Grabbing a blanket, she threw the most valuable of her belongings into it. With a scrap of thin rope she bound the blanket around these possessions. Hugging the bundle to her chest, she moved to the far side of the room.

'Sorceress!'

The voice was the village head's. Emerahl froze, then forced herself to move. Drawing magic, she swept away the dirt covering a section of the floor. A large rectangle of stone appeared.

'Come out, sorceress, or we'll come in and drag you out!'

Quickly! Drawing more magic, she sent dirt flying. A stairway appeared. She forced thick dirt out of the tunnel beyond. Stone appeared, then a cavity. Finally, with a gasp of relief, she cleared the mouth of a tunnel.

'All right. We're coming in.'

'I will enter first, for your safety,' an unfamiliar voice said. There was a weak protest. 'If she is a sorcerer, as you say, she may be more dangerous than you expect. I have dealt with her kind before.'

Emerahl fled into the tunnel. A few steps into the darkness, she turned and reached out with her mind. Dirt cascaded into the tunnel as she pulled it toward her. She could not tell if it was enough to conceal her exit.

Best get away, then. She willed a light into existence. It revealed a staircase descending into blackness. Clutching her bundle, she hurried down.

The stairs seemed endless, but at least the tunnel hadn't deteriorated too much. In places the walls or roof had given way and she had to push through carefully. The air was growing damp when she heard a faint echo of sound from behind her.

She cursed again. That tunnel had been her secret for over a hundred years. She should have chased off the smugglers when they had first arrived, but she had rightly feared that news of a fearsome sorceress living in the lighthouse would attract unwanted attention. Now she was being driven out of her home by their descendants.

A fierce anger gripped her. It was tempting to ambush them in the dark. So long as the priest didn't see her, she would be safe. She could kill him, and the rest, before they knew what had happened.

'Nothing stays the same. All you can be sure of in life is change.'

Mirar had said that. He had faced the final change: death. One mistake and she would join him. It was not worth the risk.

She ran down the rest of the stairs.

At the bottom was a stone door. No point in persuading the mechanism to work. It was probably rusted shut. Extending her hands, she channelled magic through them. Force struck the stone and it shattered with a deafening boom. She stepped out onto a narrow path to the left of the door.

It was not a path so much as a fold of rock in the cliff. She extinguished her light and continued by moonlight. Her old body was already aching from her flight down the passage.

Now she felt unsteady as she hurried along the path, one hand touching the cliff side for balance.

She did not dare pause to look behind. When the pursuit reached the end of the tunnel, she would hear it. The cliff curved around, so she was probably out of sight already.

The path narrowed and she was forced to press herself flat against the rock and edge along it, balancing on her toes. Finally she felt a break in the rock face. She shuffled to it and hauled herself into the cave.

Cupping her hand, she created another light. The cave was shallow and most of the space was filled by a small boat. She examined it closely. It was made of a single piece of saltwood, a rare and expensive timber that was difficult to work but took hundreds of years to deteriorate. The name she had painted on the prow so long ago had flaked away.

'Hello again, Windchaser,' she murmured, running her hands over the fine grain. 'I haven't got any sails for you, I'm afraid. I'll have to rig up a blanket for now.'

Taking hold of the prow, she dragged it toward the mouth of the cave. When most of it was projecting from the cliff, she gave it a firm shove with magic. It flew outward and down, guided by her mind, and splashed onto the surging sea.

Next she sent the bundle down into the boat, hoping that the more delicate of her possessions would survive the landing. A wave threatened to toss the boat against the cliff, but she held it in place with her will. She stepped to the edge and drew in a deep breath. The water was going to be *very* cold.

Then she heard voices to her right. Peering around the edge of the cave she saw moving light no more than fifty strides away.

Smothering a curse, she forced her old body to dive forward, as far out from the cliff as possible.

She fell.

Liquid ice suddenly surrounded her. Though she had braced herself for the cold, it took all her effort not to gasp out in shock and pain. Twisting around, she kicked toward the light of the moon.

As her head broke through the surface of the water she felt a wave force her toward the cliff. She reached for more magic and pushed against the solid presence behind it. Water gurgled around her as she surged forward. In a moment she had reached the boat.

It was perilously close to the land now, the sea having taken advantage of it while she was occupied with diving and swimming. Grabbing hold of the side, she hauled herself in. For a moment she lay in the bottom, gasping at the effort it had taken and cursing herself for allowing her body to grow so unfit.

Then she heard a shout. She sat up and looked back. Men clung to the rock face. The priest was nowhere in sight.

Smiling, she focused her mind on the cliff and pushed. The boat shot away, sending spray to either side. The cliff slowly receded, taking with it the villagers who had driven her from her home.

At that thought, she cursed savagely.

'A priest! *Here!* By the gods' balls, Windchaser, isn't there anywhere I can go that the Circlians haven't seeded with their poisonous stink?'

There was no answer. She looked at the mast strapped securely down in the belly of the vessel and sighed.

'Well, what would you know, anyway? You've been trussed up like a grieving widower for years. I guess you and I had best get to the task of finding you a sail and me a new home.'

CHAPTER 9

When Danjin entered Auraya's reception room he saw a now-familiar tall man by the window. *Leiard*, he thought. *On time, as always.*

The Dreamweaver turned and nodded to Danjin politely. As Danjin returned the gesture he noted that condensation from the Dreamweaver's breath marked the window. He felt the hairs on his neck begin to prickle. How could anyone stand so close to the glass, with that drop outside?

He had noticed that Leiard always moved to the closest window when entering a Tower room. Was he fascinated by the view? Danjin looked closely at the Dreamweaver, who was staring outside again. Staring quite intently, too. Almost as if he wanted to step through it and . . . and . . .

Escape, Danjin suddenly thought.

Which would be understandable. Here he was, standing in the one place where the gods' influence was strongest in the world. The gods who had executed the founder of the Dreamweavers.

Yet this staring was the only sign Danjin had ever seen of Leiard's discomfort. *I've never seen him agitated, but then I've never seen him relaxed, either. He gives the impression that his thoughts and emotions are always under tight control.*

The door to Auraya's private rooms opened. She smiled as she saw her guests. Danjin made the formal gesture of the circle. Leiard, as always, remained motionless. Auraya had never shown any hint of being offended by this.

'Danjin Spear. Dreamweaver Leiard,' she said. 'Are we packed and ready?'

Her face was aglow with excitement. She was like a child about to embark on her first journey away from home. Leiard indicated a worn bag beside a chair.

'I am ready,' he siad solemnly.

Auraya looked at the bag. 'That's all?'

'All I ever travel with,' he replied.

'Our luggage is already on the ship,' Danjin informed Auraya. He thought of the three large trunks he had sent ahead. One had been full of scrolls, gifts and other items related to their journey's purpose. Another had been full of Auraya's belongings. The third had been the largest, filled with his own clothing and possessions. Leiard and Auraya had it easy, he decided. They both wore a uniform, not the endlessly varied finery he was expected to wear as a member of Hanian high society.

'Then we should proceed to Mairae's quarters,' Auraya said. Stepping backwards, she bent down to pick up something in the other room. 'Come on, Mischief. Time to go.'

She was carrying a small cage. Inside it her veez hunched, all four legs braced against the floor.

'Cage bad,' he said sullenly.

'Quiet,' she told him.

To Danjin's surprise, the creature obeyed. As Auraya moved toward the main door, Leiard picked up his bag and looked at Danjin expectantly. Danjin left and the Dreamweaver followed.

Auraya started up the stairs. As they climbed, the cage in the stairwell descended past them. Its sole occupant was a young man in spectacular formal dress. Danjin recognised the man as Haime, one of the many Genrian princes. The prince, seeing Auraya, made a half-bow and the formal gesture of the circle. Auraya smiled and nodded in acknowledgement.

They passed the door to Rian's rooms. Danjin thought of the rumours and speculation that were rife in the city regarding Rian's recent journey south. Reports about a dangerous sorcerer attacking villages in Toren had reached Jarime and all had assumed Rian had left to deal with the impostor. When Rian had returned a few days ago, Danjin had expected some sort of triumphant announcement that a threat to the lands had been dealt with, but none came. Did this mean Rian had failed? Or had he travelled south for an entirely different reason?

Auraya reached Mairae's door and knocked lightly. It opened and the pale-haired White ushered them into her reception room.

'I'm nearly ready,' she said after exchanging quick formal greetings. 'Just make yourselves comfortable.'

Her face was a little flushed, Danjin noted. She hurried into the private rooms of her quarters. Auraya smiled, then paused and looked questioningly at Leiard. The Dreamweaver met her eyes levelly and shrugged. Auraya turned away, apparently satisfied with what she had seen in his face, or read from his mind.

Mystery surrounds me constantly, Danjin thought wryly.

A small whine drew his attention back to Mischief. The veez was restless, turning circles in his cage and stopping to stare upwards. Belatedly, Danjin looked up to find another veez clinging to the ceiling above them.

Mairae's veez . . . What is its name? Stardust.

He could see why. The veez was black with tiny white speckles all over. A female. She leapt from the ceiling to the back of a chair, then scurried down to the floor. Approaching Mischief's cage, she stood up on her hind legs and made the complex chittering noise that was the creature's natural vocalisation.

The door to the private rooms opened. Mairae walked back into the reception room. A servant followed close behind, carrying a small bag. Seeing Stardust, Mairae called the veez's name.

'Are you taking Mischief?' Mairae asked Auraya as Stardust bounded over to her.

'I have to, if I'm going to complete his training according to the Somreyans' instructions.'

Mairae bent to pet the veez at her feet. 'I'd love to bring Stardust, but ships make her ill.' She pointed at the door to her private rooms. 'Go inside.'

Stardust trotted to the doorway then sat down and gazed longingly at her mistress.

'I'll be back soon,' Mairae assured the creature.

Stardust let out a long, exaggerated sigh, then folded her paws and rested her chin on them, so that she now blinked imploringly up at her mistress. Mairae rolled her eyes.

'Little manipulator,' she muttered. 'We should go quickly, before she starts crying.'

'They do that?' Auraya asked.

'They can't make tears like humans do, but they certainly know how to mimic a good wailing.' She closed the door. 'Are you ready for your first sea journey?'

'As ready as I'll ever be,' Auraya replied.

Mairae gave them all one of her dazzling smiles. 'Then let's get ourselves to the docks before they think we've changed our minds and leave without us.'

Danjin smiled. *As if one of the White's ships would leave without the White.* He followed Mairae out of the room. As they waited for the cage to arrive, he considered the task ahead.

Would everything work out as they hoped? There was a good chance it would, he decided. He would have thought otherwise if his impressions of the Dreamweaver had been less favourable. During all the consultations on the alliance, Leiard had been refreshingly frank about the terms that would offend his people, and yet the alternatives he'd suggested had not been unreasonable. So far Danjin had seen nothing to make him suspect the Dreamweaver wanted anything more than to reduce conflict between his people and Circlians.

Yet there was definitely something strange about Leiard. For a start, his behaviour toward Auraya changed from moment to moment. Sometimes he was quiet and his manner and speech were respectful; at other times his tone was authoritative and confident. Perhaps he regained his confidence when he forgot who she was, then lost it when he remembered again.

Or was it something else? Danjin was not sure. Maybe it was Leiard's nervousness with the other White that bothered him. Though Leiard had met and spoken with Mairae several times during discussions about the alliance, he was always warily polite to her. Around Dyara he was reluctant to speak at all, though this was probably because the older woman had made no pretence of her dislike of heathens. During one of the first meetings Dyara had questioned Leiard until Mairae had protested that half of their meeting time was being taken up with 'interrogation'. Danjin suspected that Dyara found Leiard's reticence and vague answers frustrating. Her dissatisfaction only sparked more questions.

Rian had appeared once during a meeting but had treated Leiard with indifference. Juran was the only White that Danjin had not observed Leiard interact with. It would be interesting to watch. He suspected that nothing would distress Leiard more than meeting the man who had killed the founder of his cult.

As the cage rose up toward them Danjin considered whether Leiard's discomfort was simply contagious. *I am uncomfortable*

157

around him because he is uncomfortable around the people I respect.

He was certain of one thing: he was going to keep a close eye on Leiard. The White might be difficult to deceive, but he'd never wager that it was impossible.

The outer arms of the Bay of Jarime had slowly drawn closer together during the last hour, revealing tall cliffs on either side. Auraya watched with interest as the crew of the *Herald* went about their tasks, following orders relayed down a chain of command. The ship pulled out of the bay, then between the two great columns of rock known as the Guardians. The swaying of the deck changed to a deep rolling as they entered the waters of Mirror Strait.

'Ships used to make me ill.'

Auraya glanced at Mairae. They were sitting up on the stern, where wooden benches hugged the railing. Soft cushions had been placed there for them and a canopy shaded them from the bright sun. Leiard and Danjin stood near the prow and a small team of servants were down in the hull preparing a light meal.

'Seasickness?' Auraya asked.

'Yes. It affected me so badly, I'd spend most of a journey barely conscious.' Mairae lifted her hand and splayed her fingers. The sunlight glinted off the white ring on her middle finger. 'Sometimes it is the smallest of the gods' Gifts that I treasure the most.'

Auraya looked at her own ring, then at the pair at the prow.

'I hope Leiard and Danjin will be all right.'

'I'm sure the Dreamweaver has his own ways of curing seasickness, and Danjin has probably brought medicines for it. He's very organised.'

'Yes.' Auraya smiled. 'I don't know what I'd do without him.' She turned to regard Mairae. 'You don't have an adviser?'

'I did, in the beginning. His name was Wesso, but I called him Old Westie because he came from Irian Island and his accent was so strong it was hard, sometimes, to understand him. He was my adviser for nearly ten years.' Her gaze became distant. 'I didn't need him by then, but dismissing him would have hurt him deeply, so I kept him until he died. I do miss him sometimes.'

Seeing the sadness in Mairae's eyes, Auraya felt a pang of sympathy – and something akin to dread.

'Have you grown used to watching people grow old and die?' she asked in a low voice.

Mairae met Auraya's eyes, her expression unusually grave. 'No, but I have learned how best to allow myself to grieve. I give myself a measure of time to feel bad, then move on. And I don't let myself anticipate it too much. The way I see it, you can't worry overly much about the future when the future stretches endlessly before you.'

'I guess not. But sometimes I can't stop worrying. I suppose that's something I'll have to learn, among other things.'

Mairae's eyebrows rose. 'What are you so worried about?'

Auraya hesitated, then shook her head. 'Oh, just . . . small things. Nothing important.'

'You're still human, Auraya. Just because you have big matters to deal with doesn't mean the small ones don't count. Since I've taken Dyara's place as your teacher for this trip, it's my job to answer all your questions, large or small.'

'I don't discuss small matters with Dyara.'

Mairae grinned. 'I don't either. All the more reason to talk to me. So?'

'I worry about being lonely,' Auraya admitted.

Mairae nodded. 'Everyone fears that, mortal or not. You will find new friends to replace the old.' She smiled. 'And lovers, too.'

Like Haime, the Genrian prince? Auraya thought back to the morning, to the young man descending in the Tower cage. She had caught enough of his thoughts to know that he had just left Mairae's rooms – and what he had been doing for most of the previous night. It had only confirmed that the rumours about Mairae and her lovers were true.

Mairae chuckled. 'From the look on your face, I'd guess you've heard about mine.'

'Only rumours,' Auraya said evasively.

'It is impossible to keep secrets from other White, even more so from the servants.' She smiled. 'It is ridiculous for anyone to expect us to remain celibate for all eternity.' Mairae winked. 'The gods haven't said we must.'

'Have they ever spoken to you?' Auraya asked, seizing the opportunity to change the subject. She suspected that once Mairae started discussing her former lovers, she'd expect Auraya to as well – and she was sure her own experiences would never live up to Mairae's. 'They've said nothing to me yet.'

Mairae nodded. 'Sometimes.' She paused, her expression becoming distant and rapt. 'Yranna likes my taste in men. She's like a big sister.' She turned to face Auraya. 'I'm sure you've heard about Anyala, Juran's great love. Everyone talks about how wonderfully loyal Juran was. Trouble is, he hasn't had another woman since, and she's been dead nearly twenty years. That makes it look as if he expects the rest of us to remain celibate, too. You don't think so, do you?' Mairae looked at Auraya expectantly.

'No. I . . . I had heard that Juran had a wife once,' Auraya said. She wasn't having much success steering the conversation away from lovers.

'They were never married,' Mairae corrected. 'The gods have been clear about that. No marriage or children. Juran hasn't even *looked* at another woman since she died. It's not healthy.

And Dyara . . .' She rolled her eyes. 'Dyara is worse. Such a typical prudish Genrian. She's had this tragic love affair with Timare for nearly forty years. It's never been physical. I don't think she could bear the rest of us seeing her naked in Timare's thoughts. The way she behaves, so secretive, makes people think that love is something to be ashamed of.'

'Timare?'

'Her favourite priest,' Mairae said. She looked at Auraya closely. 'You didn't know?'

'I only met High Priest Timare once or twice, before I was chosen.'

Mairae's eyebrows rose. 'I see. So Dyara's keeping you two apart. She probably wants to stop you finding out her little secret.' She drummed her fingers on the bench. 'Has she said anything to you about how you should behave when it comes to affairs of the heart – and bedroom?'

Auraya shook her head.

'Interesting. Well, don't let Dyara impose her stuffy values on you. You'll only make yourself lonely and bitter.'

'What . . . what about Rian?' Auraya asked, giving up on shifting the subject and instead deflecting it toward others.

Mairae's nose wrinkled in distaste. 'I don't think he's capable,' she muttered. Then she grimaced. 'That's cruel and unfair. Rian is lovely. But he's just so . . . so . . .'

'Fanatical?'

Mairae sighed. 'Yes. Nothing could come between Rian and the gods. Not even love. A woman could live with that, but not with being constantly reminded of it.'

Am I like that? Auraya wondered. In the years she had been a priestess she'd thought herself in love a few times, but the feeling of elation and connection had never lasted more than a few months. When she thought of the gods, the feeling of awe and reverence was something completely different. If it was love, it was nothing like the earthly feelings she'd had for those mortal lovers. So how could one leave no room for the other?

'He's being a bit hard on himself for losing the Pentadrian,' Mairae added.

'Yes,' Auraya agreed eagerly. At last Mairae had turned to other matters. 'Do you think the Pentadrian will come back?'

Mairae grimaced. 'Maybe. Evil men are rarely deterred for long. If they do harm, and get away with it, they will usually try to do it again.'

'Will Juran send Rian to the southern continent, then?'

'I doubt it. This sorcerer is too close to Rian in strength. I doubt there are others like him in the south, but there are plenty of Pentadrians as Gifted as our high priests and priestesses there. With their help he might be a real danger to Rian. No, if we are to defeat him we'll have to wait until he comes to us.'

Auraya shivered. 'I won't feel quite safe until I know he's dead.'

'Don't let it bother you.' Mairae's face shifted into a wise expression Auraya had only seen on older people. 'There have always been powerful sorcerers, Auraya. Some powerful enough to achieve immortality without the help of the gods. We've always defeated them.'

'The Wilds?'

'Yes. Power has a way of corrupting people. We are fortunate that we have the guidance of the gods and the knowledge that our Gifts would be removed if we turned to evil. The sad truth of the world is that most people who have great magical power don't use it well. Their ambitions are usually selfish, and there is nobody strong enough to hold them to account for their wrong-doings.'

'Except us.'

'Yes. And by encouraging Gifted individuals to become priests we ensure new sorcerers are under our control.'

Auraya nodded. 'Is this sorcerer one of the old Wilds?'

Mairae frowned. 'A few evaded Juran and Dyara: a woman known as The Hag, a boy associated with the sea and sailors, called The Gull, and a pair known as The Twins. They haven't been seen in a hundred years. Juran thinks they may have travelled to the other side of the world.'

'None of them sound like this sorcerer.'

'No. He is a new Wild, if he is one at all. The gods did warn us that we would encounter more. A few are born every thousand years. We must deal with them when they appear. For now, you and I have an alliance to negotiate.' She grinned. 'And you must make the most of being free from Dyara's yoke.'

'She's not that bad.'

'Liar. She was my teacher too, remember. I know what she's like. That's part of the reason I insisted I couldn't do this without you. She tried to convince Juran you were too inexperienced, but he can see this is well within your ability.'

Auraya stared at Mairae and struggled to think of a reply. She was saved by a familiar cry.

'Owaya! Owaya!'

A veez scampered across the deck, nearly tripping two of the crewmen, and launched itself into Auraya's lap. Mairae laughed in delight as Mischief began licking Auraya's face.

'Stop! Enough!' Auraya protested. As the veez calmed down, she frowned at it disapprovingly. 'How did you get out?'

The veez gazed up at her adoringly.

'I believe he picked the lock of his cage again,' a male voice replied. Leiard strolled across the deck toward them. Auraya felt her heart leap at the sight of him. He had proved to be more useful in the role of adviser than she had hoped. It was so good to have his company on this journey. His presence gave her confidence.

'Cage *bad*,' the veez muttered.

'I heard the servants cursing him, and offered to bring him back,' Leiard told her.

'Thank you, Leiard.' She sighed. 'I expect he'll just do it again. He may as well stay with me.'

Leiard nodded. His gaze slid to Mairae, then his eyes dropped to the deck.

'Mairae of the White,' he said.

'Dreamweaver Leiard,' she replied.

He looked at Auraya again. 'I will tell the servants he is with you.'

As he walked away, Mairae gave a small sigh. 'I like tall men. He has nice eyes. Pity he's a Dreamweaver.'

As Auraya turned to stare at her fellow White in shock, Mairae laughed. 'Oh, Auraya. You are nearly as much a prude as Dyara. I don't seriously want to bed him, but I don't think there's anything wrong with admiring a man's finer points any more than it's wrong to admire a flower or a particularly well-bred reyna.'

Auraya shook her head reproachfully. 'Nothing wrong at all, except I don't want to be thinking of the men around me like that.'

'Why not?'

'I have to work with them. I don't need the distraction of wondering what they'd be like in bed.'

Mairae chuckled. 'One day you might, when you realise how many long, boring meetings you're going to have to sit through in the future.'

Auraya could think of nothing to say to that.

A servant hurried out onto the stern and made the gesture of the circle. 'Midday refreshments are ready,' she said. 'Shall I bring them up here?'

'Yes, thank you,' Mairae replied. She rose and looked down at Auraya. 'I guess we're about to find out how well your adviser is dealing with sea travel.'

Auraya smiled and lifted the veez onto her shoulder. 'I guess we will.'

CHAPTER 10

There is a particular kind of tension that comes over people near the end of a journey. For the crew of the *Herald* it had to do with preparing for the subtler task of directing the ship into a port already crowded with vessels. For the passengers it was anticipation of leaving the discomfort of the seacraft behind, balanced by mingled hopes and doubts for what they might experience at their destination.

Leiard considered Auraya's adviser, who was standing on the other side of the two seated White. Danjin Spear was intelligent and knowledgeable, and had been respectful toward Leiard, though occasional comments had betrayed his dislike of Dreamweavers in general.

He turned his attention to Mairae. Of all the White, apart from Auraya, she was the most friendly toward him. Her warmth appeared to be a natural part of her character rather than something practised, but it was clear she preferred highborn company. While she sympathised with the poor and praised the hard-working merchants and artisans, she didn't treat them the same way as she did the rich and powerful. He guessed she regarded Dreamweavers somewhere between the poor and artisans, and probably pitied rather than despised them.

Unlike Auraya, who neither pitied nor despised Dreamweavers. Leiard looked down at her and could not help feeling a little glow of pride. It was hard not to when he considered what she had achieved. The other White had accepted him and his advice, though some obviously did so begrudgingly.

They're relying on me to make this alliance happen. Who would have guessed? The Gods' Chosen relying on a Dreamweaver.

A gust of cold air swept over them, taking the ship ever closer to the city. Arbeem's square whitestone houses were built on a slope that dropped steeply toward the water. They looked like a jumble of oversized staircases. Occasional patches of green broke the endless white. Somreyans loved gardens.

In the centre of the port an enormous statue stood upon a massive column. The weathering it had suffered suggested immense age and rendered the face almost unrecognisable. A memory flashed into Leiard's mind, jolting him with its strength. It was of the same statue, but less weathered. A name came with it.

Svarlen. God of the sea.

This had to be a link memory – and an ancient one. Leiard gazed up at the colossus as the ship passed it, allowing the old image of a newer statue to overlay the reality of it now. He heard a horn blowing and turned to face the city again.

A boat was moving forward to meet them, propelled by rowers. It was wide-berthed and spectacularly decorated, the emblem of the Council of Elders painted on its sail.

The captain of the *Herald* called an order. The sail was furled and the ship drifted to a halt. As the council boat pulled along-side, both crews threw ropes to the other vessel and secured the craft together.

Three important-looking individuals stood on board the boat, each wearing the gold sash of a member of the Council of Elders. To the left was a robust, grey-haired high priest. His name was Haleed, Leiard recalled. To the right was a middle-aged woman in a Dreamweaver vest. This would be Arleej, the Dreamweaver elder. The leader of his people.

He had been looking forward to meeting this woman. In the messages sent between the council and the White via priests in both lands, Leiard had seen hints of a sharp-minded, proud woman. Pride was not a characteristic Dreamweavers were encouraged to display, but neither was judging too quickly, he reminded himself. The leader of the Dreamweavers would need to be strong in this age.

The third man on the boat, standing between the others, was thin and elderly, but though he carried a walking staff his eyes were clear and alert. This, Leiard guessed, was the council's Moderator, Meeran.

Rising from their seat, Auraya and Mairae thanked the captain of the *Herald* then crossed to the welcoming craft. Leiard and Danjin followed, the adviser carrying Mischief in his cage. A sulky muttering came from the veez. During the journey Auraya had taught her pet to endure imprisonment in exchange for generous rewards. Despite this, his tolerance for the cage lasted no longer than an hour.

As soon as the White were aboard, Meeran stepped forward.

'Welcome to Somrey, Chosen of the Gods.' He bowed slightly then made the formal sign of the circle. 'I am Moderator Meeran. It is our pleasure to see you again, Mairae Gemshaper, and an honour to be the first foreign land to receive Auraya Dyer.'

Arleej's eyes slid to Leiard's. Her stare was intense and questioning, and he sensed doubt and suspicion. He inclined his head, and she dropped her chin once in reply.

'We are delighted to be visiting your fair islands, Moderator Meeran,' Mairae replied, 'and I am pleased to be renewing my acquaintance with you and all the council members.' She looked at Haleed and Arleej. The pair inclined their heads and murmured a reply.

'I have been looking forward to meeting each of you,' Auraya said, smiling with enthusiasm. Arleej's lips curled upward in response, but her smile did not extend to her eyes. 'I have heard much about the beauty of your land, and hope to see some of your country,' Auraya added, 'if I have time.'

In other words, if we settle this quickly, Leiard thought.

'Then we must arrange a tour for you.' Meeran's smile was genuine. His gaze then shifted past Mairae to Danjin. 'This must be Danjin Spear. I had the pleasure of trading with your father, in my younger days.'

Danjin chuckled. 'Yes. He spoke both admiringly and scathingly of your bargaining skills many times.'

Meeran's smile widened. 'I imagine he did, but I like to think those skills are put to better use now, for the benefit of the people.' His gaze flickered to Auraya, and Leiard wondered if she had noted the subtle warning in the man's words. Then Meeran's attention turned to Leiard. 'And you must be Dreamweaver Adviser Leiard.'

Leiard nodded.

'Have you visited Somrey before?'

'I have memories of this place, but they are old.'

Arleej's eyebrows rose fractionally.

'Then welcome back, Dreamweaver,' Meeran said. 'I look forward to hearing how you came to be in this unique and promising position of Dreamweaver adviser to the White. Now,' he turned and clapped his hands, 'we shall offer you refreshments.'

The boat had pulled away from the ship, the rowers' backs flexing as the oars cut through the water. Meeran ushered the visitors to seats and made polite conversation while servants brought glasses of a warm spiced drink called ahm.

A high wall ran along the entire length of the city. On top of it was a long line of people, those in front sitting with their feet dangling over the edge. As the welcoming craft drew closer the calls of these people grew audible. Auraya and Mairae waved, rousing a cheer from the crowd.

The craft did not dock in front of this gathering, but moved on. Leiard saw armed guards keeping the people from straying beyond a certain section of the dock. After this only a line of priests and priestesses waited and it was toward these people the boat moved.

Solid wooden walkways had been built all along the dock wall. As the boat's hull settled against one, the rowers drew up their oars. Some secured the boat to the dock, while others set down a carved and painted bridge for the visitors to cross.

Meeran led them off the welcoming craft and up a stairway. At the top of the wall, the priests and priestesses stared at Mairae and Auraya, their awe and excitement strong enough for Leiard to sense without effort. Two high priests stepped forward to be introduced by Haleed. Looking beyond them, Leiard realised he stood within Arbeem's Temple. The building was a humbler style than those in Jarime and was built in the same fashion as most of the city structures – single-storey and plain.

Hearing his name spoken, Leiard brought his attention back to the introductions. The high priests regarded him with suppressed curiosity and doubt. When all had been introduced, Arleej announced that she must depart.

'I must return to the Dreamweaver House. We are performing the spring link tonight,' she explained. She turned to Leiard. 'Would you like to attend, Dreamweaver Leiard?'

His pulse quickened. A link, and a chance to consult another Dreamweaver about his strange memories. 'I would be honoured,' he replied slowly. 'I may be needed here, however.'

'Not tonight, Leiard,' Auraya said. She met his eyes levelly, and gave an almost imperceptible nod. *Meet your people,* her expression seemed to say. *Let them see that you can be trusted.* 'But we will wish to consult with you tomorrow morning,' she added.

'Then I will attend,' he announced. 'And return tonight.'

Arleej nodded. 'I look forward to meeting you all again tomorrow,' she said, nodding politely. The others murmured replies. As she turned away, a priest stepped forward and offered to guide them through the Temple.

The Dreamweaver elder was silent as they followed the priest. After a short journey they stepped out of the building into a courtyard. A covered four-wheeled tarn and driver waited nearby.

'The high priest was going to send us out of the main gates,' she said, 'but I insisted we leave this way. A crowd was bound to gather out the front, which would have made our exit difficult.'

Leiard nodded. Was she implying that the crowd was likely to be dangerous, or that it would simply block the way? While Somrey was the nation most tolerant and supportive of Dreamweavers, there were always small groups with views contrary to the majority in any country.

The tarn was simple and undecorated, and the driver a hired man. Leiard settled next to Arleej on the seat. The Dreamweaver elder told the driver their destination, and soon they were travelling along the narrow, crowded roads of the city.

As the tarn neared the Dreamweaver House, Arleej considered her companion. He was not what she had expected, but then her expectations hadn't been specific. Just someone less like a Dreamweaver and more like a Circlian.

Leiard was, if anything, more Dreamweaver-like than she.

171

The way he answered her questions reminded her strongly of her teacher. Keefler had not known his year of birth, and had lived for most of his life in a remote location. He, too, had been quiet and watchful.

The answers to her questions about his relationship with Auraya of the White had startled her into silence. He had begun teaching the woman as a child in the hope that she would become his student. She had joined the Circlians instead. If Arleej had suffered such a disappointment she doubted she would have been able to face her former student without struggling with resentment. Leiard appeared to have accepted Auraya's choice and her elevation to the White. He described her, of all things, as a *friend*.

It all seemed too good to be true. That the gods had chosen someone who had been taught by and sympathised with Dreamweavers was incredible. That they tolerated any thought of their people working with Dreamweavers was even more so. Had they finally come to accept the existence of heathens?

She doubted it. A century of persecution had lessened Dreamweaver numbers, but not eliminated them. The early years of violence after Mirar's death had encouraged the compassionate to sympathise with Dreamweavers and the rebellious to join the cult. Now, perhaps, the gods sought to woo heathens to them by appearing to be generous and benevolent.

They will fail, she thought. *So long as Dreamweavers pass link memories from generation to generation there will be no forgetting the true nature of the gods.*

The tarn turned a corner and pulled up in front of a large building. The street was busy, and people moved constantly in and out of the building. Leiard looked up at the symbols carved into the façade.

'The only Dreamweaver House still standing in Northern Ithania,' Arleej said. 'Come inside.'

He followed her into a generous hall. Three elderly Dreamweavers stepped forward to greet Arleej, speaking Somreyan. When she introduced him as the Dreamweaver adviser to the White, their expressions became wary.

Leiard greeted them in Somreyan. Arleej stared at him in surprise. 'Your grasp of our language is impressive,' she said.

He shrugged. 'I know many languages.'

'The spring link is about to begin,' a voice called.

Arleej glanced at Leiard and noted a glint of intensity in his gaze. He was looking forward to this, she decided. She started toward the corridor. Leiard followed and the three elderly Dreamweavers came after, uncharacteristically silent, Arleej thought. *No doubt it has occurred to them that he will join us, and they're deciding if that is for good or ill. It is a gamble. He may learn much about us, but they must realise that we may also learn of his, and the White's, intentions in regard to the alliance.*

Had Auraya realised this when she had allowed him to leave her side for the evening?

The corridor ended at a large wooden door. Arleej pushed it open and stepped out into a round, sunken garden. The air was cool and moist. Several Dreamweavers were already present, forming a broken ring. Leiard glanced around, a look of mild puzzlement on his face. As if he recognised the place.

Arleej joined the circle, stepping aside to allow room for Leiard. The elderly Dreamweavers from the hall took their places. Arleej waited until all was quiet, then a little longer to allow the stillness of the place to calm her thoughts before she spoke the words of the ritual.

'We gather tonight in peace and in pursuit of understanding. Our minds will be linked. Our memories shall flow between us. Let none seek or spy, or impose a will upon another. Instead, we shall become one mind.'

She lifted her arms to either side and took hold of the

hands of her neighbours. Two minds touched her senses, then dozens more as all of the Dreamweavers linked hands and minds. There was a shared feeling of elation, then a brief pause.

Images and impressions quickly overwhelmed all sense of the physical world. Memories of childhood mingled with those of recent events. Images of well-known faces followed those of strangers. Snatches of remembered conversations echoed in the thoughts of all. She didn't move to guide them; she let the mingled thoughts move where they would.

Slowly the inevitable happened. All were curious about the newcomer. As some wondered who he was, those that knew revealed his identity. Leiard's response was slow, beginning with his acknowledgement of his position as Dreamweaver adviser, then shifting to include many layers of thought. Arleej understood that he hoped to help his people. She also saw the affection and admiration he felt for Auraya. At the same time, he revealed his fear of the White and their gods.

Arleej watched with amusement as his thoughts now began to run in circles. Every time he considered his distrust and dislike of the gods and the White, the thought of Auraya brought reassurance. While he believed she would not willingly harm him or other Dreamweavers, he was not foolish enough to think she would not do so if ordered by the gods. He felt this worth the risk.

All were relieved to see he was working with Auraya for his people's benefit, not the gods' or even Auraya's. Being around any Circlian other than Auraya stirred a deep fear in him, however. Such fear came only from experience. Had something terrible happened to him? As Arleej considered this, Leiard's thoughts turned to other matters that worried him. Strange memories came to him unbidden, he revealed. Sometimes thoughts sprang into his mind that did not feel like they were entirely his own. The curiosity of the other linked Dreamweavers rose.

In response, these memories began to spill forth.

She saw the Guardian in the port. The statue was not as weathered, and she suddenly knew what it represented. A god – and not one that the Circlians now worshipped.

She saw a smaller Arbeem, with a half-constructed dock wall. She saw the Dreamweaver House as a new building painted in bright, welcoming colours.

She saw the face of an elderly Dreamweaver man and knew him to be her predecessor from centuries earlier. A thought came with it, and it was nothing like Leiard's internal voice.

A proud one, that Dreamweaver elder. I had to talk him out of withholding care from the Moderator, though the man deserved it. That was the last time I visited Somrey. Wasn't much of a kingdom then – not even considered part of Northern Ithania. Who'd have thought it would become the only refuge for Dreamweavers?

Arleej's heart was racing. *Leiard is right*, she thought. *These aren't his thoughts. They are Mirar's.*

She had encountered similar link memories before. Most Dreamweavers had fragments of Mirar's recollections, gained during links. Mirar been linked with other Dreamweavers for so long, there were plenty of his link memories still around. There was something comforting about the thought that the ritual Mirar had begun in order to encourage understanding and speed teaching should also keep part of him alive in the minds of his followers.

However, Leiard carried more than just fragments of Mirar's memories. His mind was full of so many recollections that a sense of Mirar's personality had emerged. It was like knowing someone so well, you could predict how they would behave or speak.

Arleej sensed the excitement of the other Dreamweavers.

She could feel them greedily prodding for more memories, but the flood had abated now as Leiard contemplated the source of them. Arleej could see that he hadn't known or even guessed the truth. He was not even sure who he had picked the memories up from. Probably his teacher, though he had no strong memory of the man – or woman.

And that was something that had also bothered him. Why were so many of his own memories so hazy?

:You have many link memories, she told him. *And you have spent long years in isolation. With time, it is easy to forget which recollections are yours and which are not. The boundaries have blurred, so you must reestablish them. Linking is the best method. The assertion of your identity at the end of a link strengthens your sense of self.*

:But linking will give me more link memories, Leiard pointed out.

:Yes, it will. However, the more you link, the less of a problem that will be. For now, link with only one other Dreamweaver so there is less memory transfer for every self-assertion. Link with younger people who have fewer memories to transfer. This young man you are teaching, for example, would suit you well.

:Jayim. Leiard considered how little experience of life the boy had. *Yes, he will be most suitable – if he decides to remain a Dreamweaver.*

Disappointment flowed from several of the Dreamweavers. They had realised that Leiard could not join in another link with them while in Arbeem, so they would not see more of Mirar's memories. Arleej felt a wry amusement. Her people had put aside all their suspicions and now accepted and trusted him. Was this just because he held Mirar's memories?

No, she decided. *His intentions are good. His loyalty is to us, though it would be sorely tested if he were forced to choose between his people and Auraya.* That he felt this newest of the White to be worthy of his regard was a good sign, too.

Satisfied, she began the last part of the ritual, the self-assertion.

I am Arleej, Dreamweaver elder. Born in Teerninya to Leenin Booter and . . .

She drew her thoughts in to herself as she recalled those facts that she felt most defined her. As she opened her eyes, she turned to find Leiard still involved in the ritual. The lines about his forehead deepened, then he drew in a deep breath and looked at her. She smiled and released his hand.

'You have been a surprise to us, Leiard.'

His gaze shifted to the other Dreamweavers, who had gathered in groups to talk, and were no doubt talking about him. 'Tonight's discovery was a surprise to me as well. I have much to think about. Will I cause offence if I leave now?'

Arleej shook her head. 'No, they will understand. Most return home soon after a link – though I think they would break that habit tonight if you stayed. I'll see you out, before they pounce.' She ushered him toward the door, waving away one of the elder Dreamweavers as he stepped forward.

'Leiard must return to his travelling companions,' she announced. There were murmurs of disappointment. Leiard touched his heart, mouth and forehead and each of the Dreamweavers solemnly followed suit.

As she led him down the corridor to the entrance of the House, Arleej could think of nothing to say, only a stream of questions best left for another time. They stepped out of the House to find a hired platten had just arrived carrying a family with a sick child. She hailed the driver.

'Are you free for another ride?' she asked.

'Where to?' the man asked.

'The Temple,' she instructed. 'The back entrance.'

The driver's eyebrows rose. She bartered a fair price and paid the man, then watched as Leiard climbed aboard.

177

'I expect I'll see you tomorrow,' she said.

'Yes.' Leiard smiled then turned to face the front. Taking this as a cue, the driver flicked the reins and the vehicle drew away.

Arleej shook her head slowly. It was odd, indeed, to be sending a Dreamweaver 'home' to a Circlian Temple.

When the vehicle had turned out of sight, she hurried back inside the House. As she expected, her closest confidant, Dreamweaver Neeran, was waiting for her in the hall. His eyes were wide with wonder.

'That was . . . was . . .'

'Astounding,' she agreed. 'Come up to my room. We need to talk.'

'Of all the people to have Mirar's memories,' he breathed as he followed her up the stairs, 'it had to be the Dreamweaver adviser to the *White*.'

'An extraordinary man in an extraordinary position,' she agreed. Reaching the door to her room, she pushed it open and ushered Neeran inside. He turned to stare at her.

'Do you think the White know?'

She considered. 'If he didn't, then how could they?'

'All of the White can read minds. Surely Juran will have recognised something of Mirar in Leiard.'

Arleej thought of Leiard's appearance and demeanour. He was nothing like the Mirar she had seen in link memories.

'If Juran has, then he was not bothered by it. If he hasn't, well, now that this is known by us and Leiard, the White will discover it too. I only hope this will not cause him trouble.'

Neeran's eyes widened and he nodded in agreement. 'They also know that Leiard has been working to our mutual benefit.' He looked up at Arleej. 'Which is curious in itself, isn't it?'

She nodded. 'Curious that someone with so much of Mirar in them would encourage this alliance?'

'Yes.'

'No matter what the White do about Leiard, one thing is clear.' She moved to the fireplace, where a bottle of ahm stood warming beside the hearth. 'We should consider the possibility, strange as it may seem, that an alliance between Somrey and the White is what Mirar would have wanted.'

As the dark speck in the sky grew larger, Tryss watched apprehensively. Hours had passed since the time Drilli had said she would meet him. He had strapped on his new harness three times, determined he would not wait for her. Each time he had unstrapped the harness again. She had extracted a promise from him that he wouldn't test it unless she was there to see, and he didn't want to disappoint her.

Now, watching the approaching Siyee, he felt his pulse quicken with alternating dread and excitement. Drilli had come to observe him work many times. He had expected her to grow bored, but she just sat close by and talked endlessly. To his surprise, he liked it. Mostly she spoke of their families, or the landwalkers' alliance proposal, but often she would question him about the things he had made. Sometimes she made suggestions. Occasionally they were good.

The speck had grown into a figure now. It descended toward him and he sighed with relief as he recognised Drilli's wing patterns. He picked up the harness and ducked his head through the loop of the neck strap, then began to secure the other bindings.

A whistle of greeting heralded her arrival. She landed gracefully and strode toward him, grinning.

'Look at you,' she said.

'You're late,' he told her, completely failing to sound annoyed.

'I know. I'm sorry. Mother had me plucking girri for hours.' She flexed her fingers. 'Are you ready?'

'Been ready for hours.'

'Let's go, then.'

They leapt into the air together. The wind set the straps of his harness humming. It was lighter than the last, having fewer parts. The main weight hung from just below his chest, however, so he was more conscious of this harness than the last.

'Comfortable?' Drilli called.

'Bearable,' he replied.

They swooped down toward a narrow valley. Unlike the bare sides of the mountain, which were covered with only the toughest of grasses and trees, the valley was filled with vegetation and more likely to be hiding prey. As they swooped across the treetops something launched itself into the air. Drilli gave a whoop of excitement.

'Get him!' she shrieked.

It was an ark, a predatory bird more used to hovering, swooping and stunning its prey with paralysing magic than being chased itself. It glided below them, occasionally flapping its wings.

Tryss followed it. He drew his arms together and grabbed the pipe strapped to his side, then spread his wings wide before he could fall far. Another quick movement brought the pipe to his lips. Now it was time to see if his latest adaptation proved useful.

With one end of the pipe held between his teeth, he dipped the other into the basket of tiny darts hanging below his chest. He sucked in and felt a dart lodge in the pipe. Looking up again, he saw that the ark had changed direction. He shifted his wings and pursued it.

The bird glided below, unsure what to make of its pursuers. While Siyee would happily catch and eat ark, they rarely bothered so were not familiar predators to the birds. Tryss aimed as best he could, with the pipe fixed between his teeth, then blew as hard as he was able.

And missed.

Tryss growled – the closest he could get to a curse while holding the pipe between his teeth. He bent to take another dart into the pipe, then took aim again. This time he missed by an arm's length. Sighing, he tried once more, but at the last moment the bird dived into the protection of the trees.

Frustration coiled around him like strangling vines. He gritted his teeth and felt the pipe split. This time he did curse, and the pipe fell out of his mouth into the vegetation below.

Suddenly all he wanted to do was get rid of the contraption strapped to him. He flew toward an outcrop on one side of the valley, landed heavily, then sat down and started pulling at the harness straps. Drilli dropped onto the ground in front of him.

'Stop. Let me do that,' she said, grabbing his hands.

He wanted to push her away. *Why am I so angry?* Standing up, he relaxed and let her undo the bindings. Frustration and anger bled away as the pressure of them lessened, and as he found himself standing closer to her than he had ever dared.

'So what happened?' she asked as the harness slid to the ground.

He grimaced. 'I missed. Then the pipe split. I . . . I crushed it between my teeth.'

She nodded slowly. 'I can make you another, but you'll have to get better at using it.'

'How?'

'Practice. I told you it wasn't as easy as it looked.'

'But I *have* been practising.'

'On the ground. You need to practise using it from the air. On moving targets.' She looked away and frowned. 'And I think you need to build something to help support it while you're aiming – and so if you drop it you won't lose it.'

He stared at her, then smiled.

'I don't know why you bother with me, Drilli.'

She looked at him, then grinned. 'You're interesting, Tryss. And clever. But a bit slow at times.'

He winced. 'Slow?'

'I've got a question for you, Tryss. How many times should a girl mention to a boy that she hasn't got a partner for the trei-trei before she gives up and tries someone else?'

He stared at her in surprise. She winked, took two steps back then turned and dived off the outcrop. A moment later she swooped upward on an updraught.

Shaking his head, he abandoned the harness and set off in pursuit.

CHAPTER 11

The Temple of Arbeem was a beautiful place. Though smaller and much less spectacular than the one in Hania, there was no part of it that didn't have a pleasing view. The front overlooked the port, and windows had been placed wherever possible to offer a glimpse of water.

Behind the Temple was a garden of many tiers. All rear windows offered a view of greenery. Auraya had been longing for the chance to explore it, but in the five days since their arrival in Somrey she hadn't found an opportunity until now.

Mairae walked beside her.

'I've been thinking about Leiard,' she said quietly. 'These link memories of Mirar's don't bother me. Maybe he has more than most Dreamweavers, but that doesn't make him Mirar.' She chuckled. 'Mirar was a flirt and a shameless seducer of women. Leiard doesn't strike me as either.'

Auraya smiled. 'No. You're worried about what the others will think, aren't you?'

Mairae grimaced. 'Yes. Rian won't like it, but he doesn't stick his nose in other White's business – though he'll certainly give his opinion on the subject. Dyara will probably be alarmed and worried that Mirar will somehow still work against us through Leiard. She'll want you to dismiss Leiard, despite all the help he's given us.'

'And Juran?'

'I don't know.' Mairae frowned. 'Have you ever discussed Mirar with Juran?'

Auraya shook her head.

'He doesn't talk about it in the way you'd expect. You'd think he'd be happy that Mirar is no longer making his life difficult, but instead he says it was a – how did he put it? – an "unfortunate necessity". I think he even feels guilty about it. Definitely regretful.'

'Why?'

'I don't know.' Mairae shrugged. 'But I think seeing Mirar's memories in Leiard's mind might stir more guilt and regret.'

'I see.' Auraya chewed on her lip. 'If I replace Leiard with another Dreamweaver there's still a chance Juran will be reminded of Mirar. Many of them carry Mirar's memories, though it is rare to find this many in one person. A younger Dreamweaver might not have any, but he may not be as useful to us.'

Mairae sighed. 'And just being around a Dreamweaver is going to remind him. It's a question of degree. I'm sure Juran is capable of living with reminders of the past, but confronting him with actual memories of Mirar's may be a bit much to ask.'

'What should we do?'

Mairae pursed her lips, then shrugged. 'Wait and see. I'll let Juran know about these memories so he is prepared for them. Should they prove a problem, I'll let you know. Otherwise, just keep on as before.'

Auraya sighed with relief. 'I will.' They reached a small stone pavilion and sat down. A full-sized statue of Chaia stood in an alcove. It was impressively accurate – a solid version of the glowing figure she had come face-to-face with at the Choosing Ceremony. 'I should be worn out. All that political discussion, but it never tired me.'

'Another of the gods' Gifts,' Mairae said. 'Without them I'm sure all that rich Somreyan food would have made us sick – or fat.'

Auraya grinned. 'Do you think there's a noble family here that hasn't fed us? We've eaten every meal at a different house.'

'I was beginning to suspect they'd invent new mealtimes just so we could visit more people.'

'I feel a bit guilty about it, actually. While we've been socialising, poor Leiard has been running back and forth between us and the Dreamweaver House. He's exhausted.'

'Then we'll have to hope, for his sake, that the council accept the modifications to the alliance or he'll have to go through it all again. Ah – here's your other man.'

Auraya looked up, expecting to see Danjin, but instead a furry shape bounded out of the garden and leapt onto her knee.

'Owaya!' Mischief looked up at her and fluttered his eyelashes.

She choked back a laugh. He had learned the mannerism from the many veez belonging to Somreyan families. It appeared to melt the hearts of most rich Somreyan women. *Not me*, she told herself, though she had an uneasy suspicion she might be wrong.

She hadn't intended to take him with her on her social visits, but Mairae assured her that the Somreyans expected her to take her pet everywhere, as they did. At gatherings the veez played boisterously with each other, though servants always hovered nearby to discourage unplanned amorous encounters. Mischief had learned many new words, including some that were going to scandalise Auraya's servants when he returned to Hania – if any understood Somreyan.

Now, as he realised his latest trick had failed to make a treat appear in her hands, he began to look sulky. He gave a little huff and hung his head.

'You're so mean,' Mairae said. 'I'll take him to the kitchen and find him something to chew on. I do believe this sensation I am feeling is hunger. I'd almost forgotten what that was.'

'I'll come with you.'

'Stay,' Mairae said. 'You won't be alone long.'

Auraya blinked in surprise, then concentrated on the minds around her. She found Leiard's quickly, as he was walking through the garden toward her.

'Mischief. Snack.' Mairae held out an arm. The veez looked from her to Auraya.

'Go on,' Auraya said.

He leapt from her lap and scurried up Mairae's arm to her shoulder. Auraya watched them walk away, smiling as the veez licked Mairae's ear and caused her to flinch.

Soon afterwards she heard footsteps. Leiard came around a corner and saw her. He smiled and lengthened his stride. As he reached the pavilion his eyes strayed to the statue of Chaia and his face froze for a moment, then his gaze returned to her.

'Auraya of the White,' he said formally.

'Dreamweaver Leiard,' she replied.

'It grows late,' he observed. 'Will they decide today, do you think?'

She lifted one eyebrow at him. 'I've never seen you anxious before.'

His lips twitched up at one corner. 'It would be disappointing if we came so far only to have them reject the alliance.'

'Yes, it would, but perhaps it would only take a little more negotiation to persuade them.'

'Perhaps.'

He glanced at the statue again. She turned to regard it. If Chaia was watching, what did he make of Leiard? Were the gods bothered by the revelation that the Dreamweaver adviser to the White contained Mirar's memories?

No, they probably knew all along, she realised. *They would have warned me if Leiard was a danger.*

But would they warn her if this put *him* in danger? Standing up, she moved out of the pavilion and began to stroll down the path. Leiard let out a long, quiet sigh of relief and fell into step beside her.

She felt a pang of annoyance at the sigh. It reminded her that, even if she managed to encourage tolerance for Dreamweavers among Circlians, he would never be comfortable around anything to do with the gods. That was to be expected. He had turned from the gods to become a Dreamweaver. When he died the gods would not take his soul. It would cease to exist. The thought pained her. *I am immortal. I won't ever meet him in the afterlife. It wouldn't be so bad if he simply worshipped a different god. At least I'd know he still existed somewhere.*

She shook her head. Why would someone reject the gods and their chance at eternity? She turned to regard him, and his eyebrows rose in query.

'What is it?'

'Why did you become a Dreamweaver, Leiard?'

He shrugged. 'I don't remember exactly,' he said. 'Must have been the right decision at the time.'

'What did your family think – do you remember that?'

He frowned, then shook his head. 'My parents are dead.'

'Oh, I'm sorry.'

Leiard made a dismissive gesture. 'It was a long time ago, when I was young. I barely remember them.'

Auraya laughed. 'When you were *young*? Leiard, you can't

187

be all that old. You're the only person I know who seems to get younger every time we meet.'

'That's because you've been growing up.'

She crossed her arms. 'How old are you?'

He paused and frowned. 'About forty, I think.'

'You *think*? How can you not know exactly how old you are?'

His frown deepened. 'Arleej believes my loss of memory is caused by me not linking with other Dreamweavers for many years.'

Sensing his distress, she decided to change the subject. It was clear his loss of certain memories bothered him.

'How many years has it been since you joined a link?'

'Not since before I lived in the forest near your village.'

She drummed her fingers against her arm. 'How long were you in the village before my family arrived?'

'A few years.'

'Then you haven't linked for nearly twenty years. How old are Dreamweavers when their training is finished?'

He looked at her oddly. 'Twenty, if they start young.'

She nodded. So he was right: he was about forty. For some reason that disappointed her. Maybe because the older he was, the less time she would know him for. He would only grow older while she stayed the same physical age. It gave her an uncomfortable feeling that time was running out. A few more decades and his soul would be gone forever.

'Have Dreamweavers ever served the gods?' she found herself asking.

'No.'

'Do you think they ever would in the future?'

'No.'

'Why not?'

'Because we don't want to.'

She looked at him sidelong. 'Because they had Mirar killed?'

'Partly.'

'And the other part is?'

'Because being powerful does not give someone the right to tell others how to think or live, or who to kill.'

'Not even if that someone is older and wiser than you? Like a god?'

'No.' He looked away. 'People should have a choice whether they worship the gods or not.'

'They do.'

'Without punishment or penalty?'

'So you expect them to take your soul whether you worship them or not?' she asked in return.

'No. I expect my people to be free from persecution.'

'That is in the past.'

'Is it? Then why do Dreamweavers still fear to walk the streets of Jarime? Why are they forbidden to practise their skills in order to help people?'

Auraya sighed. 'Because of what happened a century ago. And I don't mean Mirar's death.'

He said nothing to that. She was both relieved and disappointed. While she did not want to argue with him, she did want to hear his view on the events in the past that had led to the Dreamweavers' situation now.

According to records she had read, Mirar had been both admirable in his work and self-indulgent in his habits. He had taught his people everything about medicines and care for the sick or wounded. His Gift of healing had been unique and he'd been generous at applying it.

But he'd had a reputation for indulging in drink, pleasure drugs and seduction that had scandalised many. Dreamweavers, though they did not speak of it, knew that the reputation was well earned. The truth was in link memories of Mirar and

189

those who had known him, passed down through the generations. Auraya could see this knowledge in their minds. She had seen it in Leiard's.

Still, it was not Mirar's character flaws that had convinced the gods that he must be killed. He had worked openly against them, trying to prevent the formation of the White. He had seeded doubts, telling the people malicious lies about the fate of their souls in the gods' hands. He had claimed that some of the dead gods had not deserved their fate, while the Circle were guilty of terrible acts of cruelty. And the final action that had condemned him had been to send the people of Ithania powerful dreams in an attempt to turn them away from the gods.

Instead, the people had begged the gods to free them from his manipulations.

He brought about his own death, she thought.

Yet what followed Mirar's death had been terrible. The gods had never decreed that ordinary Dreamweavers should be killed, but there had been many murders of Dreamweavers after Mirar's death, carried out by overly enthusiastic Circlian followers. These fanatics had been punished, but it took a long time to discourage others from emulating them.

Most Circlians knew that no priest had ever matched a fully trained Dreamweaver in medical skills or knowledge. Now that Auraya understood the purpose and benefits of a mind link, she had realised that this was how the Dreamweavers shared and passed on so much knowledge. As far as she knew, no priest had ever attempted anything like a mind link. Except for telepathy, which did not involve opening one's mind to another, Circlians felt an aversion to having their minds messed with. Invading another's mind was a crime – a law which had been instated because of Mirar's actions.

190

Perhaps it's time for us to get over our squeamishness, Auraya mused. If the Circlian priests learned to do what Dreamweavers could, they, too, could increase their knowledge of healing. She felt a chill run over her skin. If they matched, even surpassed, the Dreamweavers, one of the most powerful attractions for newcomers to the heathen cult would be lost. The Dreamweaver cult might fade out of existence in a few generations. *Or in one, if I or other White pass on the knowledge we read from their minds.*

She shivered. *No. That would make us guilty of the crime people have always suspected Dreamweavers of: invading the privacy of another's mind and using the information to harm others.*

Yet it could be done without any linking of minds. If priests could be persuaded to work alongside Dreamweavers they were sure to pick up new skills and knowledge. It would be slow, but it would encourage tolerance and acceptance in the meantime.

Do I really want to be the cause of the Dreamweaver's demise?

No. But I can't continue to let people turn away from the gods and sacrifice their souls. Not when it isn't necessary. People believe that the Dreamweavers' healing knowledge will be lost unless some make that sacrifice. But if they could learn the same things by becoming priests and priestesses would they still become heathens?

Today, in this garden, with Leiard walking beside her, she had stumbled upon a terrible dilemma. One day she was going to have to choose between keeping his friendship and saving souls.

But not right now. Danjin had appeared on the path before them. He grinned as he saw her, and she knew without reading his mind what his news would be. She did not feel triumph, however, only a wry relief.

'They've done it!' he called. 'They've signed the alliance!'

*   *   *

191

Emerahl looked over her shoulder. Her little boat of silvery wood glowed in the moonlight. Casting her eye ove the mooring rope, she nodded to herself, then drew her shawl over her head and made her way along the dock.

She had been travelling for weeks now, sailing up the coast of Toren. Every few days she had moored at small coastal villages to sell cures in exchange for food, clean water and items such as sailcloth, a waterproof sea tawl and fishing line. The people she traded with treated her with friendly respect, though it was clear they thought it peculiar that an old woman might travel this way.

The villages had grown steadily larger and more frequent until it seemed every bay had sprouted a pier or five. This afternoon she had turned into a deeper bay where large ships slowly swayed at anchor. Buildings covered all the land, and the coast was a labyrinth of wooden docks. She had arrived at the city of Porin, capital of Toren.

A length of dried starlight weed had bought a mooring from the corrupt dockmaster. One of the village women had stolen it from her husband to exchange for a cure for a feverish child several months earlier. Emerahl had been saving it for herself and was not pleased to be losing it. The hallucinatory qualities, coupled with euphoria, made it one of her favourite pleasure drugs.

So she was not in a pleasant mood as she strode into the city's market district. In any large city there was a place where trade never stopped and shops never closed. People, when desperate, sought out cures at any time of the night.

She did not intend to trade with the customers in the market, however. The right to trade was always a jealously guarded commodity in cities. If she had wanted to sell her wares she would have had to make an arrangement with a stallholder to work outside his or her shop. Part of her profit would go toward paying for the privilege of plying her trade. She didn't have time for that.

Instead, she had a collection of items to sell to cure shops. Some she had already possessed, some she had gathered on the way. There were sacs of venom from yeryer fish to thin the blood, spines of the prickle mat which could be used to apply a shot of anaesthetic to a precise location, and antiseptic straps of seaweed. She had added to this a few bags of ground firespice, which had grown in plentiful quantities around the lighthouse, and several potent herbs.

A few items of no medicinal but high monetary value had found their way into her bag. Most were aphrodisiacs. Generally these had no genuine physical effect, but most people became so excited by the thought they were indulging in a 'cure' that stirred sexual desire that they mistook their excitement for the effect of the 'cure'. Of course, these 'cures' came either from some fierce creature, like the teeth of the giant garr she had found washed up on a deserted beach, or they looked like sexual organs, like the dried sea worms, fleshy phallic wemmin flowers and sea bell she'd found tangled in some floating weed. The latter she would consider selling only as a last resort. It was rare and valuable, and no shopkeeper was going to pay a passing traveller what it was truly worth. One day she might be in a better position to barter.

Noise and light drew her to her destination. Large awnings, each hung with lanterns, formed two tunnels along each side of a long street of shops. Musicians added a cheerful note to the voices of the thin crowd of shoppers. Some sellers bellowed out inviting descriptions of their wares. Others made bold promises of reasonable prices and fair deals.

Emerahl bought a loaf of bread, a stick of grilled ner – she was heartily tired of fish – some overpriced fruit and a cup of sweetened, fermented shem milk. As she continued along the street the smells of food were replaced by the acrid smell of smoking herbs and incense. Here she found what she was looking for.

The first shop of cures was large and busy. A counter stretched across the front of the store and jars of many sizes and shapes filled shelves along the back wall. She brought her bag to the counter and waited patiently to be noticed. The seller was a middle-aged bald man with sharp eyes. As soon as he finished selling a dubious cure for footrot to a young soldier, he turned to her.

'What can I help you with, young lady?'

She smiled at his attempt at flattery. 'My poor arm aches,' she told him. 'So I am hoping to sell some of my bag's contents.'

His sharp eyes flashed with amusement. 'Is that so? And you hope to sell them to me?'

'Yes.' She opened the bag and drew out the jar containing the sacs of yeryer venom. 'Would you have a use for these? They're fresh. I collected them no more than a week ago.'

As she opened the jar, his eyebrows rose. 'A week, you say? Perhaps I could spare a few coin for them.' He eyed her bag, which was smelling somewhat fishy. 'What else do you have?'

She drew out a few more items, then the bartering began. He was interrupted several times by a younger man, perhaps his son, who eventually disappeared into the back of the shop. Emerahl concentrated on her customer. He was selective, spending long moments in consideration, though she judged she was offering her goods at low prices. He did not meet her eyes, and she found herself wishing she had managed to keep up her skill at sensing emotions.

I'm going to have to regain it, she thought. *It will make it easier to adapt to the changes in the language, too. I'd assumed the villagers' strange way of speaking was a result of their low background, but it seems Toren speech has changed in general.*

The seller had seen only half of the items in her bag now. Growing tired of this man's slow manner, she decided to pretend this was all she had to sell, and asked for her money.

He slowly counted out coins from a purse, stopping midway when his assistant returned to have a whispered conversation.

'I'd like to get to my bed some time soon,' Emerahl interrupted. She put her hand on top of the jars he'd agreed to buy and took a half-step back from the counter. 'Aren't my prices good enough for you?'

He raised his hands in a placating gesture. 'I'm sorry, lady, but my assistant has a rather delicate and urgent matter to attend to.' He returned to the counter and counted out the rest of the coins. She pushed the jars toward him, swept the coins into her bag and cut his long farewell short.

As she left the shop, she let out a sigh of irritation. Had he been hoping she'd lower her price just to get him to hurry up? Had she *looked* like she was in a hurry?

Puzzling over this, she wandered into a nearby liquor seller's and bought a measure of spicewater. Taking a seat in a dark corner, she raised the glass to her lips and looked across the street to the cure-seller's shop.

She nearly choked as she saw two priests step out of the door. The seller appeared and pointed toward the liquor shop. As the priests headed toward her Emerahl's heart began to race.

They probably just want a drink, she told herself. But they were looking at everyone in the street. As an old woman passed them, they paused and stared at her intently. *No, it's not a drink they're looking for.*

Suddenly the seller's behaviour made sense: his evading her eyes, his delaying her. His assistant disappearing. The whispered conversation between them.

'. . . a rather delicate and urgent matter to attend to.'

The matter of an old woman selling cures? Had the shop

owner been told to watch for her? *I don't know that for sure*, she told herself. *This could be a simple coincidence.* The priests might be looking for someone else. The fact that she had just been driven from her home by one was making her suspect them all of seeking her.

Coincidence or not, I'm not waiting around to find out. Emerahl opened her bag, pulled out her oiled waterproof sea tawl and shrugged into it. Removing the shawl about her head, she replaced it with a broad-brimmed sailor hat, tucking her hair inside. Then she wrapped her bag in the shawl and put it under her arm.

The priests were only a few strides from the liquor seller's now. She stepped out of the door, paused to make the sign of the circle with one hand in their direction, then moved away, walking with the rolling, unhurried gait of a sailor.

She waited for them to call out, but only the boasting of the sellers broke the general hubbub of the market. It seemed to take forever for her to reach the end of the street. Once there, she quickened her pace a little and kept to the shadows.

Am I being pursued? If I am, how could the priests have guessed that I would come to the Porin night market to sell cures?

The answer was clear. If the priest at Corel had travelled up the coast he would have heard of the strange old woman selling cures who sailed alone in a boat. He would have recognised her and alerted priests in towns ahead by telepathy, telling them to watch for an old curer woman passing through. It was sheer luck that she hadn't been confronted by another priest before now.

But *why*? These priests couldn't possibly know who she really was.

Maybe the priest at Corel was curious to know who the cranky old sorceress was who had been living in a remote lighthouse for so long . . .

Oh. Her stomach sank. *If he asked the villagers how long I'd been there, they might have told him generations. That would make him suspect I am immortal. Even if he doesn't believe it, he's probably obliged to check.*

As she neared the docks, she slowed. Creeping closer, she searched her surroundings. In the distance she could just see her little boat tied up to the pier. Finding a darkened corner, she sat down and waited.

She did not have to wait long. As the dockmaster emerged from his shack she glimpsed the corner of a chair and the back of someone wearing something white with a blue edge.

Goodbye, little friend, she thought at the boat. *I hope you find a good owner*.

Then, with a pang of regret, she turned away and slipped into the shadows of the city.

The stranger had taken a seat at the back of the room and had spent the last two hours watching the other occupants of the drink shop. Roffin hadn't liked the look of the man from the moment he had walked in. Too well groomed, he was. Trussed up in a big tawl. A foreigner, with an arrogance to his manner that suggested highborn ways. Roffin didn't like the way the man watched everyone come and go.

'You lookin' at our mystery guest again?' Cemmo murmured.

Roffin turned to regard his companion. Cemmo was a wiry man, one of the youngest of the local fishermen. Roffin grunted quietly.

'His kind don't belong here.'

'Nope,' Cemmo agreed.

'Should be up at the high-folks' drink shop.'

'Tha's right.'

'Someone oughta throw him out.'

'Upta Garmen. He won't 'less there's trouble.'

197

'Garmen's got somethin' to lose if highborn folks take exception. We don't,' Roffin pointed out.

Cemmo looked away. 'True. But . . . I dunno. Somethin' 'bout him looks dangerous.'

'Just his starin' gettin' to you.'

Garmen, the owner of the drink shop, gave the stranger a quick, nervous glance. The man wasn't drinking much, either, Roffin noted. Cheap, foreign bastard.

As Roffin slammed down his third mug, the stranger turned to stare at him. Roffin stared right back. The man's eyebrows rose a little. He smiled.

'Well, if nobody else has got the guts.'

Cemmo frowned as Roffin rose, but said nothing; he just slid off his chair and followed, a silent supporter. As Roffin strode toward the stranger, others looked up and nodded in approval.

The stranger watched him come, apparently unconcerned. Roffin leaned over the man, taking full advantage of his bulk.

'You're in the wrong place,' he told him. 'The place for you is on the other side of the road. Uptown.'

A smile thinned the stranger's mouth.

'I like here,' he said in a deep, strangely accented voice.

Roffin straightened. 'We don't like *you* here. Go stare at your own kind.'

'I stay.' The man gestured at the seat opposite. 'You stay. We drink.'

'You drink elsewhere,' Roffin growled. He reached for the stranger's shoulders. The man's eyes narrowed but he did not move. Roffin felt scorching heat envelop his fingers. He snatched his hand away, cursed and stared at his reddened skin.

'What did . . . ?'

'You go,' the man said, with a note of warning in his voice. Roffin took a few steps backwards. The stranger was a sorcerer. No threats were going to budge him. Cemmo looked at Roffin questioningly. As Roffin glanced around the room, he realised that all the occupants were watching him. Had they seen what the man had done? Probably not. They just saw Roffin backing down to a highborn foreigner. Scowling, he turned on his heel and strode to the door.

'Take my money elsewhere,' he muttered as he left, slamming the door behind him. Once outside, however, he stopped, unsure what to do now. Cemmo hadn't followed. Long habit made him note the sound of the surf pounding at the base of the cliff below and the whistle of the wind between the buildings. It would be a rough night on the water.

His hand throbbed. He looked down and decided he ought to get someone to see to it.

The priest. Yes, he'll have a cure for it. Roffin glanced back at the drink shop and smiled. *And I'm sure Priest Waiken will want to know there's a foreign spy in town.*

CHAPTER 12

Rippling, surging water stretched in all directions. The reflected light of the rising sun formed ribbons of orange on its surface. Occasionally a seabird would soar past, seemingly oblivious to the ship or its occupants.

Looking to the west, Danjin could see a blue smudge of mountains above a thin, dark strip of land. The Sunset Range ran up the west coast of Hania to Mirror Strait, where it plunged into the water and formed a line of small islets leading to the larger Somreyan Islands. According to ancient histories some of those mountains had once spouted fire and ash, but now they were cold and silent.

'Danjin.'

He turned in surprise. Auraya rarely rose before dawn. Her long hair was plaited into a simple tail rather than the usual elaborate style. She was frowning.

'Good morning, Auraya of the White,' he said, making the gesture of the circle. 'It is a beautiful morning, isn't it?'

She glanced at the sunrise but her frown did not fade.

'Yes. It is.' She looked at him. 'I will be leaving the ship in the next hour. Would you look after Mischief and ensure Leiard reaches his accommodation safely?'

Looking along the deck, Danjin noted that four crewmen

were untying a small boat from where it had been securely tied up on deck for most of the trip.

'Of course,' he replied. She was biting her lip. He reached out but did not quite touch her arm. 'Can you tell me what calls you away?'

She turned slowly, her gaze sweeping over the crew. 'A little,' she said quietly. 'Juran has received several reports of a Pentadrian priest, probably a spy, passing through villages and towns on the north Hanian coast. He has sent Dyara to capture the man and has asked me to approach from the north in order to cut off his escape.'

He nodded, understanding her apprehension. Her training in the use of her Gifts had barely begun. This could be her first sorcerous confrontation.

The gods will protect her, he told himself. *And Dyara will probably turn it into a lesson*, he added wryly.

Her lips curled into a small smile as she read his mind. 'I will return to Jarime with Dyara, so I am leaving you in charge, Danjin Spear.'

'Does Leiard know that you are leaving, or why?'

She shook her head. 'Tell him what I have told you, but to the rest say only that I have left to deal with some matter on the coast.'

He nodded. 'I will.'

She fell silent, watching the distant coastline. As they drew closer to the land, Danjin fought a growing anxiety. *She is one of the Gods' Chosen*, he reminded himself. *She can look after herself.*

He realised it was not her safety he worried about. She might be forced to kill this spy. It was not a burden he would wish on her any sooner than necessary.

If only Mairae had returned with us, he thought, instead of remaining behind to make arrangements for trade and other delegations to visit under the terms of the alliance. As soon as this thought came he knew it was an unworthy one. Mairae might be fully trained – or so he assumed – but she was as undeserving of the burden of a death on her hands as Auraya was.

The sun crept higher and the coast closer. The dark line Danjin had seen from a distance became a weathered black cliff. A building with several stout towers was visible, built close to the edge of the wall. The boat was lowered into the water. Auraya climbed nimbly down, joining the rowers inside.

Danjin leaned on the railing as he watched them row away. Auraya sat with a straight spine and did not look back.

'Adviser Danjin Spear.'

Danjin turned to find Leiard standing behind him. He wondered how long the Dreamweaver had been there.

'Yes, Dreamweaver Leiard?'

Leiard stepped up to the railing and stared out at the boat. 'I gather Auraya will not be joining us for the morning meal.'

Danjin shook his head. 'No. She has left to meet Dyara in order to deal with a Pentadrian spy and will return to Jarime by road.'

Leiard nodded. He watched the boat a moment longer, then turned to face Danjin again. The corners of his lips twitched upward. 'Then we had best return below before the wafercakes cool.'

Danjin chuckled. Turning from the railing, he followed Leiard below deck.

As the boat neared the cliffs, Auraya wondered how they could possibly land safely. Waves crashed against the black vertical rock face, filling the air with salty spray. It was clear any craft attempting to moor here would be battered to pieces. The rowers heaved and hauled against the oars, propelling the boat around a bluff. A narrow beach of dark sand appeared, riddled with black rocks. Auraya breathed a sigh of relief as the crew headed for it.

Looking up, she made out a zigzagging line of stairs carved into the cliff face, leading to the top. The boat scraped against sand. The men pulled in their oars, jumped over the sides and, as a wave pushed the craft forward, hauled it up the beach.

Auraya rose and stepped out. As her sandals sank into the sand, water welled up and chilled her feet. She thanked the rowers, then left them dragging the boat back into the water as she started toward the base of the stairs.

The stairs were steep, narrow and worn to a dip in the centre of each tread. She started climbing and was soon breathing deeply. The higher she climbed, the more disconcerting the drop to the shore became. Wind buffeted her, and she wondered uneasily what would happen to her if she fell. Dyara hadn't taught her how to survive a fall. Would a defensive shield like the one used to protect her from a magical attack also save her from the impact of landing on the sand or rocks far below?

Perhaps it would be better not to think about it. Auraya resolutely turned her mind from the subject and continued her climb. Her thoughts soon returned to the task Juran had set her. The Pentadrian had been seen lurking about in drinking houses, perhaps hoping to overhear something of interest to his people. His description did not match the powerful sorcerer Rian had fought; he was older and dark-haired. Yet she could not help but feel a little apprehensive.

There can't be two sorcerers of such strength, Juran had assured her. *We might encounter one once a century. This man has been staying in poor accommodations. I doubt his Gifts are as strong as those of a high priest or priestess.*

When, at last, she reached the top of the cliff she was surprised to find a small crowd waiting for her. A village surrounded one side of the blackstone building atop the cliff edge.

A priest stepped forward. 'Welcome to Caram, Auraya of the White. I am Priest Valem.'

She smiled. 'Thank you, Priest Valem.'

He gestured to a well-dressed man with pale eyes and grey in his hair. 'This is Borean Stonecutter, our village head.'

She inclined her head to the man, who made the formal two-handed sign of the circle. Others in the small gathering followed suit. She noted that they were plainly dressed. One still wore the scorched apron of a metalworker. Most avoided her eyes, while a few gazed at her in awe. She smiled warmly at them.

'I am also the owner of the watch-house,' Borean said, gesturing to the building on the edge of the cliff. 'Priest Valem has arranged for you to stay there.'

'I would be honoured to visit your home,' Auraya replied. 'I hope I have not caused you inconvenience.'

'It is no trouble,' he replied. He beckoned politely and they began walking toward the house. The priest fell into step on her other side. 'I let rooms to travellers from time to time, so I am not completely unprepared for visitors,' Borean assured her. 'I cannot promise the comforts of Jarime, however.'

'Neither I, nor my fellow White, lead an extravagant life. Is the house very old?'

She did not have to feign interest as he told her of the long history of the building. It had been built by one of his ancestors many hundreds of years before, as both home and watch-tower to warn of a sea invasion.

When they reached the door she paused to thank the villagers for meeting her. Once inside she encouraged Borean to take her through the house, the priest following silently. The interior was rich in artefacts, but not overly luxurious. They finished in one of the squat towers, where he presented a suite of rooms for her.

'I have arranged for local women to serve—'

A crash downstairs interrupted him, then a woman's scream. The sound of running footsteps followed. Borean and Priest Valem exchanged puzzled glances, then the village head excused himself and moved to the entrance of the suite. As he reached it a man in a brown travelling tawl stepped into the doorway, blocking his exit. His eyes slid over the village head and the priest, and met Auraya's.

Her skin prickled as he stared at her. There was something strange about him. His skin was pale but his eyes were so black she could not make out his pupils. That was not the source of the strangeness, however. She looked closer and her stomach sank as she realised what it was.

She could not read his mind.

'Who are—?' Borean began.

The man glanced at the village head. Borean tumbled backwards. He landed heavily and clutched at his stomach, gasping for breath. Drawing magic, Auraya hastily created a protective barrier across the room between Borean and the sorcerer. The village head scrambled away from the door, still struggling to breathe. She stepped forward to take his arm and help him to his feet, not taking her eyes from the man in the doorway.

'Are you hurt?' she murmured to Borean.

'Just . . . win – ded,' he said hoarsely.

'Is there another way out of these rooms?'

He nodded.

'Good. Take the priest and go.'

:Juran, she called as the two men left via a side door.

:Yes?

:The Pentadrian spy is here.

:Already?

:Yes. She made the link stronger and let him see the sorcerer through her eyes.

205

:What can you glean from his mind?

:Nothing. I can't read his mind. Is this a common Pentadrian skill?

:I don't know. We have to consider the possibility. I will contact Dyara.

:He sought me out. There is no other reason for him to come into the house. Are you sure he's a spy? That's not spy-like behaviour.

:He must think you are a priestess of some importance and he intends to force information out of you. I doubt he knows who you are.

'You must be Auraya of the White,' the Pentadrian said.

She stared at him in surprise.

:So much for that theory, she thought at Juran. *Where is Dyara?*

:An hour's ride away, Dyara answered. *Keep him talking, Auraya, and inside the house. I will be there soon.*

'I am Auraya,' she said. 'Who are you?'

'I am Kuar, First Voice of the Gods,' he replied.

:Great Chaia! The leader of the Pentadrians? Juran said incredulously. *Why would the leader of a cult venture into the north alone? He must be lying.*

The Pentadrian started moving toward her, one slow step at a time.

'Why are you here?' she asked.

'I came to see you,' the sorcerer replied.

'Me? Why?'

'To learn . . .' He reached her barrier. As he spread his hands out before it his tawl parted to reveal black clothing and a silver star pendant. She frowned. A spy wouldn't travel in a strange land with only a tawl to hide the dress of his people.

'What do you wish to learn?' she asked.

A blast of power battered her shield, sending whips of lightning-like magic across its surface. She gasped at the strength of it. The attack stopped and he regarded her coolly.

'How strong you heathens are,' he replied.

She fixed the Pentadrian with what she hoped was a cold stare. 'Did that answer your question?'

The sorcerer shrugged. 'Not quite.'

Auraya crossed her arms and stared defiantly. Inside she was trembling with shock.

:Juran, she said. *I suspect your theory that one powerful sorcerer is born every hundred years is wrong. And I think your spy theory is wrong too.*

:I fear you are right on both counts, Juran agreed. *He is strong, but so are you.*

:But I've barely learned more than how to shield myself!

:That's all you need. When Dyara gets there she will deal with him.

The sorcerer's eyes narrowed. A second blast of magic set her barrier humming. On either side of the room, stray magic scalded paint and set furnishings ablaze. As the attack increased, she drew more and more magic to resist it.

:By the gods he's strong!

:Your shield is too large, Juran warned. *Draw it in closer to yourself. You'll find it more efficient.*

She did as he advised. With the barrier abruptly gone, the sorcerer's attack shattered paintings, furniture and windows. She felt a pang of guilt at the destruction.

The attack stopped. She watched the Pentadrian's face. His eyes were thoughtful. He took another step forward.

'There are much more civilised ways of doing this,' she told him. 'We could devise a test of some sort. Perhaps hold annual games. People would come from—'

As a brutally powerful blast battered her shield she put all her concentration into drawing and channelling magic. The man watched her intently, showing no sign of effort as his onslaught grew ever stronger. Then she found she could no longer draw magic fast enough to counter his attack. White light dazzled her as he broke down her defences. She knew a brief instant of pure agony. Staggering backwards, she gasped for air and looked down at herself. She was alive and, to her surprise, unhurt.

:Flee! Juran's communication was like a shout in her mind. *He is stronger. There is nothing more you can do.*

The knowledge hit her like a physical blow. The Pentadrian could kill her. She felt a wave of terror and hastily created another shield. Looking up at the sorcerer she saw him smiling broadly. *So much for immortality*, she found herself thinking. *People are going to remember me as the shortest-lived immortal in history!* She took a few steps toward the side door and encountered an invisible force.

'No, no,' the Pentadrian said. 'You are not leaving. I want to see if you call on your gods. Will they appear? That would be interesting. It would answer many questions.'

:Is there a window behind you? Dyara asked.

:Yes, but if I move toward it he will block me.

:Then you will have to resist him. It will take time for him to break down your defences again. Use that time to get to the window.

Auraya backed away from the sorcerer. His smile widened and she suspected he thought her afraid of him and was pleased. *I am afraid of him!* She stepped into a square of light from the shattered window behind her and felt sunlight warm her calves. The sorcerer looked down at her feet and frowned. His gaze flickered to the window and his eyes narrowed.

An invisible force struck her shield. Though she fought it, she did not have the strength to stop herself from being forced backwards against the wall. The window was an arm's length away. The Pentadrian strode forward until he stood before her.

'Where are your gods?' he asked. 'I know your strength. It will not take long to defeat you again. Call on your gods.'

The window was so close, but she could not move. The sorcerer shook his head.

'They don't exist. You are deceivers. You deserve to die.'

He splayed his fingers before her chest. She tried to shrink away, but the wall was hard against her back. If only it were possible to pass through it . . .

But of course I can! Drawing power, she sent it backwards in a great blast. The wall gave way with a deafening crack. She saw the sorcerer's eyes widen in surprise as she fell away from him. She braced herself for the impact of her shield meeting the ground outside.

But it didn't.

She continued to fall. As she turned upside down she saw sand and rocks and water rushing toward her.

I must stop!

She felt magic channel through her, answering the command of her mind. The sensation of falling ended in one wrenching jolt. For a moment she was too stunned to think. She sucked in one breath, then two. Slowly, she opened her eyes, not able to remember when she had closed them.

A wall of dark sand lay within arm's reach.

Not a wall, she corrected, *but the beach*. Looking around, she saw the cliff wall to her right and the sea to her left. She was floating.

How is that possible?

Thinking back, she considered the thought that had passed through her mind. *I wanted to stop. To stop moving.*

It was more than that. She had seen herself moving in relation to what was around her. Not specifically the cliff or sea. Everything. The *world*.

And I did. She shook her head in amazement. *And I'm still doing it. Can I make myself move again by willing myself to change position in relation to the world?*

She hesitated, afraid that by examining this new Gift she would lose it and drop the rest of the way to the beach. Not a fatal fall, but a disappointing one.

But, she reasoned, *if this ability – this Gift – had taken a lot of thought I would have been aware of it from the start.* No, this was unlike any Gift she had learned before. This was like learning to walk. Something she didn't have to think about.

If learning a Gift is like learning to play an instrument, then this is like singing.

If she could move herself, it would be like flying. That thought sent a thrill through her body.

I have to try. Me in relation to the world. I want to turn over and face upward.

She rolled over sideways in three abrupt movements. Above her was the cliff. She thought about moving higher and began to rise. Slowly, then with greater speed, she lifted herself upward. To be vertical would be better, she decided. Slowly she pivoted until she was upright. She passed the edge of the cliff and stopped as she found herself looking down on the watch-house.

Abruptly she remembered the sorcerer and her elation died. Smoke was escaping from the hole she had blasted in the side of the house. Villagers were hauling buckets of water from a well to the building. She felt her stomach knot with fear as she searched for the sorcerer. If he was still there she would have to retreat until Dyara arrived.

Moving over the village, she looked for him in vain. Then she saw a dark figure riding northward on a reyna. She searched for his thoughts and found none. She sighed with relief.

He must have assumed I'd died. And Juran and Dyara must be wondering what happened. She smiled. *They're not going to believe me.*

:Juran.

:Auraya? You're alive. What . . . ? Where are you?

:Over Caram.

:I don't understand . . .

:Neither do I. The gods couldn't make me stronger, so instead they have given me a new Gift. I can see the sorcerer. He is leaving. Should I follow him? Or meet Dyara?

:Don't put yourself in danger. Meet Dyara. You must both return.

:We can't let the sorcerer get away! Dyara protested.

:We must. You are stronger than Auraya, but we don't know if you are strong enough, and until Auraya has completed her training we should not set her against such dangerous sorcerers – even with assistance. Meet Auraya and return to Jarime.

Auraya surveyed the buildings below. Smoke was no longer curling from the house. As she watched, Borean emerged, and from his gestures she guessed he was telling the villagers the water was no longer needed.

:Where are you, Dyara?

:On the road, not far away now.

:I'll come south and meet you.

Breaking the link, Auraya willed herself into motion once again.

CHAPTER 13

The first thing Leiard noticed when Danjin Spear opened the door to Auraya's rooms was how pale the adviser was. The man's fear of heights wasn't as well suppressed as usual, but added to it was amazement and wonder.

'Dreamweaver Leiard,' Danjin said, a little breathlessly. 'Mairae said I should send you to the roof. The stairs will lead you there.'

'Thank you, Danjin Spear.'

Cool air gusted out of the room. Leiard paused and glanced over Danjin's shoulder to see a pair of workmen standing before a window empty of glass.

So that's the source of his heightened fear. He's all too aware that nothing lies between him and the drop outside. But why is the glass missing? Has someone fallen through it? He could sense nothing from the adviser or the men to suggest that.

His view of the room was obscured as Danjin closed the door firmly. Leiard shook his head and began climbing the stairs. The mystery would probably be solved when he spoke to Auraya.

The *Herald* had returned to Jarime three days ago, and Leiard to the Bakers' house. News of the signing of the alliance had travelled faster and Tanara had already had a

212

celebratory dinner arranged. She invited other Dreamweavers and sympathetic friends. Not all were as sure as she that this was the beginning of peace between Dreamweavers and Circlians, but all agreed that there had been a marked lessening of harassment of 'heathens' in Jarime during the last few months.

Jayim had been silent and thoughtful that evening. Later, he had questioned Leiard on his role. Leiard had sensed that the boy was close to deciding his future. He did not nudge him toward a choice. Jayim needed to sort this out by himself.

This morning a feeling of resolution had imbued the house. Jayim had been tense and quiet, clearly waiting for an appropriate moment to speak. At the end of the morning meal he had asked if Leiard still wanted to teach him. A few words later Leiard had gained himself a pupil.

Tanara had barely enough time to grasp what had transpired when the summons to the White Tower had come. Leiard had left the boy grinning and his mother planning another celebratory meal. Now, as he climbed the stairs to the roof, Leiard asked himself if he was happy with the arrangement. Jayim was intelligent and Gifted. With training and maturity he would make a good Dreamweaver. So why did he feel this lingering regret? Did he crave solitude? Or simply not to be encumbered by a student? Or did he still hope, deep down, that Auraya would come back to him?

I'm a fool if I do.

The end of the staircase appeared. A small door stood half-open, swaying gently. Leiard felt cool air on his face.

As he stepped outside, something swooped in and out of sight just beyond the edge of the Tower. He stopped and frowned. It had been too big to be a bird. He'd had a brief impression of human proportions. Had a Siyee come to Jarime? His heart beat faster at the thought. As far as he knew no Siyee

213

had flown this far before. He hurried toward the railing at the edge of the Tower.

Looking over the edge, he saw the figure clearly. This was no Siyee, but a human of normal proportions. Impossibly, this human – this woman – had no wings. A white circ flared out from her shoulders. She was turning slow loops in midair. As her face turned upward he felt his heart jolt.

Auraya!

He stared at her in disbelief. *How is this possible?*

With magic, obviously, a voice in his mind replied.

He had never seen it done before. Though plenty of sorcerers had tried, no one had ever achieved it. Until now he'd had no idea it was even possible, but here she was, defying the pull of the earth.

Flying!

He considered what it had cost the Siyee to be able to take to the sky, and suddenly it hurt to watch her. It was not the only pain he felt, but emptiness, as if the last of his hopes were draining out of him. No matter how disillusioned with her life Auraya might become, nothing would ever lure her away from *this*.

She was grinning widely, all her attention on the acrobatics she was performing, albeit slowly.

'Leiard!' She had noticed him. 'Look what I can do!' she called. She turned another loop. Her circ flared and he noticed she was wearing trousers beneath it rather than the usual long tunic. No doubt the latter had proved awkward to fly in – at least with any dignity.

He couldn't help smiling. The childlike glee in her voice reminded him of the girl she had been. Her gaze shifted past him and her grin relaxed into a smile. She swooped down and he turned to watch as she dropped to the roof.

A priest was walking toward them. The man had a dignified

bearing, but wore an expression of friendly concern. There was something familiar about him.

It's him, the voice in the back of Leiard's mind said.

Who? Leiard asked. No answer came, but he didn't need one. This priest's circ was plain, and there was only one White he hadn't met.

'Juran,' Auraya said. 'This is Dreamweaver Leiard. Leiard, this is Juran of the White.'

A memory flashed into Leiard's mind of Juran's face set with determination. With it came a surge of fear. Leiard managed to suppress it. There was no getting out of this meeting. *Juran has no reason to harm me*, he told himself.

The White frowned, no doubt catching Leiard's thoughts, but then his face relaxed.

'Dreamweaver Adviser Leiard,' he said. 'It is a pleasure to meet you at last. Thank you for your help with the Somreyan alliance. Auraya and Mairae tell me your assistance was invaluable.'

Leiard inclined his head in reply. 'It was a pleasure to assist them.' He glanced at Auraya. 'And it appears the gods are pleased with Auraya's efforts.'

Juran smiled. 'They could have warned us,' he said ruefully, but with no hint of reproach. His expression became serious again. 'Auraya has told me about link memories. She says you have many of Mirar's.'

Auraya's smile disappeared. She frowned at Leiard in concern.

'It is so,' Leiard replied. 'I have no idea where or from whom I picked them up. It had been many years since I participated in a memory link.'

Juran nodded. 'How recent are these memories?'

'They are fragmentary,' Leiard replied truthfully. 'It is hard to know what time they relate to. Some are old, as the landmarks within them are not as affected by time. Sometimes it is impossible to tell.'

Juran opened his mouth as if to say more, then shook his head and turned to regard Auraya. 'We have much to do today, and I'm sure your adviser would appreciate it if we chose more comfortable surroundings than the Tower roof in which to discuss your time in Somrey.'

'Then perhaps we should meet in your rooms,' she suggested. 'I have arranged for a window in mine to be made into a door. It's a little . . . draughty.'

Juran's eyebrows rose. 'My rooms, then.' He glanced at Leiard. 'Let us delay no longer.' With a polite gesture, he indicated that Leiard should walk beside him back to the stairway door.

As he fell into step beside the White's leader, Leiard felt a nagging misgiving. *Do not trust him*, the other voice in his mind whispered. Taking a deep breath, Leiard did his best to ignore it. The sooner he started teaching Jayim to link, and so could assert his own identity on a regular basis, the better.

This time the ritual words Juran recited at the beginning of the meeting in the Altar stirred gratitude as well as loyalty in Auraya. The two short phrases she contributed were spoken with more feeling than ever before.

'We thank you.'

Her thanks now included the extraordinary Gift the gods had given her. Juran had called her to the roof early, to see if he could master the skill. Though she explained it as clearly as she could, and even projected her understanding of it to him mentally, he could not emulate her.

'Perhaps I should throw myself off the Tower,' he had murmured once. As he looked over the railing to the ground, he had shuddered. 'No, I think some risks are not worth taking. It would not be a pleasant way to discover this is a Gift meant solely for you.'

Which was an interesting possibility. Would the others be given their own unique Gifts? Perhaps the gods would explain today . . .

'Guide us.'

At these words her thoughts shifted to the other reason they had gathered here and her mood darkened. They were to discuss her encounter with the Pentadrian sorcerer.

The brief ritual over, Juran regarded the other White soberly.

'Two black sorcerers,' he said. 'Both Pentadrians. Both powerful. One who claimed to be Kuar, the leader of their cult. If he is their leader, why did he come here alone? Why did the other Pentadrian come? Are they a danger to Northern Ithania?' He paused and looked at each of them expectantly.

'The answer to your last question is clear,' Dyara said. 'This man called Kuar bested Auraya in a plain battle of strength. She is stronger than Rian and Mairae. That means he is a danger to at least three of us. The first Pentadrian showed us how dangerous they are to the people of Northern Ithania.'

'Kuar did not kill ordinary people,' Juran reminded her. 'We should not judge all Pentadrians by the actions of the first sorcerer we encountered. That one may have been abusing his power while outside the control of his superiors.'

Dyara frowned and nodded. 'True.'

'We can be sure they regard us with contempt,' Rian said. 'Both called us heathens.'

'Yes,' Auraya agreed. 'Kuar urged me to call on the gods, as if he didn't believe they would protect me.'

:It's obvious that religion is their main grudge against us, and that they are dangerous, Mairae said. Even through the telepathic link Auraya could sense the woman's impatience.

:I want to know what they're capable of, and if they're planning any further attacks.

'We must send more spies,' Dyara said.

Juran nodded. 'We have some there, but it is time to increase their number. We need more priests to speed communication.'

'They don't like Circlian priests,' Rian warned. 'Every priest or priestess who has travelled to Southern Ithania has been sent home.'

'Then the ones we send now will adopt a disguise.'

'If they are discovered, they will be killed.'

Juran grimaced. 'That is the risk we must take. Find volunteers among the priests and priestesses and make sure they are well informed. I won't send anyone who does not choose to face such danger.'

Rian nodded. 'I will.'

Juran rubbed his chin thoughtfully. 'Kuar did not attract attention to himself initially. Not in the way the first Pentadrian sorcerer did. Both appeared to be testing our defences and strength. I hope they found us too powerful a people to consider any aggressive move.' He sighed. 'It is clear that none of us should face one of these Pentadrian sorcerers alone. We will have to keep our own movements less public, so only a trusted few know when one of us is separated from the others.' He frowned. 'Let's hope these two do not return together.'

Auraya shuddered at the thought, earning herself a sympathetic look from Dyara. The woman's attitude toward Auraya had changed markedly. She was less critical, and almost companionable. Auraya hoped it was her success in Somrey that had brought this about, but suspected that Dyara was simply being supportive in case Auraya was upset by her confrontation with Kuar.

'Where is Kuar now?' Dyara asked.

'He was seen travelling north for a day after Auraya's encounter, then, like the previous sorcerer, he stole a boat.'

'What of this sorceress seen in Toren?' Rian asked.

Juran shook his head. 'She is no Pentadrian. From the reports

I've had, she has been living alone in an old lighthouse, selling cures to the locals. The village head took exception to this and called on a priest to drive her out, but she fled before he arrived. The priest would have left it at that, but the stories about the woman worried him. The villagers claim she has been there for over a hundred years. He is worried she might be a Wild.'

'An old woman? Could she be The Hag?' Rian asked.

Juran shrugged. 'People can live longer than a century, and the tales of the past may be exaggerated with each generation. We are obliged to check all reports of Wilds, however, so I have given the priest the task of finding her.'

'Isn't that dangerous?' Auraya asked. 'If she is a Wild she would be more powerful than he.'

Juran nodded. 'That is a risk the priest has chosen to take. *We* certainly don't have the time to hunt for her.' He shook his head. 'If he confirms that she is, we will . . .'

His voice faded to silence and they all looked around in surprise as the five sides of the Altar began to unfold. Slowly they rose to their feet.

'What does this mean?' Auraya asked.

'The gods are here,' Rian breathed, his eyes bright with religious fervour. Footsteps suddenly echoed in the vast Dome.

Dyara rolled her eyes. 'If they are, they've taken a humble form today. No, we are about to be interrupted, and it must be important.' She nodded and looked pointedly past Rian's shoulder. As one they turned to see a high priest hurrying toward them.

'Forgive the intrusion,' he gasped as he reached the dais. 'Two ambassadors have just arrived.'

'What land are they from?' Juran asked.

'From . . . from Si.'

The Siyee! Auraya drew in a quick breath and heard Dyara

219

make a small noise of surprise. Juran glanced at her, one eyebrow raised, then stepped away from his chair.

'Then we had best meet them,' he said.

They left the Altar and hurried toward the edge of the Dome. Hundreds of priests and priestesses had gathered outside to stare upward. Following their gaze, Auraya felt her heart leap as she saw the tiny winged shapes circling the Tower.

'They probably don't know we're down here,' Dyara said. 'Should we greet them at the top of the Tower?'

Auraya smiled. 'I could save you the trouble.'

Dyara looked at Auraya, her expression unreadable. Juran chuckled.

'Every moment the gods' intent becomes clearer,' he murmured. 'Go, Auraya. Greet them on their own ground, so to speak.'

Auraya concentrated on the sense of the world around her and her position in relation to it. Drawing magic, she moved herself upwards, increasing her speed until the wall of the Tower rushed past. In the windows she glimpsed faces. The Siyee did not notice her approach until she was almost upon them. Startled, they swooped away.

Slowing to a stop, she held herself suspended in the air and watched as they began to circle her at a distance. From this close she could see that all she'd been told of the Siyee was wrong. Except what Leiard had told her, she corrected herself.

They looked like children. It was not just their small size though, but that their heads seemed large in proportion to their bodies. Their chests were broad but their arms were wiry and muscular. Their wings were not feathered or attached to their backs, as legend told. Their arms were their wings: the bones of their fingers were elongated and formed the framework for a translucent membrane that stretched from fingertip to torso.

The armholes of the vests they wore extended to their hips to allow room for their wings. Slim-fitting trousers made of the same rough cloth as their vests covered their lower halves, and thin straps bound the cloth close to their legs.

As the two circled closer, she noted finer details. The last three fingers of each hand formed the wings, leaving the fore-finger and thumb free. She found herself unable to decide if they were beautiful or ugly. Their angular, large-eyed faces were exquisitely fine, but their thinness and featherless wings did not live up to the depictions of them in scrolls and paint-ings. Yet they circled her with an easy grace that she found fascinating.

'Welcome to Jarime, ambassadors of Siyee,' she called. 'I am Auraya of the White.'

The Siyee whistled to each other, adding a spoken, high-pitched word here and there. Reading their minds, she saw that this was their method of speech.

'She must be one of the Gods' Chosen,' one of the Siyee said.

'Must be,' the other replied. 'How else could she be standing on air?'

'Nothing in their message told of their ability to . . . to . . .'

'Defy the pull of the earth?' the other suggested.

She concentrated on their thoughts, finding in them the words she needed. Mimicking their speech was more difficult, but as she repeated her greeting they circled closer.

'I am Tireel of the Green Lake tribe,' one of the Siyee said. 'My companion is Zeeriz of the Fork River tribe. We have flown long and far to speak to the Gods' Chosen.'

'We have been sent by our Speakers to discuss the alliance you have proposed,' the other added.

Auraya nodded and searched their minds for words. 'The

other Gods' Chosen wait below. Will you come down and meet them?'

The two Siyee exchanged glances, then nodded. As she descended, they followed, still circling. She understood that they could not stop in midair as she could. They relied on this continual gliding to keep them aloft. She noted the subtle shifts in their posture as they compensated for changes in the wind. When she neared the ground they swooped away toward a clear area of pavement to land. She followed.

As her feet touched the ground, Juran, Rian and Dyara came forward. The Siyee eyed the crowd of priests and priestesses nervously.

'Do not fear,' Auraya told them. 'They are just surprised to see you. They will not harm you.'

The Siyees' attention shifted to the other White. Tireel stepped forward.

'We have come to discuss alliance,' he said simply.

'You have flown far,' Juran replied, his voice softening as he spoke their strange language. 'Would you like to rest and eat first? We have rooms in the Tower for guests.' The two Siyee looked up at the building dubiously. 'Or if that is unsuitable a cloth house could be made in the gardens,' Juran added.

The Siyee exchanged a few soft whistles, then Tireel nodded. 'We will accept your rooms in the Tower,' he replied.

Juran nodded in reply. 'Then I shall escort you inside and see to your comfort. If it is acceptable to you, we will meet to discuss the alliance tomorrow.'

'That is acceptable.'

As Juran ushered them toward the Tower, Auraya realised Dyara was watching her.

'Well, that was nicely arranged.'

Auraya frowned. 'How so?'

'You gain the ability to fly a few days before the sky people arrive.'

'And you think that was my doing?'

'Not at all,' Dyara smiled. 'The gods are rarely coy about their intentions. That's where we have the advantage over these Pentadrians. We don't have to invent mysterious signs or complicated deceptions to convince our people of their existence.'

CHAPTER 14

The bare stone slopes of the Open were bathed in orange light. As the sun set, fires were lit at the centre of the clearing in a circular pattern. Snatches of song, beating of drums and the constant whistling calls of the Siyee filled the air.

All these effects combined to create an atmosphere of anticipation and festivity. Tryss felt a twinge of excitement as he surveyed the scene. Siyee of all ages were dressed in their finest. Bright colours and patterns had been painted on sun-bronzed skin. Jewellery adorned both men and women. Every face was strange and wondrous, for all were wearing masks.

As Tryss landed beside his father, he gazed around in admiration. As always, the variety and workmanship of the masks was amazing. There were animal masks, insect masks and flower masks; masks adorned with patterns and masks covered in symbols. He gasped as he saw one carefully carved to represent a Siyee with wings outstretched, smiled at a man whose head had been 'replaced' by a large hand, then laughed aloud at a woman whose mask was an enormous ear.

Girls hurried past, giggling, their masks made entirely of feathers. An old man hobbled in the other direction, his grey hair streaming out from beneath a worn representation of a fish head. Two small boys narrowly missed Tryss's legs as they hurtled past, one face hidden by a sun, the other half-covered by a crescent moon.

As Tryss followed his father to their usual place in the great circle, he put a hand up to straighten his own mask. It seemed bland and foolish next to some that he had seen – simply a repainted autumn-leaf design from a trei-trei festival a few years before. He'd had no time to make a new one, with all his spare time dedicated to practising using his new harness and blowpipes.

Drilli was pleased with his progress, though he still missed his targets as often as he hit them. She had assured him that people didn't expect archers to hit their target every time, so they wouldn't expect him to either. He wasn't so sure. When the time came to demonstrate his invention, he needed to dazzle and impress. He needed to prove that this method was *better* than hunting with a bow from the ground or setting traps.

He sighed. Tonight he wanted to forget all that. The summer trei-trei, held late in the season, was the last festive Gathering before the long winter began; a last opportunity for feasting and wasting energy in acrobatic flying.

And this year he had a partner.

As Tryss's parents took their places among their tribe, two voices rose above the general chatter.

'. . . seen it before, haven't you?'

'Yes. Three years ago, I think. A bit of fresh paint doesn't make an old mask look good again, does it? And an autumn leaf in summer! Can't even get the season right.'

Tryss decided it would be better to pretend he hadn't heard the voices, but his mother looked in their direction.

'You're not getting along with your cousins any more, are you?'

She sounded concerned. Tryss shrugged.

'They're not getting along with me,' he replied. 'Not since I got sick of them making me look stupid so they looked better, anyway,' he added quietly.

Her eyebrows rose. 'So that's why. I thought it was something else.'

He frowned at her, but her attention had shifted elsewhere. Her eyes flicked back to him, then she nodded meaningfully and looked away again. Following her gaze, he saw a butterfly-faced girl and knew instantly that it was Drilli. No other girl walked the way she did, he mused. Confident, but not showy. Her gracefulness was completely unselfconscious.

Looking at his mother again, he considered her insinuation that Drilli was the reason for his cousins' taunting. She was probably right. They were jealous. They didn't need to be. Drilli liked him and helped him with his inventions, but he had no idea if she thought he was anything more than a friend.

Except, well, she had lured him into asking her to be his partner tonight, and girls didn't do that unless they were interested in being more than friends with a boy.

The last rays of the sun had disappeared now. As Drilli and her family took their places the threads of music from instruments about the circle began to synchronise. All chatter ended. The Speaker of another tribe stepped into the circle, dressed in the traditional bright garb of the Patternmaker. He would direct the festivities, choose the order of flight patterns, and award prizes.

'For centuries since Huan declared her work complete and that we were ready to govern ourselves, we have come together every winter and summer to celebrate and give thanks,' he called. 'We hone our skills and test our abilities so that she will look upon us and be proud. In spring we celebrate the oldest and youngest of us. In summer we rejoice in the partnership of man and woman, be they newly matched or familiar companions.' He raised his arms. 'So let the couples begin the trei-trei!'

As musicians began a lively old tune, Tryss's parents exchanged a smile and took off their masks. They ran forward, leapt into the air and joined the other couples wheeling in the traditional moves of the pattern. Turning away, Tryss looked toward Drilli's tribe. She was watching him expectantly.

He started toward her, but paused as two familiar figures approached her from either side. Her smile turned to a frown as Ziss grabbed her wrist.

Her words were lost in the hubbub of voices around her, but the shake of her head made her meaning clear. Ziss scowled, but didn't let her go. She turned abruptly to stare at Trinn, standing on her other side, and her expression became angry. She shook off Ziss's hand, then stalked away.

Tryss noted that her father was watching her closely. His frown deepened as she joined Tryss.

Is that disapproval? he wondered.

'Tryss,' she said. 'You weren't going to leave me to fend off your cousins by myself, were you?'

He smiled. 'You're quite capable of defending yourself, Drilli.'

'It's nice that you think so, but it would have been much more flattering if you had gallantly come to my rescue,' she huffed.

'Then give me enough time to get there before dealing with them yourself,' he retorted.

The music changed and she looked up at the fliers above, her eyes shining with eagerness.

'I would be honoured if you would fly with me,' he said, the formal words sounding awkward.

She grinned, then took off her mask. He removed his and laid it next to hers on the ground. As she turned to face the circle, Tryss glanced back at his cousins. Both glowered at him.

Then he and Drilli were running. They moved apart and sprang into the air. He felt the heat of a fire add to the lift beneath his wings. It carried him upward, Drilli at his side. In a moment they had found a place among the couples, following the simple movements of an uncomplicated public pattern.

He had flown patterns many times before, but not like this. In early years he had flown with his mother, carefully following her every move. Later, with younger cousins, he had needed to direct them. Drilli did not direct or follow. He could read her slightest change of posture and know what she wanted or expected to do, and she responded to him the same way. It was both exciting and calming, liberating and hypnotic.

They stayed aloft for pattern after pattern, focused only on each other whether the music was lively or slow. He found he could manage complex patterns he had never bothered to attempt before. Finally the music ended and they descended to the ground to watch as hoops and poles were set up for the acrobatic tests. Soon Siyee were swooping about, gaining cheers from those watching.

During one of the louder rounds of cheering, Drilli leaned close.

'Let's slip away,' she whispered.

He looked at her in surprise. Taking his hand, she slowly led the way through the crowd toward the dark forest at the edge of the Open. They stopped now and then, sometimes to watch, once to talk to an old friend, then, after a long, careful examination of all around them, she bent close again.

'You walk uphill into the forest for fifty steps then stop and wait. I'll count to a hundred then follow.'

He nodded. Glancing around to make sure nobody was watching, he waited until one of the acrobats started an intricate move before striding away into the forest. It was dark in the trees. The immense trunks had a sinister presence that he had never noticed during the day. He could not guess why: the Siyee had lived here without doing them harm for nearly three centuries.

Realising he had lost count of his steps, he stopped. After a while he heard soft movement. As a feminine shadow appeared and he recognised Drilli's walk he sighed with relief.

'I think your cousins saw us leave,' she told him.

He turned and cursed as he saw the pair hurrying through the forest edge toward them.

'I bet they've been watching us the whole night.'

'Fools,' she murmured. 'Anyone who thinks they can win a girl over by being cruel to others is stupid. Follow me. Try not to make any noise.'

They crept through the forest. In the dark it was impossible to avoid stepping on twigs or dry leaves, but the ground had been cleared and smoothed into paths by many years of traffic. Tryss concentrated on following her and on their pursuit, so when she stopped it took a moment to realise where they were.

At the end of the path was a large bower. The walls glowed from a light within.

'That's the Speakers' Bower!' he exclaimed. 'We're not supposed to come here.'

'Shhh!' She put a finger to her lips and looked over his shoulder. 'They won't dare follow us. And nobody will be at the bower. They're all at the festival.'

'Then why's there light inside?'

'I don't know. One of the Speakers probably left a lantern burning, to guide—'

Tryss froze as three figures appeared from the trees to one side and strode toward the bower. The newcomers did not look

229

in their direction, to his relief, but marched up to the bower and went inside. The light within threw their distorted shadows up against the walls.

Drilli was breathing faster now. She turned to look in the direction his cousins had been approaching from, then abruptly crept closer to the bower and crouched down at the base of one of the huge old trees.

'If your cousins find us they'll turn us in,' she told him. 'Better we hide here and risk discovery by the Speakers.'

She looked toward the bower again. Voices could be heard now.

'We were attacked,' a man said darkly. 'But not by men. By birds.'

'Birds?' Tryss recognised Speaker Sirri's voice.

'Yes. There were maybe twenty of them. They came out of the treetops as one.'

'What kind of birds?'

'None I've ever seen before. Like a large black kiri.'

'*Very* large,' a third voice added. 'Their wingspan was almost equal to ours.'

'Truly?'

'Yes.'

'What harm did they do?'

'They tore at us with beaks and claws. We all have scratches,' the first visitor said grimly. 'Niril lost an eye, Liriss lost both. Half of us have torn wing membranes, and both Virri and Dillir may never fly again.'

Silence followed this.

'This is terrible,' Sirri replied with genuine distress. 'What did you do then? How did you escape them?'

'We didn't. They drove us to the ground. We tried to shoot at them but they scattered as soon as they saw us take our bows, as if they understood what they were for.' The speaker paused. 'We walked for a time, then those of us who could fly did so, keeping low and among the treetops in the hopes that we could land and fight if another attack came.'

There was a sigh. 'We do not need another danger to add to those we already face.'

'I have never heard of these birds before. Most likely they are an invading species. We should eliminate them, before they breed into numbers that threaten us all.'

'I agree. We need to warn all tribes and—'

'There is something else,' the third man interrupted. 'My brother here believes I was imagining things, but I am sure I saw a landwalker.'

'A landwalker?'

'Yes. I saw her as we left. She was watching us, and the birds were gathered around her.'

'I understand why your brother doubts. Landwalkers have never ventured that far into the mountains before. What did this woman look like?'

'Dark skin. Black clothing. That is all I can tell you. I only caught a glimpse of her.'

'This is strange. I must consider what you have told me. Is there anything else I should know?'

'No.'

'Then I will see you back to your tribe.'

The distorted shadows shifted to one side of the bower, then three figures stepped outside. Tryss watched them stride away, his heart pounding.

'I don't think we were supposed to hear that,' he whispered.

'No,' Drilli replied. 'At least they didn't see us.'

'No.'

'We should go back.'

But he was suddenly conscious of how close she was. He did not want to move away, and she was making no move to do so either. He could feel the warmth radiating from her skin, and smell her sweat mingled with a distinctly female scent.

She shifted closer.

'Tryss?'

Her voice was tentative and questioning, and somehow he knew no question would follow. His name was the question.

'Drilli?' he murmured.

He could barely see her in the darkness – just her jaw outlined by starlight. Slowly, he leaned forward.

Her lips brushed his. He felt a shock of exhilaration, then her mouth closed over his and he felt heat rush through his blood. Two thoughts flashed through his mind.

She wants me.

My cousins are going to be furious!

He didn't care about his cousins. She *wanted* him. There was no mistaking that. This was no chaste kiss of a friend. Her hands gripped his shoulders. He slipped his arms under her wing membranes and caught her waist. She drew back slightly.

'Promise me something,' she breathed.

All he could see were stars reflected in her eyes. 'Anything.'

'Promise me you'll show the Speakers your harness at the next Gathering.'

He hesitated at the sudden change of subject. 'My harness . . . ?'

'Yes.' She paused. 'You're surprised.'

'It was far from my thoughts,' he admitted.

She laughed quietly. 'Did I actually manage to get your full attention for once?'

He pulled her closer. As he kissed her again, her mouth opened. She mouthed his lips gently, sending shivers of pleasure down his spine. He spread his fingers out over her back, feeling the deliciously neat curve of her spine. As she nibbled at his lower lip he ran a finger down the seam of her clothes, where

232

her vest allowed the membrane of her wings to escape. He felt her stiffen in surprise, then relax and lean against him, her breasts firm and warm against his chest.

This is just too good, he thought wryly. Sliding his hands under the vest, he sighed as he felt the bare, silky skin of her back. He felt her hands follow the same course under his clothes, running from the base of his neck down to – he chuckled in surprise as she squeezed his buttocks. But as he moved to do the same, she pulled away. The sound of their breathing was loud. She drew in a deep breath and let it out slowly.

'We have to go back.'

He looked away, disappointed but knowing she was right. His cousins, annoyed at losing their quarry in the forest, would return to their parents and report what they'd seen. *They didn't see everything*, he thought smugly.

'Promise me we'll do this again,' he said, the words coming out before he could consider them.

She chuckled. 'Only if you promise me you'll show the Speakers the harness.'

He let out a long breath, then nodded. 'I promise.'

'That . . . ?'

'I'll show the Speakers the harness.'

'At the next Gathering?'

'Yes. Unless a better opportunity comes.'

'I suppose that's reasonable,' she said.

They stood in silence for several heartbeats. He found himself remembering the feel of her skin under his hands. He longed to touch her again.

She sighed. 'Do you think you could find your way back on your own?'

'No.'

She laughed. 'Liar. Of course you can. I think it would be

better if we returned from different directions. I'm going to go round the other side of the Open.'

'That's a long way. Would it be *that* bad if people saw us together?'

'My father doesn't want me to marry outside the tribe.' She paused. 'Not that I'm asking you to marry me. But he doesn't like me talking to you.'

He stared at her and felt the night turn sour.

She stepped close. 'Don't worry,' she said lightly. 'I'll change his mind.' She leaned forward and kissed him firmly. Then she slipped out of his grasp. He caught the flash of her teeth in the light from the bower before she turned and hurried away.

Emerahl had learned long ago that the easiest method of finding the secret ways of a city was to befriend the youngest and poorest residents. The grubby, cunning children of the streets could tell you more about its underside than the adults who ruled it. They knew how to be invisible and their loyalty could be bought cheaply.

She had sought them out the day after her narrow escape in the market. Finding a small square in the poorer quarter of the city she spent a few hours watching and listening to the activities around her. The locals weren't fools, and she only observed two successful pocket-picking attempts.

When one of the boys slouched past her, she met his eyes squarely.

'That's a nasty cough you've got there,' she said. 'Better lose it before the weather gets cold.'

The boy slowed and stared at her suspiciously, taking in her well-worn but mostly clean clothes.

'What you care?'

'Why shouldn't I?'

234

He stopped, his eyes narrowing. 'If you did, you'd give me some coin.'

She smiled. 'And what would you do with it?'

'Buy food – for m'sel' and m' sis.' He paused. 'She got the cough worse than me.'

'How about I buy the food for you?' she suggested.

He did not answer. She looked away. 'Only way you'll get anything out of me.'

'All right. But no weird stuff. I'm not going anywhere with you but the market.'

So she followed him to the local, smaller market and bought him some fruit and bread, and treated them both to thin pastry pockets full of freshly grilled meat. She noted him slipping the last few bites into a pocket, and guessed his story of a sister was true.

'For that cough,' she said, 'you and your sister need a bit of this.' She purchased some decongestant from a herbalist after smelling it critically to see if it did contain the herbs it claimed to. 'A spoonful of this three times a day. No more, or you'll poison yourselves.'

He stared at her as he took the bottle. 'Thanks.'

'Now, you can do me a small favour in return.' He scowled. 'Don't worry. No weird stuff. I just want some advice. I need a place to stay for a few days. Somewhere cheap. And quiet, if you know what I mean.'

That night she found herself the guest of a small gang of children living in the basement of a burned-out house on the outskirts of the poor quarter. She found that Rayo, the boy she had helped, did have a sister ill with a serious chest infection, so she brought out her own cures to treat the illness more aggressively.

It did not take long for news of the priests' search for an old healer woman to reach the children. They confronted her with the news and their suspicions the next day.

'The city's all stirred up. The priests are looking for a sor's-ress,' a younger boy, Tiro, said.

'An old woman. Like you,' a girl, Gae, added.

Emerahl grunted. 'So I heard. Priests think every old woman is a sorceress, especially if she knows a bit about herbs and things.' She pointed a bony finger at them. 'They're just jealous, you see, because we know more than they do about cures.'

'But that's stupid,' Rayo said. 'You're old. You'll be dead soon.'

She looked at the boy reproachfully. 'Thanks for reminding me.' Then she sighed. 'It *is* stupid. Like you said, what can we do, eh? Nothing but put up with them roughing us up.'

'They done that to you?' Tiro asked.

She sighed and nodded, pointing at a rip in the seam of her tawl. 'Chose a fine time to get turned out of my house, didn't I?'

'Then you not the sor'sress. You safe,' Gae assured her.

Emerahl looked at the girl sadly. 'Depends if they find what they're looking for. If they don't, they'll just keep hassling us. Or they might take someone and put the blame on her rather than admit they lost the one they're after.'

'We're not going to let that happen,' Rayo told her firmly.

She smiled. 'You're all too good to me, letting me stay here.'

The children didn't seem to mind that the few days she had said she would stay turned into a week, then two. She gave them things of hers to sell. They brought back food and even a little cheap firewater, and occasionally spied on the priests so she would know when the search ended.

'I o'erheard two of 'em,' Tiro told her breathlessly one night. 'They were talking of the higher priest who d'recting the search. Ikaro's his name. They said he c'municates with the gods, and he been giv'n the 'bility to read minds.'

'So they haven't found her yet?' she asked.

'Don't think so.'

Emerahl sighed, but her dismay was more to do with the news of her pursuer's abilities.

Of course, the people Tiro had overheard might be so in awe of their superior that they believed any rumour that came their way. However, she could not take the risk that it was true. Any priest who tried to read her mind would see nothing. It took considerable magical ability to master the Gift of hiding one's mind. He might not know this, but she wasn't intending to find out.

According to the children, anyone leaving the city by boat, tarn, platten or foot was being watched by priests. Even the secret ways of the underworld were being watched. All old women were being taken to the high priest to be examined. The Circlians were putting a lot of effort into finding her. If they had guessed who she was, the gods would be peering through every priest's eyes, looking for her. And if they found her . . .

She shivered. *They'll kill me, just as they killed Mirar, The Oracle and The Farmer, and probably The Twins and The Gull, though I never heard reports of their deaths.*

It was tempting to simply stay put and wait it out. The priests couldn't keep this up forever. They would try a few other ploys before they gave up, however. She expected a reward would be offered soon. When that happened she could no longer be sure of the children's loyalty. They were friendly, but they were not stupid. If the price was big enough she knew they would sell her with barely a second thought. She was, after all, just an old woman.

Nobody was safe company now. What she ought to do was change her appearance, and it would have to be more than a change of clothing and hair colour. She needed something much more dramatic.

237

Such a change was not beyond her abilities, but the thought filled her with trepidation. It had been a long time since she'd practised this Gift. A lot could go wrong. She needed time – perhaps a few days – in which to make the change, and she must not be interrupted as she worked.

The children could not know, of course. It would be better if they never saw her new form – or even knew she had adopted one. Getting away from them would not be easy, however. Even if she came up with a plausible excuse, where was she to go?

But perhaps she would not have to leave. A lot of her problems would be solved if they believed that she had died.

CHAPTER 15

Danjin had spent most of the last two weeks in a constant state of awe and wonder. He was not the only person to experience this, though he believed he was one of the few who had managed to keep their wits despite everything that had happened. Most of the priests either walked about in a daze or could be heard gushing out praise for the gods or speculating on what wonders might still be in store for them all.

As his platten bore him through the archway into the Temple, Danjin considered the events that had brought this about.

The first revelation had been Auraya's return. Neither ship nor platten had brought her back to the city. Instead, she had *flown* into the Temple like a great white wingless bird. Dyara's arrival had been considerably quieter, he had been told by a servant. She had returned on the Bearer she had ridden out on, looking 'as if she had a lot to think about'.

The second revelation had been less pleasant. Auraya had told Danjin of her confrontation with the Pentadrian sorcerer and that the discovery of her new Gift came only as a result of her defeat. This information was to remain a secret, however. The White did not want to cause unnecessary fear among the people by making it known that the Pentadrians had a sorcerer of such strength he had overcome one of the White.

Danjin hadn't grown used to the idea that the woman he worked for could perform aerobatics that even birds could not achieve. After the Siyee ambassadors arrived he noticed a subtle change in the other White's behaviour toward Auraya, as if the appearance of the Siyee explained why she had been given this new power.

It makes sense, I suppose, he thought. *Does that mean I will be accompanying her on a journey to Si?*

Since then Danjin had met with Auraya only once or twice a day. He had no knowledge of the sky people, and couldn't speak their language, and it had come as a blow to realise he was of no use to her at the moment. It had been obvious the few times he had observed her with them that she was fascinated by these winged people. And the Siyee seemed equally captivated by her.

Little wonder, he thought. *She has more in common with them than anyone else here.*

The platten drew closer to the Temple buildings. He noted that the few priests about at this early hour were engaged in the new unofficial pastime, which he had dubbed sky-gazing. Most were looking at the Tower, however. It had not taken long for people to learn that a window in Auraya's room had been replaced with a glass door so she and her Siyee friends didn't need to ascend to the top of the building when they wanted a little aerobatic exercise. Seeing her emerge often brought cheers from her audience.

Thinking of the window-door in her rooms, Danjin shivered. Perhaps it was just as well she didn't need him any more.

Of course she still does, he told himself. But it didn't help. Here was an opportunity to learn about one of the few peoples he knew nothing of, but he couldn't take advantage of it because she hadn't included him in her discussions with them.

The platten stopped. He stepped off and thanked the driver. Priests nodded politely at him as he strode inside the Tower. He made the gesture of the circle in reply. The cage was resting at the base of the stairwell. He concentrated on his breathing as it bore him upwards, keeping his mind from imagining the drop below it by recalling a verse of poetry he'd memorised, then translating it into Dunwayan. Arriving outside Auraya's rooms, he stepped out and knocked on her door.

She answered it herself, and greeted him with a smile. Not quite the broad grin she had worn so often in the last two weeks, but a more subdued expression. He wondered what had tempered her recent high spirits.

'Come in,' she said, directing him to a chair. As she sat down he cast a quick look at the windows. To his relief, the glass 'door' was closed.

'I know you're disappointed that you haven't seen more of the Siyee ambassadors,' she told him. 'They may appear bold and confident, but in truth they find us landwalkers intimidating – especially as most of their experiences of us are as invaders and murderers. I've tried to keep the number of landwalkers around them to a minimum.'

As she spoke, a furry bundle on a nearby chair uncurled. Mischief blinked sleepily at them, then stretched, crept onto Auraya's lap and curled up again. Auraya didn't appear to notice.

'I was hoping to make it up to you by bringing you along, but I'm afraid that isn't going to be possible now.'

'Bringing me along?'

A now-familiar sparkle entered her gaze. 'To Si. To enter into negotiations for an alliance. Juran sent them a proposal months ago, and they want onè of us to return with them to Si.' Her smile faded. 'But the journey would take months, and involves crossing difficult terrain. You would have to climb

241

mountains to get there, Danjin. Juran has decided that I must go alone.'

'Ah.' Danjin knew he would not be able to hide his dismay from her, so he did not bother keeping it from his face. 'You're right,' he told her. 'I am disappointed. I am also concerned. In Somrey you had myself, Mairae and Dreamweaver Leiard to advise you. You are still too inexperienced, if you'll forgive my frankness, to be tackling an alliance on your own. Can't this wait?'

She shook her head. 'We need allies, Danjin. More than lone sorcerers may venture north from the southern continent in the future. However, I will not begin negotiations with the Siyee immediately. I will spend a few months learning all I can about them first.'

'Then, perhaps if I left now I would arrive in time to help you negotiate.'

'No, Danjin,' she said firmly. 'I will need you here.'

She reached under her circ, then leaned forward and opened her palm. On it rested a white ring. A priest's ring. Danjin stared at it in surprise.

'You honour me beyond what I deserve,' he said. 'But I do not wish to join—'

'It's not a priest's ring.' She smiled. 'It is what we call a "link ring". Priests, as you know, can communicate with each other through their rings. They can because they are Gifted, and their rings are simple things. This,' she held the white band, 'is more refined and took some time to make. If I need to communicate with you I can, through this. But that is all that it can do. It cannot link you with anyone else.' She held it out to him. 'Wear this, and I will be able to speak to you from Si. Don't lose it. I only have the one.'

He took the ring and held it up. It was plain and smooth, and he could not guess what it was made of. He slipped it onto his finger, then lifted his eyes to meet hers.

'There is one other matter that bothers me,' he told her.

She smiled and leaned back in her chair. 'Your concern for me is heartening, Danjin, but I will be in less danger from Pentadrians in Si than anywhere else. It is a remote, sparsely populated place, difficult to traverse. The Siyee would notice and report intruders before they ventured far into their land. Why would any Pentadrian undertake such an arduous journey?'

'To find you,' he replied.

'They won't know I'm there,' she told him.

'Then . . . for the same reasons you're going.'

'The Si haven't invited the Pentadrians into their land to negotiate an alliance as far as I or the ambassadors know. Nor have the Pentadrians approached any other lands.'

He sighed, then nodded his head in defeat. 'So how long will I be at a loose end?'

She chuckled. 'You won't be, Danjin. I'll be gone for only a few months – though if I'm successful Juran is considering sending me to the Elai. The courier he sent to them has not reported his progress for months.'

'The sea people.' Danjin whistled quietly. 'Soon there'll be no mysteries left in the world.'

A troubled expression crossed Auraya's face, and she looked away. Mischief stirred. She looked down at him and her smile returned.

'There's one other matter I wanted to discuss with you, Danjin.'

'Yes?'

'Could you come by each day and spend some time with Mischief while I'm gone? You'll have to be careful. He's getting sneaky. I keep finding him crawling around on the outside of the window. I've had a lock installed, but he's already learned to open it, so I'm going to have the window nailed shut while I'm away.'

Danjin shuddered. 'You do that, and I'll take care of him.'

She chuckled. 'Thank you. I'm sure Mischief will appreciate the company.'

After Danjin left, Auraya paced the room.

I know I sounded much more confident than I feel, she thought. *It's not any particular aspect of this journey that worries me, just that I must do it all alone.*

She would not be out of contact with the rest of the world. She could communicate with the other White at any time. Juran had told her to consult with him before she made any major decisions. That was as reassuring as it was reasonable.

Dyara hadn't raised a word of protest. She had filled the journey back to Jarime with lessons in magic, but there was less of a lecturing manner in her instruction. Dyara was no longer set on holding Auraya back until she had perfected every exercise but instead appeared determined to pass on everything she knew about wielding magic as quickly as possible, telling Auraya to practise whenever she had the time to.

'The rest of us had time to learn at our own pace. It may be that you, as the last of us, will not,' she had said cryptically.

Which only made it harder to avoid worrying about the future. Some nights Auraya woke from nightmares in which she was trapped, powerless, within the grip of the Pentadrian sorcerer's magic. It was not comforting knowing that someone more powerful than her, who appeared to mean her and her people harm, existed.

She reached the window and stopped. Like any other mortal, she could only put her trust in the gods.

'Lee-ar.'

She turned to find Mischief staring at the door, his pointed ears upright and alert. Chuckling, she strode across the room.

As she opened the door, Leiard froze, his hand poised ready for knocking.

'Dreamweaver Leiard.' She smiled. 'Come in.'

'Thank you, Auraya of the White.'

'Lee-ar!' Mischief bounded off the chair. Leiard laughed as the veez dashed up the front of his clothes onto his shoulders.

'He likes you.'

'Lucky me,' he replied dryly. He flinched as Mischief began sniffing at his ear.

Thinking of the favour she'd asked of Danjin, Auraya sobered. Mischief didn't dislike Danjin, but he did seem to like Leiard better. Her first thought had been to ask Leiard to visit Mischief, but she knew how uncomfortable he felt when in the Temple. Better to spare him that.

She suppressed a sigh. How had it come about that both of her advisers had reason to fear visiting her? For Leiard it was being in a place of the gods' influence; for Danjin it was being so far from the ground.

Perhaps that was part of the reason she was enjoying the company of the Siyee ambassadors so much. Like her, they loved flying and the gods – or at least Huan. Though they were the first people she had encountered that worshipped one god over the others. That wasn't surprising, however. Huan had created them.

'I called you here to assure you I haven't been ignoring you,' she told Leiard. 'I've been so busy I've had no time for unofficial visits. I regret that, because we'll have few opportunities in the near future to talk.'

Leiard looked at her questioningly.

'I'm going to Si, to negotiate another alliance.'

His eyebrows rose. 'Si?' He smiled. 'You'll enjoy that. The Siyee are a gentle and generous people. Honest and practical.'

'What do you know of them?'

'A little.' He lifted Mischief from his shoulder and sat down. The veez immediately curled up in his lap. Sitting opposite, Auraya felt a small pang of jealousy that her own pet seemed to prefer her visitor.

'The Siyee are in my memories,' he told her. 'Since you have spoken to them at length, you will know most of what I do. What they may not have mentioned are the taboos of their culture.'

She leaned forward. 'Yes?'

'Not all Siyee can fly,' he told her. 'Some are born incapable and some lose the ability. Accidents are tragically common. Old age is particularly cruel to them. Be careful how you refer to these Siyee. Never describe them as crippled.'

'How should I refer to them?'

He shook his head. 'They have no commonly used term. If you are to meet with any Siyee, let him or her decide where it should take place. If the one you are to meet is capable of flight, he will come to you. If he is not, you must go to him. In that way, you are not insinuating that the former cannot fly, and treating the latter with respect by not drawing attention to his or her inability.'

'I understand. I've noticed they tire easily when walking.'

'Yes.' He paused, then chuckled. 'They treat landwalkers more like flightless Siyee than not. But you . . .' He frowned. 'You should not allow them to. Otherwise it will seem like you expect favours you do not deserve.'

This is valuable advice, she realised. *I would not have thought it odd if the Siyee always arranged to meet me wherever I am staying.*

'Anything else?'

He paused, then shrugged. 'That is all I can recall now. If I think of anything else before you leave, I will make sure you know of it.'

246

She nodded. 'Thank you. If you remember something after I have left, tell Danjin. He will be taking care of my affairs here while I'm away.'

'I will. When will you be leaving?'

'In a few days.'

'How long do you expect to be in Si?'

'As long as it's necessary, and I am welcome. A few months, most likely.'

He nodded. 'It is unlikely you will need my advice in that time now that the Somreyan alliance is signed.'

'Yes,' she agreed. 'Though I will miss your company.'

He smiled, his eyes flashing. 'And I yours.'

'How is your new student, Jayim?'

His expression was a mixture of remorse and determination as he replied. 'Not used to working hard,' he said. 'But he does have a natural fascination for cures and healing. I have a lot of work in front of me.'

'At least you'll have more time for it, with me out of your way.'

'But no excuse to escape from my responsibilities,' he pointed out.

She chuckled, then a faint chime drew her attention to a timepiece on the side table. 'Ah, I'm afraid I must send you back to them now. I have a lesson with Dyara next.'

She rose. He gently scooped Mischief up and set him aside, then stood and followed her to the door. As he wished her luck, she shook her head.

'I'm sure I'll find time to talk to you again before I go.'

He nodded, then turned away and started down the stairs. Closing the door, Auraya felt a pang of sadness.

I'm going to miss him. I wonder if he'll miss me. She strolled to the window and looked down at the people far below. From his thoughts she knew that Leiard regarded her as more than someone who could help his people. He felt affection. Admiration. Respect.

At that thought she felt a pang of guilt. The idea that had come to her in the garden of the Somreyan Temple came rushing back. She had struggled with it several times, unable to decide what she should or should not do. All reason told her that dissuading people from joining the Dreamweaver cult was the right thing to do. The gods did not preserve the souls of those who turned from them. By stopping people joining the Dreamweavers she would be preventing the death of many souls.

Yet she also felt that there was something wrong with causing the demise of the Dreamweavers. Those people chose to become Dreamweavers and knew what they sacrificed.

Furthering Circlian knowledge of healing *was* a good aim. Deliberately reading Dreamweavers' minds in order to gain that knowledge was wrong, however. It was stealing. Although arranging for her own people to discover that knowledge for themselves was not.

If I think of it as merely increasing the priests' healing knowledge, then I will be doing nothing wrong. How can I be blamed if it leads to the Dreamweavers' demise?

Because I saw the consequences and continued anyway.

She sighed. *It's not my responsibility to save the Dreamweavers.*

Leiard should fear me, she thought. She shook her head. *It always comes back to Leiard. Do I struggle with this simply because I'm afraid I'll lose his friendship?*

Juran's warning came back to her. '*But be careful, Auraya, that you do not compromise yourself for the sake of friendship.*' She turned away from the window. *There's no hurry. A project like this would take years. Its effects wouldn't be felt for at least a generation. Not until long after Leiard has died.*

Sitting down next to Mischief, she scratched his head. *The*

way things are going I may never have time for it anyway. Between
making alliances and avoiding a premature death at the hands of
these Pentadrians, I think I'll be occupied for some time.

'She said she'd always wanted to be buried in a box, like proper
people.'

Rayo looked at his sister, then back at the body of the old
woman. 'Boxes cost.'

'She still has money left,' Tiro said. 'Only right we use some
for a box.'

'Don't have to,' his sister said. 'When we were in the pit
we saw a box that looked like a coffin. It's what got us talking
'bout it. Might still be there.'

'Then go see,' Rayo tossed at Tiro. The boy and two others
hurried away.

Crouching down, Rayo took the old woman's hand. It was
cold and stiff. 'Thank you, Emeria. You fixed m' sis, and m'sel',
and were true gen'rous. We'll get your box, if it's still there.
I hope you don't mind us taking your money and stuff. It's
not like you'll be needing it, now you're with the gods.'

The others nodded. Rayo drew a circle on the old woman's
forehead, then got to his feet. The boys might need help if
the box in the pit was big enough to be used as a coffin. There
would be digging to do, too. It would take lots of time and
energy. He looked at his sister.

'Take her stuff,' he said. She nodded and set to work.

An hour later Emeria's body lay in the box. His sister and
the other girls had slipped up into the hills to pick flowers.
All but the woman's worn-out undershift had been removed
from the body, but with the flowers scattered over her everything looked right and respectful.

They each spoke a quick, tearful farewell, then covered the
box with a few charred planks of wood salvaged from the burned

house they lived under. Rayo and the other boys dug a hole in the small yard behind the house. The ground was hard, and it was dark by the time they finished. Finally they returned to the house, carried the box out and set it in the hole.

When all that was left was a mound of earth, they scattered a few more flowers, then returned to their cellar. All were silent and glum.

'Where's her stuff?' Rayo asked his sister.

The others gathered around as she brought a stack of clothes and Emeria's bag to the centre of the room. They all grimaced as she opened the bag and a distinctly fishy smell wafted out.

She handled the contents carefully.

'They're cures. She told me what they were for and how to use them. These ones she said she'd sell, because they weren't really good for anything, but some people thought they made them good at sex so they were actually worth a lot.'

'We can sell them,' Rayo said.

She nodded. Bringing out a small leather wallet, she tipped the contents onto the ground. The others grinned at the pile of coins.

'She kept this real close, tied round her waist. Her secret stash.'

'*Our* secret stash,' Rayo said. 'Everyone gets something, to be fair. We start with the clothes. I'm taking the tawl. Who wants the tunic?'

As they divided Emeria's belongings, Rayo felt a warm feeling of rightness. She hadn't been with them long, but so long as they each had something of hers it would be like a bit of her was still with them.

I hope she's happy, up there with the gods, he thought. *I hope they know they got the best part of her.*

CHAPTER 16

Though the morning air was growing colder each day, Leiard had chosen to hold Jayim's lessons in the rooftop garden of the Bakers' home. It had taken some time and persistence to convince Tanara not to interrupt them. She had initially assumed that she could bring them hot drinks without disrupting the lessons, so long as she didn't speak. Leiard had told her firmly that her presence broke their concentration and she wasn't to approach at all. After that she kept creeping up the staircase and peering at them every hour or so, and was disbelieving when he told her that this, too, was a distraction.

He wasn't sure if he'd convinced her yet. To be sure, he had made a mental note of the average time between interruptions and paced his lessons accordingly. It was essential that they be left alone this morning, as he intended to teach Jayim the finer points of a mind link.

Opening his eyes, Leiard regarded his new student. Jayim's chest fell in the slow, regular rhythm of a calming trance. A little of the boy's former reluctance to learn the mind skills of Dreamweavers still remained, but Leiard didn't expect all doubts to vanish overnight. Otherwise, Jayim was being attentive and working hard. His enthusiasm was for medicines and healing, and he was progressing well in those areas.

That was part of the reason Leiard had decided they would perform a mind link today: he wanted to see if they could pinpoint the source of Jayim's aversion to developing his telepathic abilities. The other reason was so that Leiard could assert control over the link memories that were overlapping his own identity. He wasn't sure what would happen to him if he didn't. Would his sense of self continue to erode? Would his thoughts become a muddle of conflicting memories? Or would he begin to believe he was Mirar?

He did not intend to find out. Closing his eyes again, Leiard held out his hands.

'We gather tonight in peace and in pursuit of understanding. Our minds will be linked. Our memories shall flow between us. Let none seek or spy, or impose a will upon another. Instead, we shall become one mind. Take my hands, Jayim.'

He felt the boy's slim fingers brush his, then grasp his hands. As Jayim sensed Leiard's mind, he recoiled slightly. Leiard heard him take a deep breath, then reach out again.

At first there was only a sense of expectation. Leiard felt his companion's nervousness and waited patiently. Soon, snatches of thought and memory flitted through Jayim's mind. Previous lessons, Leiard saw. Embarrassment at private matters revealed. He found himself thinking back, to other links with adolescent boys and similar secrets unintentionally revealed.

:Do not try to block these memories, he advised. *Blocking disrupts the link.*

:But I don't want to reveal them! Jayim protested.

:Nudge them aside. Try this: whenever you find your mind wandering in that *direction, think of something else. Select an image or subject that is neither pleasant nor unpleasant, but which will lead your thoughts away.*

:Like what?

:I list the medicines useful to babies.

252

To his credit, several such medicines sprang to Jayim's mind. His thoughts soon returned to the former subject, however.

:Does this distraction work all the time?

:Most of the time.

:Do you use the same trick to stop yourself giving away other secrets – like those that Auraya tells you?

Leiard smiled.

:What makes you think Auraya tells me secrets?

:I sense that she has.

The boy was perceptive. Leiard sensed smugness.

:Could I trust you with those secrets? he asked.

Jayim was all curiosity and eagerness now. Of course he would keep whatever he learned to himself. He would never risk losing Leiard's trust. Besides, if he did, Leiard would learn of it in the next memory link.

Then doubts crept in. What if he accidentally let something slip? What if someone tricked him into giving secrets away?

:Secrets are best kept secret, Leiard said. *The more who know, the less secret they are. It is not distrust that keeps me from telling you, Jayim.*

:You like Auraya, don't you?

The abrupt change of subject made Leiard pause. It also stirred a mixture of emotions.

:Yes, he replied. *She is a friend.*

But he knew she was more than that. She was the child he had once taught, who had grown into a powerful, beautiful woman . . .

:You think she's beautiful, Jayim stated. His amusement deepened. *You fancy her!*

:No! Her face came into his thoughts and he felt a familiar admiration suddenly sharpen into longing. Shocked, he pulled away from Jayim's mind, breaking the link.

253

The boy said nothing. Leiard sensed smugness again. He ignored it.

I don't desire Auraya, he told himself.

I'm afraid you do, another voice in his mind disagreed.

But she is young.

Not so young any more.

She is a White.

All the more reason to desire her. The attraction of the forbidden is a powerful force.

No. Jayim has put the idea into my head. I do not desire her. Next time I meet Auraya I will feel just as I did before.

We'll see.

Opening his eyes, Leiard saw that Jayim was watching him expectantly.

'Your secret is mine,' the boy said.

'There is no secret,' Leiard said firmly. 'You proposed an idea I hadn't considered. Now I have, and I believe you are wrong.'

The boy looked away and nodded, but he was obviously holding back a smile. Leiard sighed.

'Why don't you fetch some hot drinks from your mother? We'll have a rest, then begin again.'

Jayim nodded, then scrambled to his feet. Leiard watched him hurry away.

They say to teach a student is to be taught yourself. I only hope Jayim's lesson proves to be wrong.

If I had known how soon the next Gathering was going to be, Tryss thought, *I would never have made Drilli that promise.*

The day after the trei-trei, the Speakers had announced that a Gathering would be held in four days. Drilli believed that they wanted to warn everyone about the birds, and Tryss figured she was probably right. That had left him little time

254

to ready himself for presenting his harness. Now that the day of the Gathering had arrived, he could think of a thousand things he still needed to do, and another thousand that could go wrong.

He'd done all he could do in the short time he'd had. He'd practised using the harness and blowpipe every day, avoiding duties at home and ignoring the scolding he'd received in return. His father's disapproval lacked conviction, however, since Tryss always brought back meat for their dinner.

He could not bring back all of the animals he'd killed, however. It would have drawn too much attention to himself too early. Though he had managed to bring down another yern, he hadn't dared carry back meat from such a large beast. Leaving it to the scavengers was the only option, and that had dampened his elation at his success.

He could not hunt yern as part of his demonstration. The animals were too big to trap and transport to the Open. Drilli had suggested breem. They were small, quick and shy of humans, which meant they would probably stay within the half-circle of gathered Siyee, but they were still challenging enough that killing them with missiles from the air would impress most people.

Drilli had trapped several every day so Tryss could practise hunting them. She had also decorated the harness, painting it in bright colours so it would be more visible at a distance. He was finding he was not too comfortable with the idea of being the sole object of everyone's attention at a Gathering, but when she pointed out that the paint actually drew more attention to the harness than to him he felt a little better.

He had moved the harness from the cave in which he'd been hiding it to his family bower this morning, keeping it concealed in a large string-reed sack. At Drilli's urging he had explained to his parents what it was, and that he was going to show it

255

to the Gathering that night. His parents' reaction had been mixed. His mother couldn't see why ordinary hunting methods weren't good enough, but was excited by the thought of him presenting his ideas to the Gathering. His father, on the other hand, appeared impressed by the invention, but was worried about Tryss making a fool of himself – and his family.

As am I, Tryss thought wryly.

He was prepared to take that risk. Almost everything was in place, so he couldn't back out now. He didn't want to, anyway. Though the thought of the demonstration filled him with trepidation, Drilli's confidence in him was infectious. Whenever he doubted, she was full of reassurances. He was ready. All that remained was to ask the Speakers for time to address the Siyee.

He'd left this to the last moment. Once he did, word would spread that he was going to demonstrate a hunting invention. He'd be plagued by questions and probably taunted by more than just his cousins.

The sun was low in the sky when he approached the Speakers' Bower. The Siyee leaders were standing around the entrance and several regarded him suspiciously as he drew near them.

He hesitated, aware that his heart was racing and his stomach was fluttering with nervousness.

'May I talk to Speaker Sirri?' Tryss forced himself to ask. He looked through the bower entrance but could not see anything in the dark interior. A shadow moved into the opening and Speaker Sirri stepped out.

'Tryss. We have many important matters to discuss before the Gathering begins. Can this wait until tomorrow?'

'Not really,' he said, aware that other Speakers were staring at him disapprovingly. 'I'll be quick.'

She nodded, then shrugged. 'Come in, then.'

Tryss's heart skipped. He had never been inside the Speaker's

Bower before. With shaking legs he walked past her. It took a moment for his eyes to adjust to the light. The interior was plain and unadorned. A ring of stools stood at the centre. He was pleased to see the room was empty of other Siyee.

'What is it, then, Tryss?'

He turned to face Speaker Sirri. For a moment he could not find his voice. She smiled, the skin around her eyes creasing, and he remembered that she was only one of his own tribe, selected by his own people, and he had no reason to be intimidated by her.

'I've made something,' he told her. 'I want to show it to everyone tonight.'

'Your hunting harness?'

He stared at her in surprise. Her smile widened.

'Sreil told me about it. He said it had potential.'

'He did?' Tryss blurted out. He thought back to the day he'd brought down a yern with drug-tipped spikes months earlier. Sreil had said something . . . *'Good try.'* Tryss had assumed the boy had been mocking him. Perhaps he'd meant what he'd said.

'Yes,' Sirri replied. Her smile faded. 'I have to warn you. It will take a lot to convince people. Nobody likes the idea of carrying anything heavy or—'

'It's not heavy,' Tryss interrupted.

'—or being encumbered by something,' she continued. 'You are sure this invention of yours works?'

He swallowed hard, then nodded.

'Then I'll give you time to show it to us at the beginning of the Gathering. That gives you an hour to get ready. Is that enough?'

He nodded again.

'Then go.' She indicated the doorway.

Tryss hurried out. As the other Speakers turned to regard

257

him, he realised he was grinning foolishly. He schooled his expression and walked away.

An hour! he thought. *I thought I'd have to wait until the end of the Gathering. I had better tell Drilli, then get the harness.*

Once he was clear of the dense forest around the Speakers' Bower he leapt into the air. He flew down the Open to Drilli's family bower. Landing outside her home, he called her name. At once he heard voices arguing inside. After a moment she pushed through the door-hanging, grabbed his arm and drew him quickly away. He looked back to see her mother frowning at them from the entrance.

'Well? Did they say you could show the harness?' Drilli asked.

Tryss grinned. 'Yes. But at the start, not the end like we thought. We've got less than an hour.'

Her eyes widened. 'That soon?'

'Yes. You better get the breem ready while I get the harness.'

'No, I'll need your help to carry them. We'll get the harness first.'

They hurried to his family bower. Tryss was surprised to find it empty.

'My parents must have left early,' he told her. 'They said they—'

The words he had been about to speak fled his mind as he saw what lay in the centre of the bower.

Brightly coloured pieces of wood were scattered across the floor. The strips of leather and gut that had bound the harness together lay in pieces. The blowpipe, so carefully painted by Drilli, had been crushed. The bag that had held the darts had been shredded, and even the darts had been broken, each one snapped in two.

Tryss stared at the fragments of his invention and felt as if his heart, too, was breaking into pieces.

'Who did this?' he heard himself saying in a wounded, incredulous voice. 'Who would do something like this?'

'Your cousins,' Drilli said in a low voice. She shook her head. 'It's all my fault. They're jealous of you. Because of me.'

She made a little choking sound, and he realised she was crying. Amazed that she could be so upset about something he had made – though with her help – he took a step toward her, then hesitantly put an arm around her shoulders. She turned toward him, her eyes shining with tears.

'I'm sorry.'

He drew her close. 'It's not your fault,' he told her, stroking her hair. 'If you believe that, they win.'

She sniffed, then straightened and nodded. 'They haven't won yet,' she said firmly, wiping the tears from her eyes. 'We'll show them. We'll show all of them. Just . . . not tonight.'

He looked at the remains of his harness and felt hurt and disappointment harden into a knot of anger deep inside. 'Next time I'll make two harnesses. Maybe three.'

'And I'll get *my* cousins to keep an eye on Ziss and Trinn.'

'Better still, tie them up somewhere for the night.'

Drilli managed a smile. 'Hang them by their ankles.'

'Next to a tiwi hive.'

'Covered in rebi juice.'

'After removing their clothes.'

'And their skin. With a seeding knife.'

'You're scaring me now.'

Drilli's smile was feral. She bent and picked up the splintered blowpipe. 'Do you need any of this, to make another?'

'No.'

'Good.' She took a basket from a hanger, squatted and began gathering up the pieces.

'What are you going to do with them?'

She grimaced. 'One of us has to tell the Speakers you won't

259

be demonstrating your harness. If I go, they'll know someone else believes in you. And showing them this will convince them you weren't messing them around.'

Tryss felt a heavy weight settle around him as the full effect of his cousins' act became clear. The Speakers knew what he was working on. People would suspect he had blamed others for the failure of his invention – or lacked the courage to demonstrate it. He would be—

'You'd better find your parents and tell them.' Drilli straightened. 'Be quiet about it and pretend everything's normal.'

She hesitated, then stepped up to him. Her lips quirked into a smile, then she leaned forward and kissed him. He blinked in surprise, but as he began to kiss her back she moved away. She winked and pushed aside the door-hanging.

'I'll see you there.'

And then she was hurrying away.

CHAPTER 17

Watching the Siyee ambassadors closely, Auraya recognised the telltale signs of weariness. Being small in stature, they did not have a great tolerance for intoxicating drink, and, like children, they were energetic in their movements but tired quickly.

Dyara was talking quietly to Tireel. Auraya heard snatches of their conversation.

'. . . courage to cross so much landwalker territory, when your people have had good reason to fear us.'

'We flew high and mostly at night,' he replied. 'Landwalkers do not look up often. When they did, they probably thought they were seeing large birds.'

Dyara nodded. 'You will not need to take such precautions on your return. Auraya will not allow you to be harmed.'

'For that we are grateful. It seems to me that the gods must be in favour of this alliance, or they would not have given one of you this power to resist the pull of the earth.'

Auraya smiled. The Siyee ambassadors did not call her Gift flight. They saw no similarity between using magic, as she did, and riding the winds. Even so, they believed that she, of all landwalkers, might truly understand their people.

The ability to fly was at the core of what they were, both physically and culturally.

As Zeeriz yawned she looked pointedly at Juran.

:Our guests have reached their limits, Auraya told the White leader.

:I think you're right.

Juran straightened, then cleared his throat. All eyes turned to him.

'I would like to offer a prayer,' he said. 'And wish our guests a good journey one last time before we retire.' He paused, then closed his eyes. 'Chaia, Huan, Lore, Yranna, Saru. We thank you for all you have done to bring us together tonight, in order that we may bring peace and understanding to the lands of Ithania. We ask that you watch over Tireel of the Green Lake tribe, Zeeriz of the Fork River tribe and Auraya of the White as they journey to the land of Si. May you guide and protect them.'

He opened his eyes, then picked up his glass. At once servants hurried forward to add a dash more tintra to their glasses. Auraya smothered a smile as she saw Zeeriz's look of dismay.

'I wish you a safe and pleasant journey.' Juran looked over the rim of his glass at one ambassador, then the other. His grave expression softened into a smile. He raised his glass to his lips and sipped. As all followed suit, Auraya noted how Zeeriz gulped almost all of the tintra in his glass, as if to get rid of it faster.

Tireel grinned. 'We'll look after Auraya,' he assured Juran.

'She'll be treated like . . . like . . .' Zeeriz began.

'Like an honoured guest,' Tireel finished.

'Thank you,' Juran said. 'Then we'd best let you both get some sleep in preparation for your long flight.'

He pushed back his chair and rose. Auraya turned to face Zeeriz and, finding him gone, looked down. She had ordered high chairs to be made so the Siyee would sit at an equal height to any other occupants of the dining table. It was always a surprise to find herself suddenly towering over them again at the end of a meal.

Zeeriz's eyes were closed. He swayed a little, then opened them and blinked up at her.

'It's just not fair how much you landwalkers can drink,' he muttered.

She chuckled. 'Let me take you back to your room.'

He nodded and let her guide him out into the corridor. She heard Dyara and Tireel following, still talking. The ambassadors were staying on one of the middle floors of the Tower, close to the dining hall. Auraya and Dyara bade their guests goodnight, then started toward their rooms. As they reached the great staircase, Dyara gave Auraya a speculative look.

'You seem more worried about this journey than the last,' she observed.

Auraya glanced at Dyara. 'I am,' she admitted.

'Why do you think that is?'

'I must do it alone.'

'You can still consult with Juran or me,' Dyara pointed out. 'It is more than that, I think.'

Auraya nodded. 'Perhaps I didn't care quite as much whether I succeeded with the Somreyans or not. It's not that I didn't care at all,' she hurried to explain, 'but the possibility of failing with the Siyee, of giving them reason to dislike us, bothers me. They are, I guess, more trusting of us. The Somreyans weren't. So, if I fail, it will be akin to betraying their trust.'

'You didn't feel the same obligation to avoid betraying the trust of the Dreamweavers?'

Auraya shrugged. 'They never trusted us in the first place.'

'No,' Dyara replied. She looked thoughtful. 'But your friend trusts you. It was a bold move, making him your adviser. I

263

thought it unwise, but it has proved to be quite beneficial.'

Auraya stared at Dyara in amazement, then looked away. Was this approval? From Dyara? Over befriending a *Dreamweaver*?

Dyara halted at the door to Auraya's rooms. 'Good night, Auraya. I will see you at the farewell tomorrow.'

'Good night,' Auraya replied. 'And . . . thank you.'

Dyara smiled, then turned away to continue up the stairs. As Auraya entered her rooms, she considered Dyara's words.

'But your friend trusts you.'

She hadn't had a chance to speak to Leiard in the last few days. Tomorrow she would be leaving early. No chance to see him one last time.

Then tonight is my only chance to say goodbye.

She frowned. It was late. Too late to send for him. She couldn't send someone to wake him up and bring him to the Tower only to spend five minutes with him before sending him home again.

Would he really mind? She pursed her lips. What was worse: dragging him up here in the middle of the night, or not saying goodbye?

Smiling to herself, she closed her eyes and sought the mind of the priest on night duty below. After giving him her instructions, she sat down to wait.

This time tomorrow I'll be sleeping in a village Temple somewhere. She glanced around the room. Everything looked as it always did. There was no trunk of belongings, just a small pack containing spare white clothing and some gifts for the Siyee. Everything she needed would be given to her by the priests and priestesses of the Temples she stayed in.

Once she entered the mountains there would be no more Temples. The Siyee had assured her that all her needs could be met in their land. They would supply her with all the objects of a civilised culture, such as paper and ink, which they made themselves. She would be given a 'bower' of her own to stay in.

Standing up, she walked to the window and looked down. The Dome was a shadowed expanse, ringed by lanterns. A few priests and servants hurried about their business. The city below was a scattering of lights in a sea of black.

A tarn entered the Temple loaded with healer priests. Auraya watched two platten arrive, then felt her heartbeat quicken as she saw another pass under the arch bearing a single occupant. Even from so far above, she recognised Leiard. His white hair and beard stood out despite the distance.

As the platten approached, he looked up. She found herself smiling, even though she knew he could not see her.

Moving away from the window, she began pacing the room. Would he mind that she'd called him here? Suddenly her purpose for doing so – just to say goodbye – seemed silly. She could have sent a note instead. She could have visited him . . . No, that would have disturbed the whole household of the people he was staying with.

Well, there's nothing to be done about it now, she decided. *I'll apologise, say goodbye, then send him home. By the time I return to Jarime he'll have forgiven me.*

She paced the room. What was taking him so long? Perhaps she had been mistaken. She moved to the window.

I could question the priest on duty . . .

She froze as a light tapping came from the door, then let her breath out in a rush.

He's here.

Smoothing her circ, she strode to the door and opened it. Leiard regarded her with wary expectation.

'Leiard. Come in.' She ushered him inside. 'Sorry about the late hour. I haven't had a moment to myself, and no time to see you as I promised. I'm leaving tomorrow. I couldn't go without saying goodbye.'

He nodded slowly, and she was pleased to see he was not annoyed, only relieved. It dawned on her, then, that by calling him here so late she had caused him to wonder if something was wrong. Why hadn't she foreseen that?

'I guess I should have just sent a message,' she added ruefully. 'Rather than wake you up.'

His lips twitched into a slight smile. 'I don't mind.'

'I don't just need to say goodbye. I need to thank you.' She paused, then reached for his hand. He hesitated, then lifted his hand to hers. Their fingers met. She drew breath to speak, but stopped as she met his eyes. His expression was tight and wary, as if he was struggling to control some emotion. She looked closer. His thoughts were in turmoil. Her touch had roused . . .

She felt heat rush through her body. Her touch had aroused him. He was struggling to suppress desire for her.

I hadn't realised his admiration was so . . . but I guess it wasn't or I would have seen it in his mind. This is something new. This has happened tonight. Now.

Her heart was racing.

Her own body had reacted to his desire. She felt a smile pull at her lips. *I desire him. Now we've both discovered something.*

She was conscious of the tense silence between them. The only sound was their breathing. Neither of them had moved. His gaze hadn't left hers. *We should step away from each other and pretend this never happened.* Instead, she reached out and touched his cheek, then traced a finger across his lips. He didn't move away, but neither did he return the caress. She read hesitation in his thoughts.

This decision has to be mine, she realised. *He cannot forget who we are. Only I can make this choice.*

She smiled and lifted her lips to his. He returned her kiss gently, sending a shiver down her spine. Then they both moved together, reaching out to the other. She kissed him firmly and he responded with equal hunger and passion. Their bodies collided; she grasped his vest and pulled him close against her. His hands slid around her back, but his touch was dulled by the thickness of her circ.

Vest. Circ. Reminders of who they were. She didn't want to be reminded. Not now. These reminders must go.

She laughed quietly. *This is not like me*, she thought. Leiard's lips left her mouth and he began kissing her throat, and then her neck, his lips hot and firm. *This is not like him either*. She was discovering a side of him she had never suspected existed.

And I like it. She chuckled. Winding her arms around his waist, she backed toward the door to her private rooms.

Emerahl smiled and ran her hands over her body.

It worked.

But of course it had. She had never botched the change. Mirar had told her long ago that her ability to change her body was an innate Gift. He had a theory that all Wilds had a Gift that came naturally. Like musical ability came to those with true talent. Hers was the ability to change her physical age.

Opening her eyes, she saw only darkness. The air was growing stuffy rapidly. Once she had roused from the death trance, she had created small tunnels to let air into the box. They weren't enough now that she had brought her body out of the slowed state necessary to change her appearance, and she was breathing at a normal rate.

She grimaced. A death trance was never pleasant, but it had been essential to fool the children and had allowed her to survive being buried underground. She did not know how many days had passed, but one thing was sure: she had to get out of her coffin soon or she would suffocate.

She was not sure where the children had buried her, however. If they, or anyone else, saw her dig her way out of her grave, the story of it would spread faster than a winter cough, perhaps alerting the priest to her change of appearance. She would have to be careful.

Closing her eyes, she sent her mind out and was pleased when she managed to sense the emotions of others nearby. It was not easy sorting through them, but she recognised the sleepy thoughts of children. She cursed. They were somewhere close by. She would have to be quiet.

Slowly, Emerahl drew magic and used it to break through the box lid just above her head. She shifted the dirt above it down to the other end of her coffin to gather around her feet. The pale sky of near-dawn appeared above her sooner than she expected.

They ought to have buried me deeper, she thought. *But their ignorance has saved me some trouble.*

She enlarged the hole until it was big enough to allow her body through, then squirmed and pushed upward. Peering out, she saw that she was in the small yard at the back of the burned-out house the children lived under. She paused to think.

I could bury myself again and wait until they all go out for the day. She considered. *No. A few always stay behind to mind the place during the day. Better to go now while they're asleep.*

Drawing her arms up, she grabbed the lip of the hole and pulled. She had to pause to catch her breath several times, and as more of her emerged into the morning light she saw why. The change had used up a lot of her body fat. Her arms were bony and wasted, her breasts almost non-existent. As she brushed dirt off the dirty white shift the children had left her in, she felt the hardness of protruding hip bones beneath.

I'm weak and scrawny, she mused. *A skeleton reborn from a coffin womb. I wouldn't blame anyone for thinking me some unholy, unwholesome creature today.*

At last she was able to get her feet under her and stand up. To her relief she had enough strength to stand, probably to walk, too. Stepping up out of her grave, she turned and considered the evidence of her rise from death.

Better fix this mess.

Drawing magic, she shifted and smoothed the dirt until the hole was filled and all sign of her emergence was gone. She smiled sadly as she saw the shrivelled flowers scattered over the ground. She wished she could do more for the children, but she had her own survival to think of.

What next?

She looked down at herself. Her hands and arms were covered in dirt and she was wearing only a stained shift. Her hair hung down over her shoulders, still the stiff white hair of an old woman. She needed a wash, then clothes and food, and something to dye her hair with.

It was then that she realised the wallet she had strapped to her body was gone. She was not surprised; she had known there was a good chance the children would find it. After all, she could not hide *everything* inside her.

She briefly considered sneaking into the house to look for it, but dismissed the thought straightaway. It was too great a risk, and the children had probably spent most of it already. Turning her back on her 'grave', she quietly walked past the house and out into the poor quarter.

The thin grey light of morning slowly brightened. The streets were quiet but not deserted. She passed a pair of middle-aged washerwomen, who regarded her with distaste, then a younger man with a wooden leg stopped to leer at her. She felt self-conscious for the first time in over a hundred years.

And people ask me why I, who can be any age I please, would choose to be old? Emerahl thought wryly.

But then, there were definitely pleasures to be gained from being young again. She had always been attractive to men when in her younger form. Sometimes women, too. Some of her good looks obviously still showed despite her current wasted state. She only needed some regular healthy meals to regain her curves.

But food cost money. She frowned as she considered the near future. With her wallet and her body fat gone, she needed to find a source of income quickly. Theft was a possibility, but she was long out of practice and didn't have the strength to run if she was seen. Being caught might bring her to priestly attention.

Priests were looking for a woman who sold cures, so she could not consider selling her knowledge and skills in that area either. She continued downhill, heading toward the sea. The direction she had chosen amused her. She had been born by the ocean, and had always been drawn to water in times of strife. When the flat, liquid horizon finally appeared, she sighed with relief and quickened her steps.

Once she reached the water's edge she followed the road that hugged the shore, looking for a more private place to wash. Most of the small bays were occupied. When she came to a small bay with a single pier she stopped. Two fishermen were working in their boat, one young, one old, preparing their catch for market. She considered them for a moment, then walked boldly down the pier.

'Looks like a good catch,' she said as she passed.

They glanced up, then stared at her. She smiled back at them, then turned away. Reaching the end of the pier, she stepped off.

Cold water engulfed her and the shock of it drove the air

from her lungs in a rush of bubbles. She felt sand beneath her feet and pushed up again. Coming to the surface, she sucked in air, then kicked away from the pier.

'Lady?'

She rolled over, then laughed as she saw the two fishermen peering at her from the end of the pier, both wearing worried expressions.

'Don't worry,' she told them. 'I just wanted to get clean.'

'You gave us a scare,' the younger man said reproachfully. 'Thought you wanted to drown yourself.'

'I'm sorry.' She swam toward them, noting how their eyes shifted from her face to those parts of her that came to the surface. The shift was half-transparent now that it was wet. 'Thank you for thinking to save me.' She swam under the pier.

She could hear them walking along the boards above her. There had been no mistaking their interest. She pursed her lips, considering. One way to solve her current dilemma had already occurred to her, and now an opportunity had presented itself. It wasn't as if she hadn't done this sort of work before. In fact, she had always considered herself quite good at it.

Looking up, she noted how the beams of wood crossed to form a narrow, slimy shelf. Hidden by the water, she reached under her shift, probed inside herself.

This is one of the reasons some men call this part of a woman's body a whore's purse, she thought as she drew out a small bag. Among the contents was the sea bell, dembar sap pendant and some coins. The coins would not buy her much more than a few meals, and no jeweller would give her even a fraction of a fair price for such a valuable sea bell while she looked like she did now. No, she would have to work up to that. She put the bag up on the slimy shelf then swam out from under the pier.

The fishermen's attention snapped back to her. They walked alongside as she paddled toward their boat.

271

'This your boat?' she asked.

'My father's,' the young man said, glancing at his companion.

'Mind if I come aboard while I dry off?'

The pair exchanged glances, then the older man nodded. 'Why not?'

She grinned at them, then swam to the vessel's side. The younger man stepped onto the boat, reached down and took her hand, then hauled her up onto the deck. She noticed the father glancing about to see if anyone was watching, and smothered a smile. *Thinking of your wife, are you?*

Stepping back, she drew magic and sent heat and air through her shift. The younger man moved away and regarded her with new respect. Though she knew she probably looked more exciting wet, these two potential customers needed to know she could not be easily cheated of her fee.

When her shift was dry, she let out a sigh.

'You'd think with all my Gifts I wouldn't have ended up a whore.' She looked up at them and blushed. 'I only just started, mind. And I won't be doing it for long, either. Only until I can find a job.'

The two men exchanged glances, then the father cleared his throat.

'How much?'

Emerahl smiled. 'Well, I think such gallant men who thought to save a lady from drowning ought to receive a discount, don't you?'

And this, she thought wryly, *is the other reason men call that part of a woman's body a whore's purse.*

272

PART TWO

CHAPTER 18

The world was a great blanket of green tinted with the colours of autumn and rumpled where mountains burst through the fabric. Rivers glistened like silver thread. Tiny buildings, like scattered mosaic tiles, clumped here and there, connected by brown roads. When Auraya looked closely a multitude of little movements revealed minute animals – and people.

Auraya would have liked to fly closer to the ground, but Zeeriz preferred to keep well away from landwalkers, despite her presence. It was exhausting for him to remain in the air all day. Flying was not as effortless as Siyee made it appear, and Zeeriz was stiff and sore by the time dusk brought them to the ground. Auraya could not imagine how taxing Tireel's journey was: he had flown on ahead to warn the Siyee of her coming.

After several hours even the world below couldn't keep her entertained. There wasn't much to occupy her mind apart from future negotiations with the Siyee, and eventually she tired of worrying and planning for that. Instead she had learned to mimic her companion's movements – to act as if wind, momentum and the pull of the earth had the same effect on her as they did on Siyee. By doing so she could better appreciate the limitations of their physical form.

She had also drawn much from the ambassador's mind about his people. His thoughts ranged from his responsibilities, fear of landwalkers, hopes for the future and memories of childhood. Most interesting was the suppressed resentment he felt when he saw her mimicking his flight. He wondered why the gods had given a landwalker access to the air with none of the restrictions and penalties the Siyee endured.

That the Siyee had overcome the limitations and consequences of their creation was a source of pride. All Siyee were taught that their ancestors had willingly accepted pain, deformity and early death in order that the goddess Huan might create their race. They continued to pay the price even now, but the numbers of crippled babies had been decreasing over the centuries. Their population had been growing slowly. Only the Toren settlers threatened that.

Something must be done about those settlers, Auraya thought. It would not be a simple task. Huan had decreed that the mountains to the east of Toren belonged to the Siyee. Land-hungry Toren settlers interpreted 'mountains' as being any land too steep to cultivate and had slowly taken over the fertile valleys and slopes. She doubted the King of Toren knew of the activities of his people, and fully expected that if he did, he had no intention of doing anything about it.

But he will, if the White insist that he must.

She smiled grimly. The Siyee needed this alliance with the White. They wanted it, but feared they had little to offer in return. They believed they were neither strong nor skilled enough to be of use in war and had no resources to trade. It was her task to find something they could offer in return for the White's protection – or simply convince them that whatever small help they could offer in war, trade or politics would be enough.

She looked at Zeeriz again. He glanced at her and smiled.

Little was known about their people. Auraya had learned much from Tireel and Zeeriz, but she would gain a greater understanding of the Siyee by meeting leaders and observing their everyday activities. That the White made the effort to visit a country always pleased its inhabitants. The two ambassadors were delighted that she was taking the time to see their homeland, and she hoped this sentiment would be shared by the rest of their people. If all went well, she would gain their respect and confidence on behalf of the White in the next few months.

Looking toward the dark line of mountains in the distance, Auraya felt a thrill of excitement. In truth, she was as pleased to be visiting Si as the ambassadors were to be escorting her there. She was going somewhere few landwalkers had been, to learn about a unique race of people.

I couldn't be happier.

At once she felt a familiar disquiet. It was not doubt in herself or fear of failure. *No, it's the thought of the mess I've left behind.*

'*You have an interesting way of saying goodbye,*' Leiard had said. A memory of sheets bunched up at the end of her bed flashed through her mind, then one of naked limbs tangled together. Then tantalising earlier memories arose.

Who would have thought? she mused, unable to help smiling. *Me and Leiard. A White and a Dreamweaver.*

At that thought she felt her smile fade and her mood begin to sink toward a darker place. She resisted half-heartedly. *I have to face this. I have to do it now. Once I reach Si I'll be too busy to spend time agonising over the consequences.* Sighing, she asked herself the question she'd been avoiding.

How will the other White react when they find out?

Dyara came to mind first. The woman all but growled with disapproval whenever Leiard was around. Dyara would not easily accept him as Auraya's lover. Mairae, on the other hand, might not mind it at all, though she'd probably prefer it if

Auraya hadn't chosen to bed a Dreamweaver. Rian wouldn't like it. He had never suggested that the other White ought to choose celibacy as he had, but he was sure to dislike the idea of one of them bedding a heathen.

And Juran? Auraya frowned. She couldn't guess what his reaction might be. He had accepted Leiard as her adviser. Would he tolerate him as her lover? Or would he say this was pushing the White's acceptance of Dreamweavers too far?

No, he'll tell me that the people won't accept it. That it will undermine everything I've said or done to encourage tolerance of Dreamweavers. People will believe my opinion was based on love – or lust – rather than good sense, and they will remember that Mirar was a seducer of women. They will think I've been duped and make their feelings known by attacking Dreamweavers.

It was too soon to expect them to accept this. Perhaps time was the key. She chewed on her lip for a moment. If she kept her affair secret it might give the White and the people time to grow used to the idea. It was not as if she was bedding every attractive, unmarried highborn male in Northern Ithania. If Mairae could get away with *that*, then surely Auraya could get away with sleeping with one Dreamweaver.

She sighed again. *I wish that were true. What chance do I have of keeping this a secret? Everyone knows about Mairae's affairs, and if Dyara can't keep her tragically chaste relationship with Timare secret from the rest of the White, how can I keep mine?*

Fortunately she was going to spend the next few months far from Jarime. A lot could happen in that time. She could come to her senses. Leiard might come to his.

What if he already has? What if he has no intention of seeing me again? What if he has sated his curiosity and is not interested in anything more? Her heart twisted. *No! He loves me! I saw it in his mind.*

And I love him. She felt a warm glow of happiness spread

through her body. Pleasant memories returned, but were soured when she recalled an image of his Dreamweaver vest and her circ lying together on the floor. That had been a sobering sight. It seemed, somehow, blasphemous.

The gods must know, she thought.

She shook her head. *We can't do this. I should turn him away.* But she knew she wouldn't. *Until the gods make their feelings known I won't try to guess what they think of us.*

She looked over her shoulder. Jarime had disappeared over the horizon hours before. *How can I leave such a mess behind me?* She couldn't turn around and fly back, though. She made herself think of the Siyee, and how disappointed and offended they would be. How much she wanted to see their land for herself.

A few months, she told herself. *By the time I return I will have decided what we should do.*

And hopefully I'll have gathered the courage to do it.

Rain pattered against the canopy overhead. Feeling something land on his head, Danjin looked up. A patch of water had somehow made its way through the dense, oiled cloth. He dodged another drip, sliding along the seat of the platten, then reached into his pocket for a cloth to wipe his scalp.

Instead, his fingers encountered a piece of parchment. Danjin withdrew it and sighed as he saw it was his father's message.

Theran has returned. I have invited your brothers for dinner.
Your presence is required.
Fa-Spear

'When I said it would be pleasant to have some time to myself again the gods must have been listening,' he muttered.

He looked up at the canopy. 'Great Chaia, what did I do to deserve this?'

'Neglect your family?' Silava suggested.

Danjin looked at the woman sitting opposite him. The light of the lantern softened the lines on her face. They were mostly the lines gained from smiles and laughter. *Mostly.* There had been less pleasant times. Just as many as experienced by those who married for love, he had noted in recent years. They had both been unfaithful, both learned that honesty was the hardest but only path to forgiveness. While they had never been passionately in love with each other, they had, eventually, become the best of friends.

'Which family?' Danjin asked. 'Mine or ours?'

She smiled. 'You should ask that of an unbiased judge, Danjin. Just be sure that our family will always want to see more of you. Especially once your grandchildren are born.'

Grandchildren. The thought of becoming a grandparent was both delightful and dismaying. It meant he was getting old. It also made his daughters happy. They were flourishing in their new homes. He was relieved to have chosen good husbands for them, though he had mostly taken Silava's advice on the matter. Pity one couldn't choose one's parents.

'If it is my father's family you mean, then you are being punished, too,' he pointed out.

'That is true. But he ignores me at these dinners. It's you he will target.'

Danjin scowled at the reminder. Silava leaned forward and patted him lightly on the knee.

'I left a bottle of tintra on the reading-room table for you.'

He smiled with appreciation. 'Thank you.'

The platten slowed. Danjin peered out of the canopy and felt a familiar sinking sensation in his stomach as they pulled up outside his father's mansion. Then he remembered the ring on his finger. He took some strength from the knowledge that the Gods' Chosen did not think him the failure his father believed his youngest son to be.

He climbed out of the platten, then turned to help his wife disembark. The rain was falling heavily, wetting their tawls quickly. They both breathed a sigh of relief as they reached the door of the mansion.

A tall, thin man with a lofty expression ushered them inside. Danjin regarded Forin, the head servant, suspiciously. The man had an apologetic way of announcing Danjin's arrival as if it were an interruption rather than a requested visit.

'Welcome, Danjin Spear, Silava.' Forin inclined his head to both of them.

'*Adviser* Danjin Spear,' Danjin corrected. He untied his tawl and held it out to the servant.

Forin's eyes gleamed. His mouth opened, then his eyes dropped to Danjin's tawl and he hesitated. Danjin realised the man was staring at the white ring shining on his finger.

'Of course. Forgive me.' He took Danjin's tawl and Silava's, then hurried into another room.

Silava glanced at Danjin as they entered the communal room. She did not smile, but he recognised that familiar glint of triumph in her eyes. The one he normally received when *he* lost an argument.

Two of Danjin's brothers waited in the room, standing beside braziers. Seeing them, Danjin felt satisfaction from the small victory melt away. His siblings' greetings were formal and awkward. Their wives spared thin smiles for Silava, then returned to their conversation, ignoring her. The rain fell through the roof opening into a pool below. Benches covered in cushions and luxurious blankets were arranged with perfect symmetry around the walls of the room. The floor was polished veinstone and the walls were painted with murals depicting ships and trade goods.

A servant appeared with warmed Somreyan ahm. As he sipped, Danjin considered his family. No doubt Theran, the favoured brother they had all been invited here to see, was staying in the mansion and was with his father already.

All of Fa-Spear's sons had joined in the family's trading enterprises, with varying success. Theran, the second son, was a natural trader. Two of the younger brothers had died in a shipwreck twenty years before. Ma-Spear, who had never fully recovered from birthing Danjin, had sickened and died soon after. A year ago the oldest brother's heart had stopped, so now there were only four sons left: Theran, Nirem, Gohren and himself.

The seven sons were supposed to expand the Spear trading empire. Danjin had tried, but he hadn't lasted any longer than his first voyage at sixteen. Within two days of arriving in Genria he had befriended a distant nephew of the king and found himself surrounded by political manoeuvrings far more thrilling and meaningful to him than the long journeys and constant tallying and calculations of trade. Distracted, he had not been present to inspect the grain loaded onto the ship, and by the time he returned to Jarime half of it was spoiled by pests.

His father had been furious.

'Danjin?'

At his wife's murmur, Danjin looked up. Two men were walking down the corridor to the communal room. Forin moved to the centre of the room.

'Fa-Spear and Theran Spear,' he announced.

The old man's face was a mass of wrinkles and he walked with the aid of a staff. His eyes were sharp and cold and flicked from face to face. To his right walked Theran. The older brother smiled at Nirem and Gohren, but his expression became more forced as he met Danjin's eyes. Instead of dismissing his youngest brother, as he usually did, Theran raised his eyebrows.

'Danjin. I was not expecting you to come. Father says your duties at the Temple keep you from attending most family gatherings.'

'Not tonight,' Danjin replied. *And how could I miss the opportunity to be scornfully ignored or made the butt of your jokes?*

The old man moved to a long bench and sat down. The rest of the family paused, waiting to be invited to sit. Fa-Spear waved a hand.

'Sit. Sit,' he said, as if their formality embarrassed him. Yet Danjin knew any deviation from this ritual of manners always infuriated his father. They sat at places long established by family tradition: Theran on Fa-Spear's right, Nirem and his wife on his left, Gohren next to Theran, and Danjin furthest from his father beside Nirem's wife.

As a succession of delicacies were brought by female servants the conversation turned to trade. Danjin forced himself to listen, and remained prudently silent. He had long ago learned to avoid joining these discussions. Any observation or question he made on the subject of trade was examined as proof of his ignorance of such matters.

No matter how silent he remained, his father always made a point of discussing Danjin's work. As Theran finished a long description of a successful deal, Fa-Spear looked up at his youngest son.

'I do not see our adviser to the White gaining as much profit from serving the Temple.' Fa-Dyer gestured at the walls. 'If you are so important to the Circlians, why is it that a mere merchant lives in better conditions than you? You must ask for an increase in your allowance when you next see your employer. When will that be?'

'Auraya has left for Si, Father,' Danjin replied. 'To negotiate an alliance.'

His father's eyebrows rose. 'You did not accompany her?'

'The mountains of Si are not easily crossed by landwalkers.'

'Landwalkers?'

'It is what the Siyee call ordinary humans.'

His father sniffed. 'How uncouth. Perhaps it is fortunate she left you behind. Who knows what unsavoury habits these people have?' He popped a morsel of food into his mouth then wiped his hands on a cloth a servant girl held out for him.

'If the Si do ally themselves with Hania, you may see more of them here. They will install an ambassador and others will visit in order to seek education, join the priest-hood, or trade.'

His father's gaze sharpened. He chewed, swallowed, then took a sip of water.

'What do they have to trade?'

Danjin smiled. 'That is one of the questions Auraya intends to answer.'

Fa-Spear's eyes narrowed. 'There is opportunity here, son. You may not have a decent income, but if you take advantage of opportunities like this that issue may not matter.'

Danjin felt a flash of indignation. 'I cannot use my position to gain trade advantages.'

His father snorted. 'Don't be such a righteous fool. You won't be adviser forever.'

'Not if I abuse my privileges.' *Nor if I follow in your foot-steps*, Danjin added to himself, thinking of the enemies his father had made over the years. Powerful enemies who had barred him from trading in certain places.

:Why don't you remind him of that?

Danjin started at the voice in his mind.

:Auraya?

:Yes, it's me. Sorry, I didn't mean to intrude. The Siyee are asleep, and I'm . . . well . . . bored.

He started to smile, and quickly schooled his expression.

'. . . fame and glory have passed,' his father was saying, 'you will soon be forgotten.'

Danjin opened his mouth to reply.

:Your father's right about one thing. We should pay you more.

He choked.

:How long have you been listening?

There was a pause.

:I peeked a while back.

:Peeked?

:To see if you were busy.

'Are you listening?' Fa-Spear demanded.

Danjin looked up, and quickly considered whether he should explain who he had been communicating with.

:Go on, Auraya urged.

:I mean no disrespect, Danjin told her, *but you don't know my family. Some pots aren't worth stirring.*

'I was considering your advice, Father,' Danjin replied.

Fa-Spear's eyes narrowed, then he turned to Nirem. 'Have you seen Captain Raerig lately?'

Nirem nodded, and started recollecting a drunken gathering in a remote town. Relieved that attention had finally shifted from himself, Danjin let his thoughts stray, until he was brought back by the mention of the southern cult.

'He said they're good customers, these Pentadrians,' Nirem said. 'Half of their priests are warriors. He buys Dunwayan weapons and sells them on the southern continent. Can't sell enough of them. Do you think we should . . . ?'

To Danjin's surprise, his father frowned. 'Maybe. I've heard they're gathering an army down there. Your great-grandfather always said war was good for trade, but it depended on who was planning to fight who.'

'Who are they planning to fight?' Danjin asked.

His father smiled thinly. 'I'd have thought you'd know, Adviser to the White.'

'Perhaps I do,' Danjin said lightly. 'Perhaps I don't. Who do you believe they're going to fight?'

His father shrugged and looked away. 'For now I'd rather keep what I know to myself. If there's an advantage to be gained from this, I wouldn't want a stray word in the wrong place to ruin it.'

Danjin felt a stab of anger. It was not the veiled insult suggesting he'd leak information that riled him, but that his father knew he had information Danjin needed. Information that the White needed.

Then his anger evaporated. If his father hadn't wanted Danjin to know about the Pentadrians gathering an army, for fear it would ruin some trade deal, he wouldn't have mentioned it at all. Perhaps this was all the warning his father could bring himself to give his youngest son.

:Are you listening, Auraya?

No reply came. Danjin turned the ring around his finger and considered what he ought to do. *Find out more*, he decided. *Make my own enquiries*. Next time Auraya spoke to him through the ring he would have something substantial to tell her.

CHAPTER 19

A feeling of suffocation woke Leiard. He sat up, gasping for breath, and stared at his surroundings. The room was dark and he sensed dawn was not far away. He could not remember the dream that had woken him.

Rising, he washed, changed and slipped out of his room. Creating a tiny spark of light, he crossed the communal room and made his way up to the rooftop garden. He stepped outside into the chill air and approached the garden seats where he held Jayim's lessons.

Sitting down, he considered his dream. All that remained was a feeling of fear. He closed his eyes and concentrated on a mental exercise designed to retrieve lost dreams, but nothing stirred. Only the fear lingered.

The dreams he did remember were of Auraya. Some were pleasant, filled with joy and passion. He hadn't had such arousing dreams since . . . so long ago he could not remember. Unfortunately, some of the dreams were full of unpleasant consequences, of accusation and retribution and terrible, terrible punishment.

You should have left. You should have reminded yourself of what she is, a voice said in his mind.

I did.

You should have reminded yourself harder.

This other voice in his mind – the thoughts that Arleej believed were a manifestation of Mirar's link memories – spoke to Leiard often now. It was logical that, if he was going to be arguing with himself over Auraya, this illusionary Mirar would side against him having anything to do with the White. Mirar *had* been killed by one of them.

He had wondered, briefly, if Mirar had influenced him somehow that night in Auraya's room. Leiard was wary of blaming this secondary identity for any of his own actions, however. There had been no voice encouraging him to seduce Auraya. Mirar had been silent until early the next morning, not speaking until Leiard left the Tower.

Auraya had kissed him goodbye, then asked him to keep their tryst a secret. A reasonable request, considering what he was. What she was. Had anyone seen him leave? He had seen no sign of servants, but had been prepared to behave as if nothing other than a late-night consultation had occurred.

The lie sounded implausible, however. Servants liked to imagine more exciting matters than political discussion went on behind doors late at night, especially if that consultation lasted all night. If they did suspect he'd bedded Auraya, the other White would have read it from their minds. If any of the Gods' Chosen wanted to confirm it they had only to summon Leiard and read *his* mind.

No summons had arrived. He was hoping this meant his visit had not been noticed or speculated upon. When he thought of the consequences to his people if such a scandal became known, he shivered with dread. Yet whenever he wasn't worrying he found himself planning ways to visit her secretly when she returned.

If she wants me to. She might regard me as a night's entertain-

*ment. A lover she'll cast off when she realises how inconvenient he
will be to keep around. If only I could find out what she wants.*

There was a way, but it was dangerous. He could dream
link with her.

Don't be an idiot. If she reports you they'll have you stoned.

She won't tell anyone.

'Leiard?'

He jumped and looked up, surprised to find Jayim standing
in front of him. The garden was now lit by the faint light of
dawn. He had been so lost in thought, he hadn't noticed.

The boy yawned as he took the seat opposite Leiard. He had
wrapped himself in a blanket. *Winter is coming*, Leiard thought.
I should teach him ways to keep himself warm.

'Will we practise mind-linking again?' Jayim asked.

Leiard considered the boy. They hadn't linked since the day
Jayim had observed Leiard's attraction to Auraya. He had been
so disturbed by that, he had put off further lessons in the skill.

Now the thought of linking with his student filled him
with fear. If he did, Jayim was bound to learn of Leiard's night
with Auraya. He would see, too, Leiard's hopes to continue
the affair. If Jayim knew that, there would be two people in
Jarime from whom the White could read Leiard's secret.

'No,' Leiard replied. 'The air is chill this morning. I will
explain the ways the body is affected by cold, and teach you
how to counter it.'

High Priest Ikaro paused outside King Berro's audience
chamber. He took a deep breath and stepped into the room.
Attendants, advisers and representatives of the greater trades
stood about the throne. The seat was empty, however. The king
was standing before an enormous urn.

It was decorated in the new style, Ikaro noted. A black
coating covered the urn, then designs and figures had been

289

scratched out of it, revealing the white clay beneath. The king glanced at Ikaro, then beckoned.

'Do you like it, High Priest Ikaro? It is of myself naming Cimro as my heir.'

'I do indeed,' Ikaro replied, moving to the king's side. 'There is grace and skill in these lines, and the detail is exquisite. You do me a great honour, your majesty.'

The kind frowned. 'By showing this to you? I intend to place it here. You will see it each time you enter this chamber.'

'Yet I will not have an opportunity to stand and admire it, your majesty. My attention will always be on more important matters.'

The king smiled. 'That is true.' He stepped away from the urn and strolled toward the throne. 'I did not know you were an appreciator of art.'

'I am merely an appreciator of beauty.'

Berro chuckled. 'Then it is a great irony that you have turned my city upside down looking for an ugly old hag.' The king settled onto his throne. His expression became serious and his fingers drummed on the throne's arm. 'How much longer do you intend us to continue with this search?'

Ikaro frowned. He could not read the king's mind – he was only able to read minds when Huan was present – but he did not need to. The king was not hiding his impatience. The usual reassurances would not placate Berro this time. He was not sure what would, except . . .

'I will ask the gods.'

The king's eyes widened. The men and women exchanged glances, some sceptical.

'Now?'

'Unless this is an inconvenient time,' Ikaro added. 'I could use the palace Temple.'

'No, no,' Berro said. 'Speak to them, if that is what you feel is right.'

Ikaro nodded, then closed his eyes.

'Join me in prayer,' he murmured, putting both hands together to form a circle. As he spoke a familiar chant of praise he was grateful to hear many voices quietly echoing him. He drew courage from them. At the end of the chant he paused, then drew a deep breath.

'Chaia, Huan, Lore, Yranna, Saru. I ask that one of you speak to me so that I may receive instruction.'

He waited, heart racing. His skin prickled as an energy filled the air.

:High Priest Ikaro.

Gasps echoed through the chamber. Ikaro opened his eyes and glanced around. There was no sign of the owner of the voice, but he could see from the expressions of everyone in the room that they had heard it.

'Huan?' he asked.

:It is I.

He bowed his head.

'I have done as you bade, but I have not found the sorceress. Should I continue searching? Is there any other way I might locate her?'

:Let her think you have given up. Call off the searchers. Stop checking people at the port and main gate. Instead, have these exits watched by a priest in disguise. If she believes the search has ended, she may take the opportunity to leave the city. I will be watching for her.

Ikaro nodded. 'If she can be found this way, I will find her,' he replied with determination.

The goddess's presence faded. Ikaro looked up at the king, who wore a thoughtful expression.

'Is it only recently that the gods have spoken to you in this way?'

'Yes,' Ikaro admitted.

The king frowned. 'No doubt the goddess knows I am grateful that the restrictions on my city will be lifted, but I will include my thanks in my prayers to be sure. Much as I do not want a dangerous sorceress roaming free in my city, I am concerned that my people will suffer if trade is restricted. Will you need any assistance following her instructions?'

Ikaro shook his head, then hesitated. 'Though perhaps you should inform the guards that beggars around the gates are to be left alone.'

'Beggars, eh?' Berro smiled crookedly. 'Original disguise, that one.'

Ikaro chuckled. 'And if it would not be inconvenient, a few guard's uniforms might come in handy as well.'

Berro nodded. 'I'll see that you get them.'

For all of the last day and most of the morning, Auraya and Zeeriz had flown over impressively rugged mountains. She had lived most of her childhood in the shadows of the range that divided Dunway from Hania, but those mountains were mere hills compared to these high, jagged peaks.

Looking down at the steep slopes and broken ground, and the tangled limbs of trees and sharp spires of rock she could see how difficult it would be to travel into Si by foot. The 'ground' was vertical more often than horizontal, and every bit of soil had been claimed by plants, from sharp grasses to enormous trees.

Wide, rubble-filled rivers cut through the forest. High eroded banks scattered with enormous dead trees hinted at an impassable spring flow. These rivers surged toward glittering blue lakes, then spilled out to form two huge, sea-bound rivers.

They had flown directly southeast from Jarime, then turned south to fly between a gap in the mountains. That night they had camped in a cave furnished with a fireplace and simple beds, stocked with dried food. In the morning she woke to the smell of fried eggs, and was surprised to find that Zeeriz had flown out to raid a few nests at dawn. Obviously the Siyee were not squeamish about eating other winged creatures.

They had flown southeast all morning. Now, as the sun rose to its zenith, her attention was drawn to a long, exposed stretch of rock on the side of a mountain.

'That is the Open,' Zeeriz explained. 'Our main gathering and living place.'

She nodded to show her understanding.

:Juran?

:Auraya.

:I am nearing my destination.

:I will alert the others. They're eager to see it.

Auraya sensed a little of his excitement and smiled. Even Juran, normally so serious, was thrilled by the prospect of seeing the home of the Siyee.

Not long after, a shadow passed over her. Looking up, she saw three Siyee flying above. They stared at her, fascinated. She flew closer to Zeeriz.

'Should I stop and greet them?'

'No,' he replied. 'If you stop to greet every Siyee who comes to gawk at you, we won't reach the Open until nightfall.' He looked up at the newcomers and grinned. 'You're going to attract quite a crowd.'

As they continued on, she occasionally glanced up to smile at the Siyee above. Soon more joined them, and then more, until she felt as if she was being followed by a great, flapping cloud. Drawing closer to the Open, she began to make out Siyee standing on the rocky ground – and they began to notice her. Some leapt into the air to investigate. Others simply remained on the steep slope, watching.

At the back of her mind, Auraya was conscious of her continuing link with Juran. One by one the other White joined that link, and she allowed them to view what she was seeing. The steep rock face that was the Open was like a giant scar on the side of the mountain. Longer than it was wide, it was surrounded by forest. The trees of that forest were enormous, and would no doubt be even more impressive viewed from the ground.

The rock face was uneven, broken into three levels. In the middle section a group of Siyee adults were standing in a line. These, she guessed, were the tribal leaders: the Speakers.

From below a pounding began, drawing her attention to several drums arranged on either side of the Open. Suddenly Siyee began darting in front of her. Seeing that they were wearing identical clothing and were all adolescents, she understood this aerobatic display was a show put on to impress her.

They dived and swooped back and forth, their movements synchronised. The patterns they formed were intricate, yet they managed to keep pace with her as she and Zeeriz descended toward the waiting Speakers.

The drums stopped and the fliers streaked away. Zeeriz swooped down to the ground. As he landed lightly before the Speakers, Auraya dropped down beside him. A woman stepped forward holding a wooden cup in one hand and what looked like a small cake in the other.

'I am Speaker Sirri,' the Siyee said.

'I am Auraya of the White.'

The Siyee offered Auraya the cup and the cake. The cup was full of clear, clean water. Zeeriz had told her of this ritual of welcome. Auraya ate the cake, which was sweet and dense, then drank the water. She handed the cup back to the Speaker. No thanks were to be offered, Zeeriz had told her. All Siyee of all tribes welcomed visitors with food and water, since no Siyee could carry much of their own. Even enemies must give and receive refreshment, but the silence prevented words of thanks sticking in anyone's throat.

Sirri stepped back and spread her arms wide, exposing the membranes of her wings. This, Auraya read from the woman's mind, was a welcome reserved only for those the Siyee trusted. The Siyee trusted the gods, so in turn they trusted the Gods' Chosen.

'Welcome to Si, Auraya of the White.'

Auraya smiled and copied the gesture. 'I am delighted to receive such a warm welcome from you and your people.'

Sirri's expression softened. 'It is an honour to receive one of the Gods' Chosen.'

Auraya made the sign of the circle. 'And it is an honour to be welcomed by the gods' most wondrous and beautiful creation.'

Sirri's eyes widened and her face flushed. Auraya noted the other Speakers exchanging glances. Had she said something wrong? She was not sensing offence from them. She read a mixture of thoughts, and slowly came to understand that, as a people, they wondered about their place in the world. Did their existence have a purpose? Or had their creation simply been a passing folly, an entertainment for the goddess who had made them? Her words had suggested that, perhaps, part of their purpose was simply to be an expression of beauty and wonder.

She would have to be careful here. These people could read meanings into her comments that she didn't intend. She must be sure to explain that she knew no more than they when it came to the gods' deeper purposes. After all, they hadn't even spoken to her since the Choosing Ceremony.

'We have called a Gathering in order to discuss your proposed alliance,' Speaker Sirri told her. 'Messengers have been sent to all tribes asking for their Speakers or representatives to come.

It will take two or three days for everyone to arrive. In the meantime, we have arranged a small welcoming feast to take place tonight in the Speakers' Bower, beginning at sunset.'

Auraya nodded. 'I look forward to it.'

'There are many hours left before sunset. Would you like to rest, or see more of the Open?'

'I would love to see more of your home.'

Sirri smiled and gestured gracefully toward the trees on one side. 'I would be honoured to show you.'

CHAPTER 20

A s the water in the bowl stilled, Emerahl examined her reflection, tilting her head so she could see her scalp. Her natural, youthful hair colour was just beginning to show, though only on close examination. It was a less vivid shade of red than the dye she had applied a few days ago, but she would be able to hide the change by using a weaker dye solution as it grew longer.

She straightened and considered herself. A young woman with dazzling green eyes, lightly speckled pale skin and hair the colour of a sunset looked back at her. Her long tunic was a faded green that might once have matched her eyes, but the neckline was provocative – and would be more so once she put on some weight.

The small smile the girl in the mirror was wearing disappeared and was replaced by a frown.

Yes, I definitely need to regain my curves, she thought. *I'm a scrawny wretch.*

Unfortunately, she had used up almost all her small income from her first customers by renting a room for a few nights. The price of accommodation had increased quite a bit in the last hundred or so years. As had other things. She hadn't realised until it was too late why the fishermen hadn't haggled too fiercely. She had assumed desire for her had made them malleable, when the truth was they had got themselves a bargain.

Clothes had been her first priority, however. Her price for lying with the fishermen had included a dirty old tawl she had spied in the cabin. It had covered her until she could buy herself the tunic and find a room. That night, after cleaning herself up, she had ventured out to replenish her purse.

Customers did not warm to her that evening and she made barely enough money to pay for food and another night's rent. On the third night the man she brought back to her room stared at her white hair and treated her roughly. When he left, he all but reeked of vengeful satisfaction. She wondered if the woman he wanted to hurt knew how much he hated her.

She had skipped a meal so she could buy hair dye. The next night she had no trouble picking up customers. There weren't many red-haired women working the streets of Porin. She was a novelty.

Emerahl ran a comb through her hair one more time, then turned toward the door. She silently cursed the priest who had chased her from her home, then straightened her back and left.

She did not have to travel far. Her accommodation was situated in an alley off Main Street, the main thoroughfare of the low end of town. Anything could be bought or arranged here: whores, black-market goods, poison, a new identity, someone else's possessions, someone else's life. Competition was fierce among the whores and her presence had been quickly noted and challenged. As Emerahl took her place at the alley corner, she looked for now-familiar hostile faces. The dark-skinned twins standing just past the other corner of the alley had tried to intimidate her into leaving, but a small demonstration of her Gifts had convinced them to leave her alone. The sharp-nosed girl across the road had attempted to befriend her, but

Emerahl had turned her away. She was not going to be here long enough to need friends, and did not intend to share her customers or income with another.

A chill rain began to fall. Emerahl drew magic and shaped it into a barrier over her head. She noted how the dark twins huddled close under a window awning. One cupped her hands and red light began to spill from between her fingers. The other twin wrapped her hands around her sister's.

Across the street, the sharp-nosed girl quickly became soaked, turning her from a young woman into a bedraggled child. To Emerahl's amusement, the girl's clinging wet clothes attracted a customer. She nodded to herself as the pair disappeared. Though she did not want the girl's friendship, she had enough fellow-feeling for these street whores that seeing them courting illness bothered her.

The rain became heavier. Pedestrians grew fewer, and most barely spared the street girls a glance. Emerahl watched as a pair of young men swaggered down the opposite side of the road. One looked up at her, then nudged his companion with an elbow. The other began to look in her direction, but as he was about to see her something blocked their view.

Emerahl frowned at the covered platten that had pulled up in front of her. Then she saw the man looking at her from behind an opening in the cover. Middle-aged, she noted, but well dressed. She smiled. 'Greetings,' she said. 'Are you looking for something?'

His eyes narrowed and a wry smile curled his lips. 'Indeed I am.'

She then sauntered up to the opening.

'Something I can help you with?' she murmured.

'Perhaps,' he said. 'I was looking for a little company. Some stimulating conversation.'

'I can offer you stimulating *and* conversation,' she replied.

299

He laughed, then his eyes strayed to the magical shield above her.

'A useful Gift.'

'I have many useful Gifts,' she said slyly. 'Some are useful to me, some may be useful to you.'

His eyes narrowed, though whether at the warning or invitation she wasn't sure. 'What is your name?'

'Emmea.'

The opening in the platten cover widened. 'Get in, Emmea.'

'That will cost you at least—'

'Get in, and we'll negotiate out of the rain.'

She hesitated, then shrugged and climbed inside. If the price was too low, or he proved to be troublesome, she could easily use her Gifts to break free. All she would risk was a walk in the rain and, as she settled onto the soft cushions piled upon the seat beside him and noted the gold rings that graced her customer's fingers, she knew that was a risk worth taking.

The man called out and the plattern jerked into motion. It travelled slowly. Emerahl eyed her customer. He stared back at her.

'Thirty ren,' he said. She felt her heart skip. Generous. Perhaps he could be pushed further. She feigned disdain.

'Fifty.'

He pursed his lips. She began undoing the ties on the front of her tunic. His eyes followed every movement of her fingers.

'Thirty-five,' he offered.

She snorted softly. 'Forty-five.'

He smiled as she spread open the cloth of her tunic, revealing the length of her body. She lay back on the cushions and saw the desire in his eyes intensify as she ran her hands down her body, from her small breasts to the fine triangle of red hairs at her groin.

He breathed deeply, then met her eyes.

'Heybrin will not protect you from disease.'

So he had noticed the smell of the herb. She smiled thinly. 'I know, but men don't believe me when I tell them my Gifts can.'

The corner of his lip twitched. 'I do. How does forty sound?'

'Forty it is, then,' she agreed, sliding across the seat and reaching for the fastening of his finely tailored pants.

He leaned forward and ran the tip of his tongue down her neck to her nipples, and his fingers slid down into her pubic hair, caressing. She smiled and pretended to be aroused by this, hoping he wasn't thinking she would forgo the fee if he gave a little pleasure in return.

She turned her attention to his body, and soon he was more interested in his own pleasure. Once he was inside her, she let the instincts of her body keep time with his movements and focused her mind on his. Emotion, mostly lust, came to her like drifts of smoke. She was getting better at sensing it.

His movements became more urgent, then he sighed into a climax. Like most men, he drew away after only a moment's pause. She sighed and relaxed against the cushions. *This is definitely better than a hard brick wall against my back.*

When she looked up at him, he was regarding her curiously.

'Why is a beautiful young woman like yourself working the streets, Emmea?'

She managed to stop herself looking at him as if he was an idiot.

'Money.'

'Yes, of course. But what of your parents?'

'They threw me out.'

His eyebrows rose. 'What did you do?'

'You mean who – "Who did I do?"' she said lightly. 'Or who didn't I do? I guess I was meant for this work.'

301

'Do you enjoy it?'

She regarded him coolly. Why all the questions? 'Most of the time,' she lied.

He smiled. 'How did you learn about heybrin?'

She considered the motion of the platten. It was still moving slowly. They couldn't have gone far, but the more he talked the further they travelled from Main Street. Was he trying to intimidate her into forgoing her fee for the sake of escaping him? Well, it wasn't going to work.

'I . . . my grandmother knew a lot about herbs and magic. She taught me. Mother said she shouldn't have taught me how to stop babies until I was married, but . . .' Emerahl smiled wryly. 'My grandi knew me better.'

'My grandmother used to say people will always have vices, so you may as well profit from them.' He frowned. 'My father is the opposite. Very moral. He'd hatè to see me now. He took our money out of her "immoral ventures" and put it all into the eastern mountains. We've made a lot of money out of rare woods and mining.'

Suddenly she understood what was going on. He was the kind of customer who liked to talk. Well, he *had* mentioned wanting stimulating conversation. She may as well play along. If she humoured him she might learn something – and if she proved a good listener he might become a regular customer.

'Sounds like he made the right decision, then,' she said.

He grimaced. 'Perhaps. Perhaps not. The searches at the gates have slowed traffic and we've lost custom because of it. I don't know why they bother. If a priest with mind-reading Gifts can't find this sorceress, who can? Now there are rumours the White are going to ally with the Siyee, who want the land we own.'

'The White?'

'Yes. The Siyee sent ambassadors to the White Tower.

Apparently one of the White has left to visit Si. The newest one. I guess it's too much to hope that she'll mess it up out of inexperience.'

Emerahl shook her head. 'Who are the White?'

He turned to stare at her. 'You don't know? How can you not know?'

Something in his tone told her that she had revealed herself ignorant in a matter that every modern man and woman knew well. She shrugged. 'My home is remote. We didn't even have a priest.'

His eyebrows rose. 'Well, then. No wonder you ran away.'

Ran away? She hadn't said that, but perhaps he had sensed in her manner that she was lying and guessed at the reason. Running away was a likely story for a young woman on the streets.

'The White are the highest of the Circlian priests and priestesses,' he explained. 'The Gods' Chosen. Juran is the first, then Dyara, Mairae, Rian, and now Auraya.'

'Ah, the Gods' Chosen.' Emerahl hoped she had managed to hide her shock. *How could Juran still be alive?* The answer was obvious. *Because the gods want him to be.* She nodded to herself. Most likely these other White were long-lived, too. What was this White Tower? She suddenly remembered the tower dream that still occasionally bothered her. Was this the tower?

'You look . . . Did that make sense?'

She looked at the man sitting beside her and nodded. 'Yes, it jogged my memory. Grandi taught me something like that, but I'd forgotten most of it.' She looked at him. 'Can you tell me more?'

He smiled, then shook his head sadly. 'I must return to my home. First I will take you back to yours.' He called instructions to the driver and the platten began to rock more rapidly. After a few minutes it slowed to a halt.

303

Reaching into his tunic, he drew out a wallet and silently counted out small copper coins.

'Fifty ren,' he said, handing them to her.

She hesitated. 'But . . .'

'I know. We agreed on forty. You're worth more than that, Emmea.'

She smiled, then impulsively leaned forward and kissed him on the lips. A brightness flared in his eyes and she felt his hand brush against her waist as she climbed out of the platten.

He'll be back, she thought with certainty. *I knew I wouldn't be here long.*

She noted that the twins had disappeared. Turning around, she waved at her night's investment as the platten drew away. Then, with fifty ren tucked into her purse, she hurried down the alley to her room.

Tryss woke several times during the night. Each time he opened his eyes he saw only darkness. Finally, he blinked sleep away to see the palest light filtering through the walls of his parents' bower.

He rose and dressed quietly, strapping his tools to his waist. As an afterthought, he grabbed a piece of bread on the way out and by the time he had reached the Open all that was left was the burned crust, which he tossed aside. He stretched and warmed up carefully. If he was to test his new harness today, he did not want pulled muscles hampering his movements. As he ran through the exercises, he looked to the northern edge of the Open, but the White priestess's bower was hidden within the shadows of the trees.

The landwalker's presence had stirred the Siyee into a state of excitement and suspense. Everyone talked about her and the alliance offer all the time. Tryss was half sick of the subject, particularly because those people most excited by this visit by the Gods' Chosen were those who had scoffed loudest when they heard of his harness. The people who did not believe the Siyee had anything to offer the White in return for their protection.

That's because they're the least intelligent of us, Drilli had said when he voiced this observation.

He smiled at the memory, then leapt into the air. Cold wind rushed over his face and chilled the membrane of his wings. Winter was drawing ever closer. Snow already dusted the highest peaks. Many of the forest trees had lost their leaves, revealing herds of the animals he intended to hunt.

My family won't go hungry this year, he told himself.

It took him an hour to get to the cave where he now stored his new harness. He came to it by a roundabout route which would hopefully confuse anyone who might try to follow. His cousins were still gloating over their act of spite, but neither had harassed him since. His father had said something about the pair being busy with a task Speaker Sirri had set them.

Landing before the cave, Tryss hurried inside. Every time he entered and found all as it had been when he left it, he felt a surge of relief.

Not this time. A figure stood beside the harness. He froze in alarm, then felt a mix of relief and anxiety as he saw that it was Speaker Sirri.

The leader of his tribe smiled at him.

'Is it finished?'

Tryss glanced at the harness. 'Almost.'

The smile faded. 'So you haven't tested it yet.'

'No.'

She looked at him thoughtfully, then beckoned.

'Sit with me, Tryss. I want to talk to you.'

As she dropped into a squat, Tryss moved to the other side of the harness and folded himself down. He watched her closely. She looked into the distance, then turned back to regard him.

'Do you think you could have this finished and working by tomorrow night?'

Tomorrow night was the night of the Gathering. The White priestess would address them. Tryss felt his pulse quicken.

'Maybe.'

'I need a definite "yes" or "no".'

He took a deep breath. 'Yes.'

She nodded. 'Are you willing to risk demonstrating it at a Gathering this important?'

His heart was racing now. 'Yes.'

She nodded again. 'Then I will arrange for it to be part of the meeting. It should be timed well, if you are to impress everyone.'

'I'd be happy just to convince a few people,' he muttered.

She laughed. 'Ah, but we have to convince everyone.'

'Some will never believe in it.'

She tilted her head to one side. 'Do you realise that part of the reason they will not open their minds is because they fear you are right?'

He frowned. 'Why? If I'm right, they can hunt. And fight.'

'And go to war. If we go to war, many of us will never return, even if the fight is won. We are not as numerous as landwalkers and do not produce as many healthy children. A victory for the White may be the final defeat for the Siyee.'

Tryss felt himself turn cold as her words sank in. If his invention enabled Siyee to go to war, and that led to the end of the Siyee, then he would be responsible for his people's demise.

'But if we can hunt and grow crops we will be stronger,' he said slowly, thinking aloud. 'We will have more healthy children. If we can defend ourselves from invaders, more of us will live to have children. When we go to war we must attack from far enough away that the enemy's arrows can't reach us. None of us have to die.'

Sirri chuckled. 'If only that were true. We have two paths before us. Both have a price. It may be that the price is the same.' She rose. 'Come to my bower late tonight and we will discuss the timing and form of your demonstration.'

'I will.' He stood up. 'Thank you, Speaker Sirri.'

'If this works, all of the Siyee will thank you, Tryss.' She paused, then winked. 'Not to put any pressure on you, of course.'

Then she strode out of the cave and leapt into the sky, leaving Tryss with the nagging feeling she had just done him a favour he might come to regret.

CHAPTER 21

A s the black-clothed, brown-skinned landwalker climbed carefully down the rock face, Yzzi smothered a laugh. The woman moved slowly and awkwardly, choosing her foot- and hand-holds carefully. Yet there was a surety in the way the woman climbed that suggested she was well practised at this. It reminded Yzzi of a boy in her tribe who had been born without a membrane between his arms and body. He could not fly, but he could walk further and leap higher than any normal Siyee. At first his efforts had been comical and pitiful, but she and the other children came to respect him for his determination to be as mobile as possible.

The woman had reached the bottom of the slope and paused at a thin stream to drink. She would have to be familiar with climbing, Yzzi decided, since she must have crossed plenty of terrain like this to get so far into Siyee lands.

Yzzi shifted her weight from one leg to another, keeping her balance easily on the branch. The woman rose, then looked up . . . directly into Yzzi's eyes. A chill ran down Yzzi's spine, but she did not move. It was possible the woman hadn't seen her. She might be hidden by the foliage.

'Hello,' the stranger called.

Yzzi's heart stopped. *She's seen me! What do I do?*

'Don't be afraid,' the woman said. 'I will not hurt you.'

It took a moment before Yzzi made sense of the words. The woman spoke the Siyee language haltingly and the pitch of her whistles was a little off. Yzzi considered the stranger. Should she talk to the woman? Her father had told her that land-walkers could not be trusted, but he had changed his mind when the White priestess visited their tribe this morning.

'Will you come down and talk to me?'

Yzzi shifted her weight again, then came to a decision. She would talk, but she would do so from where she was.

'I'm Yzzi. Who are you?'

The woman's smile widened. 'I'm Genza.'

'Why are you in Si?'

'To see what's here. Why don't you come down? I can barely see you.'

Once again, Yzzi hesitated. The landwalker was so large. She cast about, looking for a place she might perch that was closer to the woman, but from which she could fly away easily. A ledge on the steep slope the woman had just climbed down looked good enough. Diving from the branch, she swooped down and landed neatly on her new perch.

She turned to regard the landwalker. The woman was still smiling.

'You're so pretty,' she murmured.

Yzzi felt a flush of pleasure.

'You're strange,' she blurted. 'But in a good way.'

The woman laughed.

'Would you pass on a message from me to your leader?'

Yzzi straightened. Passing on messages was important, and children weren't often given important messages to deliver. 'All right.'

The woman took a few steps closer and looked deep into Yzzi's eyes.

'I want you to tell them that I am sorry about the harm the birds did. It was not meant to happen. They were trying to protect me and I did not realise what was happening until it was too late. I came here to see if we could be friends. Will you remember all of that, Yzzi?'

Yzzi nodded.

'Then repeat it back to me now, so I can see how well you'll—'

A distant whistle snatched Yzzi's attention away. She looked up and exclaimed as a large group of Siyee flew overhead. At the centre was a white-clad figure conspicuous among the rest for its size and winglessness.

The White priestess, Yzzi thought. She turned back to see Genza crouching beneath the fronds of a large felfea tree. The woman's expression was terrible – wavering between anger and fear.

'How long has *she* been here?' she snarled.

'A few days,' Yzzi replied. 'She's nice. You should come and meet her. She'll want to be your friend, too.'

Genza straightened and her expression softened as she looked at Yzzi. She muttered a few strange words Yzzi didn't understand, then sighed. 'Can you tell your tribe leader one more thing, Yzzi?'

Yzzi nodded.

'Tell your leader that if the Siyee ally themselves with the heathen Circlians, they will gain an enemy more powerful. Now I know she is here, I will not stay.'

'You don't want to meet the Speakers?'

'Not while she is here.'

'But you came so far! It can't have been easy.'

Genza grimaced. 'No.' She sighed, then looked at Yzzi hopefully. 'You wouldn't happen to know of an easy way back to the coast?'

Yzzi grinned. 'I haven't been that far, but I'll help you as much as I can.'

Genza smiled with warm gratitude. 'Thank you, Yzzi. I hope one day we'll meet again and I can return the favour.'

As Danjin entered Auraya's rooms, he heard a shrill cry of joy. 'Daaaa-nin!'

He immediately ducked and looked up. The ceiling was bare. He cast about, searching for the owner of the voice. A grey blur streaked across the room and leapt up into his arms.

'Hello, Mischief,' he replied.

The veez gazed up at Danjin, blinking adoringly. Mischief had taken quite a liking to Danjin now that the adviser, Auraya's servants and the occasional visit from Mairae and Stardust were the only company he had. Auraya's pet also found it amusing to drop onto Danjin's head from the ceiling, a trick that was only slightly less unnerving than the view from the windows.

Danjin scratched the veez's head and spoke to it for a while, but soon his thoughts returned to the discoveries he had made over the last few days. He had visited friends and acquaintances all over the city, in high and low places. What he'd heard had confirmed his worst fears. The Pentadrians of the southern continent were raising an army.

Military training was a part of their cult and he had hoped his brother and father had come to the wrong conclusions about the trade in weapons. However, both the retired sailor Danjin had befriended during his early years of travelling and the Dunwayan ambassador had told him of active recruitment of soldiers and smiths within Mur, Avven and Dekkar, the lands of the southern continent.

Mischief squirmed out of Danjin's arms, clearly dissatisfied with the amount of attention he was getting. He jumped up onto a chair and watched as Danjin began pacing, the veez's small, pointy head moving back and forth.

Was Northern Ithania the Pentadrians' target? *Of course it is.* Other landmasses lay to the northeast and west, but they were so far away as to be almost regarded as legend. If the Pentadrians had their sights set on conquering some other place, the closest was the continent to their north.

:What's wrong, Danjin?

He let out a gasp of relief.

:Auraya! At last!

:It's nice to be missed, but that's clearly not what's bothering you. What is this about Pentadrians conquering Ithania?

He quickly related what he had learned.

:I see. So this is what people are saying. I don't think the possibility of war will remain a secret much longer.

:You knew all this?

:Yes and no. We've only just begun receiving reliable reports of what's going on in the south. They're the observations of people who are being careful not to be noticed. The sort of information you have unearthed – purchases of materials and a change in their military behaviour – are new to me. Tell Juran what you have learned. It will help him see the bigger picture.

:I will. How is your work in Si going?

:It's a fascinating place. I can't wait to tell you all about it. These people have such gentle natures. I was expecting some kind of internal conflict – like the ancient grudges between the Dunwayan clans – but there's only a mild sort of competition between tribes that they channel into aerial contests. They look for matches between young men and women of different tribes, and marry quite young, which encourages adolescents to mature quickly. Have you heard from Leiard at all?

Danjin blinked in surprise at the sudden change of subject.
:No. Not once since you left.

312

:Could you . . . could you visit him? Just to let him know I haven't completely forgotten about him.

:I'll do it tomorrow.

:Thank you. And how is . . . Ah, here's Speaker Sirri. I will talk to you again soon.

The sense of her presence faded, then suddenly returned.

:And give Mischief an extra scratch for me.

:I will.

Then she was gone. Danjin moved to the chair, crouched and scratched the veez's head.

'There, that's from your mistress.'

Mischief closed his eyes, his pointy face a picture of bliss.

Danjin sighed. *If only I was so easily soothed*, he thought. *Auraya knows of the Pentadrian army, but that doesn't make it any less frightening. I just have to hope that the White are doing all they can to prevent a war – or at least to win if it is unavoidable.*

'Sorry, Mischief,' he said to the veez. 'I must leave you. I need to tell Juran what I know.'

He gave Mischief one last scratch, then rose and hurried from the room.

After Speaker Sirri left, Auraya slowly walked around the bower the Siyee had made her. It was a marvellous creation, so simple yet so beautiful. They had made hers twice the size of a normal bower, measuring it against the landwalker named Gremmer who had delivered the offer of an alliance to them.

It was dome-shaped, made of long, flexible supports, with one end buried in the ground and the other secured against the trunk of an immense tree. A thin membrane stretched between the supports. Auraya could not guess if it was of animal or plant origin. During the day, light filtered through, filling the room with a warm glow. Membranes had also been stretched between the outer frame and a pole sunk into the ground near the trunk of the tree, dividing the house into three rooms. She ran her fingers lightly over the walls and their flexible supports, then turned to regard the simple furniture.

Chairs made of wooden frames with woven material slung between filled the main room. A single slab of rock lay in the centre of the floor with a depression in the centre for cooking in. Most Siyee families had a member with enough magical ability to learn the Gift of heating stone. The bed in the second room was a length of material slung between a sturdy support wedged into the floor and a loop around the trunk at the centre of the room. The blankets on the bed were woven from the fine down of a small domestic animal and were deliciously soft. They beckoned to her. It was late. Tomorrow would bring a new challenge: speaking to the Siyee at their Gathering.

Stripping off her white circ she changed into a simple tunic she had brought for sleeping in. Since leaving Jarime she hadn't bothered trying to dress her hair in the typically elaborate Hanian fashion, since all her hard work was soon blown undone when she was flying. Instead she plaited it into a single tail, which she now undid.

She managed to get into her sling bed without too much trouble. After arranging the cushions and blankets comfortably, she relaxed and let her thoughts wander. Time passed and sleep would not come. Danjin's news had only added to her disquiet over the communication she'd had with Juran earlier that day. Every day it seemed more likely that Northern Ithania was facing the threat of war with the Pentadrians. And Juran had brought Mirae back from Somrey for fear she was vulnerable to an attack by one of the black sorcerers.

And here I am, trying to convince the Siyee to ally with us. If they do and war comes, they will have to join us in the fight. They are not a strong or robust people. How can I ask them to fight when it is likely some of them will die as a consequence?

She sighed and shifted a little. It would be unfair to the Siyee to keep the possibility of war from them until after they made their decision. Telling them of it might dissuade them from an alliance with the White, however. She would have to make them see that turning down the alliance and avoiding involvement in a war would not save them from the Pentadrians. If the Toren settlers could present a threat to them, so could invaders.

The Siyee might decide to take that risk. After all, the Pentadrians might not invade Northern Ithania. However, she couldn't gamble that war wouldn't come and that she didn't need to warm the Siyee. Even learning that she had kept the *possibility* of war from them would anger them.

It almost seems as if the Pentadrians have spread the idea they're planning a war in order to dissuade anyone from allying with the White, she thought. Then she shook her head. *That is too devious to be true. The Pentadrians haven't even visited Si. They've shown no signs of wanting the Siyee, who worship Huan, as allies.*

She shifted again, her sling bed rocking with the movement.

I will have to tell the Siyee of the threat of war eventually, she thought. *If I choose the right time, perhaps I can still convince them the alliance is beneficial to them. After all, with the gods on our side we can't lose.*

Holding onto that thought, she finally surrendered to the call of sleep.

:*Auraya.*

The voice was a whisper in her mind.

:*Auraya.*

This time it was stronger. She struggled awake and blinked at the darkened room. It was empty, and when she searched for minds, she found none close by. Had it been a mental call?

No, it had the feel of a dream about it, she decided. *I think I dreamed that someone called me.* She closed her eyes. Time stretched out, and she forgot about the dream.

:Auraya.

She felt herself rising toward consciousness, like floating up to the surface of water. Her awareness of the caller's mind faded. She opened her eyes, but did not bother searching for the speaker. He was limited to the dream.

He? She felt her heart skip a beat. Who else would be calling for her in a dream but Leiard?

Abruptly, Auraya was wide awake, her heart racing. *Should I answer? If I did would we be dream-linking? Dream-linking is a crime.*

So is using a Dreamweaver's services, she thought. *A ridiculous law. I want to know what dream-linking is. What better way than to join one?*

But if I engage in a dream link, I will be breaking a law. And so will he.

It's not as if I'm a helpless victim. I could make him stop at any time.

Or could I?

She lay awake for some time. Part of her longed to speak to Leiard, but another hesitated to. Even if she wanted to, she was too *awake* now. She doubted she would fall asleep again easily.

Some time later she heard her name called and knew simultaneously that she *had* managed to fall asleep, and that she *had* to talk to Leiard.

:Leiard? she ventured.

A sense of personality grew stronger, flowing around her like thick, sweet smoke. It was Leiard and yet it was not. It was the man she had glimpsed on her last night in Jarime. The warm, passionate man hidden beneath the dignified Dreamweaver exterior.

:I cannot be anything but myself in this state, he told her.

:Nor can I, I am guessing, she replied.

:No. Here you can show the truth, or hide it, but not lie.

:So this is a dream link?

:It is. Do you forgive me this? I only wished to be with you in some way.

:I forgive you. But do you forgive me?

:For what?

:For that night we . . .

Memories flashed through her mind, more vivid than they were when she was conscious. She not only saw their limbs entangled, but felt the slide of skin against skin. From Leiard came amusement and a deep affection.

:What is there to forgive?

More memories washed over her, this time from a different vantage point. What this revealed was startling. To experience pleasure from his point of view . . .

:We both wanted it. I think that was clear, he said.

:What is happening? she asked. *These memories are so vivid.*

:They always are, in the dream state.

:I can touch, taste . . .

:Dreams are powerful. They can bring solace to the grieving, confidence to the weak—

:Justice to the wrongdoer?

:Once, yes, they had that role. No longer is it so. Dream links still allow loved ones to meet when they are parted. They are the Dreamweavers' alternative to the priest ring.

:I would have given you a ring, but I didn't think you'd accept it.

:Do you accept this? We are breaking a law.

She paused.

:Yes. We must talk. What we did – wonderful though it was – will have consequences.

317

:I know.

:I should not have invited you.

:I should not have accepted.

:Not that I regret it.

:Nor I.

:But if people find out . . . I would not like this to cause you harm — or your people.

:Nor I.

She hesitated, then made herself say what she ought to say.

:We won't do it again.

:No.

They both fell silent.

:You're right, she said. *We can't lie in this place.*

He reached out to touch her face.

:But we can be ourselves.

She shivered at his touch. It awoke more memories.

:I wish you were here.

:So do I. I am, in one form at least. Memories, as I said before, are more vivid in the dream state. Are there any you wish to relive?

She smiled.

:Just a few.

CHAPTER 22

The sun was a bright ball softened by the mist shrouding the city. Few people were about, and those who were hesitated before they passed Leiard, no doubt wondering what a Dreamweaver was doing wandering through the docks on such a morning.

What he was doing was thinking. Remembering dreams of remembering . . . and feeling guilty about them.

He had decided days ago that he would not reach out to her in dreams, but last night his subconscious had decided otherwise. By the time he had realised what he was doing, it was too late. She had answered him.

Even then, he should have had the will to stop, but Auraya had embraced the dream link so naturally and completely. She was impossible to deny, and the night's pleasures had been too good to resist.

She has a good imagination, that one, a voice in his mind murmured. *It is a pity she's a tool of the gods.*

Leiard frowned. *She is more than just a tool.*

No? Do you think that if the gods ordered her to kill you, she'd refuse?

Yes.

You are a fool.

319

Leiard stopped and looked out over the water. Ships swayed in the water, ghostly in the mist.

I am a fool, he agreed.

Well, it's been a while.

Leiard decided to ignore that. *I shouldn't have done it*, he thought. *We broke the law.*

A stupid law.

A law nonetheless. A law that is punishable by death.

I doubt she'll be punished. As for you . . . once again, you were clever enough to ensure it was her decision. She'll blame herself for encouraging you to break that law, if she has any conscience.

It wasn't her fault.

No? So you think you're so charming she lost all will and couldn't resist you?

Oh, be quiet! Leiard scowled and crossed his arms. This was ridiculous. He was arguing with a memory of Mirar. Which was happening more often now. He hadn't been linking with Jayim for fear of the boy learning of his night with Auraya, but Arleej had said he must in order to regain his sense of identity. Was this why Mirar's personality had become so . . . so . . .

Protective? Because I know you and Auraya plan to sneak away to secret locations in the city to rut yourselves silly once she gets back. Because you're a Dreamweaver, and when your affair is discovered my people will pay the price.

They won't discover it, Leiard replied. *Not if the other White never get a chance to read my mind. I will have to give up the role of adviser.*

Which will make them suspicious. They'll want to question you. To ask why.

I'll send a message. I'll tell them I need more time to train Jayim.

A likely story.

They won't spare me a second thought. I'm just an ordinary

Dreamweaver. They'll probably be relieved to get rid of me. They'll—

'Leiard?'

The voice came from close by. Leiard blinked as he realised he was at the end of a pier. He turned to see Jayim standing behind him.

'Jayim?' he said. 'What are you doing here?'

The boy's forehead crinkled. 'Looking for you.' He glanced from side to side. 'Who were you talking to?'

Leiard stared at his student. Talking? He swallowed and realised his throat did feel as it did when he had been speaking for some time.

'Nobody,' he said, hoping that he didn't look as disturbed as he felt. He shrugged. 'Just reciting formulas aloud.'

Jayim nodded, accepting Leiard's explanation. 'Are we going to have lessons today?'

Leiard looked out at the ships. The fog was thinner now, rising in drifts. It was impossible to tell how long he had been standing here. A few hours, from the position of the sun.

'Yes. More cures, I think. Yes, you can never know too many by heart.'

Jayim grimaced. 'No links?'

Leiard shook his head. 'Not yet.'

Emerahl was dragged, protesting, from the depths of sleep by a persistent hammering. Reaching a state of befuddled awareness, she recognised the sound as that of a fist making contact with a door. She opened her eyes and muttered a curse. The one advantage of staying up late and sleeping all morning was that she did not have the tower dream, but occasionally the landlord came early for the rent.

'I hear you,' she called. 'I'm coming.'

With an effort, she pushed herself upright. Immediately she felt the cloying ropes of sleep loosen. She blinked and rubbed her eyes until they remained open, yawned several times, then, throwing on her dirty old tawl, went to the door.

As soon as the latch clicked the door swung inward. Emerahl stumbled back, gathering magic quickly to form an invisible shield. The intruder was a large middle-aged woman dressed in fine clothing. Behind her stood two broad-shouldered men, obviously hired guards.

No feeling of violent intent came from this rich stranger and her guards, only curiosity and the arrogance of people with wealth or power. Emerahl stared at the woman.

'Who are you?' she demanded.

The woman ignored the question. She glanced around the room, eyebrows rising with disdain, then gave Emerahl an assessing look. 'So you're the whore Panilo's discovered.' She pursed her lips. 'Take off the tawl.'

Emerahl made no move to obey. She met the woman's eyes levelly. 'Who are you?' she repeated.

The stranger crossed her arms and thrust out her generous bosom. 'I am Rozea Peporan.'

She obviously expected Emerahl to know the name. After a short silence, the woman frowned and uncrossed her arms, placing her hands on her hips instead.

'I own and run the richest brothel in Porin.'

A brothel? Opportunity comes knocking quickly in Toren. Or hammering, as it was.

'Is that so?' Emerahl said.

'Yes.'

Emerahl put a knuckle to her lips. 'Panilo is the trader who bought my services the last few nights.'

'That's right. He's a regular customer. At least he was until recently. He has an eye for quality so I'm always suspicious if my spies tell me he's been visiting Main Street.'

'So you're here to tell me to move on, then?'

322

Rozea smiled, but her eyes remained cold. 'That depends. Take off your tawl. *And* your shift.'

Emerahl shrugged out of the garments and tossed them on the bed, then drew her shoulders back and turned to display her naked body. She didn't have to strain her senses to detect the guards' interest. The way the woman examined her body was impersonal and calculating. Emerahl turned full circle and tossed her head.

'Skinny,' Rozea said. 'Good bones. I can always work with good bones. No scars . . . What is your natural hair colour?'

'Red.'

'Then why dye it?'

'To make it redder. So I stand out.'

'It looks cheap. My establishment isn't cheap. My girls can strip it back and redye it a natural shade. Were any of your customers diseased?'

'No.'

'You?'

'No.'

'Good. Get dressed.'

Emerahl moved to her chair, where she had draped her green tunic after washing and drying it last night. 'What makes you think I want to work in your establishment?' she asked as she donned it.

'Safety. A clean room. Better clients. Better money.'

'I have Gifts. I can protect myself,' she stated. She gave Rozea a sidelong look. 'What kind of money are we talking about?'

Rozea chuckled. 'You'll earn no more than fifty ren to start with.'

Emerahl shrugged. 'Panilo paid me that. I want a hundred.'

'Sixty, with new clothes and some jewellery.'

'Eighty.'

323

'Sixty,' Rozea said firmly. 'No more.'

Emerahl sat on the edge of the bed and pretended to consider. 'No rough customers. I hear people like you let rich men get nasty with their girls if they offer enough money. Not with me. I have Gifts. If they try anything, I'll kill them.'

The woman's eyes narrowed, then she shrugged. 'No rough types, then. Are we agreed?'

'And no diseased ones. No money's worth sickness.'

Rozea smiled. 'I do my best to keep my girls safe,' she said proudly. 'Customers are encouraged to bathe beforehand, which gives us the opportunity to examine them. Any customers known to be diseased are banned from the house. All girls are given cleansing herbals. If you are Gifted enough, there are other methods you can be taught.' She gave Emerahl a lofty look. 'We have a reputation to uphold as the cleanest brothel in Porin.'

Emerahl nodded, impressed. 'Sounds reasonable. I'll give it a try.'

'Fetch your things, then. I have a platten waiting.'

Looking around, Emerahl recalled that her purse was in a pocket of the tunic and the sea bell was sewn into her sleeve. She rose and walked to the door. Rozea glanced at the discarded tawl and shift, then smiled and led her out.

'We tell our customers our girls are from good families that fell on hard times,' Rozea said as they descended the stairs. 'You have an old-fashioned way of talking which will support that illusion. You'll be taught all the social graces of high society. If you prove an apt student we'll teach you a language or two.'

Emerahl smiled wryly. 'You'll find I'm a fast learner.'

'Good. Can you read?'

'A little.' She hoped she was right. If the language had changed over a century, how much had writing changed?

324

'Write?'

'A little.'

'Sing?'

'Well enough to frighten birds from the crops.'

Rozea laughed quietly. 'No singing, then. What about dancing?'

'No.' Which was probably true. It had been a long time.

'What is your name?'

'Emmea.'

'Not any longer. Your new name is Jade.'

'Jade.' Emerahl shrugged. 'The eyes, right?'

'Of course. They are your best feature at the moment. My girls will teach you how to enhance your better features and hide your worst by selecting clothing, modifying your posture and, as a last resort, applying paint.'

Reaching the bottom of the stairs, Rozea pushed through the door. A plattern waited in the alley. The two guards climbed onto the seat next to the driver. Rozea gestured for Emerahl to join her inside. Emerahl glanced to either side as she climbed in. Main Street was empty but for a few sleeping beggars. Nobody was going to witness her 'disappearance'. Not even her landlord, which wasn't a bad thing.

At an order from the driver, the arem pulling the plattern started forward, carrying Emerahl away. *A brothel*, she thought. *Are the priests more or less likely to find me there? Probably neither. At least it will be more comfortable. It might even be profitable.*

325

CHAPTER 23

The sky was the blue-black of early evening. Stars blinked and shivered all around, but the cause of their disturbance was only visible when looking west, where hundreds of winged forms could be made out against a sky still aglow from the sunset.

These forms glided down to the Open, to the level area at the middle of the rocky slope known as the Flat. Fires had been lit in a large circle and their light set the faces of the Siyee aglow.

Auraya recognised many of these faces now. She had talked to Siyee of all ages, positions and tribes. Not far from her stood the trapper of the Snake River tribe who had described how his people had been driven from their fertile valleys by Toren settlers. Further away stood the old matriarch of the Fire Mountain tribe who had shown Auraya the forges her people used to make arrowheads and knives from the abundant mineral deposits in their homeland. Landing now were three young men from the Temple Mountain tribe who had approached her to ask what they must learn to become priests.

'There has never been a Gathering this large in my lifetime,' Speaker Dryss murmured to her, 'and I have attended them all.'

She turned to regard the old man. 'Speaker Sirri explained to me that only Speakers or those chosen to represent them are required to attend a Gathering. I am not surprised more have come, however. What you decide tonight could change your way of life. If I was Siyee, I'd want to be here to hear their decision.'

'True, but I'm sure a few are here just to catch a glimpse of the Gods' Chosen,' he replied, chuckling.

She smiled. 'Your people have been welcoming, Speaker Dryss. I confess I'm half in love with this place, and wish I did not have to leave.'

His eyebrows rose. 'You do not miss the comforts of your home?'

'A little,' she admitted. 'I miss hot baths, mostly. And my friends.'

He opened his mouth to reply, but at that moment Speaker Sirri turned to the line of Speakers.

'It is time, I think. If we wait for stragglers, the night will end before we do.'

The others nodded in agreement. As Sirri stepped up onto Speakers' Rock the Siyee below stopped talking and looked up expectantly.

Sirri lifted her arms. 'People of the mountains. Tribes of the Siyee. We, the Speakers, have called you here tonight to hear the words of Auraya of the White, one of the Gods' Chosen. As you know, she has come to us to discuss an alliance between Siyee and the Circlians. Tonight we will hear her words and voice our thoughts. In seven days we will gather again to make our decision.'

Sirri turned and looked at Auraya expectantly. Stepping forward to stand beside the woman, Auraya looked down at the Siyee people. Since she had arrived she hadn't needed to read their minds to discover their doubts and hopes. They had

327

spoken of them openly. Now she let her mind skim over theirs.

They were hesitant, sure that there would be a penalty whether they agreed to an alliance or not. They were a timid people, who rarely resorted to violence. They were also a proud people. While they did not want to go to war, where it was likely some would be killed, if they did they wanted to be seen as valuable and effective. It was this pride that she must appeal to now.

'People of Si, Huan's creation, I have come to your land at your invitation to learn about you, to tell you something of my own people and to explore the possibility of an alliance forming between us.

'I have learned much about you and have come to admire you for your tenacity and peaceful ways. I find myself no longer unbiased – I would dearly love for there to be a link between my people and yours. I am dismayed by the Siyee deaths at the hands of landwalkers. I can also see many ways we may enrich each other's lives through trade and an exchange of knowledge. I find myself thinking, selfishly, that an alliance would be a wonderful excuse to neglect my duties as a White and visit Si more often than needed.'

This brought smiles to many faces. She paused, then made her expression serious.

'An alliance requires agreement on several issues, and the first I will address is war. If we, the White, have an agreement with you to protect your lands, we can end this incursion of settlers without bloodshed by demanding the King of Toren take action to stop it. For such assistance, we ask for your promise of help in return, should we and our allies be threatened by invaders.'

She saw grim expressions on all faces, and nodded. 'I know you do not believe you can be of much assistance in war. It would be as ridiculous for Siyee to engage landwalkers in hand-

328

to-hand combat as it would be for me to do so. My strength is in sorcery, yours is in flight.

'Your ability to fly makes you more suitable as scouts. You can report on the positions and movements of enemy troops and warn of traps and ambushes. You can carry and deliver small precious items – cures or bandages for the wounded, messages to fighters who have no priest to relay orders to them.'

The mood of nearly all Siyee was the same now. They had responded well to her words, some with enthusiasm, some with a cautious acknowledgement that she was right. She nodded to herself.

'It is difficult to ask something of you that may one day bring death and grief to your families, just as it will be difficult should I ever have to ask the sons and fathers of my own people to fight in our defence. I hope never to see the day when a threat forces such terrible choices upon us.

'So you may wonder, then, how this alliance will benefit your people in times of peace. We can offer you trade, knowledge, and access to the Circlian priesthood. Many of you have expressed doubt that you have anything of value to sell. This is not true. You manufacture unique items that will be of both practical and artistic value outside Si. You have deposits of minerals that could be mined. You have rare plants that have curative properties. Even the soft blankets in the bower you have built for me would fetch a high price in Jarime. These commodities are but those that I have noticed in the few short weeks I have been here. An experienced trader would see more.

'Then there are the benefits that come with the exchange of culture and knowledge. We have much to learn from each other. Your methods of governing and of resolving disputes are unique. The Circlian priesthood offers education and training in healing and sorcery. In return we only ask you to

329

share your healing knowledge with us so that we may better help our own peoples.'

Auraya paused and let her gaze run over the hundreds of faces. 'I hope that our lands may be united in a pledge of friendship, respect and mutual prosperity. Thank you for listening, people of Si.'

She stepped back from the edge of the outcrop and looked at Sirri. The Speaker smiled and nodded, then raised her arms again.

'The Speakers will now talk with their tribes.'

Auraya watched as the line of Speakers broke. Each leapt off the outcrop and glided down to their people, leaving her alone. She sat down and watched as the crowd separated into tribes.

Once again, she let her mind touch those of the Siyee, listening in as they argued and debated. Though they had been stirred by her words, they were still naturally cautious. The changes she had spoken of both excited and frightened them.

They should consider this carefully. It is unlikely their world will ever be the same, even if war never comes. Landwalkers would come here and leave their ideas behind – both good and bad. They would want to carve a road into Si in order to make the journey easier. The Siyee would need to be careful; they could exchange invading settlers for greedy, unscrupulous merchants – especially if they decided to set up more mines.

I will have to make sure that never happens.

She was surprised at the strength of the protectiveness she felt. It had been only a few weeks since she had arrived. Had these people charmed her that much?

Yes, she thought. *I feel like I belong here. I keep forgetting how different I am, and when I do I almost wish I could shrink to half my size and grow wings.*

She looked up at the enormous trees, but caught a sliver of

330

thought and quickly looked away. Someone was up there. A boy, waiting anxiously for his moment to appear. Auraya had already glimpsed enough of Sirri's thoughts to know the Siyee leader was planning a surprise for later in the Gathering.

Some sort of demonstration, Auraya thought. *Something she believes will convince the Siyee to agree to an alliance.*

She resisted the temptation to read the boy's mind, instead concentrating on the Siyee. Time passed and gradually the Speakers left their tribes and flew back to their former positions. When the last of them had returned, Sirri came back to the outcrop and the Siyee quietened.

One by one the Speakers talked, expressing the opinions of their tribe. Most of the tribes were in favour of the alliance, but a few were not.

'All tribes must agree on this,' Speaker Sirri stated. 'We have not. Before I call an end to this Gathering, I ask you to listen to me. I believe our reluctance to open our lands to the landwalkers stems from our inability to fight them. Why should we risk our own lives in war when we cannot harm our enemies? Why should we allow landwalkers into our land when we can't drive them out if their intentions prove to be malicious?'

Auraya regarded the Speaker thoughtfully. She knew Sirri wanted the alliance, but these two points would only dissuade the Siyee from agreeing to it.

Sirri raised her arms. 'We *can* fight. We *can* defend ourselves. How? Let me show you.'

She looked up at the tree the boy was waiting in, then into the edge of the forest, and nodded.

From high in the tree, Tryss could hear the voices of the people below, but he could not make out their words. He had given up trying to and instead had searched the crowd for Drilli. He found her standing with her parents.

He hadn't spoken to her for over a week. Her father had sought Tryss out and ordered him to stay away from her. She was not going to marry a boy from another tribe, he had declared, and certainly not one with strange ideas who spent his time in idle daydreams. She could do better.

His cousins had made it clear who had revealed his and Drilli's liking for each other, but they could be lying just to annoy him. Anyone watching Tryss and Drilli at the trei-trei would have had to suspect they were growing close. They had flown together for most of the night.

He looked down at his invention. Would Drilli's parents change their minds about him if he abandoned inventing and started acting more like other Siyee boys? Would he give it up if that was the only way he could see Drilli?

The question bothered him. He pushed it away, but kept finding himself considering it. He looked at Drilli. She was beautiful and smart. Surely he would do anything . . .

Hearing Speaker Sirri's voice again, he dragged his attention away from Drilli. The Speaker looked up at him, then down at the Siyee holding the cages of breem, and nodded.

The signal. Tryss's heart leapt and started to pound. He searched the ground, looking for movement. *There!*

He dived. Pushing thoughts of the watching crowd out of his mind, he thought only of the small creature that he had spotted. He had to concentrate. His harness was new and a bit stiff, he had only lamplight by which to see the animals and breem were *fast*.

Leaves whipped past his ears. He spread his arms and swooped out from between the branches of the tree. Drawing a dart into his blowpipe, he took aim and blew.

The breem squeaked as the dart hit its leg. It continued limping on but the poison would soon finish it. Tryss had spotted a second breem and turned to follow it. This time the dart sank into the centre of the creature's back. He felt a surge of triumph and flapped his wings to gain a little height, looking for more of them.

Two darted out of the crowd from the other side of the Flat. He missed the first one, but hit the second. Curving around, he blew a dart at the first again, but it swerved at the last moment and the dart bounced off the ground harmlessly. The creature disappeared between the legs of the watching Siyee.

Frustrated, Tryss gained altitude again. He saw the last two breem scamper into the Open and turned quickly. Diving toward them, he tightened his grip on the thumb straps of the new addition he'd included with this harness. He'd only had a few hours to practise with it and it was much harder to aim.

The two breem stopped in the middle of the Open, aware only of the Siyee that surrounded them. Tryss took aim, flexed his thumbs and felt the springs snap open, realising too late that he'd unintentionally released both. Small arrows shot forward. One speared a breem, the other skittered over the ground and wedged itself into the wall of the outcrop . . .

Which he was about to fly into. He arched his back and felt rock brush his hip as he barely managed to avoid a collision. The manoeuvre had lost him height, however, and he was forced to land abruptly, in a way he hoped looked intentional.

The Siyee were utterly silent. Then someone in the crowd began to whistle enthusiastically, as the crowd did during the aerobatic contests of the trei-trei. Others joined in and Tryss found himself grinning as the Open echoed with the sound. He looked up at Speaker Sirri. She smiled and nodded with approval.

The Speaker raised her arms and the whistling subsided.

'People of the mountains. Tribes of the Siyee. I believe you, like me, can see the potential in what Tryss has shown you tonight. What he has invented is a weapon. Not the kind of weapon suited to landwalkers, like those we discarded long ago. One made for *us*. Not only is it an excellent hunting tool, but it is a weapon that will allow us to fight with pride and effectiveness, whether that be in our own defence or that of our allies.

'It is late, tonight, for us to discuss the potential of this weapon and how it may alter our views of the White's proposal of alliance. I suggest we do so in another seven days, when we gather to make our decision. Are you in favour of this?'

A shout of assent came from the Siyee. Sirri looked at her fellow Speakers. All nodded.

'Then it will be so. This Gathering is ended. May you return safely to your homes.'

The Siyee erupted into excited conversation. Tryss looked up at the priestess, suddenly curious to see what her reaction was. She was looking at Sirri, however, wearing a thoughtful frown that soon disappeared as one of the other Speakers turned to address her.

He felt a tug on his arm and turned to find Sreil grinning at him.

'That was fantastic! Why don't you ever join the aerobatic team each trei-trei?'

'I, um . . .'

Someone saved him from answering by shaking his arm. 'Is it heavy? What's it made of?'

He found himself standing in the centre of a crowd of Siyee who wanted to examine the harness. Their questions were endless, and often repeated, but he made himself stay and answer them.

It's not just about demonstrating it, he told himself. *I have to convince them to try it themselves.*

But he longed to get away from them and find Drilli. Whenever a gap formed around him, he searched for her, but in vain. She and her family had gone.

CHAPTER 24

Not long after Danjin entered Auraya's room there was a knock at the door. Mischief was asleep on his lap, his usual energy suppressed by a bout of a common veez illness. Putting the creature aside, he went to answer the door. To his surprise, Rian was standing outside.

'Adviser Danjin Spear,' the White said. 'I wish to speak to you.'

Danjin made the gesture of the circle. 'Would you like to speak to me here, or somewhere else, Rian of the White?'

Rian nodded. 'This will do.'

Up close, Rian appeared to be no older than twenty, and Danjin had to remind himself that this man's true age was nearer to fifty. It was not so easy to forget who Rian was, however. He carried himself as if conscious and proud of his position, and, unlike Auraya, he was always serious and formal. His way of looking at others without blinking was uncanny.

'The observations of your family in regard to the sale of weapons to the Pentadrians have proved accurate,' Rian said. 'Do you believe they may have other useful information?'

Danjin pursed his lips. 'Perhaps.' *But whether they would tell me is a question I can't answer*, he added.

Rian's eyebrows rose. 'Do you believe they would be willing to act as spies for the White?'

Spies? Danjin realised he was staring at Rian and lowered his eyes. *Would they?* He considered how his father and brothers might react to the idea and felt his heart sink. *Of course they would.* They'd be delighted at this confirmation of their worth. Merchants of information as well as goods.

'I believe they would.' *But you'll have to use those mind-reading skills to make sure they're telling you all they know*, he couldn't help thinking. *They might hide information they can reap an income from, or if it might damage their current business.*

Rian nodded. 'I will arrange to meet them, then. Do you wish to be involved?'

Danjin considered, then shook his head. 'My involvement would complicate the arrangement unnecessarily.'

'Very well.' He turned toward the door, then paused. 'What do you know of Sennon, Adviser?'

'Sennon?' Danjin shrugged. 'I have visited the land several times. Mostly by sea, but I have crossed the desert twice. I speak Sennonian. I have a few contacts there.'

'The Sennon emperor signed a treaty of alliance with the Pentadrians yesterday.'

Once again, Danjin found himself staring at Rian, this time in dismay. He recalled Auraya's first meeting with the Sennon ambassador. The man had invited her to visit. It had been ridiculous to expect a new White, untrained and not yet familiar with her position, to travel all the way to Sennon. Perhaps one of the other White should have gone. Reminding the emperor that a powerful alliance backed by the gods lay beyond the mountains to the west might have prevented him from signing an alliance with the Pentadrians.

'You think we should have made greater efforts to befriend the Sennon emperor and his people,' Rian said, frowning.

Danjin smiled wryly. 'Yes, but what can you do? There are only five of you – only four until recently. You've only just allied with Somrey, and now Auraya is working on Si. You didn't have the time or resources to woo Sennon as well.'

The corner of Rian's mouth twitched. 'No, we didn't. Control of time is not one of the Gifts the gods have bestowed on us.'

'Perhaps the emperor will not like his new friends and change his mind. I imagine he will be as thrilled to meet those black vorns as the Torens were.'

Rian's expression darkened. 'Unless he desires his own hunt to train. He has advised all Circlian priests to leave, claiming it is for their own safety.'

Danjin grimaced. 'Oh.' He shook his head. 'The emperor has always maintained that he does not want to favour one religion over another.' Abruptly, Danjin thought of the Dreamweavers. He felt a pang of guilt. Auraya had asked him to visit Leiard, but he had been too busy hunting rumours of Pentadrians to do so. 'Do you think I should warn Dreamweaver Adviser Leiard?'

Rian shrugged. 'If you wish. All reports I have received suggest that Pentadrians are tolerant of the followers of small heathen cults. It is only Circlians they despise, no doubt because they know our gods are real.'

Jealous, eh? Danjin smiled grimly. If this all led to a conflict, at least the Circlians had this one advantage: their gods were real and would protect them. He only feared the damage these Pentadrians might do in the process. In war there were always casualties.

A light had entered Rian's eyes. He regarded Danjin with approval.

'Thank you for your assistance, Adviser.'

Danjin inclined his head and made the gesture of the circle. 'I am glad to be of help.'

He followed Rian to the door and opened it. The White stepped through, then paused and looked back.

'When I speak to your family, I will not mention I consulted you.'

Danjin nodded in gratitude. He watched Rian walk away, then closed the door. Mischief looked up at him, blinking sleepily.

'That,' he told the veez, 'was *very* interesting.'

Auraya opened her eyes. The room was dark, and she could barely make out the walls around her. Had something woken her?

Well, it hasn't done a good job. I still feel like I'm mostly asleep . . .

She opened her eyes a second time. This time the darkness was absolute. Except . . . a familiar figure wearing Dreamweaver robes appeared.

:Leiard?

:Hello, lover of dreamers; dreamer of love.

His lips moved as the words came to her.

:Is . . . is this a memory? It feels like it is you, speaking to me now, and yet it doesn't.

:Yes and no. It is me speaking to you, dressed in your memory of me. My mind given a form by yours. You are learning fast. It seems you have a natural flair for this.

:Perhaps I should have been a Dreamweaver.

:But your heart is the gods'.

:My soul is the gods'; my heart is yours.

Leiard smiled – a sly, secretive smile. It was an expression she had never seen him wear before. Was this just her mind embellishing the mood she sensed from him?

:I've always suspected souls were a concept the gods invented to encourage people to serve them. In fact, I once had a conversation with a god in which he admitted that—

339

She jolted awake and found herself staring at the roof of the bower. Daylight filtered through the walls.

'Auraya?'

The voice came from the entranceway. She rose, wrapped a blanket around her shoulders and moved into the main room. Opening the flap that covered the doorway she found Speaker Sirri standing outside.

'Yes, Speaker?'

The woman smiled. 'Sorry to wake you so early. We have just received a message that we feel we must urgently discuss with you.'

Auraya nodded. 'Come in. I will be with you in a moment.'

She hurried to her room and closed the hanging divider. Undressing, she splashed water from a large wooden basin over herself and quickly dried off with magic. Once she had dressed again she ran a comb through her hair and began plaiting it as she returned to the main room.

Speaker Sirri stood beside the entrance, tapping her forefinger against the frame of the bower. Auraya would never have guessed the woman's mood from her face, but this small sign of impatience made her look closer. At once she sensed that the Speaker was resisting a growing alarm at the news of a landwalker woman seen in Si. The woman had apologised for the attack on a tribe by black birds that Sirri had told Auraya of.

'There will be food at the meeting,' Sirri said as Auraya stepped outside.

The Speaker took to the air and Auraya followed. Sirri caught an updraught and glided up to the top of the Open, where she landed neatly. The forest was cluttered with undergrowth here, keeping the bower hidden from view.

Auraya had visited the Speakers' Bower several times already, but she was sure she had been led down a different forest path each time. She resisted the temptation to read the Speaker's mind, sensing that Sirri wanted to wait until they joined the other Speakers before revealing the contents of the message that had so disturbed her.

I trust her, she mused. *Or perhaps it's just that I know she is not keeping something from me, and has her reasons for waiting.*

They reached the bower. Sirri said nothing as she stepped up to the entrance and pulled the flap aside. Inside, the Speakers of the other fourteen tribes waited. They stood to greet her and she sensed a new caution in the way they regarded her. Sirri ushered her to one of the short stools then took her place. She glanced at the other tribe leaders before she turned her attention back to Auraya.

'Auraya of the White,' she began. 'Do you remember me telling you of the large black birds that attacked the Sun Ridge tribe a month ago?'

'Yes. One of the hunters claimed to have glimpsed a land-walker nearby.'

Sirri nodded. 'The birds have not been seen since, though some of us have looked for them cautiously, but the woman has been seen again recently.' She glanced at the leader of the Twin Mountain tribe. 'By a child. We have no reason to doubt this girl's story; she is not prone to making up fanciful tales.

'She says she encountered the woman close to her village. The woman asked her to deliver a message. It contained an apology for the attack on the hunters. She claimed it was an accident, that she did not know what her birds were doing until it was too late. Her true intentions were to befriend us.

'Then she saw you fly past,' Sirri met Auraya's eyes levelly, 'and changed her mind. She decided to leave Si, after telling the child to give her tribal leader a different message. She said if the Siyee ally themselves with Circlians they will gain an enemy even stronger.'

341

Auraya felt a chill. 'What did this landwalker look like?'

'Her skin was dark. She looked young and strong.'

'Her clothing?'

'She was dressed in black and wore a silver pendant.'

The chill became a shiver of cold that ran down Auraya's spine.

'Ah.'

'Have you heard of this woman before?'

Auraya shook her head. 'No, but I have encountered people like her. She may be a member of a cult from Southern Ithania. I must tell Juran about this.'

Closing her eyes, she called out Juran's name.

:*Yes?* he replied.

:*I think a Pentadrian has been snooping around in Si.* She told him what she had learned.

:*A woman with birds; a man with vorns. The five leaders our spies named include two women.*

:*Yes. What shall I tell the Siyee?*

:*Everything. All of Northern Ithania will know of these sorcerers soon enough. This might nudge them into signing an alliance.*

Auraya smothered a sigh and opened her eyes. *What am I getting these people into?* she asked herself, yet again. *What would I be abandoning them to, if I didn't try to persuade them to seek our protection?* She looked around at the anxious faces of the Speakers.

'Juran and I believe we know *what* she is, just as she recognised what I am. She is a Pentadrian sorcerer,' she told the Speakers. 'We have encountered two others. The first entered Toren with a hunt of vorns. The creatures were larger and darker in colour than their wild relations and appeared to obey mental orders. Their master's only intention in entering Toren appeared to be to cause terror and death. Rian found and confronted the man, who fled when it was clear he could not win the fight.

'The second sorcerer was not accompanied by vorns,' she continued. A memory of being pinned agaisnt a wall by the black sorcerer's power brought an echo of fear. Auraya drew in a deep breath, pushing aside both the memory and the dread that came with it. 'Or any other creature but an ordinary reyna. He did not harm anyone as far as we know. I was sent to help Dyara find him but he, too, escaped us.'

'What do these sorcerers want?' a Speaker asked.

Auraya grimaced. 'I don't know. One thing is sure, they hate Circlians. They call us heathens.'

'What do they worship?'

'Five gods, as we do, but theirs are not real gods.'

'Perhaps this is why they defend their beliefs so ferociously,' Dryss murmured.

'Why did this sorceress enter Si?' another Speaker asked.

'For the same reason Auraya has: to seek an alliance,' someone replied.

'By *attacking* us?'

'She said it was a mistake. She said she wanted to befriend us.'

'Until she saw Auraya.'

Several of the Speakers glanced at Auraya. She met their eyes, hoping she looked more confident than she felt.

'She threatened us,' Dryss reminded them. He grimaced. 'I fear we are being forced to choose between two great powers. No matter what we do, we face changes we can't avoid.'

'You don't have to choose either,' Auraya pointed out. 'You can choose to remain as you are.'

'And be slowly starved and hunted out of existence by these landwalker settlers?' another replied. 'That is no choice.'

'We can fight the invaders now,' a younger Speaker declared. 'Using this dart-thrower. We don't need to ally with anyone!'

Voices joined in argument. Auraya raised her hands and the

Speakers quietened again. 'If you wish it, I will leave Si. Once I am gone you can invite this sorceress to return. Find out what she wants from you and what she offers in return. But please be cautious. Perhaps she did not mean to harm your hunters, but I do know that one of her fellow Pentadrians is a cruel man, who deals out death and pain for the sheer enjoyment of it. I would hate to see the Siyee suffer at his hands.'

'Maybe he was an outlaw. Maybe he came to Northern Ithania because he had been thrown out of Pentadrian lands,' the young Speaker argued.

'At least these Pentadrians have never taken our land from us,' someone else murmured.

'That may only be because they do not have a border with our lands,' Sirri pointed out.

Auraya winced. 'They do now.'

The Speakers turned to frown at her.

'What do you mean?' Dryss asked.

'The Sennon emperor signed a treaty of alliance with the Pentadrians yesterday. Sennon shares a border with you, albeit a small one.'

'On their side there is only desert.'

'Except where the desert ends and the mountains begin.' This came from a Speaker who had not joined the debate so far. 'There are several landwalker settlements along the coast.'

The Speakers fell silent. Their gazes dropped to the floor. Auraya felt a pang of sympathy as she sensed them struggling with their fears.

'Good people of Si,' she said quietly. 'I wish that you were not facing such hard times and such difficult choices. I cannot make these decisions for you. I cannot tell you who to trust. I would never dream of forcing you to choose one way or another. I believe that when the gods asked me and my fellow White to seek allies throughout Ithania they simply wished to see us all united in peace. Perhaps they foresaw some future conflict. I don't know. I do know that we would be honoured to have the people of Si standing beside us, in times of conflict or peace.'

She rose, nodded once, then left. As she walked from the bower she heard muffled voices. She could not distinguish the words, but her Gifts told her what was said.

'We are caught up in this – whatever it is – whether we like it or not. I say we choose a side, because on our own we are sure to perish.'

There was a pause, then: *'If we must choose who to trust, then will it be the one who came in secret, bringing dangerous birds, or the one who waited to be invited?'*

And finally: *'Huan made us. Do these Pentadrians worship Huan? No. I choose the White.'*

CHAPTER 25

In the shadows around Leiard and Jayim only the faint shapes of trees and plants could be made out. They might have been in the middle of a forest. It was the lack of familiar noises that ruined the illusion, telling Leiard plainly that they were on the roof of the Bakers' house.

I miss the forest, he realised suddenly. *I miss being calm. Being undisturbed in heart and mind. Safe.*

Then go back, fool.

Leiard ignored the tart words in his mind. *This voice in my head is merely an echo of a long-dead sorcerer*, he reminded himself. *If I ignore him, he'll go away.* He looked at Jayim. The boy was waiting patiently, used to Leiard's long pauses.

'Magic can be used for healing in many ways,' Leiard said. 'The Gifts that I will teach you are divided into three levels of difficulty. The first level involves simple actions: the pinching of a blood tube to stop bleeding; cauterisation; the realignment of broken bones. The second involves more complex interventions: encouraging or discouraging blood flow; stimulation and guidance of the body's healing processes; blocking pain.

'The third level involves using Gifts so difficult they take years to learn, if that is at all possible – as only one or two

Dreamweavers in every generation has the ability to achieve this level. These Gifts require a trance of concentration and a sure knowledge of all the processes of the body. If you learn them, you will be able to realign any tissue within a body. You will be able to make a wound disappear, leaving no scar. You will be able to give a blind man sight and make a barren woman fertile.'

'Can I revive the dead?'

'No. Not those who are truly dead.'

Jayim frowned. 'Can someone be dead, but not truly dead?'

'There are ways to . . .'

Leiard stopped, then turned toward the stairway. He could hear faint footsteps drawing closer. Two sets. A lamp appeared and light flooded out. Tanara climbed out, followed by a familiar, well-dressed man.

'Leiard?' Tanara called tentatively. 'You have a visitor.'

'Danjin Spear.' Leiard stood. 'What brings you—'

'Before you get talking, come inside,' Tanara interrupted. 'It is too cold out here for entertaining guests.'

Leiard nodded. 'Indeed, you are right.'

Tanara ushered them down the staircase into the communal room, where braziers provided warmth, then dragged Jayim away with her to help prepare hot drinks. Danjin settled into a chair with a sigh.

'You look tired, Adviser,' Leiard observed.

'I am,' Danjin admitted. 'My wife and I hoped I would have more free time while Auraya was in Si, but I'm afraid the situation has been quite the opposite. How have you been?'

'I spend all my time teaching Jayim.'

Except for at night, when you indulge in illegal erotic dream links with one of the White, Mirar whispered. *Wonder what he'd think of that? The mistress he loves like a daughter lying with a Dreamweaver . . .*

Tanara entered the room again, carrying two steaming mugs of hot spiced tintra. Danjin took a sip and smiled.

'Ah, thank you, Ma-Baker. This is most welcome. It is cold outside.'

'It is, isn't it?' she replied, sending Leiard a meaningful look. 'Especially on a day too cold for anybody to be sitting on a roof.'

'Mother!' Jayim's protest echoed through the doorway. 'I've told you a hundred times already: he taught me how to keep myself warm with magic.'

She sniffed, then smiled at Danjin. 'Just call out if you need anything.'

When the door had closed behind her, Leiard turned to regard Danjin. Mirar's comment had reminded him that he knew little about how Auraya's work was progressing. Little of the dream links had involved any discussion of her work in Siyee. Their attention had been on . . . other matters.

'So how is Auraya?' he asked.

Danjin smiled. 'She is enjoying herself immensely. As for whether she will be successful at her task,' he shook his head, 'that is unsure. Their leaders, the Speakers, want all tribes to agree to an alliance before they sign anything, and during the first Gathering a few tribes spoke against it. She hopes that new revelations will change their mind. The threat of war is one. The other is a fortunate coincidence. One of the Siyee has created a new weapon that will allow them to strike at the enemy while in flight, making them an effective force in battle. They will hold another Gathering in a week to decide.'

What is this weapon? Leiard wondered. The idea that the Siyee might become warlike dismayed him. He had always been heartened to know there was at least one non-violent race in the world.

A non-violent people created by Huan. Now there's an irony for you, Mirar muttered.

'She asked me to visit you,' Danjin added. He drained the mug of tintra.

Leiard smiled. 'So she hasn't forgotten us yet.'

'No.' Danjin chuckled. 'I suspect that if it wasn't for her commitment to her position she would settle in Si.'

'She is infatuated,' Leiard said. 'It happens to some new travellers. They discover a place and fall in love with it. They believe everything there is done as it should be. Eventually they come to see that place for what it is – both the good and the bad.'

Danjin regarded Leiard with an odd expression. Leiard sensed surprise and a reluctant respect. 'In my early years as a merchant, and later as a courier and negotiator, I noted the same phenomenon.' Danjin looked at the empty mug in his hands, then set it aside. 'I must continue home. It is late and my wife is expecting me.' He rose. 'Please pass on my gratitude for the warm drink.'

'I will,' Leiard assured him.

Leiard walked with Danjin to the main entrance. As they reached it Danjin hesitated, frowned and glanced at Leiard almost furtively. Leiard sensed a sudden shift in the man's mood. Danjin wanted to say something. A warning, perhaps.

Danjin turned back to the door.

Ask him if there is anything else, Mirar said.

No, Leiard replied. *If he was able to tell me, he would have.*

You can't be sure of that. We both know his family have always hated Dreamweavers. If you won't ask him, I will.

Leiard felt something slip away, like the sensation of not quite catching a falling object in time and having it slide through his fingers. His mouth opened, though he hadn't willed it to.

349

'There is something else, isn't there?'

Danjin turned to regard Leiard in surprise.

Not as surprised as I am! Leiard thought. He groped for control of his body, but he had never lost it before and had no idea how to regain it.

'Something is bothering you,' Mirar repeated, holding Danjin's gaze with Leiard's eyes. 'Something important. A possible threat to my people.'

Danjin was silent and thoughtful, obviously considering what he would say, and oblivious to the change within Leiard. He let out a small sigh and looked up.

'If your people have any reason to fear the Pentadrians, I would have them leave Sennon,' Danjin murmured. 'That is all I can say.'

Mirar nodded. 'Thank you. For the warning and for the visit.'

Danjin's shoulders lifted. 'I would have come sooner, if I could have.' He inclined his head. 'Good night, Dreamweaver Adviser Leiard.'

As Leiard heard his name he felt Mirar's hold over his body fade. Back in control, he swayed with shock. Danjin was looking at him expectantly.

'Good night,' he said.

Leiard watched Auraya's adviser walk up to a covered platten and climb inside. As the driver urged the arem into a trot, Leiard closed the door. He set his back against the wall and let out a long breath. His heart was racing.

What just happened?

Mirar did not reply.

I just lost control of my body to a memory echo, Leiard answered himself. *Can this happen again? Can Mirar take over permanently?* He realised he didn't know. *I must find someone who does. But who?* He smiled grimly. *Dreamweaver Arleej. If the leader of the Dreamweavers can't tell me the answer, nobody can.*

A movement in the doorway made him jump, but it was only Tanara. She peered at him in concern.

'Are you well, Leiard?'

He drew in a deep breath. 'Yes. I am tired. I . . . I will go to bed now.'

She nodded and smiled. 'I will tell Jayim. Pleasant dreams, then.'

Leiard expected a cheeky reply from Mirar, but the presence in his mind remained silent. As he passed Tanara, he paused.

'Danjin asked me to give you his thanks for the drink,' he told her.

She smiled. 'He seems like a nice man. Nothing like what I've heard about the Spear family.'

'No,' Leiard agreed.

'Good night.'

He entered his room, took off his vest and lay down on his bed.

All Dreamweavers learned mental exercises designed to speed the transition to the dream state. Even so, more than an hour passed before the Dreamweaver elder responded to his call. He guessed she had only just fallen asleep.

:Leiard?

:Yes. Do you remember me?

:Of course. One does not forget a Dreamweaver with so many of Mirar's memories.

:No, one does not. I am beginning to wish it were not so.

:Oh? Why is that?

He explained what had happened and felt her rising concern.

:How often have you linked with your student?

:Once or twice, he replied evasively. *It is a little early to be doing so.*

:You are avoiding it, she stated, not fooled by his excuse.

:Yes, he admitted. *I have . . . I have found myself the holder of a secret I dare not risk revealing to him.*

:I see. Then you must find someone else to reveal it to. Someone you trust. Otherwise I fear you will lose your identity. You will be neither yourself nor this manifestation of Mirar, but a half-mad mixture of both.

:I know of no one . . .

:There are other Dreamweavers in Jarime. Will one of them suffice?

:Perhaps. He paused. *There is one other matter I should tell you of. I spoke to Danjin Spear this evening. He warned me that the Dreamweavers in Sennon may not be safe.*

:He speaks of the alliance between Sennon and the Pentadrians.

:Ah!

:Yes. We have nothing to fear from the Pentadrians. They have always treated Dreamweavers well. When you speak to this adviser again tell him to remind the White that we Dreamweavers do not take sides in war. If there is a conflict we will tend the wounded of all nations, as we have always done.

:I will. Is there to be a war?

:The more I learn of these Pentadrians, the more I fear a conflict is inevitable. She paused. *What do you know of them?*

:I have no link memories on the subject, Leiard replied. *What I know is based on comments from Auraya and the rumours circulating around Jarime. Are their gods real?*

:Nobody knows. The Circlians assume not, of course. Even if they are right, that makes the Pentadrians only a little less dangerous.

:A little is something, at least.

:Yes. I must go now. I have more Dreamweavers to contact. Take care, Leiard. Consider what I have said.

The link ended as she turned her mind away. Leiard drifted in the nothingness, knowing her advice was sound, but fearing the consequences. If he allowed another Dreamweaver to know his secret, then the next Dreamweaver he or she linked with would discover the truth. Soon all Dreamweavers would know . . .

:Leiard?

His heart leapt as he recognised Auraya's mental voice and he eagerly reached out to meet her.

There is no undoing what we have done, he thought. *We may as well enjoy it while we can.*

As Emerahl returned to her room, warm and relaxed from an hour-long soak in hot water, she considered how her situation had improved. She was still a whore, but at least she was a well-fed one, with customers of better quality than before. She was earning more money, though Rozea insisted on holding most of it in credit.

While she had played the prostitute twice before in her long life, it was not a role she particularly enjoyed. Thinking back to the first time, more than five hundred years ago, she grimaced. A triad of powerful sorcerers had hunted her across Ithania, determined to extract the secret of immortality from her, even though they were too weak to achieve it. Singly they were no match for her, but together they were a potent enemy. In desperation she had changed her appearance and taken on a role they believed she was too proud to consider.

They had been right. Her pride had smarted with the touch of every customer. How could she, one of the immortal ones, be reduced to selling her body to men who saw her only as a moment's entertainment?

The three sorcerers eventually fell out, one killing the other two. She didn't learn of it for two years. Two years of self-imposed humiliation she hadn't needed to endure. *What else could I have done? People on the streets don't care about foreign sorcerers. That sort of news travels slowly.*

She sighed. People often assumed that just because she was

immortal she must know a great deal. They expected her to be able to describe momentous historical events to them as if she had witnessed them. For most of her life she had kept quietly to herself, staying away from power games and the people who played them.

Which was how she preferred to live. Fame and power had lost their charm within the first hundred years of her life. She had turned to prostitution the second time to escape both. Settling in a remote village, she had begun healing the locals as she always did. What started as a trickle of visitors come to see the healer sorceress had turned into a flood and the village had rapidly become rich. She was flattered at first, and reasoned that she was doing more good for more people this way. Her protests that she was just an old hag earned her an affectionate nickname: The Hag.

A few people had offered to help organise housing for the visitors. Soon they were extracting money from the sick. Tiring of their greed and fanaticism, she had slipped away. She had underestimated how famous she had become. People in even the most remote places knew of The Hag. Her followers kept watch for her everywhere and whenever she was sighted the news quickly spread.

It was the anonymity of prostitution that attracted her the second time, but she had not remained a whore for long. Mirar found her. She smiled to herself as she remembered how popular he had been with the girls and his surprise at finding her there. Though he understood why she had retreated from humanity in that way he insisted it was bad for her. He took her away into the Wilds, long before they were colonised by the Siyee. They'd been both lovers and friends, but she had never been infatuated . . .

'Jade,' a breathy voice called.

She looked up. Two women stood at the end of the corridor.

One was Leaf, a friendly middle-aged woman who organised the girls for Rozea and had given Emerahl a tour of the brothel when she first arrived. The other was the brothel favourite, Moonlight, a curvaceous beauty with dark hair, pale skin and clear violet eyes. Those eyes were travelling up and down Emerahl's body, and the fine nose was wrinkled in distaste.

'Panilo just arrived,' Leaf said as Emerahl reached them. 'He's asking for you.'

Moonlight's eyebrows rose. 'So this is the street whore Panilo took a liking to.' She met Emerahl's eyes. 'Don't get too attached to him. His attention never stays on one girl for long.' A sense of bitterness emanated from the woman.

'You speak from experience, then?' Emerahl asked mildly.

Moonlight's eyes flashed with anger. 'Panilo's kindness is the only part of my early years that I have in common with you.'

Emerahl smiled, amused that this woman had taken offence so easily. 'I doubt your early years were anything like mine,' she replied. 'Excuse me, but I . . .' She paused. Her senses were telling her something else about this woman. She focused them on the woman's belly. Something stirred there.

'I have a customer to attend to,' she finished. Turning away, she strode back to her room. Before entering she paused and looked back. Moonlight had bent close to murmur to Leaf. One hand rested lightly on her stomach and her face was tight with worry.

So she's pregnant, Emerahl mused. *I could use that to gain her trust, or to weaken her position if she proves to be a problem for me.* She shook her head. *Better to ignore her. I don't want to attract too much attention to myself.*

As she stepped into her room she saw that both of her room companions were awake.

'Look, Jade. Tide's in,' Brand said, pointing to the other woman.

355

Tide rolled her eyes at the joke. 'Are you ever going to stop that? It's not funny any more.'

Emerahl chuckled and sidled past the beds to a line of long, feminine tunics hanging from hooks on the back wall of the room. She took down a new green tunic, made of a cloth invented some time in the last century that shone like polished metal but was luxuriously soft to touch.

'Panilo's back?' Tide asked.

'Yes.'

Brand made a face and flopped back onto the bed, her bright yellow hair spreading over the pillow. 'I've heard he's nice, but he visits too early for my liking.'

Emerahl took off her bathing robe and slipped into the tunic. 'I'm not used to sleeping all day and staying up all night, so it suits me fine.'

Tide stepped forward to pluck a piece of thread from the tunic. 'You keep him as long as you can,' she advised. 'He's nice *and* rich.'

'I'll do my best.' She moved to the door, then paused to look back at them. 'How is my hair?'

'Magnificent,' Brand replied. 'Get going, Jade, before some other new girl catches his eye.'

Emerahl grinned, then hurried down the corridor. A few turns, stairways and doors later she entered a large, richly decorated communal room. The high ceiling and tasteful decorations on the walls and columns gave the room a feeling of formal respectability. The roof aperture allowed a view of blue sky, also reflected in the pool below. Paintings on the walls depicted men and women engaged in lovemaking. She rarely had time to examine them, but during each visit had glimpsed intriguing scenes, including some that looked quite improbable.

Panilo looked up at her as soon as she entered, and was instantly on his feet, smiling.

'Emmea.'

'Jade,' she corrected, putting a finger to his lips.

'Jade, then,' he said. 'I preferred Emmea.'

She glanced at the other two men in the room. One lounged on a bench with the air of someone waiting expectantly. A crowd of girls surrounded the other, flirting expertly. Both men had paused to stare at her.

Their unconcealed admiration sent a shiver of both pleasure and anxiety up her spine. *Perhaps I should make myself look a little dowdy*, she thought. *I must not draw too much attention . . .*

'Don't let them frighten you,' Panilo murmured. 'Galero over there couldn't afford you, and Yarro wants only the house's best, which, fortunately for me, is a position you haven't yet attained.'

She smiled at him, appreciating the compliment and wondering how much Rozea was charging him. 'Let's get out of here, so I can have you all to myself.'

She drew him through a door into a complex of rooms. Leaf had told her to use one of the luxurious suites whenever she was with Panilo, and a smaller, humbler room when with other customers. It made Emerahl wonder just how highly placed in Toren society Panilo was.

'Bath?' she asked. Each of the luxurious rooms had a large tub.

He shook his head. 'After.' Reaching out, he ran his hands through her hair. His eyes roamed over her face. 'You are so beautiful, Emmea. I'm glad Rozea brought you here, even if it does cost me twice as much to have you.'

She smiled and drew him toward the bed. 'I'm glad she did, too. It's a lot more comfortable than a wooden seat in a platten. Here I can take my time . . .' She began to loosen the ties of her tunic, undoing them with exaggerated slowness.

357

He chuckled. 'Not too much time,' he said as he reached out to help her. 'I have yet another meeting to attend.'

Another meeting? Emerahl reined in her curiosity, trying to smother it by concentrating on her work. His comment lingered in her memory. He had visited her nearly every night since she'd arrived at the brothel and each time he had mentioned a meeting. She was growing more and more certain that something important was happening in the city – something that only high-ranking nobles and the whores that attended them knew about. By practising her mind-reading abilities constantly, on both customers and fellow whores alike, she had regained her ability to pick up emotions. The dominant feelings she had been sensing around the brothel were anxiety and anticipation.

She was sure Panilo knew what was going on and it was time he told her.

Later, when he was relaxing in the bath, she considered how best to nudge the information out of him. He was not one for word games. He preferred honesty to trickery. A direct question might be all he needed.

'So what's got the city all stirred up?' she asked lightly.

He looked at her in dismay and she began to apologise, but he silenced her with a gesture.

'I'm not offended that you asked, but . . .' He sighed. 'It's not a pleasant subject. This last week . . .' He suddenly looked tired.

'I'm sorry,' Emerahl murmured. 'I've spoiled your night – reminded you of the things that worry you. Here.' She moved behind him and began massaging his shoulders.

'You haven't spoiled my night,' he told her. 'That will come after I leave your company.' He paused, then shrugged. 'I suppose you'll find out eventually. Will you promise to keep this to yourself?'

'Of course – but don't tell me if you don't want to,' she said.

'I do want to. I have to tell somebody, and my wife isn't the sort of woman who listens.'

Wife, eh? 'Then I have to warn you about something.'

'What?' he asked sharply.

'I think half the girls here have sworn to keep the same secret.'

He laughed. 'I don't doubt it.' He hummed quietly. 'That is good, what you're doing.' A long pause followed, then she felt the muscles in his shoulders tense.

'The White have asked us to prepare our army for a war,' he told her.

'A war?' She felt a mingled dismay and hope. Wars brought danger, but also opportunity. Perhaps an opportunity for her to escape the city. 'Who with?'

'With the Pentadrians.'

She paused. He had been astonished that she didn't know who the White were. Should she admit that she didn't know who these Pentadrians were either?

'You're wondering who they are, aren't you?' he asked. 'Well, I can't tell you exactly. All I know is that they're a cult based on the southern continent. They've managed to persuade Sennon to ally with them.'

'They plan to invade Toren?' she asked.

'They plan to invade all of Northern Ithania. To get rid of all Circlians. They hate Circlians.'

'Why?'

'I don't know. I don't think anyone does.'

I could think of a few reasons, Emerahl thought. *They've given plenty of so-called 'heathens' reason to hate them. Who knows what they did to these Pentadrians.*

'So it looks like I'll be marching to war in a few weeks,'

Panilo continued. 'With my own men to command. What do I know about war? Nothing.'

All that anyone ought to know, she thought sadly. *Poor Panilo. Looks like my best customer won't be around for a while – and might never return.*

'You probably won't have to do anything more than relay commands to your men,' Emerahl said soothingly. 'The king will be making all the decisions for Toren.'

He nodded. 'And he'll be following the directions of the White.'

The White. Of course. All the priests and priestesses will be called forth to fight. The watch over the gates will be called off. I'll be free to leave the city. Just a few weeks.

Panilo straightened. 'How can we fail when we have the gods on our side? These Pentadrians are only heathens, after all.'

'That's true.' She smiled, leaned against his back and wrapped her arms around his chest. 'When you get back you can tell me all about it.'

CHAPTER 26

Since demonstrating his harness, Tryss had been waking up early. Sometimes he rose quietly and slipped out to hunt; at other times he stayed in bed, listening for the sounds of his family starting their daily routine. Today he had decided to stay in bed. He'd stayed up late and all he felt like doing was dozing.

His thoughts strayed to conversations of the previous evening. Sreil, Speaker Sirri's son, had told Tryss that the young men of other tribes were all eager to try out his invention, but their Speakers had ordered them to leave Tryss alone. They wanted to ensure no tribe was seen to be given favour over the others. Speaker Sirri had suggested that one man from each tribe be chosen to form the first group Tryss would teach. Those men would pass on what they learned to their tribe.

Tryss wasn't sure if that was a good idea. It certainly wasn't the fastest way to teach others and it might not be the most reliable. If one of those men didn't understand him, mistakes might be passed on.

Nothing would happen until the alliance with the White had been signed, anyway. Last night the Siyee had held a second Gathering. This time all the tribes had agreed to an alliance with the White. The mood had been grim rather than celebratory. While most Siyee were happy with the decision, some clearly felt they were being forced to make a choice between the White and the White's enemy in order to save themselves from the settlers. As if the priestess was to blame for the Siyee's situation.

She isn't, Tryss had decided. *The White are as much to blame for having an enemy as the Siyee are for having their land stolen by invaders.* It felt right that White and Siyee could now help each other out.

A faint noise drew Tryss's attention. He listened carefully and decided that what he was hearing was his mother in the main room, probably preparing the morning meal.

I could go out and help her, he thought. *Doesn't look like I'm going to go back to sleep.*

He swung out of bed and washed himself before dressing. Stepping out into the main room, he grinned as his mother looked up at him. She smiled, then turned her attention back to a stone bowl.

'You're up late.'

He shrugged. 'It was a long night.'

'I saw you talking with Sreil,' she said approvingly. 'He's a smart boy, that one.'

'Yes.'

The water in the bowl began to steam, then bubble. She dropped nutmeal and dried fruit into it and the liquid stopped simmering. Tryss watched as she stared at the porridge until the liquid began to boil again. *If Siyee were more Gifted, we might never have needed the harness*, he thought. Most Siyee could manage this heating his mother was doing, but little more. From what he'd heard, most landwalkers had small Gifts too.

'I haven't seen much of Ziss and Trinn lately.'

'Me neither,' he agreed. 'Thank Huan.'

362

She glanced at him. 'You shouldn't let that little prank of theirs ruin your friendship.'

'It wasn't a *little* prank,' he retorted. 'And they were never my friends.'

One of her eyebrows rose. 'Just be careful how you treat them now. You're going to be getting a lot of attention, and they'll resent you for that. It's always better to avoid making enemies out of—'

'Hello? Anybody awake?'

The words were spoken quietly and came from beyond the bower entrance. Tryss recognised Speaker Sirri's voice, and exchanged a glance with his mother.

'Yes. Come in, Speaker Sirri,' his mother called.

The door flap opened and the older woman stepped inside. She nodded respectfully at Tryss's mother, then smiled at Tryss.

'The Speakers will be meeting to witness the signing of the alliance this morning. I would like Tryss to attend.'

His mother's eyebrows rose. 'You would? Well, I can't see why not. Does he have time enough to eat?'

Sirri shrugged. 'Yes, if he does not take too long.'

'And you?'

The older woman blinked in surprise. 'Me?'

'Would you like some nut mash? It is ready and I have plenty.'

Sirri eyed the bowl. 'Well, if it is no trouble . . .'

Tryss's mother smiled and spooned out the hot mash into four bowls. Sirri sat down to eat. From the look of relief on her face, Tryss guessed the Speaker had not found the time to eat anything this morning. The hanging across the door to his parents' room opened and his father stepped out, his hair sticking up in all directions. He looked at Sirri in surprise.

'Speaker,' he said.

'Tiss,' she replied.

'Is that breakfast I can smell?' he said, turning to Tryss's mother.

'It is,' she replied, handing him a bowl.

'You must be proud of Tryss,' Sirri said.

Tryss felt his heart swell with pleasure as his parents nodded. 'He's always been a clever boy,' his mother said. 'I thought he would do well, perhaps become a bowermaker or arrowforger. I never guessed he would help bring about such changes for our people.'

'We couldn't stay as we were,' his father added. 'My grandfather always said adapting to and embracing change was the Siyee's greatest strength.'

'Your grandfather was a wise man,' Sirri said.

Tryss's mother nodded in agreement, then glanced at Tryss. 'I only fear what any mother fears: that such changes will have a terrible price.'

Sirri grimaced. 'I know that fear well. If we go to war with the White, as I suspect we will, I doubt I could keep Sreil here. Nor should I. It will be a difficult time.'

Tryss's parents nodded again. They all ate in silence, then Sirri set her empty bowl aside and looked at Tryss.

'Change awaits no one, but alliance signings can't happen without the Head Speaker. We must go. Thank you for the meal, Trilli. It is much appreciated.'

Tryss's mother gathered the empty bowls and ushered them out. As Tryss and Sirri emerged into the sunlight he caught a movement from the next bower. His heart leapt as Drilli emerged. She saw him and grinned, but the smile faded as her father stepped out. He gave Tryss a warning look then strode away, Drilli following.

Tryss sighed, then turned to find Sirri regarding him.

'Your neighbours have been spending a lot of time with the Fork River tribe's representatives. I did not think much of it until I remembered that a family from their own tribe had settled with the Fork River folk. I suspect Zyll hopes to persuade his daughter to marry into this other Snake River family. He's keen to prevent the Snake River tribe becoming absorbed into other tribes.'

Tryss felt as though his heart was shrivelling up. When Sirri looked at him he shrugged, afraid that if he spoke his voice would betray his feelings.

'Of course, he can't force her to if she is already pledged to another.' She shook her head. 'I always thought that law a foolish one. It forces young people to choose who they marry too early. I don't like the idea of fathers marrying their daughters off to young men they hardly know, either.'

She glanced at Tryss. 'Come on.' Together they broke into a run, leapt and spread their arms wide. As Sirri's wings caught the wind and she swooped upwards, Tryss followed. Her words repeated over and over in his mind as they flew toward the top of the Open.

'. . . he can't force her to if she is already pledged to another.'

Was she aware that he and Drilli had been seeing a lot of each other until Drilli's father intervened? She obviously disapproved of what Zyll was doing. Was she suggesting he and Drilli exchange a pledge of marriage?

It might be the only way he would see Drilli again.

But . . . marriage. It was such a grown-up thing to do. He would have to move out of his parents' bower. The tribe would build them their own. He considered what it might be like to live with Drilli.

He smiled. It would be nice. A bower all of their own. Time together. Privacy.

Was she the right girl for him? He thought of the other girls he knew. The ones in his tribe, who he had grown up with, were like family members. A few were friendly, but they weren't anything like Drilli. She was . . . special.

Ahead, Sirri landed and paused to wait for him. He dropped down beside her, then followed her along one of the trails to the Speakers' Bower. Thoughts of Drilli were chased away as he realised he was about to participate in an event that was likely to become part of Siyee history.

'Wha – what will I have to do?' he asked.

'Nothing. Just sit at the back and stay silent unless you're spoken to,' Sirri told him.

Suddenly his mouth was dry. His stomach began to flutter disconcertingly. Sirri strode up to the entrance and pulled the hanging aside. As she stepped through, Tryss swallowed hard and followed.

The room was crowded with Siyee. All had looked up at Sirri when she entered, and were now regarding him with interest. The priestess was present, looking larger than ever in the close room. She met his eyes and smiled, and he felt blood rush to his face.

Sirri moved to an unoccupied stool. As she sat down, Tryss glanced around the room. There were no other stools. He sat on the floor, where he could see Sirri between two of the Speakers.

'Last night every tribe considered again the White's proposal for an alliance,' Sirri said. 'Last night all tribes made a decision, and all decided the same. We, the Siyee, will make this pact with the White. We will become allies of the Circlians.

'We debated long into the night the exact words of this commitment between us.' She looked at Auraya. 'This morning Auraya of the White has scribed these words onto parchment in the languages of both Si and Hania. These two scrolls have been inspected by all.'

The White priestess held up two scrolls. Tryss noted that the wooden rods attached to the parchment were carved with Siyee patterns.

'All that remains is for each of us to sign it on behalf of our tribe,' Sirri finished.

She reached behind her stool and lifted a flat board into view. A small container of black paint sat within a recess of the board and a brush lay in another. Sirri placed the board across her knees.

The White priestess held the scrolls before her. She closed her eyes.

'Chaia, Huan, Lore, Yranna, Saru. Today your wish to see Northern Ithania united in peace comes a step closer to realisation. Know that the people Huan created, the Siyee, have chosen to ally with the people you chose to represent you in this world, the White. We do so with joy and great hopes for the future.'

Tryss felt his skin prickle. He had no time to wonder at this as Auraya opened her eyes and handed Sirri one of the scrolls. The Speaker unrolled the parchment, picked up the brush and loaded it with paint.

As the brush-tip moved across the scroll, the bower was utterly silent. A shiver ran down his spine. He watched Sirri paint her name sign and tribe sign on the second scroll, then pass the board to the next Speaker.

Tryss realised this was no ritual refined by centuries of repetition. The Siyee didn't have a ceremony for an event like this: they had never signed an alliance before. This was a new ritual, begun today.

The silence continued as the scroll passed from Speaker to Speaker. The White priestess watched all patiently. Tryss noticed that her gaze occasionally grew distant, as if she was listening to something beyond his hearing. Once she smiled faintly, but he saw nothing in the room to explain her amusement.

Finally the scrolls were returned to her. She signed slowly, obviously not used to using a brush to write with. When she was done, she handed the board and one of the scrolls to Sirri. The Speaker put the board aside, but kept hold of the scroll.

'Today our peoples have joined hands and hearts in friendship and support,' Sirri said. 'May all Siyee, and our descendants, honour this alliance.' She looked at Auraya.

'Today the White have gained an ally we will value for all eternity,' Auraya replied. 'In accordance with the agreement we have just made, our first act will be to effect the return of Toren settlers to their homeland. This will take time if it is to be achieved without bloodshed, but we are determined it will be done within the next two years.'

This brought triumphant smiles to the faces of the Speakers. The air of formality dissolved as one asked her how this might be done without spoiling future prospects of trade with Toren. The Speakers began talking with each other, and some rose and moved to Sirri's side to inspect the scroll.

Tryss watched it all silently, but it did not take long before one of the Speakers noticed him. As the old man began to ask him questions about his harness, others joined in, and soon Tryss found himself unable to answer one query before another was thrown at him. He felt overwhelmed.

'Fellow Speakers, have some pity on the poor boy.' Sirri's voice cut across the questions. She shouldered her way into the circle of men and women surrounding Tryss. 'What you all want to know is when your tribes will get their own harnesses and when they will be trained to use them.' She looked at Tryss. 'What do you think, Tryss?'

He glanced at the Speakers, then drew in a deep breath and considered.

'The harnesses have to be made first. I can teach two makers from each tribe, so one can correct the other if mistakes are made. I'll start teaching them as soon as they arrive.'

'How does that sound?' Sirri turned to regard the Speakers. The men and women nodded.

'Good.' Sirri patted Tryss on the shoulder. 'Now, tell us what they'll need to bring.'

As Tryss listed the tools and materials that he'd used to make his harness, a feeling of wonder began to grow. He'd done it. He'd convinced them, thanks to Sirri. She had listened to him when he had first wanted to demonstrate the harness. She'd seen the potential of his invention. She'd given him a chance. He glanced at the Speaker and felt a surge of gratitude. She even sympathised with him about Drilli – and had told him of a way they could be together again.

He owed her a lot. One day he hoped he might repay her. For now, the best he could do was train his fellow Siyee to hunt and fight.

Though now that he thought of it, he had never used the harness in battle. He had only his imagination to tell him it would be an effective weapon.

It's not over yet, he thought. *Even I have more to learn.*

Since hearing how she had flown right over the Pentadrian sorceress weeks before, Auraya had paid more attention to the forest below her whenever she was flying. She had seen no black-clad landwalkers, thankfully, just an abundance of wildlife and a lot of trees.

The sorceress was long gone – or so the Siyee believed. She looked up and around at the mountains. Great spires of rock and snow rose on all sides. Forests clung to their steep slopes. In the valleys and ravines below, glittering threads of water wound down toward the sea.

Magnificent, she thought.

She felt buoyant. Lighter than air. It was not just her peculiar Gift, it was a mood that had stolen over her since she had first arrived, reaching its peak this morning when she had succeeded in her task of uniting Siyee and White.

That was not all. This morning she had woken from dreams of Leiard so full of love and passion that she had not wanted to wake at all. She longed to return to Jarime, yet sometimes she wondered if reality would prove to be disappointing in comparison to their shared dreams.

No, it will be better, she told herself.

Sirri changed direction slightly, so Auraya altered her course to match. The Speaker had been gradually gaining altitude for the last hour and the air had grown icy. Auraya drew magic constantly in order to keep herself warm. The Siyee seemed unaffected by the chill.

They had been flying for most of the day and the sun was dropping toward the horizon. Looking ahead, Auraya saw that they were heading toward a mountain peak slightly lower than the others. She had seen glimpses of their destination in the woman's mind, and from them knew that they were heading for this peak and that she would find a Temple there.

Auraya had been intrigued to learn that the Siyee had their own Temple. Though they worshipped Huan, they were not true Circlians. They did not follow – or even know of – the rituals and traditions landwalkers had invented in order to express their worship of the five gods.

She had wanted to visit the Temple, but Siyee law forbade anyone to approach unless invited by the goddess or accompanied by a Watcher, the closest thing to a priest or priestess the Siyee had. This morning, Sirri had passed on one such invitation. Since then Auraya's stomach had been fluttering with excitement. Did this mean they were finally going to speak to her?

If they are, why don't they just speak to me? Why this invitation passed through others? Auraya found herself wondering, not for the first time. *Maybe because they want the Siyee to note it. Had the gods simply spoken into my mind the Siyee would not know, or would have to trust that I told the truth. And if the gods appeared in the presence of the Siyee that takes some of the holiness out of this place, since it's where they go when they commune with Huan.*

They drew closer to the peak and Auraya began to make out details. The highest point was oddly shaped – cylindrical and rounded at the top. She saw a sliver of sky within the shape, and realised that it was hollow. Suddenly what she had glimpsed in Sirri's mind made sense. A small pavilion Temple had been carved out of the stone peak.

She wondered how it had been built. Below the circular base, on all sides, was a near-vertical drop. Perhaps if a hollow had been made first, the structure could have been gradually carved from the inside. None but Siyee could have reached such a high, inaccessible place, however. She had not realised the Siyee stone-carvers were so skilled. As she drew closer she could see that it was a simple, undecorated structure. Five columns supported a domed roof. The proportions were flaw-less, the surfaced polished to a shine.

Sirri flapped her wings to gain a little more height, then tilted them so that she landed neatly between two columns. Auraya abandoned all pretence of being subject to the forces of wind and the pull of the earth. She straightened and stopped, floating in midair, then moved herself forward until her feet met the centre of the Temple's floor.

Only then did it occur to her that the Temple had been made to landwalker proportions. She did not need to duck her head to avoid the ceiling.

'This is the Temple,' Sirri said quietly. 'It has always been here. Our records say it was here long before the Siyee were created.'

'The Siyee didn't create it?'

Sirri shook her head. 'No.'

'Then who did?'

'Nobody knows. Huan, perhaps.'

Auraya nodded, though she was still mystified. The gods could only affect this world through humans, and then only through willing humans, so at least one human must have been involved. Perhaps Huan had given a stone-carver the ability to fly in order to have this place created.

'This is a sacred place. Even those of the Temple Mountain tribe, who keep watch over it, rarely visit.' Sirri gave Auraya a quick smile. 'We don't want to distract Huan from her work unnecessarily.'

Auraya ran a hand over a column. There was no sign of wear or age. 'It is amazing.'

'I have one question, before I leave,' Sirri said. 'The Speakers wish to know when you want to depart for Borra?'

'Want to? Not ever.' Auraya sighed. 'But I need to – and soon. I must see if I can persuade the Elai to join us.'

Sirri smiled. 'I wish you luck, then. The Elai distrust outsiders.'

Auraya nodded. 'So you have said. Yet they trade with you.'

'We creations of Huan like to keep in contact. The Sand tribe trades with the Elai. You should meet with their Speaker before you go. I'm sure he can tell you more about the sea people than I can.'

'I will.'

The Speaker's expression became serious. 'For now, Auraya of the White, I must leave you.' She moved to the edge of the Temple and pointed downward. 'See that river?'

Auraya moved to Sirri's side and looked down. A ribbon of reflected sky wound down a narrow ravine.

'Yes.'

'When you are done, fly down there. The Temple Mountain

tribe live in caves along the ravine.' She turned to give Auraya a smile, then leaned out over the edge and glided away.

:Auraya.

Her heart seemed to stop. The voice had spoken in her mind. It was distinctly feminine.

:Huan?

:Yes.

The air before her brightened. Auraya stepped back, her heart pounding, as a figure of light formed before her. She dropped to her knees, then prostrated herself before the goddess.

:Rise, Auraya.

As Auraya obeyed she felt herself trembling with a mixture of joy and terror. She was standing, alone, before one of the gods. *Even though I am one of their Chosen, before them I am just another ordinary human.*

Huan smiled.

:You are no ordinary human, Auraya. We do not choose ordinary humans. We choose those with extraordinary talents, and you have certainly proved to have more of those than we initially detected.

The goddess's tone was approving, yet Auraya sensed a note of irony. She did not have time to wonder at Huan's meaning as the goddess continued speaking.

:We are satisfied with your success in unifying Northern Ithania so far. I am particularly pleased to see the Siyee united with the White. You will find they are the easier of my two races to befriend, however. Your flying skills will not impress the Elai. They will be a greater challenge for you.

:How can I impress them?

:That is for you to discover, Auraya. The choice must be their own, so we will not interfere either by giving you instructions, or giving the Elai direction.

:I understand.

Huan's lips twisted in a wry smile.

373

:I doubt it. You are young and have much to learn — particularly in matters of the heart. I do not disapprove of you enjoying the Dreamweaver, Auraya. It is up to your fellow White to decide what is acceptable or unacceptable to the people. However, heed this warning. Only pain can come of this sort of love. Be prepared for it. Your people need you to be strong. Falter, and they may suffer.

Auraya felt her face warming as surprise was followed by embarrassment.

:I will, was all she could think to say.

Huan nodded. The figure dissolved into a column of light, then shrank, faded and vanished.

Kimyala, high priest of the followers of Gareilem, donned his many-layered octavestim slowly, following the ancient ritual of his forebears with great care. As he arranged and tied each garment he murmured prayers to his god. It was important to remember every stage of the ritual, and every ritual of the day.

He had asked his master, the former high priest, why this was so. The great Shamila had replied simply that it was important to remember.

Kimyala had not comprehended at the time. He suspected he hadn't wanted to, because of his youthful impatience with the endless and complicated rituals. Now he understood better. It was important to remember, because there were too few who did.

Too few believed. The Circlians thought Gareilem dead and scorned his followers. The Pentadrians believed this too and pitied Kimyala. The Dreamweavers agreed with both, but at least they treated him with respect.

Kimyala was sure of one thing: gods cannot die. This was one of the ancient secrets of the followers of Gareilem. Let the others doubt, but he and his people knew the truth. The gods were beings of magic and wisdom. They existed as long as magic existed, so Gareilem must still exist somewhere, in some form. Perhaps, one day, he would return. His silence may even be a test of their faith. He was letting his followers dwindle until only the most loyal remained.

The dressing ritual over, Kimyala left his room and climbed to the roof of the old temple. Gareilem was the god of rock, sand and earth. His temples had always been built high on the sides of mountains. Here, near the southern coast of Sennon, there were only a few hills. The temple was built on a small rocky outcrop in the midst of a sea of dunes, but the lack of vegetation taller than a saltbush meant it had an uninterrupted view of the surrounding area.

Reaching the roof of the temple, Kimyala let his gaze move across the land. The sun hung just above the horizon, calling for his attention. The ritual chant for the end of the day crowded his thoughts, but it was not yet time. There wasn't much to see to the west. Just the swell of a few more hills along the coast. The Gulf of Sorrow stretched, blue-grey, before him. A little to the left he could see the Isthmus of Grya reaching toward the southern continent. At its base was the dark smudge that was the city of Diamyane.

The city was close enough that he could see the scribble of roads and the sprawling low houses between them. On a clear day he could make out the city's denizens without even the use of a lens. Today a slight but persistent wind had raised enough dust to soften the details of the city. There was nothing interesting to see. Except . . . as he looked beyond he noticed something unusual.

'Jedire!' he bellowed. 'Bring my lens! Quickly!'

He heard hurried footsteps as his acolyte, studying in the room below, responded. Glancing at the sun, Kimyala judged he still had several minutes before it touched the horizon. Soon all light would be gone and the land would disappear in darkness.

The sound of sandals slapping against the stone stairs heralded the arrival of Jedire. The boy reached the top and handed Kimyala the lens. The high priest held the tube up to his eye.

He searched for the city and from there found the Isthmus. The dark smudge he had seen took form. Columns of figures marched toward Sennon, some holding banners. In the centre of each length of black cloth was a white five-pointed star.

'Pentadrians,' he said in disgust, handing the lens back to his acolyte.

The boy raised the tube to his eye.

'What are they doing?'

'Don't know. A pilgrimage, maybe.'

'They're carrying weapons,' the boy said in a hushed voice. 'They're going to war.'

Kimyala snatched the lens from the boy and turned to face the city. Raising the tube to his eye, he sought the Pentadrians again and examined the line of marchers closely. Sure enough, some were wearing armour. Heavily laden carts trundled in their midst. As he watched, the head of the black column reached the city.

He muttered a curse. He had already lost two boys to the Pentadrians. It was not easy keeping them when the Pentadrians were always about, flaunting their riches and powers. If that wasn't enough to lure young men away, there were always the rumours about their fertility rites. It was said that they held orgies in which all participants were masked, and that some-times their gods joined in.

'It's an army, isn't it?' Jedire asked. 'Have they come to take over Sennon?'

Kimyala shook his head. 'I don't know. Nobody is trying to stop them.'

'If they aren't here to invade us, who are they going to invade?'

He turned to regard Jedire. The boy's eyes were bright with excitement.

'Don't get any foolish ideas about running off to join Ewarli and Gilare,' Kimyala warned him. 'Boys die in battles. They die horribly, in terrible pain. Now take this lens below quickly. I have a ritual to perform.'

As the boy hurried away, Kimyala turned his attention to the sun. The fiery disk was about to touch the horizon. It was time to ignore the ominous presence of the army below, and begin the ritual.

CHAPTER 27

*T*he window was open. Danjin cursed the servants. How had they
let this happen? Mischief might get out – could be out there
clinging to the wall right now, oblivious to the risk of falling.

He ought to call the servants and get someone else to deal with it,
but he found he could not stop himself walking toward the opening.
Cold air surrounded him. He moved to the edge. Felt his toes curl
over the sill, chilled by the wind.

I am on the brink, he thought. Then he frowned. Why aren't I
wearing shoes?

He looked beyond his feet at the ground far, far below, and everything began to spin.

Suddenly he was standing at the base of the White Tower, looking
up. He ought to have felt better now that he was outside on good,
firm ground, but this only terrified him more. The tower loomed over
him, leaned over him. Too late, he saw the cracks form.

He saw it crumple, saw the fragments fall toward him. He could not
move. Rubble pelted down upon him, beat him to the ground, covered
him, smothered him. He fought the terror. Told himself to lie still . . .

'Danjin.'

He felt hope. If he could hear someone, perhaps he was close enough
to the surface that they could dig him out. His throat was dry and
full of dust, and he could not make a noise.

Patience. There can be no fast way out of this.

But he must also hurry. He had to decide how to use his remaining strength carefully . . .

'Danjin. Wake up.'

A hand grasped his arm. Rescue!

'Danjin!'

He woke with a start and took in his room, the blankets wound tightly around his body – but not his feet – and his wife staring down at him.

'What?'

Silava straightened and placed her hands on her hips.

'There is an army outside.'

An army? He untangled himself from the blankets and followed her to one of the windows. This side of his house faced one of the main streets of the city. He looked down and stared in surprise at the lines of troops marching past.

It was strangely thrilling to see them. Hanian soldiers were always visible in the city, from the clean roads of the noble families to the low streets of the rougher parts, but never this many at once. The steady tread of their sandals sounded so confident and *organised*.

'They're not wasting time,' he muttered to himself.

'For what?'

'At the meeting last night, Juran announced that the Pentadrian army have entered Sennon and declared their intention to rid the world of Circlians,' he explained. 'It's been so long since Hania faced a military threat. A few nobles expressed their doubt that our army was up to it. This will convince them.'

She looked down at the troops. 'Where are they going?'

He considered. 'Probably to the Temple to seek the gods' blessing.'

'All of them at once?'

'Between them and the priests they'll put on such a show that our young men will flock to join the army and be part of the great adventure. So will the forces of other lands, though they have no choice. They're bound by the terms of their alliances with the White.'

She considered him speculatively. 'So you're allowed to tell me all this now?'

'Yes. It's public knowledge, as of last night.'

'You didn't tell me when you got home.'

'You were asleep.'

'News of this importance is worthy of being woken up for.'

'One is reluctant to interrupt another's sleep when so deprived of it oneself.'

She gave him a withering look.

He spread his hands. 'Would it have made any difference if you had learned of this five hours earlier?'

Her nose wrinkled. 'Yes. I probably wouldn't have slept at all.' She sighed. 'So I guess you will be accompanying Auraya on this great adventure?'

He looked down at the soldiers marching past below. 'Probably, though I am no military expert or soldier. I'll probably end up doing much the same sort of duties as I do now – which was something my father insisted on mentioning numerous times last night.'

She chuckled. 'I'm sure he did. Did you tell him you know they're all spying for the White?'

'No. I changed my mind. He was so insufferably smug. Auraya and I find it much more amusing to let him think I don't know.'

Silava's eyebrows rose. 'She's back?'

He shook his head, then tapped his temple with one finger. 'She wanted to see the reactions of the other nobles and ambassadors. They're much more outspoken when they believe they're not in the presence of a White.'

She paused. 'Is she in your head now?'

'No.' He took her hand, recalling other occasions when the mention of Auraya seeing through his eyes had disturbed her. 'It's not like that. She doesn't take over my mind. I'm still me. All she can do is hear what I hear and see what I see.'

Silava drew her hand away. 'I understand that. Or at least I think I do. But I can't help not liking it. How do I know whether she's watching me or not?'

He chuckled. 'She's discreet.'

'That makes her sound like your mistress.'

'Are you *jealous*?'

She moved away, avoiding his gaze. 'Don't flatter yourself.'

He smiled and followed her. 'I think you are. My wife is actually jealous of Auraya of the White.'

'I . . . she gets more time with you than I do.'

He nodded. 'It's true. She gets all that dry information about customs and politics and law that I know you love so much. Is that what you miss? Shall I tell you all about the laws laid down by the King of Genria fifty years ago? Or the many traditions and rituals for the serving of techo in Sennon high society?'

'There's a lot more of *that* in you than anything else,' she retorted.

He caught her hand and turned her to face him. 'That may be true, but everything else there is to have, I give to you. My friendship, my respect, my children, even my body – though you probably see nothing of worth in this sad, neglected form.'

Her lips thinned, but he could tell from the way the lines around her eyes deepened that she was pleased and amused by his words.

'If I didn't suspect you were hoping I'd convince you otherwise, I'd be a bigger fool than you,' she said.

He grinned. 'Can't you at least pretend to be a fool for me?'

She pulled away and strode toward the door. '*I* don't have the time, and my husband no doubt has more dry information to hurry off to gather and deliver to his mistress.'

He sighed loudly. 'How can I face the world believing such things about myself?'

Reaching the door, she glanced back and smiled. 'I'm sure you'll manage.'

If Auraya hadn't known that there were many times more Siyee than those now waiting in the Open, she might have thought the entire race had come out to see her off. Most had gathered together into a large crowd standing under the outcrop from which the Speakers had addressed them during the two Gatherings. Others filled the branches of the enormous trees on either side. Still more glided above, and their constant movement cast distracting shadows on the ground.

As she emerged from the trees, faces turned toward her and a shrill whistling began. This was their way of cheering. She smiled at them all, could not have stopped if she had wanted to.

'Your people are so friendly,' she told Sirri. 'I wish I could stay a little longer.'

The Speaker chuckled. 'Be careful, Auraya. While we would like to keep you for ourselves, we know how important you are to Northern Ithania, and to our own future. If you like it too much here, we may have to stop being so nice to you.'

'It would take a lot to change my opinion of you and your people,' Auraya replied.

Sirri paused to regard Auraya thoughtfully. 'We have won you over, haven't we?'

'I've never been so happy as I have been here.'

'You're the only landwalker I have found myself constantly forgetting is a landwalker.' Sirri frowned. 'Does that make sense?'

Auraya laughed. 'Yes, it does. I keep forgetting I am a land-walker, too.'

They reached the first of the Speakers, who were standing in a line along the edge of the outcrop. Auraya spoke to each, thanking them for their hospitality if she had visited their tribe, and promising to visit their home in the future if she hadn't. The Speaker at the end of the line was the leader of the Sand tribe, Tyrli. The sombre old man and the few members of his tribe who had travelled to the Open for the Gathering would be guiding her to the coast.

'I look forward to your company on our journey, and seeing your home, Speaker Tyrli,' she said.

He nodded. 'I am honoured to be of assistance to the Gods' Chosen.'

She sensed that he was a little overwhelmed. Moving on, she stood beside Speaker Sirri as the Siyee leader turned to face the crowd.

'People of the mountains. Tribes of the Siyee. We, the Speakers, have called you here to bid farewell to a visitor to our lands. She is no ordinary visitor, as you all know. She is Auraya, one of the Gods' Chosen, and our ally.' She turned her head to regard Auraya. 'Fly high, fly fast, fly well, Auraya of the White.'

The crowd murmured the words. Auraya smiled and stepped forward.

'People of Si, I thank you for your warm hospitality. I have enjoyed every moment of my time among you. It saddens me to leave you, and I know as soon as I depart I will be impatient to return. I wish you well. May the gods watch over you.'

She made a circle with both hands. A few of the children in the crowd copied her gesture. The air vibrated with enthusiastic whistling again. Tyrli moved to her side.

'Now we go,' he murmured.

He leaned forward and, spreading his arms wide, leapt off the outcrop. The wind bore him upward. Auraya lifted herself into the air to follow. As she did, Siyee flew out of the trees and joined her, some still whistling. She grinned and laughed as these young escorts swooped playfully around her.

As they flew further from the Open some began to glance backwards. Gradually their numbers dwindled as Siyee fell back, some giving one last whistle in farewell. Eventually only Tyrli and his people remained.

Time seemed to slow then. The Siyee mostly remained silent while flying. If they communicated at all, the words they were most likely to use during flight – directions, commands – had long ago been replaced by whistles. To speak to each other while in the air involved flying closer together in order to make out words. Siyee did not feel comfortable flying close together. They felt crowded.

So Auraya was surprised when Tyrli slowed and moved close to her in order to talk.

'You wished to know more of the Elai,' he stated.

She nodded.

'They are ruled by a king,' he told her. 'One leader instead of many.'

'Do they have tribes?'

'No. They did, once. One for each island. Few live anywhere but the main island now. In their city.'

'Why is that?'

'For many years, landwalkers have attacked them. It is not safe to live on the outer islands.' He glanced at her, his expression grave. 'The Elai do not like landwalkers for this reason.'

384

Auraya frowned. 'Why did these landwalkers attack them?'

'To steal from them.'

She scowled. 'Raiders.'

'Yes. The Elai are in a much worse situation than the Siyee. Many have been killed by these landwalkers. There are many thousand Siyee, but barely a few thousand Elai.'

'All living in this city. Have you seen it?'

He looked almost wistful. 'None but Elai have seen it. Only they can go there. It is a great cave reached by swimming through underwater tunnels. They say it is very beautiful.'

'An underwater city. That would keep them safe from raiders.' How was she going to talk to the Elai if they lived under-water? Were the gods going to give her the Gift of breathing water?

'Not underwater,' Tyrli said. He almost appeared to smile. 'They may live in water, but they still breathe air. They can hold their breath for a long time, however.'

She looked at him in surprise. 'So the legends are wrong. Are they covered in scales? Do they have a fishtail instead of legs?'

He laughed. 'No, no.' She caught a glimpse of a figure in his mind: a near-naked, hairless man with dark, shiny skin and a broad chest. 'Huan gave them thick skin so they can stay in the water for many hours, and big lungs so they can hold their breath for a long time. She gave them fins, too – but not like the fins of fish. Their fins are as much like fish fins as our wings are like bird wings. You will understand, when you see them.'

She nodded. 'Has any landwalker befriended them before?'

He considered. 'One. Long ago. He used to visit us, too. I heard he knew a secret route into Si, though not even Siyee know where it is now. Many people liked him. He was a Gifted healer. He could heal wings that were damaged beyond repair.'

'He must have been a powerful sorcerer. What was his name?'

He paused and frowned, then nodded his head. 'His name was Mirar.'

She turned her head to stare at him. '*Mirar?* The founder of the Dreamweavers?'

He nodded. 'A Dreamweaver. Yes, that is right.'

Auraya looked away, but barely noticed the landscape below as she considered this revelation. Was it so surprising that Mirar had roamed these mountains long ago? Then she remembered: Leiard had told her he had memories of the Siyee. Were they Mirar's memories? And if they were, did Leiard also have memories of the Elai?

She pursed her lips. Perhaps tonight, if he spoke to her in a dream link, she would ask him about the sea people. Though it sounded as if the Elai were in even greater need of the White's help than the Siyee, she suspected their resentment toward all landwalkers would make negotiating with them difficult. Perhaps Leiard knew how best to gain their confidence. She needed all the information she could get.

Turning back to Tyrli, she smiled.

'So how long has your tribe been trading with the Elai?'

Drilli sighed and followed her parents out of the bower. They were going to yet another meeting of the fragmented Snake River tribe. The families living among other tribes were using the Gatherings as an opportunity to meet in one place and plan for their future. She glanced at Tryss's family bower, despite knowing he would be away training other Siyee in the use of the harness. Not even his cousins were hanging about.

As she turned back, her father caught her eye and frowned disapprovingly. She looked away, despite the temptation to glare at him, and obediently followed as he set off along a forest path.

How could he do this to me?

For months they had danced around each other. It had been a good-humoured game at first. He would ask what she thought of some young man, and she would give some polite but dismissive answer. He would nod in acknowledgement and leave it at that.

Then she had met Tryss. He was no stronger or better bred than any of the matches her father had proposed, but he was *interesting*. Most of the young men in her tribe sent her delirious with boredom. Most of the older men did too. Except her grandfather . . . but he had died during the invasion of her home.

Like her grandfather, Tryss was clever. He thought about things. *Really* thought. He didn't pose or boast to get her attention. He just looked at her with those deep, serious eyes . . .

Her father had lost all patience with her when he learned that she had been spending so much time with Tryss. He couldn't come up with any good reason for his disapproval of their neighbour's son, except that Tryss wasn't of the Snake River tribe.

To Zyll, the need to keep his tribe from being absorbed by others was more important than anything else – even his daughter's happiness, she was discovering. He had forbidden her to speak to Tryss. He was taking advantage of these meetings to look for a husband for her.

There was nothing she could do about it. Siyee law stated that parents could arrange their offspring's first marriage. Marrying young had been essential in the past in order to increase the chances of more healthy children being born.

I can always insist on a divorce, she thought. *We only have to stay together for two years.* That seemed like an eternity. *By then, Tryss might have found someone else. And I might have children.*

She grimaced. *I don't even know if Tryss wants to get married. The trouble with being attracted to quiet types is that they aren't good at letting you know what they want.* She had no doubt that he liked her a lot, and that he was attracted to her – she was sure of that!

A flicker of light caught her attention. Looking beyond her father she saw that several lamps surrounded a clearing ahead. Though it was only mid-afternoon, the trees here were so close together that little sunlight penetrated to the forest floor.

One lamp stood in the middle. Several men and women were sitting in a circle around it. She recognised Styll, the Speaker of her tribe. Beside him sat her father's latest proposed suitor for her, Sveel. The boy smiled at her and she felt a pang of guilt. He was obviously enthusiastic about the match.

She looked at the woman sitting beside Styll and felt a mild surprise. Speaker Sirri and her son, Sreil, sat among her tribe. A mad thought came to her. Perhaps Sirri had come seeking a wife for her son, too. Perhaps Sreil and Sveel would have to battle for her. Drilli smothered a laugh at the thought. *Too bad, Sreil. My father won't accept anyone born outside the Snake River tribe, not even the son of the leader of all Siyee.*

Her family joined the circle, her father managing to direct her to the place beside Sveel. She made herself talk to the boy. There was no point being rude. If she must marry him, she may as well try to get along with him. He wasn't a dislike-able person, just not interesting or particularly smart.

'So why have you joined us, Speaker Sirri?' her father asked. 'I have heard you do not agree with our marriage traditions.'

Sirri smiled. 'It is not that I disagree with them, Zyll, but that I think it is foolish for Siyee to marry so young. They haven't fully developed as individuals at fourteen.'

'Which is why it is best that their parents select a partner for them.'

She shook her head. 'If only that were so. I have observed parents make bad matches as often as good ones. While they may take great care with their choice, they are hampered by the fact that their sons or daughters haven't yet become the person they are going to be. How can they decide who will make a suitable mate when they don't yet fully know their offspring's character?'

Zyll scowled. 'This is not just about character. It is about bloodlines and tribal connections.'

She frowned. 'Huan released us from our interbreeding laws over a century ago.'

'Yet we don't want to regress to a state where half of our children are born—'

'There is little danger in that now,' Sirri interrupted, her eyes suddenly cold. Drilli suddenly remembered hearing that the Speaker's first child had been born wingless and shrivelled, and had died an infant. 'There are enough of us now that such occurrences rarely happen.'

'I was not talking of inter-tribal connections,' Zyll said. 'I was talking of links within a tribe. My tribe is scattered. If we are not careful, it will vanish in a few years.'

Sirri's expression changed subtly, somehow becoming thoughtful and dangerous at the same time. 'You need not be worried about that any more. The White will return your land to you, and you now have an effective means to defend it, thanks to young Tryss.'

Zyll's jaw tightened at the mention of Tryss's name. 'Even so, we need to strengthen the bonds between our families, or we will return only to find we are strangers to each other.'

Her eyebrows rose, then she nodded respectfully. 'If you must go to such lengths to reassure yourselves, then that is what you must do. I will miss your family's presence here in the Open.' She looked at Sveel. 'You've been training with the warriors, haven't you? How are you finding it?'

Sveel straightened. 'It's hard, but I'm practising every day.'

She nodded. 'Good. You'll need those skills to defend your land after you return. Which is what I wanted to talk to you all about.' She paused, then turned to look at her son. 'Sreil, did you bring that basket?'

The boy blinked, then his eyes widened. 'No, I forgot. Sorry.'

She shook her head and sighed. 'Well, go fetch it then. Bring some water, too.'

'How am I supposed to carry all that?'

'Take Drilli with you.'

Drilli blinked in surprise, then looked at her father. He nodded his approval, though he did not look happy. She got to her feet and hurried after Sreil.

Speaker Sirri's son set a rapid pace, and soon the voices of her tribe had faded beyond hearing. He glanced back, then slowed so she could catch up.

'So you're going to be married,' he said.

She shrugged. 'Looks like it.'

'You don't sound too enthusiastic.'

'Don't I?' she asked dryly.

'No. You don't like Sveel, do you?'

'He's all right.'

'But not who you'd like to be marrying, right?'

She frowned at him. 'Why are you asking?'

He smiled. 'It was pretty obvious who you favoured at the trei-trei, Drilli. So why aren't you marrying Tryss? He's more famous than the founders.'

Her stomach twisted. 'Because I don't have a choice.'

'Of course you do.'

She scowled. 'Do I? I haven't spoken to Tryss for weeks. He hasn't even tried to talk to me. I don't even know if he wants to get married.'

'I could find out for you.'

Her heart skipped. 'You'd do that?'

'Of course.' He smiled, then chuckled in a self-satisfied way. At once she felt a stab of suspicion. She stopped and crossed her arms.

'What's in it for you, Sreil? Why help us?'

He turned to face her, still smiling. 'Because . . .' He paused and began to chew his lip. 'I shouldn't say.'

She narrowed her eyes at him.

'Well . . .' He grimaced. 'All right then. Your father is a tribal snob. It's not just that he won't even consider letting you marry someone whose invention might save our people and get him back his lands – though that just tops everything – it's other things he's said and done since coming here.' His expression changed from angry to apologetic. 'Sorry.'

She nodded. What he'd said was fair, though she did feel a little offended that this was how her family was regarded. Surely after all they'd been through . . .

'Mother also thinks you probably contributed to Tryss's success,' he added. 'He might need you in some way, so it's foolish to take you away from him.'

She blinked in surprise and was about to deny it when she remembered that she was the one who had shown him how to use blowpipes. He had come up with the idea of using them as part of the harness, but if she hadn't been there . . .

'Ask him,' she said. 'But don't tell him why. I don't want him to marry me just to save me from marrying someone else. He has to want to marry me because he wants to.'

Sreil grinned. 'I'll get back to you on that.'

CHAPTER 28

Millo Baker was a quiet man. Leiard had come to understand that Jayim's father knew the value of being content rather than happy. Millo might not be overjoyed with his life, but neither was he unhappy with it.

He rarely joined his wife, son and guest for the morning meal. Today, however, a bout of the usual winter head infection had forced him to rest. He had surprised Leiard by being unusually talkative, telling them of the news, official or speculation, that he had heard. But then the cure Leiard had given him sometimes had that effect on people.

'Have you been to the Temple?' he asked Leiard.

'Not since Auraya left.'

Millo shook his head. 'I've never seen so many soldiers. Must be the whole army in there. Didn't know it was so big. The lines of men – and women – looking to join are so long they go out the arch and two blocks down the main road.'

Tanara frowned and glanced at Jayim. 'Just as well they don't take Dreamweavers.'

Jayim's expression was guarded. Leiard sensed that the boy's feelings were a mixture of relief, guilt and annoyance.

'What do you know of these Pentadrians, Leiard?' Millo asked.

Leiard shrugged. 'Not much. Only what other Dreamweavers have told me. They are a young cult, only a few hundred years old at the most. They worship five gods, as the Circlians do.'

'Real gods, or dead ones?' Millo asked.

'I do not know. Their names are unfamiliar to me.'

'What are their names?'

'Sheyr, Ranah, Alor, Sraal and Hrun.'

'Perhaps they are old dead gods who had different names in the southern continent,' Jayim suggested.

'Perhaps,' Leiard agreed, pleased that Jayim would think of this.

The boy's eyes brightened. 'Or the same gods as the Circlians follow, known by different names.'

'That wouldn't make much sense,' Tanara pointed out. 'They'd be sending their own followers to fight their own followers.'

Leiard looked at her thoughtfully, then shook his head. 'No, I can see no profit in it for them.'

She frowned. 'You think they'd do that, if there was profit in it?'

'Possibly.'

'But that would be unspeakably cruel.'

'The gods aren't as noble and fair as the Circlians would have us believe,' Leiard found himself saying. 'We Dream-weavers remember what they have done in the past, before this charade of concern for mortals began. We know what they are capable of.'

Tanara stared at him in horror.

Mirar, Leiard thought sternly. *I told you not to do that.*

Yes, you did. But what can you do to stop me? the other voice replied.

Leiard ignored the question. *What did you hope to achieve by frightening her?*

Now another knows the truth.

And how will that benefit Tanara?

Mirar didn't reply. Tanara looked away. 'Then we'd best hope they continue to want to keep up the charade,' she murmured.

Jayim was watching Leiard through narrowed eyes. 'What do these memories of yours tell you about the Pentadrians?'

'My memories tell me nothing. I have learned what I have learned from Dreamweavers in Sennon.'

'Through dream links?'

'Yes.'

Jayim frowned. He opened his mouth to speak, then sighed and shook his head. 'What do they think of them?'

'That Dreamweavers have nothing to fear from the Pentadrians. The southern cult regards us with pity, not fear or dislike. Which proves that their gods are not the same as the Circlians',' he added.

The boy nodded slowly and thoughtfully. 'Will we join this war?'

'Dreamweavers do not fight,' Leiard replied.

'I know, but will we go as healers?'

'Probably.'

Tanara's eyes widened. She glanced at her son and bit her lip. Millo frowned.

'We will be quite safe,' Leiard assured them. 'The Pentadrians understand that we tend to all, no matter what race or religion. Our Gifts will protect us from mishaps or misunderstandings.' He looked at Jayim. 'It will be a good opportunity for Jayim to hone his healing sk—'

A knocking interrupted him. They all looked up at each other, then Millo stood and moved to the door.

Leiard finished his drink, then left the table. Jayim had finished his meal long before. Like most boys his age, he was perpetually hungry. He stood and followed Leiard toward the stairs to the rooftop garden.

'Wait, you two,' Millo called.

He stepped back from the doorway. A woman moved past him, and as Leiard took in the Dreamweaver robes and familiar face he blinked in surprise.

'Dreamweaver Elder Arleej,' he said, touching heart, mouth and forehead.

She smiled and returned the gesture. 'Dreamweaver Adviser Leiard.'

'It is good to see you again. Are you well?'

She shrugged. 'A little tired. I have only just arrived.'

'Then you will be wanting some food and a hot drink,' Tanara said. 'Sit down.'

Tanara ushered Arleej to a seat then bustled out. Leiard sat down next to the Dreamweaver elder and gestured for Jayim, who was hovering uncertainly by the stairway, to join them. Millo shuffled away to his room.

'What brings you to Jarime?' Leiard asked.

Arleej smiled crookedly. 'Haven't you heard? There is to be a war. You and Auraya talked us into an alliance just in time, it seems.'

Leiard smiled. There was no resentment in her voice, only irony. 'No wonder you are tired. Did you share a ship with hundreds of soldiers, or did the Somreyan Dreamweavers manage to claim one for themselves?'

She shook her head. 'We are travelling in small numbers on merchant ships, arriving before and after the Somreyan army. Memories of the massacres of Dreamweavers on the mainland are still strong. We will attract less attention this way.'

'I do not think you would have been in any danger, had you arrived with Somreyan troops.'

'You are probably right. Seeing the troops of another land

395

valuing Dreamweavers might have encouraged Hanians to do the same. Old habits and fears are hard to defeat, however, especially for us.' Arleej looked at him, her direct gaze unsettling. 'How are you, Leiard? Has linking with Jayim helped you control your link memories?'

Leiard sensed Jayim's surprise and alarm. 'I am making some progress on my—'

'He doesn't link with me,' Jayim interrupted. 'He teaches me everything except mind links or dream links.'

Arleej looked from Jayim to Leiard, her brows lowering into a frown.

'And he mumbles to himself all the time,' Jayim added, his voice strained. 'Sometimes it's like he's not aware of me. Then he says odd things in the voice of a stranger.'

'Leiard,' Arleej said, her voice quiet but filled with suppressed alarm. 'Do you know . . . ? Are you . . . ?' She shook her head. 'I know you understand what you risk. Is this secret of yours so great you would sacrifice your identity – your sanity?'

He shivered. *My sanity. Maybe I've already lost it. I am hearing voices – one voice, anyway.*

You think you're going insane? Mirar injected. *Living inside your mind is enough to drive anyone mad.*

If you don't like it, go away.

'Leiard?'

He looked up. Arleej was frowning at him. He sighed and shook his head.

'I can't link with Jayim.' He turned to regard his student. 'I am sorry. You should find another teacher. One of the Somreyans will surely—'

'No!' Jayim exclaimed. 'If what Ar – Dreamweaver Elder Arleej says is true, you'll go insane without my help.' He paused to catch his breath. 'Whatever secret you have, I'll keep it. I won't tell anybody.'

'You don't understand,' Leiard said gently. 'If I tell you this secret you can never link with another Dreamweaver. I would not restrict your future that way.'

'If that's what it takes to save you, then I'll do it.'

Leiard stared at Jayim in surprise. When, in the last few months, had this boy become so loyal?

Arleej made a small, strangled sound. She let out her breath in a rush. 'I don't know, Jayim. That is a heavy price for you to pay.' She turned to Leiard, her expression tortured. 'How . . . how long would Jayim have to keep this secret?'

Forever. Leiard looked away and shook his head. It was unfair, but he could not unlive the past.

You know this affair can't last, Mirar whispered. *Eventually it will be discovered so you may as well tell Jayim.*

Why do you want me to stop? You seemed to enjoy dream-linking with her.

She is one of the gods' pawns. I enjoy the irony. In fact, next time I might have a little play with her myself.

Leiard felt his stomach turn. Could Mirar interfere with the dream link?

I might show you a few things you thought you didn't know.

You wouldn't dare. If Auraya knew you had this much control . . .

She would do what? Kill me? But that would mean killing you. I suppose that might not be so hard if she knew her lover could turn into the hated Mirar at an inappropriate moment.

Leiard sighed. *What do you want me to do?*

Leave Jarime. Find somewhere remote where Auraya won't find you. Train Jayim in mind-linking.

If Arleej is right, it will mean the end of your existence.

I don't want to exist. This is the Age of the Five. My time is in the past, when there was a multitude of gods, and immortals roamed freely – what they now call the Age of the Many – and perhaps the far future, but not now.

Leiard was amazed by this admission. If this shadow of Mirar did not want to exist, why was it so concerned about Leiard's safety?

The other voice did not answer.

Very well, he thought. *But I will join the Dreamweavers going to the war first.*

He waited, expecting Mirar to protest, because following the army meant being near the White – and Auraya – but the voice remained silent. Relieved, he looked up at Arleej.

'I can only do this if Jayim and I leave Jarime,' he told her. 'I will join you in tending the wounded after the war, then we will disappear for a while. We will meet with other Dreamweavers in the future, when it is safe to do so.' He turned to Jayim. 'You must never allow yourself to come into the presence of the White. They can read minds more thoroughly than any sorcerer has before.'

Jayim frowned. 'If they can read my mind, won't they read the secret from yours?'

'Yes.'

'But you're the Dreamweaver adviser.'

'Not for much longer. I will be resigning as soon as I am ready to leave.'

'Why not now?'

'They may attempt to meet me in order to learn the reason. I want to be long gone when they receive my message.'

Jayim's eyes were wide. 'This must be quite a secret.'

Arleej smiled grimly. 'Yes. I hope it is worth all this trouble.'

'What trouble?'

They all looked up to see Tanara standing in the doorway, holding a platter of food. As Arleej explained, Leiard felt a pang of guilt. He would be taking Jayim away from his family, probably never to return. Then something else occurred to him and he groaned.

'What is it?' Arleej asked.

He looked at her apologetically. 'The White could learn from you and the Bakers that I have left because I have a secret I wish to keep from them.'

She grimaced. 'Which would be enough reason to send people out to find you and bring you back.' She shrugged. 'I don't intend to go anywhere near them anyway.' She looked at Tanara. 'I doubt the White will seek out you and your husband. They're too busy organising a war. Just in case, can you be somewhere else for a few weeks? If you need money for accommodation, we can provide it.'

'Millo has a brother living in the north,' Tanara said. 'We haven't visited in a while.'

'Then visit him,' she said. 'I think I can keep away from the White so long as they still have a Dreamweaver adviser to consult.' She turned to Leiard. 'Do you have anyone in mind to take on the role?'

He shook his head. 'That would be your decision, or Auraya's.'

She pursed her lips, then her eyes narrowed. 'Since Auraya is absent and the other White are busy with war preparations, the matter will probably be put off until she returns – unless I can offer a few candidates. Hmm, this will take some consideration.' She rapped her finger on the table and paused to think. 'My people will be leaving in advance of the army. We will always be more than a day's ride from the Circlians. The White won't know you're with us, and even if they find out they'll be too busy with their preparations to seek you out. I would like to remain close at hand while you sort this out. You may need my help.'

Leiard bowed his head. 'Thank you. I hope I won't need it.'

The eastern horizon brightened steadily, casting a thin, cool light over the sea.

As Auraya walked along the beach with Tyrli she considered her first impressions of the Sand tribe's home. She had come to associate the Siyee with high mountains and forests, but seeing their bowers among the treeless dunes of the coast yesterday had caused her to reassess her assumptions about them. They lived well here on the beaches of Si, which only highlighted what they had lost when Toren settlers had stolen the fertile valleys of their homeland.

'You have everything you need?' Tyrli asked.

'Everything except enough time,' she replied. *Or Leiard's recommendations*, she added to herself. He hadn't dream-linked with her in days, which had made it easier to rise before dawn this morning. She had been waking up early, worrying about the reason for his silence, for the previous two mornings.

'If you had more time I would introduce you to the Elai who trade with us, but they will not meet us for nearly a month.'

'I would like that, even if just to see more of your tribe,' she told Tyrli truthfully. She had only glimpsed how his people lived and would have liked to learn more about them. 'Juran is pressing me to meet with the Elai as soon as possible.'

'There will be another opportunity,' he replied.

'I'll make sure of it.' She turned to face him. 'I will return to the Open in about ten days.'

He nodded. 'We will be ready.'

She smiled at his grim confidence. He had sent messengers back to the Open with her news of the Pentadrian invasion and Juran's request for help in the coming battle. She sighed and looked across the water.

'You should be there by midday,' he assured her.

'How do I find my way?' she asked.

He turned to face the mountains and pointed. 'See the mountain with the double peak?'

'Yes.'

'Fly away from it, keeping it aligned with this beach. You'll see the coast on your right. If you don't see it after a few hours, keep bearing right until you do. Follow it to the end of the peninsula. Then head directly south. There are a lot of little islets around Elai. If you fly for more than an hour without seeing one, you've missed Elai and should head northwards again.'

She nodded. 'Thank you, Tyrli.'

He bowed his head. 'Good luck, Auraya of the White. Fly high, fly fast, fly well.'

'May the gods guide and protect you,' she replied.

Turning to face the sea again, Auraya drew magic and sent herself directly upward. The beach dropped away from her feet until Tyrli was a small dot in a great arc of sand stained gold by the rising sun. She glanced behind at the mountains and noted the position of the double peak. Turning her back, she sent herself in the opposite direction.

For the last few months she had become accustomed to flying in imitation of the Siyee. Now that she was alone she did not feel the need to pretend what she could do was limited by physical strength or the pull of the earth. She began to experiment. The Siyee could only fly as quickly as the wind and their stamina allowed. She had no idea how fast she could move so she began to increase her speed.

Wind was already a problem and she guessed this would be the factor that limited her. As she flew it buffeted her face, dried her eyes and chilled her. She could use magic to generate warmth, but as she flew faster she found that this warmth was quickly stripped away. Curiously, she also began to find it hard to breathe.

She created a magical shield in front of her. It slowed her abruptly, like an oar dragging in water. The shield acted like

401

an oar because of its shape, she guessed. She didn't need an oar, she needed . . . an arrowhead. Inspired, she changed the shape of her shield to a pointed cone. Now it cut through the air easily. It diverted the wind around her and she found she could breathe again.

By now she was moving quicker than she had ever moved before, on land or in the sky, but the only way she knew this was because of the wind rushing past. The sea was too far below to give her any true feeling of speed, and there were no Siyee or reyna riders to compare herself to.

Looking ahead she saw that a shadow had appeared on the horizon – the coast Tyrli had described. If she skimmed over land she might get a better idea of how fast she was flying. She watched the coast impatiently as it drew closer. A rocky face appeared. Cliffs. When she finally reached them she curved to the left and began to follow this rocky, vertical road.

As she did she felt a thrill of excitement. The rock wall rushed past. The air hissed. She was flying faster than she had imagined. Exactly how fast she couldn't guess. As fast as falling, perhaps?

It would have been faster to fly in a straight line, but she found herself following the curves of the wall. It was exhilarating. She swooped into bays and ducked around points. An archway of rock appeared ahead. She flew through it and found herself weaving between several spires of rock that had survived the slow erosion of the cliff face. Ahead, she could see one huge spire standing like a defiant sentinel just beyond the next point. She flew out and circled it.

Coming back around to face the coast, she felt a wry disappointment. From here the cliffs turned sharply northeast. The sentinel marked the end of the peninsula. Her flirtation with the coastline must come to an end.

Circling back around the sentinel, she slowly rose until she reached the top, then set herself down on a flat area of rock. The thin whistling of the wind through the cracks and crevices of the spire was unnaturally quiet after the roar of air passing her during flight. She considered the coastline then turned to regard the sea.

Borra was too far away to be seen from the coast. She had made good time so far. Perhaps if she continued to fly as quickly she would reach it in the next hour. Drawing more magic, she started the final leg of her journey.

The first of the islets appeared after several minutes. Soon more followed, then she saw bigger islands ahead. By the time she had reached these islands even larger ones had appeared on the horizon.

Unlike the smaller islands, which looked like the tops of sand dunes that had accumulated vegetation with the tides, the larger islands appeared to be small, half-drowned mountains. The first she passed was a pair of mountains linked by a rocky ridge. To her left she could see a single smaller peak, and to her right a high rocky crescent rose out of the sea. These landmasses, and the smaller islands between them, formed an enormous ring the size of one of the Si mountains.

Tyrli had told her to look for Elai on the beaches of the largest island. That would be the cresent-shaped island, she decided. She flew toward it, descending slowly. When she was low enough to make out the shrubby vegetation near the coast, she began to search for signs of the sea people.

She found them moments later. Dark-skinned men and women roamed every beach. They were laying strips of glistening seaweed out on the sand, and she could see human forms swimming underwater around the dark shadows of the vegetation, cutting more.

Most were working steadily, though one Elai in each group appeared to be there only to direct the others. A few

403

individuals had climbed to higher ground and stood looking out to sea. One appeared to be looking directly at her and she sensed his amazement. He did not wave or alert the others to her presence. From his thoughts she saw that he didn't believe what he was seeing.

Then there was a bellow of anger, and the watcher jumped and turned to look down at the nearby beach. The leader of the working Elai waved a fist threateningly. The watcher pointed at her. The leader glanced up, then took a step back in surprise.

Time to introduce myself, Auraya thought wryly.

As the leader continued staring at her, other Elai stopped working and looked up to see what he was gazing at. She descended slowly, as she was now sensing both fear and awe from them. Though she dropped toward a place several paces from them, they backed further away.

Then, as her feet touched the ground, they threw themselves onto the sand.

She blinked in surprise, then searched their minds. At once she saw the reason for their reaction. They thought she was Huan.

'People of Borra,' she said slowly, picking the words in their language from their minds. 'Do not abase yourself before me. I am not the goddess Huan, but one of her servants.'

Heads rose. The Elai exchanged glances, then slowly got to their feet. She could see them clearly now. They were only slightly shorter than landwalkers and completely hairless. Their skin was a smooth, glossy blue-black, similar to the skin of the sea-ner she had seen swimming next to the ships on her return from Somrey. Their chests were broad and their hands and feet large and flat with membranes between the fingers and toes. As they stared at her, she noticed that their eyes were rimmed with pink. When they blinked she saw that this

404

pinkness was another membrane, which slid over their eyes like a second set of lids.

All eyes were fixed on her. She skimmed their thoughts. Several had quickly concluded that, if she was no goddess, and clearly not Siyee, then she was a landwalker and not to be trusted. These Elai regarded her with unconcealed suspicion and a hint of simmering hatred. The rest were still confused, their thoughts sluggish. These were the lowest of the Elai society, she guessed. The slow or the unfortunate. They did this menial work because they could do little else. She looked at their leader. He was no smarter, but his bullying temperament had earned him this higher position.

As she met his eyes, the man squared his shoulders. 'Who are you?' he demanded.

'I am Auraya of the White,' she replied. 'One of the Gods' Chosen. I have come on behalf of the gods to meet the leader of all Elai – King Ais.'

The leader narrowed his eyes. 'Why?'

'To . . .'

It was hard to find the right words when these Elai workers' thoughts were full of words they associated with landwalkers – killing, raping, stealing. The words for peace, negotiation or alliance did not pass through their minds so she changed tack. The leader did not expect her to explain herself.

'That is for the king's ears only,' she said.

The leader nodded.

'Will you send one of your people to the king for me?' she asked.

He scowled. 'Why?'

'I would not enter your city without permission,' she replied.

He paused, then looked around at his workers. He pointed to the man who had first seen her – the watcher. The man's shoulders were slumped and his skin looked dull. She read

405

thoughts of discomfort and realised he was dehydrated from spending too much time out of the water. As he received his orders he cheered at the thought of a decent swim.

'Go tell Ree,' the leader said. 'He'll send someone to the palace.'

As the man splashed into the water the leader looked at Auraya. 'It will take time. The palace doesn't take much notice of harvesters. We have work to do now. You wait here, if you want.'

She nodded. He said no more, but raised his voice and hounded the workers back to their tasks. Auraya watched them for a while, but when she caught several resentful thoughts about her staring she moved further away and took care to appear as if her attention was elsewhere.

The sun climbed to its zenith, then began to descend. The Elai did not pause for rest, though they stopped now and then to wet their skin. From their minds she learned more about Elai customs.

Their city was crowded, and most Elai lived in tiny rooms. Living in such close quarters made them respectful of each other's space. Strong taboos about touching or meeting another's eyes existed, and were based on a strict social hierarchy.

They couldn't have been more different to the Siyee.

Despite these divisions of class and power, there was a strong sense of duty toward all other Elai. These men and women willingly emerged from the city to harvest the seaweed, be bullied by men like their leader, and risk being attacked by raiders, in order to help feed their people. She read concern from many of them for a worker who was ill and to whom they had brought food.

Even the wealthy and powerful contributed to the city's safety. If the king knew his people were starving, he would distribute food to them. Four times a year he held a feast to which all Elai were invited. He even took his place in the roster for manning the lookout above the city, climbing the long staircase in order to help watch for raiders.

Staircase? Above the city? Auraya smiled. *So there is another way into the city other than the underwater one.*

It was an interesting piece of information, but not one she intended to use. To do so would be to ensure she never gained the Elai's trust. Reading the workers' minds had shown her the terrible impact the raiders had made on the sea people's lives. It was no surprise to see how deeply they loathed landwalkers. Being a representative of the gods might get her an audience with the king, but it would not ensure anything more. She was going to have to prove herself trustworthy.

She sighed. *And I don't have time for that.*

'Landwalker woman.'

She started at the gruff voice and turned to see that the leader was approaching. Standing up, she walked forward to meet him.

'The king sent a reply to your message,' he said hesitantly. She realised with dismay that he was gathering his courage. He expected her to be angry and feared how she would express it. 'He said: "The King of Elai does not want to talk to the landwalker claiming to speak for the gods. Landwalkers are not welcome here – not even to stay on the smallest island. Go home."'

She nodded slowly. There was no sign of deceit in his mind. The message might have changed a little with repetition, but not the general meaning in it. The man regarded her warily, then hurried away.

:Juran?

:Auraya? Juran replied immediately.

:The King of the Elai refused my request to meet with him. I don't think he believes that I am what I say I am. She repeated the

407

message. *That is not all. These people's hatred for landwalkers is strong. I think we will have to prove ourselves trustworthy. I wish that we could do something about these raiders . . .*

:That would remove a potent incentive to ally with us.

:I don't think a promise of dealing with the raiders some time in the future will impress them at all. Unlike the Siyee, help will have to come before, not after an alliance.

:You can't be sure of that until you meet the king. Be persistent. Come back tomorrow and every following day. You can, at least, impress him with your determination.

She smiled. *I will.*

Looking down at the workers, she saw that they were now tying huge bundles of seaweed on their backs. Some were wading into the water and swimming away. She caught snatches of thought that told her they were leaving early and that some suspected this was because her presence frightened their leader.

She sighed in frustration. How was she ever going to win over the Elai, when just her presence on the beach had an adverse effect on these people?

Huan did say this would be a challenge, she reminded herself.

Smiling wryly, she gathered magic and lifted herself into the sky.

CHAPTER 29

As the dark folds of sleep slipped away, Emerahl became aware of voices.

'Jade. Wake up.'

'That's probably not her real name.'

'I don't know her real name. Do you?'

'No, she wouldn't tell me.'

'You *asked?*'

'Didn't you?'

'No. It's not polite.'

'I used to know a girl named Jade.'

'It's a nice name. Not like Brand. Who'd call their daughter Brand? I hate my name.'

Who are these women? Emerahl felt her mind rise toward full consciousness and memory return. *They're just my room companions.* She frowned. *They're awake before me? That's unusual . . .*

'Who'd call their daughter Tide? Or *Moon*light?' Tide asked.

Brand giggled. 'My little brother used to have a pet moohook called Moonlight.'

Tide chuckled. 'Moonlight. Diamond. Innocence. Names best suited to whores or pets. Only an idiot would curse their child with them. Jade isn't too bad, I suppose. Look, she's awake at last.'

Emerahl found herself looking at the two attractive young women. She yawned and sat up.

'What are you two doing up this early?'

Brand smiled ruefully. 'Rozea's called a meeting. You'd better get dressed. Quickly, too.'

Emerahl swung her legs out from under the blankets and stretched. The other two girls were wearing older tunics rather than their best. Emerahl chose the worn, plain tunic Leaf had given her to wear outside of working hours or during lessons and quickly changed into it.

As she dressed she saw and heard other girls passing in the corridor. Brand and Tide waited quietly but she could sense excitement and expectation from their minds.

'What's this meeting all about, then?' she asked as she quickly combed her hair.

'Don't know,' Brand replied.

'Probably something to do with the war.'

'Hurry up and we'll find out sooner,' Brand urged.

Emerahl smiled and moved to join them at the doorway. They stepped out into the corridor, Brand in the lead. Emerahl took note of the turns they made, and after climbing the third staircase guessed that their meeting place was on the top floor of the brothel.

A few steps later she followed her companions through a pair of large open doors into an enormous room. Windows lined opposite walls. A wide screen painted with scenes of love-making stood on a raised floor at the end of the room. The main floorspace was filled with girls.

Emerahl looked around, surprised to see so many. Some she had only met briefly since arriving at the brothel, others had introduced themselves and welcomed her warmly. There were girls here she had never seen before. As she scanned the faces she saw a distinctly masculine one, and realised that there were young men in the room as well as women. She hadn't seen male whores here before, either.

'This is the dancing room,' Tide murmured. 'Rozea has two or three big parties in here each year. Sometimes the king attends. Last year he—'

Her words were lost behind the clang of a bell. Faces turned toward the raised floor. Rozea had appeared. The madam waited until the room was quiet, then handed a large gold bell to Leaf.

'It is good to see you all in one place again,' she said, smiling. 'So many lovely faces in one room.' Her gaze flickered around the room, then her expression became sterner.

'You will have all heard by now that Toren's army will be leaving in a week to join the fight against the Pentadrian invaders. Many of our customers will be going to war to risk their lives for our sakes.' She paused, then smiled. 'And we will be going with them.'

Emerahl felt her stomach sink. The last thing she needed to do was tag along after the very priests who wanted to find her. She would have to leave the brothel.

'Well, not all of us,' Rozea corrected. 'Some of you will stay here. I'll leave the choice up to you. We will travel as comfortably as we can. I have already arranged for tarns and tents to be made. Our customers will still be of the same quality and they expect a certain degree of luxury for their money.'

She smiled. 'For some of you this will be a rare opportunity to travel outside Porin. You will also witness a great event. It is not every day you have the chance to see the White in battle. You may even, if you are lucky, meet one of them.'

Emerahl resisted a smile. Rozea was making tagging after an army sound like a wonderful adventure. There would be a lot of work, in rough and dangerous conditions. Surely none of these girls – and boys – were fooled by this pretty speech.

411

Her senses told her that the room was buzzing with excitement. Emerahl sighed. *These young women and men know nothing of war*, she reminded herself. *There hasn't been one in over a hundred years, from what I've heard.*

One pair of eyes was not shining with excitement, however. Moonlight was standing to one side, her expression aloof. Emerahl sensed mild envy from the woman. Rozea's voice became businesslike again.

'Those of you who wish to go, come to the front of the room. Those who want to stay behind, move to the back. Go on now. There is no shame in either. I need people to come and people to stay.'

Brand strode forward confidently. After a moment's hesitation, Tide followed. Emerahl stayed where she was, near the back. As the room began to settle, Rozea scanned the faces of those closest to her. She frowned, then looked up at the back of the room. Seeing Emerahl, her lips thinned in disappointment. Emerahl felt her stomach knot. She tried to think of a reason Rozea might want her to come on this trip, but she could find none.

The woman's attention returned to the small crowd before her.

'Thank you. Stay here and Leaf will write down your names. You may all have a day free to visit family before you go, if you wish to. Once again, thank you.'

She stepped down from the raised floor and strode toward a pair of doors. As she reached them, she paused and looked at Emerahl.

'Jade. Come with me. I want to speak to you.'

Emerahl smothered a sigh and followed Rozea into a large room furnished with an enormous bed fit for a king. *In fact*, she thought, *it probably is for the king*. The woman closed the doors quietly, then turned to face her.

'Why don't you want to come with us, Emerahl?'

Emerahl sighed and looked away. 'I only just got here. I feel comfortable and safe for the first time in . . . well, a long while.'

Rozea smiled. 'I see. What if I told you I have plans for you? What if I said that by the time you returned to Porin you would be the richest, most sought-after lady of pleasure in all of Toren?'

'What do you mean?'

Rozea's smile widened. She took Emerahl's arm and gently drew her to the bed. They sat down. 'Moonlight is pregnant. I can't take her with me, and I'll need a new favourite soon anyway. The comments customers have made about you have proved me right. You're good at your work. You have a quality about you that intrigues men. I want you to be the new favourite. Since you must be seen to earn the position, you will leave with the girls and take on your new role when we—'

'I don't want to be the new favourite,' Emerahl interrupted.

Rozea's eyebrows rose. 'Why not? You will have fewer customers, and then only the best of them. You will earn ten times as much as you do now.'

'But Panilo—'

'If you have a special place for him in your heart, then you may still see him.'

'I don't want to leave Porin.'

Rozea straightened and crossed her arms. 'I'll give you a few days to think about it. I have to warn you, Jade. The comfort and safety you have here must be earned. I expect you to come with me, favourite or not.' She inclined her head at the door. 'Go.'

Emerahl bowed her head and walked out of the room. The knot in her stomach had grown into a hard lump of anxiety. She looked around at all the whores talking excitedly and sighed. *I thought I'd found a place to lie low and hide. Instead I'm to become the city's favourite mistress. So much for the anonymity of prostitution!* She considered the options she had. She could leave the brothel now and remain in Porin, alone, unprotected, with limited money in a city half-empty. *If Rozea pays me.* Emerahl chewed her lip. *Or I could leave the city with Rozea and the girls.*

Rozea would probably follow behind the army, after the supply carts. The priests would travel at the front of the column, leading the army. Their attention would be elsewhere. But the priest searching for her might guess she'd take the opportunity to leave. He might stay behind to watch for her. *This is so frustrating. I don't even know if the priest is still watching the gates.* She did not like taking even tiny risks. One small mistake could mean her death. She had lived a long time, and the longer she had lived, the more fond of living she had become.

Either that, or I've just become a bigger coward.

Then I must get over it. Sometimes risks have to be taken, or one ends up trapped and miserable. So which risk is worse?

Leaving the city with the whores might be a smaller risk than leaving by herself. If she was one girl among many the priests might not look closely. Then again, she might stand out as the only one whose mind was unreadable.

Unless, of course, they think there's a good reason for my lack of thoughts. A good reason, like being dead . . . or unconscious.

She felt a shiver of cold run over her skin. Playing dead was not something she wanted to do again if she could avoid it. Reaching an unconscious state, however . . . There were many ways to do it, and not all of them were unpleasant.

'What's wrong, Jade?'

Emerahl turned to find Brand approaching. 'Rozea ordered me to go.'

Brand snorted. 'So much for giving us a choice. Are you going to visit your family before you go?'

414

'No, are you?'

The girl shrugged. 'Probably. I don't like them much, but I may as well take the chance to leave the brothel for a day.'

Emerahl frowned. She doubted Rozea would allow her to go out. How was she to get the substances that would make her fall unconscious?

Then the obvious solution came to her. She lowered her voice. 'Could you do me a favour, Brand?'

The girl smiled. 'Depends what it is.'

'I'll probably need a little something to help me relax on this journey. Could you do some shopping for me while you're out?'

Brand's eyebrows rose, then she grinned. 'Sure.'

The warm updraught from the ravine bore the young Green Lake tribesman upward. He tilted his wings and landed lightly on the cliff top. His face was flushed with embarrassment and anger.

'It's not easy, is it?' Tryss asked the man, smiling wryly. 'Think of what it was like when you first learned to use a bow. This is even harder. Both you and your target are moving. If you had the dedication to learn the bow, then you have what it takes to learn this.'

The man's expression softened a little. Tryss turned to the next young warrior, a sullen-looking man, and frowned.

'Your harness is loose.'

The man scowled. 'It is uncomfortable.'

Tryss met the man's eyes. 'I'm not surprised. Fitted properly, it should move with you. Hanging like this it will only hamper you. When you first carried a bow you would have been conscious of its weight. You would have been taught that you must strap it tight against your body or it could be dangerous in flight. The same is true for this harness. Like

415

your bow, you will soon grow used to the feel and weight of it. Fit it properly and I'll—'

A loud whoop and laughter smothered his words. Tryss turned to see a group of boys, led by Sreil, land nearby. Small packs were strapped to their backs. Seeing them, Tryss sighed with relief. The packs were filled with replacement darts and arrows for the harnesses. The Siyee too young or too old to fight were making them in great numbers. He knew these Green Lake tribesmen would be more enthusiastic about learning to use the harness if there was the prospect of actually killing something.

The boys distributed the darts and arrows while Tryss gave instructions on how to set them into their harnesses. He noted that the sullen man had tightened his harness straps at last. Sreil sent the boys home, then turned to regard Tryss.

'Can I talk to you for a bit?'

Tryss nodded. He turned to the warriors. 'Find me something worth hunting,' he told them. 'I'll catch up.'

Several of the men grinned. They turned away and leapt off the cliff. Tryss watched them, making sure all the harnesses were working well. Three days before, a badly made harness had seized up. Its owner had not been far from the ground but he had broken both legs in the fall. Since then Tryss had recommended that harnesses be inspected carefully every day by a member of each tribe proficient in their use and making.

'I spoke to Drilli again,' Sreil said.

Tryss's heart skipped a beat. He turned to regard Sreil expectantly.

'And?'

'It wasn't easy,' Sreil added. 'Her father practically keeps her locked up in their bower all the time now. I think he suspects something. Mother wasn't all that subtle about what we were

416

up to that day we met with the Snake River tribe. I wouldn't be surprised if—'

'Sreil! What did she say?'

The boy grinned. 'You *are* tense today. Anyone would think you were about to get married.'

Tryss crossed his arms and glared at Sreil. Since Tryss had started training the Speaker's son, he had been pleased to find he got along well with the boy. Nothing bothered Sreil. He found something funny in every situation. Sometimes his sense of humour was deliciously dark, at other times infuriating. Like now.

Sreil put up a hand as if to ward off a blow. 'Stop that glaring. You're scaring me.'

Tryss continued glaring.

'All right. She said "yes".'

Two emotions swept through Tryss: relief and a giddy terror. Drilli wanted to marry him. She was willing to defy her father and leave her tribe to become his wife.

He was going to get married.

It's not like we can't change our minds in a few years, he told himself. *If she decides she doesn't like me after all.*

Still, it meant the end of their childhood. They would be adults, expected to contribute to the tribe to the fullest. Not just the simple chores he did every day for his parents, but the work of gathering food, making bowers and fighting.

Which I'm already doing now anyway. Instead of going home to my parents I'll go home to Drilli . . . and maybe a child too, in a year or so.

He smiled, picturing himself playing with his own little son or daughter. The thought was appealing. The things he could teach them . . .

I just have to survive this war first – and she has to survive having the children.

He turned his mind from that thought. He could not go through life always afraid the worst would happen. People overcame their troubles as they came to them. For now, all he needed to deal with – other than training warriors – was getting Drilli away from her father so a marriage ceremony could take place. For that he needed Sreil's help.

'So who is going to do the ritual?' he asked. 'Your mother?'

Sreil grinned. 'No,' he said. 'She doesn't mind people suspecting she had a hand in this, but she doesn't want anyone knowing for sure. Performing the ritual would make it obvious that she planned it. Once we get Drilli away I'll fetch one of the other Speakers. The head of the Temple Mountain tribe is still here. I bet he doesn't know what's going on.'

'What if he refuses to do it?'

'He can't. He has to do it. It's law.'

Tryss took a deep breath. 'So when?'

Sreil grimaced. 'That depends on Drilli's father. We'll have to wait until he and her mother leave her alone in the bower.'

'Can't we arrange something? Give them some reason to leave?'

Sreil smiled. 'Of course. Yes, that's what we'll do.' He rubbed his hands together gleefully. 'This is going to be so much fun.'

'For you, maybe,' Tryss retorted. 'I'm going to be dying of nerves.' Then he grinned. 'I'm glad you're enjoying helping us, Sreil.'

The other boy shrugged. 'I'd better go and start plotting. I think your students have found something worth hunting.'

Tryss searched the sky until he saw the Green Lake warriors. The men were flying in circles, and as he watched one dived down into the trees.

'I had better make sure they're being careful.' He nodded at Sreil, then leapt off the cliff and flew toward his latest group of trainee warriors.

CHAPTER 30

Danjin's new clothes – the uniform of an adviser – were stiff and tight. Until now he hadn't thought it possible that anything could be less comfortable than the fancy garb a nobleman was expected to wear in public. The thick leather vest of the uniform, designed to emulate armour, fitted too closely over a white tunic that looked like a frugal attempt to mimic a priest's circ. Clearly, whoever had made the uniforms could not decide whether advisers were military or priestly, so they'd mingled elements of both styles of clothing.

The door to his bedroom opened. He turned to find Silava staring at him.

'Appalling, isn't it?'

She nodded. 'If you have an opportunity, lose the vest rather than the tunic. I suspect you'll look fine in just the tunic, but you haven't got the body for wearing only the vest.'

He patted his chest and stomach. 'What do you mean? Aren't I manly enough?'

She smirked. 'I'm not answering that. If you do rid yourself of both the vest and the tunic, be sure to time it well. Your adversary will probably be blinded by all the white skin. Or laugh so much he drops his sword. Either way, it might give you a chance to run away.'

Danjin huffed with indignation. 'Me? Run away?'

He expected a quip about his fitness, but instead her expression became serious.

'Yes,' she said. She walked up to him and gazed into his eyes. 'Run away. I'm too young to become a widow.'

'I'm not going to . . . wait a moment. Too *what*?'

She pinched his arm, somehow managing to hurt him despite the thick cloth.

'Ow!'

'You deserved that. I'm trying to tell you how much I'm going to worry about you.'

Several cheeky replies sprang to mind but he pushed them away. He gently wrapped his arms around her shoulders. The material of the vest resisted the movement and he felt a stab of resentment that even embracing his wife was difficult in this ridiculous garb.

Silava sniffed. He drew away, surprised. She wiped her tears and turned from him, embarrassed.

'You will . . . you will be careful?' she asked quietly.

'Of course.'

'Promise me.'

'I promise I will be careful.'

She nodded and drew back. 'I'll hold you to that.' The sound of footsteps approaching drew their attention to the doorway. Their servant appeared, breathing heavily.

'Fa-Spear has arrived.'

Danjin nodded. 'I'll be down to join him in a moment.'

He turned to his wife and kissed her. 'Goodbye for now, Silava.'

Her eyes glistened, but her voice was normal as she replied, 'Goodbye for now.'

He hesitated, reluctant to leave her when she was upset, but she waved a hand impatiently.

'Go on. Don't keep your father waiting.'

'No, that would never do.'

She managed a smile. He winked at her, then left the room. As he started down the stairs to the ground floor he drew in a deep breath and steeled himself for his father's scorn.

It was cold outside, despite the bright morning sunlight. Fa-Spear was waiting in a covered platten. Danjin stepped out of his house and into the vehicle.

'Father,' he said in greeting.

'Danjin,' his father replied. 'What a beautiful day to set out for war, eh? I wonder if the gods arranged it.'

'Whether they arrange it or not, every rain-free day will be appreciated,' Danjin replied.

His father leaned back in his seat and called to the driver to move on. As the platten sprang into motion, he regarded Danjin in his typical calculating manner.

'You must be feeling proud today.'

'Proud?'

'You are risking your life for your country. That is something to be proud of.'

Danjin shrugged. 'I will not be in any great danger, Father. Certainly nothing equal to what my brothers have faced recently. It takes a braver man than I to venture into the south at this time.'

His father's eyes gleamed. 'Indeed, their job is one that involves taking many risks.'

Danjin chuckled. 'Yes. Though it didn't surprise me when Rian observed that Theran has a habit of taking unnecessary risks.'

'Rian said that?'

'Yes. He also said Theran is not good at following orders either, but I guess that doesn't come easily to a man who is used to having a free rein.'

Fa-Spear stared at Danjin, his eyes slowly narrowing.

'What do you know of Theran's travels?'

Danjin shrugged. 'Everything he bothered to report. Nirem and Gohren were much more reliable. And careful.'

'You . . . you knew all along.'

Danjin met and held his father's eyes. 'Of course I did.'

Fa-Spear stared at Danjin, his expression neither approving or disapproving.

'Was it your idea?'

'No,' Danjin answered truthfully. 'Even if it had occurred to me, I would not have suggested it. I could not have deliberately sent family members into danger. Rian raised the matter with me beforehand and kept me informed of their activities.'

'I see. Why didn't you tell us you knew?'

Danjin smiled, 'It wasn't necessary. These sorts of matters are best left undiscussed. For everyone's sake.'

'So why are you telling me now?'

'Because Rian and his people are too busy preparing for war to tell you the latest news, so I offered to pass it on myself.' Danjin paused. 'Theran *was* taken captive as we suspected, but our people managed to rescue him. He, Nirem and Gohren are on their way home.'

His father nodded, the relief clearly written in his face. The same relief Danjin had felt at the news. While he might not get along well with his brothers, he did not want to see any of them enslaved or killed.

Then he took a deep breath and forced himself to go on. 'There is something else you should know, Father. When Theran was captured he was tortured. He revealed many names, including Nirem's and Gohren's. Because of this, neither Theran, Nirem or Gohren will be safe if they sail in southern waters. The White have released them from their duties. I recommend you do not send them—'

'No!' Fa-Spear's eyes blazed. 'Theran would never—!'

'He did,' Danjin said firmly. 'No man can guess how well he, or another, will stand up to torture. The White know this and do not judge him. They are grateful for all he endured in order to bring us information about the Pentadrians.'

His father looked away, his brow a mass of wrinkles. *How forgiving will you be, Father?* Danjin thought. *You never did have any tolerance for weakness, especially not in your sons.*

Fa-Spear was silent for the rest of the journey. The Temple grounds, once neatly scythed grass, were now a mess of mud, tents, carts, soldiers and animals. A long line of platten had formed along the road to the Tower. As the occupants of each disembarked, the vehicles were driven away to a waiting area behind the main Temple buildings.

When their platten finally stopped before the Tower, Danjin waited for his father, as the head of their family, to step out, but the old man did not move. He looked at Danjin, his expression serious.

'Take care of yourself, Danjin,' he said quietly. 'You may not be my favourite son, but you *are* my son, and I do not want to lose you.'

Danjin stared at his father in surprise as the old man rose and climbed down from the platten. He shook his head, then followed.

So this is what it takes. Well, I don't intend to go to war every time I want him to show he values me in some small way.

'I must take my place,' Danjin said as the platten moved away. 'Take care of yourself, Father. And my brothers.'

'I'll probably have to spend the next year recouping losses from the trade deals we've lost in Sennon,' Fa-Spear grumbled quietly. 'Go on, then. Go take your place in this unprofitable but necessary war.'

Danjin smiled. *Back to his old gruff self.* He nodded politely, then turned away to look for his fellow advisers.

The White's advisers would travel in a tarn together, once the parade left the city. Danjin hadn't been told where to meet them, but he had a good idea how to find them. After searching for several minutes he saw a small group of men and a few women wearing the same uniform as his own. They looked about as comfortable as he felt, he noted.

They stood in a rough circle beside the platform that had been built for the White to address the army from. Their attention was on something or someone in their midst. As Danjin reached them he saw that Rian was talking to them. He stepped into a gap in the circle.

'Adviser Danjin Spear.' Rian glanced at him, then around the circle. 'Now that you are all here there is someone I must introduce.'

Rian glanced over his shoulder, then stepped back. To Danjin's surprise, a Dreamweaver woman stood a little apart from the group. Rian beckoned and she stepped forward, her gaze wary.

'Dreamweaver Adviser Raeli. She replaces Dreamweaver Leiard, who has resigned in order to dedicate himself to training his student.'

The advisers nodded politely, but the woman did not smile or return the gesture. She met Danjin's gaze and he realised he had been staring at her out of surprise.

'Then I wish him well,' Danjin said to her. 'I found him a useful and reliable fellow adviser.'

The woman acknowledged this with a shallow nod, then looked away. Danjin glanced at Rian. Did Auraya know of this turn of events? She hadn't mentioned it last night, when she had spoken to him through the ring. He considered asking Rian, but the White had turned abruptly to stare in the

425

direction of the platform. A crowd of high priests and priest-esses had gathered before it. Beyond them were the rest of the priesthood. Beyond that was the army. Danjin could just see the plumes on their helmets – blue for the Hanians and red and orange for Somreyans.

'I must leave you now,' Rian stated. 'We are nearly ready to begin.'

He made the one-handed gesture of the circle, which all advisers apart from the Dreamweaver woman returned, then hurried away to join Juran, Dyara and Mairae at the platform. After a brief exchange of words, the four White ascended the stairs.

The crowd immediately began to quieten. The White formed a line. As the third strongest, Auraya would normally have stood in the middle of that line, Danjin noted. was she watching now?

Of course she is, Danjin thought. *But she will be linking with the other White. They'd have the best view from up there. It must be quite a sight.*

Juran stepped forward and raised his arms. When the last few voices had dwindled to whispers and murmurs, he let his arms fall to his sides.

'Fellow Circlians. People of Hania and Somrey. Loyal friends and allies. I thank you all for answering my call to arms.

'Today we will set forth for the Plains of Gold. There we will meet with the forces of Genria, Toren and Si. We will form a vast army. It will be a sight to inspire awe. Never before have so many nations of Northern Ithania united in one single purpose.

'It will also be a terrible sight, for what brings us together is war – and not a war of our making. A war brought to us by a foolish and barbaric people, the Pentadrians.' He paused. His voice had been dark with contempt when he had spoken the name of the heathen cult.

'Let me tell you what I know of these Pentadrians. They claim to worship five gods, as we do. But these gods are false. The Pentadrians must enslave and seduce men and women into worshipping them, and they have set forth for Northern Ithania with the intention of forcing us to do so as well. But we will not!' His voice rang out, strong and angry.

Several voices in the crowd rose in reply, shouting denials.

'We will not exchange our gods for these corrupt sorcerer priests!' Juran continued.

'*No!*' came the reply.

'We will drive them back to their heathen temples.'

'*Yes!*'

'We will show them what it is to worship real gods, with real power.'

The crowd began to cheer. Juran smiled and let them yell their enthusiasm for a while before speaking again.

'The gods have entrusted us, the White, with great power in order that we can protect you. We have called together an army of our own. We Circlians are not a violent people. We do not relish bloodshed. But we *will* defend ourselves. We *will* defend each other. We *will* defend our right to worship the Circle of Gods. And we *will* win!'

He raised a fist and shook it at the crowd. The response was deafening. Danjin resisted a smile. With the sun shining and Juran's confidence infecting all, it was hard to imagine them losing this battle. *Not that I can imagine us losing the battle anyway*, he mused. *How can we fail, when we have the gods on our side?*

'Follow us now!' Juran called over the cheering. 'Follow us to war!'

He stepped off the platform and mounted his Bearer. The other White followed suit. They urged their magnificent white reyna toward the crowd. High priests and priestesses stepped back to allow their leaders through.

427

Gradually, everyone began to follow. Danjin edged toward the platform, then climbed a few steps so he could watch as the great mass of people shuffled inward to become part of a column marching out of the Temple. Hearing a distant roar, Danjin looked over their heads. The White had just passed through the archway into the city. He took another step up, and saw that the streets beyond were lined with people.

The stairs vibrated from another's steps. Danjin looked down to see Lanren Songmaker, one of the military advisers, climbing toward him.

'We should move closer,' the man murmured. 'I doubt the army will wait for us if we aren't ready to step in behind the priests.'

'Yes,' Danjin agreed. He descended to the ground and joined the other advisers. As the last of the priests and priestesses joined the column, Lanren ushered them forward to take their place.

Auraya looked at the remains of the previous night's meal and grimaced. She liked fish, but the only species she had been able to catch last night was woodfish. They were notoriously bland and she had found no spices or herbs with which to add flavour. She had resigned herself to this tasteless fare only to be tormented by impressions of the fine feast Danjin was enjoying during their mental conversation last night.

If I had known I'd be camping on an uninhabited cliff top for days I would have brought a bit of food with me. And some soap.

She had just washed herself in a small pool of rainwater she'd found the day before. Her circ was far from its former dazzling white, though she used her Gifts every day to help remove dirt and stains. Sometimes it seemed the only use she had for magic was everyday chores.

Well, apart from flying and reading people's minds, she amended.

428

Moving to the cliff edge, she looked out toward the islands of Borra. She had returned there every day for the last four days. Each time her request to meet with the king had been denied. Yesterday, however, the message the courier had memorised had been different.

'Tell her that I will meet her only if she comes to the palace.'

Was he afraid she was trying to trick him into emerging from the safety of his underwater city? Surely the Elai who had seen her would have reported that she had always come alone. Or had he made the condition out of spite, thinking that she would not be able to reach the city, or would drown in the attempt?

She smiled and leapt off the cliff. While she could easily enter it via the secret path to the lookout, that was no way to earn their trust. If she was to meet the king's challenge she must enter by the underwater way. Her arrival would generate as much curiosity as fear. They'd be as interested in knowing how she had managed to get to their city without drowning as frightened that a stranger had reached their home.

While waiting for Elai messengers to deliver her request for a meeting to the king she'd had plenty of time to think about how she would get to the palace. She had watched these strange sea people, noting how quickly they could swim and for how long they could hold their breath – which was not as long as she had expected. They could remain underwater for only about three to four times as long as a landwalker. They could swim remarkably fast, however. Her experience of swimming had only ever been a little paddling in a quiet bend of the river near her village. That should not be a problem, though. She was not intending to swim.

The air was moist today. Wind teased the waves, sending spray upward. It buffeted her, forcing her to slow down, so she arrived an hour later than she had the previous days. Once

429

she sighed the islands she headed for the one with the two peaks. She descended slowly, noting that the beaches of this island were deserted. Searching with her mind she found several pairs of Elai keeping watch from the highest peak and more in the water. As she landed on the sand she caught a thread of thought from the watchers. She had been seen. She smiled and walked toward the water.

Just before she reached the waves lapping the sand, she stopped. She created a magical shield about herself and then, still upright, lifted herself a little above the ground and moved forward. When she was above deeper water she allowed herself to descend. The shield dipped into the water. The water resisted the intrusion, but she had practised this many times now. The bubble of air around her wanted to bob to the surface, but she didn't let it. She strengthened her shield, sent herself down-ward, and entered a ghostly world.

Ripples of sunlight produced an illusion of movement all around her. The waves, whipped up by wind, in turn stirred the sea floor into clouds of sand. In the gloom she could see bizarre shapes. Structures in the form of trees or fungi or huge patterned eggs loomed around her, all fringed by sea-grasses and weeds whipped back and forth by the waves. Fish hid in this strange sea garden. She suspected they were the same species of fish she had been dazzled by during her experiments at travelling underwater, but their colours were muted in the diminished light.

This fantastic underwater forest ended abruptly. She moved over the edge of a cliff and looked down into an endless gloom. The sea floor could be a few hundred paces down, or several thousand. She shivered and began to descend. From the Elai minds she had read, she knew her destination was not too far distant.

As she dropped down a dark shape veered around her and

stopped. The Elai – a woman – turned back to stare at her. Auraya smiled, but this only startled the woman out of her shock, and she fled.

More Elai appeared. They too stared at her then flitted away. Faint lights drew Auraya to a great hole in the cliff side. Elai were swimming in and out of this constantly, but as they saw her the flow stopped. Some rushed around her and away, others turned and disappeared back into the hole.

The light, Auraya saw, came from the ugliest fish she had ever seen, imprisoned in small cages. The cages were positioned in pairs, and their occupants appeared entranced by each other. As she entered the hole, she passed a pair. One darted toward the other, but the cage prevented its sharp teeth from meeting the flesh of the other fish.

The air within her shield was growing a little stale now. She resisted the temptation to move faster, not wanting to frighten the Elai any more than she already had. After what seemed like an eternity of travelling along the slowly ascending tunnel, she reached the first pocket of air.

It was only shallow, but it was wide enough that several Elai could dart up for a lungful of air when they needed to. She knew from the Elai that narrow vents and cracks between the rock and the surface above kept the air in the pocket fresh.

She opened the top of her shield and let fresh air in. It was cold. When she could feel cold air touch her ankles, she sealed the shield and descended again.

Though she could not see them, she was aware of Elai minds in front of and behind her. If they had wanted to, they could have fled. Instead they remained close enough to watch her. *That's good*, she decided. *They're not as skittish as they first appear. Their eyesight must be better than mine, too.*

She stopped for air eight more times, then the sides of the tunnel widened abruptly and numerous lights appeared above

431

the surface. She moved herself upwards. As her shield broke the surface of the water she found herself at the edge of an enormous cavern.

Thousands of holes had been carved into the walls, and more than half of them were filled with light. At the other side of the lake was a wide archway. The floor of the cavern sloped upward from the water like a giant ramp, and a crowd of Elai milled about by the water's edge, staring at her. As she watched, more hurried up out of the water to join them.

A horn sounded, filling the cavern with echoes. The Elai scattered to either side of the ramp. From behind them appeared a group of Elai men, carrying spears and wearing proud expressions. They stopped at the edge of the water and formed a defensive line.

Auraya moved forward slowly until she was floating just before them.

'I am Auraya of the White. As the king requested, I have come to the Elai city to meet with him.'

The warriors did not move, but several frowned. From one side came a voice.

'So I did. Come, then. These men will escort you to the palace.'

Auraya searched, but could not see or sense the owner of the voice nearby. Intrigued, she moved forward and set her feet on the ground. The warriors moved apart and formed a double row on either side of her. She drew her shield in close and followed her escort into the underground city of the sea people.

CHAPTER 31

L eiard looked down at the snow collecting on the tufted ears and stubby horns of the arems before him. The plodding gait of the large, spotted beasts pulling the four-wheeled tarn was soothing. Arems were strong, placid creatures well suited to hauling vehicles or ploughs. He could remember seeing carvings of arems hauling carts in ruins from ages long past, so he knew they had been tamed thousands of years before. They could be ridden, but were slow to walk and respond to instruction, and too broad of back to make a comfortable ride. No noble man or woman would ever deign to ride an arem. The fine-boned, flighty reyna that nobles rode did not make good harness beasts, however, though they could be trained to draw racing plattens.

Unlike other animals, arems didn't appear to have any Gifts. Most animals or plants used magic in small ways that helped them find food, defend themselves or search out a mate. If arems had a Gift, he suspected it was the ability to sense the destination in their driver's mind. They had an impressive memory of the roads and places they had visited, and many stories were told of them bringing drivers who had fallen into a doze, due to drink or illness, home. Or to the houses of their mistresses.

The Dreamweavers were taking turns driving the three four-wheeled tarns they had purchased in Jarime to carry their food, tents and supplies. Some walked ahead to melt or sweep away snow where it had blocked the road. All Leiard could see of the cart before him was the oiled cloth covering the large bundles of supplies strapped onto it. There was no point looking over his shoulder; his view was blocked by his own equally loaded tarn. He could hear the voices of the Dreamweavers that made up Arleej's group.

'Do you think the army will catch up with us?' Jayim asked.

Leiard looked at the young man sitting beside him, then back at the arems.

'No. Most are travelling on foot.'

'Why?' Jayim asked.

Leiard chuckled. 'There aren't enough trained reyna in Hania for half the local army, let alone for the Somreyans as well.'

Jayim chewed his lip. 'We're hardly travelling much faster than a walk, and we keep having to stop because of the snow, so we won't get much further ahead of them.'

'We might. Remember, we don't have an army to keep in order. Imagine the time and effort it will take for them to camp each night, to arrange distribution of food and fuel for fires, settle disputes, rouse everyone in the morning, get them to pack up and start marching. Even when these last snows stop and the weather warms, there is much to do.'

Jayim looked thoughtful. 'It would be interesting to watch. I almost wish we were travelling with them, though I understand why we aren't.'

Leiard nodded. During a mind link a few days ago he had shown Jayim a few link memories of previous wars. Because Dreamweavers did not take sides, and treated the sick and injured no matter what the nationality or creed of their patient, this often caused resentment. In the past, more than a few

434

Dreamweavers had been killed for 'helping the enemy'.

Dreamweavers did not travel with armies. They travelled before and behind, in small groups. They waited at a distance during the folly of battle, then, afterwards, they entered the battlefield and the camps of both armies simultaneously to offer their assistance.

Jayim glanced at Leiard, then quickly away.

'What is it?' Leiard asked.

'Nothing.'

Leiard smiled and waited. It was unusual now for Jayim to hesitate to speak. After a few minutes, Jayim looked at Leiard.

'Do . . . do you think you'll meet with Auraya at some point?'

At her name, Leiard felt a thrill of hope and expectation. He took a deep breath and reminded himself why he was here with Arleej.

'You'd have to meet in secret, wouldn't you?' Jayim persisted.

'Not necessarily.'

'I guess you'll be safe so long as the other White aren't around to read your mind.'

'Yes.'

'Do you think you will . . . get together? One last time?' Jayim asked.

Leiard glanced at Jayim. The boy grinned.

'This is no small matter, Jayim. I've put us in great danger. Don't you understand that?'

Don't be such a bore. The poor boy is a virgin. What he saw in your memory was more interesting than anything he's imagined before.

Leiard frowned at the familiar voice in his head. *Not quite gone yet, are you, Mirar?*

It'll take a few more mind links to get rid of me. Maybe a lot more.

'Of course I understand,' Jayim replied, his expression

435

serious. Then he grinned again. 'But you have to see the funny side, too. Of all the people you had to pick. It's like one of those plays the nobles enjoy. All scandalous affairs and tragic love.'

'And their consequences,' Leiard added.

I like the boy's attitude, Mirar said. *He has a sense of humour, this one. Unlike the man I'm stuck inside . . .*

'Sometimes the lovers get away with it,' Jayim pointed out.

'Happy endings are a luxury of fiction,' Leiard replied.

Jayim shrugged. 'That's true. Of all the secrets you could have had, I wasn't expecting something so . . . so . . .'

'Risqué?' Leiard offered.

Jayim chuckled. 'Yes. It was a surprise. I don't know why, but I thought the White wouldn't be . . . um . . . they'd be celibate. I suppose if you're immortal it's a bit much to expect. Perhaps that's why Mirar was like he was.'

Leiard choked back a laugh. *Well? Was that the reason you were so badly behaved?*

I don't know. Maybe. Does any man know why he does the things he does?

You've had plenty of time to work it out.

Sometimes answers can't be found, even when you have all the time in the world. Immortality doesn't make anyone all-knowing.

'I wonder if all of the White are like that?' Jayim wondered. 'If immortality makes them . . . you know. Surely people would have heard about it if the other White were bedding everyone in sight.'

Leiard scowled in indignation. 'Auraya has not been bedding everyone in sight.'

'She might be. How would you know?'

'Enough gossip,' Leiard said firmly. 'If you've time for gossip, you have time for lessons.'

Jayim made a disappointed sound. 'While we're travelling?'

436

'Yes. We're going to be travelling a lot for the next few years. You'll need to become accustomed to receiving your training on the road.'

The boy sighed. He half turned to look over his shoulder, then changed his mind.

'I can't believe I'm not going home after this,' he murmured, almost too faint to be heard. Then he straightened and looked at Leiard. 'So what am I going to learn today?'

Something has happened, Imi decided as she followed Teiti, her aunt and teacher, along the corridor. First there had been the messenger, panting from exertion as he hurried up to Teiti, whispered something in the old woman's ear, then limped away. Then Teiti had told her she must leave the pool and the other children, and would not listen to any of Imi's protests as she dragged her home.

They had taken one of the secret routes, which instantly made Imi suspicious. When they had reached the palace the guards hadn't smiled at her like they usually did. They ignored her completely, looking stiff and serious. The guards who always stood beside the doors to her room smiled, but there was something in the way they then glanced up and down the corridor that told her that they, too, were nervous about something.

'What's going on?' she asked Teiti as the doors closed behind them.

Teiti looked down at Imi and frowned. 'I told you, Princess, I don't know.'

'Then find out,' Imi ordered.

Teiti crossed her arms and frowned disapprovingly. Unlike the rest of the palace servants, Teiti wasn't easily intimidated. She was a family member, not a hireling, and of a status only a little lower than Imi.

Teiti did not scold Imi, however. Her scowl of disapproval changed to a frown of worry.

'Sacred Huan,' she muttered. 'Wait here. I'll go and see if I can learn what is happening.'

Imi smiled and pressed her palms together. 'Thank you! Please hurry!'

The old woman strode back to the doors. She laid a hand on the handle, then turned to regard Imi suspiciously.

'Be a good girl, Imi. Don't go anywhere. For your own safety, stay here.'

'I will.'

'If you're not here when I return, I won't tell you anything,' she warned.

'I told you, I will stay here.'

Teiti's eyes narrowed, then she turned away and left the room. As the doors closed behind the old woman Imi raced into her bedroom. She ran to a carving on one of the walls and slipped her hand behind it. After a little groping around she found the bolt. She pulled it back and the carving silently turned outward like a door.

Behind it was a hole. Her father had shown her this hole many years ago. He had told her that if any bad people should invade the palace, she should crawl through the hole and wait until they were gone.

He hadn't told her that this hole was the beginning of a tunnel. She had discovered this one night when boredom overcame her fear of venturing into an unknown dark place. Pushing a candle before her, she had only managed to crawl a short way before encountering a wall of stone and mortar.

It wasn't a completely solid blockage, however. The adult who made it must have had little room to move, and had done a poor job. She had been able to hear voices beyond it, filtering through cracks and holes in the barrier. Voices she couldn't quite understand.

So for a month she slipped into the hole every night, long after she ought to have been asleep, and chipped away at the blockage. The dust and crumbs of mortar she tipped into the privy. The larger stones she smuggled out in her clothing.

Now, as she climbed up into the hole, Imi congratulated herself again for her discovery. Once the blockage had been removed she had crawled on to find a small wooden door, latched on the tunnel side. She had opened it to find herself in a small cupboard. Beyond that was a room lined with pipes.

She had guessed at once what this was. Her father had told her that he had a device that enabled him to speak or listen to people in other parts of the city. He had described the pipes that carried sound.

He didn't know that she knew where it was, or was using it herself.

Coming here was the most delicious fun. She always made sure she knew he was busy somewhere late at night before she crawled through to the room. There she pressed her ear to the ear-shaped openings in the pipes and listened to conversations between important people, quarrels between servants, and romantic exchanges between secret lovers. She knew all the gossip of the city – and the truth as well.

Reaching the wooden door, Imi listened for voices then pushed through. She hurried to the pipe she knew came from the king's audience chamber and pressed her ear to the opening.

'. . . of the benefits of trade. The art I see here in this room, the jewellery you wear, tell me you have talented artisans here. These artisans could make goods to sell outside Borra. In exchange you might enjoy some of the luxuries of my people, like the beautiful cloth produced in Genria that sparkles like stars, or the bright red firestones of Toren.'

The voice was a woman's and was strangely accented. She spoke slowly and haltingly, as though searching for and considering every word. Imi caught her breath at the description of sparkling cloth and burning stones. They sounded marvellous, and she hoped her father would buy some.

'There is also a world of spices, herbs and exotic foods that you might like to try, and I know there are people in the north who would pay a fortune for the opportunity to try new flavours and produce from Borra. Do not think we have only luxuries to trade. My people have many cures effective in treating all kinds of diseases, and I would not be surprised to discover that you have cures we have never encountered. There is much that we could exchange, Lord.'

'Yes, we have.' Imi felt her heartbeat quicken as she heard her father's voice. 'It is a fair speech you make, but we have heard it before. Landwalkers once came here claiming that they wished only to trade with us. They stole from us instead, taking sacred objects from this very room. We hunted them down and retrieved our property, and swore never to trust landwalkers again. Why should we break that vow and trust you?'

Landwalker? Imi thought. *This woman is a landwalker! How did she get into the city?*

'I understand your anger and caution,' the woman said. 'I would do the same if I had been betrayed in such a manner. I would urge you to retain that caution if you were to open your doors to traders. They are not always the most honest of people. But I am no trader. I am a high priestess of the gods. One of the five chosen to represent them in this world. I cannot stop duplicity in this world any more than you can, but I can work to prevent it, or make certain it is punished. An alliance with us would include an agreement of mutual defence. We would help you protect your lands from invaders, if you would agree to help us in return.'

440

That seems a bit silly, Imi thought. *There are only a few of us and lots of landwalkers . . .*

'What help could we possibly offer you, a sorceress of great strength, in command of great armies of landwalkers?'

'Whatever help you could give, Lord,' she answered calmly. 'The Siyee have just made such an agreement with us. They may not be large or strong in body, but there are many ways they can help us.'

Silence followed. Imi could hear her father clicking his tongue against the roof of his mouth, as he always did when thinking hard.

'If you are what you say you are,' he said suddenly, 'then you should be able to summon Huan now. Do that, so that I may ask her if you speak the truth.'

The woman made a small noise like a smothered laugh. 'I may be one of her representatives, but that doesn't give me the right to order a god around.' She paused, and her voice became so quiet that Imi could barely hear her. 'I have spoken to her of your people recently, however. She said this was for you to decide. She would not interfere.'

Another silence followed.

'You know this already, don't you?' she added in a tone of mild surprise.

'The goddess has said as much to our priests,' the king admitted. 'We are to decide this ourselves. I see it as a sign that she trusts my judgement.'

'It would appear so,' the woman agreed.

'My judgement is this: I do not know enough about you, landwalker. I see no reason why we should risk our lives for the sake of a few trinkets. Your offer of protection is tempting, as I'm sure you know it is, but how can you defend us when you live on the other side of the continent?'

'We will find these raiders and deal with them,' the woman

replied. 'Any other threat can be tackled by ships sent from Porin.'

'They would never get here in time. Next you'll suggest mooring a ship here. Then you'll want to start a settlement for the crew. That is unacceptable.'

'I understand. An alternative will be found. If we discuss this—'

'No.' Imi recognised the stubborn hardness that came into her father's voice when he had made a decision. She frowned, disappointed. It had sounded so exciting, all this talk of trade. Surely the easiest way to get rid of the raiders was to pay someone else to do it.

'Imi!'

She jumped at the voice. It was Teiti's, and it was not coming from within the pipe. It was coming from the hole in the cupboard. Her teacher had returned. Imi's heart skipped. The only reason Imi could hear the woman was because she had left the carving – the door to the hole – open! If Teiti discovered the hole, Imi's visits to the pipe room would end.

Imi dived into the cupboard. She closed the door behind her, then climbed into the hole. The wooden door was harder to close; she had grown a bit lately and there wasn't much room to reach back and close the latch.

Crawling forward as fast as she could, she stopped just within the hole and looked out. Teiti was in the next room, roaming about. As the woman looked under a chair, Imi choked back a laugh. Teiti thought she was hiding.

'Imi, this is naughty. Come out now!'

The woman started toward the bedroom. Imi froze, then, as Teiti paused to look inside a cupboard, quickly reached out and pulled the carving back over the hole.

She listened as Teiti roamed around the bedroom, her voice all trembly. Imi frowned. Was Teiti angry? Or just upset? The voice faded as her teacher returned to the main room. Then Imi heard a quiet snuffling sound. She flushed with guilt. Teiti was crying!

Pushing aside the carving, she slid out of the hole as quietly as she could, then carefully bolted the carving back in place, before running into the other room.

'I'm sorry, Teiti,' she cried.

The woman looked up, then gasped with relief.

'Imi! That was not funny!'

It wasn't hard to look guilty. Teiti might be a strict teacher, but she could also be fun and generous. Imi liked to play tricks on her friends, but only to make them laugh. She didn't want to hurt anybody.

'This must be serious,' she said.

Teiti wiped her eyes and smiled. 'Yes. There's a landwalker in the palace. I don't how she got here, or why, but we'd better stay put in case there's trouble.' Teiti paused and frowned. 'Not that I think you're in any danger, Princess. She doesn't even know about you, so I think you're quite safe.'

Imi thought about the woman she'd overheard talking to her father. A sorceress and priestess of the gods, who wanted the Elai and her people to be allies – which was another word for friends. She didn't sound like someone to fear.

Imi nodded. 'I think so, too, Teiti.'

The moon was a cheerful grin of white. When Tryss had first seen it, he could not help thinking how it was a good omen. Now, several hours later, the pale crescent seemed more like a mocking smile.

Or a murderous blade, he thought. He let out a long breath, sending mist billowing around him, then shook his head. *Superstitious nonsense, this. It's just a big rock stuck in the frozen water of the upper sky. Nothing more, nothing less.*

'I don't believe it. He's pacing. Calm, serious Tryss is pacing.'

Tryss jumped at the voice. 'Sreil!' he whispered. 'What happened?'

'Nothing,' the older boy said. 'It just took a little longer to cut through the wall than I thought.'

Two figures emerged from the shadows, their footsteps dulled by the snow. Moonlight lit both faces, but Tryss saw only one. Drilli, wrapped in a yern pelt. His heart flipped over as he saw her face. Her eyes were wide. Her expression . . . hesitant. Anxious.

'Are you sure—'

'—about this?'

They'd spoken the same words, together. Drilli grinned and he found he was doing the same. He stepped forward and took her hands, then touched her face. She closed her eyes briefly, smiling blissfully. He pressed his lips to hers. Her answering kiss was strong and confident. He felt his entire body flush with heat. All the chill of winter seemed to retreat from around them. When they parted, his heart was racing and every doubt had evaporated.

Or I've completely lost my senses, he added. *It's what they say about young men, after all.*

He turned to Sreil.

'Where now?'

Sreil chuckled. 'In a hurry, are we? I still think Ryliss is the best choice. He has camped a little further from the Open than everyone else. You know what these Temple Mountain types are like. All serious and seclusive. Follow me.'

Tryss took Drilli's hand and they followed Sreil through the forest. It was a long journey; they had to skirt around the top of the Open. The dark shadows of the trees blocked the moonlight and snow blanketed all. Tryss and Drilli tripped over obstacles.

Drilli made a small sound.

'What's wrong?' he whispered.

'My feet hurt.'

'Mine, too.'

'Couldn't we have flown?'

'I'm sure if we could have, Sreil would have chosen to.'

'I guess this is hurting him as much as us.'

She fell silent, then after a few minutes squeezed his hand.

'Sorry. How romantic of me to complain about sore feet on my wedding night.'

He chuckled. 'I'll give you a romantic foot-rub later, if you like.'

'Mmm. Yes, I'd like that.'

When a bower appeared among the trees ahead, Tryss felt a surge of relief. Sreil told them to wait while he checked to see if Speaker Ryliss was alone. Tryss felt his stomach beginning to flutter. Sreil moved to the entrance of the bower. A shadow within came to the doorway. The hanging was pulled aside, then Sreil turned and beckoned to them.

Drilli's hand was tight around his as they hurried toward the bower. They stopped just outside the door. Speaker Ryliss regarded them thoughtfully, his eyes shadowed by thick grey eyebrows. He waved a hand.

'Come in.'

They went inside. A fire was burning to one side, the smoke rising to a hole in the roof. Its heat was welcome. Ryliss gestured to log seats, and as they sat down he settled into a hammock chair.

'So you two want to get married tonight,' he said. 'That is no small thing. Are you both sure of it?'

Tryss glanced at Drilli, then nodded. She smiled and murmured a 'yes'.

'I understand this is against your parents' wishes.'

445

'Drilli's parents,' Tryss answered. 'Mine wouldn't protest.'

The old man regarded them soberly. 'You both should know that while you may choose to marry each other without permission from your parents, doing so means your tribe is not obliged to provide a feast or give you any gifts. Your parents are not obliged to accommodate either of you in their bower.'

'We understand,' Drilli replied.

The Speaker nodded. 'I cannot refuse you this rite, if you request it formally.'

Tryss rose and Drilli stood by his side. 'I am Tryss of the Bald Mountain tribe. I choose to marry Drilli of the Snake River tribe. Will you perform the rite?'

'I am Drilli of the Snake River tribe. I choose to marry Tryss of the Bald Mountain tribe. Will you perform the rite?'

Ryliss nodded. 'By law I must grant your request. Tryss must now stand behind Drilli. Please take each other's hands.'

Drilli grinned as they did as they were told. Her eyes were bright as she looked over her shoulder at him. She looked both excited and a little frightened.

'Last chance to get out of it,' she whispered.

He smiled and tightened his grip on her hands. 'Only if you can get loose.'

'Quiet, please,' Ryliss ordered. He frowned at them both. 'This is a serious undertaking. You must remain together for the next two years, even if you come to regret your decision. Raise your arms.'

He opened a small pouch strapped to his waist – the pouch all Speakers wore – and drew out two brightly coloured pieces of thin rope. He began to tie one pair of their hands together.

'I am Ryliss of the Temple Mountain tribe. I bind Tryss of the Bald Mountain tribe and Drilli of the Snake River tribe together as husband and wife. Fly together from this day.'

He moved to their other clasped hands. 'I am Ryliss of the

446

Temple Mountain tribe. I bind Drilli of the Snake River tribe and Tryss of the Bald Mountain tribe together as wife and husband. Fly together from this day.'

Tryss looked at their hands. If they had been flying this close together, they'd have to be conscious of each other's every movement.

I guess that's the point.

Ryliss stepped back and crossed his arms.

'In choosing to bind yourself to each other, you have committed yourselves to a partnership. You are responsible for each other's health and happiness and for the upbringing of any children produced from your union. As this is your first marriage, you have also chosen to step into the responsibilities of adulthood. You will both be expected to contribute to whichever tribe you choose to live with.'

He paused, then nodded. 'I declare you married.'

It's done, Tryss thought. He looked at Drilli. She smiled. He wrapped his arms around her, drawing her arms across her body.

Sreil cleared his throat. 'There remains only one last step.'

Tryss looked up at Sreil in dismay. What could there possibly be . . . ?

'That is true.' The corner of Ryliss's mouth twitched, the closest he had come to a smile all night. He looked at Tryss, then Drilli. 'I will be back in the morning. Please do not make a mess.'

With that, he strode out of the bower and disappeared. Tryss looked at Sreil, confused.

'What step?'

Sreil's grin widened. 'I don't believe you asked that.'

'Oh!' Tryss felt his face beginning to heat as he realised what Sreil had meant. Drilli giggled.

'Sometimes I wonder how someone so clever can be so silly,' she said.

'Me too,' Sreil agreed. 'Well, then. I'm sure you'll have no problems finishing off the ritual. You don't need my help, so I'll head back.'

'Thank you, Sreil,' Drilli said.

'Yes. I owe you,' Tryss added.

Sreil feigned innocence. 'I had nothing to do with all this.'

'Nothing at all,' Tryss replied. 'Go on, then. We won't say a word.'

Sreil chuckled, then backed out of the bower and pulled down the hanging. Tryss listened to his footsteps crunching in the snow. They faded into the distance. Drilli lifted a hand and regarded the ropes, then raised an eyebrow.

'I do hope Ryliss hasn't tied these too tightly.'

CHAPTER 32

The brothel's caravan was an impressive sight. Twelve tarns stood before the building, each pulled by two arems. The first six tarns were brightly painted, their sides bearing Rozea's name. The sturdy covers were trimmed with matching colours. The last six were plainer and servants hovered around them, the women waiting beside one of the vehicles, the men adding a few sacks and boxes to another.

Brand and Tide made appreciative noises, their breath misting in the air. They started toward the fourth cart with Emerahl and three other girls. An hour before, waiting in the dance hall, they had been asked to form groups of six, then Rozea had selected cart numbers for them by taking marked tokens out of a bag.

Our employer does like to appear to be fair, Emerahl mused. *I wonder if Moonlight agrees. Does she know that Rozea intends for me to return as the brothel favourite? Does she hate me? Or is she happy to be relieved of the position?*

It didn't matter. Emerahl didn't intend to return. She planned to slip away from the caravan as soon as she was free of the city.

That is, if I can get out of the city unnoticed, she amended.

She resisted the temptation to run her fingers over the hem

449

of her sleeve. Tucked into it were small nuggets, each a compressed lump of formtane. Taken in this form the drug took effect slowly and lasted about an hour.

It was not an unheard-of drug in Porin. The usual method of taking it was as a tea or burned in a pipe. It produced a blissful calm, quashed nausea, and in strong quantities put one to sleep.

Sleep wasn't enough for Emerahl. She needed it to render her unconscious.

The knot in her stomach tightened as she considered the risk she was taking. If this didn't work – if the priest who could read minds was watching at the city gates, noticed that he couldn't read the mind of one of the whores, decided to investigate, thought it suspicious that she had drugged herself into unconsciousness, and held them back until she woke up – then her unnaturally long life was about to end.

To make her taking of the drug less suspicious, she had prepared several nuggets of formtane. These she would give to the other girls. They were a weaker dose, so they would only experience the delicious calming effects. A tarn full of unconscious women was bound to raise suspicion rather than avoid it.

Emerahl was the last to climb into the tarn. They were all dressed in heavy tawls and carrying blankets. The tarn covers would protect them from rain, but not from cold. Winter was far from over, and would grow harsher as they travelled northward.

It was cramped inside, with six women squeezed onto the hard bench seats.

'They looked roomier from the outside,' Brand muttered. 'Watch where you put your shoes, Star.'

'It smells like smoked ner,' Charity complained.

'I doubt Rozea bought them new.' Bird kicked her heels

backwards, making a solid thud. 'There's something under the seat.'

Emerahl peered under the seat opposite. 'Boxes. I think some of our supplies are in here. Our seats are closer together than they need to be. I wouldn't be surprised if there are compartments behind them.'

'Why would there be?' Tide asked. 'Is Rozea too stingy to buy enough tarns?'

'No,' Brand said. 'I bet they're secret compartments to store things, just in case we get robbed.'

The others stilled and looked at her.

'Anyone who robs us will think the supply carts are all we have,' Brand explained. 'If they look in here they'll see us, and nothing else.'

'Nobody's going to rob us,' Star declared. 'We'll be with the army.'

'But we might fall behind,' Bird said in a small voice. 'Or even be separated.'

'We won't,' Star assured her. 'Rozea won't let us.'

A high-pitched whistle sounded outside. The girls exchanged nervous glances, and all remained silent until the tarn jerked into movement.

'Too late to change your minds now,' Tide murmured.

'We could all jump out and run back inside,' Charity suggested half-heartedly.

Emerahl snorted. 'Rozea would send someone in to drag you back. I thought everyone but me was eager to set out on this glorious adventure.'

The other girls shrugged.

'You don't want to go, Jade?' Star asked. 'Why not?'

Emerahl looked away. 'I think robbers will be the least of our problems. It's the soldiers we'll have to watch out for. They'll think fighting earns them a free roll with us whenever they want, and we don't have enough of our own guards to prevent them. This is going to be rough, dirty work.'

Charity grimaced. 'Let's not talk about it any more. I'd rather delude myself that we're going on a great adventure, during which we'll witness great events. Events I can tell my grandchildren about.'

'Just as well grandmothers are allowed to edit out the bad parts,' Brand said, chuckling. 'And embellish the good parts. The soldiers will be brave, the generals handsome, and the priests virtuous and even more handsome . . .'

At the mention of priests, Emerahl felt the knot in her stomach clench. She leaned past Tide and lifted the door flap. They were halfway to the gates. Her mouth went dry. She resisted the urge to reach for the formtane. *Soon.*

'Have you ever bedded a priest?' Tide asked Brand.

'A few.'

'I haven't. What about you, Star? Charity?'

Star shrugged. 'Once. And he wasn't handsome. He was fat. And fast, thank Yranna.'

'Quite a few,' Charity admitted with a grin. 'I think they like me for my name. They can go back to their wives and say they spent the evening in Charity work and be telling the truth.'

Brand burst out laughing. 'Rozea certainly knows how to pick names. What about you, Jade?'

'Me?'

'Have you ever bedded a priest?'

Emerahl shook her head. 'Never.'

'Perhaps you'll bed your first one on this trip.'

'Perhaps.'

Brand wiggled her eyebrows suggestively. 'They're supposed to be quite good at it.'

'About as good as any nationality or creed that is supposed to be good at it, I'm guessing.'

'You're too serious, Jade – and why do you keep looking outside?'

Emerahl let the flap go. She sighed and shook her head. 'Travelling makes me sick.'

Star groaned unsympathetically. 'You're not going to throw up, are you?'

Emerahl made a face. 'If I do, I'll be sure to lean in your direction.'

'You're cranky. Here.' Tide stood up, bracing herself against the flexible cover. 'Sit by the window. If you feel sick you can open the flap for some fresh air.'

'Thank you.' Emerahl managed a smile and slid across the seat. Tide sat down in the middle and patted Emerahl's knee sympathetically.

Looking outside again, Emerahl judged they were not far from the city gates. She let the flap fall and turned to the other girls.

'I brought something,' she told them. 'Something for the nausea. It wouldn't be fair if I didn't share it.'

Brand smiled knowingly. 'The formtane?'

'Formtane!' Star exclaimed. 'Where'd you get that?'

'I took a little side trip to the market on the way to visit my family,' Brand told them.

Emerahl held out her left arm and eased the first of the nuggets out of her sleeve hem. She popped it into her mouth and swallowed, then began to push the next one free.

'So who wants some?'

The other girls leaned forward eagerly.

'I've never tried it before,' Tide admitted.

'It's wonderful,' Charity whispered. 'Time seems to slow down and you feel all light and floaty.' She accepted a nugget of formtane. 'Thank you, Jade.'

A wave of dizziness swept over Emerahl. She worked

another nugget out of her sleeve and gave it to Brand. She had to concentrate hard on removing three more nuggets for Tide, Bird and Star. Then she let herself relax against the seat back. Waves of delicious dizziness were rolling over her now.

'Have you got any more?' Star asked dreamily.

Emerahl shook her head, not trusting herself to speak. She thought about checking how close they were to the gate, but could not rouse herself to do so.

The other girls were smiling blissfully now. Such silly expressions. Emerahl felt a laugh bubble up and out of her. They grinned at her in surprise.

'What's so funny?'

'You'll look s' happy,' she slurred.

Tide giggled, then they all burst into lazy-sounding, breathless laughter.

'Feeling better now, Jade?' Brand asked. 'Not so *Jaded*?'

Emerahl laughed, then leaned forward. She swayed. Her vision blurred.

'Ma' mine li'l strong'r,' she managed.

Then she slipped into a comfortable, delirious blackness.

Time stopped, but she felt too lazy to care. She let her mind relax into the safe, warm darkness. Out of it a tower appeared. The sight of it disturbed her. She felt a flash of annoyance.

Oh no. Not again.

The tower stretched impossibly high. It tore clouds as they drifted past. She couldn't stop herself looking at it. It captured her attention.

Where is this place?

The tower flashed out of existence. She looked down. A different building stood in its place. The old Dreamweaver House in Jarime. The one that Mirar had been buried under after Juran, high priest of the circle of gods, had killed him.

I'm dreaming. I shouldn't be. I should be unconscious. This isn't good . . .

She tried to break free, but the dream tightened its grip. Suddenly the high white tower loomed over her again, even more menacing than before. She wanted to flee, but couldn't move. Once again she knew she would be seen if she stayed. She couldn't stop herself looking. They had only to see her and . . .

'What's wrong with her?'

. . . know who she was . . .

'She took formtane. She gets sick when she travels. I think she made it a bit too strong.'

. . . and when they saw . . .

'She certainly has. She should be unconscious, but instead she's been caught in a dream.'

. . . they would kill her . . .

'Caught? You can see that?'

'Yes, I'm a priest.'

'In a guard's uniform?'

'Yes.'

'Will she wake up?'

. . . the tower loomed over her. It seemed to flex. She felt a stab of terror as cracks ran down the surface . . .

'Yes. She will break free of the dream when the drug wears off.'

. . . and the tower began to fall . . .

'Thank you, Priest . . . ?'

'Ikaro.'

The voices barely registered in Emerahl's mind. The dream was too real. Perhaps the voices were a dream and the dream was reality. She heard the roar of the collapsing tower, felt the pain of her limbs being crushed, of her lungs burning as she slowly suffocated. It went on and on, an eternity of pain.

'Jade?'

I don't like this reality, Emerahl thought. *I want the dream. Perhaps if I convince myself the dream is real, I will escape this pain.* She struggled to hear the voice better, concentrated on the words. The pain faded.

'Jade. Wake up.'

Someone forced her eyes open. She recognised faces. Felt the radiating concern from familiar minds. Held onto that and pulled herself clear of the dream.

She gasped in a lungful of wonderfully clean air and stared at the five girls leaning over her. Their names ran through her mind. She could feel the movement of the tarn. She was lying down. *The tower dream*, she thought. *I had it again. There were voices this time. Another dream inside the dream.*

'What happened?'

The relief on the girls' faces was touching. They had good hearts, she decided. She would miss them, when she left.

'You took too much formtane,' Brand told her. 'You fell unconscious.'

'A priest at the gates came over to see,' Charity added. 'I don't know how he knew.'

Emerahl felt a stab of alarm. She sat up. A priest! So the dream within the dream had been reality? 'What did he say?'

Tide smiled. 'He had a look at you and said you were fine, just dreaming.'

'I think he could read minds,' Star added.

He could see me dreaming? She frowned. *I must have let my guard down.*

'We were worried you'd made a mistake with the dose,' Brand told her. 'Or that you had tried to kill yourself.'

'You weren't trying to kill yourself, were you?' Tide asked anxiously.

'No.' Emerahl shrugged. 'Just thought it would last longer if I took more.'

456

'Silly girl,' Brand scolded. 'You won't make that mistake again.'

Emerahl shook her head ruefully. She swung her legs over the end of the seat. Brand sat down beside her.

'You look a bit dreamy still,' Brand said. 'Lean on me and have a nap – if you can sleep with all this rocking.'

Emerahl smiled in gratitude. She rested her head on the shoulder of the taller girl and closed her eyes.

So the priest read my mind, she thought. *And dismissed everything he saw there as a dream.* She thought of the fear of being seen that always lurked in the tower dream. A fear similar to her own fear of discovery. She silently thanked the Dreamweaver who was projecting these dreams. He or she had probably saved her life.

As Auraya woke she realised she had not dreamed of Leiard, and she sighed in disappointment.

He hadn't visited her dreams since she had left Si. She had nursed a faint hope that the reason had something to do with her travelling and being hard to find, and that he would link with her again when she came back to the Open, but her sleep hadn't been interrupted last night.

That's only one night, she thought. *He won't know I've returned yet, and now I'm leaving again.*

She rose and began to wash. *Surely he checks to see if I've returned each night. Perhaps he is too busy – or maybe dream-linking is too tiring to spend each night at it.*

I shouldn't be thinking about this. I should be thinking about taking the Siyee to war.

There had been a lot to arrange. She had spoken to the Speakers until late last night, discussing what they would need to bring, and what they would have to rely on the landwalker army to supply. The Siyee could not carry a lot of weight. They would bring their weapons, small transportable bowers and enough food to get them to the Plains of Gold, but no more. Auraya had spoken to Juran and received assurances that food would be provided for the Siyee once they'd joined the army.

Auraya examined her clothing closely and used magic to remove as many stains as she could. She combed out the knots in her hair, which she'd gained while flying yesterday. *The Siyee definitely have the right idea keeping their hair short*, she mused. *I wonder what I'd look like with short hair . . .*

She braided her hair into a long tail then moved into the main room of her bower. A Siyee woman had brought her a small basket of food the night before. Auraya drank some water then began to eat.

This may be my last night here for many months. After the war, Juran will want me to come back to Jarime. The thought brought a pang of sadness. She did not want to leave. But she also felt a stirring of curiosity. *What will my next challenge be, I wonder? Another alliance to negotiate? Will I return to Borra to appeal to the Elai king again?*

It would take more than words to persuade King Ais to consider an alliance. She had seen much suspicion and hate of landwalkers in the Elai's minds. Dealing with the raiders might help gain the sea people's trust. If not, it would at least remove the main reason the Elai hated landwalkers. In a few generations their hatred might diminish to the point where they wouldn't consider contact with the outside world to be so dangerous. She had told Juran as much and he had agreed.

If her next task was not the Elai, then what? She considered the possible consequences of the war. Sennon was backing the Pentadrians. If the gods still wanted Sennon to ally peacefully with the rest of Northern Ithania, there would be work to do there after the war, not least encouraging forgiveness from the White's allies. By uniting with the enemy, Sennon would cause the deaths of many Northern Ithanians. Many would want to see Sennon punished, but that would only cause ongoing resentment and more hatred.

She frowned. Persuading the Sennons to sign an alliance would be best handled by Juran. She and the other White would probably work at convincing Circlians to accept it, but that wouldn't keep her completely occupied.

There's always the Dreamweavers.

Her stomach sank at the thought. For months she had barely thought about her ideas for improving Circlian healing knowledge in order to prevent people being lured into becoming Dreamweavers.

It's not as if my intention is to harm Dreamweavers, she told herself. *I only want to save the souls of those who have not yet become Dreamweavers.*

'Auraya of the White. May I come in?'

She looked up at the door eagerly, grateful for the distraction.

'Yes, Speaker Sirri. Come in.'

The hanging over the door moved aside and the Siyee woman stepped in. Sirri was dressed in clothing that Auraya had never seen Siyee wear before. A hard leather vest and apron, crisscrossed with straps, covered her chest and thighs. One of the new dart-throwing contraptions was bound to her chest, and a bow and a quiver of arrows were strapped to her back. At her hip she wore a pouch and two knives.

'Don't *you* look prepared for a fight,' Auraya exclaimed.

Sirri smiled. 'That's good. My people need to think their leader is prepared to fight beside them.'

'You certainly are,' Auraya said. 'I'd flee if I were a Pentadrian.'

Sirri's smile became grim. 'More likely you'd laugh. In truth, I think we're going to learn a lot from this war.'

Auraya felt her grin fade. 'I won't pretend there isn't going to be a cost,' she said. 'I do hope that it will not be a high one. I promise I will try to ensure it isn't.'

The Speaker acknowledged Auraya's promise with a nod. 'We know what we face. Are you ready?'

Auraya nodded. 'Are your people already assembled?'

'All loaded up and ready to fly. They just need a speech or two.'

Putting her empty mug down, Auraya stood and glanced around the room one last time, then picked up the small pack she had brought with her to Si and followed Sirri outside. She could hear the gathered Siyee long before she saw them. The chatter of so many voices combined was like the sound of water cascading over rocks. As she and Sirri approached the outcrop above the crowd, whistles filled the air. Auraya smiled down at the largest crowd of Siyee she had seen so far.

The tribes ranged in size from a few dozen families to over a thousand individuals. Of the thousands of Siyee, more than half formed this army. Not all were warriors, though. For every two Siyee dressed as fighters she could see one that was not. Each tribe was bringing their own healers and domestic helpers, who would also carry portable bowers and as much spare food as possible.

Sirri's appearance was the cue for the other Speakers to come forward and form a line. Auraya took her place – a few steps from the end of this line – and watched as Sirri stepped onto Speakers' Rock and spread her arms wide.

'People of the mountains. Tribes of the Siyee. Look at your-selves!' Sirri grinned. 'What a fierce sight we make!'

The Siyee shouted and whistled in reply. Sirri nodded, then raised her arms higher.

'Today we are leaving our homes and flying to war. We do so in order to keep a promise. What was that promise? It was a promise to help a friend. Our allies among the landwalkers need our help. They need us, the Siyee, to help them defend themselves against invaders.

'We know what *that* is like.' Sirri's expression was hard now. 'We know the pain of losing land and lives to invaders. No longer will that pain be ours, for our new allies are also keeping their promises. Last night Auraya of the White gave me the welcome news that the King of Toren has ordered his people out of our lands.'

The whistling that followed this announcement was deafening. The noise continued on and on. Sirri turned and beckoned to Auraya. As Auraya moved to join the Speaker, the crowd slowly quietened.

'People of Si, I thank you,' she said. 'By giving your support and strength to my people you help us defend against a terrible enemy. For many years we have heard rumours about these barbaric peoples of the southern continent, but they were too distant to be of concern. We heard that they enslave men and women, and that these followers of the Pentadrian cult force strange and perverse rites on their people. We know that they worship war for the sake of violence itself.

'Now these Pentadrians wish to spread their vile ways. They wish to destroy my people and enslave all of Ithania.'

She paused. The crowd was silent now and she sensed the beginnings of fear.

'They will fail!' she declared. 'For men and women who worship war for the sake of violence are not true warriors, as we are. Men and women who invade another land are not driven by a passion to defend their homes, as *we* are. Most importantly, men and women who follow heathen cults do not have the protection of true gods . . .' she paused, then spoke each word quietly but firmly '. . . as we do.'

She put her hands together to form the symbol of the circle.

461

'As one of the White I am your link to the gods. I will be your translator and interpreter. I am proud to be the link between such a people and the gods. I am proud to accompany such an army as this.'

:And I am proud to have created such a people.

The faces below Auraya changed as one. Eyes widened, mouths opened. She felt their awe, like a gust of wind, at the same time as she sensed the presence at her side. The crowd, as one, dropped to the ground as she turned to face the glowing presence of the goddess. Huan lifted a hand, indicating that Auraya should remain standing.

:Rise, good people of Si, Huan said.

Slowly the Siyee climbed to their feet. They gazed at the goddess in awe.

:It pleases me to see you gathered here today. You have grown strong and plentiful. You are ready to take your place among the peoples of Northern Ithania. You have chosen your allies well. You have a loyal friend as well as an ally in Auraya. She loves you more than duty requires. All the White will protect you as best they can. But it will be your resilience as a people that will ensure you survive in the future, not Auraya or I. Be strong, but also be wise, people of Si. Know your strengths and your weaknesses, and endure.

The goddess smiled, then her glowing form faded and disappeared. Sirri looked at Auraya, her eyes still wide, then at the gathered Siyee.

'We have heard the words of the goddess Huan. Let us wait no longer. Let us fly to war!'

She nodded to the Speakers. They immediately moved to the edge of the outcrop and flew down to join their tribes. Sirri turned back to Auraya.

'I had a stirring final speech planned, but I completely forgot what I was going to say,' she confessed quietly.

Auraya smiled and shrugged. 'A visit from the gods can have that effect on a person.'

'It doesn't matter. What matters is we set off in a confident state of mind, and Huan certainly arranged that nicely. Now, it looks like my tribe is itching to get into the air. Would you like to fly with us?'

Auraya nodded. 'I would, thank you.'

Sirri grinned, beckoned, and they both leapt off the outcrop. The Speaker's tribe immediately surged into the air to join them, followed by tribe after tribe of Siyee. Auraya looked back at the cloud of flying figures and felt a thrill of amazement.

But it was followed by a stab of concern. *This will be their first war*, she thought. *There is no way they can be fully prepared for what they will face.* She sighed. *And there is no way I am either.*

PART THREE

CHAPTER 33

Plains are supposed to be flat tracts of land, aren't they? Danjin thought as he climbed the face of the hill. The Plains of Gold were better described as 'undulating'. They were a little less undulating in the western part, but here in the east they could be described as flat only in comparison to the rugged mountains at their edge.

They weren't living up to the other part of their name, either. The plains were gold only in summer when the grasses turned yellow. Now, in the aftermath of winter, they were a mix of healthy green new shoots growing up among older, darker plants.

Danjin reached the top of the hill and paused. His heavy breathing sounded loud in this quiet place. He turned around and his quibbling and discomfort were forgotten. Below was the largest army camp he'd ever seen.

The only *army camp I've ever seen*, he corrected himself. *But this is certainly larger than any I've read of.*

Men, women, animals, tarns, platterns, and tents of all sizes covered a large valley surrounded by low hills. The grass that earned the plains their pretty name was now trampled into mud. The light of the late-afternoon sun touched a line of brown that led into the valley on one side and continued to the mountains on the other. A wider band of crushed grass around the western part of this road showed the direction the army had come from. In the centre of the valley was a large tent, which had somehow managed to remain white despite being pitched beside the muddy main thoroughfare of the camp each night. This was where the White's councils of war were held.

It was hard to imagine any force could match this army. Danjin looked to the mountains in the east. Even at this distance they looked fierce and unassailable. He was too far away to see the road winding up to the pass. Somewhere beyond those peaks was another army, and by all reports it was even larger than the one before him.

He took some reassurance from the fact that the Circlian army was not yet fully formed. So far it was made up of only three nations: Hania, Somrey and Genria – the latter had joined them a few days out of Jarime. The Toren army was due to arrive in a few days, the Dunwayans were not much further away, and the Siyee . . . the Siyee were due any moment.

Turning his back on the army, Danjin gazed at the southern sky. It was cloudless apart from a dark smudge near the horizon. *She said they had reached the plains*, he thought. *So where are they?*

He stared at the sky until his eyes began to water from the brightness. Looking away, he dabbed at his eyes with a sleeve. Footsteps brought his attention abruptly back to his surroundings and he turned to find a soldier approaching. The man was one of the many guards patrolling the hills around the camp.

'You all right, sir?' the man enquired.

'Yes, thank you,' Danjin replied. 'Just the brightness of the sky.'

The man glanced southwards then stopped and shaded his eyes. 'Will you look at that cloud?'

Danjin followed the man's gaze. The dark smudge had grown larger and . . . fragmented into many tiny specks. He felt his heart skip a beat.

'It's them,' he muttered.

Danjin left the soldier looking puzzled and hurried down the hill. It seemed a longer journey back to the camp despite being all downhill – though it didn't help that he kept glancing behind, worried he wasn't going to make it in time. When he reached the first of the tents he slowed. Soldiers watched him pass, always alert for signs of nervousness among the army's leaders and their advisers.

Reaching the main thoroughfare, Danjin saw that Juran, Dyara, Rian and Mairae were already standing outside the white tent, their attention on the sky. The elderly Genrian king, Guire, stood nearby with his advisers and attendants. Meeran, the Moderator of the Somreyan Council, stood with the Circlian elder, Haleed. A Dunwayan ambassador, Jen of Rommel, stood beside the Dunwayan priest who always accompanied him, and whose main role appeared to be to provide the White with a way to communicate with the absent Dunwayan leaders.

Danjin quietly joined the small crowd of advisers. He noted that the new Dreamweaver adviser was present. Raeli rarely attended war councils, and when she did she remained aloof and apparently uninterested. Sensing him looking at her, she turned to meet his eyes. He nodded politely. She turned away. Danjin suppressed a sigh.

I think I may actually miss Leiard. He wasn't much more talkative than this woman, but he was . . . what, exactly? Approachable, I suppose.

Raeli's attention was on the sky. He turned just in time to see the first of the Siyee appear over the top of the hill he had just climbed. A pair of them circled the valley once, drawing murmurs from the onlookers, then suddenly a great mass of them poured over the crest of the hill. Danjin heard gasps and exclamations as thousands of Siyee swooped down to fill the valley. He realised his own heart was beating fast with excitement. The Siyee wheeled and turned then began to drop to the ground. The sound of their wings was like a rush of wind, and the smack of feet on the ground was like the patter of heavy rain.

Once they had landed, their small size was suddenly obvious. Their childlike appearance was tempered by their clothing and weapons, however. Unlike the two messengers who had come to Jarime, these Siyee had bows, quivers of arrows, knives, and what looked like blowpipes and darts strapped over leathery vests and trousers. Both men and women had short hair, muscular bodies and a proud demeanour. These were warriors, small but fierce.

'Interesting. Very interesting.'

Danjin turned to look at the speaker. It was Lanren Songmaker, the military adviser the White now favoured above the others. The man glanced at Danjin and smiled grimly.

'I can see how these people might be useful to us.'

'Auraya certainly thinks so,' Danjin replied.

'Here she is.'

Danjin turned back just in time to see Auraya descend to the ground before the White. A Siyee woman swooped down and landed beside her.

Auraya smiled. 'This is Sirri, Speaker of the Bald Mountain tribe and Head Speaker for the Siyee.'

Juran stepped forward and made the two-handed sign of the circle. 'Welcome, Speaker Sirri, and all Siyee. We are pleased and grateful that you have come so far to help us defend our lands.'

Auraya turned to the other woman and uttered a string of whistles and sounds. *Translating*, Danjin realised.

As Sirri replied, Auraya translated for the benefit of the audience. Danjin examined the faces of the people around him. Most were staring at the Siyee. Some looked fascinated, others amused. The Dreamweaver adviser looked as uninterested as ever, while Lanren Songmaker was all suppressed excitement.

The Siyee were reacting to this scrutiny in different ways. Some eyed the humans warily, others kept their gaze on their leader and the White. Danjin noted the similarities and differences in their garb and realised they were standing in groups – each one was probably a different tribe.

The exchange ended with Juran raising his voice to speak to the Siyee in their own tongue. Danjin smiled crookedly. It almost annoyed him that a simple Gift bestowed by the gods could make irrelevant a skill he might spend years learning.

As the Siyee began to move away, following their leader along the thoroughfare to make camp, Auraya stepped forward to join the White. Her eyes shifted to Raeli, who stared back expressionlessly, then she looked at Danjin and smiled.

:Hello, Danjin Spear.

:Welcome back, he thought at her.

:Thank you. We've got a lot of catching up to do.

:We have indeed. I have to warn you, Juran has a habit of forgetting that mortals need food or sleep. We may have trouble finding time to do this catching up.

:Then I'll have to make sure he remembers.

Once the Siyee moved away to make camp, Juran invited all into the tent. Lanren Songmaker watched as the hierarchy of power asserted itself. The White's leader looked to the King of Genria first, as the man was the only royal personage present. Then the Somreyans entered, as the Moderator was the closest to a ruler that his country had. The two Dunwayans followed, as representatives of their country. Lanren was eagerly waiting

471

to see how the King of Toren would fit in, since the two kings were of equal position. Guire was a sensible monarch, but Berro was known for being rude and troublesome.

Next the advisers entered the tent, in no particular order. The White discouraged them from behaving as if one was more important than another, yet Lanren still felt it wise to give way to the White's personal advisers. They were much closer to the White and had been working for them far longer.

He followed Danjin Spear to the tent entrance. Lanren had found the youngest of the Spear brothers an intelligent, well-educated, cautious man – nothing like his brothers in regard to the latter. Danjin had seemed a bit lost so far, and Lanren guessed this was because Auraya had been absent and the adviser had no more knowledge of war than history books might offer.

In matters of strategy and fighting, Lanren was the 'expert'. He felt he was hardly that, but there were few other choices. Nobody could be an expert on war when there had been no more than a few minor confrontations in Northern Ithania for the last hundred years. He had studied war and strategy since he was a child, witnessed most of the small skirmishes or uprisings that had happened in the last fifty years, lived in Dunway some years in order to study their warrior culture, and spent a few months in Avven over a decade ago, during which time he had observed the military cult of the Pentadrians – albeit from a distance.

As he entered the tent he noted that everything was arranged the same way it had been each night before. Around the room, several chairs of equal size and plainness had been arranged in a rough circle. A large five-sided table stood in the centre of the room. On it lay a beautiful map. It was a fine work – the best he had ever seen – painted in rich colours on vellum.

Juran looked at Auraya. 'The Dunwayan forces have reached their southern border and await our decision. Before you arrived we were discussing what they should do: join us or remain in Dunway.'

She looked down at the map. 'I was considering this question during my journey. Either choice is a risk.' She glanced at the Dunwayan ambassador. 'As I understand it, Jen of Rommel, if the Dunwayans join us on this side of the mountains they will leave Dunway vulnerable to attack should the Pentadrian army veer north. It seems unfair to ask your people to leave their borders unprotected in order to help us.

'From all reports,' Auraya continued, 'the Pentadrian army is enormous. Dunwayan fighters are famed for their skills in battle, but our spies have reported that these Pentadrian warrior sects also produce exceptional soldiers. We know from our encounters with these black sorcerers that they are more powerful than any in Dunway. Even if all the Dunwayan fighters remain to protect their home, I fear the land would still fall.'

The Dunwayan ambassador frowned as he nodded in acknowledgement.

'If they did remain at home,' Auraya added, 'and the Pentadrians did not fight them but continued through the mountains, there is the possibility that our army will be no match for the Pentadrians' trained warriors. I must pose this question: if this army fell, how long would Dunway stand?'

'So you would have us cross the mountains?'

Auraya nodded. 'Yes, but . . .' she paused and looked at Juran '. . . perhaps not all. Perhaps leave some Dunwayans at home. If the Pentadrians invade Dunway, your warriors can slow their advance, giving us time to cross the mountains and engage the enemy.'

Those people will make no difference, Lanren thought. *But . . . I think she knows that. She simply wishes to allow the Dunwayans to feel a little safer. It won't work, however. They're too well versed in warrior lore to deceive themselves into believing such an illusion.*

Juran glanced at Lanren and shook his head. 'A few fighters would not slow an army of the size of the enemy's.'

'He is right,' the Dunwayan ambassador agreed.

'May I make a suggestion?' Lanren interjected.

Juran looked at him and nodded.

'We know that the Pentadrians are not far from the mountains,' Lanren said. 'The more time we have to reach and fortify our position in the pass, the better. If the Dunwayan army should come through the mountains, they can set traps along the way, slowing the Pentadrians' progress.' *And they'll enjoy doing it*, Lanren added silently.

Juran smiled. 'Indeed, they might.' He looked at his fellow White. Each nodded once. He turned back to the Dunwayan ambassador. 'Please convey our assessment and suggestions to I-Portak. Tell him we would prefer it if he joined us here, but respectfully acknowledge the risk that would entail. We leave the decision for him to make.'

The ambassador nodded. 'I will.'

Juran looked down at the map, pursed his lips, then straightened. 'This evening's reports on the Pentadrians' position have not yet come. Let us have an early meal, then return to consider our journey to the pass. I would like to include the Siyee in that discussion.'

Many of the room's occupants looked relieved. Lanren suppressed a wry smile. While none had walked more than a few steps of the journey from Jarime, they were all tired. They had had little sleep each night, since discussions usually continued long past midnight. Lanren was not the only one who had adapted to sleeping while sitting upright in a rocking, jolting tarn.

As always, Lanren hung back and noted who left the tent with whom. He saw Auraya catch Danjin Spear's eye. The man already looked a little less lost. Then something small dashed into the tent and launched itself at Auraya.

'Owaya! Owaya!'

All turned to see a small grey creature run up Auraya's circ and onto her back. He began to race from one shoulder to another, panting with excitement.

'Hello, Mischief,' Auraya said, her eyes bright with amusement. 'I'm happy to see you, too. Here, let me – I'll just – *will* you stay still for a moment?'

He dodged her hand, then paused to lick her ears.

'Argh! Mischief! Stop that!' she exclaimed. She winced and lifted him down, then held him firmly against her chest with one hand, while scratching his head with the other. The creature gazed up at her adoringly.

'Owaya home.'

'Yes, and hungry,' she told him. She looked up at Danjin. 'You?'

'Yes,' Danjin replied.

Her smile widened. 'Then let's see what we can rustle up. You can tell me what Mischief has been up to while I've been gone.'

'Plenty,' Danjin told her wryly.

As they walked out of the tent, Lanren felt a familiar nagging feeling. It was a feeling he had when he had just seen something that might prove to be important. Something about the exchange he'd witnessed.

Or was it simply the possibilities inherent in the veez itself that nagged at his thoughts. The creatures could be useful as scouts or couriers.

His stomach grumbled. Shaking his head, Lanren put the thought aside and left in search of dinner.

Long past midnight, Auraya paced her tent. The war discussion had lasted hours. At first the time had flown by, but as the night lengthened, the presence of the new Dreamweaver adviser had reminded Auraya of the questions she wanted to ask Leiard.

She knew from reading Raeli's mind that the woman had no idea why Leiard had resigned from the position. Auraya could easily guess the answer to that. Any of her fellow White could learn of their affair just by seeing into his mind. He must have resigned to prevent that.

She felt a pang of guilt. If she'd realised the consequences of taking him to bed that night . . . but one wasn't meant to think twice in moments of passion. That's how it was in folk-tales of love and heroism. Even in those tales there was a cost to forbidden love. Obviously it hadn't occurred to Leiard how much trouble they would cause, either. Even if they had restrained themselves that night, there would still have been the revelation of their love for each other. The White would have read that from his mind anyway.

Is there a chance they might accept my choice of lover? I doubt they'd be happy about it, but they may come to support us in time. We could become a symbol of unity between Circlians and Dream-weavers.

It was all very fine dreaming of becoming a symbol of unity when she didn't know where he was or – she felt her stomach twist – if he still felt the same way about her. During dinner she had asked Danjin if he had seen Leiard. He had no idea where Leiard or any of the Dreamweavers were. She knew they preferred not to travel with armies or to show preference for any side in a battle, but they could not be too far away. Their destination was the same as both armies: the battlefield.

She ought to be sleeping, but she knew she would not. Tomorrow Juran would expect her to join the other White leading the army to war. The only time she had free to seek Leiard was these few spare hours of night.

As she reached the tent entrance she heard a small, muffled voice.

'Owaya go?'

She looked back at the basket Mischief had taken to as his bed. A small head and two bright eyes appeared among the blankets.

'Yes,' she said. 'Mischief stay.'

'Msstf Owaya go.'

Auraya paused, not sure of the veez's meaning. The creature jumped out of the basket and bounded past her. He stopped a few strides away and looked back at her.

'Msstf Owaya go,' he repeated.

He wanted to come with her. She smiled, then shook her head.

'Auraya fly,' she told him.

He looked up at her.

'Msstf Owaya fly.'

Did he truly understand what she was saying? She focused on his mind and saw a bright mix of adoration and eagerness. She tried to communicate a sense of rising above the ground. He quivered all over with excitement, then squeaked and rushed up her body to her shoulder.

If he truly understood, she didn't know. Perhaps if she lifted herself into the air a little he would take fright and jump off. Then he would understand the meaning of the word 'fly' and know he couldn't come with her.

She moved outside and slowly lifted herself upward. The veez's claws tightened on her shoulder, but she sensed no fear from him. *Of course not*, she mused. *He climbs up walls and across ceilings all the time.*

She moved higher, testing his confidence. The only change in his mood was a growing anticipation. When she was looking down at the tops of the tents, she began to move forward.

477

Mischief settled against her back, enjoying the breeze ruffling his fur.

He likes it, she marvelled. *Who would have thought? I'll hope his understanding of heights includes knowing when he's too high to jump off safely . . .*

She had reached the edge of the camp now. Flying on, she followed the curve of a hill upward. At the top she paused to look around.

Then she began to search for Leiard.

CHAPTER 34

Tryss looked down at the hundreds of campfires below, and smiled. From a distance it was easy to feel superior to these landwalkers. He and Drilli had talked about it last night. For a start, these people hardly ever looked up. He supposed they had rarely needed to before now. If the Pentadrians had the same weakness, it would be easy to exploit in the coming battle.

Another landwalker weakness was their *slowness*. The Siyee could travel in an hour or two the distance the rest of the army walked in a day. It had quickly become clear that the Siyee would not be *following* the Circlian army to the battlefield. There was no point in flying around in circles while the land-walkers made their slow but tireless way across the plains, so Sirri had offered to take the Siyee ahead to find a good place for the army to camp the next night. Juran had agreed.

There had been no need to hurry, so they had had plenty of time to inspect the territory. The plains were a different kind of terrain than they were familiar with. Flying low, they stirred up flocks of birds or herds of small, fine-boned animals the landwalkers called lyrim. These creatures provided an excellent opportunity for harness and blowpipe practice. Tryss and Drilli had led one of the many teams of hunters. So many

479

of these animals were brought down that by the end of the day they had killed more than enough to feed themselves. The excess meat was cooked and presented to the landwalker army when it arrived that evening.

It made them popular with the army. The landwalkers had lifted their cups and dedicated their ration of drink to the Siyee after the meal. It was another amusing custom of theirs.

However, the hunt made the Siyee unpopular with a small group of landwalkers who appeared early the next morning. It appeared that these herds of lyrim had belonged to them. Juran had given these men bags of the metal coins the landwalkers used for money, and the lyrim herders had left looking grim, but no longer angry.

All feelings of superiority Tryss enjoyed soon disappeared whenever he was among the landwalkers. Their size was enough to intimidate any Siyee, but watching them at weapons training was truly sobering. Many of these fighters were quite arrogant. Once one sneered openly at Tryss and a group of Siyee. Later, Auraya heard of the incident and was angry. She explained that some landwalkers felt that killing a man at a distance, rather than face-to-face, was a dishonourable and cowardly act. They disdained landwalker archers for that reason. It was all right for them, Auraya had said. They were born large and strong. If only large and strong people fought in wars, armies would be small indeed.

'Tryss!'

Startled out of his thoughts, Tryss looked around. Speaker Sirri was riding an updraught toward him. She landed on the hill beside him.

'The war council is about to begin,' she called. 'I want you to come with me.'

'Me?' he exclaimed.

'Yes. I can probably take a few companions, but I doubt I

could get away with bringing all fourteen Speakers with me. I'd rather not choose between them, so I'll take someone else instead.'

His heart was racing. 'I don't know anything about planning a war!'

She laughed. 'Neither do I! I know one thing though. You're clever. You think differently to me. There's no point bringing someone who thinks like me, because they'll probably only see the same problems and have the same ideas that I will. I need a companion who'll understand what I *don't* understand.'

'I might not understand anything.'

'I doubt that. So, are you coming?'

He grinned. 'Yes!'

'Good!'

She swooped downward and he followed. They glided toward the white tent, where a small crowd of landwalkers had gathered. Only one of the group glanced upward and saw Tryss and Sirri approaching. As they landed the rest exclaimed in surprise and turned to stare at them. The one who had noticed them stepped forward and placed a hand on his chest.

'Lanren Songmaker,' he said. Opening his hand, he gestured to Sirri. 'Hed Speekr Seerree?'

Sirri nodded. She looked at Tryss and spoke his name. The landwalker's eyebrows rose. He waved a finger across his chest, then mimed shooting an arrow. Sirri nodded again. The landwalker pointed to his head and made a signal with his thumb that looked vaguely silly, but seemed to imply approval.

Tryss smiled and nodded to indicate he understood. Being praised so publicly ought to have embarrassed him, but instead he felt a growing dismay. These landwalkers didn't know the Siyee language, and he didn't know theirs. How was he going to help Sirri if he couldn't understand a word spoken at the war council?

481

The man named Songmaker turned and introduced the others. He managed to make himself clear, despite the language difficulties. By saying 'Hed Speekr' and pointing to one of the others, he told them that the person was a leader. Pointing to his head and mouth and then another person told them that the man or woman was present to provide thoughts and words to the leaders.

Advisers, Tryss thought. *Like me.*

A quiet woman in a leather vest smiled faintly as she was introduced. Sirri murmured to Tryss that this was one of the legendary Dreamweavers. Songmaker made the head and mouth gesture. *Another adviser*, Tryss concluded.

Songmaker then pointed at himself, patted the scabbard at his hip, then tapped his head.

So he is a warrior and adviser. A good man to be friends with during a war . . . if only there wasn't this language problem. I wonder how long it would take to learn their tongue. The Siyee language had evolved from a landwalker one, so it might not be that difficult. Some words might be the same, or at least similar.

The attention of the landwalkers had shifted now. Tryss could not see past them to the source of their distraction, however. Then leaders and advisers alike stepped back and the White appeared.

They were impressive figures. Five handsome men and women, all dressed in white. The man who began to address the crowd – Juran – greeted the group in sober but warm tones. Auraya caught Tryss's eye and smiled.

Juran turned to Sirri. 'Welcome, Speaker Sirri – and this is Tryss the inventor, isn't it?' he said in the Siyee language.

Tryss felt his face warm. He wasn't sure what to say to this powerful, formidable man. Auraya chuckled.

'Yes, this is Hunter Tryss.' She said something else in the landwalker tongue, and Tryss realised she was translating. He sighed with relief when he knew his fears were unfounded. If Juran or Auraya translated everything, the war council would not be incomprehensible.

He watched as the White ushered the leaders and their advisers into the tent. The man named Moderator Meeran paused just before the entrance. Auraya beckoned to Sirri. Tryss followed as Sirri stepped forward to join the landwalker as he entered. Tryss guessed there was some significance in this. He would ask Auraya about it later, if he had the opportunity.

Inside the tent was a large table too high for Tryss to see what was on top. All but the White moved to chairs arranged in a circle around the walls of the tent. Two of these chairs were empty. Tryss frowned as Auraya gestured to them. They were landwalker-sized chairs. The seats were as high as Tryss's chest.

They could have brought some smaller chairs for us, he grumbled. *It seems a bit rude . . .*

Sirri didn't complain, however. She moved to one and sprang easily up onto the seat. Tryss was conscious of the many eyes on him as he leapt up onto the second chair. He turned to face the room and saw that he could now see the top of the table.

Ah, that's the reason they didn't.

A large sheet of thin material lay on the table. On it had been painted a colourful shape surrounded by blue. Looking closer, Tryss felt a thrill of amazement. This was a map – and he had never seen a map of such detail or scope. It was a map of the entire continent of Northern Ithania.

He stared at it, trying to work out where Si was. Eventually he realised the lines of scribbly upside-down 'v' shapes were mountain ranges. The great mass of 'v's near the bottom must be Si – it was the most mountainous part of Northern Ithania. He could not make sense of the placement of the individual mountains, however. Since no landwalker had ever charted Si,

483

as far as he knew, the mapmaker had probably guessed their placement.

The White's leader, Juran, began to speak. As he did, Auraya moved away from the table and slipped between Sirri's and Tryss's chairs.

'He says that we will begin by discussing how the Siyee can assist us before and during the battle,' she murmured. 'Since he'll be mainly talking to you, he'll speak your language as best he can, and Dyara will translate to the others.'

Sirri nodded. Juran turned to face her.

'Welcome to the war Gathering, Head Speaker Sirri,' he said, forming the words slowly and carefully. The woman, Dyara, translated for the others in a murmur.

'Thank you, Juran, leader of the White,' Sirri replied. 'I am eager to help in any way I can.'

He smiled. 'How you may help us is what we will discuss tonight. What do you wish your people's role to be?'

Sirri paused. 'As archers of the air,' she said. 'As eyes in the sky.'

'Indeed, that is how I imagine they would be best employed,' Juran agreed. 'I do not think it wise to send you out to randomly attack our enemy during the battle. That would be risky and a waste of your potential. We should use every opportunity to surprise the enemy and work together on land and in the air to our best advantage.'

'How might that be done?' Sirri asked.

'Our war adviser, Lanren Songmaker, has many suggestions on this matter.'

Sirri looked at the man who had greeted them. 'I am eager to hear them.'

'Then he will describe them now. Lanren?'

The friendly landwalker rose from his seat. At a nod from Juran he began to speak. Auraya translated. Tryss listened in fascination as possible encounters with the enemy were described, and how they might be resolved with the Siyee's help. He had imagined the two armies clashing in one great confrontation, not in these carefully planned complex stages and layers of attack.

The man's understanding of the Siyee's limitations in flight was surprisingly good. It seemed Tryss had not been the only person watching and assessing the strengths and weaknesses of his allies. Then the man made a blunder, an assumption that the wind conditions in the mountains would be the same as on the plains. Tryss found himself interrupting. Too late, he realised what he had done and fell silent, his face burning.

'Don't stop, Tryss,' Auraya murmured. 'Speak up. This is what we are here for: to correct each other's mistakes. Better now, than after they have caused deaths on the battlefield.'

He looked up at her, then at Sirri. The Speaker nodded encouragingly. Tryss swallowed hard.

'Air moves differently in the mountains,' he said. 'Sometimes to our advantage, sometimes not.'

Auraya translated. The man spoke.

'Can you predict how these winds will move?'

'Only in a general way. We won't know until we get there if the air will flow as we expect it to.'

From there, the discussion became more detailed. Sirri joined in, but often looked to Tryss when the scenarios Songmaker described became complex. The war adviser was full of enthusiasm, but after a while he stopped and spoke to Juran. Auraya translated.

'We could talk about this for hours, even days. May I suggest that we continue in my tent? All interested in the fine details would be welcome to join us.'

'Yes,' Juran agreed. 'First I would like to consider how the Siyee might be of use before the battle as our "eyes in the sky".' He looked at Sirri and returned to the Siyee language. 'We have no spies in the Pentadrian army. The sorcerers who lead it are able to read minds and discovered our spies who had infiltrated their forces. The only reports of their position we are receiving are from scouts observing from afar, and their last report was to tell us that the army has entered the forests of the foothills. Would you be willing to send some of your people over the mountains to learn more?'

Sirri nodded. 'Of course.'

'How long would they take to cross the mountains and return?'

She shrugged. 'A day, perhaps two, to get across, and the same in returning. How long they spend scouting once they're there depends on how many Siyee I send and how difficult it is to see into this forest. How large is the area they need to search?'

Juran pointed at one of the mountains ranges on the map. Sirri nodded as he circled his finger over the map to indicate an area.

'I'll send twenty pairs. That should reduce the searching to a day.'

Juran nodded. 'Can they leave tonight?'

'There is no moon tonight. It is dangerous flying in the mountains during times of such darkness. They can leave before dawn, however. By the time they reach the mountains there will be enough light to fly by.'

Juran smiled. 'Then we must wait. Thank you, Speaker Sirri.'

Sirri chuckled. 'I should thank *you*, Juran of the White. I have too many energetic young men itching for excitement and adventure. This will keep some of them occupied.'

The landwalkers smiled as Dyara translated this.

'Perhaps you should choose the more sensible of them,'

Auraya suggested. 'Ones who won't reveal themselves unless they have to. We're hoping your people will be a nasty surprise for the enemy.'

Sirri nodded resignedly. 'You're right, unfortunately. I will have to be careful in my choosing.'

'Are there any other changes or decisions we need to make for your benefit?' Juran asked. 'Are your people happy with the arrangements made so far?'

'Yes,' Sirri answered. 'I do with to apologise again for our mistake in hunting the lyrim. If we had known—'

'There is no need to apologise,' Juran soothed. 'If we'd encountered these herds I would have ordered them caught and slaughtered myself. Herders and farmers have always understood that such things happen in times of war. If they did not, they would never have had the courage to come to me and ask for compensation.'

'I see.' Sirri looked thoughtful. 'Should we continue hunting, then?'

Juran smiled. 'If you wish, but take only half from each herd you encounter, and leave the males and the pregnant females so that the lyrim may quickly replace their numbers through breeding.'

Sirri grinned. 'We will.'

'Do you have anything else you wish to discuss?'

She shook her head. Juran glanced around the room. He spoke to the other landwalkers.

'He's asking if anyone has any questions,' Auraya translated.

None of the landwalkers spoke, though a few of them looked as if they'd like to. As the discussion turned to other matters, Tryss felt himself relax as everyone's attention moved away from him. Now, with Auraya translating, he would learn more about how these landwalkers planned to wage this war.

* * *

487

A young Hanian soldier stared into his campfire. He saw in the flames the shapes of fierce warriors and great sorcerers. *What is it going to be like?* he wondered. *I only joined the army last year. That can't be enough training, can it? But the captain says a disciplined fighting spirit is all that I'll need.*

:And a great deal of luck, Jayim added.

:Move on, Leiard told his student. *You look in order to learn, but if you linger for the sake of entertainment you are abusing your Gift.*

Jayim was learning fast. He had achieved the trance state needed for mind-skimming the night before, but had not been able to converse with Leiard at the same time without losing concentration. Now he was faring better.

The next mind was more lively. A Siyee male, his thoughts distorted by tintra. He and two others of their tribe had invited a few Somreyan soldiers to their bower. They had not been prepared for the effect the alcohol had on their small bodies.

:I hope the Somreyans don't take advantage of them, Jayim worried.

:They may, they may not. You cannot help them without revealing that you looked into their minds. They will not understand why we do this. Move on.

The thoughts they caught next were less verbal and more physical. This Siyee's attention was entirely on her partner, on touching and feeling. She thought neither of fighting nor of the coming battle. Jayim was finding this all very, very interesting.

:Move on.

Jayim felt a rush of embarrassment at his hesitation. He turned his mind from the lovers.

:The Siyee have women fighters. So do the Dunwayans. Why don't Hanians?

:Why do you think?

:Because our women are weaker?

488

:They could be as strong as Dunwayan women if they wanted to be. It only takes training.

:Because someone has to look after the children and homes?

:What of the Siyee children and homes? You know from the many minds we have touched that they have left their offspring in the care of the elder Siyee.

:I don't know, then. Perhaps Hanians just don't need to. We have enough men to fight for us.

:Or so we hope.

:There'd be no point bringing women if they were untrained. Women don't have time to train if they marry and have children young.

:The Siyee marry young, too.

:So what is the reason?

:I don't know for certain. We can't read the mind of a race like we are reading the minds of individuals tonight. Customs and traditions accumulate over time and are resistant to change. Only a great need for change can alter the way a people live, or their sense of morality.

:So if we didn't have enough men to fight, women would learn to?

:Probably. The trouble is, by the time the situation forces women to fight there is no time to train them. Now, seek another mind.

Leiard followed Jayim. The boy brushed past the minds of Dreamweavers camped around their tent. From one came a sharp jolt of alarm, but not at their touch. Something else. A shape in the darkness beyond the camp . . .

:Wait. Go back.

Jayim paused, then returned to the alarmed Dreamweaver's mind. Through her eyes they saw a figure walking out of the darkness. A priestess. A high priestess. As the woman drew closer, the Dreamweaver recognised her and felt a wary relief. *It's the friendly one. Auraya.*

:Auraya. Leiard felt a thrill of both pleasure and fear rush through his body. *She has come looking for me.*

:Looks like my lessons will have to end early tonight, Jayim said smugly.

:We'll make up for lost time tomorrow, Leiard replied.

:Then I expect you to make sure my sacrifice is worth it.

Leiard sighed. The boy was as bad as Mirar.

:Enough, Jayim. Assert your identity.

As Jayim followed the ritual, Leiard concentrated on his sense of self. *I am Leiard, Dreamwe—*

And a fool, a voice in his mind interrupted. *You knew she would join the army, yet you still tagged along with your fellow Dreamweavers when you should have run in the other direction.*

Mirar. Leiard sighed. *When am I going to be rid of you?*

When you regain your senses. It's not your identity you're having problems with, it's your loins.

I am not here to see Auraya, Leiard thought firmly. *I am a Dreamweaver. I have a duty to treat the victims of this war.*

Liar. You have a duty to protect your people, Mirar retorted. *If these Circlians whom you feel a duty to treat discover you seduced their high priestess, they'll pick up their swords and slaughter every Dreamweaver they can find. It'll be a nice little warm-up to the battle with the Pentadrians.*

I can't just disappear, Leiard protested. *I have to explain to her why I must leave.*

She already knows why you must leave.

But I have to talk to—

And say what? That you know of a nice little remote spot, perfect for those times she fancies a bit of rough and bumpy? You can tell her that in a dream, just as you can explain why you can't—

'Leiard?'

It was Jayim. Leiard opened his eyes. The boy was staring at him.

'It hasn't got any better, has it?'

Leiard rose. 'I have not lost control to him in weeks. That is an improvement. I expect it will take time.'

'If there's—'

'Hello? Leiard?'

The voice sent a shiver down Leiard's spine. Auraya's voice. He had not heard it in months. It brought memories of dreams they'd shared, echoes of that first night together. His heart began to race.

All he need do was invite her in. He drew breath to speak and paused, waiting for Mirar to protest, but the other presence remained silent. Perhaps out of caution. If Mirar spoke, Auraya would hear him and . . .

'Leiard?'

'I am here. Come in, Auraya.'

The flap opened and she stepped inside. He felt his chest slowly tighten, realised he was holding his breath, and exhaled slowly. Her hair was pulled back into a plait, but wisps of it had blown free in the wind – or more likely in flight – and hung about her face. She was even more beautiful like this, he decided. Tousled, like after that night of . . .

'Greetings, Auraya of the White,' Jayim said.

She looked at the boy and smiled.

'Greetings, Jayim Baker. How is your training progressing?'

'Well,' the boy replied.

Her smile was warm, but it faded a little when she turned to regard Leiard.

'I heard you had resigned.'

Leiard nodded.

'It was nice to meet you again, Auraya,' Jayim inserted. 'I'd best be going.'

She watched as he hurried from the tent, then turned back to Leiard.

'He knows.'

'Yes. A weakness of our mind-link teaching methods. I trust him.'

She shrugged. 'Then so do I.' She took a step toward him. 'I understand why you resigned. I think I do, anyway. You had to in case we were found out and my people reacted badly.'

'I did not resign only to protect Dreamweavers,' he told her, surprising himself with the force of his words. 'I also did it so that we might . . . we might continue to meet.'

Her eyes widened, then she smiled and her face flushed. 'I have to admit, I was a little worried. The dream links stopped and it's taken me two nights to find you.'

He walked to her, then took her hands. Her skin was so soft. She looked up at him, and her lips curled into a small, sensual smile. The scent of her was teasingly faint, making him want to breathe in deeply.

What was I going to say? He blinked and thought back. *Ah, yes.*

'I had to make some decisions,' he told her. 'Decisions best made alone.' He could feel the tension within her through her hands.

'And what did you decide?'

'I decided . . .' He paused. Until this moment he hadn't realised how close he had been to giving in to Mirar. Life would be easier if he simply ran away. Now that he was with Auraya again – seeing her, touching her – he knew he couldn't run from her. She would haunt him day and night.

'I decided that what mattered was that we be who we are,' he told her. 'You are one of the White. I am a Dreamweaver. We are lovers. To be otherwise would be denying who we are. To allow others to be harmed because of our love would be wrong. We both know that. So . . .'

'So?'

'We can only meet in secret.'

'Where?'

'Far from Jarime. I have a place in mind. I will send you the location in a dream.'

The corner of her lips twitched. 'Just the location? Nothing else?'

He chuckled. 'You were getting a little too fond of those dreams, Auraya. I was afraid you would put me aside for them.'

Her fingers tightened around his. 'No, I still prefer the real thing. Or . . . at least I think I do.' She looked over his shoulder, in the direction of the bed. 'Maybe I had better make sure.'

He glanced toward the tent flap. Jayim had closed it well, he noted. No gaps.

'Don't worry,' Auraya murmured. 'Nobody will hear a sound. I've already made sure of it.'

As she drew him toward the bed, Leiard could not help wondering at the irony. What did the gods think of one of their most favoured priestesses using her Gifts to hide her secret affair with a Dreamweaver?

He sobered. There was little chance they didn't already know. If they'd disapproved, they would have done something about it long ago.

Then Auraya kissed him and all thought of the gods fled his mind.

CHAPTER 35

Emerahl pulled the fur collar of her tawl close. Turning to face the tent's entrance, she sighed deeply, then straightened her back and strode outside.

At once she felt eyes upon her. The first were those of the guards charged with watching her. They were supposed to be her protectors but their role was more akin to jailors. She had endured their polite attention since the day the brothel had left Porin.

When Rozea had heard of Emerahl's 'accident' with formtane she had decided that she must announce her new favourite that day to prevent any more 'foolish and destructive habits'. Since then Emerahl had travelled in Rozea's tarn and was given the best of everything – including her own personal guards.

The other whores stood further away. Emerahl had barely spoken to them since leaving Porin. She knew from short snatches of conversation with Tide that they believed she had planned her little 'accident' with formtane in order to get an audience with Rozea and persuade the madam into promoting her.

It didn't help that Rozea wouldn't let Emerahl visit Tide or Brand, or allow them to see her. She knew that Brand had purchased the formtane for Emerahl, and didn't trust either of Emerahl's friends not to smuggle something else to her.

There was one dubious benefit to her new position. Her customers were always the richest nobles of the army. The few priests who did visit the brothel's tents could not afford the services of the favourite. So far.

Emerahl almost wished she hadn't told Rozea she didn't want to go on this trip. Once Star had related Emerahl's gloomy predictions for the trip, Rozea had decided there was a chance her favourite's fears might get the better of her. The tents were arranged each night in a way that ensured Emerahl's was watched from every direction. No sharp tools were allowed, and her customers were asked to remove all weapons before visiting. Rozea loved fanciful adventure stories and knew that a stolen knife and quiet slash of an unwatched tent wall had given many a fictional heroine the means to escape her captors.

None of these precautions were keeping Emerahl from leaving, however.

It's not the guards or the tent walls, she thought as the servants deftly removed the tent poles and the structure collapsed. *It's been the neighbours.*

She looked around at the empty field they had camped in. The remnants of an already harvested crop had been trampled well into the ground – first by the army and now by Rozea's caravans. She felt a twinge of anticipation. So far they'd managed to keep up with the Toren army. The troops often disappeared into the distance during the day, but the brothel caravan always managed to catch up late that night.

Last night they hadn't. A small party of wealthy customers had ridden back to visit them and had left in the early hours of the morning. Emerahl's customer, a second cousin of the king, had told her that the army was now travelling as fast as men could be driven so that they would join the Circlian army in time for the battle.

Every night of the journey before this last, the brothel had camped among the troops. Every night priests wandered among these soldiers, bolstering spirits and keeping the general sense of purpose high. It was this that had prevented Emerahl from leaving. Any confrontation between herself and her guards was bound to draw attention. Even if she did manage to slip away unnoticed, the news that Rozea's prize whore had run away would fill many soldiers' heads with ideas of a free roll with a coveted beauty, and a reward when they brought her in. She could defend herself easily enough, but doing so would, again, attract attention, and she didn't have much chance of avoiding that if the entire army was looking for her.

Now that the army had moved ahead of the caravan the danger was gone. Soon the brothel would be too far behind for nobles to visit it at night. She had only to arrange a distraction for her guards and slip away, and with no customer in her bed all night her absence probably wouldn't be noticed until morning.

'Jade.'

Emerahl looked up. Rozea was walking toward her, her high boots caked with mud. The woman was obviously relishing this travelling lifestyle and always spent each morning stomping around the camp issuing orders.

'Yes?' Emerahl replied.

'How are you feeling?'

Emerahl shrugged. 'Well enough.'

'Come along, then.'

Rozea led her to the lead tarn and ushered her inside. A servant handed them goblets of warmed spicewater. Emerahl drank hers quickly, intending to lie down and sleep as soon as she was finished. She was in no mood for conversation with Rozea today, and if she had the chance to escape tonight she wanted to be as rested and alert as possible.

496

'You're quiet this morning,' Rozea noted. 'Too early for you?'

Emerahl nodded.

'We have to start early if we're going to catch up with the army tonight.'

'Do you think we will?'

Rozea pursed her lips. 'Perhaps. If not, at least we'll keep ahead of Kremo's caravan.'

Kremo was one of Rozea's competitors. The man's caravan was larger and he catered to all but the poorer soldiers, who could only afford the lone, sick-looking whores that trailed the army like carrion insects.

'I'd better get some sleep, then,' Emerahl said.

Rozea nodded. Emerahl lay down on the bench seat and fell asleep straightaway, waking only briefly when the tarn jerked into motion. When she woke next, the tarn had stopped. She looked up and discovered Rozea was gone.

Closing her eyes, she started to drift into sleep again. Shouting male voices jolted her awake. She opened her eyes, cursing the noisy guards.

Screams erupted somewhere beyond the tarn.

Emerahl scrambled upright and yanked the door flap of the tarn-cover open. Trees crowded the road. Men she did not recognise were rushing through them toward the caravan. Emerahl heard Rozea somewhere in front of her tarn, bellowing orders to the guards, who were already moving to meet the attackers.

They were wearing the armour and brandishing the swords and spears of Toren soldiers, Emerahl realised. She stared hard at one of them. His emotions were a mix of greed, lust and a gleeful exultation at being free of endless orders and restrictions.

Deserters, Emerahl guessed. *Turned thief and outlaw most likely*.

She looked around, heart racing. There didn't appear to be

497

many attackers, but more could be hiding in the trees. She paused as she noticed the fallen tree lying in front of Rozea's tarn. The trunk had been hacked at; this was no natural obstruction.

A stranger suddenly stepped in front of her. She recoiled in shock, shrinking back into the tarn. He grinned up at her and ripped the flap aside. As he started to climb into the tarn, Emerahl gathered her wits. She drew magic, then hesitated. Best make it look like a physical blow. She sent it in a ball of force at his face.

His head jerked backwards and he grunted with surprise. Blood began to pour from his nose. He growled in anger and heaved himself into the tarn.

Tough bastard, she thought. *And stupid, too.* Drawing more power, she directed it at his chest. The blow threw him backwards out of the tarn. As he fell, his head struck a tree trunk with an audible crack.

Emerahl crept toward the doorway. She jumped as another figure stepped into view, then relaxed as she recognised the face of one of the brothel guards. He bent and she heard a chopping sound.

'He won't be bothering you again, lady,' the guard called cheerily.

'Thanks,' she replied dryly.

'Now keep out of sight. Kiro and Stillo need a bit of help.'

The whores' screaming had changed to a panicked shrieking. As the guard moved away, Emerahl ignored his order and peered out the door.

Three of the deserters were backed up against one of the tarns. They were fighting two guards – now three as her rescuer joined them. The girls inside the vehicle sounded hysterical. As she watched, the skinny, wasted-looking attacker lashed out – faster than he looked capable of moving – and the guard that had been fighting him sagged to the ground.

The skinny man paused to regard his remaining two comrades. Instead of joining them, he stepped behind them, swung around and hacked at the tarn cover. The frame broke and the cover collapsed inward. The girls started screaming again.

At the same time, one of the two fighting deserters fell. The skinny man reached inside the tarn. Emerahl held her breath, then her heart sank as the man pulled out a slender arm. He yanked at it and Star toppled out of the tarn and onto the ground at his feet.

He put his sword-point against her belly.

'Stand back or she dies!'

The fighters paused, then backed away from each other. The remaining deserter was bleeding heavily from a leg wound.

'That's right. Now, bring us your money.'

The two guards exchanged glances.

'Bring us your money!'

Emerahl shook her head sadly. *There's only one way this will end. If the guards ignore Skinny's demands he'll kill Star. If the guards give in, Skinny will take her away as insurance against the guards following him and retrieving the brothel's money. He'll most likely kill her as soon as he feels he has escaped them.*

Unless I intervene. But I can't. Not without revealing I'm powerfully Gifted.

Or would she? Rozea already knew her favourite had a few Gifts. If Emerahl kept her use of magic basic – just a weak blast to knock the sword from the man's hand, for instance – nobody would be more than a little surprised. She would have to wait for the right moment, when Skinny was distracted. The slightest hint of a magical attack and he'd push that sword into Star's belly.

Emerahl drew magic and held it ready.

'You're not getting a coin from us, you cowardly lump of

arem dung.' Rozea stepped into view from between two tarns.

The wounded deserter chose that moment to collapse. Skinny didn't glance at his fallen companion. He only pressed his sword harder into Star's belly. The girl cried out. 'Make one move and I'll kill her.'

'Go on then, deserter,' Rozea challenged. 'I've got plenty more like her.' She nodded to the guards. 'Kill him.'

The guards' expressions hardened. As they raised their swords, Emerahl sent a bolt of magic forth, but even as it left her she saw Skinny's blade stab downward.

Star screamed in pain. Emerahl's magic knocked the sword aside at the same moment a guard's sword sliced through Skinny's neck. Star screamed again and clutched at her side. Emerahl realised with dismay that her blast had ripped the sword out of the girl and caused even more damage. Blood gushed from the wound.

Emerahl cursed and leapt out of the tarn. The guards stared at her as she passed them and crouched at Star's side. She heard Rozea say her name sharply, but ignored it.

Kneeling down beside the injured girl, Emerahl pressed a hand firmly over the wound. Star cried out.

'It hurts, I know,' Emerahl said quietly. 'We have to prevent your blood escaping.' Pressure alone wasn't going to stop the flow, however. She drew magic and formed it into a barrier beneath her hands.

She looked up at the guards. 'Find something to put under her so we can carry her to my tarn.'

'But she's—'

'Just do it,' she snapped.

They hurried away. Emerahl looked around. Rozea was still standing several strides away.

'Do you have a kit of cures and herbs?' Emerahl asked.

The madam shrugged. 'Yes, but no point in wasting them.

She's not going to survive that.'

Cold-hearted bitch. Emerahl bit her tongue. 'Don't be so sure. I've seen worse fixed by Dreamweavers.'

'Have you now?' Rozea's eyebrows rose. 'You become more interesting every day, Jade. When did a poor runaway like you get the chance to observe Dreamweavers at work? What makes you think you can do what takes them years of training to learn?'

Emerahl looked up and met Rozea's eyes. 'Perhaps one day I'll tell you – *if* you get me the kit and some water. And some bandages. Lots of bandages.'

Rozea called to the servants. The door flap of the last tarn opened and fearful faces appeared, then one servant emerged and hurried to Rozea. The guards appeared with a narrow plank of wood. Emerahl rolled Star on her side. The girl made no sound. She had fallen unconscious. The guards slid the plank underneath her. Emerahl kept her hands pressed against the wound as she rolled Star back onto the plank. The guards took the ends of the makeshift stretcher and carried the girl toward Rozea's tarn.

Rozea followed. 'You're not putting her in there. You can treat her just as well outside.'

The sooner I get away from this woman the better, Emerahl thought. 'She shouldn't be moved once I've sewn her up, so we have to get her somewhere warm and comfortable first.' She looked at the guards. 'Put her in.'

They obeyed her. As they climbed out again, Rozea stepped into the doorway. Emerahl grabbed her arm.

'No,' Emerahl said. 'I work alone.'

'I'm not letting you—'

'Yes, you are,' Emerahl growled. 'The last person she will want to see when she wakes up is *you*.'

Rozea winced. 'She would have died either way.'

'I know, but she needs time to accept that. For now you'll only agitate her, and I need her calm.'

Rozea frowned, then stepped aside. Emerahl climbed inside and crouched next to Star. A moment later servants deposited a large bowl of water, scraps of material and a pathetically small leather bag on the floor near the entrance.

Emerahl didn't touch them. She placed her hands on the wound again.

'Nobody is to disturb me,' she called out. 'Do you hear me?'

'I do,' Rozea replied.

Emerahl closed her eyes. Forcing her breathing to slow, she turned her attention inward.

She reached the right state of mind quickly. This healing technique was similar to her own method of changing her physical appearance but not as demanding of time or magic. Her mind must alter its way of thinking in order to grasp the world of flesh and bone. In this state of consciousness everything – flesh, stone, air – was like a vast puzzle made up of a multitude of pieces. Those pieces formed patterns. They *liked* to form patterns. When healing, she need only to realign pieces roughly in their proper pattern and old links would re-form.

That was how she liked to work, anyway. Mirar had tried to encourage her to hone her skills beyond what was necessary. He had made an art of this healing method and would always continue refining his work until the patient was back to his or her original state – or better – with no scarring and no need for rest in order to recover strength. Emerahl hadn't seen the point of spending so much time and effort on healing just for the sake of aesthetics. Besides, if Star didn't end up with a scar the others might realise Emerahl had done something exceptional. Tales of her work would certainly draw the attention of priests.

Slowly, the broken inner edges of the wound realigned. Fluid no longer spilled out, but flowed along appropriate channels. When nothing remained but a shallow wound, Emerahl opened her eyes.

Reaching for the water and bandages, Emerahl heated the former and used the latter to clean the wound. She reached for the kit and took out a needle and thread. Using a little magic, she heated the needle as Mirar had taught her, to help prevent infection. The thread smelled of a herb oil known to fight festering of wounds. The kit might be small, but its contents were good.

When she turned back she found Star staring at her.

'You're not what you seem to be, are you, Jade?' the girl said softly.

Emerahl regarded her warily. 'Why do you say that?'

'You just healed me with magic. I could feel it.'

'That's just the cure I gave you making you feel strange.'

Star shook her head. 'I was watching you. You didn't do anything but sit there with your eyes closed, while I could feel things moving inside me. The pain is less, when it should be worse.'

Emerahl considered Star carefully. She doubted the girl would believe a denial.

'Yes. I did use a little magic trick I learned from a Dreamweaver to ease the pain. Don't think you're all properly healed. You could come apart again if you're not careful. I have to sew you up now, to help stop that happening. Do you want medicine to make you unconscious?'

Star looked at the needle and went pale.

'I . . . I think you'd better give me some.'

Emerahl put the needle down and looked through the kit. She found a vial of liquid labelled 'to force sleep – three drops', which smelled of formtane and a few other sedatives.

'This will do.' Emerahl looked at Star and sighed. 'Will you promise me something?'

Star paused, then nodded. 'You don't want anyone to know you used magic.'

'Rozea already knows I have a few Gifts. I don't want her to know *how* Gifted I am or she'll have me doing things with customers I don't want to do. So let's pretend that you weren't as hurt as you appeared to be and that I only used magic to stop the blood flowing and to hold things together while I sewed you up.'

Star nodded. 'I'll tell them that.'

'You promise you'll tell them no more?'

'I promise.'

Emerahl smiled. 'Thank you. I miss you all, you know. Sitting up here with Rozea is so boring. She won't even let Brand come and talk to me.'

'Now you'll have me to talk to,' Star pointed out, smiling.

Not if I leave tonight, Emerahl thought.

She put a hand behind Star's head and lifted it so she could tip a few drops of the cure into the girl's mouth. Star swallowed, grimaced, then continued talking.

'You were right, about this trip being dangerous. We are so far behind the army now. How many of the guards are dead?'

'I don't know.'

'Some are. I know that. What if this happens again?' Star looked at Emerahl, her eyes becoming glazed. 'I'm so glad yr with 's. If yr powrs'r strong, y cn help pr'tect 's. We need y'.'

Emerahl looked away, turning her attention to threading the needle. Of the guards she had seen fighting only two had been alive at the end. Others might have been keeping watch for further attack, out of her sight, but if not then the caravan was now badly under-protected.

And two guards can't watch me effectively.

504

She began sewing the edges of the wound together. Star made a small whimpering sound at first, then her breathing slowed and deepened.

Star's right. The whores need protection, Emerahl thought. *Especially if the caravan doesn't meet the army again for days.*

Days in which she was in no danger of being discovered by the priests.

She muttered a curse. Finishing the stitching, she put the needle and spool of thread back in the kit. Then she called Rozea's name.

The madam peered into the tarn. She looked at Star and her eyebrows rose.

'She lives?'

'For now.'

'Well done.' Rozea climbed inside and sat opposite the sleeping girl. 'Nice stitching. You're full of surprises, Jade.'

'Yes,' Emerahl replied. 'Including this one. I'm leaving. I want the money you owe me.'

Rozea paused. Emerahl could sense the woman's indignation turn slowly to annoyance as she realised she could not keep her pet whore from escaping. 'If you leave now, you go without a coin.'

Emerahl shrugged. 'Very well. But don't expect to see me again. Ever.'

The madam hesitated. 'I suppose I can give you some food and a few coins. Enough to get you back to Porin. When I return we'll talk about the rest. How does that sound?'

'Reasonable,' Emerahl lied.

'Good – but before you do, tell me why you feel you must abandon us. Was it today's unpleasantness? It was a bit of bad luck, but surely travelling with us is safer than travelling by yourself. You've seen the lone workers, how ill and beaten they look.'

505

'I don't intend to sell my body. I can get work as a healer.'

'You? Why would people pay you when they could get the services of a priest or Dreamweaver for free?'

'When people don't have a choice they'll take any help they can. There can't be many priests or Dreamweavers left in the villages between here and Porin. They've all joined the army.'

'Of course there are. There are plenty of healers too old to travel who stayed behind.' The woman's voice softened. 'Are you sure about this, Jade? I would hate for anything bad to happen to you. You think a few Gifts make you safe, but there are men out there with cruel minds and stronger powers.'

Emerahl lowered her eyes.

'What are your chances of attracting unwanted attention alone, a girl of your looks? Here, with us, you are safer. As soon as we catch up with the army I will hire new guards. How does that sound?'

'Perhaps if . . .' Looking away, Emerahl chewed her lip.

Rozea leaned forward. 'Yes? Tell me.'

'I want to be able to refuse a customer I don't like the look of,' Emerahl said, raising her eyes to meet Rozea's. 'I want every third night off.'

'So long as you don't refuse them all the time, I suppose that is reasonable for a favourite, but resting every third night is unreasonable. What about every sixth night?'

'Fourth.'

'Fifth, and I'll raise your fee.'

'What point is there in that? You won't pay me.'

'I will, when you need it – and I have enough to pay new guards.' The woman paused. 'Very well,' she said slowly. 'I will accept your limitations.' She leaned back in her seat and smiled. 'So long as you give me your word you will stay with me for the next year.'

Emerahl opened her mouth to give her acceptance, then paused. She should not give in too easily.

'Six months.'

'Eight?'

Emerahl sighed and nodded. Leaning forward, Rozea patted her on the knee. 'Wonderful. Now stay here while I see if the boys have managed to move that tree yet.'

As Rozea climbed out of the vehicle, Emerahl looked at Star and smiled grimly. She had no intention of keeping her word. As soon as the caravan neared the army and the girls were safe, she would leave. The conditions she had set would only help to ensure her safety until then.

And perhaps I can arrange for us to fall too far behind the army for nobles and priests to ride back to visit us, she thought.

As soon as Auraya's feet touched the ground, Mischief leapt off her shoulder and ran into her tent. Auraya approached slowly. She had seen the light within as she'd flown closer to the camp, and the lack of any sense of a mind there had told her that one of the White was waiting for her.

'Mrae! Mrae!'

'Hello, Mischief.'

Auraya relaxed a little, though she wasn't sure why finding Mairae waiting for her was different to finding any other White. It was probably because Mairae had admitted to enjoying many lovers. She, of all the White, would be the least bothered by Auraya having one, too.

The tent flap was open. Auraya peered inside to find Mairae sitting on one of the chairs. In the lamplight she appeared even younger and more beautiful. She looked up at Auraya and smiled.

'Hello, Auraya.'

Auraya entered the tent. 'Has something happened?'

'Nothing new.' Mairae shrugged. Her smile became more forced. 'I couldn't sleep, so I decided to visit you. Seems like I never get a chance to talk to anyone. It's always war and politics. Never just talk, between two people.'

It was more than that, Auraya guessed. Something was bothering Mairae. Auraya didn't need to read the woman's mind to know it. She moved to the chest that Danjin had packed for her. Opening it, she lifted out two goblets and a bottle of tintra.

'Drink?'

Mairae grinned. 'Thank you.'

Auraya filled the goblets. Mairae took one and drank deeply.

'So where did you go tonight? Just flying about?'

Auraya shrugged. 'Yes.'

'Juran seems eager to face the Pentadrians. Have you noticed?'

'I wouldn't have said he was "eager". More like . . . if he has to do it, he'll do it well. How do you feel?'

'I . . . I'm dreading it,' Mairae admitted with a grimace. 'You?'

'Definitely not looking forward to it,' Auraya smiled wryly. 'I have no doubts, though. We'll win. The gods will make sure of it.'

Mairae sighed and took another gulp of tintra. 'It's not defeat that I'm worried about. I dread the killing . . . the bloodshed.'

Auraya nodded.

'You don't seem worried, though,' Mairae commented.

'Oh, I am. When I find myself thinking about it, I think of something else. It's going to be horrible. Of that we can be sure. There's no point tormenting myself now by imagining *how* horrible. It'll be bad enough when it happens.'

Mairae considered Auraya thoughtfully. 'Is that why you

spent the last few nights flying around? Are you distracting yourself?'

'I suppose I must be.'

One of Mairae's eyebrows lifted suggestively. 'Is this distraction a "he"?'

Auraya blinked in surprise, then laughed. 'If only!' She topped up Mairae's goblet, then leaned forward. 'Do you think I could persuade Juran to revoke the law against using a Dreamweaver's services?'

Mairae's eyebrows rose. 'I'm surprised you haven't attempted it already.'

'If I hadn't been in Si I would have.' Auraya met and held Mairae's eyes. 'Do you think he would revoke it?'

'Perhaps.' Mairae frowned as she considered. 'If he's reluctant to, suggest lifting the ban for a set time after the battle.'

'I will. I would rest a little easier if I knew those that survive the battle might survive their injuries.'

'I don't think it would make me rest any easier,' Mairae said glumly.

Auraya smiled. 'Sounds like *you* need to find yourself a distraction, Mairae. Surely, in the greatest army Northern Ithania has ever seen, there's a man or two who has caught your eye.'

Mairae's eyes brightened. 'Yes, quite a few actually, but with so many of my former lovers here as well I have to be on my best behaviour. It wouldn't do if I was seen to favour one ally over another.' She paused, and a thoughtful look came over her face. 'Though there is one race I haven't tried . . .'

Auraya felt a stab of horror as she realised what Mairae was considering.

'No!'

Mairae grinned. 'Why not? They might be small, but—'

'It's forbidden,' Auraya told her firmly. 'By Huan. Matings with landwalkers produce deformed children.'

'But I won't conceive.'

'No, but if you seduce any of them into breaking one of their most serious laws, you'll mar or even destroy this new friendship between Siyee and landwalker.'

Mairae sighed. 'I wasn't all that enchanted by the idea, anyway.' She lifted her goblet to her lips, then hesitated. 'Do you think anyone will mind if I don't choose from the nobility? There's a good-looking war-platten driver in the Genrian army. A real champion, that one.'

Auraya smothered a sigh. The rest of the night was not going to pass quickly.

CHAPTER 36

Not long after Danjin had drifted into sleep he was startled awake again by someone poking at his legs. He opened his eyes just as the sensation became a warm weight, and looked down to find Mischief curling up on his lap.

He sighed and shook his head. No matter how carefully he locked the veez's cage, the creature always managed to escape. He ought to put Mischief back, but the cage was underneath the opposite seat, behind the legs of Lanren Songmaker. The military adviser was asleep and Danjin did not want to disturb the man.

The veez was a welcome extra source of warmth, anyway. *Wouldn't my father love to see me now? I was hired for my intelligence and knowledge of the world, but all I have been useful for so far is as a pet's guardian.*

He looked around the tarn. All of the other occupants were asleep, even the new Dreamweaver adviser, Raeli. Her face had lost much of its rigid wariness. She was not a beautiful woman, but without the constant frown of tension marking her forehead she was not unattractive either.

Last night, over dinner, Auraya had told him that Raeli's aloofness stemmed from fear and suspicion. The woman was afraid of ill-treatment and of making mistakes that might harm her people. She hesitated to make friends lest they betray her. Auraya assured him that Raeli noted and appreciated every friendly gesture made toward her. She had pointed out that he would find it easier to befriend the Dreamweaver than she would, as one of the White. He had taken that as a hint that she wanted him to befriend Raeli for her.

It wouldn't be easy. Raeli responded to most questions as briefly as possible. This morning, when he had entered the tarn with Mischief, a hint of warmth had entered Raeli's gaze, and he began to consider whether the veez would provide common ground between himself and the Dreamweaver. She was Somreyan and keeping veez as pets was a Somreyan habit. Though he had no idea when he was supposed to find time to befriend her, when every moment of his day was taken up with war councils, attending to Auraya, or obeying the unspoken rule against chatter in the advisers' tarn.

Danjin closed his eyes and sighed. *It would be so much easier if Leiard hadn't resigned.* He hadn't seen Leiard since the day he had visited the Dreamweaver in Jarime. Last night Auraya had mentioned speaking to Leiard the previous night. She told Danjin how, while flying about two nights ago, she had noticed an encampment of Dreamweavers in the distance. She had visited them, and found Leiard there.

That would have to have been after the war council. Doesn't she need sleep?

He yawned. *Perhaps not. But I do.*

For a while his thoughts drifted. Weariness overcame the discomfort of sleeping upright and the jolting of the tarn as it trundled along the road. Then something kicked him in a way that made him grateful for the heavy leather vest protecting his groin. He started awake with a curse, and the first thing he saw was the veez slip under the flap covering the opening of the tarn and disappear. Next he realised he was the object

512

of several reproachful stares. Throwing off the last vestiges of sleep, he leapt up and went in pursuit of the creature.

It was raining outside the tarn. The army was a long line of men, women, animals and vehicles. The column in front was more like a procession. The leaders of each nation had brought or been provided with spacious, decorated tarns and a regiment of elite troops. Ahead of all these was a large, covered tarn painted entirely white.

He could see no sign of Mischief, but he knew from experience that the best place to look first was wherever Auraya might be. *If only I still had her ring*, he thought. *I could ask her*. She'd taken the ring from him to give to the leader of the Siyee scouts. Knowing what the sky people saw was clearly a much more important use for the ring than allowing him to find her wily pet a little faster.

Ah, but I hadn't realised how useful it was until it was gone.

He frowned as he considered what to do. If Auraya had returned from accompanying the Siyee to the next camp she would probably be with the other White. He started jogging toward the white tarn.

As he drew closer he saw that Juran was riding beside the tarn on one of the famous Bearers. The leader of the White spent most of the day in the saddle. He was always somewhere in the long column, talking to people. Danjin had seen grooms tending to the other four Bearers, but the only other White he had observed riding were Dyara and Rian. Mairae seemed to prefer the comfort of the tarn, or perhaps remained there so that anyone who wanted to speak to the White was always sure of a place to find one.

Auraya, he knew, had never learned to ride. Danjin was not sure why a Bearer had been brought along for her. Perhaps the White didn't want her lack of riding ability to be known, although surely her flying ability more than made up for that.

Flying was how she preferred to travel now. She had flown with the Siyee yesterday, far ahead of the army. In part this was to provide protection and a voice of authority if herders decided to retaliate against the Siyee hunting their stock. Partly it was to ensure the White could communicate with the sky people, since the Siyee had no priests to relay messages telepathically. Danjin also suspected it was to ensure the camping grounds the Siyee chose were suitable for landwalkers and accessible for vehicles.

Danjin knew that Juran had been reluctant to allow Auraya to stray far from the other White at first. When she had demonstrated just how quickly she could return to the army, Juran had changed his mind. Her ability allowed her to travel at incredible speeds.

Danjin, however, was puffing as he neared the white tarn. He was relieved to see Mairae and Auraya inside. Juran glanced back at him.

'Adviser Spear.'

'Is Mischief . . . ?' Danjin panted.

'Yes, he's here.'

As Danjin drew level with the tarn he slowed to a walk. Auraya turned to smile at him.

'Ah, Danjin.' She chuckled. 'You could have sent one of the servants for him. Come aboard. He'll settle down after a bit, and you'll be able to take him back.'

Danjin climbed up into the vehicle. Mairae was lounging in one of the seats with her legs curled up beside her. Auraya's feet were planted firmly on the tarn floor, her boots and the hem of her circ stained with mud. Mischief was perched on one of her knees, and had left small pawprints on her circ.

'Fly!' the veez said insistently. As Danjin sat down beside Auraya the creature looked at him suspiciously. 'No cage.'

'No fly,' Auraya replied. 'Fly later.'

The veez sagged in dejection. It gave a sigh and looked away.

'Hello, Danjin.' Mairae smiled sympathetically. 'He's a handful, but don't worry. He won't see you as an adversary so long as you feed him.'

Danjin opened his mouth to reply, but hesitated as he noted a Bearer approaching swiftly, ridden by Dyara. Mairae looked over her shoulder at the woman, then back at Auraya.

'I can't see the point in this,' she murmured. 'What could you possibly learn in the next few days?'

Auraya shrugged. 'Perhaps something useful. At least I'll get some battle practice in.'

Mairae turned to Juran. 'You said yourself, so long as Auraya follows your lead – so long as we all do – she'll be fine. She's not going to pick a fight with one of these black sorcerers on her own. Not after what happened before.'

Juran shook his head. 'Should Auraya be separated from us – which is possible since she so often joins the Siyee – she may be cornered by one of these sorcerers. It may be her skills rather than her strength that save her.'

He turned to watch as Dyara's Bearer drew up on the other side of the tarn. 'Hello, Dyara. Did Guire agree?'

The woman smiled thinly. 'Yes. He's always reasonable, but how long he'll remain so will depend on Berro. Things are going to get interesting once the Torens arrive.' She looked at Danjin and nodded politely, then turned her attention to Auraya. 'I thought we might head north and put some distance between ourselves and the army.'

Auraya smiled. 'That would be wise. We don't want to frighten anyone, or break anything.' She looked at Juran. 'You will consider what I suggested before?'

Juran nodded. 'Yes. As you said, the fighters will resent us if we don't allow them the choice.'

Auraya rose and placed Mischief in Danjin's lap. Danjin looked from her to Juran, wondering what they were referring to.

'Fly?' Mischief said hopefully.

'No fly,' Auraya replied firmly. 'Stay with Danjin. Behave and we'll fly later.' The veez's head swivelled in impossible angles to follow her as she climbed out of the tarn.

Dyara dismounted. A groom hurried forward to take the halter. As she and Auraya walked away from the road, Danjin felt Mischief sigh heavily.

Juran looked over his shoulder abruptly, then smiled. 'My presence is needed yet again.'

'Go on, then.' Mairae chuckled. 'Don't enjoy yourself too much.' As Juran rode away, she turned to Danjin. 'It wouldn't be fair to ask you to stay and keep me company. You look like you need a good night's sleep. You and Auraya both.'

He smiled wryly. 'I was beginning to think the White did not need to sleep.'

Her expression became rueful. 'We do as much as any mortals, though our Gifts enable us to overcome the effects for a while. It is not easy to find time to sleep right now. Or when any of us find the time, we can't.'

Danjin regarded her in surprise. None of the White were showing any signs of anxiety, but perhaps they were merely good at hiding it. There had been something both disturbing and reassuring in the way Juran and Mairae had calmly analysed Auraya's chances of surviving a confrontation with one of the enemy sorcerers.

Mairae shrugged. 'We all have our ways of dealing with our fears. Juran stays up all night planning and plotting. Rian prays. Auraya flies around.' Mairae suddenly smiled coyly. 'Or so she says.' Her eyes slid sideways to regard Danjin. 'I did wonder if she had found another distraction. Perhaps she is spending time with someone close to her heart.'

Danjin frowned. Then he realised what she was inferring and felt a mix of embarrassment and shock. Auraya take a *lover*? It was possible, of course. She would have told him, surely. She trusted him enough to . . . but then again, if she wanted to hide it from the other White she couldn't tell him . . .

He shook his head. 'How am I supposed to sleep now? I'll be wondering the same thing all day.'

Mairae laughed. 'I'm sorry, Danjin Spear. I did not mean to add another source of disturbance to your rest. Go. You had better return to your tarn before I give you more unsettling ideas.'

He rose and made the sign of the circle, then climbed out of the tarn. Mischief rode on his shoulders as he walked past the procession. The veez appeared to have forgotten Auraya now. Danjin rubbed the creature under its chin, as he'd seen Leiard do.

Leiard!

Danjin stumbled to a halt. Auraya had found the Dreamweaver encampment two nights ago while 'flying around'. Was this where she had been last night? Was there more to her visits than catching up with an old friend?

Surely not. He knew she considered Leiard as much a friend as an adviser, but what if the feelings she had were stronger than friendship?

That would explain the secrecy, he thought.

What secrecy? Danjin shook his head and continued walking. *All I know is that Auraya visited Leiard once and that she flies about at night. That is far from proof that she has a lover, let alone that the lover is Leiard.*

As he neared his destination, he stopped and looked back at the white tarn.

Besides, he thought. *Auraya's no fool. She'd never risk all she's achieved by taking a Dreamweaver as a lover.*

* * *

517

The sun was low in the sky when Dyara and Auraya began to walk back to the road.

'So how am I doing?' Auraya asked.

Dyara glanced at her and smiled grimly. 'Well enough. You have a natural talent for magic, but that's no surprise. The gods would not have chosen you otherwise.'

'I thought it was my charming personality.'

To Auraya's surprise, Dyara chuckled. 'I'm sure they chose you for that as well. You won't survive this war on charm alone, Auraya – and I know you understand that.'

Auraya nodded. 'We covered almost everything I've learned since being chosen. What will we do tomorrow?'

Dyara frowned. 'I have been thinking of ways that your flying ability might be used to your advantage. You know that when you draw a great deal of magic to yourself, you lessen what exists in the world immediately around you. Magic flows in to replace what is used, but too slowly if what you are doing uses a great deal of power quickly. To compensate, you need to draw magic from further away from yourself, which takes more effort, or move yourself physically to where magic isn't as depleted.'

'And avoid moving to where my enemy has been standing.'

'Yes. You are not restricted to moving across the surface of the land as we are. You have the entire sky to move through. Your source of magic will always be fresh so long as you remain airborne and in motion.'

Auraya felt a small thrill. 'I see. I hadn't thought of that.'

'The trouble is, Juran will want you with us as it will be easier to—'

:Auraya? Are you watching?

Auraya stopped. The mental call was weak and hesitant, but clear enough that she recognised the sender. Tireel, the Siyee ambassador who had come to Jarime, had volunteered to lead the scouts over the mountains. She had given him her link ring so he could contact her when they arrived.

:Tireel. Where are you?

:The other side of the mountains. We've found the Pentadrians. They're a lot closer than you said they'd be.

She could feel his excitement and fear. Reaching out to Dyara, Juran, Mairae and Rian, she told them what was happening and channelled Tireel's communication to them.

:How close are you? Show me what you're seeing.

It took him a few tries before he was able to convey a clear image of his surroundings. When he did, he sent an impression of a narrow valley seen from high above. Two rivers wound down the centre, one blue, one black. Then she realised that the black river was a flow of people, not water.

The Pentadrian army.

The sight of it was no surprise, yet it was a shock. Until now she had only heard of the enemy through reports and only encountered it in the form of lone black sorcerers. Seeing this endless column marching steadily toward the pass and her own country made the threat of invasion real and chilling.

:Can you get closer? Juran asked.

:I'll circle around and drop down with the sun at my back.

Tireel directed some of the other Siyee to inspect the neighbouring valleys, then instructed others to wait out of sight of the army. Any Pentadrians who happened to look up would dismiss the flying shape as that of a large predatory bird. Predatory birds were solitary, however. Several large birds would attract attention, and it would not take much speculation before someone realised they might not be birds, but humans.

Satisfied that his instructions were being carried out, Tireel began to descend. He did so in stages, copying the flying habits of predatory birds. Details of the Pentadrian army became visible. Auraya noted that the column was divided into five sections. Each was headed by a lone rider and followed by supply carts.

:Are these leaders the five sorcerers and sorceresses we've been told of? Juran asked.

:I'll try to get a closer look at one, Tireel offered.

Tireel dropped lower until Auraya was able to see that one of the lead riders was a woman. On the woman's arm perched an enormous black bird. Unlike the trained hunting birds of the Genrian nobility, this one was unhooded. Its head swivelled about, looking into the trees on either side of the road. Then it abruptly cocked its head and spread its wings. Its screech echoed through the valley.

The woman's head snapped up. Tireel could see the oval of her face, but not judge her expression. She moved her arm. The black bird leapt into the air, its wings beating strongly.

:Get away, Auraya urged.

Tireel circled away. Looking back, he glimpsed several more birds fly up from among the Pentadrians. Fear lent him strength and Auraya registered a little of the strain he felt as he beat his wings.

:Do you think she recognised what he is? Mairae asked.

:If she is the only Pentadrian with birds then she is probably the one who entered Si, Auraya answered. *So she has seen Siyee before.*

:We'd best assume our hopes of surprising them have been dashed. Juran's thought was quiet, and only heard by the other White.

:I doubt we would have surprised them anyway, Dyara replied. *This woman saw Auraya with the Siyee. She will have considered the possibility that the Siyee would join us.*

:So these are the black birds that—

Impressions of shock and pain cut Mairae's question short. A confusion of thoughts and sensations followed. Tireel, stunned, could only wonder what had happened. His head and shoulders felt battered. He felt as if he'd flown into a cliff, but

520

he could see he was still in midair. He wasn't falling. He was lying on something. When he looked down he saw nothing but the ground below.

The Pentadrian army had stopped. Hundreds of upturned faces watched him. The sorceress stood with arms raised, stretched in his direction. Black birds circled between him and the ground.

Auraya felt her stomach turn over.

:The sorceress has him. Dyara's thought was tense with dismay.

:This is not good, Juran murmured.

The support that had held Tireel fell away and he dropped. Spreading his wings, he stopped his fall, but not before he reached the birds.

They swooped in close, jabbing him with their beaks and slashing with claws. He drew his arms in close, instinctively protecting his wings, and dropped like a stone. An instant later he realised this might be a way to escape them. Drop below and arc away . . .

Auraya felt a rush of hope.

The birds followed. He saw their sleek shapes beside him. Wings drawn close into a dive. The ground rushed up toward him. He spread his arms again.

At once they darted in to claw and rake. He gritted his teeth against the pain and resisted the urge to protect himself. The ground was not far below now. He could not drop any further.

:Get away, Auraya whispered, even though she knew he could not escape.

Glancing down, Tireel saw the enemy. Hundreds of faces watching. Then claws ripped through his wings. He screamed in agony and fell. The knowledge that he would never fly again was like an extra weight dragging him down. He closed his eyes and prayed that death would be instant.

521

The ground did not come like a last merciful blow. It curled around him and slowed his fall. As he felt the texture of it against his back he could not help feeling hopeful. He was alive. His wings might be torn, but he was still . . .

Then he opened his eyes and saw the ring of black-robed men and women surrounding him.

:This is not good, Juran repeated.

:No, Dyara agreed. *They will learn much about us from him.*

:What can we do? Mairae asked.

:Nothing.

:Perhaps the other Siyee will kill him.

:If they try, they will be captured too, Auraya told them. *They can't get close enough without being caught themselves.* Her heart ached. *This is my fault. I should have gone with them. I should have gone* instead *of them. I could have been there and back in less than—*

:No, Auraya, Juran said firmly. *If you had gone, we would have lost a White instead of Tireel.*

:He's right, Auraya, Mairae added.

:We did *not know these birds would be there, or that they would see Tireel and be able to alert the sorceress to his presence*, Dyara pointed out.

:I know it is hard to watch, but we must know what Tireel reveals, Rian said. *Keep the connection, Auraya.*

She focused on Tireel's mind. His vision was blurry. He was losing a lot of blood. The sorceress was beside him. She took his hand and drew it closer to herself. The movement stretched his wing membrane and sent fresh rips of agony through him. He felt something sliding from his finger.

:The ring! Dyara exclaimed in dismay. *She is taking the ring.*

:It is a loss that cannot be helped, Juran murmured. *But perhaps worth it if we glimpse her thoughts . . .*

As the ring left Tireel's finger, the sense of his mind

disappeared. In its place came a feeling of regret tempered by a ruthless determination. *The Siyee chose to ally with the heathens*, the woman thought. *Best remember that. What is this, then? A trinket, or something more? Perhaps a magical device. What if I . . . ? No!*

The sense of her thoughts disappeared as she threw the ring away. Auraya opened her eyes. For a moment she stared at the grassy hills around her, disoriented. Dyara stood beside her.

:Did we learn anything useful? Mairae asked hopefully.

:No, Juran replied wearily. *At least not from her. Tireel has shown us much that we did not know. The size of their army. How close they are to the pass. We will have to hurry, if we are to meet them there. Then there is this new threat that these birds pose, especially to the Siyee. There is much to discuss tonight. I will send your Bearer back for you, Dyara. What about you, Auraya?*

:I will fly.

:Then I will see you both soon.

As the other White broke their link with her, Auraya looked at the line of mountains to the east and sighed.

'I had not thought the first death would be a Siyee,' Dyara murmured.

'No.'

'Would you like me to tell Speaker Sirri?'

Auraya glanced at Dyara, then shook her head. 'No, I will tell her.'

Dyara nodded. 'Then go. I will be fine walking alone. In truth, I'll enjoy – relatively speaking – a bit of solitude. I'm sure Juran won't mind if you take your time, too.'

Their eyes met, and Auraya suddenly understood that Dyara's toughness was not absolute. She was cold, but not uncaring. The death of Tireel had distressed her greatly.

Stepping away, Auraya drew a deep breath and sent herself into the sky.

CHAPTER 37

Tryss woke to find his face pressed against the membrane of his portable bower. Muffled voices penetrated the thin walls. He rolled away and felt the pressure of a warm body behind him.

'Hmph, you woke up,' Drilli observed as he turned over. 'I was expecting to have to shake you. You came back so late last night.'

He smiled, moved closer and rested a hand on her bare waist. 'I'll always wake up early when you're next to me.'

She caught his hand as he began to slide it up toward her breast. He pouted, and she laughed. 'It's not *that* early,' she told him. 'I'm surprised Sirri hasn't come to see why we haven't packed up yet.' She kissed him then pulled away. Sitting up, she grimaced and rubbed her belly.

'Still feeling sick?' he asked.

'A little,' she admitted. 'It's just the food. Too much meat and bread. Not enough fruit and vegetables.' She looked around the bower. It was barely big enough for them to sit up in. But her attention was on the sounds beyond the walls.

'Something has stirred everyone up.'

He listened to the muffled voices. From one side came an exclamation of dismay. Somewhere close to the front of the tent two Siyee were having a rapid discussion. He couldn't quite make out the words.

'Let's get dressed and find out.'

She was already reaching for her clothes. They quickly shrugged into their vests and wriggled into trousers, then strapped on harnesses and weapons. Drilli finished first, but she waited until Tryss was ready before crawling out of the bower.

Siyee had gathered into groups. From their expressions Tryss guessed that something serious had happened. Some looked frightened, others angry.

'Tryss, Drilli,' a familiar voice called.

He turned to see Sirri step out of a group and start toward him. Drilli hurried toward her, Tryss a step behind.

'What's happened?' Drilli asked.

'The scouts found the Pentadrian army. Their leader, Tireel of the Green Lake tribe, has been captured.'

Tryss felt his heart sink. 'How?'

'He flew too close to them. He didn't see until it was too late that the sorceress with the black birds – the birds that attacked the men of the Sun Ridge tribe – was leading that part of the army. The birds saw him, and the sorceress brought him down.'

'Is he dead?' Drilli asked in a low voice.

Sirri grimaced. 'We don't know. He wasn't killed by the fall, but was in a bad state when Auraya's link with him was broken.'

'If there's a chance he's alive, we should find out.' Tryss felt a spark of hope. 'We must rescue him.'

The Speaker sighed and shook her head. 'If only we could, Tryss. He is in the middle of the Pentadrian army and imprisoned by sorcerers. We would only get ourselves captured as well.'

'Of course.' Tryss felt his face flush. The answer was obvious. 'Auraya will rescue him.'

'No.' Sirri put a hand on Tryss's shoulder. 'She'd have to fight five powerful Pentadrian sorcerers and all their priests and priestesses. Alone, she would not survive either. We might be able to win this war with one less Siyee, but I doubt we'd have a chance with one less White.'

Tryss stared at her in disbelief. 'So we just give up?' He felt a pang of frustration and anger. 'It could have been me. I wanted to lead the scouts, but you said I'd be more useful here, working with Songmaker.'

'Tryss . . .' Drilli murmured.

'And you are,' Sirri told him firmly. 'I'm as grieved as you are, Tryss, but all the same I'm glad you didn't go. I need you here. Tireel may have saved many more of us. We know about the black birds now. We have time to invent ways to fight them.'

He looked at her sharply. Something about the way she had said 'invent' suggested that she had used the word deliberately to distract him. *Of course she did*, he told himself. *She's trying to drag my attention away from Tireel's fate to something more pressing – the safety of us all.*

He managed a smile of sorts. 'We had better start making plans, then.'

She squeezed his shoulder. 'That's why I've called a Gathering. The landwalkers can leave without us today. We'll catch up later, after we've discussed this among ourselves. Tonight you and I will tell the war council our plans.'

Her gaze shifted away from him. She looked over his shoulder and narrowed her eyes.

'There's Speaker Vreez. I must go now. When I join my tribe to discuss ideas, Tryss, I hope you'll have plenty of them.'

'I will,' he promised.

526

She nodded, then managed a half-smile for Drilli. Walking past him, she strode away toward a trio of older men.

Tryss felt Drilli's hand curl around his. 'If I complain about you spending all night talking with Songmaker again, kick me,' she murmured.

As the last massive tree trunk was lowered into place across the road, Kar heard footsteps behind him.

'That is my favourite so far.'

Kar glanced back at the approaching man. Fin, Lem of the Tarrep warriors, was tall for a Dunwayan. He was handsome, though, and kept his beard short. The tattoos on his face accentuated slightly tilted eyes and an intelligent gaze.

'I see that the hidden dartfly nest is the true obstruction, but why did you set fires at either side?' Fin asked.

'Smoke subdues dartflies,' Kar explained. 'The wood is mytten. It burns slowly and makes much smoke when green. The smoke will keep them within the hive until the logs are disturbed.'

'Lessening the chance a few stray dartflies will warn of the trap's nature.' Fin nodded. 'I see.'

He barked out orders to the fire-warriors and his clan members, then turned away. Kar followed as his leader started along the road to the pass. The rest of the men followed silently, the last driving an open tarn carrying tools and materials for their traps.

The way twisted and turned. Parts of it were steep. Kar considered every feature for potential. He still had a few trap ideas he wanted to try, but they needed the right sort of terrain. When they had been walking for an hour they turned a corner and Kar came to a halt.

'Ah.'

Fin smiled. 'I thought you'd like this.'

The road continued steeply between two rock walls. The walls leaned inward, nearly touching. Wedged between them, several paces along the 'passage', was an enormous boulder.

Kar stroked his beard, then started walking again. He moved to the walls and examined them. There were plenty of seams and creases running the length of the passage. He looked up at the boulder as they passed beneath it, then continued his inspection of the walls. At the end of the passage the walls drew back from each other again, forming the sides of a narrow ravine filled with rocks and huge boulders. The road wound onward.

He turned around and walked back. Coming out of the passage he saw what he was hoping for.

Just above the turn, in the place he had been standing when he first saw the suspended boulder, was a wide ledge. Sighing happily, he beckoned to the fire-warriors and told them what he wanted them to do.

Less than an hour later they had finished. The fire-warriors looked tired. Their task had demanded constant concentration. Their brows glistened with sweat despite the cold and their gold brow-bands were dulled with dust. He hoped they would not be too tired for their next task.

Looking up at the walls, he could just make out the two thin ropes following the creases in the rock. Their path was guided by small iron rings set into the stone. He followed the ropes to the ledge, where they were attached to sand-filled sacks supporting a carefully arranged pile of rocks.

He then traced the strings back along the wall, his assistants following as he marched up the steep passage between the walls. He did not even glance at the boulder above. When he reached the end of the passage, he found Fin waiting for him.

The clan leader was frowning, but he said nothing as Kar ordered the sorcerer-warriors to roll the nearest of the huge boulders across the passage entrance. Fin remained tense and silent as small iron rings were set into the boulder's surface and the strings attached. Only when Kar declared the trap set did Fin call Kar over to explain.

'You did not use the suspended boulder.'

'I did,' Kar assured him. 'It is a distraction.'

'How so?'

'The enemy will be too busy worrying that the suspended boulder is a trap to notice the ropes.'

Fin nodded slowly. 'And when the enemy's sorcerers move this boulder out of the way, they will trigger the fall of the massed rocks on the ledge back at the turn. You strike not at the head of the army this time, but at its guts.'

'They will put their fire-warriors at the front of their army, to shield against traps or remove blockages.'

Fin chuckled. 'What will you come up with next, I wonder?'

Kar smiled. 'We still have not used the acid.' He looked at the fire-warriors. 'That will require alert and rested minds for safe handling.'

'Yes. We all need a rest. Let us find a place to sit.' He gestured to the man driving the tarn. 'Bring us food and water.'

As the men settled onto rocks to rest and eat, Kar gazed at the road ahead. The pass and Hania were still many hours' walk away. He, Fin and their assistants had fallen far behind the rest of the Dunwayan army, but they would catch up eventually. In a day or two they would enter the pass and join the Circlian army.

He smiled. Then they would join in the greatest battle between mortals ever to take place in Northern Ithania.

The Plains of Gold were crisscrossed with roads. Those the Dreamweavers had been taking were smaller and less maintained than the main east-west road the army was following.

Sometimes they ran parallel to the main road and sometimes they took a different direction, but in general the Dreamweavers were able to keep pace with the army fairly easily.

Today they had been forced to travel along an uneven grassy track that wandered far from the army's path. Arleej was unconcerned, however. Local farmers had told them that the track would soon meet with a more frequented road, which ran directly south to meet the east-west road. At that point the Dreamweavers would begin following the army at a cautious distance.

Leiard glanced at his student. Jayim was watching the ground before the arem, a crease between his eyebrows. He had grown more confident and skilled at driving the tarn now, but still needed to concentrate at the task. It was too much to expect the boy to receive lessons at the same time.

Jayim now had a tendency to stray away from lessons into speculation about Auraya or the coming war. When Leiard grew tired of fending off the boy's questions he simply gave his student the reins.

'I have a question,' Jayim said suddenly.

Well, it works most of the time, Leiard thought wryly.

'Yes?'

'You've been teaching me the same sorts of things you did back in Jarime – apart from the mind links. I'd have thought you'd concentrate on teaching me to heal with magic. After all, that's what we're here for.'

Leiard smiled. 'Teaching magical healing always presents us with a dilemma. How can I teach you to heal when you have no injuries to practise on? We Dreamweavers do not harm others or ourselves in order to provide subjects to heal.'

The boy was silent. 'So I won't learn to heal until we get to the battlefield.'

'No.'

'I was expecting . . . I thought I'd be . . . well, ready by the time I got there.'

'Nobody is ever ready to face a battlefield for the first time.' Leiard looked at Jayim and chuckled. 'You will learn a lot quickly when you do. Do not fear the learning. I will guide you.'

Jayim shook his head. 'No point in worrying about something you can't avoid; you'll have enough worries when it happens.'

Leiard looked at Jayim in surprise. 'That is an old saying.'

The boy shrugged. 'My mother says it all the time.'

'Ah. I imagine you've given her many reasons to . . .'

The tarn before them slowed to a stop. As Jayim pulled on the reins, Leiard peered around the side of the vehicle before them. Another vehicle stood side-on to the lead tarn, blocking its path, and four Dreamweavers Leiard did not recognise stood beside it.

'Looks like our numbers have just grown a little,' Leiard said. 'Stay here. I will greet the newcomers.'

He climbed down from the tarn and strode forward. As he drew closer to the strangers he saw that Arleej's caravan had reached the end of the track. Three vehicles waited on the side of a wider road. Arleej was talking to one of the newcomers, a stocky male Dreamweaver with pale hair. She saw Leiard and beckoned him forward.

'This is Dreamweaver Leiard, former Dreamweaver adviser to the White,' she said. 'Leiard, this is Dreamweaver Wil.'

The man was Dunwayan, Leiard noted. Wil's eyebrows had risen when Arleej had mentioned Leiard's former position.

'Adviser to the White,' he said. 'I had heard something of this.' He paused, then snorted. 'I had best tell you now that I have my doubts about the wisdom of it. These White are mind-readers. They could rob us of much of our knowledge.'

531

'Only that which is valuable and acceptable to them,' Arleej replied. 'Which, when you remember that they consider our use of herbs quaint and our mind-linking skills taboo, is little.'

Wil shook his head. 'Attitudes change.'

'And they have, to our benefit, for now.' She smiled. 'You will find Auraya of the White surprising, Wil. She visits us every night. She and Leiard are old friends, since before her Choosing.'

Wil's eyes widened slightly. He stared at Leiard for a moment, then shrugged. 'I look forward to meeting her.'

'We had best return to our tarn,' Arleej said firmly. 'We have much travelling to do before we draw close to the army again.'

Wil nodded, then headed toward the first of his group's tarns. As Leiard turned away, Arleej spoke his name. He looked back. She gestured to her tarn.

'Join me for a while?'

He followed as she climbed up onto the seat. The newcomers waited while she urged her arem forward and took the lead along this new road. After several minutes Arleej looked at Leiard and smiled.

'The White have told Raeli that they have lifted the ban on people using our services for a day after the battle.'

'That is good news.'

'Yes. It appears some good has come from your friendship with Auraya.'

He nodded in reply.

'I expect she does not reveal any of the White's plans for the army?'

Leiard shook his head. 'Nothing we don't already know.'

'Has she mentioned the new Dreamweaver adviser at all?'

'Once.' He grimaced. 'She finds Raeli's aloofness disappointing, but understands the reason for it. She hopes there will be time later, after the war, to befriend Raeli – or at least gain her respect.'

'I see. What else does she talk about?'

Nothing you could repeat now, Mirar muttered.

Quiet, Leiard thought sternly.

'Reminiscences.' He shrugged. 'Stories of her visits to Si and Borra.'

Liar.

'Has she noticed this trouble you have with Mirar's link memories taking on a personality in your mind?'

He frowned and looked away. 'I'm not sure. She hasn't mentioned it.'

Because you block me out too effectively when you're with her, Mirar growled. *Nothing like pure lust to make a man take full possession of his body.*

Then she is the key to getting rid of you!

No. You can't be with her all the time.

A feeling of threat came with the reply. Leiard felt his control slip and found himself looking at Arleej.

'I have a confession to make,' he found himself saying. 'This fool of a Dreamweaver has been . . .'

No!

Leiard fought Mirar and managed to regain control. Arleej was frowning at him in puzzlement.

'What's wrong?'

Leiard shook his head. He dared not speak for fear that the words that came out would not be ones he'd planned to utter.

'It's Mirar, isn't it?'

He nodded.

Her eyes widened in understanding, then she frowned again in concern.

'Jayim told me he thought things had been getting

533

worse lately. He said it started after Auraya first visited you.'

Leiard looked at her in alarm.

'Don't worry, he kept his promise. Though he could not hide his concern for you.'

Arleej took his hand and held it firmly when he tried to pull away.

'There's more to this than you're willing to tell. I would leave you your secrets, but I suspect they're destroying you. Tell me, Leiard. Obviously Mirar wants you to.'

He shook his head.

'I am already avoiding the White so they do not learn you are keeping something from them. I may as well know the whole truth.'

He looked away. Arleej fell silent. Then she sighed.

'Mirar.'

The name was spoken like an order. A summons. He felt control melt away.

'At last.'

His own voice was different: higher and with an authority and arrogance he'd never possessed. He found himself straightening and turning to regard Arleej.

She stared at him and he saw a hint of fear in her face.

'Why are you doing this to Leiard?'

'For his own good. He cannot continue this affair with Auraya. It will destroy him, and my people.'

Her eyes widened. 'Affair?'

'He loves her. She probably loves him, too. It's pathe – er, sweet. But dangerous.'

'I see.' She looked away, her gaze intense as she considered what she had just learned. 'I do not think Leiard would do anything to harm our people,' she said slowly. 'He must believe there is no danger.'

'He is wrong.'

'How so? If this secret remains hidden there is no imme-diate—'

'Even if accident does not reveal it, you can be sure the gods know.'

She shuddered. 'Obviously they don't disapprove or they would have put a stop to it.'

'They will when it brings them the greatest advantage. You can be sure it will not be for our benefit. Never think that they don't hate us. We contain memories of darker times, when they were not so benevolent. They do not want their followers to know what they are capable of.'

Arleej had turned a little pale. She grimaced, then shook her head. 'Leiard, Leiard. What are you doing?'

Suddenly Leiard had control of himself again. He gasped and raised shaking hands to his face.

'You're back!' Arleej exclaimed. 'I did speak your name,' she added thoughtfully.

'If that is how it works then please don't speak his name again,' Leiard choked out.

She patted his knee apologetically. 'I won't. I'm sorry.' She paused. 'What are you *doing*, Leiard? The risks you're taking—'

'Are small,' he finished, taking his hands from his face. 'When this war is over, I will retreat to an isolated place. No one need ever know about us.'

'No one? Mirar is right. The gods must know. He may be right about them waiting for the right time to retaliate. You . . . you have a duty to protect your people. You *should* end this affair, Leiard.'

Leiard looked away. 'I know. When I'm with her, I can't even think of it.'

Slowly Arleej's expression softened. She leaned back in her seat and sighed.

535

'Oh, that's love all right.'

She stared ahead, her forehead deeply creased. Leiard watched her closely. What would she do? Would she tackle Auraya? Would she order him to stop seeing Auraya?

Would you obey her? Mirar asked.

Probably not, Leiard admitted. *If she wants me to leave now, I will.*

'I don't know what to do with you,' Arleej said softly, without looking at him. 'I must think on it for a while. From now on we will not camp as close to the army as we have in the past. I would rather it was a considerable inconvenience for the White to visit us. If Auraya comes . . . I will not interfere. I will do all I can to ensure this secret remains undiscovered.'

'Thank you,' Leiard murmured.

Her gaze shifted to his. 'I will do this thinking better alone.'

He nodded, then, feeling like a chastised child, climbed down from the tarn and made his way back to Jayim.

CHAPTER 38

Auraya fastened her circ and walked back to where Leiard was still rolled up in blankets on the floor. She smiled down at him. He smiled back and she felt his hand grab her ankle.

His thoughts were wistful. He wished that she could stay longer – that she would be here when he woke up in the morning. He knew they couldn't risk that.

Everyone here believes these quick visits in the middle of the night are merely official business, she heard him think, *undertaken late because she's too busy or because we don't want the new adviser knowing she's still consulting me.* He sighed and thought of Arleej. *Everyone believes that but two.*

Auraya frowned. His smile faded as he realised she'd read his mind. She felt him let go of her ankle.

'Arleej knows about us,' she said.

'Yes.'

Auraya chewed on her lip. This could prove awkward. Someone in such a high position in Somrey and among Dreamweavers was likely to meet one of the other White at some time. One stray thought from Arleej and their affair would be discovered.

'We can trust her not to say anything.'

Auraya looked at him closely. 'You aren't entirely sure of that.'

He frowned and sat up, the blankets falling from his bare shoulders.

'She is concerned about Mirar's presence in my mind.'

'The link memories?' Auraya shrugged. 'Why?'

He hesitated. 'You haven't noticed . . .' He looked away and frowned. 'He remains silent when you are here.'

Auraya shook her head. Leiard wasn't making much sense. 'He?'

'Mirar, or the echo of his personality in my mind. He speaks to me sometimes. Occasionally he has . . . spoken through me.'

Looking closer, she began to understand. Sometimes this manifestation of Mirar's memories had spoken using Leiard's voice. He had found it disturbing, understandably. He was afraid she would be repelled by it.

'I have always managed to regain control,' he assured her.

'I see. I can understand why that would worry you, but why does it concern Arleej? I would have thought she'd be happy to have this link with your former leader.'

'It's just that . . .' He paused. 'It doesn't bother you?' he asked hesitantly.

Auraya shrugged. 'They're only memories. They've been quite useful to me, actually. What you told me about the Siyee was invaluable.'

He looked away and she sensed he was still troubled.

'It bothers me,' he said. '*He* doesn't like us together. He says we endanger my people.'

Auraya felt a small stab of hurt. A part of him didn't want her. *That's not entirely true*, she told herself. *These memory links are from a man who hated and feared the gods and who was killed by Juran at the gods' bidding. Of course I spark an echo of fear in his mind.*

538

'I don't agree with him,' Leiard said.

'So you argue with him?'

He looked at her in surprise. 'Yes. But . . . not when you're here.'

She smiled, relieved. 'Then I am good for you.'

His lips curled up at the corners. 'Yes.'

Yet she sensed a hesitation. She looked deeper and understood. To give in to this other personality would also bring peace. It was tempting, sometimes. She sat down and wound her arms around him.

'We'll fight him together then. I'll help you any way I can. When this war is over,' she added. 'Can you wait that long?'

He ran his fingers through her hair. 'I'd wait centuries for a moment with you.'

She grinned. 'There you go, getting all romantic on me again. You'll only have to wait a day, not centuries. I'll be back tomorrow night.'

She leaned forward and kissed him. His lips were warm. Pleasant memories rose. She wanted to touch him, but resisted. Instead she pulled away and stood up.

'You had better get dressed and see me out.'

He pouted, then grinned and threw off the blankets. Naked, he began to gather his clothes from the floor. She watched him dress. There was something both fascinating and sobering about this reclothing. As if he was putting on an identity at the same time. When he had finished, he ushered her to the entrance like a respectful and attentive host.

'It was pleasant meeting with you again, Auraya of the White,' he said formally.

She nodded. 'As always, I hope. Give Dreamweaver Elder Arleej my assurances.'

'I will.'

He held open the tent flap and she stepped outside.

Lamplight from within spilled out, illuminating the dark shapes of other tents. Then the flap closed and all was darkness.

She looked up at the sky, then concentrated on the world around her. It was so easy now. She drew magic and moved herself upward.

Cold wind ruffled her hair. A few strands, wet from a quick wash in a basin of water, chilled her neck. She dried them with magic. Rising higher, she saw lights in the distance. The army camp.

Were there more lights than usual, or was she imagining it?

Drawing more magic, she created a shielf to protect her body from the wind and sent herself speeding toward the camp. It did not take long before her suspicions were confirmed. She could see lines of torches moving through the tents. At the point where the line fragmented, near the edge of the camp, she could make out tents being erected.

Newcomers. This must be the Toren army.

As she drew closer she saw four pale figures standing outside the war-council tent. Facing them was a small crowd, lamplight reflecting from an abundance of polished metal and shining cloth. Nobles and other important personages, she guessed. One figure stood a few steps in front of the rest.

Berro. The Toren king. Why didn't Juran call me when they first arrived?

She hovered above the gathering. The sound of the king's voice drifted up to her. Deciding it would be rude to interrupt, she sent Juran a quiet communication.

:Juran? Should I join you?

He made a small, surprised movement, then glanced upward.

:Yes, he replied. When I indicate.

She heard him say something. Then he made a small beckoning gesture. She dropped down and landed beside Mairae.

540

The king turned to stare at her in astonishment. He looked up at the sky, as if expecting to find she had jumped from some structure, then at her again.

'Auraya,' Juran said. 'I believe you met King Berro just after your Choosing?'

'Yes,' she said. 'A pleasure to meet you again, your majesty.'

The king drew in a deep breath and appeared to gather his wits.

'It is an honour to see you again, Auraya of the White. You have settled into your new position with impressive speed and confidence. I had heard of your Gift of flight, but did not quite believe it until now.'

She smiled and made the sign of the circle. 'The gods give us what we need in order to do their bidding.'

His gaze flickered, and she was pleased to see his thoughts turn to the Siyee. By pointing out that the gods had given her the Gift of flight, she had hinted they had done so in order that she might convince the Siyee to become the White's allies. Hopefully he would think twice about contesting the removal of Toren settlers from Siyee lands. No monarch dared to defy the gods.

The king's attention returned to Juran. 'I have travelled at the fastest pace my troops could sustain in order to join you in time. We are, I believe, two days' travel from the pass. Will there be time to rest?'

Juran frowned. 'I can only give you a shorter day's travel tomorrow. Your troops may have more time to rest once we reach the pass, however.'

'That will be sufficient.'

'You are also weary,' Juran stated. 'It is late to be discussing war plans. If it is agreeable to you, I will travel with you tomorrow in order to relate to you all that has been discussed and decided.'

Berro smiled with relief. 'That would be most agreeable. Thank you.'

Juran nodded and made the formal gesture of the circle. 'I will speak to you in the morning then, your majesty.'

The king returned the gesture, then moved away, the crowd of nobles following. Auraya turned to regard her fellow White. Juran looked relieved, Dyara resigned. Rian and Mairae appeared to be pleased.

'At least they're here,' Dyara murmured. 'The Dunwayans are in the pass, setting traps. When they join us we will be quite a force.'

'Indeed we will,' Juran replied. 'For now we should return to our beds.'

The others nodded. Mairae and Rian strode away. Dyara paused, then headed toward the Genrian army camp. Seeing that Juran hadn't moved, Auraya approached him. He looked at her.

'What is it?'

'I was surprised you didn't call me,' she said.

He looked relieved. 'No. Mairae said you were doing an aerial patrol. That you have been doing so for the last few nights and I should leave you to it. Actually, I'm surprised you hadn't told me.'

Auraya shrugged. 'It's just my way of pacing when I can't sleep.'

He smiled, then suddenly became serious. 'Well, just remember that effects from lack of sleep have a way of sneaking up on you when you least need them to. I don't imagine an unintentional nap would be beneficial if you happened to be airborne.'

'No,' Auraya grimaced. 'Not very. But . . . don't hesitate to call me if you do need me here.'

He nodded. 'I will.'

'I'd best be off to bed then.' She paused. 'You too.'

He sighed. 'Yes. You're right.'

She moved away. Hearing a quiet yawn, she glanced back to see Juran cover his mouth with a hand. She nodded to herself. Perhaps he would rest a little easier now that the Torens had arrived.

Emerahl jolted awake. For a moment she felt panic rising. Was the caravan being attacked? Then a lingering feeling of suffocation sparked her memory and the dream came flooding back.

The tower dream. She felt a flash of irritation. Had the Dreamweavers become so unskilled they could not teach one of their own to stop projecting his or her dreams?

'Are you all right, Jade?'

Emerahl looked at Star. A mattress had been brought into Rozea's tarn for the girl. Star was managing to pretend her injury had been bad, but not potentially fatal. Unfortunately, being mostly healed meant she easily grew bored with lying about all day. Sometimes Emerahl pretended to fall asleep to escape the girl's chatter. Right now, Star was looking up at Emerahl in concern.

'A dream, that's all,' Emerahl replied.

'What were you dreaming? It wasn't about a tower falling down, was it?'

Emerahl blinked in surprise. 'Why do you ask?'

Star shrugged. 'A few of my customers have told me about it. Said they had the same dream many times.'

'How many?'

'I don't know. They didn't say.'

Emerahl shook her head. 'I mean, how many customers told you they had the dream?'

Star considered. 'Three or four.' She looked at Emerahl. 'So did you have it?'

Emerahl nodded. 'Yes.'

'Is it the first time?'

'No, I've had it a few times.'

'What's it all about then?'

'There's a tower. It falls down.'

Star grinned. 'I mean, why are people having the same dream? What does it mean?'

'"A dream's meaning depends on the dreamer",' Emerahl quoted. She frowned, considering her theory that the dream was about the death of Mirar. Something about this didn't quite fit.

'To be crushed under a building . . .' Star shuddered. 'Nasty way to die.'

Emerahl nodded absently. If the dreamer was dreaming about the death of Mirar, they couldn't be reliving their *own* experiences. They were reliving Mirar's. To do that they must have link memories of his death, which meant that someone must have linked with him as he died.

That was extraordinary. The thought of it sent a shiver of cold down her spine. No wonder the dreamer could not stop experiencing the dream over and over.

'Maybe it means the White will fail.'

'Dreams aren't predictions, Star,' Emerahl said.

Not this one. This one was historical. Mirar's experience of death must have passed from Dreamweaver to Dreamweaver for the last century. Now, in the mind of a powerful Dreamweaver, it was being projected to every man or woman Gifted enough to receive dreams.

I wonder if that's deliberate. Is somebody trying to remind the world who killed Mirar?

'Jade?'

Emerahl raised a hand to stall Star. *The gods made Mirar a martyr. This dream is no doubt touching the minds of priests and priestesses, too. Surely the gods are trying to put a stop to it.*

'I have to tell you something,' Star said in a quiet voice. 'I told . . .'

Maybe they can't. Maybe this dreamer is protected. By whom? Someone powerful. An enemy of the gods. The Pentadrians! Maybe—

'. . . I told Rozea you healed me with magic.'

Emerahl turned to stare at Star. 'You did *what?*' she snapped.

Star flinched away. 'I'm sorry,' she whimpered. 'She tricked it out of me.'

The girl looked frightened. Emerahl began to regret her harsh response. She softened her expression.

'Of course. Rozea's cunning enough to talk a merchant out of his ship. I was wondering why she's being so nice to me all of a sudden.'

'I've never been much good at keeping secrets,' Star admitted.

Emerahl looked at Star closely. She sensed enough to guess that 'tricking' the girl hadn't been difficult. *What should I do now?*

I should leave.

Emerahl smiled. Now that Rozea knew she was a sorcerer there was no reason to hide the fact. She was free to take the money Rozea owed her, by force if necessary. Yet once the caravan did join the army Rozea was bound to tell of the sorceress who'd robbed her. Her story might attract priestly attention. *No, I should just leave. The money isn't worth the risk.*

Yet Emerahl still felt a foolish obligation to protect the girls for as long as possible. Once the caravan drew close to the army and Rozea hired new guards, the girls would be safe enough.

And then? Emerahl considered her idea about the dreamer being protected by Pentadrians. She had made no plans beyond escaping the priest, then Porin, and now the brothel. Perhaps she would seek out this dreamer. Perhaps he or she could offer Emerahl protection from the gods and their servants.

If that meant joining the Pentadrians, so be it. For all she knew, they might actually win this war.

CHAPTER 39

During the afternoon the east-west road met a wide, stony river. It continued along the banks, the constant din of water rushing over rocks drowning out all but raised voices and the occasional honk of an arem or the call of a reyna. The road entered a wide valley. It passed small villages where the army was greeted by smiling adults and excited children. Then, as the last rays of the sun disappeared over the horizon, they arrived at the end of the valley and Juran called a halt.

I guess this means we've left the plains and entered the mountains, Danjin thought as he stepped into the war-council tent. *From here it's all uphill.* He looked around, noting the haughty expression on King Berro's face, the stiff posture of Speaker Sirri and the concerned and sympathetic looks King Guire was giving the Siyee leader.

He moved to one side to wait. The tent remained unusually silent until the arrival of Auraya and the Siyee scouts.

Auraya made the sign of the circle. 'Greetings all. This is Sveel of the Snake River tribe and Zeeriz of the Fork River tribe. They are the first of the Siyee scouting expedition to return.'

Juran stepped forward. As he spoke to the two Siyee in their language, Dyara translated for the rest of the council.

'I thank you, Sveel of the Snake River tribe and Zeeriz of the Fork River tribe, for undertaking this dangerous journey. Without your help we would know much less about our enemy. It grieves me, however, that this information cost us the life of one of the Siyee.'

The two Siyee warriors nodded. They looked exhausted, Danjin noted.

'Auraya has told me you hastened to return in order to report something you suspect may be of importance. What is that?'

The Siyee named Zeeriz straightened. 'After Tireel was captured we tried to stay close enough to see what happened, but the birds came for us and we had to fly further away to avoid them. They kept us away from the army until night, when they finally left and we were able to search for Tireel. We found him beside the road. Dead.'

He paused and swallowed audibly. Danjin noted that Sirri's head was bowed and her eyes closed. He could not help feeling admiration for her. *I can't imagine the Toren king shedding a tear for a lost scout.*

'I was chosen to lead in his place,' Zeeriz continued. 'I left four behind to bury Tireel, and took the rest with me to pursue the army. We could not find them. They were no longer following the road and we could not locate them in the surrounding land.'

Juran frowned. 'No tracks?'

'None that we could find, but we are people of the air and have little skill at tracking. The land there is stony and hard and feet do not leave much imprint.'

'Perhaps they travelled faster than you expected,' Dyara suggested.

Zeeriz shook his head. 'We circled a large area. Further than they could have travelled in a day. When we could not find them I decided we should return here at first light.'

King Berro leaned forward. 'It was night when you were searching, wasn't it?'

When this was translated, the Siyee scout looked at the monarch and nodded.

'Then it's obvious what happened. They knew there'd be more of you watching, so they travelled without torches. Most likely they were right under your noses, but you didn't see them.'

'Large groups of landwalkers make a lot of noise,' Speaker Sirri pointed out. 'Even if my scouts did not see them, they would have heard them.'

'Unless the troops were ordered to keep quiet,' Berro countered.

Zeeriz straightened his back. 'I am confident that I would have heard them if they had been there. An army of that size cannot travel silently.'

'Oh?' Berro's eyebrows rose in disbelief. 'How would you know? How many armies of that size have you encountered before?'

'We heard yours coming half a day before it arrived,' Sirri answered tartly. 'Even if your men had kept their mouths shut, we'd still have heard them.'

King Berro opened his mouth to speak, but another voice cut in.

'It is possible the Pentadrians were sheltering in the old mines for the night,' Jen of Rommel, the Dunwayan ambassador, said mildly.

Danjin heard someone close by suck in a breath. He turned to see that Lanren Songmaker's eyes were wide with realisation.

'Mines?' Juran frowned. 'You mean the ancient mines of Rejurik?'

Jen shrugged. 'Perhaps. My guess would be the more

549

recent ones. They're just as extensive as their famous predecessors, but less likely to have collapsed. There are caverns deep inside them that are large enough to hide an army. Why you would want to, however . . .' He spread his hands. 'Bad ventilation, so no fires and no hot food. They had a cold sleep that night.'

'Could they travel through the mountains into Hania?' Lanren Songmaker asked.

Jen shook his head. 'Impossible. The mines never extended that far.'

'They have plenty of sorcerers. They could *make* the mines extend that far.'

'No,' Juran said. 'It would take months, if not years, to carve a tunnel large enough. The rock and debris removed would have to go somewhere. Ventilation shafts would have to be created and sorcerers posted to pull air inside, as natural circulation wouldn't be enough for that many people.'

As this was translated for the Siyee, Zeeriz looked relieved. Danjin felt a pang of sympathy for the young man, who'd rushed back only to have his abilities questioned so derisively by the Toren king.

'It sounds as if they sheltered in the mines for the night,' Berro said, waving a hand at Zeeriz. 'Perhaps they feared an attack from our little spies.'

Little spies. Danjin suppressed a sigh. Berro was known for his habit of antagonising the Genrians. It looked as if he was set on insulting the Siyee as well.

'If the army emerged the next day we'll find out when the rest of the scouts return tomorrow,' Sirri replied.

'If they saw them.'

'An army that size is hard to miss from the air,' Auraya pointed out. 'Even if they deviate from the road, doing so would slow them down and they would eventually have to return to it to approach the pass. There is only one road through the mountains.'

Berro nodded respectfully. 'That is true, Auraya of the White.'

His unquestioning acceptance of her words only highlighted his disparaging attitude toward the Siyee, Danjin noted. Auraya looked at Juran, who met her eyes and nodded.

'Are there any further questions for Sveel of the Snake River tribe and Zeeriz of the Fork River tribe?' Juran asked.

Silence followed. Auraya turned to the two scouts. 'Thank you for coming to us to report. You are tired and hungry. Allow me to escort you back to your people.'

As Auraya left, Danjin realised that Mairae was watching him. He smiled and inclined his head. The corners of her lips curled up, her expression unmistakably speculative. She turned to watch Auraya leave.

At once he remembered his conversation with her the day before. As her gaze snapped back to him and her eyebrows rose questioningly he realised what she wanted him to tell her. *I don't know if she has a lover*, he thought at her. *Do you?*

She smiled and nodded.

He blinked in surprise.

Who?

She shrugged.

He looked away, both disturbed and curious. Imagining someone bedding Auraya was like imagining his daughters engaged in the act with their husbands – not something he was ever comfortable thinking about. Yet he also wanted to know who had caught her attention.

He glanced around the room, but even as he considered the men there he realised it could not be one of them. Mairae could read their minds, so she would know if any of them was

Auraya's lover. So it could only be someone whose mind she couldn't read – or someone she hadn't met.

As far as he knew, the White couldn't read each other's minds. He looked at Mairae. So it was possible . . .

Mairae's eyes widened in horror. She shook her head, a movement akin to a shudder. He smiled. She obviously found the idea of bedding a fellow White appalling, but that did not mean Auraya would. He turned his mind from the possibility anyway, not wanting to cause Mairae discomfort.

If Auraya's lover wasn't one of the White, he would have to be someone Mairae never encountered. If that was so, and she was visiting him regularly, he must be in the army.

To his surprise, Mairae shook her head. How could she be sure? She smiled. *So someone outside the army*, he thought. *But close enough for Auraya to visit.*

His stomach sank as the possibility he had considered before wormed itself back into his mind.

The Dreamweavers. Leiard.

No, he told himself firmly. *They are friends. No more than that.*

It made sense that Auraya would visit Leiard. Mairae must be assuming there was more to Auraya's night excursions than there was. He looked at Mairae. She was frowning, but as he met her eyes she smiled, shrugged and nodded.

Then Juran announced a break for dinner and Danjin sighed with relief. He'd been half afraid Auraya would return and find him speculating about her private life. Hopefully, by the time she saw him again, his mind would be preoccupied with something else.

It had been a long day, but now that Auraya had finally escaped the war council she felt her weariness replaced by a growing anticipation. Soon she would be with Leiard again. All that was spoiling her mood was the absence of Mischief. She had found his cage open when she had returned to her tent. No doubt a servant was being led a chase around the campsite.

She didn't dare leave without him. He might lead a servant a long way, right up to the Dreamweaver camp. That could prove awkward to explain.

'Auraya?'

Recognising Danjin's voice, she moved to the tent entrance. In his arms was a squirming, struggling ball of fur. She sighed with relief.

'Thank you, Danjin.' She beckoned him inside. 'Now, Mischief, where have you been?'

'Owaya. Owaya. Bad man. Take Msstf away. Bad.'

She looked at Danjin, alarmed by the words. He grimaced and let the veez squirm from his arms and bound into hers. Mischief curled up around her neck.

'Not so tight,' she gasped. She looked at Danjin. 'What happened?'

His expression was a mix of concern and guilt. 'At dinner a servant came to tell me Mischief was gone. It's taken me hours to find him. Or rather, he found me.' Danjin sighed. 'He's been saying "bad man" over and over. I fear someone may have taken him.'

Auraya could feel the veez's heart racing. Stroking his back, she gently probed his mind. Memories flashed through his thoughts. A human face, the lower half covered with something. The cage opening and a hand grasping the veez's neck. Scratching, biting, the taste of blood. Being trapped inside something. Chewing through and the relief of freedom.

Bad man! he said into her mind. She started. He'd never spoken to her telepathically before.

'I think you're right, Danjin,' she said. She looked at him and sensed guilt again. Surely *he* hadn't . . .

She looked closer and was relieved to see the true source of his guilt. Mairae had asked if she had a lover days ago and he had forgotten about it until she had posed the question again tonight. He felt ashamed of himself for speculating about her private life. Then Leiard's name flashed into his thoughts and she felt her relief evaporate. Danjin believed she was merely visiting Leiard out of friendship, but suspected Mairae thought there was more to it.

Her whole body went cold. She knew Mairae was inclined to speculate about such things, but she hadn't thought the woman would go so far as to lure her adviser into considering possible lovers. If Mairae was prepared to do this, how much further would she go to satisfy her curiosity? It would only take a few hours' riding and a little mind-reading for speculation to become known fact. Her heart began to race. Mairae might already be riding toward the Dreamweaver camp.

I can't take that risk. Leiard has to leave now. Tonight.

Unwinding Mischief from around her neck, Auraya handed him back to Danjin.

'Stay here. Keep him company. He's had a fright. I want to find out what I can. Which servant told you to look for him?'

'Belaya.'

She nodded, then strode out of the tent. Her heart was pounding. She glanced around with both eyes and mind, but detected no watchers. Drawing magic, she sent herself up into the sky, created a wind shield and drove herself through the air.

The Dreamweaver camp was further away than before, but she reached it in moments. A lamp burned within Leiard's tent. She landed in front of it and walked to the door flap.

'Dreamweaver Leiard?'

The flap opened, but no hand held it aside. She looked beyond and felt her heart stop. Juran stood within.

554

He knows. The knowledge rushed over her like a blast of cold wind. She saw the anger in Juran's face. His entire body was tense; his hands were clenched at his sides.

She had never seen him so angry before.

'Come in, Auraya,' he said in a low, tight voice.

To her surprise his fury did not frighten her. Instead, she felt a surge of affection for him. She knew him well enough to be sure he would never allow anger to override reason. He did not like violence. The few times he had referred to killing Mirar, he had always expressed regret at the necessity.

I trust him, she thought. *I even trust that he would never harm Leiard, despite what he now knows.*

But Leiard wasn't in the tent, and the bag that he kept with him at all times was missing.

'Juran,' she said calmly. 'Where is Leiard?'

He drew in a deep breath, then let it out slowly.

'I sent him away.'

She looked at him; held his gaze. 'Why?'

'Why?' Juran's eyes narrowed. 'Do you think I haven't discovered your affair? Or do you think I'd allow it to continue?'

Auraya crossed her arms. 'So you get to approve my lovers, then?'

His gaze wavered. 'When I learned of . . . this . . . I asked myself the same thing. The answer was simple: my first duty is to our people. As is yours.' He shook his head. 'How could you do this, Auraya, when you must have known what the consequences would be when you were discovered?'

Auraya took a step closer to him. 'I can accept that our people do not embrace change quickly, that improvement in attitudes happens over generations. I intended to keep our affair private only to avoid testing the people's tolerance. I knew I could not keep it from you forever. Nor did I intend to. You have long disliked Dreamweavers, and I did not know how long I should wait before telling you. I doubted you had put aside all prejudice. How long would I have needed to wait before you did? Years? Decades? Centuries? I am in love *now*, Juran. Leiard is growing older. He will die one day. I cannot wait for you to get used to the idea that a Dreamweaver might be worthy of me.'

He gazed at her intently. 'My views are not the issue here, Auraya. You are one of the White. Your first duty is to guide and protect the people. You may have lovers, but they must not come between you and the people. If they do, you must give them up.'

'He won't come between—'

'He will. He already has. I saw it in his mind. You have broken the law against dream-linking. What next?'

'I've accepted Dreamweaver healing before, Juran. There is a similarly ridiculous law against that too. You're not so foolish as to think this is a sign that I do not respect the laws in general.'

'You must appear to be lawful,' he replied. 'Or you will lose the respect of the people. Just learning of your affair will damage your standing in their eyes.'

'Not as much as you think. Not all people dislike Dreamweavers.'

'The majority distrust them.' He paused, then sighed. 'Auraya, I wish I did not have to ask this of you.' He grimaced. 'I do not wish to cause you pain. But you must give up Leiard.'

Auraya shook her head. 'I can't, Juran.'

'You can,' he said firmly. 'Eventually you will look back and see it was the right thing to do, even if it was painful at the time. You have to trust me on this.'

Trust? This has nothing to do with trust. Everything he's said comes from fear. Fear that a Dreamweaver will have too much influence over me. Fear that if I offend just one prejudiced Circlian, the rest will stop respecting us all. Most of all, he fears change.

She managed a smile. 'I do trust you, Juran. I expect you to trust me in return. I will not let Leiard come between me and the people. They will barely know he exists.'

She turned away and strode to the door flap.

'Auraya.'

Pausing in the entrance, she looked back.

'He can't come back,' Juran told her. 'I gave him an order, and I don't think even he will disobey it.'

She smiled. 'No. He wouldn't. Doesn't that tell you something, Juran? Doesn't that tell you he isn't someone to be afraid of?'

Turning away, she stepped outside and launched herself into the air.

CHAPTER 40

Clouds were slowly creeping down from the north, blotting out the stars one by one. Bellin yawned, then turned his attention back to the gowts. Most had folded their long, spindly legs beneath themselves and were dozing. A few remained alert, their slender heads moving from side to side as they kept a watch for predators.

They were clever animals. They accepted him as an extra form of protection, and allowed him to milk them in return. Yet they never lost their natural wariness. Despite his presence, they took turns as lookouts throughout the night.

Which is just as well, he thought. *I can't help falling asleep or being distracted now and then.*

He leaned back against the rock wall and drew some magic. Converting it to light, he sent a glow into the space before him, then he began to shape it.

First he created a gowt. That was easy; he spent all his time with them so he knew how they looked. Moving the gowt was harder. He got it to walk, then run, then leap from rock to rock.

When he grew bored with that he started shaping another familiar form. Old Lim. The wrinkled old face looked right, but the body was too straight. Old Lim was bent like a wind-twisted tree.

There. That's better. Bellin made the figure scratch its rear – something Old Lim did all the time. He chuckled, then felt a small pang of guilt. He shouldn't make fun of Old Lim. The man had found him abandoned in the mountains and raised him. Lim didn't know who Bellin's real parents were. Bellin didn't even look like most of the people who lived in these parts. The only clue he had to his past was a scrap of material with a symbol stitched onto it. It had come from the blanket he'd been wrapped in when Old Lim found him. There had been a gold amulet, too, but Lim had sold it to pay for food and clothes for Bellin.

Bellin occasionally wondered where he had come from, and even thought about setting off on an exciting journey to find his parents. But he liked it here. He didn't have to work hard, just watch the gowts and gather their wool when they moulted. When Old Lim died the safety of these gowts would be his responsibility. He couldn't leave them unprotected.

Bellin sighed and considered what he could make next. Old Lim had taught him how to make the light pictures. They helped keep away predators as well as kept Bellin awake.

The pictures weren't the only Gift the old man had taught Bellin. If fanrin or leramer were bold or desperate enough to approach the gowts, he chased them away with little balls of fire.

'You're lucky you've got me,' Bellin told the gowts. At the sound of his voice, several of the sleeping gowts started awake. Which was odd. They were used to his voice.

'Old Lim can barely sting them, but I could kill one if I wanted to,' he said in a soothing voice, hoping to reassure them. 'I could . . .'

He paused, then frowned. His back felt odd. The rock wall he was leaning against was vibrating.

Leaning forward, he discovered that he could feel the same

559

vibration beneath his buttocks and feet. The gowts were climbing to their feet. Their narrow ears were twitching in fear.

Slowly, Bellin stood up, turned and placed his hands on the rock wall. The vibration seemed stronger now. Something struck his head lightly. He yelped in surprise and looked up. Dirt and bits of stone were raining down. He backed away hastily.

When he was several strides away he found he could see a crack widening at the top of the wall. He stared at it and slowly realised that the rock wasn't splitting; the dirt that had accumulated in the crack was spilling out. It cascaded down, forming a growing mound of earth where he had just been sitting.

The vibration under his feet was growing stronger. Then he heard and felt a concussion of air. A plume of dust and stones escaped the crack. He ducked and threw his arms up to protect his head as they scattered over the surrounding area.

The sound stopped, then a whistling began. He looked up to see that the grasses atop the rock wall were all bent toward the crack. Air appeared to be rushing *into* the fissure.

The ground had stopped vibrating. He glanced behind and felt his heart freeze.

The gowts were gone.

Forgetting the disturbing behaviour of the mountain, and the strange whistling of air being sucked into the crack, he created a ball of light and started to search for the tracks of his beloved gowts.

Leiard looked back at Jayim and felt a pang of guilt and sympathy. The boy was pale and in obvious discomfort. Arems were not the most pleasant of mounts, and even less so without a saddle. Free of the tarn harness and urged to a faster pace, they had settled into a trot that they could keep up for hours, but which made for an unpleasantly jolting ride.

It could not be helped, though. Juran had ordered them to leave immediately, and remained to ensure they did. They had grabbed some food and their bags but it was clear Juran's patience would not stretch to them dismantling the tent, packing the tarn and harnessing the arems.

Leiard felt another pang of guilt. The arems had been bought by Arleej. She had also bought a few spare arems in case one became sick or lame, so she would not be forced to abandon the tarn.

He'd had no time to see her, or even leave a note to explain his sudden absence. Watchers in the Dreamweaver camp would have seen Juran arrive and had probably seen him leave again soon after Leiard and Jayim. Arleej would guess what had happened. She would be worried. *So am I*, he admitted. *What will this mean for the rest of the Dreamweavers? Will they be safe?*

One thing is sure, he thought. *Juran won't want the world knowing that one of his own was bedding a Dreamweaver, so he'll keep that a secret.*

Leiard was surprised that he had been singled out. He had expected Juran to order all of the Dreamweavers to leave, even if only to conceal the fact that his ire had been directed at a single man. Perhaps even Juran recognised that he would need the Dreamweavers after the battle. The army was huge. Though Circlians were supposed to refuse Dreamweaver healing, they rarely did when desperate. There would be too many injured soldiers for the priest healers to deal with when the battle was over.

Jayim will miss a great opportunity to increase his learning, he thought. He looked at the boy and felt guilty again. Jayim had been terrified by Juran's anger. Leiard knew the boy had been all too aware that the man who had come to deal with

561

his teacher was also the man who had killed Mirar. Jayim's relief when Juran had ordered them to leave had been obvious.

When fear passes, he will be angry, Leiard thought. *He will ask what right Juran has to send us away when my only crime is loving Auraya.*

He'll blame you, a familiar voice added. *He'll wonder why you let yourself get into this situation in the first place. He'll wonder why you didn't get out of it when you realised what it would lead to. When it becomes clear that you still plan to see Auraya, he'll wonder if you care about your people at all.*

Mirar, Leiard thought wearily. *You must be happy at this turn of events.*

Happy? No. This is what I was afraid of. Do you really think Juran will be content with sending you away? You've reminded him of what he hates most about Dreamweavers. Our influence over people. Our abilities. I was known as a great seducer. You will replace me in his eyes. If you continue the affair, he will know. He will find other ways to punish you, through harming our people.

Leiard shivered. *No. Auraya will not allow it.*

He is her leader. She is a servant of the gods. If they command her to obey him, she will. You know this.

She will do anything to prevent bringing harm upon Dreamweavers.

Anything? Would she leave the White? Give up power and immortality? Would she defy the gods she loves? You know she would never disobey them.

Leiard shook his head, but he knew the last was true. The air had become heavy and cold, and he was not surprised when it began to rain. He allowed the drops to fall on him and soon his clothes were saturated.

Far ahead he saw lights. He pulled his arem to a stop and stared at them. He had been following the road for hours. The army was far behind. Who were these people? Had Juran changed his mind? Were there priests waiting here to apprehend him?

As he watched he caught the sound of galloping hooves in front. As the rider drew near, Leiard opened his palm and created a small light. The stranger wore the uniform of a high-ranking member of the Toren army. The man grinned as he passed. His mood of smug contentment touched Leiard's senses like a waft of heady scent.

Leiard understood, then, that the lights were those of a travelling brothel. He sighed with relief and urged his arem back into a trot.

Auraya loves you, Mirar whispered. *And you love her.*

Leiard frowned, wondering at this change of tack.

You say she will give up anything to protect our people. I don't believe you, but if it is true then consider this: should you ask her to? Should you demand that she give up what she has?

The road descended. Leiard felt his heart sinking with it.

It might not come to that.

It will. I know Juran. He will demand she make a choice. Do you think you're a fair exchange for the gods she loves so much? Can you give her what they do?

Leiard shook his head.

Do you want to see her grow old and die, and know it is your fault?

Each of Mirar's words felt like the job of a knife.

Love is thrilling, especially forbidden love, but passion fades and becomes familiarity. And familiarity becomes boredom. When the thrill has gone between you, do you think she will never look back at what she was, and what she might have been, and wish she had never met you?

Leiard felt his throat tighten. He wanted to argue that it wouldn't be like that, but he could not be sure.

If you love her, Mirar urged, *free her. For her own sake. Let her live on to love again and again.*

And if she doesn't want to be freed?

563

You must convince her. Tell her you do not want to see her again.

She won't believe me. She can read my mind, remember.

Mirar was silent for a moment. The lights ahead were brighter now.

Then let me do it.

Leiard shivered. He was cold all over, and he knew it was not just the rain soaking his clothes that was chilling him.

She is bound to track you down tonight. I will remain only as long as it takes to convince her to leave you.

He was so tired. Tired of the risk and the secrecy. He looked up at the dark sky and felt the rain sting his face.

I'm sorry, Auraya, he thought. *There can be no happy ending for us. Mirar is right: the longer this goes on the more harm it will bring.*

He drew in a deep breath, then breathed out a summons.

'Mirar.'

When the first rays of dawn lightened the eastern sky, Auraya felt her hopes dim. She had flown in every direction from the Dreamweaver camp as far as a rider could travel in a day. She had returned to the Plains of Gold. She had roamed the foothills of the mountains. She had followed the road almost all the way to the pass.

She had found no sign of Leiard.

As she had flown, she had kept her senses open for human thoughts. While she had sensed the minds of soldiers and villagers, herders and prostitutes, she hadn't caught even a glimpse of Leiard's mind. He had all but disappeared.

Like the Pentadrians, she thought wryly.

She now hovered high above the ground, unsure what to do next.

Perhaps I missed something. I could return to the Dreamweaver camp and start again. This time I'll fly in circles, moving steadily outward . . .

564

Before she had even finished the thought she was speeding across the sky again. When she reached the place the Dreamweavers had camped, they were already gone. She could see them in the distance, travelling along a narrow, overgrown track.

A lone figure followed them. She caught weary thoughts and a familiar personality.

Jayim.

The boy crested a rise and reined in his arem. As he saw the Dreamweavers far ahead, he felt a rush of relief. It was followed by guilt and uncertainty. He looked over his shoulder to the southeast.

I shouldn't have left him . . . but he wouldn't listen to me. The way he spoke . . . something's wrong. I have to get help.

He urged the arem into a trot, thinking that if he caught up fast enough Arleej would be able to return to the brothel camp before Leiard moved on. He pushed all thought aside but the need to reach them. Auraya watched him go, fighting a rising dismay.

The *brothel* camp?

She had flown over more than a few. The presence of prostitutes was an accepted consequence of having a large army travelling across the country. She had mixed feelings about them. While she could see that bedding a whore might boost a soldier's confidence, or soothe an agitated mind, there was the spread of disease to worry about. She also didn't like how some of the men believed they weren't being unfaithful to their wives by sleeping with a whore during a war.

Which was why she hadn't looked too closely at the minds in these camps. Which probably made the camps the perfect place to hide from her. Did this mean Leiard was hiding from her?

No. He's hiding from Juran.

565

She started flying toward the closest of the camps she could remember encountering last night. As she did she forced her mind away from unpleasant possibilities. *I trust him. He went there to hide from Juran, not me.*

He was not in the first of the camps, nor the next two. She remembered the direction of Jayim's backward glance and flew further southeast. A half-day's ride from the army she found another. Searching the minds of those below, she glimpsed Leiard's face in one of the whores' thoughts.

And reeled from the thought that accompanied it.

. . . at those buttocks. And I thought him scrawny last night. Definitely not scrawny. If I had my way, I'd give him this night for free. Who'd have thought a Dreamweaver would be so good at . . .

Auraya tore her mind away. Hovering above the brothel, she stared down at the tents in disbelief.

I must be mistaken. The girl must have been thinking of another Dreamweaver. One who looks like Leiard.

She looked into the thoughts of those below her again. This time she skimmed over the feminine minds, searching for a masculine one. When she found Leiard, it took her a moment to recognise him.

His thoughts were not those of a man exiled from his love. They were those of a man relishing unexpected freedom.

It isn't that I don't think Auraya's attractive or smart or good-natured, he told himself. *She's just not worth all this trouble. Better we slip away with no explanation.*

Gone was the affection and respect she had always seen in his mind. There was not even the slightest ember of love left within him. Instead he regarded her with a mild regret.

She gasped and recoiled, but there was no avoiding the pain that ripped through her. *So this is how it feels to have your heart broken*, she thought. *Like someone has stabbed you and twisted the knife. No, like someone has gutted you and left you to die.*

566

Tears sprang into her eyes, but she fought them. He *had* loved her. She knew that. Now he didn't. Just a few words from Juran had killed it.

How can that be? How can something that was so strong be killed so easily? I don't understand. She wanted to look again, to search for an explanation, but couldn't bring herself to. Instead she began to ascend slowly. She caught the thoughts of the whore again. Leiard had just shaved his beard away completely. The girl thought he looked much younger and more handsome. She told him so, and that he was welcome in her tent any time. Would he be returning tonight? No. Perhaps if he visited Porin in the future . . .

Figures emerged from the tents below. Auraya moved herself higher, aware that anyone looking up might notice her. She continued ascending until the camp was a tiny mark on the landscape below. When she reached the clouds the world disappeared behind a wet, cold blanket of white.

CHAPTER 41

Emerahl lifted the repaired flap of the tarn cover and peered outside. According to the customer she'd attended to last night, the army was a few hours' ride ahead of them. He'd shaken his head when she'd expressed a hope that they'd catch up. The army was travelling fast, he told her. It would reach the pass before them. It was safer for them to remain at a distance anyway. Who knew what dangers lurked in the mountains?

He had then set about comforting and reassuring her. She'd realised that he was the kind of man who needed a woman to be weak in order to feel strong and manly. He was not one who felt comfortable around capable women so it was easy to get rid of him in the morning by striding about her tent assertively and making clever conversation. She pitied his wife. Men who needed women to be weak and stupid could be unpleasant to be around when they felt the natural order of things was being upset.

'What can you see, Jade?'

She looked at Star, then shrugged. 'Rocks. And grass. And more rocks. Oh, look, there's more grass,' she added dryly.

The girls smiled. Rozea had declared Star well enough to travel with the others last night, though Emerahl was sure the decision had more to do with avoiding another day of incessant chatter. Emerahl had insisted on riding with Star in case sitting up for hours proved too much for her. This gave her an opportunity, at last, to talk to Brand and Tide.

All of the girls appeared to have forgiven her for becoming the favourite. This might be because they had realised that their grudge was ridiculous, but Emerahl doubted that. She suspected it was her healing of Star that had brought her back into their favour.

'I had the most amazing night last night,' Charity said.

Brand, Tide and Bird groaned. 'Do we have to go through all that again?' Brand complained.

Charity gestured at Star. 'She hasn't heard yet.'

Brand sighed. 'Go on, then.'

Charity's eyes were bright as she leaned toward Star. 'Last night a Dreamweaver came by. It was late and not many of the girls saw him. He wasn't bad-looking, so I was rather pleased when he chose me.' She paused and grinned widely. 'If that's what all Dreamweavers are like in bed, I'll take one any time.'

Star's eyebrows rose. 'He was that good?'

'Oh, you wouldn't believe me if I told you.'

Star grinned. 'Tell me anyway.'

Intrigued, Emerahl found herself searching Charity's mind for any hint of deception. She could detect nothing more than wistfulness, gratitude and, most of all, smugness.

It was rare, but not unheard of, for a customer to make more than a token effort to pleasure a whore in return. As Charity talked, Emerahl felt a pang of sadness. This night of pleasure reminded her of a few she had experienced herself, long ago, with another Dreamweaver. *The* Dreamweaver. She smiled as she imagined what the girls would say if she told them of *that* liaison.

'Any time he wants to sneak into my tent he can have the night for free,' Charity told them.

'They don't call her Charity for nothing,' Brand said, rolling her eyes.

'What did he look like?' Star asked.

'Tall. Skinny. I thought he was a bit scrawny at first. Very pale blond hair. Almost white. He had a beard, but he shaved it off the next day. Looked much better without it, too.'

Emerahl turned her mind from the girls' chatter. Thinking of Mirar brought her back to her plans to find the source of the tower dream. It seemed a fanciful thing to do, hunting down a dreamer for no real reason other than curiosity. Although what else was there to occupy her? After a hundred years Northern Ithania had filled up with priests and priestesses. That restricted what she could do to almost nothing.

She was growing more and more convinced that the dreamer was on the other side of the mountains. The closer she got to the range, the stronger and more vivid the dream became. If that meant he or she was among the Pentadrians, so be it.

'You were right about the secret compartments,' Tide whispered into Emerahl's ear, making her jump.

She turned to regard the young woman. 'Compartments?'

'Under the seats,' Tide said, gently tapping her heel against the underside of her seat. 'I saw Rozea putting things in here a week or so ago. She does it in the morning, when we're all still asleep. I woke up and watched her through a hole in our tent.'

Emerahl smiled. 'Aren't you a clever thing?'

Tide grinned. 'Not that I'm stupid enough to take anything.'

'No, that would be foolish,' Emerahl agreed.

Foolish for anyone who needed to stay in the brothel or couldn't fend for themselves outside of it, she amended. In just a few days the Circlians would clash with the Pentadrians. She would wait and watch, and when the right moment came she would take her money and head for the pass.

And she would leave whoring, priests and Northern Ithania behind her.

As the final strut sprang into place, Tryss stood up and gave the bower one last critical examination.

'It's fine,' Drilli said. She rose from her crouch and handed him a leg of roasted gowt. 'So who did these new soldiers turn out to be?'

He looked at her in surprise. It was easy to forget that information did not always filter through to everyone. They had been flying together when the soldiers had been spotted marching down from the pass. Sirri had told him to fly back and inform the White, and though he had returned hours ago he had only just rejoined Drilli.

'Dunwayans,' he told her. 'They live on the other side of the mountains, but further north. The men who came down to meet us are tribe leaders, war planners and priests. Most of their army is in the pass, waiting for us to join them.'

She nodded and chewed slowly, her expression thoughtful. 'Have you seen Auraya?'

He shook his head. 'Songmaker says she practises magical fighting techniques with Dyara for most of the day.'

'She always spends some time each day with us, too, though. Nobody's seen her at all since yesterday.'

Tryss took a bite of roasted gowt. It was interesting but not surprising that information about the Dunwayans didn't spread quickly among the Siyee, yet they noticed Auraya's every movement.

'I'm sure she's occupied with something important. I might find out what it is tonight.'

Drilli made a small noise of protest. 'Another war council?

571

Am I ever going to have you all to myself for an entire night – without you sleeping through it all?'

He grinned. 'Soon.'

'You always say that.'

'I thought you were tired.'

'Yes. I am.' She sighed and crouched beside the fire. 'Exhausted. It makes me cranky.' The firelight bathed her skin with a warm orange glow, highlighting her cheekbones and the lean angles of her body.

She's so beautiful, he thought. *I'm the luckiest Siyee alive.*

'Father still won't talk to me,' she said gloomily.

He moved to her side and rubbed her shoulders. 'You tried again?'

'Yes. I know it's too soon, but I can't help trying. I wish Mother was here. She would talk to me.'

'She might not. Then you'd feel doubly worse.'

'No,' she disagreed with conviction. 'She *would* talk to me. She knows things can be more important than . . . than . . .'

'What things?' he asked absently.

'Just . . . things. Here's Sirri.'

He looked around to see Speaker Sirri land on an outcrop above their camping place. She smiled.

'Hello, Drilli. That smells delicious.'

Drilli rose. 'Hello, Sirri. You're not skipping meals again, are you?'

Sirri laughed. 'I ate something before.'

'Here.' Drilli stood up and tossed something in Sirri's direction.

The Speaker caught it neatly. 'A spice cake. Thank you.'

'She makes them hot,' Tryss warned.

Sirri took a bite, chewed, then winced. 'They certainly are. Well, we'd best fly or the meeting will start without us.'

Tryss nodded. He rose as Sirri leapt into the air, but paused as he felt Drilli's arms wind around his middle. He turned to face her. Her kiss was warm and lingering and he pulled away reluctantly.

'Soon,' he promised.

'Go on, then.' She patted his rear. 'Before she comes back looking for you.'

He grinned, then turned and leapt into the air.

They had camped on a small ledge overlooking the road. Most of the Siyee had set up their bowers on ledges and outcrops, whereas the only accessible space for the landwalkers to camp on was the road itself. From the air the landwalkers' many lamps and fires looked like giant, looping glitterworm larvae.

Tryss caught sight of Sirri and flapped hard to catch up. She glanced back at him as he neared. 'How are your meetings with Songmaker going?'

'I'm learning faster than he is. He has a big disadvantage, you see. Our spoken language is similar to his, but our whistling words are all new.'

'How close are you to understanding landwalkers?'

He shook his head. 'A long way off. I sometimes recognise a few words. That tells me what they're talking about at least.'

'That could be useful.'

The white tent appeared around a curve of the road. They both descended toward it. The crowd they usually found waiting outside wasn't there. As they landed, they heard voices inside.

'Well, better late than not at all,' Sirri murmured.

He followed as she strode forward. The discussion halted as they entered.

'Please forgive us our late arrival,' Sirri said.

'Don't apologise,' Juran replied. 'We were just making introductions.' He gestured to the four Dunwayans Tryss had seen only briefly before. They were small for landwalkers, but their bulging muscles gave the impression of formidable strength and the patterns drawn on their faces added to their fierceness. As Juran introduced them, Tryss found himself thinking it was probably fortunate that Dunway wasn't a neighbour of Si. If these people ever decided they wanted more land he doubted even poisoned darts and arrows would stop them.

When the introductions finished, Sirri moved to her usual chair. Tryss took his place beside her and looked around the room. All of the White were present except Auraya. As Juran returned to a landwalker tongue, Dyara moved between Tryss's and Sirri's chairs and began to translate in a murmur.

'Mil, Talm of Larrik, has reported that the Dunwayan force has settled in the pass at a place well suited to defence,' Juran said. 'Hundreds of traps have been set along the road in order to slow and weaken the enemy. Scouts report that the Pentadrians have not yet reached the first of them. It appears the enemy has fallen far behind.' Juran paused. 'Unexpectedly far.' He turned to regard Mil. 'Any news?'

Mil glanced at a priest standing nearby, who was clearly of the same race. The man shook his head.

'Our scouts have seen no sign of them.'

'There have been no sightings to indicate that the army has diverted to the north either,' Mil added.

To the north? Tryss frowned, then understanding came in a rush. The Dunwayans were afraid the Pentadrians would turn north to attack them. Their forces were, after all, waiting in the pass rather than at home ready to defend their land.

'There is no sign of the army at all,' the priest added. 'The Siyee were the last to have seen them.'

There was a pause, and many of the people present were frowning.

'Surely they're not still in the mines,' Guire said.

'Waiting, perhaps,' the Somreyan leader muttered. 'But for

what?' He looked at Juran. 'Are you sure they can't be tunnelling through the mountains?'

Juran smiled and nodded. 'Very sure.'

Mil nodded. 'I am more concerned that the Pentadrians are taking a different route *over* the mountains.'

Juran frowned. 'Is there one?'

'There is no road,' Mil replied. 'The mountains are full of gowt-herder paths, however. It would be a slow and difficult journey crossing by these paths, but not impossible.'

'We must know what they are doing,' Juran said firmly. 'If the Pentadrians emerge on the plains while we are in the pass we will end up chasing them across Hania, and beyond.'

'If they are crossing the mountains, my people will find them,' Sirri said.

Juran turned to regard her. 'That would be dangerous – more dangerous than before.'

She shrugged. 'We know about the black birds now. We will be careful. I will call for volunteers – and this time they will be armed.'

Juran hesitated, then nodded. 'Thank you.'

Sirri smiled. 'They will leave at first light. Do you want one of them to carry a link ring?'

Juran exchanged a quick glance with Dyara. 'Yes. One will be brought to the leader of your volunteers before he or she leaves.' He paused, then looked around the room. 'Is there anything else that needs to be discussed?'

The settling of the matter felt a little abrupt to Tryss, but perhaps he only imagined it. He watched the four White closely, particularly Mairae and Rian. Tonight Rian looked . . . well . . . *unhappy*. He occasionally stared out of the tent and scowled. Not an angry scowl, but it was clear something was annoying him. Or perhaps he was disappointed about something.

He'd noted before that Mairae was more inclined to give

away hints of her feelings. As he watched, her gaze became distant and she frowned. He chewed his lip. Perhaps all they were anxious about was the coming battle, and the apparent disappearance of the Pentadrian army. He could not help wondering about Auraya's absence, though. It was odd that nobody had mentioned where she was.

Then, suddenly, the answer came to him.

Of course! Auraya is missing because she's already out looking for the Pentadrian army! Mairae was worried about her. Rian was annoyed because . . . perhaps he'd wanted to go instead. Or perhaps he'd thought it too dangerous.

Either way, it made sense that this was why she was missing. His pleasure at having worked this out faded quickly, however, and was replaced by the realisation of the risk she was taking. If she stumbled upon these Pentadrian sorcerers on her own she would be outnumbered. What if she were killed? What would the Siyee do without her? No other landwalker understood them like she did.

Be careful, Auraya, he thought. *We need you.*

CHAPTER 42

The servant dismantling Auraya's tent untied the ropes at each corner one by one. As the structure slumped to the ground, Danjin sighed heavily.

She's been gone two days, he thought. *It's all my fault.* He shook his head in an attempt to dispel the gloom that had come over him. *I can't be sure of that. She might have disappeared for a good reason.*

Yet he didn't believe so. The White were behaving as if there was nothing untoward about Auraya's absence. They'd given no reason for it, and if anyone had suspicions they hadn't dared to voice them. However, Danjin knew the White well enough to notice the small mannerisms that betrayed worry and anger.

Which was why he had been trying to talk to them. Danjin thought it wise not to approach Juran, since the White leader was the one giving away hints of anger at the mention of Auraya. Dyara's response to his questions had been to find him something to do. Rian just shrugged and said it was not a convenient time to discuss it.

And Mairae? She was avoiding Danjin. For someone whose role was to be approachable when the other White were busy, she was amazingly effective at this.

He looked down at the cage beside him. Even Mischief wasn't inclined to talk. He'd entered his cage without protest, as if he hoped good behaviour would bring back his mistress.

Or had his kidnapping frightened him out of roaming around the camp? Danjin felt a pang of sympathy for the veez. After Auraya had left, Mischief had curled up in Danjin's lap. He hadn't slept; he'd huddled there for hours, staring at his surroundings and starting at the slightest noise.

'Can you keep a secret?'

Danjin jumped at the quiet, familiar voice behind him. Recognising it, he turned to stare at Mairae in surprise. She looked more serious than he had ever seen her appear before.

'Would Dyara have hired me if I could not?' he replied.

She moved to his side and looked down at Mischief.

'It was a bit mean having him taken, but we didn't have time to think of anything else,' Mairae murmured. She met his eyes. 'All I can say is it wasn't my idea.'

Danjin stared back at her. 'Mischief? He was a diversion, wasn't he? To keep me away from the war council.'

She shrugged non-committally. *Or my guess is not quite right.*

'And Auraya. It was to keep me away from Auraya.'

Her chin dropped slightly in a subtle nod.

Why? He had his suspicious, but he made himself consider other reasons. *Either they wanted to conceal something from me, or prevent me from telling Auraya something. If they wanted to conceal something from me there was no need for deception. They only had to ask me to leave the war council. There was no need to have Mischief abducted.*

So it is more likely they wanted to prevent me telling Auraya something. Or prevent Auraya reading my mind. Foremost in my mind had been Mairae's suggestion that Auraya had a lover.

He drew in a deep breath. 'So. Is it true? Were my suspicions right?'

Mairae smiled crookedly. 'I thought you believed they were just friends?'

'So they weren't?'

Her smile faded. 'No. This you must swear to tell no other.'

'I swear I will not.'

Auraya and Leiard. Why hadn't I seen it? Did I so badly need to believe her judgement was faultless that I could not see what I didn't want to see?

Mairae looked away and sighed. 'I feel for her. One can't force the heart to choose wisely. It has a way of choosing for itself. Juran sent him away. It'll take a while before she forgives Juran, I think.'

'Where is she?'

She turned to regard him. 'We don't know. She refuses to answer our calls. I believe she isn't far away. She will return when the war begins, if not earlier.'

'Of course,' he agreed. For some reason saying it aloud made him feel better. She would come back. Perhaps only at the last moment, perhaps full of accusations, but she would come back.

Mairae chuckled. 'Don't blame yourself, Danjin Spear. If anyone is to blame for this it is me, not the least for urging you to consider who Auraya might be visiting. I think you have to agree that separating them will be for the best. For her *and* Northern Ithania.'

He nodded. She was right, yet he couldn't help feeling a fatherly disappointment in Auraya. Of all the men of the world, she couldn't have chosen a more inappropriate lover. Leiard, too, should have seen the consequences of their affair and ended it.

His respect for the Dreamweaver had diminished. *Apparently even wise heathen healers can be fools in the face of love*, he thought wryly.

The servant was now packing the last of Auraya's tent and

579

belongings onto a tarn. As the man turned to regard them expectantly, Mairae took a step away from Danjin.

'I'm glad we talked about this,' she said. 'Take good care of Mischief. We should reach the pass tonight. I'll see you in the war-council tent.'

He made the sign of the circle, then watched her stride away. When she moved out of sight he picked up Mischief's cage, told the servants to join the procession and started toward the advisers' tarn.

Auraya paced.

The grass she was trampling grew on a stony ledge that ran along the steep side of a valley. The valley ran roughtly parallel to the one the east-west road followed in order to reach the pass. She imagined explorers of ancient times wasting days following this valley in the hope of crossing the range. They would have been sorely disappointed when they reached the sheer cliffs and difficult terrain at the end. A climber might have managed to cross the mountains from here, but no ordinary traveller and certainly no platten or tarn could have.

She ought to be in the next valley, not here.

Why can't I bring myself to return? Juran's not responsible for Leiard's faithlessness. Even if he was, I can't punish the whole of Northern Ithania for his actions.

Yet she couldn't bring herself to rejoin the army. At first it had seemed reasonable and sensible to spend a few hours alone. Her mind was a whirling mess of anger, pain and guilt and she was afraid that if she returned she would either scream her anger at Juran or turn into a tearful mess. She needed to get a grip on herself first.

Those hours had turned into a day, and the day into three. Every time she thought she had regained control of her feelings and started flying toward the pass, she soon found herself reversing direction again. The first time it was seeing the Dreamweavers in the distance that had caused her to veer away; the next it was a caravan of whores. Last night it had been nothing but the thought of facing Juran again. All brought up intense feelings that she was not sure she could keep hidden.

They'll reach the pass tonight, she thought. *I'll rejoin them then. Perhaps I'll simply be there when they arrive. Yes, they'll be too relieved to have reached their destination to pay much attention to me.*

She sighed and shook her head. *This shouldn't be happening. It wouldn't be happening if it weren't for Juran.* Perhaps she ought to be grateful to him, as his actions had caused her to see Leiard's true nature.

It was like looking into the mind of a different person, she thought, shaking her head. *I thought I knew him so well. I thought having a mind-reading Gift meant nobody could deceive me. Obviously that isn't true.*

She'd always sensed something mysterious about Leiard. He had hidden depths, she'd told herself. She'd attributed this difference between Leiard's mind and the mind of ordinary people or other Dreamweavers to the link memories he had. Now she knew that there was more to it. She knew he was capable of hiding a part of himself from her.

Leiard had told her the link memories sometimes manifested as another mind within his own. He had even told her this shadow of Mirar didn't like her, but she had never sensed this other personality. Never heard it speak.

She had to accept that she might not have been able to. The trouble was, if Leiard was capable of hiding a part of himself, he also might be capable of lying to her. It was possible this notion of another personality in his mind was simply an explanation he hoped she'd believe if she ever sensed his true feelings.

She groaned. *This is going nowhere! I've been tormenting myself about it for days. If I could just think about something else . . .*

Looking around, she considered her surroundings. The ledge continued to her left and right. Some time in the distant past the surface of the slope had slipped downward, leaving rock exposed and a ledge that ran down to the valley floor in one direction and up toward the peaks in the other.

Most of the ledge was hidden behind trees and plants, but with the vegetation cleared and the surface levelled it could easily become a narrow road.

Maybe it was an old abandoned road. A road to where? Curiosity aroused, she decided to follow it. She made her way through the trees and vegetation choking the ledge. After a few hundred strides the path ended. A steep slope fell to the valley floor on one side. The wall on her right was a jumble of rocks, half hidden behind grasses that had grown in the soil between them.

She turned to retrace her steps, and froze in surprise.

A glowing figure stood a few feet away. Tall and strong, but not heavily built, he was the picture of athletic maleness. His perfect masculine mouth curled up into a smile.

:Auraya.

'Chaia!'

She dropped to the ground, heart racing. *I left it too long. I should have returned sooner.* Suddenly her self-pity seemed foolish. Selfish. She felt ashamed of herself. She had forgotten her duty to the gods and their patience had run out . . .

:Not yet, Auraya. But it is time you forgave yourself and your fellow White. Rise and face me.

She climbed to her feet, but kept her eyes downcast.

:Do not be ashamed of your feelings. You are but a human, and a young human at that. You have an empathy for those not like yourself. It is only natural that your empathy can become love.

He moved closer, then reached a hand toward her face. As his fingers met her cheek she felt a tingling sensation. There was no sense of pressure. He was insubstantial. His touch was the touch of pure magic.

:We know you have not abandoned your people. You should not linger here alone any longer, however. You are in danger and I would not like to see any harm come to you.

He stepped close. She looked up at him and felt sadness and anger slip away. There was only room for awe. He smiled as a parent might smile at a child, with indulgent affection. Then he leaned down and brushed his lips against hers.

And vanished.

She gasped and took two steps backwards. *He kissed me! Chaia kissed me!* She touched her lips. The memory of the sensation was strong. *What does it mean?*

The kiss of a god could not be the same as the kiss of a mortal. She remembered how he had smiled at her like a parent amused by a child. That was how she must appear to him. A child.

And parents don't kiss their children when they are angry, she reminded herself. *They kiss to comfort and to convey their love. That must be it.*

Smiling, she moved to the end of the ledge. It was time to go. Time to return to the army. Drawing magic, she sent herself upward. The valley shrank beneath her. She turned to fly in the direction of the pass.

A rumble brought her attention back to the ground. Dust was wafting up from the rocks below. Then grass, soil and rocks began to stir. Chaia's words echoed in her mind.

You should not linger here alone any longer, however. You are in danger . . .

If she was in danger, then whatever was happening was enough to threaten even a powerful sorceress. She felt a flash of fear, but it was followed by an equally strong surge of curiosity. Stopping in midair, she looked down. The rocks were now tumbling down the slope into the valley. Clouds of dirt were gusting from behind them. From somewhere inside the earth, something – or someone – was about to emerge.

She had heard tales of mountains exploding and bleeding out molten rock, causing devastation for great distances. If that was about to happen, she probably shouldn't be hovering right above these shifting rocks. She should fly away as quickly as possible.

The area of disturbance below her was small, however. The mountains around her showed no signs of upheaval. The only area of strangeness was the place she had been standing.

Chaia didn't say I had to return to the army, just that I should not linger here alone. Would I be safe if I watched from the other side of the valley?

Moving away, she flew to a rock formation on the other ridge and looked back. She could see a cave forming as more rocks spewed out of the ground.

Tales of great monsters living in caves under the mountains came to mind. Considering how exaggerated the tales of the Siyee were – describing them as beautiful humans with bird wings attached to their spines – it was likely those tales were as inaccurate. However, if such a beast was about to emerge, she wanted to see it.

But I had better make sure it doesn't see me.

She searched the rock formation for possible hiding places, then dropped down into a shadowy crevice. It was barely wide enough for her to stand in sideways and the air within it was damp and cold, but it concealed her and gave her a view of the valley.

A boom brought her attention back to the opposite slope. Rock and soil sprayed out of the cave. Silence and stillness followed. All vegetation around the ledge was gone. Grass, trees and creepers had been blasted away along with soil and rocks. What remained was clearly man-made.

She saw that the rocks she had assumed were natural were stone bricks. The exposed face had been made up of collapsed walls. A massive lintel stood across the top of a gaping hole. On it she could make out a simple carved design: a pick and a shovel.

It was the entrance of a mine.

Her stomach sank as she recalled the possibility being discussed and dismissed in the war council that the Pentadrians were traversing the mountains via mines. According to the Dunwayan ambassador the mines didn't reach as far as Hania.

Clearly they did. As a black-robed figure emerged from the darkness, star-shaped pendant glittering, she began to understand how badly she and her fellow White had underestimated their enemy. The sorcerer's face tilted up to greet the sunlight and Auraya went cold all over. It was the one who had attacked and defeated her months before. Kuar.

She sought a familiar mind.

:Juran?

The response was immediate.

:Auraya! Where are you?

:Here.

As she let him see what she was watching, more of the Pentadrians began to emerge. They blinked in the sunlight as their leader moved out onto the ledge. She could see now that the dirt had been swept away to expose large squares of flat stone – paving.

The black sorcerer reached the edge and looked down the steep slope. He held his hands out, palms down. Grass and soil flew into the air, slowly revealing a steep staircase leading to the valley floor. When the entire flight was clear, the Pentadrian leader stepped aside and his followers began to descend.

:Where are you? Juran repeated, his question more alarmed than accusing this time.

:A valley running parallel to the one you are following. Let me show you. She sent him what she remembered of the view from above.

:How far are they from the mouth of the valley?

:A day's walk, she guessed. *If they have been travelling all night they may stop now to rest.*

The sound of voices and marching feet filled the valley, and grew steadily louder as more and more Pentadrians spilled out of the mine. All looked intensely relieved. Some paused to breathe deeply and gaze up at the sun. Once on the valley floor, they stopped to wait and watch their companions emerge. Their leader remained on the ledge, smiling with obvious satisfaction.

And well he should, Auraya thought. *What he has achieved is amazing.*

:This changes everything, Juran said. *We must hurry if we are to meet them. The Dunwayans will have to travel even faster in order to join us.*

:The traps they set in the pass are useless now.

:At least they will slow or stop other Pentadrians sneaking through to bite at our heels.

:How long will it take you to head them off? she asked.

:A day. Maybe more. We will have to face them on the plains.

And lose the advantage of fighting in the pass. Auraya sighed. The mass of black robes gathering in the valley below was like a steadily growing pool of ink.

:How did you find this place?

The question came from Dyara. Auraya could not help smiling.

:Coincidence. I was walking along that ledge. Chaia appeared and warned me not to linger. As I left, the ground began to stir.

586

:Chaia told you they were about to emerge? Juran asked.

:No, he told me I would be in danger if I stayed where I was. I thought at first that he meant I should leave the valley, but when I saw that the disturbance was restricted to one place I decided to hide and watch.

Another figure joined the man on the ledge. A woman this time. She looked familiar.

:You will be in danger if they find you, Juran told her.

Screeching echoed out of the passage.

:Yes, Dyara agreed. *Leave now. We have seen all we need to see.*

Flapping forms spilled out of the passage. Auraya shrank deeper into her hiding place as black birds began to circle the valley.

:I don't think that would be wise right now, unless you don't mind them knowing they've been seen.

There was a pause.

:Stay, then, Juran agreed. *Wait until they move on.*

:And hope they don't decide to camp for the night, Dyara added.

The pool of black robes had become a lake. After several minutes sinuous black forms flowed out. Vorns. Auraya frowned as she watched the murderous sorcerer Rian had fought join the two on the ledge.

Three black sorcerers. Two more to go. She could do little more than wait and watch as the rest of the Pentadrians emerged. She sensed her fellow White's attention shift away. No doubt they were busy organising their own army's retreat down the pass road.

Another woman and man joined the trio on the ledge. To Auraya's relief, the pair brought no other sinister animal companions with them. The birds and vorns were bad enough. Each column of the army was made up of several hundred Pentadrian sorcerers and soldiers. A hundred or so men and women wearing plain clothes and carrying heavy burdens always followed. A few robed men walked alongside them, each carrying a short whip.

Slaves, Auraya thought, and shuddered with disgust and pity. There were no tarns and no arems. All the supplies were carried by these slaves.

Finally the flow of people ended. As the last of the slaves descended the stairs, the five black sorcerers formed a line across the front of the ledge. The leader began to speak. His voice boomed out, but Auraya could not understand him or read his mind. She looked down at the men and women below and concentrated on their thoughts. An understanding of the words came.

Kuar spoke of bringing truth and justice to Northern Ithania. He jeered at the Circlians for believing in dead gods. Only the new gods existed. They would soon know the truth.

Auraya drew away and shook her head. The adoration and unquestioning belief of these people was disturbing. As the Pentadrian leader raised his voice, she reluctantly sought his followers' minds again. To her surprise, he was calling for his gods to appear. She smiled grimly, wondering what sorcerous effect he would use to dazzle his followers.

A glowing figure appeared beside him.

Auraya stared at the apparition. It was an image of a man wearing exotic armour. Her senses vibrated with the power that radiated from this being. But how could this be?

:*Juran.*

:*Auraya. Can it wait?*

:*No, I think you should see this.*

She let him see what she was witnessing and communicated what she was sensing. The black sorcerers had prostrated themselves before the apparition. So had the entire Pentadrian army. Even the slaves.

:*It is an illusion*, Juran assured her.

:If it is, then it's the first that ever radiated power. I have never felt this except in the presence of the gods.

:The circle of five are the only gods that survived their war, Juran said firmly.

:Then perhaps this is a new god, Dyara suggested.

The five sorcerers had climbed to their feet. They moved aside as the apparition stepped forward. No sound came from the glowing man, but the people below began to cheer at intervals as if responding to his words.

:If this is a god then there is reason to fear there are more, Rian said. *We know these people worship five gods. Why would this god tolerate them worshipping four additional gods if they were false?*

:Five new gods? Juran said disbelievingly. *All undetected by ours?*

:We have to consider the possibility, Mairae said.

:We know the black sorcerers are strong, Rian pointed out. *How else can they rival us in strength without the assistance of gods?*

:Either way, we know this will not be an easy battle, Dyara added.

:No, Juran agreed. *Our people do not need to hear of this. They would become . . . disheartened. Auraya, get out of there as soon as you can. We must meet and reconsider our own strategy.*

:I will, Auraya told him. *I assure you, the last place I want to be right now is here.*

One loud cheer burst from the Pentadrians. The apparition disappeared. Auraya felt a surge of relief.

:It's gone, she told them.

The sorcerers descended the stairs. The lake of black robes stirred and separated into five columns. Auraya murmured a prayer of thanks to Chaia as the Pentadrian leader moved to the head of a column and began to lead the army down the valley.

CHAPTER 43

Leiard opened his eyes. He was riding an arem and he was alone. Mountains rose before him. The road wound toward them. He felt a flare of panic and reined in the arem.

I'm heading toward the pass. What's going on? I should be going in the other direction.

Yes, Mirar replied, *but that fool student of yours ran away and we have to find him.*

Jayim? Why would he run away?

I don't know. When I went to find him he was gone.

Find him? Were you separated?

I thought he'd appreciate his privacy.

Leiard felt suspicion growing. *Why? What have you done?*

I bought him a gift, to keep him distracted. You wouldn't have wanted him to witness a confrontation with Auraya, would you?

What gift?

A whore. Who'd have thought a young man like Jayim would take fright at that?

Leiard groaned and pressed his hands to his face. *You're supposed to be wise and skilled in understanding the mind and heart. How could you have made such a mistake?*

Nobody's perfect.

If you were wrong about Jayim, you might also be wrong about Auraya.

590

No, Mirar replied firmly. *Only a lovestruck fool cannot see the danger you were putting our people in. Arleej agreed. So did Juran.*

And Auraya? Leiard felt his heart sink with dread. What did you say to her?

Nothing. Haven't seen her. Which is a pity. I was looking forward to it.

Gazing up at the mountains, Leiard sighed. *You may still get your chance. We do have to find Jayim.* Juran had made it clear that Leiard must ensure his and Auraya's affair remained a secret. Jayim could not learn from anyone but Leiard, since he could not link with another Dreamweaver without the risk of passing that knowledge on.

Except Arleej, he thought. *She knows.* He nudged the arem into a walk. *She could teach him.*

Ah! Of course! Mirar exclaimed. *I gave control back to you because I thought you'd find Jayim more easily than me. I didn't need to. We don't need to return at all.*

Yes we do. I am Jayim's teacher. I cannot abandon that obligation to another without his consent – or theirs.

Of course you can. Juran ordered you to leave. He will be angry if you return. Your duty to avoid bringing trouble onto your people outweighs your obligation to Jayim.

Leave what? Leiard argued. *The tent? The mountains? Northern Ithania? No, he ordered me to leave Auraya. So long as I avoid her company, I am obeying his order. I will return and find Jayim.*

No. I will fight you.

Leiard smiled. *I don't think you will. I think you agree with me on this.*

How can you be so sure?

You set down these rules. You're even more obliged to follow them than I.

No answer came to that.

Leiard considered how he might find Jayim. First he should

contact Arleej. But if it was daylight she'd be awake and impossible to reach with a dream link. She might sense him seeking her, however. Sometimes powerfully Gifted Dreamweavers could, if there were no other distractions. Leiard dismounted and led the arem to the side of the road where a large, elongated boulder stood on its end. Numbers had been carved into the surface. These markers were a new feature of the east-west road, placed there by the Circlians at intervals of roughly a day's march.

Sitting with his back to the rock, he closed his eyes and willed himself into a dream trance. It was not hard, since he felt as if he hadn't slept in days.

We haven't.

Quiet!

Leiard slowed his breathing and sought a familiar mind.

:Arleej?

He waited, then called again. After the third call he heard a faint reply.

:Leiard? Is that you?

:Yes, it is me.

:You sound different. This is you – not Mirar?

:Yes, it is me. Is Jayim with you?

:Yes.

He sighed with relief.

:Where are you? he asked.

:On the east-west road. We're backtracking. Raeli says the Pentadrians have been seen emerging from mines on this side of the mountains. The Circlian army is hurrying back to confront them. Where are you?

:The east-west road. I doubt I overtook you, so you're probably heading toward me. I'll wait here for you.

:Good. Jayim will be glad to see you.

Leiard opened his eyes. He rose and led the arem on to a

place where he could see the road ahead, then sat down again. His stomach rumbled with hunger, but he was too tired to get up and see if the arem was carrying any food.

How long has passed since I let you take control? he asked Mirar.

A day and a half.

What did you do in all that time?

You don't want to know – though in truth I mostly searched for Jayim.

Leiard sighed. *You're right. I don't want to know.*

He let the arem's lead-rope go. It took the opportunity to graze. Carrying a rider was easier for the beasts than hauling a well-laden tarn. So long as they had plenty of water and a bit of grass to eat by the side of the road each night they could be ridden for days at a steady pace. Leiard examined the beast critically. She wasn't ill or injured. Mirar had not abused her.

Though all he wanted to do was lie down and sleep, Leiard stood up and tended to his mount.

The sun had climbed higher in the sky by the time the Dreamweavers appeared. Arleej, as always, was driving the lead tarn. Leiard mounted the arem and waited.

'Dreamweaver Leiard,' Arleej said as she drew close. 'I'm glad you have returned to us. It saves us the trouble of finding you later.'

'It is good to see you again, Dreamweaver Elder,' he replied. 'Surely you would not have come looking for me?'

As the tarn reached him he directed the arem to walk beside it. Arleej looked at him critically.

'After what Jayim told me? Definitely.' She frowned. 'You look tired. Have you slept? Eaten?'

He grimaced. 'Not for a while, I think. I do not recall anything of the last day and a half.'

'Then Jayim was right. Mirar did take control of you.'

'He worked that out?'

'Yes. He was afraid it might be permanent and came back to us for help. Which put me in a difficult situation. Should I search for you or fulfil my duty as a healer?'

'You made the right choice.'

'Jayim did not think so.' She glanced at him. 'The Circlian army is racing down the road behind us. We must get out of their way and still manage to remain close enough to be of help. I would never have thought anyone could find their way under the mountains.'

Leiard shrugged. 'It has been done before. The way is not all underground. Mines lead to limestone caves, which lead to hidden valleys used for grazing by gowtherders. There is another old mine on this side of the mountains, though last I heard the entrance had caved in. Nothing a powerful sorcerer couldn't unblock, however.'

Arleej stared at him, then shook her head. 'If you had not resigned from your position, you would have been part of the war council. They discussed the possibility that the Pentadrians might follow the old mines under the mountains. You could have warned them of this.'

'If I'd warned them, would they have believed me?'

The corners of her mouth twitched upward. 'Auraya would have.'

'You haven't mentioned them discussing this before.'

Arleej frowned. 'Raeli told us of it two nights ago. The night you left.'

'So if Juran had not sent me away, I would have told you it was possible, and you would have warned Raeli, and the White could have disbelieved her instead.'

Arleej threw back her head and laughed. 'I will have to point this out to Juran one day.' She looked thoughtful. 'That is what I will do if Juran learns you returned to us and protests.'

'I can't stay, Arleej.'

She gave him a serious, determined look. 'You *must* stay with us, Leiard. What is happening to you is unnatural and dangerous. Only we can help you. I intend to take you back to Somrey with me when this foolish war is over. I doubt Juran will object to having a large stretch of sea between you and Auraya.' She lifted an eyebrow. 'Will you agree to that?'

Leiard looked away. What she wanted was much more sensible than running blindly with no destination in mind. Surely Mirar would see that. He felt a sudden rush of gratitude to Arleej and turned to meet her gaze.

'It seems the more I try to leave, the more reasons I find to stay. Thank you, Dreamweaver Elder. I will remain with you.'

She looked relieved. 'Good. Now go back and see to your student. He's been worried about you.'

'Jade.'

The voice brought Emerahl out of a deep sleep. A sleep her body surfaced from reluctantly. She scowled with annoyance, drew in a breath and opened her eyes.

Rozea was leaning over her, smiling.

'Quickly. Sit up. I've sent the servants for some things. We've got to get you presentable.'

Emerahl sat up and rubbed her eyes. The tarn was motionless. 'Presentable? Why?'

'The army is coming. It'll pass us at any moment. It's the perfect opportunity to show you girls off. Come on. Wake yourself up. You look terrible.'

The flap of the tarn opened and a servant passed Rozea a bowl of water, a towel and Emerahl's box of grooming tools, paints and ointments. Emerahl could see that the caravan had pulled over to the side of the road. Then she noticed a rhythmic sound in the distance. The sound of many, many feet marching to the pace of drums.

'The army? Coming back?' Emerahl's heart skipped as the full meaning of Rozea's words came to her. The army was returning from the pass. For Rozea this was an opportunity to put her wares on display that was too good to miss. For Emerahl, being put into the sight of hundreds of priests could be disastrous.

'Yes,' Rozea said. 'They're coming back down the road. I don't know why. We'll find out when they get here, which will be in a matter of moments. Tidy yourself up. I'm going to see to the other girls. I'll send a servant back to you.'

Emerahl took the bowl and towel. As Rozea left she began to wash her face. *I have to find a way to avoid this – and quickly.* She looked down at the box and pushed off the lid with a toe. If she was less than presentable, Rozea might let her remain unseen. The reason would have to be convincing, but then Emerahl had seen enough sick people in her long life to know how to pretend to be unwell, and healing powers could be used for other purposes.

Picking up the water bowl, she closed her eyes and began to concentrate on her stomach.

When the door flap opened again, Emerahl was lying across the seat, this time with her head by the door. As bright light streamed in, she cringed away and buried her head in her arms. The servant stared at her, then at the contents of the bowl, and hurried away. A moment later Rozea appeared.

'What's this?' she asked, her voice strained.

Emerahl shifted her head slightly so Rozea could see the paint-darkened skin under her eyes. 'I tried,' she said weakly. 'I thought I could pretend . . . I'm sorry.'

Rozea called back the servant and had the girl take the bowl away. She climbed inside the tarn.

'What's . . . what's wrong with you?'

Emerahl swallowed and rubbed her stomach. 'Bad food, I think. When I sat up before . . . Urgh. I feel sick.'

'You look a sight.' Rozea scowled in frustration. 'I can't have you scaring customers off, now can I?' She drummed her fingers on her sleeve. 'That's fine. You're my favourite, not to be seen by just any common soldier. Only by those who can afford to pay for a glimpse of rare beauty.'

Emerahl made a small noise of resignation. The madam smiled, then patted her on the shoulder. 'Get some rest. These things don't last long. I'm sure you'll be well by tonight.'

When she had left, Emerahl raised her head and lifted the door flap a little. She could see nothing, but the sound of marching was louder now. The faint giggle of the other whores close by made her smile. This would be exciting for them. Then a male voice – one of the guards – called out, 'Here they come!'

A rider came into view and her heart all but stopped.

Juran.

At first glance he looked no different to the man she had seen a hundred years before. She looked closer and realised this was not true. The years showed in his eyes – in the hard, determined expression on his face. He still looked handsome and confident, but time had changed the man. She could not say exactly how, and did not care to find out.

As he moved out of sight, two more riders came into view. A woman and a man, both good-looking. They wore the same undecorated white robes. Two more of the White. The woman also wore a hard expression. She looked about forty. The man beside her, in contrast, appeared to be much younger. He had a disturbingly intense gaze. As his attention fell on the brothel's caravan, he frowned with disapproval, then lifted his chin and looked away.

A tarn followed. Within this sat two young women. Again, both wore white and both were attractive. The blonde's expression was more open than the other. When she saw the caravan her lips twitched into a faint, wry smile that made her look older and wiser than her physical appearance suggested.

Immortals, Emerahl thought. *You can tell, once you've met a few. I wonder if I'm so easy to read.*

The other woman wore her hair unbound. She had large eyes and a triangular face. She stared at the caravan, then quickly looked away. Not out of disdain, Emerahl saw. The woman looked pained.

The pair passed out of sight. Another tarn followed. It was highly decorated and surrounded by elaborately uniformed soldiers. Emerahl recognised the current Toren king's colours and symbols. Several more fancy tarns followed. Genrian. Somreyan. Hanian. Then the priests and priestesses began to file past. She let the door flap fall and rolled onto her back, heart pounding.

So those are the ones they call the White, she thought. *The ones the gods chose to do their dirty work among mortals.*

She listened to the sound of the army passing and the calls of the girls. It was disturbing knowing so many of the gods' followers were filing past her, separated only by the tarn cover. *I should not have stayed with the brothel after the ambush*, she decided. *I should have taken my money and left.*

She would have felt bad about leaving the girls unprotected, however; she could not have known that they would be safe. *And if I'd left, I would never have been in this unique position to see the Gods' Chosen without being seen myself.* She smiled at the thought. *I do believe I'm gaining an adventurous spirit*, she mused. *What next?*

She sighed. The caravan had caught up with the army, though in an unexpected way. Rozea could find herself new guards now. There was no reason for Emerahl to stay. *I can leave . . . or can I?*

The caravan would probably follow at the rear of the army and camp beside it tonight. She faced the same danger she had before – that the news Rozea's favourite had run away would inspire an entire army to search for her.

Yet there was a new danger if she stayed. Rozea might mention her favourite's amazing powers of healing to the wrong person. Emerahl might find herself facing curious priestly visitors.

She cursed.

The door flap opened. She looked up to see Rozea regarding her. The woman moved to the opposite seat, her expression serious.

'It seems the enemy has found another way through the mountains. The Circlians are rushing to stop them.'

'Will we go too?' Emerahl asked, keeping her voice weak.

'Yes, at a distance. We don't know if the Pentadrians intend to ambush the army. I don't want to end up in the middle of a battle.'

'No.'

'You rest now,' Rozea said soothingly. She lifted the door flap, revealing lines of ordinary soldiers, to Emerahl's relief. 'I doubt we'll have customers tonight. It sounds as if the army will march all night. We'll catch up with them tomorrow – ah, there's Captain Spirano.'

She leapt up and climbed out. Emerahl turned onto her back and listened to the sound of marching. It went on and on. By the time it had stopped she was sure hours had passed.

The girls fell silent, probably taking the opportunity to sleep without the constant rocking of the tarn. Emerahl heard the guards challenge Rozea to a game of counters. She listened for a while, gathering her courage, then sat up and used the damp towel to clean her face.

As she stepped out of the tarn, Rozea looked up.

'You look better. How do you feel?'

'Much better,' Emerahl replied. She moved over to the table and looked down at the game. 'Counters. You would not believe how old this game is.'

The guard playing Rozea moved a piece. Emerahl chuckled. 'Bad move.'

The man gave her a hurt look. It was the same guard who had 'rescued' her from the deserter she had thrown out of her tarn during the ambush.

'What would you have done?' Rozea asked.

Emerahl looked at the guard. 'It is his game.'

'Go ahead,' he said. 'Win it for me, and you can have half the takings.'

She laughed. 'Rozea won't let me keep it.'

'Of course I will,' the madam said, smiling. She moved the man's piece back to its former position.

Emerahl met the woman's eyes, then looked down at the board. She drew a little magic and sent it out. A black counter slid across the board and flipped on top of another.

The two guards jumped, then grinned at her. 'Clever trick, that,' the friendly one said.

'Yes.' Rozea was staring at the board. 'Very clever.'

'Yield?' Emerahl asked.

'Can't say I have any choice,' Rozea admitted.

'What?' The guard turned to stare at the board. 'Did she win the game for me?'

'She did.' Rozea pushed a few coins in his direction. 'I believe half of that is hers.'

'Oh, you owe me much more than that, Rozea,' Emerahl replied. 'And it's time you paid up. I'm leaving.'

600

The madam leaned back in her chair and crossed her arms. 'We had an agreement.'

'I'm breaking it.'

'If you leave now, you go with nothing.'

Emerahl smiled. 'So you've said. That's hardly fair. I've earned you quite a sum. If you will not give me the wages I've earned, I will take them.'

Rozea uncrossed her arms and set her hands on her hips. 'What are you going to do? Fling counters at me with magic? Your sorcery does not scare me. If you were able to force me into giving you money, you would have done so before now.'

'Your weakness, Rozea, is that you think others are as selfish and greedy as you. I only stayed to protect the girls. Now you've caught up with the army you'll be able to hire new guards. You don't need me any more.'

'*Need* you?' Rozea laughed. 'You flatter yourself.'

Emerahl smiled. 'Perhaps. It's been a long time since I had to use magic to hurt anyone. I don't like to. I prefer to find ways around it. So I'll give you one last chance. Give me my wages. Now.'

'No.'

Emerahl turned and strode toward the tarn in which Brand and Tide were sleeping.

'Where are you going?' she heard Rozea demand.

Emerahl ignored her. She reached the tarn and opened the flap.

'Wake up, girls.'

The girls started awake and blinked at her in surprise as she climbed inside.

'Jade?'

'What's going on?'

'I'm leaving,' Emerahl told them. She turned to the front seat. 'Stand up.'

Tide and Star rose. Emerahl felt under the seat and found a tiny latch. She pulled and the compartment opened. Behind was a collection of boxes.

Rozea's face appeared in the doorway. 'What are you . . . stop that!'

Emerahl drew out one of the boxes. It was encouragingly heavy.

'Give that to me!' Rozea demanded.

Emerahl opened the box. The girls hummed with interest as they saw the coins inside. Rozea cursed and started to climb into the tarn.

With a gesture and a small shove of magic, Emerahl pushed the madam out of the tarn. Rozea toppled backwards and was caught by the guards.

'Stop her!' the woman shouted. 'She's robbing us!'

'I'm not robbing you,' Emerahl corrected her. 'Now, Panilo said you were charging twice what he originally paid me. That's a hundred . . .' she paused as the guards reluctantly tried to enter the tarn, and gently pushed them out again '. . . ren per customer. Since coming to your establishment I've had forty-eight customers, many who were richer and more important than Panilo. Let's make it a nice round five thousand ren, which makes ten gold. I'll subtract one gold for a month's food and board – and for the clothing – which I'm sure you'll give to another girl anyway. I'll need some change, of course, so . . .'

Emerahl began counting, aware that Rozea was standing a few steps away, glaring at her. The girls in the tarn were silent – too surprised to speak.

'Jade? Jade? Are you sure about this?' Brand asked suddenly, her voice low and urgent with concern. 'There's a battle about to happen. You'll be all alone.'

'I'll be fine. It's you girls I'm worried about. Don't let Rozea take any risks. Get yourselves back to Toren as soon as you can.'

'I don't understand.' This came from Star. 'If you've got Gifts enough that you can heal me and take your wages off Rozea, why'd you end up in a brothel?'

Emerahl looked up at her, then shrugged. 'I . . . I don't know. Bad luck, I suppose.'

The question made her uncomfortable, and not just because it might get them thinking of reasons why a healer sorceress might have resorted to prostitution at a time when the priests were searching for someone of that description. She counted the rest of her earnings out in silver and gold, to quicken the task.

When she had finished, she looked at each of the girls. They still looked confused. She smiled.

'Take care of yourselves. And take this advice: if you all demand it together, Rozea will have to give you your earnings. Don't squander it all; put some aside for the future. Never think you don't have a life outside the brothel. You're all talented, beautiful women.'

Brand smiled. 'Thanks, Jade. You take care of yourself, too.'

The others murmured farewells. Emerahl turned away and climbed down out of the tarn. She caught the eye of a servant.

'Get me a pack, with food and water. And some plain clothes.'

The man glanced at Rozea. To Emerahl's surprise, the woman nodded. He hurried away.

'I guess I shouldn't force you to stay when you're so set on leaving,' Rozea said resignedly. 'I'm not happy about this, but if you must go, you must go. Should you decide to return to the business at some stage, don't think you're unwelcome in my house. I'm not such a fool that I wouldn't consider employing you again.'

Emerahl regarded the woman thoughtfully, sensing a sullen

respect. *Why so friendly now? Perhaps I didn't take as much money as she expected. I still can't get used to the way prices have inflated over the last century.*

'I'll remember that,' she replied. The servant appeared. He thrust a bag into her arms. She gave the contents a quick examination, then hoisted it over her shoulder. 'Look after those girls,' she told Rozea. 'You don't deserve them.'

Then she turned her back and started along the road toward Toren.

CHAPTER 44

As the sun rose above the horizon, light spilled over the Plains of Gold. The shadows of the Circlian priests, priestesses, soldiers and archers stretched out like fingers pointed in accusation toward the mass of black-robed invaders.

The last shred of lingering weariness disappeared as Tryss watched the two armies draw closer.

Of the entire Circlian army, only the Siyee had rested the previous night. It had been a restless sleep even so. Few were able to keep their minds from the coming battle. He suspected that if the landwalkers had stopped their march they might not have gained much rest from the long night either. Even from the air he had seen signs of agitation and nervousness among them.

Black flapping shapes rose from among the Pentadrians – an evil cloud of potential death. Tryss heard exclamations of dismay around him. He glanced at the men and women nearby. People of his own tribe. Not his family or wife – the Speakers had decided it was too much to ask a flight leader to take his relations into battle – yet tribes were never so large that a Siyee didn't know every member. It was still hard to think that these people might die if he made a mistake in judgement.

His stomach clenched. He ignored it and took a deep breath.

'These black birds have beaks and claws,' he called. 'But they must get near us to use them. We have darts and arrows. We will kill them before they reach us.'

He did not know if his words had any effect. Perhaps their expressions were a little less grim and a little more determined. The birds circled above their masters, waiting for the battle to begin.

The coming together of the two armies was excruciatingly slow. Tryss watched as landwalker advanced on landwalker, creeping over gently undulating grassland. The Pentadrian army reached the top of a low ridge on one side of a valley and stopped. The Circlians marched up the far side of the valley. They, too, halted.

The two armies were still.

Then a lone black-clad figure stepped forward from among the Pentadrians. Sunlight glinted off something hanging about his neck. Tryss noted the five white figures standing before the Circlian army. One moved forward.

The two met at the bottom of the valley.

How I wish I could hear that *conversation*, Tryss thought. *Are they offering each other a chance to back off? Are they tossing threats and boasts of strength back and forth like children?* This was supposed to be a religious war, he reminded himself. *Perhaps they're having a theological argument.* He began to imagine how it might go.

'My gods are real.'

'No they're not; mine are.'

'Yours aren't real.'

'Are too!'

He choked back a laugh. *I'm being silly now. This is serious. People are going to die.*

All humour fled at that thought. As the two figures parted,

Tryss's stomach clenched again. He watched them rejoin their armies.

The distant sound of horns rang out. The Pentadrian army surged forward and the Circlians followed suit. As the roar of voices reached Tryss, Sirri's whistle pierced the air. It was time for the Siyee to join the battle. As one, the Siyee dropped into a dive.

The two armies had not yet met, but Tryss could see the air in the valley twist and glow as magical attacks met magical shields. Strange tearing, shrieking noises reached him and the occasional boom sent a vibration through the air.

It must be deafening down there, he thought.

The black cloud spiralling above the Pentadrian army fragmented and rushed upward. Part of it sped toward Tryss. He forgot all else as the black birds drew rapidly closer. Whistling orders, he directed his flight to fly straight for them, then set his fingers firmly on the levers of his harness.

'Attack!'

The spring of his harness sang. He heard the twang of others. A swarm of darts enveloped the black birds. Tryss cheered as the creatures shrieked and fell. He gave the signal to veer aside, grinning as his people whooped with triumph and indulged in a few fancy acrobatic moves.

Then he heard a shriek of pain and his heart sank like a stone. He twisted around to see that some of the birds had survived and had latched onto the legs of one of the Siyee. Their weight was dragging her down and they were clawing along her trousers toward her wings.

Not sure what he could do but hoping he would think of something, Tryss dived toward her. He could hardly use his hands to remove the birds. Instead he clenched his teeth, folded his arms and barrelled into the girl's legs. He heard squawks and a yell of surprise, and felt himself falling. Extending his arms, he caught the wind and turned back to see what had happened.

The Siyee woman was free. Her legs were bleeding. He could see a bird flying below them, unharmed but clearly stunned. Tryss quickly caught his blowpipe between his teeth, sucked in a dart and let it loose.

The bird gave a squawk of protest and surprise as it was hit. Tryss did not wait to observe the poison take effect. He looked up and called to his flight. They moved closer. Aside from scratches they were all alive and uninjured.

Relieved, he looked past them and caught his breath in dismay. The sky was full of Siyee and birds, some locked in savage struggles. As he watched he saw three Siyee fall.

He also saw that two other flights as well as his had managed to get past the deadly birds. They now flew above the battle. He remembered Sirri's instructions.

'The birds will try to keep you occupied. Don't let them distract you. Aim for their masters, the black priests and priestesses. They control the birds, so try to kill them first. Once their source of control is gone, the birds may become harmless.'

With an effort he turned away from the battle and called for his flight to follow him. They did not argue, but their expressions were grim. Tryss looked down at the Pentadrian army below and considered how he should best direct their first attack.

Blood was everywhere. The air was full of the spray and reek of it. Faces, clothes and swords were slick with it. The grass was no longer yellow, but an evil orange-red.

Another black-clad monster came. The soldier lifted his shield to block the attack and swung his sword. The motions were familiar and comfortable. Years of training finally proving to be useful. His sword was an extension of his arm. He felt his blade glide through flesh and shatter bone. It was a much more satisfying feeling than the resistant bounce of padded wood.

The Pentadrian dropped to his knees, gurgling as blood filled his lungs. A yank released the sword. A stab through the neck stilled the hand groping for a knife.

Sudden panting to his left. The soldier ducked and spun about, catching the attacker in the stomach. The man's eyes bulged in surprise. Coward, attacking from behind. He left that one to die slowly.

A glance told him that the fighters around him were now mostly of his own side. He turned and searched for the enemy. A distant growling caught at his attention. Far to the right he saw Toren soldiers fall beneath impossibly large creatures. Vorns. He stared in disbelief, and turned to run.

Then his foot caught on something. He fell and landed face down and cursed into the mud. Heat seared his ears. He reached up to cover them. The touch of his muddy hands was wonderfully soothing, but it did not muffle what came next. Screaming. Unearthly screaming that just went on and on.

Something terrible had happened.

He lifted his head. Painfully dry, smoky air filled his lungs. It set him coughing. He dragged himself into a crouch and looked around.

The grass was gone . . . no, it had become shrivelled, black-ened tussocks. Black shapes covered the ground. Some of them were moving. Twitching and writhing. The source of the screaming. He tasted bile as he realised what they were.

Men. The fighters he had been walking with a moment ago.

He hauled himself to his feet. At once he understood what had happened. The burned grass and dead – dying – men formed a long, wide line back toward the enemy. A sorcerer's strike. Deadly magic.

No training could save a soldier from this.

He had been fortunate to have been at the edge of it. His armour and heavy clothing, and falling face down in the mud, had saved him, though his ears burned fiercely. Looking down, he saw the outstretched hand of the Pentadrian who had tripped him. The man's face was charred as black as his clothes.

Setting his jaw, he picked up his sword, still warm from the strike, and started toward his less-fortunate comrades.

No link between Auraya and the other White had ever been this strong or complete.

They worked as one, their powers directed by Juran. It was surprisingly easy. There was no imposing of will. They simply opened their minds to him and followed his instructions. In return, he had four extra minds and pairs of eyes to call upon when making decisions, and four extra positions from which to attack.

It was proving to be an effective way to coordinate their efforts. And it was almost thrilling to work so smoothly with the others. No misunderstandings. No mistakes.

Yet they still had limitations. The enemy had already found Mairae's, and at one point she had been forced to leave soldiers vulnerable in order to protect herself. Their deaths had distressed Mairae, and shocked them all, but their linked sense of purpose ensured they did not falter.

Rian, too, was struggling. Juran was constantly forced to intervene whenever one of the more powerful black sorcerers attacked Rian or Mairae. Auraya had managed to defend herself against all attacks by the enemy sorcerers so far, but she knew the Pentadrian leader was stronger than her. She, too, would need help if he threw all his power at her.

He hadn't, however. Perhaps he did not have enough strength

to protect himself as well as attack her. He might still do it if the other black sorcerers shielded him.

She looked at her fellow White, all standing calmly, then at the Pentadrian sorcerers far across the valley.

Five black sorcerers, Auraya thought. *Five White. A coincidence? No, more likely they waited until there were enough of them to face us.*

At Juran's instruction, Auraya let loose a blast of power at one of the sorcerers. She sensed a shift in the man's shield as the other sorcerers helped him protect himself.

:He is the weakest of them, Juran observed. *From our spies' descriptions, he is the one called Sharneya. We might take adva—*

The Pentadrian leader sent a blast up toward the Siyee. At Juran's instruction, Auraya threw up a barrier to intercept it. She sensed Speaker Sirri's relief through Mairae; the Siyee leader was wearing Mairae's link ring.

The attack increased and Auraya strained to hold her barrier against the blast as the speed and ease with which she could draw magic to herself lessened. She took a few steps forward and was able to strengthen her barrier once again. It was not the first time she had thinned the magic around her. In the hours since the attack began, they had moved several steps into the valley from the ridge as the magic around them diminished. So had the black sorcerers. It was incredible to think how much magic had been used already, but she had no time to feel awe.

From somewhere close by came an animal snarl and a cry of pain and terror. No mere man or beast could reach her, but she was all too aware that the most Gifted of Circlian priests and priestesses stood behind and beside her and the other White, adding their strength when directed. She turned to see a huge black vorn tearing at the throat of a priestess. It must have slunk around the back of them in order to attack without warning.

:Kill it, Auraya, Juran ordered.

She blasted it. It howled as her magic sent it tumbling away from its victim, then lay twitching. Other black shapes darted away from the priests and priestesses around her. They wound between Circlian fighters, too fast for her to strike at without endangering her own people.

:Do you think the Pentadrians attacked the Siyee in order to keep us distracted long enough for the vorns to sneak behind us? she asked.

:Yes, Juran replied. *And they sent those beasts in to attack the people around you, not us. I think they were testing you, to see if you are inclined to protect the sky people in preference to the rest of the army. Let them believe that for now. Later we will use it to our advantage.*

:Yes, she replied, though she could not help feeling a twinge of doubt. *Perhaps I am inclined to be protective of the Siyee more than others?*

:You aren't, Dyara assured her.

But Auraya could not shake a growing feeling of dread. Would Juran have one of the others protect the Siyee instead? Or would proving otherwise mean leaving the Siyee vulnerable to attack?

CHAPTER 45

Though the sun was high, a chill wind kept the watchers on the ridge wrapped in their tawls. Danjin looked to either side, at the peculiar mixture of camp servants and important personages that had gathered to watch the battle. They formed a long line along the edge of the valley. Most of it was made up of crowds of servants, cooks and other camp helpers. At the centre was a pavilion. Carpet had been laid over the grass and chairs placed for those of highest rank: the two kings and the Moderator of the Somreyan Council. Advisers, courtiers and servants stood around the outside of this, entering only when summoned, and grooms stood nearby holding mounts at the ready.

The White had insisted that the two monarchs remain out of the battle. Danjin smiled as he remembered that argument.

'We are quite willing to fight alongside our men,' King Berro had said indignantly, when told he and King Guire didn't have a place in the fight.

'Be assured we know that,' Juran had replied. 'But if you enter the battle you will die. The moment the Pentadrians find a gap in our defence – and they will – they will strike at anyone who looks important to us.' He paused. 'You could disguise yourselves as ordinary soldiers to increase your chances of survival, but I would prefer you did not. You are too important to risk.'

Berro had scowled at that. 'Why, then, do you send the Siyee Speaker into battle?'

'She is difficult to distinguish from the other Siyee, and as the Siyee elect their leaders, another Speaker has been chosen to take her place if she dies.'

'I have chosen my heir,' Berro reminded Juran.

'A child,' Juran pointed out bluntly. 'Who will take some years to grow into his responsibilities.' He crossed his arms. 'If you wish to venture onto the battlefield, we will not stop you. We will not protect you at the cost of victory. If you seek glory, it *will* cost you your life – and weaken your country.'

At that point, Moderator Meeran had cleared his throat.

'I am an elected ruler, yet you have no place for me either.'

'No,' Juran replied, turning his attention to the Somreyan. 'Forgive me for pointing this out, but you are old and have no experience in fighting. You are of greater value to us for your ability to negotiate with and unite others.'

He had then asked Meeran to take charge of the non-fighters during the battle, and to negotiate on behalf of the army should the Circlians lose the battle. Nobody had asked why I-Portak, the Dunwayan leader, was joining the battle. All knew that the leader of the warrior nation was required to fight alongside his people. If he did not, he would lose the leadership to another. Several Dunwayan sorcerers – their fire-warriors – accompanied him.

Danjin looked at Lanren Songmaker. The military adviser was standing a little forward of the watchers, staring intently at the battle. His whole body was tense, his hands clenching and unclenching. Sunlight glinted off a white ring on the middle finger of his right hand.

The ring linked Songmaker to Juran, giving the White

614

leader a view of the battlefield from afar. Looking down into the valley, Danjin frowned.

The Pentadrian sorcerers and the White had blasted at each other for hours, but neither side appeared to have an advantage. When so much of the magic loosed was all but invisible at this distance, it was hard to work out what was happening. All he saw was the effect of it when one side managed to harm the other.

That harm was most often inflicted on the fighters. Neither side appeared to have killed more or less of their enemy's army, but Danjin had noted that it was always the soldiers, priests and priestesses protected by Mairae or Rian that suffered. Two of the enemy's sorcerers appeared to have the same difficulty. Both sides used the strength of their Gifted followers to shore up the weaker sorcerers' defence.

The rest of the fighting forces were not so equally matched. The advantage, to Danjin's dismay, lay with the Pentadrians.

It had not appeared so at first. There were fewer Pentadrian fighters. They had no war plattens or mounted soldiers. As the two armies came together, however, it became clear that most of the Pentadrian foot soldiers were trained and prepared to face both.

And then there were the vorns.

The huge beasts brought death and devastation wherever they roamed. They moved so fast, only luck or a concerted effort by many archers could bring them down. The beasts seemed to enjoy killing. As Danjin watched, four of them drove a group of soldiers from the main battle. They tore out the throats of those that tried to face them, then chased the rest out of the valley, loping easily after the runners and nipping playfully at their heels.

'Why don't we have creatures like that? Why don't we have vorns to fight for us?' King Berro muttered.

'I guess the White didn't have time to breed their own,' Guire replied mildly.

'They are an abomination,' a woman growled.

Heads turned to the speaker. Dreamweaver Adviser Raeli stared back, her gaze cold. 'If your White created such evil beasts, would they be any better or nobler than these Pentadrians'?' she asked.

The two kings looked thoughtful, though it was clear Berro was not completely convinced by her words.

'They have bred Bearers instead,' Meeran said. 'And my people have provided them with little helpers.' He nodded to the cage Danjin was holding.

Danjin looked down at Mischief. The veez had remained quiet throughout the battle so far. Danjin hadn't dared to leave Mischief behind, sure that if he did the veez would escape and go in search of Auraya.

'Reyna and veez?' Berro snorted. He looked to the left, where grooms held the five white Bearers ready in case the White needed them. 'Only the White have Bearers and they aren't even using them – and what use is a talking pet during war?'

'Out,' Mischief said.

The weight in the cage shifted. Danjin looked down. 'No. Stay.'

'Out,' Mischief insisted. 'Away. Run.'

'No. Auraya will come back later.'

The veez began to turn circles inside the cage, setting it rocking. 'Run! Bad coming. Run! Hide! Run!'

Danjin frowned. The veez was growing more and more agitated. Perhaps the abductor was near. he turned and scanned the faces around him. Those closest were looking at the veez in curiosity. He looked further away, to the left and right and over his shoulder.

And saw four black shapes loping up the other side of the ridge toward them.

He shouted a warning. Screams rang out as the vorns were seen. There was a moment of hesitation as people clutched at each other in terror, or collided with others as they turned to flee. The line of watchers broke. Most of it spilled down the hill toward the battle, leaving a few individuals frozen in terror on the ridge. The centremost watchers remained still, held together by a strong, confident voice.

'Everyone into the pavilion, and stay there,' High Priest Haleed said, striding forward to place himself between the vorns and the pavilion. 'I will deal with this.'

Danjin frowned as he realised the Somreyan elder was the only magically trained person among the watchers, apart from Raeli – though he had no idea how Gifted she was. Not all Dreamweavers are strong sorcerers.

All squeezed into the dubious cover of the cloth pavilion. Outside, the grooms were hastily covering the heads of the reyna with cloth, including the Bearers, in the hope that the mounts wouldn't take fright and break free. They drew them as close to the pavilion as they could.

Songmaker was still standing outside, his back to the pavilion and his attention on the battle. Danjin saw the man look around at the people fleeing into the valley in puzzlement. He called the man's name. Songmaker turned and his expression changed from puzzlement to alarm as he took in the scene. As he walked toward the pavilion, Danjin heard an animal yowl of pain close by.

He looked out to see one of the vorns lying, twitching, on the ground. The others were scampering backwards, dodging this way and that to avoid Haleed's attacks.

'Ah, magic,' Songmaker murmured. 'A soldier might lose form as he ages, but a sorcerer remains useful.'

So long as he keeps his reflexes sharp, Danjin added silently. Haleed managed to injure another of the vorns, but most of his strikes had missed the fast-moving creatures. He did not seem able to anticipate their rapid changes of direction.

'Your pet turned out to have a use after all,' a voice whispered in Danjin's ear. 'Don't worry about him. He'll return.'

He turned to stare at Raeli. She looked down. Following her gaze, Danjin realised the cage he was still holding was empty, the door open. He felt a stab of alarm. He cast about, searching for the veez.

'Don't bother. He can look after himself,' Raeli assured him.

'Against vorns?'

'They aren't after veez, they're after—'

Her words were drowned out by a scream of pain followed by an inhuman screeching. Looking out, he saw Haleed swaying under the weight of a mass of black-feathered shapes. The priest's white robes were splattered with blood.

'The birds!' someone exclaimed. 'Help him!'

'His eyes,' Songmaker hissed. 'They went for his eyes.'

Meeran barked orders. Servants hurried forward, then stopped and retreated hastily back into the pavilion. Danjin saw a black shape launch itself at Haleed, knocking the old man over. He felt a rush of terror as two more black shapes leapt past the priest. The small crowd surged back and he felt himself shoved sideways.

Losing his balance, he began to fall, but someone grabbed his arm and steadied him. All was chaos: screams, yells, shouted orders and the screech of birds. How could so few people make so much noise? A hand grasped his arm and spun him around.

He found himself facing Raeli. He stared at her in surprise. Over her shoulder he saw a reyna gallop away, King Berro in the saddle.

618

'Stay close to me,' Raeli said. 'I'm forbidden to kill, but I *can* shield you.'

He nodded. As she turned to face the pavilion there was a loud crack and the structure collapsed. The awning was covered in birds. Raeli spread her hands. The air sparked, then filled with flapping wings as the flock took off.

The sound of galloping hooves drew Danjin's attention. He saw the Bearers racing away. Each bore two riders. Danjin was relieved to see Moderator Meeran among them.

'Good,' Raeli said. 'Less trouble for me.'

Then a black shape wriggled out from under the pavilion and streaked away in pursuit.

Raeli grimaced. 'I hope those Bearers can run as fast as people say they can.'

'They can,' Danjin assured her. 'Though whether—'

As a chilling snarl came from under the pavilion, he jumped. He backed away as the cover began to shift and writhe, but Raeli stayed still. She stooped and grabbed the edge of the cloth.

'Don't free it!'

She ignored him and hauled it aside. Danjin winced as he saw the bloodied bodies underneath. A black shape reared up and launched itself at Raeli. She made a quick gesture and the vorn jerked aside. It regarded her with chilling intelligence, then slunk away.

A familiar voice cursed vehemently. Looking down, Danjin was amazed to see Songmaker struggling to his feet. His left arm was bleeding badly from deep gouges.

'I can heal you,' Raeli offered, stepping closer to examine the wound.

Songmaker hesitated, his gaze becoming distant for a moment, then frowned.

'Thank you, Dreamweaver Adviser,' he said, his tone formal, 'but I must decline. A bandage will do for now.'

619

Her lips thinned. 'I will see what I can find.'

Danjin felt a stab of sympathy for her and, surprisingly, anger. *It seems I agree with Auraya that the ban on using Dreamweaver services is ridiculous.* The vorn still lurked nearby. Raeli did not turn her back on it as she tore a strip of cloth from one of the dead servant's tunics and used it to bind Songmaker's wound.

'If the White want you to remain here, they had best send you a priest – and soon,' she said. 'I can ward off one or two of those creatures, but I doubt I could manage more.' Her gaze hardened. 'Tell your leader my people will be here in a few hours. Remind him that we do not take sides; that we will offer our help to all. Should the Pentadrians accept us, but not the Circlians, that is none of our doing.'

Lanren stared back at her, then nodded. 'Several priests are already on their way.'

The sun hung low in the sky by the time the Dreamweaver caravan stopped. Their numbers had grown to a hundred or so. Leiard knew there were more Dreamweavers coming to the battle than those he travelled among. Other caravans had stopped in nearby valleys. Scattered, they lessened the risk that the Circlians – if seized by some crazed fanatical urge after the battle – could rid the world of hundreds of Dreamweavers in one strike.

They had halted an hour's walk from the battle and Arleej had gathered a group of twenty to accompany her to the scene. Most of the others would come when the battle was over. A few would stay to defend the tarns should opportunists decide to loot them.

Leiard had joined Arleej's group. He had brought Jayim with him, knowing that the boy would sneak after them if he was left behind. Now, as they reached the scene of devastation, he sensed Jayim's curiosity and anticipation change to horror.

620

The valley was dark with churned mud, charred grass and corpses. A constant roar, muffled by distance, reached them. It was made up of screams, yells, the clash of weapons and shields, and the boom and crack of magic. Five white figures faced five black ones across the valley. The air between them flashed and writhed. Great scorch marks littered with corpses indicated where their sorcerous battle had spilled past protections.

Leiard remembered other battles. Smaller ones, but just as gruesome. They were not his memories, but they were vivid. Sorcery and death. Waste and pain. He saw that there were new elements to this battle. Black beasts – the vorns Auraya had once described – roamed through the Circlian army, deadly and hard to kill. Siyee wheeled and dived above the heads of soldiers and sorcerers. Smaller black shapes harried them, tearing their wings or attacking in numbers to drag their victims to the ground.

As he watched, three Siyee dived out of the aerial battle to swoop over the heads of the Pentadrians and send down a faint rain of missiles. One Siyee then fell as archers sent a volley of arrows in reply, but they had left several victims behind them.

Yet each death was devastating to the Siyee. There were so few of them.

I have to hope the Circlians win, he thought suddenly. *Or this may be the end of the Siyee.*

The greatest tragedy is that they are here at all, Mirar said darkly. *This will be your former lover's greatest crime: to make a peaceful people warlike and lead them to extinction.*

'So here we are. What do you make of this, Leiard?'

He turned to find Arleej standing beside him.

'Foolishness,' he replied. 'Waste.'

She smiled grimly. 'Yes, and I agree. But what do you make of the two armies? What are their strengths and weaknesses? Who will win?'

621

Leiard frowned and considered the battle again.

'It is a typical confrontation. The sorcerers fight from the back, protecting their army from magic as well as themselves. The stronger of the minor sorcerers remain with them, adding their strength.'

'You mean the White?' Jayim asked. 'And the priests and priestesses.'

'Yes,' Leiard replied. 'Those whose role is more physical than magical fight their own battle, hoping always that the sorcerers will protect them. Soldiers, archers, mounted fighters, war-platten drivers, Siyee, vorns, the black birds. They may not have strong Gifts, but they will use what they can.'

'The Siyee are like archers,' Jayim said. 'Flying archers.'

'Yes,' Arleej agreed. 'They're relying on surprise to attack and get away before the Pentadrian archers have time to retaliate.'

'Which is the same strategy the vorns are using,' another Dreamweaver noted. 'But they don't have anything like the black birds to deal with.'

'The Siyee are holding their own against the birds,' Leiard stated. 'The birds don't appear to attack when they're alone, only as groups, but that makes them more vulnerable to missiles.'

'What happens if the Circlian army loses, but the White win?' Jayim asked.

Leiard smiled grimly. 'If the White defeat the Pentadrian sorcerers they can then kill the remaining Pentadrians – or demand they surrender.'

'Would they abandon their own soldiers in order to use all their magic to kill the black sorcerers?'

'Perhaps as a last resort.'

'I . . . I don't understand. Why do they bother bringing soldiers into battle at all? I can see how the priests help the

White by giving extra magical strength, but I can't see how soldiers make any difference.'

Arleej chuckled. 'You must look to the motive for war. It is nearly always about taking control so the maximum reward can be reaped from the defeated. An invader is thinking beyond the battle. After victory they must maintain control. Even if they are powerful sorcerers, they can't be in more than one place at once, so they bring helpers. Minor sorcerers. Fighters. People who are lured by the prospect of loot and land.

'The defenders know this and so raise an army as insurance in case they lose. If the defenders' army kills as many as possible of the invaders' army there are fewer of the potential conquerers left to impose control on their people. The conquered people have a better chance of rising up against their conquerors later.'

Jayim nodded slowly. 'And if they wait until the sorcerers finish their fight, and their side loses, the enemy's sorcerers will kill them anyway. So they may as well fight now.'

'Yes.' Arleej sighed. 'Though most soldiers do not realise this. They do what they're ordered to do, trusting in their leaders' judgement.'

'Sorcerers have been known to give the remaining fighters the opportunity to surrender,' Leiard added.

Jayim stared out at the battle and frowned. 'Are we . . . are the Circlians winning or losing?'

Looking at the valley again, Leiard considered the two sides carefully. He had noted that the ordinary soldiers were struggling, but hadn't been concerned because, as he'd told Jayim, victory or failure did ultimately depend on the White.

The Circlian priests and priestesses appeared to be suffering greater losses than the sorcerers supporting the Pentadrian leaders. There were far more white-robed corpses than black. As he watched, he gradually saw why this was so.

The vorns. They were so quick and effective at killing that

from time to time they were able to get behind the Circlians' defences and surprise a priest or priestess. In addition, none of the Circlian forces were as effective at removing the enemy's sorcerers. The Siyee were the only fighters able to attack them, but the black birds were keeping the Siyee in check.

'The Pentadrians have the advantage,' he said.

Arleej sighed. 'The hardest challenge a Dreamweaver can ever face isn't prejudice or intolerance, but to stand back and watch your own country lose in a war.' She looked at Jayim. 'We do not take sides. If you step in and fight, you are no longer a Dreamweaver.'

Jayim nodded. His young face was creased with tension and unhappiness – and resolution. Leiard felt a mingled pride and sorrow. The boy would not falter, but he would not like himself for it.

Arleej turned and gave Leiard a direct, assessing look.

'And you?'

Leiard frowned at her. 'Me?'

'Not tempted to rush in and rescue anyone?'

Her meaning came to him in a rush. Auraya. Could he stand back and watch Auraya be defeated? Could he watch her die?

Suddenly his heart was racing. He looked out at the battle-field – at the five White. Why hadn't it occurred to him before? *She always seemed so strong, so confident*, he thought. *I might not have liked that she was one of the Gods' Chosen, but it meant she was safe. Immortal. Protected by magic and the gods.*

The gods . . . Surely they wouldn't allow their chosen human representatives to lose?

If you believe that, you are a fool, Mirar whispered.

'What could *I* do to save them?' Leiard said honestly. 'One single sorcerer? I doubt I'd make the slightest difference.' Aware that his voice was betraying his distress, he looked at Arleej. 'Except, as always, as a healer.'

624

Arleej gave his shoulder a sympathetic squeeze. 'And a fine one at that.'

As she walked away, Leiard sighed heavily. He no longer wanted to watch the battle. Not if it meant watching Auraya die and not being able to do anything about it.

I could spare you the ordeal, Mirar offered.

No. I am here to heal, Leiard replied.

I can do that for you.

No. When this is over with we will go to Somrey and I will be rid of you.

You think Arleej can fix you? I'm not sure you'll like having her poking around in your mind. I'm not sure I like the idea, either.

I thought you wanted to be gone?

That depends on whether the White win this battle or not. If they do, I'll let you go to Somrey. We'll see if Arleej can do something about our situation.

And if the White lose? Leiard asked.

Mirar did not answer.

CHAPTER 46

Tryss glided in a wide circle in the hope of getting a chance to view the battle. Without an immediate target, a black bird to contend with, or something else to occupy his attention, he was suddenly aware of how tired he was. Every muscle ached. He realised he was bleeding from several cuts and scratches, though he could not remember how he'd got them. They stung.

Half of his flight followed him. He looked at them critically, noting wounds and signs of weariness. Tyssi was bleeding heavily from a deep cut that worried him. The rest looked fit but tired. He surveyed the battle in the sky. The number of black birds was noticeably smaller – he gained a grim satisfaction from that – but the number of Siyee had also diminished. By about half.

Some had flown away to rest or replenish their supply of darts, but not the majority. His stomach sank. Most of the missing were dead. People he knew. People he liked. People he didn't. His heart ached with loss. It all seemed so stupid now.

Why did we agree to come here? Why did we sign the treaty? We could have stayed at home. Given up the southern lands to the settlers. Retreated to the highest peaks.

And starved.

He sighed. *We fight because the Circlians were the better choice of ally at a time when we could no longer hope that world events weren't going to affect us. Better to be part of them and suffer the consequences, than not be and suffer the consequences of them anyway.*

A whoop of triumph drew his attention down. He saw a flight of Siyee swoop upward, having unleashed a rain of poisoned darts and arrows on the enemy. The leader, he saw, was Sreil. Remembering that Drilli was with Sreil's flight, he searched for her. She was flying close behind Sreil, grinning fiercely.

Relief and gratitude washed over him. Just seeing her lifted his mood. She was still alive. *And so am I*, he thought. *And while I am, I will fight.*

Looking down at the rows of darts and arrows attached to his harness he estimated that less than a third remained. He would use them up, then take his flight out to the camp to collect more. Glancing at his companions, he gave the signal to follow. Then he dived toward the enemy below.

He'd learned to read from the landwalkers' posture and movements what their attention was on. The Pentadrians' pale faces were easy to see against the black of their robes, especially when they looked up. He aimed for a group looking intently toward one of the black sorceresses.

Suddenly all of the faces turned toward Tryss in unison. He glimpsed hands in the same position holding bows and whistled a warning while dodging to the left. The rush of arrows was frighteningly close. Something scraped past his jaw. He arched away, heart pounding.

So they've learned to watch for us, he thought. *And to pretend they haven't until we get close. Clever.*

He looked down and felt a shock as he realised how low he was flying. Fortunately the men and women below him now had their backs turned to him. Their attention was on something ahead. He looked up and felt his heart stop.

The black sorceress. He was about to fly over her into the magical battle. Twisting away, he flapped frantically and managed to reverse his flight and gain some height.

Only then did he realise he was alone.

Casting about, he forgot about potential archers below. Where was his flight? Had they turned in the other direction to avoid the archers. Or had they . . . were they . . . ?

Looking down, he saw broken, winged bodies lying on the ground. All but one was still. Tyssi was feebly dragging herself away from advancing Pentadrians, an arrow protruding from one of her thighs.

Several men reached her and began kicking.

A fury flared inside Tryss. Ignoring any danger from below, he set himself on a straight path toward her attackers. He concentrated on their backs. When he was just within range he sent two darts flying. Two of the Pentadrians fell. Tryss saw the others turn toward him and dodged away. When he looked back, Tyssi lay still, blood spreading rapidly from a wound over her heart. He felt his eyes blur with tears. Blinking them away, he turned toward the front and realised he was flying toward the black sorceress once more.

He began to turn, then stopped himself.

Even as he straightened and took aim, he knew what he was doing was utterly pointless. He did not give himself time to think. Darts shot from his harness. He saw them fly through the air. He expected them to scatter away from a magical shield.

Instead they embedded themselves in the back of the black sorceress.

Disbelief was followed by delight. He gave a whoop of glee as the woman staggered forward. Circling away, he looked back. She had turned to stare at him. As her hand moved his stomach began to sink with realisation.

Something smashed into him.

It knocked the breath from his lungs. The world rushed past, faster than he had ever flown before, then something else hit his back. The ground. He heard a crack and almost blacked out at the pain that ripped through his body.

What did I just do? he thought as he lay there, gasping. *Something really, really stupid*, he answered. *But I've killed her. I poisoned the black sorceress. We'll win now. I've got to see that.* He opened his eyes. Lifting his head sent bolts of pain down his back, and what he saw made him feel queasy. His legs were bending in places they shouldn't.

That should hurt, he thought. *But I can't feel anything at all. Nothing below my waist.* He knew he was badly hurt – probably dying – but he could not quite believe it. Black-clothed men and women loomed over him. They looked angry.

He smiled. *I killed your leader.*

One said something. The others shrugged and nodded. They walked away.

Gritting his teeth, Tryss raised his head again. Through the black-robed figures he could see the sorceress. As he watched she reached back and pulled one of the darts out, then another, and tossed them aside.

She should have been affected by the poison by now.

Instead, she turned back to rejoin the battle.

If he could have made his jaw work, he would have cursed. Instead he closed his eyes and let his head drop. *Drilli's going to be so angry with me.*

And he let blackness take him.

Throughout the day the White had moved slowly toward the centre of the valley, always seeking a fresh source of magic.

The black sorcerers, too, had advanced step by step. The army between them grew ever smaller, as if diminishing due to their unrelenting advance.

Auraya could see the faces of her adversaries now. To move forward, however, meant stepping over or around dead and injured men and women. The link with her fellow White kept her mind focused on fighting, but she was conscious of a growing tension at the back of her thoughts. She had begun to fear the end of their link, when she was no longer protected from the bleak and terrible reality that surrounded her.

Perhaps she would not have to endure it for long. She knew that the Circlian army was losing. She knew that the vorns had taken too many priests and priestesses and that this was finally tipping the balance of magical strength in the Pentadrians' favour. She knew that there were too few Siyee left flying above.

Juran's frustration imbued them all. He clung to the hope that the enemy would make one mistake. A single error that they could take advantage of.

When it came, the source was so unexpected they did not see it at first.

The more powerful sorceress faltered. At once Juran directed an attack on the weaker of the Pentadrian sorcerers, hoping his companions would not shield him in time. The man protected himself but left his own people vulnerable. Auraya felt relief and triumph as several of the enemy fell.

Then bodies rained from the sky.

She gasped in horror. The enemy had sacrificed their own in order to spare enough magic to strike at the Siyee. But why the Siyee? They were only a minor threat now.

She realised the Pentadrian leader was looking upward. He was directing the attacks. He glanced at her and smirked. Hatred welled up inside her.

:He still believes Auraya will ignore an opportunity in favour of protecting the Siyee, Juran said. *I'll protect them, Auraya. You strike at the leader.*

She gritted her teeth and drew magic faster than she had attempted before. It came to her, swift and potent. She could feel it around her, feel it respond to her will and her anger, feel it gathering and gathering within her. She closed her eyes, overwhelmed by a new sense of awareness. Time stopped. She understood that this sensing of the magic around her was not unlike the sense she had of her position in relation to the world.

:Now, Auraya!

Juran's mental shout brought her back to the physical world with a jolt. She opened her eyes and blasted the power within her at the Pentadrian leader.

The Pentadrian's smug expression vanished. She felt his defence fail. He flipped backwards, knocking men and women behind him to the ground.

Auraya waited for him to rise again. Waited for Juran's next instruction. Slowly she grew aware of the other White's surprise and the diminished force of the enemy. Pentadrians crowded around their leader. A cry went out.

:They're saying he is dead, Dyara said. *Kuar is dead!*

Auraya stared at her fellow White.

:Surely not. He must be unconscious. They must think him dead. He is trying to trick us into lowering our guard.

:No, Auraya, Rian said. *I doubt anyone could survive that blow.*

:But . . .

:He made the mistake we were hoping for, Juran decided, his words laced with triumph. *He didn't anticipate such a powerful attack and didn't put all his strength into defending himself. Maybe he was protecting something else. Something we aren't aware of.*

:We've won! Mairae exclaimed. Yet her smile quickly faded. *What do we do now?*

:Kill them, Rian answered. *If we don't they will always be a danger to us.*

:Rian is right, Juran agreed. *We have no choice. But there is no need to kill any other than the leaders. The rest of them may live . . .*

:So long as they surrender, Dyara added.

Auraya felt Juran and the others gathering magic. She did the same.

:No!

The voice boomed through Auraya's thoughts. Shocked, she nearly let her protective shield fall.

:Chaia! Juran replied.

:It is I. Do not kill the enemy leaders. If you do, others will take their place. You know these people now. You know how they fight. They know you are superior to them. Let them go.

:We will, Juran replied. Auraya could sense his relief and puzzlement. As the god's presence faded, Juran turned to regard the enemy sorcerers. The four were expressionless, but they were no longer attacking.

:We will move forward to meet them, Juran decided.

As they walked through the remaining Circlian army a stillness slowly spread over the battlefield. Fighting stopped and the two sides retreated from each other. The four Pentadrian sorcerers drew closer together.

Then Auraya became aware of a new sound. Yelling and shouting. She looked around, afraid this was a new attack.

And realised the Circlians were cheering.

CHAPTER 47

As the two armies stopped fighting and retreated to either side of the valley, Emerahl let out a long sigh.

I knew it was too good to be true, she thought. *For a while there I thought these Pentadrians were going to solve my problem with the Circlians for me.*

But the gods would never allow invading heathens to wipe out their followers. No doubt they had intervened in some way to ensure the White's victory.

Why they had waited until the end of the day was a mystery. The low sun bathed the valley with a gentle light. It glinted off weapons and shields and turned white robes to gold. Most of those were on the ground, the belongings of the dead, dying and wounded.

Soon the Dreamweavers would begin their work.

She could sense a growing tension among the men and women standing nearby. They were waiting for the two armies to leave. She had never known Dreamweavers to be so hesitant or so fearful. Link memories of the slaughter of their kind had taught them to be cautious, she guessed.

After leaving the brothel caravan she had continued back down the road toward Toren for a few hours before leaving it and starting across the plains. Even if Rozea decided to keep the loss of her favourite to herself, stories of the whore who turned out to be a sorceress were bound to spread – and become exaggerated with each telling. If a Circlian priest decided to investigate, Emerahl wanted searchers to think she'd headed back to Toren. The last move they'd expect from her would be to continue following the army. At least she hoped that was the last move they'd expect.

Looking at the tense men and women nearby, she smiled. They didn't know what to make of her. She was a young woman dressed in plain clothes roaming alone near a battlefield – too good-looking to be a solitary whore. When she had told them she was seeking the source of the tower dream and her theory that the dream was a link memory of Mirar's death, the two men leading the group had moved away to have a long, private discussion.

'There is one among our kind who may be the dreamer you seek,' they had told her when they returned. 'He has many link memories of Mirar's. After we have done our work, we will take you to him.'

So she had waited with them and had seen the conclusion to the biggest battle ever waged on Northern Ithanian soil. It was hard to resist the opportunity. She had spent so much of her life avoiding conflict that she had rarely witnessed events that were likely to become legends.

Now I have something to relate around dinner tables and camp-fires, and my audience will never fail to be impressed, even millennia from now, she thought wryly.

Below, the White and black sorcerers parted. They moved slowly out of the valley. The body of the Pentadrian leader was lifted and carried away.

'They let them surrender,' one of the Dreamweavers said, clearly surprised.

'Perhaps even they acknowledge that there has been enough slaughter today.'

'I doubt it.'

Emerahl was inclined to agree with the last speaker, but she remained silent. Many of the Circlian fighters, priests and priestesses had remained in the valley and were moving among the dead and dying. So were some of the Pentadrians.

'It is time,' the leader of the Dreamweaver group said.

Emerahl felt the tension ease. Determination replaced it. The Dreamweavers started down the valley carrying bags of medicines, followed by students laden with sacks full of bandages and skins of water.

She could not join them. There were priests and priestesses still down there. If she roamed about, the only healer not wearing a Dreamweaver vest or Circlian circ, she would attract attention.

Then I need to blend in. I need Dreamweaver robes . . .

She turned to look at the tarns. There were bound to be a few spare garments in them. Surely the Dreamweavers wouldn't mind if she borrowed a set?

Standing up, she strode back toward the Dreamweaver camp.

Priest Tauken stepped over a headless corpse and stopped. A young soldier lay a few strides away, arms wrapped tightly around his chest. He could hear the man gasping for breath. Moving to the soldier's side, Tauken dropped into a crouch. The young man looked up at him, eyes wide with hope.

'Help me,' he gasped.

'Let me see,' Tauken replied.

The young man's arms parted reluctantly. Clearly the movement caused him pain, but the only sound he managed was a whimper.

The soldier was wearing an iron chest-plate, but even that could not stop a blow by a good sword. A large gash in the plate glistened with blood.

'We have to get this off.'

The soldier allowed him to remove the armour. His gaze was growing dull. Tauken ripped away the clothing around the wound and bent close. He could hear a faint sucking sound. It came in time with the man's breathing. His heart sank. There would be no saving this one.

As he rose, the two camp servants sent to help him regarded him expectantly. He looked at them and made a small gesture with his hand to indicate they would not be stopping. They nodded and looked away, and their expressions suddenly brightened with hope.

Tauken turned to see what they were looking at. A Dreamweaver woman stood nearby, watching him. From her looks he guessed she was Somreyan.

'Are you finished?' she asked.

Juran had decreed that the law against using Dreamweaver services had been lifted for the day. Tauken opened his mouth, then hesitated. To say 'yes' aloud would be to tell the dying soldier he was done for. Instead, he nodded.

She moved forward and looked down at the man. 'A chest wound. His lungs have been penetrated.'

As she kneeled before the soldier, Tauken turned away. He took a few steps then stopped as the woman gave a piercing whistle. Looking back, he saw a younger Dreamweaver hurry to her side. She took bandages from him, and lifted a small bowl for him to fill with water from a pitcher. As the young man hurried away again, answering another whistle, she took a small jar from her vest and tipped powder from it into the water.

Tauken knew he should move on, but curiosity kept him still. Her hands moving with practised speed, the Dreamweaver bathed the wound then put the bloodied cloth aside. She paused. Tauken saw her shoulders rise and fall as she drew in and let

636

out a deep breath, then she placed a hand on the wound and closed her eyes.

There was something wrong about all this. Seeing her using her Dreamweaver magic, Tauken finally realised what it was.

'You did not ask if he wanted your help,' he said.

She frowned, opened her eyes and turned to regard him.

'He is unconscious.'

'And so can hardly decide for himself.'

'Then you must decide for him,' she said calmly.

He stared at her. Once he would have told her to leave. Better the young soldier die than risk his soul by being healed by a Dreamweaver. But he knew he would want to live if he was the young man. If Juran could lift the ban for a day then the gods must intend to forgive those who chose to use Dreamweaver services.

Who am I to deny this man life? Accepting a Dreamweaver's help does not mean a man or woman becomes one. And we could learn a lot from them.

He just hoped the young man agreed.

'Heal him,' he said. Beckoning to his helpers, he led them away.

'Gods forgive me,' he muttered to himself.

The Circlian camp was lit by a thousand torches. It ought to have been a cheerful sight, but those lights illuminated a grim scene.

Toward the end of the battle vorns had attacked the camp, killing defenceless servants and animals. Auraya could see survivors doing their best to tidy up the mess. Some were carrying corpses away, others were seeing to the wounded. Reyna that had lost their riders had been caught and were being used to carry others less fortunate to the edge of the camp.

637

Seeing this, Auraya almost wished she and her fellow White had finished the Pentadrians off.

The gods were right to let them live. I don't like unnecessary slaughter. I don't like necessary slaughter either, but killing a defeated enemy is too much like cold-blooded murder.

They had wanted to rid the world of the black sorcerers. Now, on reflection, she could see what the consequences might have been. The battle would have continued for a while longer and more people would have been killed.

She could also see that allowing the four black sorcerers to return to the southern continent might still be a decision they'd come to regret in the future. If the Pentadrian leader was replaced by an equally powerful sorcerer, Northern Ithania might face another invasion. However, it was extraordinary that five powerful sorcerers had been born in the last century or so. It was unlikely that another would be soon.

These southerners will think twice before confronting us again, Auraya told herself. She thought of the glowing figure she had seen after the Pentadrians had emerged from the mines. Whether illusion or new god, he clearly hadn't ensured their victory. *That, too, will give them reason to hesitate if they consider attempting another conquest.*

Whereas our gods, through us, have protected Northern Ithania successfully. She smiled, but felt the smile fade. Since the moment the Pentadrian leader had died, she had replayed the scene over and over in her mind. Not to gloat at having dealt the fatal blow, but to work out what had happened.

She remembered it all clearly. There had been a new awareness of magic. She could sense it just as she could sense her position in relation to the world. If she concentrated, she could return to that state of awareness. Somehow it had enabled her to take and use more magic than ever before.

The other White had been surprised at the strength of her

attack. From time to time she caught Juran regarding her with a puzzled frown. Perhaps she had learned to use her Gifts faster than he had expected her to. The others hadn't been forced to gain skills quickly by war, however.

Or perhaps Juran was just surprised that she, rather than he, had been the one to deal the killing blow. If he was, he was not resentful about it. He seemed pleased with her. She accepted this approval a little warily, wondering if it extended to forgiveness for her affair with Leiard.

At the thought of Leiard she felt a stab of pain and was glad she was no longer closely linked with the other White. She straightened her back. He was a mistake of the past. A lesson in the perils of love. Now, after the battle, her infatuation seemed childish and foolish. It was time to think of more important things: the recovery of her people – and of the Siyee.

A lone mounted rider galloped back to the White. Auraya watched him, welcoming the distraction. The advisers had reported that King Guire and Moderator Meeran had returned a few hours after fleeing the vorns' attack. King Berro, however, had not been seen.

The rider reined in before Juran. 'No sign of him yet, Juran of the White. We could send a second group of trackers.'

'Yes,' Juran replied. 'Do that.'

The man hurried away. The White continued down the slope toward the camp. When they had nearly reached it, Auraya heard a familiar high-pitched voice call her name. She let out a relieved sigh as Mischief leapt down from the roof of a tarn and bounced over the muddy ground toward her. Two more veez followed him, one black, one orange. As Mischief ran up Auraya's robe onto her shoulders, the other veez raced to Mairae and Dyara.

'Little escapee,' Dyara said, scratching the bright orange

head of her pet. She looked at Mischief suspiciously. 'Is he teaching Luck bad habits?'

Auraya smiled. 'Probably. Does he—?'

Hearing the sound of wings, Auraya felt her heart skip. She looked up eagerly, and sighed with relief to see Speaker Sirri and two other Siyee circling down. As they landed, Juran stepped forward to meet them.

'Speaker Sirri. We are indebted to you and your people. You have been invaluable to us today.'

Sirri's smile was grim. 'It was our first experience of war. We have learned much today, at great cost, although our losses are nothing to yours. When the vorns attacked our non-fighters, they were able to escape.'

'All losses are equally terrible,' Juran replied. 'Our healer priests will tend to Siyee wounded as well as landwalker.'

Sirri looked bemused, and Auraya saw images of the hundreds of Dreamweavers that had descended upon the battlefield in the woman's thoughts.

'Then I will send the non-fighters of my people, who are fresh and able to carry small loads quickly, to help them.'

Juran nodded. 'Their help would be most welcome. Is there anything else you need?'

'No. I just learned something that *you* may be interested to hear. One of my people noticed a man sitting in a tree to the northwest of here. My hunter said she was attracted by his shouting, but dared not land as she could hear one of those large predatory creatures of the enemy nearby.'

Juran's eyebrows rose. 'That is interesting. Could you send this hunter to us so that we may locate this man?'

'Of course.'

'Thank you, Speaker Sirri.'

She nodded, then stepped away. 'I will gather my people and send as many helpers as I can to you.'

Her companions followed as she ran down the hill, leapt into the air and glided away. Juran turned to Auraya.

'I think it would be best if you accompanied this hunter.'

:Just . . . don't rub it in too much, he added. *There's a fine line between earning gratitude and resentment.*

:I imagine that for King Berro the line is fine indeed. I will be careful.

'This poor man will need a mount to carry him back,' she said aloud.

Juran smiled. 'Yes, and familiar faces to ease the shock of his situation.'

She nearly laughed aloud. With a few landwalkers present to witness the rescue, everyone would know the Toren king owed the Siyee his life.

And that couldn't be a bad thing.

CHAPTER 48

Areas of depleted magic were everywhere, but that was normal for a battlefield. To compensate, Leiard only had to concentrate on the sense of magic around him and draw from less depleted patches.

He channelled magic through himself into the injured man, shifting bone and flesh until a sense of rightness began to form. Liquids returned to their correct channels. Flashes of energy shot up and down repaired pathways. He heard the man gasp with pain and quickly blocked the nerve thread again, this time in a way that could be easily reversed.

Working along the leg, Leiard repaired the rest of the damage. He passed a hand over the man's skin, feeling a deep satisfaction at the scar-free result, then unblocked the man's nerve pathways and went in search of another patient.

He had only to open his mind and any lingering thought of the wounded or dying would guide him. Befuddled, dim thoughts drew him to a Pentadrian sorcerer. The woman had been dealt a blow to the head that had left a bloody crater.

I can't save this one, he thought. *Her mind will be damaged.*

Yes, you can, Mirar whispered. *I will help you.*

Leiard crouched beside the woman and placed his hand over the wound. He let Mirar guide him. The work was so fine he scarcely dared to breathe. Mirar's will blended with his as it had so many times this night, so that he almost began to feel he was losing himself. That brought a sense of panic, but he held it back. For the woman's sake.

Leiard felt the crater in the woman's skull expand under his hand. Bone knitted. Liquids and swelling within the brain drained away. Damaged areas were repaired.

Will she return completely to normal? Leiard asked.

No, she will have some memory loss, Mirar replied. *Not necessarily a slice of her past. More likely she will have to relearn something, like how to talk, or dance – or see.*

I did not know that was possible.

You did. You have just forgotten.

The woman was healed. She opened her eyes and stared at Leiard in surprise. Then she rose to her feet and looked around the battlefield. Leiard turned her to face the Pentadrian side of the valley, then pointed. She nodded, then started walking.

Leiard turned away. Pain and grief drew him to a young Siyee man, his legs and arms bent in places and directions that they would not naturally go. A young female Siyee kneeled beside him, sobbing.

Another victim of a fall, Mirar observed. *His back may be broken, too.*

This would take a lot of magic and concentration. Leiard ignored the crying girl, kneeled beside the Siyee and began to draw in magic.

Danjin woke with a start. He was lying beside a fire. Flames licked at a fresh piece of wood. From the shape he guessed it was a piece of broken shaft from a war platten.

How long have I been asleep?

He sat up. A servant was walking away from him, probably the man who had brought the wood. He looked around

643

at the camp. Fewer lamps burned now. A handful of people still moved about, but quietly. There was a stillness to everything. No wind. Little sound.

Then he looked beyond. The sky was glowing faintly in the east.

Dawn. It's dawn. I slept most of the night.

He hadn't meant to. He had only stopped for a warm drink and a little food. Sleeping on the ground had left him feeling stiff and sore. Without any destination in mind, he rose, stretched and began to walk.

His legs took him to one side of the camp. He was cheered to see a dead vorn there, a variety of arrows, knives and even splinters of wood embedded in its side. A long line of bodies lay beyond it – the servants who had died. It was a grim sight, but nothing in comparison to the battlefield on the other side of the ridge.

Looking toward the valley, he saw a row of servants standing at the edge of the camp. As he watched, a figure walked out of the darkness. A Hanian soldier, covered in blood. Two servants stepped forward, wrapped a blanket around the man and guided him to a fire.

As a pair of Dunwayan warriors appeared, Danjin realised what was happening. These were the survivors of the battle who had been healed by priests and Dreamweavers.

I have to see this.

Walking past the waiting servants, Danjin started up the slope. The sky brightened slowly. By the time he neared the top of the ridge, he was able to see men and women coming back to camp. Some walked, some limped. Some were supported by servants. A few were being carried.

At the top of the ridge stood a familiar figure. He felt a stab of guilt as he saw her. She turned to regard him, then beckoned.

'Good morning, Danjin Spear,' Auraya said quietly.

'Auraya,' he replied. 'I must apologise.'

'If you feel you must, then do so. But you are not to blame. They would have discovered it anyway. I did intend to tell them, and you, eventually.'

He looked down at the ground. 'You must know I think you could have made a better choice.'

'Yes.'

'Good choice or not, you must be . . . disappointed at the result.'

She smiled tiredly. 'So tactfully put. Yes, I was disappointed. It is in the past now. I have more important things to do.'

He smiled. 'Indeed you have.'

Her attention shifted to the valley. Following her gaze, he saw movement among the fallen. Dreamweavers and priests were at work.

'The change I've long considered starting has begun by itself,' she murmured.

'Change?'

She shook her head. 'The healer priests and priestesses, instead of ignoring or scorning Dreamweaver healing, are paying attention. They will learn much today.'

Danjin stared at her. Priests learning from Dreamweavers? Was this what she had been aiming for all along? As the implication of this dawned on him he felt dazzled by her brilliance. If the priests could offer the same services as Dreamweavers there would be no more need for Dreamweavers.

Did Leiard know? Had he ever guessed?

Danjin doubted the man would have liked the idea. And being his lover must have made Auraya hesitate to work toward bringing about the end of his people, even if it did mean she would save the souls of those she prevented from joining the heathen cult in the future.

645

How long had she been planning this? Had making Leiard the Dreamweaver adviser been a step in the process? Now that Leiard was gone she was free to continue her work.

Auraya sighed and turned around. Glancing back toward the camp, Danjin saw that the other four White were approaching.

'We're going to have a little conversation with the gods now,' Auraya said lightly. 'Go back to camp, Danjin. I'll join you for breakfast soon.'

He nodded, then watched as she walked down the slope to join her fellow White.

A soldier limped out of the valley toward him. He glanced at Auraya again, then hurried over to help the man.

For a long time now, Tryss had struggled to make sense of it. For hours he had lain in a daze, listening to the sounds of men and women murmuring in languages he didn't understand. There was a desperation to their voices. Only much later did he realise that what he was hearing was praying.

It went on and on. Eventually most of the voices faded away. He wondered if the gods had answered. He hoped so.

A new voice had started, but this one did not speak the names of gods. It spoke a more familiar name.

'Tryss! You're alive! Tryss! Wake up! Talk to me!'

It was so familiar. And comforting, somehow. Yet he wasn't about to do what it said. Waking up meant pain. He'd had more than enough pain today.

'Tryss . . .' There was a long pause, then a choking sound. 'Tryss. I have something to tell you. Wake up.'

He felt a stirring of curiosity. It wasn't enough. The memory of pain was too frightening. He let himself drift.

Then pain came seeking him.

It was not like before – a distant, constant ache. It came in brief stabs. Each time it shot through his body it was followed by a sudden absence of pain. He felt himself dragged out of the comfortable place. *The voice will be happy*, he thought grumpily. *I'm waking up; just what it wants. I'll open my eyes and . . .*

Suddenly he was staring up at a face. A man leaned over him, frowning with concentration. The face didn't match the voice.

'Tryss! Oh, thank you!'

The exclamation came from Tryss's left. He began to turn his head, but it hurt too much. So he rolled his eyes. He could see a blurred face. A female face.

She leaned forward and recognition came like a bolt of lightning.

'Drilli.'

I spoke, he thought. *Perhaps I'm not dying after all*. He looked at the man again. A Dreamweaver. Tryss felt another stab of pain followed by numbness. Rolling his eyes to the right, he saw and felt the Dreamweaver's hands on his arm.

He felt movement inside his arm. Bones and flesh shifting. The sensation was peculiar and nauseating. Tryss decided it would be better not to watch. He looked at Drilli. She was so beautiful – even covered in mud, sweat and blood. She was grinning at him, her eyes all glittery.

'So what is it?' he asked.

She blinked and frowned. 'What is what?'

'That you have to tell me.'

To his amusement, she paused. 'So you heard that.' She bit her lip. 'Perhaps we should wait until later. When you're healed.'

'Why?'

'It's . . . too early.'

647

'Too early for what?' He tried to lift his head and gasped as pain ripped down his back.

'Tell him,' the Dreamweaver said quietly.

Drilli looked at the man, then nodded. 'Just remember that these things often go wrong in the first few months.'

Tryss sighed and rolled his eyes. '*What* things?'

She bit her lip. 'I'm – we're – going to be parents.'

'Parents?'

'Yes. I'm carrying . . .'

A baby. She's pregnant. Tryss felt a thrill of excitement. The next stab of pain hardly bothered him. He grinned at Drilli.

'That explains why you've been sick all the time. I thought it must be all those spices you like in your food.'

She pulled a face.

Tryss opened his mouth to speak, but stopped as the Dreamweaver slid his hands behind Tryss's neck. Pain shot down his body, then numbness. The Dreamweaver remained still for a long time. Slowly, feeling returned, but no pain. The Dreamweaver's hands finally slid away and Tryss felt the man turn his attention to his other arm.

'That was . . . amazing,' Tryss managed.

'Keep still,' the Dreamweaver said.

Drilli shifted position to Tryss's right side. He found he could move his arm. Lifting it, he was amazed to see there wasn't even a scar left to mark his skin.

He was able to turn his head now, so he began to watch the Dreamweaver working. The sight of his other arm bent at a strange angle was disturbing, but as the Dreamweaver's hands slowly moved over it his elbow bent back in the right direction. Tryss felt a growing awe. He had heard of Dreamweavers' legendary abilities, but nothing like this.

I was dying, he thought. *And this man has done what should have been impossible: made me whole again. He has saved my life.*

The Dreamweaver sat back on his heels and regarded Tryss critically. Then he rose and turned away.

'Wait.'

Tryss hauled himself to his feet. Belatedly he realised what he had done, and paused to look in wonder at his arms and body. Then he hurried after the Dreamweaver, Drilli following.

'Wait. Thank you. You've saved my life.'

The man's eyes roved about. He muttered something. Tryss frowned and moved closer.

'No. Not safe there. But Jayim. No. Forget. You must leave before he returns with Arleej.' The Dreamweaver paused and his voice became thin and weak. 'One more. One more.' Then he shook his head. 'Enough. The sun is rising. It is time.'

The Dreamweaver was talking to himself. Were they always like this? Perhaps only when they were working. Tryss hoped so. There was something disturbing about the idea of being healed by a madman. Shaking his head sadly, Tryss returned to Drilli.

'I don't know if he heard me. I don't know if he can,' he told her.

She nodded, and her eyes roamed over his body. 'What he did . . . it was amazing. Do . . . do you think you can fly?'

He grinned. 'Let's find out.'

She frowned with concern. 'Wait. What if it's too soon . . .'

But he was already running. Racing across the battlefield with his arms spread wide. He felt a light wind catch his wings and he leapt into the air.

As Drilli joined him, he whooped with joy and soared up into the sky.

After walking for an hour the White stopped on top of a low hill. Auraya looked back. Thin trails of smoke were the

649

only clue to the camp's location. They moved to form a wide circle.

'Chaia, Huan, Lore, Yranna, Saru,' Juran spoke. 'We thank you for giving us the means to defend Northern Ithania. We thank you for protecting our people from the Pentadrian invaders.'

'We thank you,' Auraya murmured with the others.

'We have fought in your names and we have won. Now, as we face the aftermath of this battle, we need your guidance even more.'

'Guide us.'

'We ask that you appear now, so that we may ask for wisdom.'

Auraya held her breath. She could not help it, even now. A glow filled the circle. It coalesced into five figures.

All five, she thought. *I haven't seen them all together since my Choosing.*

The gods' features appeared. They were smiling. She could not help smiling too. Chaia stood facing Juran.

: We are pleased at your victory, he said. *You have all done well. And, Auraya . . .* The god turned to regard her. *You have surpassed even our expectations.*

Auraya felt her face warming. She lowered her eyes, amused by her own embarrassment at his praise.

: What is it you wish to ask? The question came from Huan.

'We have allowed the remaining Pentadrians to surrender and return to their lands, as you instructed,' Juran told them, 'but we fear the consequences of doing so.'

: The Pentadrians may regain their strength and invade again, Lore said. *If they are determined to, they will. Killing this army would not stop another coming.*

'Then if they invade again, perhaps we should not only drive them away, but rid the world of their cult,' Rian said.

650

: There may come a time when that is unavoidable. You are not yet ready for that battle, Chaia replied.

'When Auraya witnessed the Pentadrian army emerge from the mines, she saw what appeared to be a god,' Dyara said. 'But that is impossible. What was it? An illusion?'

: It is not impossible, Yranna replied.

'But there are no other gods.'

: None of the old ones survived but us, Yranna agreed. *But new ones can arise.*

'Five of them?' Dyara asked.

: It is unlikely, Saru murmured.

'But not impossible.'

: No. Chaia looked at the other gods. *We will investigate.*

They nodded.

Chaia turned back to Juran.

: For now, return to Jarime and enjoy the peace you have fought so hard for. We will speak to you again soon. He glanced at Dyara, then his eyes met Auraya's. His smile widened for a moment, before his attention moved to Rian and Mairae.

Then the five glowing figures vanished.

Juran sighed and broke the circle by moving toward Dyara. 'Let's hope they find nothing.'

'Yes,' Dyara agreed. 'Though if the Pentadrians do follow real gods, they must be feeling a bit unhappy with them now. They lost.'

'Mmmm,' Juran replied. 'Will they again?'

'Of course they will,' Mairae said lightly. She smiled as they all turned to regard her. 'We have Auraya.'

Auraya sighed. 'Will you stop saying that, Mairae? I didn't do anything extraordinary. The Pentadrians made a mistake, that's all.'

Mairae grinned. 'The enemy is going to take back stories of the ferocious flying priestess who killed their leader.'

'I didn't fly during the battle.'

'That hardly matters. Think what a deterrent for invasion that will be. Your name will be used to frighten children into obedience for generations.'

'How wonderful,' Auraya said dryly.

'If I don't get some breakfast soon you'll find out how ferocious a priestess can be,' Dyara growled.

Juran gave Dyara a bemused look. 'That must be avoided at all costs. Come on, then. Let's go home.'

The Dreamweaver robes Emerahl had stolen were a bit big for her, but they had kept her sufficiently safe from priestly notice while she tended the sick. She had kept to the Pentadrian side of the battleground, which reduced the number of Circlians she treated. There had been no sign of the White for hours. They were probably discussing the battle among their allies.

She had no bag of medicines, but managed well enough with magic. It was satisfying work. She hadn't been free to use her Gifts in this way for . . . a long time. Just before dawn she had decided it was time to leave, but at the edge of the battlefield she had discovered a Siyee still clinging to life and stopped to help him.

By the time she had finished the sun had risen. Delicate light filled the valley. She had wanted to leave the field when it was still dark, but it shouldn't matter if anyone saw her go. The Dreamweavers might wonder why one of their kind was abandoning the field, but they were probably too involved in their work to notice. No one else would know enough about Dreamweavers to wonder why she was leaving.

She glanced around. Only one Dreamweaver stood nearby, his back to her. He was looking up at the sky. She frowned. There was something familiar about him. Perhaps he was one of the Dreamweavers from the group she had run into.

A voice reached her, low and strained. She moved closer and felt a shiver run down her back.

I know that voice.

But it could not belong to the man she had known. What was he saying, anyway? She stepped over a corpse and crept closer.

'—must go. No. She can help. No. She will only make it worse. I can't—'

The voice changed from high to low, weak to forceful, stranger to familiar. He was ranting at himself like a madman. As he cast about he turned to face her and she gasped.

'Mirar!'

It was impossible. He was dead. But as she said his name his gaze cleared and she saw recognition in his eyes.

'Emerahl?'

'You're . . . you're . . .'

'Alive? In a way.' He shrugged, then his gaze became keen. 'What are *you* doing here?'

She smiled crookedly. 'Long story.'

'Will you . . . can you help me?'

'Of course. What do you need?'

'I need you to take me away from here. No matter who I turn into. No matter how I protest. Using all your magic, if you need to.'

She stared at him. 'Why would I have to do that?'

He grimaced. 'Long story.'

She nodded, then closed the distance between them. He had aged. She had never seen him so thin and wrinkled. His hair was so light it was nearly white, and she could see from the untanned skin around his jaw that he had only recently removed a beard. If it weren't for the recognition in his eyes, and the little mannerisms she had once known so well, she might not have recognised him at all. But here he was, changed but alive. She would ponder the impossibility of this later.

Taking his arm, she led him away.

EPILOGUE

Auraya walked the battlefield.

Around her were twisted bodies. The pale, staring eyes of the dead filled her with horror. She was afraid to look into them, yet she could not stop herself. Blue lips opened and rasping voices pleaded for life. She tore her gaze away only to be caught by another corpse ranting at her. Accusing.

'It's your fault I'm dead.'

She hurried away, but the sea of corpses was endless. They lay thick on the ground. She had to step over them. They tried to grab her ankles.

'We had to fight! We had to!' she protested. 'You know that!'

Ahead she could see a light. Suddenly she was standing before it. A table and two stools had been set in a gap between the bodies. On the table was a game of counters – a game already begun. The set was beautifully made of black and white veinstone.

The corpses had fallen silent. She stepped over the last of them and looked down at the board. The two sides were caught in stalemate. No wonder they had abandoned the game.

A figure stepped out of the shadows. She felt a stab of pain as she recognised him.

Leiard.

He looked at her searchingly, then down at the board.

'What an interesting dream you're having. Why did you feel the need for me to join you?'

She shook her head. 'I don't want you here.'

'You called me.'

'I didn't.'

'You did.'

She glared at him. 'Why did you answer then? I thought you preferred whores.'

He blinked in surprise. 'So you know about that?'

'Yes.'

He looked thoughtful. 'Probably just as well. You won't be tempted to look for me.'

She felt a stab of hurt. 'Oh, there's no chance of that now.'

'You might find this hard to believe, but I didn't want to hurt you. My people were in danger. Leiard's weak and humble nature was meant to protect us, not lead us into danger.' He looked down at the board. 'There are five white pieces and five black left. Which side do you want to take?'

She looked at the board. 'White, of course.'

'Then you have won.'

One of the pieces had changed. It had been engraved with a gold circle, representing a priest, which made it a stronger piece than it had been.

'What happened? That's not how it was before.'

Leiard smiled. 'No?'

'Why did it change?'

'I don't know. This is your dream, Auraya of the White, and I want no part of it. Goodbye.'

She looked up.

He had vanished.

GLOSSARY

VEHICLES
platten – two-wheeled vehicle
tarn – four-wheeled vehicle

PLANTS
dembar – tree with magic sensitive sap
felfea – tree of Si
florrim – tranquillising drug
formtane – sophoric drug
fronden – fern/bracken-like plants
garpa – tree. Seeds are a stimulant.
heybrin – cure believed to protect against stds
mytten – tree with wood that burns slowly
rebi – fruit found in Si
saltwood – wood that is resistant to decay
shendle – plant on forest floor
velweed – cure for haemorrhoids
wemmin – fleshy flower
winnet – tree that grows along rivers
yan – tubers on forest floor

ANIMALS

arem – domestic, for pulling platten and tarn
ark – predatory bird
breem – small animal hunted by Siyee for food
dartfly – stinging insect of northeast mountains
fanrin – predator that hunts gowts
garr – giant sea creature
girri – wingless birds, domesticated by Siyee
glitterworm – insect that glows in the dark
gowt – domestic animal bred for meat and milk, resides in mountains
kiri – large predatory bird
leramar – predator with telepathic ability
lyrim – domestic herd animals
moohook – small pet
ner – domesticated animal bred for meat
reyna – animal for riding and pulling platten
shem – domestic animal bred for milk
tiwi – insects that make a hive
veez – cute, telepathic pet that can speak
vorn – wolf-like animals
woodfish – tasteless fish
yern – deer-like, limited telepathy
yeryer – venomous sea creature

CLOTHING

circ – circular overgarment worn by Circlian priests and priestesses
octavestim – garb of the Priests of Gareilem
tawl – overgarment worn draped over shoulders fastened at throat
tunic – dress for women, shirt for men
undershift – undergarment for women

FOOD
wafercakes – fried, flakey pastry
firespice – spice from Toren
nutmeal – paste made from nuts, Si
flatloaf – dense bread

DRINK
ahm – drink of Somrey, usually warmed and spiced
teho – drink of Sennon
tintra – Hanian drink
tipli – Toren drink

DISEASES
lungrot – disease that, funnily enough, rots the lungs
woundrot – the festering of a wound

BUILDINGS
wayhouse – place for travellers to stay in
safehouse – place where Dreamweavers can stay
blackstone – stone that is dark coloured
whitestone – stone that is pale coloured

*The Age of the Five trilogy
continues with . . .*
Last of the Wilds
and concludes with . . .
Voices of the Gods